**"I AM ONLY A STRIPLING,
I AM AFRAID,
IT IS BEYOND MY POWER!
I AM A COWARD.
I WOULD BE TERRIFIED
AND FLEE,
SHAMING MYSELF
AND MY TRIBE,
ACCOMPLISHING NOTHING!"**

Dead Eagle's visage clouded. "Make no excuses, warrior! You are of the Eagle Clan! I put my mark on you, and I take from you your fear; never while you live will you experience it. Accept the mission, and do not return until it is done." He reached down, and his hand passed through Hotfoot's injured shoulder.

Abruptly the fear was gone. "I accept the mission, O Spirit," Hotfoot said. "I will not dishonor you."

**"A wide-ranging, picaresque adventure . . .
combining myth, fantasy and history"**
Publishers Weekly

PIERS ANTHONY

TATHAM MOUND

AVON BOOKS ◈ NEW YORK

AVON BOOKS
A division of
The Hearst Corporation
1350 Avenue of the Americas
New York, New York 10019

First Avon Books Printing: October 1992

AVON TRADEMARK REG. U.S. PAT. OFF. AND IN OTHER COUNTRIES, MARCA REGISTRADA, HECHO EN U.S.A.

Printed in the U.S.A.

RA   10   9   8   7   6   5   4   3   2   1

CONTENTS

INTRODUCTION

In 1983 Brent Weisman of the University of Florida (UF) was searching for Seminole Indian sites relating to the Second Seminole War. One was believed to be in Citrus County, near the sweeping bend of the Withlacoochee River called the Cove of the Withlacoochee. He had assistance from a team of volunteers from the Withlacoochee River Archaeology Council (WRAC). They hoped to locate the secret stronghold of the famed Seminole leader Osceola in the nineteenth century, when he hid from the white man's troops and conducted the war that the United States was never quite able to win. Instead, to their surprise, they discovered an unnatural hill in the level swampy area near the river. It was two meters (six feet) high and twenty meters (sixty feet) across, and overgrown with brush and small trees. It looked very much like an earlier Indian burial mound, hidden in the wilderness of the Cove.

Brent returned with Jeffrey Mitchem, also of UF, and conducted a "shovel test": they selected appropriate spots and started digging a square hole. Less than a foot down they encountered pay dirt: part of a human skull and some long-bone fragments and pottery sherds. This was enough to confirm the mound as a Safety Harbor site. Historically the Safety Harbor peoples of the Tampa Bay region are known as the Tocobaga Indians, who were first contacted by Spanish explorers early in the sixteenth century. Relatively little is known about them because they disappeared before Florida was settled by the Europeans.

The mound was on land that had been safeguarded in its

natural state by Mr. Tatham. Thus the mound was titled Tatham (TAY-tham) Mound, and preparations were made for its archaeological excavation by the University of Florida. One might consider such a project to be hardly worthwhile, because available evidence suggested that this region was a relative backwater even in Indian terms. Certainly little money was available for such things. However, the parents of one of the girls in WRAC got interested and decided to underwrite the excavation of Tatham Mound. Thus this project became viable at an early date, and the work proceeded.

There is a question about the excavation of burial mounds that needs to be addressed. The disposition of the dead was a serious business to the Indians, as it is to us of the contemporary world, and for similar reason. We do not bury our lost beloved for the purpose of having some stranger muck about in the grave and play with the remains. If you believe, as many in both cultures do, that there is a spiritual association with the physical body, the desecration of those remains assumes a greater significance. Have we of one culture the right to interfere with what those of another culture set up? Shouldn't we honor their beliefs and practice, as we wish others to honor ours? In short, shouldn't that mound have been left alone?

On the other hand, our approach to the mound is not one of disrespect. Little is known of the Indians of southeastern America, and almost nothing of those of central Florida, and less yet of the Tocobaga. Their heritage was in danger of being entirely lost—unless it could be recovered through research and fieldwork. This mound represented perhaps the last significant opportunity to learn about these Indians, and if it was not excavated, their culture could indeed be lost. If the burial of the dead is intended to maintain the memory of the lives and culture of the tribe, this memory can better be facilitated by study of those burials. In fact, in this age of literacy and of computer technology, the museum may be a better repository for those bones than the ground.

I remember when I was young, reading James Fenimore Cooper's *The Last of the Mohicans,* and being struck by the horror of an entire tribe dying out. I lived at that time in Vermont, where the Mohicans (or Mahicans) once were, and was deeply moved by that notion, though the novel itself may have been unrealistic adventure. Now I live in Citrus County, Florida, and this mound showed that there were Indians here too. To me it would seem a crime to let their memory perish.

Perhaps these views balance out: the sanctity of the original mound versus the preservation of the knowledge of the culture. But there is a practical factor. Once a mound is discovered, it will not be left alone. It will be looted by unscrupulous scavengers, who will sell the beads and other native artifacts, put the pottery on mantels, and carelessly scatter the bones. No respect for law stops these lawless; they simply come and take what they can find. After they have passed, what remains has diminished value as either sacred burial or for research. Also, many mounds have been bulldozed flat by developers or farmers clearing their fields for planting. That was why Tatham Mound might be the last chance: of the many other Safety Harbor mounds known in the state, only this one remained intact and unlooted. Those of us who care for either Indian heritage or the sanctity of the dead may be outraged, but it was a fact: *the mound would not be left alone.*

Therefore there was only one answer: it had to be excavated now, carefully, under competent supervision, so that its record of this tribe, and therefore of the Indians of this section of the country, could be salvaged. Perhaps ideally it would have been better to leave it alone, untouched—but that was not a viable choice.

What was found in that mound? Several hundred burials, perhaps the largest collection of early sixteenth-century Spanish artifacts associated with the North American Indians, and convincing evidence that these natives had had contact with the explorer Hernando de Soto. The face of local archaeology was significantly changed. Much more is now known about these obscure Florida Indians than was available before. There is a longer discussion of such matters in the Author's Note at the end of this book.

But what of the people buried there? These folk lived and died, and their demise as shown by the evidence of the mound was tragic. What was their personal story? We can never know precisely, but this novel represents one conjecture. This is a vision of the living folk of the region, whose bones were found in Tatham Mound. It could have happened this way.

We do not know the language of the Tocobaga Indians, but assume it was affiliated with the large Timucuan group to its immediate north. For convenience, the language employed to tell this story is modern, with place names usually rendered as their meanings. Thus, for example, the Withlacoochee River is the Little Big River. Where the Indian concepts do not align perfectly with ours, approximations or vernacular terms are used, though this may seem anachronistic. The point is that these were living, feeling human beings whose vanished culture is worthy of respect, as is our own. We honor them to the best of our ability by coming to know and understand them, and by living for the time of this novel in their world. Let them not be completely unknown or forgotten.

CHAPTER 1

SPIRIT

I am the Tale Teller. I am dying. But before I join the realm of the spirits, I must tell my final tales, that those I love who are buried here may be properly introduced.

O Spirit of the Mound, I begin with you, for it was you who warned me, you who would have saved us, had I been able to honor your stricture. You were right, you spoke truly, and now the grief you prophesied has come to pass. I always believed you; it was only my failing as a man, my grievous misunderstanding, that prevented me from doing what you urged. How great is my grief for that failure, for now those I love are dead, when they should have lived. I beg you to welcome their spirits, for they are blameless. Only I am guilty, and only my bones will not join yours, and only my spirit will be lost. The wild animals will drag my body away and defile it. In this way I will pay for my failure, as I deserve. But the others are worthy, O Spirit, and they should be fit company for you, though they died too soon.

I count on my hands, my fingers, the winters since we met: it was ten, and ten more, and ten more, and five more. I was a stripling of ten and five winters, in quest of my manhood. I still used my childhood name, for I had not yet earned a worthy title. How long ago that seems, how far away, though time is as nothing to the spirit realm and this is the very place it happened. It is as though it was a different person, that innocent youth; I am embarrassed for him, for his naiveté, his innocence, and his ignorance. I must speak of him as if he were another person, but you will know the truth, O Spirit of the Mound.

You will know it as you have always known it. I must tell it, and make known the tragedy his error allowed, for my words are all I have remaining to give. Then my onus will be abated, and you will remember me though my spirit is gone. You will know the good people I have known and loved, not only here but elsewhere. I do not ask your forgiveness, only that you listen.

O Spirit, here is how it started, when Hotfoot came to meet you.

They had laughed when the child ventured onto the sun-heated sand, to dance madly as his bare feet burned, and ran mincingly back to his mother, crying. Hotfoot, they called him, and that became his youth-name. Hotfoot, who had not heeded his mother's warning, and had strayed too far. It was derisive, yet also apt, for he grew to be swift on his feet, and to wander far, and to get into much trouble, even as he had started.

When he was fifteen winters old he was the fastest runner of the village. No one could catch him, not even grown warriors. When they held contests among the clans, it was the Eagle Clan who won, because of Hotfoot. He could maintain it too, for he liked to run, and the more he did it the farther he was able to go without tiring. He became a messenger between villages as far as a day distant, for he could reach them and return in the time it took another to walk there. Sometimes he was several days away, and had contact with tribes that spoke other tongues. He had proved as swift with language as with his feet, and had learned the tongues of the Cale to the north and the Calusa to the south. Not perfectly, but well enough to get by, with the help of sign language and pictographs in the sand.

But he was not yet a man, and that was an increasingly grievous fault. He was not entitled to wear body paint or to speak at a ceremony. He wore his hair loose, in the manner of a woman, not permitted to tie it back in the manner of a man. He could not marry or, indeed, have a woman for sex, because none would touch a boy. With manhood several would be available; they had ways of letting him know. But mostly it was pride: he needed the status of a man.

That was why he teamed up with Woodpecker and Alligator

to make their first genuine war-party raid. They had of course indulged in many mock raids; virtually the whole of a male's youth consisted of just such games. First they had learned to hunt the simplest creatures, bringing down squirrels with their small arrows, and worked their way over the years up to deer. Then they had approached the most difficult prey: man. They matched clan against clan, and threatened each other fiercely, but never seriously, for the clans were all parts of the great tribe of the Toco. They believed they were ready, and they were certainly eager. They had gone to Chief Slay-Bear for permission, and it had been granted.

For this the clans united, and the respect they had learned for each other in the mock contests could be acknowledged in this real one. For courtesy, and the sharing of a taste of adult honor, they referred to each other by their clan names. Thus Woodpecker, rather than the child-name that would soon be lost, and Alligator, and Eagle rather than Hotfoot. This gave them each a sense of importance and responsibility, for it was not merely themselves they represented, but the honor of their clans. The youths of the other clans, the Rattlesnake, Tortoise, Deer, Bear, and Panther, would be envious of the honor these three won this day. Hotfoot's father was a Rattlesnake, but he would not begrudge the Eagle Clan this day, though in any tribal function he would support his own. A person's clan was determined by that of the mother, and no one could marry into his own clan, for all were brothers and sisters in name. Thus every father had to watch the success of his son without applause, but with secret pride.

Now they were crossing the Little Big River in their canoe, to Cale territory. It would have been extremely bad form to raid an affiliated village, but the river was the cultural and political boundary between tribes. The Cale were suitable enemies; they spoke a different tongue, used different pottery, and made similar raids into Toco territory. Therefore it was only fitting that prior grievances be redressed. He was not on business now, as a messenger, so had no protection from assault, and no need to honor any truce.

They had prepared with suitable ceremony, performing the Preparation Dance, enduring an overnight vigil, drinking and vomiting the White Drink to purify themselves, fasting,

and accepting the painful ritual scratching on their forearms
and calves without flinching. But that was merely the preparation; manhood came only with verified heroism in war. They
would serve as witnesses for each other, and were bound to
tell the truth; to do otherwise was to risk correction by the
spirits, and bring shame not only on them, but on their families
for rearing them, and on their clans, and on their village, and
on their tribe. To deceive an enemy was a great feat, but to
deceive a friend was evil.

Now they were dressed in their loincloths with leggings to
enable them to get through the thorny brush, and armed with
bows, arrows, and knives. Spears were too long and clumsy
to carry on a secret raid; if they could not strike at arrow distance, or defend themselves with their knives, then they were
not fit to be warriors. They had made their bows themselves,
finding the best saplings, molding them in the hot ashes of a
fire, carving them carefully and stringing them with deer ten-
dons, and had cut their own arrows similarly. They had good
knives, their stone blades chipped from the quarry to the west
and bound to secure wood handles. But Hotfoot hoped he
would not have to use his knife, because that would mean he
was within reach of an enemy warrior's knife, and he could be
stabbed and die even if he managed to kill the man. He hoped
that this thought did not make him a coward. The priest had
told them that fear was natural, but that a warrior did not yield
to it. So now his fear was not so much of getting hurt or killed,
but of yielding to fear itself and disqualifying himself as a warrior. Humiliation was worse than death: as a child he had
doubted, but now he knew.

Hotfoot had the lead paddle, and Alligator the rear; both
stroked swiftly and silently as Woodpecker knelt in the center,
bow ready, watching for enemies. If they were careless they
might be attacked before they had a chance to strike, or the
enemy might wait and steal their dugout canoe, so that when
they returned they would be stranded. Either would be disaster. Their objective was to come upon the enemy unobserved,
strike, and escape unscathed, leaving behind only the Toco
arrows they used. Those arrows would make clear what tribe
had inflicted this devastation on the Cale, completing the honor
for the raiders and the dishonor for the victims.

Hotfoot had been nervous during the vigil, and probably would not have been hungry even if he were not fasting. So many things could go wrong! But as he started out on the mission he felt only excitement. Now his mood was level and grim: he intended to accomplish his heroism no matter what the cost, and be a man at last. He knew his companions felt the same.

They had justification, of course. The Cale had severely wounded an elder tribesman of Atafi half a moon before, and gotten away cleanly. Retribution was required, and the three of them had volunteered to achieve it. To their surprise, this mission had been granted. Perhaps it was because most of the men were currently hunting deer, to get a supply of flesh for drying and smoking. More likely it was because the elders judged it was time for these boys to become men.

The crossing was uneventful. No enemy spied them. Hotfoot had not entirely trusted Woodpecker's alertness; he had peered closely at the riverbank between paddle strokes, verifying it. He had glanced into the dawn sky too, to make sure no bird of prey passed over them; that would have been a sure signal of mischief, unless it was an eagle. But all was well.

They coasted in to their landing at a spot hidden by over-hanging palmetto. They stepped out singly, and drew the canoe up, hiding it under old palmetto fronds. It was important that it be both invisible to outsiders and ready for instant launching, for the pursuit could be close on their return.

Now they set out on foot toward the nearest Cale village. They knew its location because it was on the trade route, as was their own town of Atafi. They were not following the trade path now, for that would have invited discovery. Instead they cut through the oak hammocks, stepping carefully so as to leave little or no trace.

But the hammocks were like islands in the swampy region, and they had to venture through marsh and even some stand-ing water. This was nervous business because of the poisonous water snakes, but they moved slowly, made it through, and stepped out without leaving footprints. Then higher ground, and a deer trail, so progress was easier.

But they did not approach the village closely. Instead they circled around it. It would be foolish to raid the closest one;

pursuit would be too certain and swift. They had to raid a more distant one that did not anticipate this, and whose inhabitants would at first be confused. By the time the Cale oriented, the raiders could be far away, and perhaps would never be tracked. To get away cleanly—that was the ideal.

They scouted their route more carefully as they drew closer to their objective. Haste was not necessary; they took the time required to spy out the best unobvious trail so that they would know it and use it without hesitation on the return, while the pursuers floundered. The ideal was a network of trails with divides and dead ends that would cause the pursuers to get lost following them. Since this was enemy territory, they had to use what existed, but could change from one trail to another according to a pattern they decided on. That way they could move rapidly on trails, instead of slowly through brush and brambles, while the pursuers could not do the same for fear of losing trace of them. The thoroughness with which they prepared for their escape was critical, because they were on man's business now. All that they had rehearsed in play, all their lives, was about to be put to the proof. Any mistake could forever deny them the manhood they sought, because those who were caught raiding were enslaved or killed. The same was true for the Cale raiders caught by the Toco.

There was one other complication: it was now late afternoon. They would have to make their raid and escape by night. That would help them hide, but would also make it easier for them to lose their way. This would be a test of their ability to retrace their set route—in changed circumstances.

Now Hotfoot got nervous again. They had undertaken the mission, and they had reached the vicinity of the village. What now? They could not simply charge in and start clubbing enemy warriors; they would be overwhelmed in short order.

"We'll ambush the first warrior to use this path," Woodpecker said as they spied a heavily traveled trail. "Then we'll kill any who pursue."

Woodpecker was the nominal leader of this party, being sixteen winters old. If any of them did not get home, it would be his responsibility. He had made his decision; now they would discover whether it was good.

Almost immediately someone came. They drew on their

bows—but it was only a child, a naked little girl, running toward the village with her hair flying back. She was not fair
game, and they let her pass. She never knew they were there,
for they were well concealed.

Then a warrior came, a grizzled veteran, leading his old woman. Woodpecker was entitled to the first shot. He loosed his
arrow—and it flew true. It caught the man in the left shoulder.

The warrior grunted and staggered. The woman screamed.

But the man was only wounded; the shot had not killed him.
That meant that Alligator had the next turn. He fired—but the
warrior was twisting forward and down in his agony, and the
arrow missed. Meanwhile there were answering shouts; the woman's scream had alerted the people of the village. In a moment
the warriors would be here.

The three boys knew what to do. They fled. They had drawn
blood, and that was the most they could hope for. Now they
had to get away, before their own blood was spilled.

They ducked down and followed their escape route, which
was the one they had scouted on their way in. In their games
of youth they had learned to remember the details of landscape
and vegetation well, so that it was natural to retrace any trail,
and Woodpecker was especially good at this. Behind them, the
cry intensified; there were whoops as the Cale warriors arrived
on the scene and recognized the arrows.

At first the three of them gained, exactly as planned; the
confusion of the Cale worked to their advantage. With the favor
of the spirits they would get so far ahead that the pursuit would
never get close.

They lacked that favor. Cale warriors were spreading swiftly
out, cutting off their escape. Hotfoot could hear them; they
were not bothering to be quiet. They were forming a line that
crossed the marked route.

There seemed to be three choices: duck down and hide,
hoping the Cale would not spy them before dark; proceed forward, hoping to slip past the line of enemies; or make a mad
charge for it before the line was tight. All three were dangerous,
because the Cale were now aroused and alert and had a fair
notion where the fugitives lurked.

Woodpecker elected to try the first. This was not cowardice,
but a sensible appraisal of their chances; it would be their vic-

tory if they escaped undetected. If they were found, they could still make their break for home. He ducked below palmetto fronds, disappearing into the thicket. The others followed. In a moment they were lying together, absolutely quiet, while the Cale closed in.

Soon a warrior came close, peering this way and that. There seemed to be little chance that he would overlook their hiding place. Indeed, the moment he spied the palmetto clump he strode directly toward it, his war club ready.

It was Hotfoot's turn. He had his bow ready, held horizontally at ground level, the arrow nocked. It was a technique he had practiced; he could shoot an arrow accurately from this position. The point quivered, and Hotfoot realized how nervous he was. He didn't want to do this! But he had to. Slowly he drew back the string, lifting the point. If the warrior turned aside and passed beyond them, then there would be an excellent excuse not to shoot. It was better to escape detection than to start the commotion all over.

The warrior did not pass. He poked at the fronds with his club, his head moving so that he could see beyond them. No chance now to escape unnoticed!

Hotfoot lifted the point and loosed his arrow at point-blank range. It happened before he realized it was going to. It was as if his arms and hands belonged to someone else, someone with twice the nerve he could ever have. The arrow passed through the warrior's neck. The man did not cry out; he could not, for it was his voice the arrow had transfixed. He simply collapsed, looking surprised.

"I never saw a neater kill!" Woodpecker breathed, awed. "No sound at all!" He was speaking of animal kills, of course; none of them had seen a warrior die in battle before.

Hotfoot did not answer. He was stunned. He had killed squirrels and rabbits, and was reckoned to have a good arm for the bow. But this was a *man*! He had known this was no game excursion they were on, but still had not until this moment appreciated the full seriousness of it.

"Take his scalp!" Alligator said.

Hotfoot just stared at the dead man, making no move. *The death of a man!*

"We must run," Woodpecker whispered. "They'll find him soon. No time for the scalp."

They moved out, silently, into the closing dusk. But Hotfoot was in a kind of trance, seeing only that warrior, the arrow through his neck, his eyes widening as he sank down. There was no glory in this kill, only horror. How could he have done it? Why couldn't he have missed, as Alligator had, or hit the shoulder, as Woodpecker had?

Because the man would have cried out, and attacked them, and then they would have had to try to kill him more messily, and if they had succeeded, by that time the other Cale would have been there, and that would have been all. He had had to do it; he knew that. Yet still he was appalled.

In this numbed time of flight and thought, Hotfoot knew that he was no warrior. Woodpecker had covered for him, giving him a pretext not to take the scalp, though of course he should have. None of them had experience in cutting heads; they would have bungled it, and indeed, they had no time. But it was more than that. Hotfoot knew with absolute certainty that he never wanted to kill again. *That* was why he was no warrior.

They gained distance, because the Cale did not at first discover the death of their warrior. They assumed that no outcry meant no discovery, so the rest were still searching their own sections of the closing net. That was good fortune for the raiders, for every moment that passed now made escape more likely. It was almost impossible to track fugitives in darkness, if the fugitives had any skill at all in silent travel.

Now they heard the outcry behind as the Cale discovered the slain warrior. But the night was near; as long as they kept quiet, they were safe.

The problem was that the same factors that inhibited the pursuit also inhibited the three of them. They could no longer see the signs they had left, or judge the lay of the land they had noted. What had been reasonably familiar was now unfamiliar. Also, the creatures of the night were emerging, including mosquitoes. The biting blackflies of day could be squeezed off when they alighted; they tended to come in swarms, and lost interest when motion stopped. But mosqui-

toes were inexorable, and invisible in the dark. The three of
them had put on no fish oil to repel these, because its odor
would give away their location. Unfortunately, the bloodsuck-
ers had no trouble locating them.

They kept moving, regardless. Their progress became noisier
as they made missteps, and they blundered into brush and
muck, surely leaving a trail that would be obvious by daylight.
But they knew that the pursuers would make similar noise,
unless they used familiar paths.

"Let's use the paths!" Hotfoot urged. "We can move faster
and quieter, and that is less risk than this."

"But they'll be watching the paths!" Woodpecker protested.

"Not if they're searching for us in the brush. They won't
expect us on the paths."

Woodpecker considered a moment, then agreed. They cut
across to the nearest established path, paused to listen for pursuit, then got on it. They were alone; either the Cale had given
up the pursuit, or they were not in this vicinity.

This helped greatly. They proceeded at almost daytime ve-
locity, for there was no danger of going astray here. In fact
they were now traveling faster than they had by day, for they
were no longer establishing an escape route.

They reached the river. Now they had to cut through the
brush again, for their canoe was hidden well away from the
regular path. This slowed them down, for the thickest of the vegetation was near the river. There were brambles and dense
thickets, and the ground was marshy. They feared for snakes
and alligators. But they were getting close to their canoe, and
once they recovered that, they would have an easy time getting
the rest of the way back to Atafi.

But they couldn't find it in the dark. They ranged back and
forth along the slushy bank, searching for the particular palmetto thicket they had used, but they had hidden the canoe
too well. In the night they were baffled.

Finally they consulted, and decided to wait for dawn, when
they should be able to spot it readily. They took turns sitting
guard, one always alert while two slept.

Now Hotfoot became thoroughly aware of the incidental injuries he had taken: the scratches that were not of the ritual
preparation, the insect bites, the bruises from stumbling in the

darkness. He was also hungry, for he had not eaten in a day and two nights, and tired, for he had not rested in that time either. The excitement that had sustained him on the mission was now exhausted. He was not sleepy, just phenomenally weary.

But the worst thing was the image of the slain warrior, the arrow through his neck. That man's spirit was surely orienting on Hotfoot now, seeking retribution. The living men could be avoided, if one was clever enough, but not the spirits of the dead. The spirits could only be diverted by the intercession of a priest—but until Hotfoot got home, the priest could not intercede. He was vulnerable now. The horror of his action rose like a dark mass before him, seeming to take animate form, and he was afraid. Afraid because of his coming shame. Because he was no true warrior, having no joy of killing. Too late, he had learned that he was a coward.

But the spirit did not attack immediately. At least, not tangibly. That was not the way of spirits, though. They did not make physical mischief, they acted more subtly. They seeped into the body of the offender, entering through his nostrils, his mouth, his anus, and spreading out within, taking time to choose their targets. Often it was the joints, which slowly coalesced, so that they operated only with decreasing range and increasing pain, making a cripple of a man without leaving a mark on him. Sometimes it was more subtle yet, so that he sickened and died, and no priest could cure him. One could never be sure that a malignant spirit had not intruded; one had to be always on guard against it, and free of pollution. Hotfoot knew that he was not free; he was now an easy target for the spirit's wrath.

Dawn came, and he gazed about, for his watch had been last. Now the locale became increasingly familiar; they were not far at all from the place they sought. Had the night not changed things so much, they should readily have found their canoe.

The others stirred. Silently, Hotfoot indicated the direction, and they nodded.

They moved to it, and it was there, exactly as they had left it. Their hiding place had been secure—almost too secure. Next time, they would be sure to memorize the position in such a way that they could find it by night as well as by day!

They launched the canoe and climbed carefully into it. Alligator took the rear paddle this time, and Hotfoot the lead, while Woodpecker knelt in the center as before. They would trade off at intervals, for now they were tired and would be traveling upstream.

They glided into the center, and beyond, seeking the familiar channel that lacked the main current. The Little Big River was gentle, easy to ride, but still it was pointless to oppose the current unnecessarily.

The river narrowed—and disaster struck. Abruptly a canoe shot out from the bank ahead, to intercept them. It carried six Cale warriors. The Cale had been watching the river—as the three of them should have anticipated.

Immediately Hotfoot and Alligator spun the canoe about, heading downstream, stroking with suddenly renewed strength. But the Cale craft followed, and it had four paddlers. It was overhauling them rapidly.

"Shore!" Woodpecker snapped. Indeed, they were already turning to get to it; it was their only chance to escape.

They cut close to the dense foliage of the bank, heedless of whatever landing they might make. On land they would have a chance to hide, to lose themselves in the thickets. This was Toco territory; the war party would not dare remain long, for fear of discovery by Toco warriors.

The canoe crashed into an overhanging oak branch—and Hotfoot felt a stunning blow to his left shoulder. His left arm went numb, and his hand lost its hold on the paddle. It didn't matter; he had to scramble out of the canoe as it halted, and splash to the shore behind the other two.

Alligator and Woodpecker were fighting their way to land as the enemy canoe came close. An arrow whistled past Hotfoot's head to graze Woodpecker's thigh. Woodpecker seemed not to notice it as he scrambled through the brush. Then they were all through, and a screening of foliage protected their rear for the moment. The Cale would not shoot blindly; arrows were too precious to waste.

Alligator turned to speak to the others—and paused, staring at Hotfoot's shoulder. Hotfoot looked, and was amazed.

An arrow was projecting from his shoulder. The head was deep in the flesh, the shaft and feathers behind. That was the blow he had felt!

"Hold him!" Woodpecker whispered.

Wordlessly, Alligator grabbed Hotfoot from the front, clasping him in an embrace that held him anchored. Hotfoot clenched his teeth and stood still, not resisting, knowing what was coming. He could not afford to make a sound, for that would show unmanly weakness, and could attract the Cale.

There was a wrench, and a terrible flare of pain. Woodpecker was yanking the arrow out, as he had to, but it wasn't coming readily. It tore at the muscle and sinew, the agony of it radiating out through Hotfoot's whole body. He clenched his teeth, making no sound, though all his world was agony. Then the arrow snapped.

Woodpecker held the shaft up. It had broken off, leaving the arrowhead embedded. Hotfoot knew that was bad; it meant the malignant Cale spirit of the arrow remained in him, and it would surely cause him much grief.

As the surge of pain abated, he felt the wetness on his back, and knew it was his blood flowing down. That, too, was bad, for it was good blood that leaked from this region, not bad blood.

Now there was a clamor behind. The Cale were landing!

The three ran, Woodpecker leading the way, weaving through the brush. But Hotfoot found that he could not keep the pace; his shoulder was throbbing and his feet were tiring.

In a moment Woodpecker realized what the problem was. The wound was weakening Hotfoot. "Hide," he said. "We will lead them away from you."

"They will follow the blood," Alligator pointed out.

Woodpecker scooped his hand along Hotfoot's back, soaking it in warm blood. "I will lead them with blood!" Then he was away, his hand extended, the blood dripping from it.

Hotfoot stumbled to the side, hunched over so that more blood would not drip, and crawled between low palmetto fronds. As he heard the Cale charging, he stretched out under the fronds, facedown, his left arm dragging. If the ruse worked, he would be safe; if not . . .

It worked. The Cale warriors paused only to inspect the blood at the spot where the three had stopped, then charged on after the drops Woodpecker had planted.

But Hotfoot knew he had to move on, because it would not take long for the Cale to realize that they now pursued only two, and that the blood had stopped. They could come back, rechecking the trail, and then they would find the offshoot. They would be after Hotfoot, and he could not outrun them.

Indeed, he could hardly run at all now. He hauled himself to his feet, and almost collapsed. He staggered on, away from the direction of the other path. He knew he would have to stop soon. He was defenseless, for he had lost his bow and arrows in the chase. Where could he go, where he would not be followed?

Here.

He gazed blearily about, trying to identify what he had heard. Who had called? Had he really heard anything?

Then he realized that he was close to the ancient holy place, where youths like him never went. The spirits of the dead were here, guarding their burial ground. There would be terrible retribution against almost any living person who defiled this site. Only a priest could come here.

Yet he had heard a call. Where could it have come from, except here?

Was he about to die, and the spirits knew this? But he was a mere stripling, a boy, not worthy to share their habitat. They should have only contempt for him.

No. He was now a man. He had made his first kill, and received his first serious wound. If he died of it, he died a man, even though he had not yet been awarded a man's name. The spirits would know that. They did not make mistakes; they knew who was worthy and who was not.

He staggered on toward the low mound, knowing where it was. The scene seemed to be tilting crazily, and the trees were whirling around him, but somehow he kept his feet until the sacred hill was there.

It was not high, only up to his belly, but it spread out widely. It was just a small rise, overgrown with brush and small trees, undisturbed. But everyone knew what it was. No one ever confused a burial site.

Hotfoot felt his consciousness fading. "O spirits of the mound," he gasped. "I come to you as a supplicant. Accept—"

Then he fell, his invocation unfinished. He lay sprawled on the mound, the light of the day dimming in his awareness.

Hotfoot never moved, but somehow he saw. A man was standing over him, looking down at his still form.

"Who are you?" Hotfoot asked without speaking.

"Do you address your elders thus?" the man demanded in the same manner.

Then Hotfoot knew that this was no mortal man. "I abase myself," he said. "O Spirit of the Mound, I apologize abjectly for this intrusion, and beg your indulgence, for I cannot rouse my body. I am Hotfoot, a boy of the Eagle Clan of Toco Atafi."

"A boy? Do not seek to deceive me thus! You have made your first kill."

"It was only in desperation. I take no joy in it. I am sickened; I wish I had missed. I am no warrior."

The Spirit considered. "You judge yourself too harshly. No sensible man truly joys in killing; he does it because he must, as you did. You are a man; you will assume the title of a warrior, and be a credit to the Eagle Clan."

"O honored Spirit, I think not, for I am dying. But if it is enough for you to accept me here, then I shall be satisfied."

"I am Dead Eagle, chief spirit of this mound," the man said. "I am of the Eagle Clan, and your ancestor. I do not accept you here, for you must not yet die."

Hotfoot received this news with confusion. "You are of my clan, but you refuse to let me be here?"

"I will accept you here only when your mission is complete."

"My mission?"

Dead Eagle nodded. Hotfoot saw this, though his face was to the ground. "There is a terrible danger coming. You must warn the living, and seek the means to avoid it. Only when you succeed in this may you join us here."

"O Spirit, what danger is this?"

"I do not know its nature, for I can foresee only imperfectly with the quartz crystal. The threat is too great and distant for such magic. It can only be accurately seen with the most potent crystal of all, the Ulunsuti, the great blazing transparent diamond on the forehead of the Uktena."

"The Uktena!" Hotfoot cried, appalled. "The terrible snake!"

"The same," Dead Eagle agreed. "You must go to the monster, and take the crystal, and use the crystal to see the exact nature of the threat. Then you will be able to warn your tribe, which is our tribe too, and to devise some stratagem to counter it. Then you may die and join us here."

"It is too much!" Hotfoot protested. "I am only a stripling, I am afraid, it is beyond my power! I am a coward. Even to see the Uktena as it sleeps is death to a hunter's family! It is almost impossible to wound the monster, and only a great hero can kill it and take the Ulunsuti! I would be terrified and flee, shaming myself and my tribe, accomplishing nothing."

Dead Eagle's visage clouded. "Make no excuses, warrior! You are of the Eagle Clan! I put my mark on you, and I take from you your fear; never while you live will you experience it. Accept the mission, and do not return until it is done." He reached down, and his hand passed through Hotfoot's injured shoulder.

Abruptly the fear was gone. "I accept the mission, O Spirit," Hotfoot said. "I will not dishonor you." Then his consciousness faded again.

CHAPTER 2

⚛

TRADER

O Spirit of the Mound, I have told you of the stripling Hotfoot who came to you so long ago, whose fear you took and to whom you gave the quest for the Ulunsuti. Now I will tell how he started that quest, and how the proof was made of his loss of fear, and of the girl he met who was to change his life. Already your wisdom was manifesting, O Spirit!

He woke again within his own lodge; he recognized the individual smell of it immediately. He was on a raised pallet of pine needles, his head on a cushion of moss. The heat of the small cooking fire warmed his right side, and the aromas of the smoke and the pot were comforting.

As he stirred, his mother heard and came immediately. "Do you know me, my son?" she asked, her voice anxious.

"I know you, my mother," he said weakly.

For a moment she just held his hand and gazed at him. But he felt the emotion in her, and knew that his survival had been uncertain. He could guess what had happened: the other boys had returned to the village and told of his injury, and warriors had come to search for him, and had traced his trail to the mound. They had carried him back, but he must have seemed dead, for he had no awareness of anything between his communion with Dead Eagle and this moment.

The Spirit of the Mound had saved his life, for the sake of the mission. Otherwise he surely would have died.

His mother fed him soup and acorn bread, and his strength returned. The priest came to the lodge, and was pleased to see

that his curative dance had worked. Hotfoot did not have the
heart to tell him that his recovery owed more to Dead Eagle
than to the dance, for the decision had been made before his
body was recovered.

Woodpecker and Alligator came, explaining that they had
been unable to double back because of the pursuit, but that
they had been successful in leading the Cale war party so far
afield that Hotfoot had been forgotten. Then the Atafi warriors
had emerged, and it had been the Cale's turn to retreat. "And
we told of your heroism," Woodpecker said eagerly. "How you
slew that warrior with a single arrow through the throat!"

As with the priest, he lacked the will to tell them that he
took no pride in that shot. He confirmed their own heroism,
bearing witness to the manly deeds they had done, especially
in leading the Cale away from him. There seemed no point in
telling about the protection the Spirit of the Mound had given
him, as that would only diminish their accomplishment. He
was glad enough to be alive!

But there were two things that remained from the experience,
that changed his life in ways that none of them had anticipated.
The first was immediate and obvious: his left arm no longer
functioned fully. His uncle of the Eagle Clan had drawn out
the arrowhead and stanched the bleeding, but the damage had
been done. The pain gradually subsided, but his shoulder was
immobile. He could still flex his elbow, and his hand worked
perfectly, but his upper arm was locked against his side. It was
no longer possible for him to use a bow or to do anything that
required the extending of that arm. The Spirit of the Cale warrior he had killed had achieved its vengeance by destroying his
ability ever to kill again with that weapon.

The second was the mission that Dead Eagle had given him.
He had to find the Ulunsuti, the great transparent crystal. He
had to use it to avert the terrible danger to the tribe. But he
had no notion of how to go about such a quest. This question
preyed on his mind during his physical recovery. What was he
to do?

So it was that when he was able to go about again, and to
function as before, except for his arm, he sought the priest. "I
am to be a warrior now, but I have no stomach for it," he

confessed. "I want never to kill another man, and I have a mission whose pursuit baffles me. I need your counsel."

The priest stared at him and through him in the disconcerting way he had. "You met with the Spirit of the Mound," he said.

Hotfoot was startled. "How do you know that?"

"How could I not know? The mark of the dead is on you."

"What mark?"

The priest tapped him on the shoulder, just beyond the healing scar of his wound. "*This* mark. In the shape of a ragged eagle. Did you not know?"

Hotfoot was startled again. "I did not know. I thought it was only a scar." He twisted his neck to look, but could not get a clear view. Yet now he remembered: Dead Eagle had said that he put his mark on Hotfoot, when he took his fear.

"The mark of the dead," the priest repeated. "And you would be dead too, if the Spirit had not accepted you. No man could spend the night at that holy site and live, otherwise."

Hotfoot realized that it was true. He had defiled a holy place, and instead of being struck dead, he had been saved. "The Spirit Dead Eagle spoke to me, and gave me a mission. I am forbidden to return until it is done. But I do not know how to do it."

"And what did the Spirit take from you?" the priest asked cannily.

"Take from me? He gave me back my life!"

"What a spirit takes is always equivalent to what it gives. Dead Eagle gave you life; what did he take? That will suggest how you should proceed."

Hotfoot was flustered. "He took nothing! He only gave me my life and the mission, and said I should not return until it is done. I accepted, and now I must do it."

The priest considered. "What was the mission?"

"He said there is a terrible danger coming, and that I should warn the living and seek the means to avoid it. It can only be seen accurately with the Ulunsuti—"

"The great transparent crystal!" the priest exclaimed. "No one can find that! The monster snake would kill any who tried!"

"I told him that. I said I was afraid, but he said he would take my fear—" Hotfoot broke off, startled.

"Dead Eagle took your fear?"

"Yes. He said I would experience it no more while I lived. But—"

"So you are not afraid to seek the Uktena?"

"Well, not afraid, but I have no idea how—"

"Truly he means you to accomplish this mission! Only the bravest of men would dare undertake such a thing, knowing he will very likely die without success."

"But I am not brave! I never want to kill again!"

"And you with only one arm!" The priest shook his head. "The spirits have little regard for mortal weakness!"

"I was a fool to accept it," Hotfoot said. "But when he took my fear, I had no caution."

"When a spirit commands, no mortal man denies," the priest said. "Now it is clear: you will assume your warrior's name, and go on your mission. You must travel until you find the Ulunsuti, and bring it back and use it to see the danger."

"But where should I search for it?"

"No mortal man knows. But perhaps the spirits know. You must seek the places of the dead, the sacred mounds, and consult with them. This does not frighten you?"

"I do not wish to profane the sacred places!" Hotfoot protested.

"You fear to?"

"I have no fear, only proper respect."

"Then you have only to ask permission for the intrusion. If you truly have no fear, they will grant it, and perhaps will help you if you tell them who sent you."

Hotfoot brightened. "They will honor Dead Eagle's mission?"

"Surely they will. The spirits know their own. If they do not, show them your mark."

"Then this is what I shall do. I thank you, priest, for this good counsel."

"I could do no less, for one the spirits have honored." But he looked doubtful about the nature of the honor.

Next day they had the Ceremony of Manhood for the three youths. They had spent the night secluded from the village, remaining alert after purifying themselves with deep draughts

of the White Drink and vomiting. Now they stood forth in turn
as the elders spoke of their deeds and presented them with
their adult-names. Woodpecker became "Striker of Warriors"
because of his first shot at the Cale. Alligator became "Deceiver
of Enemies" because of his clever ruse with the blood, leading
the enemy away from his wounded companion. And Hotfoot
became "Throat Shot" because of his single kill; this was so
dramatic a deed that it needed no qualification.

Now the village turned to celebration, with feasting and
dancing and congratulations all around. The three were men
now, and could participate in the duties and privileges of men,
including the council deliberations and the smoking of the village pipe. On this day, Throat Shot's dead arm was a badge of
honor instead of a liability; it was a serious injury taken in battle.
But privately he wished that he had not experienced either the
killing or the injury; the one had wounded his self-esteem as
much as the other had wounded his body.

That night a maiden came to him, in his corner of the barracks
lodge used by unmarried males. It was Deer Eyes, whose eyes
were indeed great and dark. He had always found her attractive, but as a boy had been entitled to no sexual privileges.
Now he was a man, and she had come to complete his initiation.
She smelled of honey.

But the memory of the killing he had done was on him, and
of the loss of the use of his arm, and he was aware that he
would soon be leaving the tribe. He felt ashamed and unworthy. Deer Eyes was a nice girl; she could do better, and perhaps
share her favors with a warrior who might in due course marry
her. Throat Shot could not; he would be gone from the tribe a
long time. He doubted that it was right to do this with her.

He tried to explain this. She was surprised, then angry. "You
say you are too good for me?" she demanded.

"No, I am beneath your notice," he explained.

"You were waiting for some other girl?" Her mixed outrage
and injured pride were manifest.

"No, no other girl! I have always wanted you! But look at
me." He touched his slack left arm with his right hand.

"Or for a man, perhaps?"

This was worse yet. There were men who wore women's
clothes and lived in the way of women. He was definitely not

one of them! "No, no man! I want you! But I am unworthy."

She gazed at him for a moment, and he knew that if she simply refused to go, and lay down with him, he would forget his unworthiness and do what he desired. But then she turned away in disgust, and his chance was gone. He had managed to misplay this most important occasion, and generate only misunderstanding and anger. Why had he even opened his mouth?

No maiden came to him the following nights. The word had gotten around. They thought him less than a man now, and not because of his arm. Steeped in the shame of their belief, he slept alone. It was indeed best that he depart this tribe; he had won his honor as a warrior, only to lose it as a man.

At the next council meeting he spoke of his mission. The warriors nodded; he had been visited by a spirit, and had to do as that spirit directed. They all saw the twisted eagle mark on his shoulder. He must go in search of the Ulunsuti so that the terrible danger might be discovered and averted. It was a worthy mission. Especially, it was left unsaid, for one who could no longer effectively fight or hunt. His absence would cause the tribe no significant loss.

The Trader came down the Little Big River in his canoe. His hair was tied back in a roll, through which were struck two bones which were sharpened at the ends like arrowheads. He was of the Ais tribe, far to the east, but he was known to all the other tribes of the region, and none offered him harm. This was because he brought marvelous items for trade, and took the more common local items in exchange. The women, especially, eagerly awaited his arrival.

He did not speak the Toco tongue. On other trips he had had an assistant who translated during the bargaining; evidently something had happened. But they knew him, and sign language was enough for this purpose. They could see what he had, and show him what was here for trade.

This time he brought fine feather cloaks and small dishes made of copper, that strange and wonderful stone that was so unlike clay pottery. But copper was precious, and all they had was chert for arrowheads. The Trader looked at that with scorn; he had fine flint already.

But the Chief was clever. "I note you have no front paddler for your canoe, no carrier for portage," he said via sign language, pointing to the empty place in the canoe and making a gesture as of paddling, then of carrying. "We will trade the services of a man for that, all the way back to your home, for six of these feather cloaks." He pointed to a heavyset warrior, and to the cloaks.

The Trader was outraged. "These are the best cloaks in the mortal realm! See their fine craftsmanship! I had to pay dearly for each one!" His gestures indicated the cloaks, and he picked one up to spread it out and show its qualities. Every feather had been split at the base of the quill, and turned back in a loop so that it could be firmly fastened to the material. "Why should I let any go for the sake of another mouth to feed?" His glance at the warrior, who had obviously eaten well, was disdainful. No one wanted an appetite like that along!

The Chief pondered. "Then an interpreter, a man good at speaking." He made the gesture to his mouth. "Who will facilitate your bargaining, and also help portage."

Now the Trader was interested. "A slave?" He made the signal of subservience.

The Chief shook his head in negation. "No slave. A warrior. To translate and portage."

The Trader nodded. "One cloak."

Now it was the Chief's turn to laugh, and the warriors laughed with him. "Three cloaks."

"Two."

The Chief sighed. He had never been able to best the Trader in dealmaking. "Two," he agreed.

"Show me the man."

The Chief beckoned Throat Shot. He stepped forward.

"A mere stripling!" the Trader protested. "A child!" He made a gesture as of patting a toddler on the head.

"A man," the Chief insisted. "He killed a Cale warrior with one arrow through the throat." He jammed at his own throat with the point of an arrow.

The Trader gazed at Throat Shot with increasing respect. "He is that one? They speak of him there!" He was talking as he made the signals, and Throat Shot, who had been listening intently all along, was beginning to pick up the words. He remembered some he had learned from the Trader's prior visits, and was beginning to get a feel for the tongue. There were points of similarity between the Ais speech and the Cale, and the man was echoing his words with sign language, so that anyone could follow his gist.

"They came after him," the Chief said. "They shot him in the shoulder." Now he put his hand on Throat Shot, and turned him so that his scar tissue showed. "He can no longer fight, but he can speak."

The Trader was quick to pick up on the arm injury. "How can he paddle? How can he portage? This is no good!"

"I can paddle," Throat Shot said in the Trader's tongue.

The man, amazed to hear the words, watched as Throat Shot got into the canoe, lifted the paddle with his right hand, bent his left arm at the elbow, and caught it with his left hand. Then he moved the paddle in the air, in a vigorous paddling motion, his right arm doing most of the work. It was relatively clumsy, but he could do it. "I can carry too; my legs are good." He had to demonstrate for the legs, because he had not yet picked up that word.

"What tongues do you speak?"

"Cale, Toco, Calusan. Ais, if you teach me. I learn quickly." Words and gestures made that clear.

"You learned this much of Ais just by listening now?" This time the Trader's hands were still; he was deliberately avoiding sign language, so that only the speech counted.

Throat Shot caught his meaning as much by his attitude as by his words. He repeated them, changing only the first. "I learned this much of Ais just by listening now."

"You will serve me loyally while you travel with me?" the Trader asked in bad Cale. "No stealing, no cheating?"

"I am a warrior," Throat Shot replied in good Cale. "I do not steal or cheat. I will serve you loyally."

The Trader lifted two feather cloaks and gave them to the Chief. It was done.

The Trader spent the night at the village, enjoying the hospitality, now that the business had been completed. No one bothered his loaded canoe; it was a matter of honor to safeguard such things, once hospitality was extended, and of course everyone in the village wanted him to come again. He sat with them by the evening fire and told of his recent experiences in his stumbling Cale, and Throat Shot translated to Toco, already serving in the agreed capacity. Everyone loved to hear of far places and events.

Naturally a maiden visited the Trader in the evening, completing the hospitality. It was Deer Eyes. She made sure Throat Shot knew. He tried to show no emotion, but he felt it. She was wasting herself on a man she might never see again, for the sake of some trinket he might give her. She could as readily have wasted herself on Throat Shot. He had been a fool.

Yet he had done what he thought was right. All he could do now was to learn from the experience, and make sure he was never again such a fool. Dead Eagle had taken his fear, but his other emotions remained, and shame was the one that ruled him now.

In the morning they started off down the river. Throat Shot took the front, paddling only on the left side. But he paddled well; he had worked at this, adapting his technique so that he could travel by canoe alone if he had to, and it was easier with another.

He was prepared for a long journey, for he did not know when he would return. His pack contained parched acorn flour to make bread in case he could not find other food, a fishhook he had carved himself from a large hollow bird bone (after ruining three prior bones), a root digger stick, his stone knife, three stone spear points, a length of fiber cord, and a small firepot whose punk, buried in ash, hardly smoked at all. With these he could do well enough, when he had to.

But soon after they were beyond the village, the Trader called a halt. They let the canoe drift in the slow current. "Turn about," the Trader said. "Face me, Toco Atafi warrior."

Throat Shot shipped his paddle and turned, careful not to rock the canoe. It continued to move, drifting with the will of the spirit of the river. What did the man want?

"You agreed to serve me," the Trader said.

The words were becoming more familiar with repetition. Also, he had picked up a number during the evening, when the Trader had had to hunt for Cale terms he did not know;

he had expressed the concepts in Ais, and Throat Shot had offered words in Cale until the right one was found. Then Throat Shot knew the equivalent Ais word too. "Yes."

"Then you must know my language better. Before we reach the next village."

Throat Shot was happy to learn it. The Trader named every item that he had to trade, and Throat Shot repeated each name, getting it straight. He knew now that another person could not have done this; there were many terms, and he had to concentrate to fix them in his mind. Then the Trader covered key concepts, and a number of these related to terms Throat Shot already knew, so it was easier. The syntax of Ais was similar to that of Toco; once he had the words, the statements settled into place.

"It is good," the Trader said at last. "It was a fair trade." By that he meant that he believed he had gotten the best of it, because an apt translator was more valuable than two feather cloaks.

"Yes," Throat Shot said in Ais, still practicing to make it seem natural.

But the Trader was no fool. "Then why did Chief Atafi think he had done better?" he demanded.

Throat Shot, caught by surprise, did not answer.

"Remember, you promised to serve me," the Trader repeated. "The trade was made, it is done. Now you must tell me the truth. I will not be angry; I just want to know."

"I was going to travel," Throat Shot said. "I have a mission. I did not want to travel alone."

The Trader slapped his knee. "So I could have charged to take you! The Chief made me pay to do him a favor!" He was using the sign language again, helping Throat Shot to pick up the words.

"I will serve as agreed," Throat Shot said somewhat stiffly, still augmenting his own words with signs to cover concepts he did not yet know in Ais. "All the way to your home. We did not cheat you."

The Trader laughed. "No, you did not cheat me. No one cheats me; I am too clever. I knew there was a reason for you to go, but I did not know what that reason was. I feared it was to betray me to thieves."

"I gave my word!" Throat Shot said, annoyed.

"Yes, you did, and you did not lie. I know; I can tell. But Chief Atafi thought he was getting the better of me, and I had to know why. If he told an ambush party to watch for a warrior with one arm—"

"He would not! That would be an act of treachery!"

"I did not think he would. I have dealt with him before, and he has never betrayed me. But this time there was something hidden; he thought he was being clever, and I had to find out why. It is a cruel world, young warrior; a traveling man has to be alert. Not every person I meet is honorable."

Throat Shot nodded. "I have heard of dishonor. But never here."

"I will teach you how to spot it, if you wish to learn. It will help you serve me better. I will show you the signals of a man who is lying."

"I would be most pleased to learn that!" Throat Shot said. "But surely they are not like the sign language I know!"

"Surely they are not!" the Trader agreed with another laugh. "They are made with the eyes, the mouth, the body, and the liar does not know he is making them. You are clever, and you are honest; I will teach you what I would not teach another."

Throat Shot was inordinately pleased by this compliment. He tried to conceal this, but could tell from the Trader's smile that he was failing. He was in effect trying to lie, and could not.

"But I would like to know the nature of your mission," the Trader said. "Why must you travel? Is it to find a cure for your sick arm?"

"I must seek the Ulunsuti," Throat Shot said. "Only that powerful crystal can enable me to save my village from great harm." And he told the interested Trader the whole story, using Cale terms when he lacked Ais terms.

The Trader stared into the water. "You know that even the bravest warrior, with both arms and the finest weapons, would fear to approach the Uktena, for it is almost certain death. How can you, with one arm, dare to do this?"

"I have no fear of the Uktena, only a concern about failure," Throat Shot said. "Dead Eagle took away my fear. If I die, then I fail, and the danger comes upon my people. But I shall try to enlist the spirits of the dead to help me, and with their help perhaps I will succeed."

"I have never met a man with no fear."

"I have not made proof of it," Throat Shot admitted. "Perhaps I misunderstood the Spirit."

The Trader shrugged. "Surely the proof will come, in due course. Serve me well, and I will introduce you to another trader with whom I meet, who travels far to the north. Perhaps you will find what you seek there."

"I will serve you as well as I am able," Throat Shot said gratefully.

"Now we are ready to proceed. You surely know the folk of the next village."

"Yes, I have been there on occasion; they are Toco, like us, on this side of the river. What do you wish me to say to them?"

"Only translate what I tell you, and tell me what they say. I shall not cheat them, but I shall drive the best bargains I can. Remember that you serve me now, not them, though they be your friends."

"I shall remember," Throat Shot agreed.

They resumed rowing. It was now afternoon; they had eaten some bread during their long talk, and were refreshed. The canoe moved rapidly along.

They drew to shore near the village of Ibi Hica, the River Village, and the Trader put a conch to his mouth and blew a loud note to signal his presence. In a moment children were running down the path to the water, eager to guide the visitors in. This was much smaller than Atafi, but the people were compatible, and relations were good. That meant that the two villages did not raid each other. The river was the boundary; beyond was raiding territory.

In due course the trading commenced. The Trader brought out one of the beautiful feather cloaks. "What have you to trade for this fine item?" Throat Shot inquired of the Chief.

The Chief answered with a question. "You, with the bad arm—are you not Throat Shot, who killed the Cale warrior?"

"Yes. But now I am translating for the Trader, as he does not speak Toco."

"He needs slaves?"

"I am not a slave!" Throat Shot said indignantly. "I help him because I travel with him."

"But does he trade for slaves?"

Throat Shot put the question to the Trader. "Not ordinarily," the Trader replied cannily. "It depends on what is offered."

The Chief summoned a girl, by the look of her barely into her first moss skirt. Children normally ran naked except in cold weather; modesty was a quality limited to adolescents and adults. Her face was pretty, but her breasts and thighs were undeveloped. "Wren is a good girl," the Chief said. "But she is growing up, and we have no need for another woman in our tribe right now. Five cloaks for her."

The Trader squinted at Wren, then spoke in the Ais tongue. "Five of these valuable feather cloaks for one unnubile child? He must think me an idiot! One Cloak, if she's healthy."

Throat Shot spoke to the Chief in Toco: "The Trader appreciates your offer, but feels that you ask too much for one so young. One cloak, if she's healthy." He knew that the Trader knew enough of the language to follow the dialogue, but the bargaining could proceed faster and better this way.

"He must think me an idiot!" the Chief exclaimed, echoing the Trader's sentiment in the standard fashion. "This girl will soon be a fine young woman, beautiful, worth a phenomenal price as a bride. Look at her lines; she is without blemish. Four cloaks."

Throat Shot relayed this offer to the Trader, who had surely understood it, but preferred to pretend otherwise. "She probably eats like a bear," the Trader said. "Suppose she runs away before I can place her? Two cloaks."

Throat Shot relayed this to the Chief, who was already primed for the next offer. "She eats like a chickadee," he said. "She's a good, obedient girl who will not run away if not mistreated. Three cloaks."

The Trader considered this. It was obviously the figure they had both been heading for. "Ask her if she will run away."

Throat Shot addressed the girl in Toco. "Will you run away if you are not mistreated?"

She looked at him, but did not reply.

"Wren, you must answer," Throat Shot said. "Do you understand what the Trader wants?"

The girl shook her head as if confused.

Suddenly Throat Shot caught on. "She does not speak our language!" he exclaimed. "She is a captive from afar!"

"She is still a good girl!" the Chief countered. "She can grow corn, she can make pots, she can do the things a woman does."

"Find out what language she speaks," the Trader said.

Throat Shot addressed the girl in Cale, but she did not respond. Then he tried Calusan. At this she reacted, and answered, but haltingly.

"What is your native language?" he asked.

She said something completely alien, but with such finesse that it obviously was a language. This intrigued him; how could she speak a language whose like he had never before heard?

He relayed the information to the Trader, who again had picked it up pretty much for himself. "Ask her where her homeland is," the Trader said.

Throat Shot asked. The girl glanced at the sun, oriented, and pointed southwest. "Far, far," she said in Calusan.

"I'll take her," the Trader said. "Three feather cloaks." He brought them out and proffered them to the Chief.

Throat Shot was amazed. "But there *is* no tribe there!" he protested. "Far, far in that direction is the great sea!" He was also privately nettled that the child had fetched a better price than Throat Shot himself had. Of course, she was a slave, while he was giving service for only a limited time. Still . . .

"Don't you want to visit the local burial mound?" the Trader asked him. "Have the girl show you the way—and learn her language. I will bargain here for lesser trades. I can do that well enough in sign language. She may be more valuable than we know."

Still dazed by this sudden settlement, Throat Shot asked the Chief if he could be permitted to visit the mound, with the girl to show him where it was.

This surprised the Chief. "That is a holy place, and a dangerous place for the uninitiate. Why do you want to go there?"

"When I was wounded," Throat Shot explained, touching his bad shoulder, "I fell in a faint on an ancient mound, and the Spirit of the Mound spared my life so that I could go on a mission. He told me to inquire of other spirits."

"Are you not afraid to approach so hostile a region? They will not be the spirits of your own town there; they may do you mischief."

"I have no fear."

The Chief shrugged. "Then go; the girl knows the way."

"I thank you." Throat Shot turned to the girl. "Take me to the burial mound," he said carefully in Calusan.

Wren understood. Her eyes went round. "Bad spirits!"

"They will not harm us. Take me there."

Reluctantly, she led the way down the appropriate path. The mound was some distance away, so there was time to talk.

Throat Shot pointed to an oak tree. "Name?" he asked in Calusan.

"Oak," she said in the same language.

"No, in your tongue."

She glanced at him, surprised. She said a word in the strange language.

Throat Shot repeated it. That surprised her again.

He pointed to a palmetto clump. "Name?"

She gave it in her language, and he repeated it.

He pointed to himself. "Man. Name?"

She gave another strange word. She was quick enough to understand, and that was a good sign. She was no idiot, just a girl whose language was foreign.

He took her through the words for girl, arm, leg, hand, foot, head, eye, mouth, nose, and so on, getting the basics down. The strangeness of her tongue was a real challenge for him, but this was his talent: to remember tongues. Once he had a term, he remembered it. He also acquired the words for interaction, so that he was able to make simple sentences in her tongue. Her perplexity gradually became joy; it had been a long time since someone had spoken her tongue, even haltingly.

Then they were at the mound, and her fear returned. "Wait here," he said in her tongue. "Do not move; the spirits will not hurt you. I must talk to them."

Wren stopped, glad to advance no farther. He was already assured that she would not run away; the Trader had perhaps understood that she would not flee someone who tried to communicate with her.

He went to the mound. "O spirits of this mound," he intoned. "I come from Dead Eagle, and I beg your help. Will you speak to me?"

He waited, but there was no response. The spirits of this mound would not talk to him.

"I apologize for intruding on you," he said with regret. "I will not return."

He left the mound and walked to Wren, who stood staring at him. "You speak to the dead?" she asked, having to use the Calusan term for "bones" to convey the concept.

"The dead, yes," he agreed. "Name?"

She gave the name for the dead in her tongue.

"But they did not speak to me," he concluded. "The spirits speak only to whom they choose to. But I know they listened, because they did not try to harm either of us."

"Yes!" she agreed, relieved.

They returned to Ibi Hica, where the Trader was concluding his business. Then they were invited to share the hospitality of the village, as was the custom.

The Trader turned to Throat Shot. "She will not run away?" he asked in his own tongue.

"She will not run," Throat Shot agreed.

They spent the night, the Trader with a nubile girl of the village, Throat Shot in a separate house with Wren. It was now his job to watch her; if she fled it would be his responsibility. He was satisfied; they talked late in the darkness, exchanging words. He found in her a mind as quick as his own. He assured her early that warriors did not seek female favors of children; it seemed she had some doubt, but he did not pursue that aspect. She was after all a captive, and captives had no rights; she could have suffered anything. He preferred to assume she had not, without asking. She became increasingly friendly as she gained confidence in him, until he had to remind her that he served the Trader, and it was the Trader who would decide what to do with her. She would probably be traded away when a profitable opportunity came. That reminder seemed to sadden her, but it was necessary.

In the morning they emerged quickly and took care of routine needs: they washed in the river, scrubbed their bodies with fine sand, urinated, and reset their hair. They would not eat until noon, after getting a fair morning's traveling done. Wren fitted in perfectly, evidently quite satisfied to be traveling with these two men. The Trader led the way to the loaded canoe, which was undisturbed. He slid it into the water. About to step into it, he paused, dismayed. "Bad omen!" he muttered.

Throat Shot looked. There was a rattlesnake curled within the canoe, just waking from its sleep. Evidently it had crawled into the dry place for the night, and would move on when the day warmed.

"He means no harm," Throat Shot said. "The canoe is protected and warm. I will move him."

The Trader backed away, evidently thinking this was a joke. Wren stood her ground, but she was not as close to the canoe. Throat Shot leaned over and put out his right hand, slowly. "Brother rattlesnake, you are in our canoe," he said soothingly. "We do not begrudge it to you, but now we must travel downriver, and you would not wish to go there. Let me help you on your way." He put his hand on the snake, just behind the head, and lifted, gently.

The snake felt the warmth of his hand, and understood that this was not an attack. It was lethargic from its cooling of the night, and not eager for a quarrel with a creature the size of a man. It slithered forward, but not aggressively. Throat Shot let it slide, moving his hand to guide its head to the edge of the canoe where it still touched the land. When it saw the solid ground, it slid on beneath his hand, and soon was out of the canoe and moving gracefully into the brush.

"I bid you good hunting, brother rattlesnake," Throat Shot called. "We had no quarrel, and hope for none tomorrow."

He straightened up and turned to the others. Both the Trader and Wren were staring at him—and now the others of the village were there too, similarly astonished.

"He meant no harm," Throat Shot said, feeling defensive. "There was no reason to kill him. Indeed, I would not want either his spirit or my friends of the Rattlesnake Clan angry with me for doing such a thing."

The Trader recovered. "You are right," he said briskly. "It is a good job. We must be on our way." He checked the canoe carefully, then stepped into the rear. Throat Shot followed, stepping into the front, and then Wren stepped into the middle. They pushed off and started paddling.

The villagers were still standing silently, staring after them, as they moved out of sight of the village.

"You spoke truly," the Trader said. "You have no fear." He was evidently impressed.

"You picked up a rattlesnake!" Wren exclaimed. "And it didn't bite you!"

Then Throat Shot realized what he had done. In all his prior life he had been highly wary of poisonous snakes, as were all the folk he knew. Such snakes were like gods, and their presence could signal deep trouble, and even when it didn't, they remained dangerous. It had been his dread to tread on one by accident. Yet he had been conscious of none of that at the time; he had simply done what needed to be done. He had handled it as he would have handled a stranded burrowing tortoise, with concern for the welfare of a totem. Dead Eagle had indeed taken away his fear.

"Ibi Hica will never forget you," Wren said. "They thought you had been lucky in battle. Now they know how great a warrior you are."

"I am no warrior," Throat Shot said, shrugging his left shoulder to remind her of the arm. He suffered a surge of pain, and resolved not to do that again. "I do not like killing. I took the easy way out."

"You could have fetched a net, or poked it out with a long stick," Wren said.

"Brother rattlesnake would not have liked that." But she was right: any other person would have done it that way.

"You may not be a warrior," the Trader said. "But you are a man like no other. I would have paid all five cloaks for your service, had I known."

Throat Shot could make no answer. Now, in retrospect, he was amazed at this verification of what Dead Eagle had done. He had never doubted, yet he was surprised.

They continued downstream. Wren had nothing to do in the middle, and talked with Throat Shot in her own language, continuing to acquaint him with the words, while the Trader listened with approval. A talking girl was worth more than a mute one, and a smart one more than a stupid one. Also, she showed animation and prettiness when she spoke, and that, too, added to her value.

Throat Shot knew the thoughts of the Trader, and was not at ease with them, for Wren was rapidly becoming a person to him, rather than an item of trade. But what she told him was fascinating, and he couldn't help himself: he had to encourage her, and listen. The Trader required him to translate it periodically, and he did so to the best of his ability. The Trader, too, was interested, and it seemed not purely for commercial reason. His motive might differ from Throat Shot's, but he was interested in learning new things.

During the next several days, they moved down the river to the sea, traveling slowly, trading at every village. This was the Trader's main region for business, and he evidently enjoyed the hospitality of the villages. In this period Wren told them the story of her mother and herself. It was an amazing tale.

CHAPTER 3

❧

MAYA

O Spirit of the Mound, I have told you how the stripling Throat Shot began his journey at your behest, and made proof of the fear you took from him, and met the girl called Wren. Now I will tell you her history, as she told it to him, and as I remember it these three tens and five winters since. She told first of her mother, in her wonderful distant land, and then of herself, among the primitives. Finally she told of her impressions of Throat Shot himself, though it was at a later time that she did this. I put it together for you in the form of this tale, O Spirit, so as not to be tedious.

The Lady Zox was the daughter of the noble Jaguar Hide, and was the latest in a long line of beauteous women. Her body was exquisitely tattooed in the most devious and symbolic patterns, with only her fine breasts unmarked. Her front teeth were filed to sharp points. Her hair was so long it touched her knees even when intricately braided. She wore a richly woven dress and a necklace of ornate stone and shell so heavy that it bruised her shoulders. Precious gems were set in her pierced ears. She bathed daily at the public bath, and perfumed herself on the shoulders and breasts with fragrant oils. There was an irregular purple mark on her spine just above the buttocks of unusual color and definition, considered to be her most lovely aspect. She painted her face red, symbolic of blood. She always carried a few pretty flowers, and sniffed delicately from time to time. Even her sandals were of the highest-quality tapir hide.

She was without a doubt the most splendid woman of the region.

Indeed, this was no surprise, for her nobility extended beyond this state. Her mother was full Maya, from the capital city of Utatlan of the southern highlands, brought here as a signal of political favor and alliance. With her she had brought the culture of the highest class, and it showed in every aspect of her life. Her father was directly descended from the Toltec princes, but even he deferred to the enormous knowledge of the Maya. The Toltecs were the rulers, but the Mayan women had established their culture, subtly, steadily, until even the language was theirs. This was the true way of conquest, which the men did not understand.

But times were hard for her father and for the people of the State of Ceh Pech. They had suffered recent reverses in war, and many of them had been captured and taken for living sacrifice. They needed strength, and so the chief was forced to make an alliance with the barbarian Aztecs of far Mexico. That meant the marriage of a noble's daughter to an Aztec chief. The Lady Zox was selected for this honor because she was the youngest and most beautiful of those available.

But she was her father's only girl-child, and he had hoped for a better position for her. An alliance with one of the other Mayan states would have been excellent; one with the distant Aztecs might be good for the Maya people as a whole, but not necessarily for Ceh Pech or this family. So Jaguar Hide arranged for a delay. He bribed a trader from the great commercial center of Xicallanco to carry her away to a far Mayan city in disguise, where she would remain until some other bride was found for the Aztec. Then she could return, and a few well-placed bribes would make it all right.

Jaguar Hide had good reason for his caution. The Aztecs were comparatively new to civilization, and their manners were uncertain. They had in their early days been wife stealers, and now they made many thousands of human sacrifices each year. Such sacrifice was proper, of course, but it was best kept in proportion; the gods could hardly appreciate a horrendous mass of living hearts all at once. The Mayan priests were experts, but surely the Aztec priests were butchers who tried to make up in quantity what they lacked in quality. Who could know how many beating hearts they wasted by incorrect ritual?

For example, there was the story of the Aztec uncouthness in a former liaison. They had served as mercenaries to the more powerful tribes of their region, before they assumed dominance by expertise and treachery. They had displayed such valor in one such war that their sponsor proffered a boon. They asked for the daughter of the chieftain himself, so that through her they could fashion a more worthy lineage. Pleased with this request, the chieftain agreed, and sent to them the beautiful girl.

In due course the chieftain arrived with his entourage, gloriously garbed for the festive occasion of the wedding. It was then that he learned that the Aztecs had sacrificed the girl, cut out her beating heart, flayed her, and made her skin into a garment to drape over their high priest so that he might impersonate the Nature Goddess.

That had been an unfortunate move on the part of the Aztecs. The girl's father was most annoyed. Few of that group survived the bereaved chieftain's expression of that annoyance. But there were other Aztecs, and they grew in power until they were dominant. Now they could flay beautiful women when they chose, and they chose increasingly often. Jaguar Hide did not want to risk having his own daughter among them. Sacrifice was important and necessary, but there were limits.

Accordingly, Zox was spirited away before the liaison with the Aztec chief could be completed. What price her father might have paid for this device she never learned, for she never returned. The trader told her that he knew of no Mayan city where she would be safe from discovery, so he took her to a region no one would know of, across the sea to a strange, primitive land. And there, abruptly revealing his perfidy, he robbed her of her jewelry and fine shawl and sold her to the natives for a basket full of pretty conch shells.

Zox was stranded in this hostile land across the sea without even what remained of her clothing, for the Calusa savages quickly stole it. She knew no word of their tongue. But because she was the most beautiful woman they had seen, they did not mistreat her. She was made a concubine of the cacique. When she refused to indulge his sexual appetite voluntarily, he did not strike her, he simply did not feed her. It was not as if he lacked for women; he had several wives already, one of whom was his sister. He wanted to make Zox come to him and ask for what he desired of her. She had to live on only those scraps she could somehow find herself. She lost weight, and her beauty suffered. They fed her then, but only enough to keep her functioning, waiting for her to claim a better life by agreeing to please the chief. All this was done without verbal communication, for she refused to learn their primitive tongue, let alone speak it. She spoke only her own, civilized dialect, aloud and to herself. She kept her heritage fresh for the day when she should be rescued and returned to her father's domain. Surely he was looking for her now!

Finally the cacique gave up on her. He was no longer very interested in her as a concubine, for she had become extremely thin and dirty, and she refused to give him any hint of accommodation. He cut off her hair and traded her to a rival chieftain to the north, where life was more primitive.

There they were not as scrupulous. She was given to a warrior, who promptly raped her. She waited until he slept, then took his flint knife and tried to cut out his heart. Unfortunately, she was not strong enough or skilled enough to lift it beating from his chest; she only made a mess of his chest, splattering blood all around, and it took some time for him to die.

The folk thought her possessed of an evil spirit. No ordinary woman would stab a man simply because he exercised his sexual rights to her. They put her in charge of the priest, to exorcise the spirit. He performed his rituals, and she seemed to respond. Actually, she had realized that she was not suited for killing people; she had not liked the experience at all. Though she refused to speak the local dialect any more than she had the Calusan tongue, she was beginning to understand it. These folk were genuinely confused, and were trying to do what they understood to be right. It was also evident that if the treatment was not effective, they would kill her.

She began to eat. When the priest worked with her, she smiled at him. Each day they made a little more progress, and each day the flesh returned to her body, and her beauty re-manifested. By the time she was cured, the priest was thoroughly enamored of her.

But he did not seek to use her sexually, for that would have been an abuse of his office. He had to return her, cured, to the chieftain, though it was evident that he desired her. The chieftain then gave her back to the priest as a reward for his success—and perhaps also out of caution, for she might relapse and kill someone else.

Now the priest was free to indulge with her. He gazed at her, and she smiled at him, and went with him to his hut. Even so he hesitated, asking her whether she wished it, and she knew he would not force her. She had made her point, and was satisfied. She made him very happy, and she did not offer him any violence. He was a more important man than she might otherwise find herself with, and she had resolved to make the best of her situation until such time as her father was able to rescue her.

In the privacy of their home, she now spoke to him, in his language, showing that she had learned it well enough. But it was her desire that no other member of the tribe know this. She had ways of demonstrating her pleasure as well as her displeasure, as he well understood; he kept her secret, and was fittingly rewarded.

Thus it remained for some time.

In due course she bore him a baby. The priest was inordinately proud, for it demonstrated his manhood and proved that he had tamed the madwoman; it was known what she did to those who forced their attentions on her. The child was female, and tiny, like her, and beautiful, lacking only the purple mark on her spine. This birth, more than anything else, caused the women of the tribe to accept the Lady Zox: she had contributed to the strength of the tribe.

She named the girl Tzec, and lavished attention on her. But the call of necessary woman's work meant that she had to leave Tzec in the care of others at times. She still would not speak, to any outside the family, but her daughter grew up among the girls of the tribe, and she had no reservation about the language. Indeed, Tzec was an apt student, learning rapidly and well. But she concealed the full extent of her ability, in deference to her mother.

Still, Lady Zox spent much time teaching Tzec her own language and culture, for she wanted the child to be prepared for that day when they returned to the land of the Maya. She told her of the splendid cities there, and the phenomenal buildings and pyramids, great and golden in the sunshine. She told of Dzibilchaltún, the city so old it might have existed from the beginning of time, but now was falling into ruins. She promised to take Tzec there one day, after they returned to their people, for it was within the territory of Ceh Pech. They would walk down the ancient central avenue to the Temple of the Seven Dolls, with its vaulted corridor, its windows, and the inner chamber which showed the key alignments of the sun. The priests there had always known when the seasons and holidays were coming, without having to leave the temple. She narrated the great histories of the sacred text of her people, the Book of the Community. She taught Tzec the unique Calendar, with its eighteen months and the Uayeb, the five unlucky days left over. Each month had its special name and symbol, and the girl learned these, pronouncing the syllables and scratching the symbols in the sand. Indeed, her name was Tzec because she had been born in the fifth month, Tzec. This was not normal practice; usually a person was named for the specific day of his or her birth, rather than the month. But in the horror of her betrayal and captivity, the Lady Zox had lost track of the exact days, and did not care to gamble on an inaccurate one. So it was simply Tzec.

But that was only the "vague" calendar, so-called because it was not exact; it tended to creep up on the seasons, interfering with the planting and harvest dates, which was a nuisance. There was another, more precise ceremonial calendar, consisting of the same twenty days, but these were not arranged into months. Instead each was preceded by a number, one through thirteen, and the men were named by these numbers and days, according to the dates of their birth. The thirteen numbers and twenty days cycled through until all had been cross-matched, and this required two hundred and sixty days. The ceremonial calendar was thus out of alignment with the vague calendar; only once in fifty-two years did they coincide, and this was a time of the greatest significance, when temples were rebuilt and special sacrifices made.

Zox taught Tzec how to mark such numbers in the Maya

system, in vertical columns, with a shell for zero, dots for one to four, horizontal lines for five, and their placement denoting whether each should be multiplied by twenty, three hundred and sixty, seven thousand two hundred, or a hundred and forty-four thousand. Such concepts were difficult, but the child was bright and she mastered them. She appreciated immediately that such feats of numbering could not be matched by the savages who had to count on the fingers of their hands. More than that, it represented proof that the wonderful world her mother described was real, for here were its numbers, unknown among the local natives.

Tzec was eager to learn this mystic lore, and the pictographs too, understanding that very few, even among the Maya, had such knowledge. Thus, even as a child of six summers, she was becoming literate, and spoke the exotic language of her ancestry. The priest allowed this, on condition that the tongue be spoken between them only privately, and the symbols shown to no others. He allowed it because he had become dependent on the favor of the Lady Zox, and she asked only this; he limited it because he knew that others of the tribe would not understand, and he could become a laughingstock and perhaps lose his position if it were known. If that happened, the Lady Zox and her daughter would have no protection, and could suffer. So he compromised, and Zox made him glad that he did, for she remained beautiful and increasingly useful to him. She could count well and record numbers of any size, and there were ways in which such records facilitated his business. By day, outside, she was a completely subservient wife; by night, in privacy, she had things her own way.

The truth was that the priest was a gentle man, and he treated Tzec well, liking her for herself and for her potential as another person who could record numbers. This was not always the case with fathers and daughters in the tribe, and Tzec understood this. She learned the ways of concealment and privacy early, and so no other people in the tribe knew how this family differed from others. Tzec's life was happy, with the approval of her father and the marvelous lore of her mother, and her friendships with the other girls of the tribe. The fact was, she was willing to wait for the return to her mother's land, across the great sea to the southwest. The life she knew here was satisfactory.

Then the terrible Toco raided. Suddenly the houses of the village were ablaze and women were screaming in the night. The warriors tried to fight, but most were out on a hunt, and those remaining were no match for the attacking war party.

Two painted men burst into the priest's house. The priest tried to challenge them, but he died in an instant, a spear through his heart. One warrior drew a knife and carved at the priest's head, scalping him. The other turned on the woman and her daughter, speaking unintelligibly, menacing them with another knife.

"Make no resistance!" Zox whispered to Tzec. "You must survive alone!"

The warrior caught Zox by her hair, which had regrown to its full natural lustrous length, and hauled her in to him. He ripped open the blanket she had wrapped about herself against the cool of the night, and gazed at her body. He grunted approval. He gestured with the knife, and Zox walked where he pointed, saying nothing. In a moment they were gone outside.

Tzec remained where she was, hoping the other warrior would not notice her. She was horrified by what was happening, but part of her was numb; she knew that she was helpless, and could only watch.

The other warrior completed his circular cut and ripped the blood-soaked scalp from the priest's skull. He tucked it in a pouch, then looked up. He saw Tzec. He gestured at her with the dripping knife.

Tzec stood, wrapped in her own blanket. The warrior grunted, and she opened the blanket to reveal her naked torso, as her mother had. She knew what men did to women, but normally they did not do it to children. But she had no certainty that this barbarian honored such customs. The warrior grimaced, but decided to take her captive anyway. He produced a cord and looped it about her neck, drawing it just tight enough to make her understand that it would throttle her if she tried to escape.

In this manner she was brought to the village of her captor. Once there, she knew there was little hope of escape; she could

hardly make it back to her own village alone, and realized that
there was little remaining there for her anyway. Her father was
dead, her mother was gone.

She was turned over to the warrior's squaw, who cuffed her
to let her know her place, then offered her some gruel. Tzec
neither cried nor resisted; she kept quiet and ate.

She slept huddled where they left her, her life desolate. She
knew the way of captivity; her mother had described her own
early days, and she had seen the captives of the Calusa. Grown
males might be tortured to death; grown females were made
into concubines; children were slaves. Slavery could become
ordinary status in time, if the slave worked well and made
friends in the tribe. No one remained a slave forever; once she
knew the ways of the tribe and honored them, she was adopted.
It had happened for her mother.

But now her mother was gone, and with her the wonderful
world across the sea. Tzec doubted she would ever see the
Lady Zox again, because she knew her mother's nature, and
the nature of warriors. The warrior who had captured Zox
would rape her, and in the morning he would be dead. The
Toco were violent barbarians; everyone knew that. They would
kill her immediately. That was why Zox had told Tzec she must
survive alone.

She understood it all. Nevertheless she cried herself to sleep.

It did not take long for the warrior to conclude that it was
too much trouble to maintain a child who could not speak the
Toco tongue. It was not something he had thought about before;
otherwise he might simply have slain her instead of taking her
captive. So he did the next best thing: he traded her to a warrior
of another village to the north, for a good bag of corn. Corn
was precious among the Toco, for they grew little of it themselves, yet it was useful for bread when mixed with acorn meal.

The new master was willing to have his wife teach the slave
child the tongue, but Tzec was not willing to learn. The Toco
had destroyed her pleasant life, killed her father and probably
her mother too. She wanted nothing to do with them. Before
long she was traded off again.

In this manner, over the course of a summer and a winter,
Tzec traveled north to the village of Ibi Hica. There she stopped,

because the Little Big River barred the way beyond. She could not be casually traded with the Cale, for they were in a state of chronic war with the Toco. They would have to wait until some ignorant trader passed; then perhaps they could get rid of her. Meanwhile they treated her well enough, and she behaved well enough. They thought her mute, because by this time she could have learned at least a few words otherwise. But they recognized her incipient beauty, and knew that in due course her value would grow, if a warrior who did not care about speech came looking for a woman.

These Toco were truly primitive. They wore little clothing, and the children none. The adult men had only loincloths, and they painted their bodies according to their status. That in itself was not primitive, for her mother, Zox, had been well tattooed and painted, but the patterns of the Toco were mere decorations, rather than symbolic of the great deeds of antiquity. The women wore moss from the trees, which they had to hang in the smoke of a fire to abolish the tiny mites which otherwise would raise uncomfortable welts in their private places. They ate mostly shellfish from the river. But they were all right as people.

Now she had been traded, for a better price than anticipated. She did not know what her future would be. Was Throat Shot interested in acquiring her? She saw that he had a bad arm, and that diminished him, but she knew now that he had an ability to learn and speak other tongues quickly, and that enhanced him. He was not cruel, and he was smart; these were compelling arguments. Most positive of all, he was marked: the discolored scar on the back of his left shoulder vaguely resembled an eagle. Primitives put great store by such marks, believing them to indicate the favor of spirits, but to Tzec it had a different appeal. Such a mark was beautiful. Her mother was marked, so she knew. It was as if this man had some affinity to her mother, being similarly set apart from ordinary folk.

She smiled at him, and her beauty manifested; she was indeed a lovely child, as the surface of calm water assured her. She was now nine winters old, and soon enough would verge on womanhood; it would be best if she caused a good man to choose her, rather than taking a chance on who else might purchase her from the Trader. She had seen and understood how her mother managed men; she knew what to do. Throat Shot was a good man; he had a ready mind, and he knew tongues she did not, including the way of talking swiftly with his hands. She was too young as yet, but whatever appeal she could generate would be worthwhile, to make him understand what she would offer as she matured. Actually, she now realized that the sexual treatment she feared from a strange man would not necessarily be onerous from this man, if it served to make him value her. A girl had to use whatever she had.

"Why do you smile?" he finally inquired, practicing her Maya tongue, which made their dialogue private. He had finally realized that she was signaling him. Men could be slow about such things, but persistence could get their attention. He was facing away from her at the moment, paddling the canoe, but anytime he turned she caught him with a smile.

"I wish you would buy me. I will do anything you want, as well as I am able, and I will get better as I grow older."

Now indeed he understood, and she saw an unmanly flush at his neck. He paddled for a while, facing forward, evidently uncertain what to say. But in time he figured it out.

"I cannot buy you, Tzec. I have no shells, no beads, no fine feather cloaks to pay for you! I am just a young man, serving the Trader so that I may travel with him and seek to fulfill my mission. Even if I had wealth, I—you—"

Tzec sighed inwardly. He was pleading poverty, and this seemed to be the case. Still, he might have something he was not admitting to, and demurred because she had not sufficiently impressed him. Probably he was not sexually attracted to an undeveloped girl, and while she was glad of that on general principles, she regretted it in this case. She might be sold to a brute of a man who would use her and throw her away damaged.

In such a circumstance, her mother would be gracious. "I understand. Of course you do not want a child. I should not have asked you."

"Oh, that was all right," he said, as he had to. "I—" Then he ran afoul of the implications again, and lost his words. At least now he would be aware of her in this respect, and judging her as a prospective future sexual partner. That was a significant gain.

Increasingly she assumed the chores of women, for she was female: preparing meals, cleaning utensils and putting the canoe in order, gathering edible mushrooms and anything else she spied. One night there was not a woman for the Trader, so Tzec went to him and massaged his shoulders, which were tired from the day's paddling. A good woman was a useful one, and she had learned what she had to, to survive in this society, even though she did not speak its language. The Trader acquiesced approvingly, seeing that she was young but competent. That meant that he would not be in a rush to trade her away. That meant, in turn, that she would have more time to impress Throat Shot.

She talked to him whenever she could, and that was often, because she was learning his tongue. She tried her best to interest him, and since he was interested in the dead, she searched for whatever she knew that related to that. She found something.

"How many souls do your people have?" she asked.

"One for each person," he replied. "How could it be otherwise?"

"The Calusa have three souls for each person."

"Three?" he asked, suitably astonished. "How can that be?"

"One is in the shadow he makes when he walks in the sunlight," she said. "I think it hovers just inside his skin near where the shadow should be, when he has no shadow, looking for its lost home, so he has to be careful then. Another is in the clear water when he looks down into it and sees it; it looks just like him, but backwards. So he must not go too far from water, or that soul suffers. The third is in the pupil of his eye, and that one is always with his body, even when he dies."

"The third soul!" he said, considering it. "The one that remains in the burial mound!"

"For the Calusa, anyway," she agreed. "So if you go to talk to a Calusa spirit, that would be the one you find."

"But Toco have shadows and reflections too!" he said. "Is it possible that we too have three souls?"

She shrugged, pleased to have amazed him with this. "I don't know, but I think they may, because I have seen Toco get sick."

"What does that have to do with it?"

"Among the Calusa, when a person loses one of his souls,

he gets sick, and the priest has to go look for it and herd it back to him so he can be well again. Sometimes the soul is unwilling to return, and many people must surround it and drive it, like a fleeing deer, so that it has nowhere else to go. He is sick until they drive it back. When they finally do, they put a fire at the door of his lodge, and at the windows, so that the soul is frightened and will not dare go out again, until it is content to stay in him where it belongs, and he is well.''

"How do they put the soul back into him?"

"The medicine man makes a ceremony to squeeze it in through the top of the man's head. But it doesn't like to go in, once it is out. If two souls leave his body, then he is like one of the dead, and will surely die if they don't return. They enter some animal or fish, and if the people kill that animal, that soul enters a smaller creature, and so on, until if they keep killing, the things it comes to vanish. But if the soul realizes that it will die, because every animal it takes will be killed, then it may decide to return to the man."

Throat Shot shook his head. "I thought all souls were like ours. Now I am not sure. I think I will watch my shadow and my reflection, just to be safe."

"I do," she admitted. She was quite pleased with herself for being able to help him in this way. Indeed, she was rewarded, for now he smiled at her as if he really cared about her. She had been inadequate to impress him with her body, but was having better success with her mind.

They reached the mouth of the river, and saw the great sea. Throat Shot gazed at it with open amazement; it was evident that he had never seen it before. He was an inland dweller. That was all right.

They followed the coast south, staying close to the land. This was no seagoing craft, certainly, and she knew that a storm could rise at any time.

Throat Shot became nervous, but not about the sea. There was something else on his mind. He spoke to the Trader, and in due course the Trader nodded. They followed another river inland, and in due course came to a series of huge mounds by the shore.

Ah! Throat Shot visited every burial mound they passed. He must have known of these, and insisted on seeing them. That was all right. The spirits of the mounds refused to talk with him, so his visits did not take long.

They landed the canoe, and Throat Shot went ashore. Tzec followed, preferring his company to that of the Trader. This was not because the Trader had been in any way unkind to her, but because he was her owner, and regarded her as merchandise. Throat Shot saw her as a person. Perhaps it was because his physical handicap gave him tolerance for her linguistic one. Or because she had tried so hard to flatter him and impress him. Or maybe he was just a more feeling person. She needed a feeling person.

The mound rose steeply to about six times her height. Tzec fancied that it suggested the pyramids her mother had described, though they were of stepped stone and larger, with lime plaster on the walls and hieroglyphic patterns on the plaster. The whole of a city's history could be read from its illustrated walls, in that magic land. Still, this was impressive enough, and it was right here where she could see it. Her mother surely would have been interested in this, primitive as it was in comparison with those she had known among the civilized Maya.

Throat Shot paused at the base. Then he resumed walking, north.

Tzec hurried after him. "Aren't you going to talk with its spirits?" she asked in Calusan, their common language.

"It's a temple mound," he said gruffly. "No spirits remain."

Oh. She wondered how he knew. But of course he had known that this mound was here, so he must know which mound was which.

Soon they came to another mound, which was lower and longer than the first. He remained at this one, his eyes closed, his face blank. He was finding spirits here.

Tzec did not know whether she believed in his ability to commune with the dead. The dead existed, certainly, but they seldom had interest in the affairs of the living. She wanted to learn more about him, and why he sought the dead, but she was hesitant to ask. So she stood silent, some distance behind him, so as not to disturb him in any way. She did not have to believe or understand; she could support him regardless, and be here when he finished.

Throat Shot stood for some time. He must be doing it! He had not remained this long at any of the other mounds. But was he truly talking with a spirit, or was he merely imagining it?

At last he turned. He walked toward her. "Your people have been here," he said.

Tzec's mouth fell open. "Mine?"

"A long time ago. Their boats—they traded here."

"The boats still come here," she said. "My mother—"

"Regularly. Before my tribe was separate. Some went to your land. But then it stopped."

"There were wars," she said.

"The spirit recognized you. He did not want to talk to me, until he saw you. I am a barbarian, but you are of the lineage of civilization."

She had told him that. It needed no spirit to account for his knowledge. But she did not care to argue. "Yes."

"Tell me of Little Blood."

Tzec jumped. She had not told him that! "I will. But why?"

"The spirit says it will change my life and help me search for the Ulunsuti."

Tzec began to believe. "It—it is a long story. My mother took many days to tell me. It will take me many days to tell you."

He nodded. "While we travel, then. I must know all you remember of it."

"But you must not laugh," she said. "It is sacred to my people, and not like the tales your folk tell."

"I would not laugh at anything the spirits of the mounds told me to do. Only through them can I achieve my quest. I do not have to understand what they ask of me. Perhaps they knew I would meet you, and that you would have something to help me."

She liked that notion very well. She hoped that her story would be what he needed. She hoped he would like it so well that he decided that he must acquire her and keep her. Perhaps he would change his mind about seeking his magic crystal, and work for the Trader for a longer time in order to purchase her.

So it was that she shared with him the lore of the Book of the Community, the sacred text of the Quiché Maya. She remembered the effect it had had on her when her mother told it, and she hoped it would work the same magic on him. If she had anything that was capable of fascinating him, at this young age of hers, this was what would do it.

The joy of it was that he had asked to hear it. The spirit had told him of it. The spirit must have decided to help her as well as him. She was coming to appreciate the spirits of the dead.

CHAPTER 4

LITTLE BLOOD

O Spirit of the Mound, I have told you of the girl, Wren, whose real name was Tzec, and how she came to live among the Toco folk. Now I will tell you of the tale she told of her people, of whom the spirit of the great mound near the sea knew. This was the tale that changed the young man's life, as surely you knew would be the case. But at the point Throat Shot did not realize this, and even when he did realize it, he knew only the half of it. But you knew, O Spirit; you always knew. You could have saved us all, if only I had not failed you, if only I had been as worthy as you hoped.

This is the story of the traditions of Quiché, the land of many trees, as recorded in the sacred Book of the Community. But there is too much to tell at once, so this is only part of it: the adventures of two men who were cruelly betrayed, and of a woman who enabled them to achieve vengeance on those who had betrayed them. This was the time before there were true men; indeed, at the dawn of the world there were many wooden men, who walked and spoke like men but were not. But after this adventure, the real men lived.

In the long night before there was truly sun, moon, or man, two ancestors lived. These were Xpiyacoc and Xmucane, or Shpiyacock and Shmucanee in this tongue, and they had two sons, whom they named after the days of their birth, as is the custom of our people. One was One-Hunter, and the other Seven-Hunter, or in our language Hun-Hunahpu and Vucub-Hunahpu. Hunahpu is the twentieth day in both our calendars, and it means chief as well as hunter, and is an auspicious day.

One-Hunter grew up and married a woman called Xbaqui-yalo, or Shbakeeyalo, her name meaning "of the uneven bones." They had two sons, named after their birth-days Hun-Batz, meaning One-Monkey, and Hun-Chouen, meaning also One-Monkey. This is because they were twins, born on the same day, and so one was named for the Quiché name of the day and the other for the Maya name of the day. There is no conflict in this, because the Quiché are both Maya and Toltec, with roots in the south and the north, and both traditions are honored among them.

One-Hunter did not stay home with his family, for that was the duty of a woman. But when the twin boys grew, he and his brother, Seven-Hunter, taught them all things manly and artistic. All four of them were great flautists, singers, painters, sculptors, jewelers and silversmiths, and also excellent shooters with blowguns. The four would get together to play the ball game of tlaxtli, one pair against the other pair, and there were none to match them. It seemed they hardly noticed when the mother of the twins, Xbaquiyalo of the uneven bones, died; the twins' grandmother, Xmucane, assumed the household responsibilities. Xmucane's husband also died, but she was competent to carry on.

The news of their proficiency spread far. One day Voc the hawk came there to watch them, and Voc told of their ability, until even the chiefs of Xibalba, or Shibalba, the underworld, heard about them. The lords of Xibalba were Hun-Camey and Vucub-Camey, One-Death and Seven-Death, and they were fearsome enemies of the living.

"What are they doing up there on earth?" these dread chiefs demanded, for they were resentful that any living folk should achieve such notoriety. Also, they coveted the ball-playing equipment of these people: their leather leggings, which protected their legs against the blows of the heavy ball: their rings, which were collars to protect their necks; their gloves for the hands and wrists; their crowns, which adorned their heads during the game; and their masks, which protected their faces. All this gear was necessary because the ball game was extremely violent. The equipment was excellent, and of considerable value, for anyone who used it would be a better ball player than otherwise, and might achieve great honor in victory. So these nether lords planned to kill the players and take their equipment.

The lords of death sent their messengers, which were four great owls. One was swift as an arrow, another had only one leg but was very large, another had a red back, and the last was distinguished by its head, for it had no legs. These owls flew out and went to the men, and told them that the lords of death wished to play ball with them.

One-Hunter and Seven-Hunter were amazed. "Did the lords One-Death and Seven-Death really say that we must go with you to their domain?"

"Yes," the four owls replied. "They said to bring all your playing gear, and your rubber balls too, and come quickly to play ball with them and impress them with your skill, for they have heard wonderful things of you."

The two men looked at each other. This was certainly a rare honor! "We must say good-bye to our mother," they said. They meant their grandmother, who was now assuming the role of their mother.

Then they went home, and told Xmucane about the invitation. "But those are the dread lords of death!" Xmucane protested. "You must not stay there!"

"We shall not stay there," they reassured her. "We are going only for a while, only to play ball with them. Here, we will leave our ball here, so that you know we will come back to play." They hung the ball in the space under the rooftree.

Xmucane was not very much reassured, but there was nothing she could do. She burst into tears as they departed. This was of course a woman's privilege, and her way of reminding them that she had misgivings about this adventure.

"Don't worry," they called back. "We have not died yet." Then they accompanied the four owls to the dread underworld.

The road there was strange and wonderful. First they went down some very steep steps, like those of the great temple, only these went down deep into the valley. At the bottom they came to the bank of a river which flowed rapidly between narrow ravines. They had to leap across it, and if they had fallen in they would have been swept away to their doom. Beyond this was a second river, which flowed among many thorny calabash trees, and they had to walk carefully lest they get hurt by the thorns. Then they came to a third river whose waters were poisonous, but they did not drink from it, being cautious, so came to no harm.

The owls led them to an intersection of four roads. One was red, another black, another white, and the fourth green. Which one were they to take? They did not know, for the owls flew away.

The black road spoke to them. "I am the one you must take," it said. "I am the way of the lord of death." But that was not the whole truth, for all the roads led to the region of death, but the black one allowed no return to the region of life. They did not know this, and walked on the black road, and therefore they were doomed.

They arrived at Xibalba, where their doom awaited them. They entered the council room of the chiefs of the underworld, not realizing what cruel tricks they would suffer. There they saw the two lords of death, seated on their thrones.

"How are you, One-Death?" they said to one. "How are you, Seven-Death?" they said to the other, politely.

But the figures did not answer. Perplexed, the men approached, and finally touched the unmoving figures—and discovered that they were made of wood. They were only carved figures.

Instantly the assembled lords of Xibalba burst into laughter. They considered the ruse great sport, and there was nothing the men from the surface could do. Of course a good host would not have ridiculed his guests, but the lords of death were not nice folk.

At last One-Death spoke. "Very well, you have come. Tomorrow you shall prepare the masks, rings, and gloves, to play the ball game." But this was further mockery, for the lords of death had no intention of letting them play. All was deceit, in this terrible realm.

"Come and sit down on our bench," Seven-Death said.

The two men went and sat on the bench. But it was of heated stone, and when their weight came down on it they were burned. They squirmed in discomfort, and then had to stand,

for otherwise their rumps would have been scorched. As it
was, they were most uncomfortable. It had been all they could
do to avoid leaping up with a yell.

The lords of death burst out laughing again, harder than
before. They had never had such a good joke. They laughed
until they doubled over, they laughed until they writhed with
pain in their stomachs, they laughed until their bones twisted,
until it seemed that they were the ones who had sat on the hot
seat. One-Hunter and Seven-Hunter could only stand and wait
for the laughter to die away; they were helpless, for they had
been fooled, and they did not wish to seem impolite.

In due course One-Death recovered enough to speak. "Go
now to that lodge," he told them. "There you will get your fat
pine torches and your cigars to smoke, and there you will
sleep."

This seemed more positive. Perhaps the jokes were over.
The two men went to the indicated lodge, which was closed
up and without windows or vents for light; there was only
darkness within it. Indeed, it was called the Lodge of Gloom,
and was no nice place to sleep. They crouched in the darkness, ill at ease until the porter arrived with their torches and
cigars.

The fat pine sticks were round and resinous, so that they
would burn a long time and make light. The lords of death
sent each of them a lighted cigar, from which they could light
the pine torches. The pine blazed up, and the gloom was
dispersed.

Then the porter said: "The lords of death have told me to
tell you that you must return your pine sticks and cigars whole
at dawn, or you will forfeit your match."

"What?" One-Hunter demanded. But the porter was gone,
and the door was closed and barred behind him.

They were confined within the Lodge of Gloom, with an
impossible requirement, because their torches and cigars were
already partly burned and could not be rendered whole again.
This was the land of death, and death's laws governed; they
could not change that. So they burned up the fat pine sticks,
keeping the gloom at bay, and smoked their cigars, which
were really very good. It seemed that the lords of death knew
how to enjoy tobacco. They hoped that this was merely another

cruel joke, and that they would be allowed to play ball in the morning.

But when dawn came, and they were let out to stand before the lords of the underworld, One-Death demanded, "Where are my cigars? Where are my sticks of fat pine?"

"They are all gone, sir," One-Hunter replied.

"Well. Then you have forfeited the match, and today shall be the end of your days. Now you both shall die. You will be destroyed; we will break you into pieces and your faces will remain hidden. We shall sacrifice you." And the lords of death were pleased.

The two men tried to protest, but it was no use. The lords of death lifted the sacrificial knives and cut out the beating hearts of One-Hunter and Seven-Hunter, and they were dead. They were buried together by the ball court. But first the minions of death cut off One-Hunter's head, for they wished to heap further indignity on him despite his being dead.

"Take that head and put it in that tree which grows on the road," One-Death said. So they put the severed head in the tree, as if it were fruit. They had another good laugh over its comical appearance. Imagine a tree growing a head!

Now this was a calabash tree, which had never borne fruit. But in a moment their laughter faltered and faded out, for now the tree was covered with fruit, and ever after it bore fruit, in honor of that head.

One-Death and Seven-Death gazed in amazement at the fruit on the tree. It was round like the head, and covered with a hard rind. They thought to remove the head from the tree, realizing that special magic was operating here, but they could not distinguish it from all the fruit. Every item on that tree looked the same. It was almost as if the tree were laughing at them, and they hated that.

Then they feared it, for they could not fathom its magic. So they tried to protect themselves from this magic. "Let no one come to pick this fruit," Seven-Death said. "Let no one come to sit under this tree." And they resolved to keep everybody away from it, lest its magic come to harm them in some way. For though they were the lords of death, their power was not complete; they could be vulnerable to magic they did not understand.

* * *

But the thing that had happened to the tree was so remarkable that news of it spread widely. The animals spoke of it, and the birds, laughing behind their wings, for none of them liked the lords of death. In due course the folk of the living realm heard about it.

In time a living girl heard the wonderful story. Her name was Xquic, or Shkeek, and she was the daughter of a Chief named Cuchumaquic. She was a maiden, unmarried, and interested in strange things. She was also somewhat willful, but she got away with this because she was beautiful. So when she heard the story of the fruit of the calabash tree from her father, she was amazed and intrigued.

"Why can't I go see this tree they tell about?" she exclaimed, but not in the hearing of her father, who would have told her why not. "The calabash has never borne fruit before; surely this must be the most wonderful harvest! I would love to go and eat some of it!"

The notion preyed on her mind, for she was without a man and had time to think about things. Finally she left the lodge, and traveled alone to the place of the ball game. It was a daring thing she did, because of the long steps, and the treacherous rivers, and the colored roads. But she went carefully, keeping out of sight, lest someone see her and report her to her father, who would then stop her. So it was that no one saw her. At last she came to the crossroads, and went along the green road because she distrusted the other colors. The lords of death were not around, because they were staying away from the tree, and she arrived at it unobserved.

"Ah!" she exclaimed, thrilled. "What is this fruit which this tree bears? How wonderful it is to see it! Oh, I must pick one of these special fruits! Surely it will not kill me!"

Then the skull hidden in the branches of the tree spoke up: "What is it you want, woman? These round objects are nothing but skulls. Surely you don't want one of them!"

Xquic was startled. "Who is it, up there hidden in the branches?" she asked, afraid she had been discovered.

"I am the skull of One-Hunter, put here by the lords of death who betrayed and slew my brother and me. The tree protects me from discovery, so that I may in time obtain our vengeance."

Xquic believed the skull, though it frightened her. "Tell me what happened," she said bravely.

So the skull told her the whole story, and more it had learned by listening to the words of the lords of death when they passed this way checking to be sure the tree remained undisturbed. "We were fools," it concluded. "If I had known then what I know now, I would defeat the lords of death and bring ruin upon them. But alas, I am dead and decapitated; it is too late."

"But I am not dead," Xquic said. Listening to the skull's story, she had come to love the bold man it had been. "How can I help you?"

"I can give you something that will make vengeance possible," the skull said. "But it will not be easy, even with the help of my magic. It will bring a hard time for you, and danger, and it will take twenty winters to accomplish. I think you would be happier if you turned around and went home and married a man your father will choose for you and bore his sons, and nurtured them, in the manner allotted to women."

"I do not want that man's sons," Xquic said. "I want to help you achieve your vengeance." She really had a somewhat strange notion of the proper place of a woman. She preferred adventure to subservience.

"Do you really want what I offer?" the skull asked again, not quite certain of her constancy.

"Yes, I want it," the maiden answered.

"Then stretch up your hand to me, and touch me." And now she saw which one was the skull. It was hideous, with little of the flesh remaining, and moisture caught within it.

But she resolved to see this thing through. "Very well," she said, and reached up and touched it.

In that moment a few drops of liquid, the saliva of the skull, fell into her palm. It tingled, and she drew her hand quickly away and looked at it, but there was nothing there.

"In my spittle I have given you my descendants," the skull said. "Now my head has nothing on it anymore; it is nothing but bone. This is true for all the great princes; it is only the flesh on their skulls that gives them a handsome aspect. When they die, men are frightened by their bones, which are no prettier than mine. So, too, is the nature of their sons, who are conceived of the spittle of their loins. Men do not lose their substance when they go; they bequeath it to the sons and daughters they beget. This I have done with you. Go, then, lovely woman, to the surface of the earth, that you may not die. Believe in my words, that it may be so." Then the skull was silent, for it had done all it could do.

Xquic believed. And so it was that the spittle entered her body through her hand, and coursed through it to the region of her womanhood, and the maiden was impregnated by One-Hunter, by the will of the eldest gods.

She returned home, having immediately conceived the sons in her belly just as if she had lain with the living man and had his seed directly. This was the first of the magic that was to enhance those sons. In this manner were Hunter and Little Jaguar begotten, Hunahpu and Xbalanque. But she did not tell her father, fearing his reaction. She tried to pretend that she had only taken a walk, which was a small part of the truth. Women in those days, as now, were excellent at deception.

But after six months had passed, her father, Cuchumaquic, noticed her condition. He remembered how her mother had been before birthing Xquic, and understood that she was pregnant.

He was extremely upset, and sought to discuss the matter with the lords of death, with whom he was on reasonable terms. The old tend to be closer to death than the young. He went to the underworld and held council with One-Death and Seven-Death.

"My daughter is with child, sirs," he exclaimed when he appeared before the lords. "She has been disgraced! She is nothing more than a prostitute." This was of course the very reaction Xquic had anticipated in him.

Now, the lords of death had a notion of what had happened, having pieced together certain hints. They had seen the maiden's footprints near the calabash tree, and understood how such an event might occur, for there had been precedents elsewhere. They knew they had to be rid of Xquic and her offspring, or there would surely be mischief to come. But they did not care to tell this to Cuchumaquic, who might have been no better pleased with them than he was with his daughter.

"Very well," One-Death said after due pause for thought.

"Command her to tell the truth, and if she refuses, punish her."

"How should I do that?" he asked.

"In an honorable manner, for she is, after all, your daughter and of noble blood, though she be a whore. Let her be taken from your lodge and sacrificed."

"Very well, honorable lords," he said, grateful for this good advice. Had he known the full story, he might have been less grateful. He departed the underworld and made his way home.

Promptly he braced Xquic: "Whose is the child you carry, my daughter?" he asked firmly.

The woman knew that the truth would damn her more surely than a lie, for she had seen where Cuchumaquic had gone. Yet it was not in her to lie to her father. "I have no child, my father, for I have not known the face of a man." Indeed she had not, for the expression meant the face and portions below, and she had touched only a skull. And she had no child, but rather two sons.

"You really are a whore!" he cried, enraged. Then, to the four great owls who were the messengers of death: "Take her and sacrifice her; bring me her heart in a gourd and return this very day before the lords of death."

The owls assumed human form, took the gourd, and set out carrying the girl in their arms. They brought with them the flint knife with which to open her breast and cut out her heart. They were not evil folk, these messengers, but they served the lords of death.

But when they came to the altar for sacrifice, and bared Xquic's breast for the terrible stone blade, she pleaded with them most winsomely. "It cannot be that you will slay me, oh loyal messengers, because you must know that what I bear in my belly is no disgrace. It was begotten when I went to marvel at the wonderful calabash tree with its sudden fruit, and communed with the severed head of One-Hunter. You know how he and his brother were tormented and betrayed when they came to play a ball game. You know that the lords of death did not deal honorably with them. By the will of the gods I have One-Hunter's sons within me, and they must not die before their time. So you must not sacrifice me, oh messengers!"

They were moved by her plea, for they had indeed seen the

fate of the two Hunters. The four owls had led the men to the underworld, but they had not known that the lords of death would trick them and cheat them of the ball game. They had lost respect for the lords of death, but had not known what to do, for they were only messengers, of little consequence.

"Then what shall we put in place of your heart?" they asked, gazing at her bared bosom where her heart lay ready for the sacrifice beneath her full breasts. "Your father told us to do this thing and to return quickly to the lords of death with your heart in this gourd. We do not wish you to die, but we dare not return without that heart."

"Very well," she said, considering. "You must have something in the gourd, but my heart does not belong to the lords of death. Neither is your proper home in the underworld, and you must not let them force you to kill folk like this. Later, I swear, the real criminals will be at your mercy, and I will overcome One-Death and Seven-Death. So then, only the blood shall be given to them, and my heart shall not be burned." For she knew that the lords intended to burn her heart in the fire, as they had burned the hearts of the two Hunters. "Gather the product of this tree," she told them, indicating a nearby tree.

They were doubtful, but they went to the tree. It was as tall as an almond tree, and the leaves and stems were white. They cut into the trunk, and the sap came out, as red as the blood of a dragon. Now part of the magic of the woman showed, bequeathed to her by the saliva of One-Hunter: her name contained blood, and the tree she designated, which had been ordinary, now also contained blood. From that day on it was known as the Tree of Blood, because of this quality, and in its way became as remarkable as the tree with the fruit like skulls.

They gathered this sap in the gourd, and it looked so much like real blood that they were astonished. When they had enough they brought it to the altar, and it clotted, and they made a ball of it in the shape of a heart. It was as if they had cut out Xquic's heart and put it with its blood into the gourd.

"Now we have the heart," they said. "But in time the lords of death will surely learn how they were deceived, and then it will be *our* hearts in the fire!"

"There is no need for that," she said. "Come to me when you are done. Here on earth, among the living, you shall be beloved, and you shall have all that belongs to you."

They took one more look at her bared breasts, and were convinced. It would be a shame to cut into that perfect flesh! "So shall it be, girl. We shall go there to complete our mission; then we shall return to serve you. Meanwhile you go on your way, while we present the sap instead of your heart to the lords of death."

"I shall," she agreed, and she got down off the altar, donned her shawl, and walked away, seeking a lodge she knew of where she would be safe.

The four messengers resumed their owl forms and flew rapidly down to the underworld, carrying the gourd. When they arrived, all the lords were waiting.

"You have done the job?" One-Death asked.

"All is done, my lords," said the first owl. "Here in the bottom of the gourd is the heart."

"Excellent! Let us see it!" exclaimed One-Death. He grasped the gourd and raised it, squeezing it with his fingers. The shell broke, and the blood flowed bright red from the interior of the heart.

One-Death smiled, believing that the enemy of death had been destroyed. "Stir up the fire and put it on the coals," he said.

They did this, and the heart heated and burned and was rendered into ashes. The lords of Xibalba drew near and sniffed it, and found the fragrance of the heart very sweet. They believed that once the heart was gone, no life or magic could remain in the body. They had been mistaken in the case of One-Hunter, who had retained his essence in his skull, but they knew that the maiden's skull would not impregnate anyone.

And as they sat deep in thought, savoring their seeming victory with the fumes of the burned heart, the four owls quietly departed. They flew like a flock of birds up from the abyss to the realm of the living, to become the servants of the maiden. But they did not do this in an obvious manner, for they knew that the course of these events had not yet been completed, and there was as yet much danger.

In this manner the lords of death were tricked and ultimately defeated by the woman Little Blood, whose association with blood was more special than they knew.

Meanwhile One-Hunter's mother, Xmucane, lived with One-Hunter's two sons by Xbaquiyalo of the uneven bones. The two boys were named Hun-Batz and Hun-Chouen, both meaning One-Monkey, but we shall simply call them Batz and Chouen.

It was to this lodge that Xquic came for shelter and sustenance, for this was the line of her twin sons, who were to be born not long after. She approached the old woman and introduced herself. "I am your daughter-in-law and therefore your daughter, mother," she said, entering the lodge.

Now one might expect a somewhat negative response from the old woman, who had been taken by surprise. Indeed, this was the case. "Where did you come from?" she cried, outraged by such impertinence. "Where are my sons? Did they not perchance die in the underworld? Where is my daughter-in-law? Did she not die and leave her children to me to raise? I know her face, and it is not your face! Do you not see these boys who remain, of the blood of my son and his wife, these two called Batz and Chouen? Do you think you are their mother? Get out of here, you impostor! Go away! Go away!" She was screaming at this point.

But Xquic had anticipated a certain amount of trouble, and was prepared for it. The skull of One-Hunter had told her of his mother, and how she was. But the skull had assured her that his mother was a good woman, who would relent once she was satisfied, and would do what was right by Xquic and the sons she bore. So Xquic remained calm and polite, and made her case in a persuasive manner.

"Nevertheless it is true that I am your daughter-in-law, good woman," she said. "I have been for some time. I met with One-Hunter, and pledged to him, and I regard myself as his wife, and I carry his children. One-Hunter and Seven-Hunter are not truly dead; they live in my womb, and when my children are born you will see your sons clearly in them, my mother-in-law. You will recognize your sons' image, and be satisfied."

Batz and Chouen overheard this dialogue, and became angry. They did not want children the image of their father and their father's brother in the lodge, claiming the attention of their grandmother. The two of them did nothing but play the flute and sing, paint and sculpt all day long; they contributed little to the upkeep of the lodge, and only grudgingly had planted corn for bread. Despite this, they were the consolation of the old woman, and she treated them well. They saw no reason to change things. But they did not speak, or make their presence known, for they believed that Xmucane would dispatch the impostor quickly enough.

Indeed, it seemed she would. "I do not wish you to be my daughter-in-law, because though I see you are with child, what you bear in your womb is the fruit of your disgrace. Furthermore you are an impostor, because my sons are already dead, and have been for some time."

But then Xquic told the woman how she had received the saliva from One-Hunter's skull, and conceived thereby, though she had never known him in life. She repeated some of what the skull had told her, including details of the family that were not known to others, and this sowed belief in the old woman, against her will.

"I still think it is a disgrace, and I do not consider you married to my son, and that's the truth," Xmucane said. "But, well, it may be so, and you are my daughter-in-law despite the disgrace. You may become part of this lodgehold if you assume the duties of it."

"I shall be glad to, mother," Xquic agreed, relieved. But she knew from what the skull had told her that her trial was not yet over. The woman would test her, to prove what she was, and would reject her if she failed to pass the test.

"Go, then; bring the food for those who must be fed. Go and gather a large net full of corn from the field, and return at once, as a proper daughter would."

"Very well," Xquic replied. She took the net and went immediately to the cornfield that the two young men had planted. There was a path there through the jungle, and the girl followed it until she came to the cornfield.

But when she got there, she found only a single stalk of corn growing. Now she understood just how lazy the boys had been, for there should have been hundreds of stalks, and there weren't even two or three. The one stalk had one ear on it, and that was hardly enough to feed the family.

Yet she had been sent here to fetch back a net full of corn, and if she failed, she would be found wanting, and perhaps thrown out of the lodge. Probably the old woman did not know how little there was here; Xquic had come just before the corn ran out, and now the blame would seem to be hers. Certainly the boys would not confess their dereliction; Xquic had seen them lurking near, and had noted their scowls. This was an ideal way to get rid of her. Maybe they had even run on ahead and stolen away all the other corn, to make her fail.

"Ah, woe is me!" she exclaimed, weeping. "Innocent that I am! Where must I go to get a net full of food, as she told me to do?"

But Xquic remembered that she had been magically impregnated, and had acquired some of the magic of the gods, so that she could do what was right by the sons she carried. Maybe the gods would help her through this pass.

"Oh Chahal, guardian of the cornfields, I beg you to give me the corn I must have!" she prayed. "Oh Xtoh, goddess of rain, and Xcanil, goddess of grain, and Xcacau, goddess of cacao, you who cook the corn and guard the field Batz and Chouen planted—I beg you to grant me what I need, for it is the will of the gods I serve!"

Then there was a light sprinkling of rain, though there was no cloud in the sky, and drops of water appeared on the red silk tassels of the single ear of corn. Xquic knew this was a magical effect, and hoped that the gods had answered her. The four owls who served her were there, and they understood what was happening. "Go pull on the strands of silk, one by one," they told her.

She approached the ear of corn, and saw that every strand of the silken beard glowed and was separated from the others. She put her fingers to one strand, and drew on it, and it came out of the ear—and lo, at its base was a full ear of corn, though the original ear remained untouched. Then she knew that the gods had answered, and she gave thanks.

She touched another strand, and drew on it, and brought out a second ear. Then a third, and a fourth, and more, until she had tens of ears, and the large net was completely filled.

She tried to lift it, to carry it back to the lodge, but the net was now so heavy it was beyond her strength. So the four owls went out into the field and forest, and spoke to the wild creatures there, saying, "It is the will of the gods that Little Blood be helped to carry her burden." Then the animals of the field came, the little squirrels and rabbits and rats and others of that type, and they grasped the edges of the net with their teeth and lifted and pulled, many of them surrounding it, and carried it along toward the lodge. Xquic, astonished, walked along with them, marveling at the manner in which the gods were helping her.

When they reached the lodge, the little animals set the net in a corner of it, as though the girl might have carried it there. Then they dispersed, each running quietly to its accustomed place in the distant field, not waiting for her thanks. This might have been generous of them, but it could also have been because quite a mound of kernels of corn had fallen on the ground during the harvest, and more had spilled from the basket as it bounced along, and they were hungry for these. They had helped Xquic; now they helped themselves.

The old woman had been out on an errand, and had seen none of this. She came in and saw the corn in the large net, and her eyes slitted with surprise and distrust. "Where have you brought all this corn from?" she demanded. "Did you, by chance, take all the corn remaining in our field, so that there will be none for the future? I shall go at once and see."

Without further word, Xmucane stalked off down the road to the cornfield. But she discovered that the one stalk was still standing there, with its lone ear. She had, after all, known of the condition of the field. She saw where the weeds had been pressed down by the net at the foot of the stalk. She saw the spilled kernels, which the animals had not yet eaten. She saw the path made by the dragging of the heavy basket. She saw the footprints of the little animals.

The old woman had intended no good for the girl she believed was an impostor. But now she recognized the intercession of the gods, and knew that she had been mistaken. A miracle had happened here, and she had to accept the situation.

She quickly returned to the lodge. "This is proof enough that you are really my daughter-in-law. I shall now acknowledge your little ones, the offspring of my son you carry. They shall be magicians."

Xquic was gratified. She took up residence in the lodge, and the old woman treated her well enough, yet she remained infected by irritation that these new boys should be chosen by the gods, instead of her grandsons who already lived with her. Why couldn't *they* have been the ones? She knew in her heart that they were unworthy, being lazy and mean-spirited, but still it rankled and clouded her vision.

When the time came, Xquic went out into the forest alone, in the fashion of women, and gave birth to Hunter and Little Jaguar. The four owls went out to the north and south and east and west, warning the animals away, that none disturb Little Blood. Both of the babies were sorcerers; indeed, the name Xbalanque meant not only jaguar, but also sorcerer. The magic of their father had indeed come to them, as it had not to the two older boys.

When the birthing was done, Xquic got up and carried the two babies to the lodge. Then she lay down and slept, for she was very tired, and had lost more than just a "little blood," as her name suggested.

The two baby boys were lusty and hungry. They screamed for milk, but their mother was in a sleep near death, and could not hear them.

"Go throw them out," old Xmucane told the older boys. "They make too much noise." Actually, she spoke with annoyance rather than intent, meaning only that the babies should be put where the sound of their constant crying would not disturb her. There was nothing to be done for the babies until their mother recovered from her deep sleep and was able to nurse them.

But the boys chose to interpret the old woman's words literally, because they wanted to be rid of this competition for attention in the lodge. So they took the two babies out and put them on an anthill, where they thought the ants would tear away their flesh and kill them. But the four owls spoke to the ants, and the ants ignored the babies, and the sand of the hill was soft, and now the babies slept peacefully.

When Batz and Chouen saw this, their hatred and envy

increased, for they realized that the babies were magically protected. So they lifted the babies from the anthill and laid them on thistles, hoping the thorns would stab them and cause them to bleed to death. But again the four owls interceded, speaking to the plants, and the plants heeded them. Still the babies slept unharmed, as if the thistles were soft pine boughs. The boys did not dare do more, because they wanted the babies to seem to die by accident, so there would be no blame.

Xquic recovered her strength and woke, and went out and found the twins. She brought them in and nursed them, and her milk was magically good, so that they prospered immediately. But the older boys refused to let the babies stay in the lodge, or to recognize them as brothers. Rather than have dissension, Xquic made a place for the babies in the forest, and tended to them there. The animals of the wild would not harm them, knowing they had the favor of the gods, and that the four great owls were watching. So it was that Hunter and Little Jaguar were brought up in the fields. This was not a bad thing, for the animals and birds and fish communed with them, encouraged by the owls, and worked with them, helping them to achieve their potential. For though they were sorcerers, they were young, and had to learn step by step how to use their powers. These powers were great, and many years were required for their perfection.

Now, Batz and Chouen were talented young men, being great musicians and singers. They had grown up in the midst of trials and want, because of the death of their mother and later of their father, and their grandmother's lodge was poor. But their father, One-Hunter, and their uncle, Seven-Hunter, had taught them to play the flute and to paint and carve and play ball. They had learned much, and become wise. The two knew about the heritage of their two younger half brothers, for they were diviners who could see through to the truth when they tried.

Nevertheless, because they were envious, their wisdom was suppressed and their hearts were filled with ill will, though Hunter and Little Jaguar had not offended them in any way, other than existing. There was nothing but hostility in that lodge, for their mother, Xquic, was not the head of it, and she did not try to oppose the will of the old woman. Xquic knew that her sons belonged in their father's lodge, where they could learn all that they needed to. So she kept silent, in order to see that the destiny of her sons was fulfilled.

Hunter and Little Jaguar were not loved by their grandmother, or by their older brothers. They were given nothing new to eat; only when Batz and Chouen had eaten their fill, and nothing but scraps were left, were the younger brothers allowed to come and take what they could find. This was true despite the fact that the younger boys now did all the hunting for the family. All day they were out shooting their blowguns, bringing down game birds, which they brought in for their mother, Xquic, to dress and cook. Neither the young boys nor the mother received any thanks for their services; it was as if all three were mere servants of the other three.

Yet the young boys did not become vexed or angry. They suffered silently, because they knew their rank and heritage, and understood everything clearly. So while Batz and Chouen played their flutes and sang, Hunter and Little Jaguar honed their hunting and foraging skills, and learned the magic of the wild places, taught by the owls. Though they were younger and smaller than their brothers, they became far more effective hunters and campers, and they could do things their brothers never suspected. Though still boys, they knew more of manhood than most men ever learned. Had Batz and Chouen not been overcome by envy and arrogance, they would have understood what was happening, and been on guard. But they were, in the end, fools, and that was to be their undoing.

The time came when Hunter and Little Jaguar had had enough. "It is time to be done with this nonsense," Hunter said. "We must be rid of these parasites."

"Yes, but how shall we do it without alienating our grandmother?" Little Jaguar asked. "For we are not yet ready to fulfill our main mission and achieve the vengeance of our father. We must remain a few more years with Grandmother Xmucane, and she is bitter enough with us already."

"That is an excellent point, my brother," Hunter said. "But perhaps our mentors the owls have an answer."

So they consulted with the owls, and the owls told them how to do it. They were impressed with the wisdom of the great messenger birds, and resolved to put the plan into effect immediately.

That day they returned to the lodge without bringing any bird, and no other game. When they entered, Xmucane saw them bare-handed and was furious. "Why did you bring no birds?" she demanded.

And Hunter answered: "What happened, grandmother, is that our birds were caught in the tree, and we could not climb up to get them. Dear grandmother, if our elder brothers, who are so talented, wish, let them come with us to bring down the birds."

Xmucane was out of sorts, having no fair retort. She didn't want the birds to go to waste. She glanced at the older brothers.

"Very well," Batz said, taking the hint. "We shall go with you at dawn to fetch down the birds. But they had better be good ones!"

Chouen nodded. It was in his mind, and in his brother's mind, that they would find some way to repay the younger boys' impertinence by arranging their deaths in the forest. They knew this was some kind of plot to embarrass them, and they were angry, though they hid their feelings.

But the younger boys had anticipated this. "We shall only change their appearance, not their nature," they said to themselves. "They want to die, and our heritage to be unfulfilled. In their hearts they really believe that we have come to be their servants. For these reasons we shall overcome them and teach them a lesson."

The older brothers would have laughed if they had heard this dialogue. But they would not have laughed had they understood how carefully the younger brothers were planning.

In the morning the four went out to the foot of the tree called Cante, the tree of yellow wood and yellow dye. It was not possible to count the birds that sang in the tree, and the elder brothers marveled to see so many. This was certainly a good hunting spot! The younger brothers shot their blowguns, but no birds fell.

"Our birds do not fall to the ground," Hunter said.

"That's because your aim is bad!" Batz said, laughing.

"I don't think so," Little Jaguar said. "Go and fetch those birds down."

"There aren't any dead birds up there," Chouen said. "But we'll go up and prove it. We'll shake every branch, and you'll see what bad shots you are." And, laughing to think how they would show up the younger boys, the two climbed the trunk of the tree.

But this was no ordinary tree. The higher they climbed, the larger the trunk swelled. Realizing that they were in trouble, the two wanted to come down from the top, but they were unable to without falling.

"What has happened to us, our brothers?" they called down. "How unfortunate we are! This tree frightens us! How can we climb down when it frightens us just to look at the awful trunk?"

Hunter and Little Jaguar well knew how bad the tree was to climb, and had known better than to try it themselves. This was the first part of their plan. "Loosen your breechcloths," Hunter called up. "Tie them below your stomach. Let the long ends hang down, and pull them from behind. In this way you can walk easily." For a breechcloth was actually a length of cloth or fiber almost as long as a man when unwound, and could be tied in more than one way.

This did not make a lot of sense to the older brothers, but they were willing to try anything that might help them get down safely. They remade their loincloths, pulling the ends back so that they dangled.

Instantly these were changed into tails. Indeed, the older brothers assumed the appearance of monkeys. Horrified, they hopped over the branches of the trees, having no trouble climbing down now, and buried themselves in the forest among the great woods and little woods. They swung from branch to branch, making faces as they went.

Hunter and Little Jaguar had not lied. They had enabled their older brothers to climb down, as they had promised. But they had done it in a way the others had not expected. They had used sorcery to change them into a form that could climb better. In this manner they overcame their enemies. They could not have done it without the magic they had learned.

But that was only the first part of their plan. Now they implemented the rest of it. They went home and spoke to their grandmother and their mother. "What could it be that has happened to our elder brothers?" Hunter said innocently. "Suddenly their faces are those of animals!"

"If you have done any harm to your elder brothers," old Xmucane said severely, "you have hurt me and filled me with sadness."

"Do not do such a thing to your brothers, oh my children," Xquic said, not wishing anyone to suffer. She was still young, so retained the softheartedness of a maiden.

They were ready for this. "Do not grieve, grandmother," Little Jaguar said. "You shall see their faces again, if you want to. But we must warn you that it may be a difficult trial for you. Be careful that you do not laugh at them."

Then the two brought out their musical instruments and made the song of the monkey. They played the flute and drum, and continued until their older brothers were compelled to come to the lodge, drawn by the music.

Batz and Chouen came, and began to dance to the music. But when the old woman saw their ugly faces, she laughed, unable to help herself. Embarrassed, the two ran away.

"Now you see, grandmother," Hunter said. "You have made them flee! You must not laugh at them, for they do not find this situation at all funny." He was speaking the truth.

"We can play this theme only four times," Little Jaguar said, and this, too, was true.

They played again, and again Batz and Chouen came, right to the court of the lodge. They grimaced, and were really very amusing with their monkey faces, their broad bottoms, their narrow tails, and their bare stomachs, until Xmucane could not refrain from laughing again. At that point they fled, as they had before.

Again the boys reproved her. They played a third time, and the grandmother managed to contain her laughter. The monkeys went to the kitchen and scrubbed their noses and frightened each other with the faces they made. Their eyes seemed to give off a red light. This was too much for Xmucane, and she burst into laughter once more.

"We can call them only once more," Hunter warned.

Yet again they played their music, and the sound was sweet, but this time the monkey brothers, three times humiliated, did not return. Instead they fled into the forest and were gone.

"We have done everything we could, grandmother," Little Jaguar said. "Your laughter drove them away. But do not grieve; we remain here, and we are your grandchildren too."

The old woman realized that it was done, and that she herself was in part to blame. She resigned herself to the situation, for she did not wish to live alone.

In this manner Batz and Chouen were disgraced and overcome, becoming animals, because of their arrogance and the way they had abused their brothers. They had been excellent musicians and artists, and could have done great things had they not allowed unworthy emotions to rule them.

Now Hunter and Little Jaguar moved into the lodge, and began to work there, for they wanted their mother and grandmother to think well of them. The first thing they did was prepare the cornfield, which had been sadly neglected by the older brothers. They took axes, picks, and their wooden hoes and went there, each carrying his blowgun on his shoulder.

"Bring us food at midday, grandmother," they said as they departed.

"Very well, my grandsons," Xmucane said, accepting the new order stoically.

When they came to the field, they used their magic to animate the tools. Hunter plunged the pick into the earth, and it continued to work by itself. Little Jaguar struck a tree with his axe, and after that it chopped the trees and branches and vines by itself. It was magically sharp, so that no fire was needed to char the hard wood and make it manageable, as was ordinarily the case. So it was that their work progressed, with little effort on their part, for they were sorcerers coming into their full power.

But next day they discovered that all the ground was whole again, and all the trees were standing as if they had never been felled.

"Who has played this trick on us?" they asked, annoyed. But there was no way to tell. They would have been suspicious of their older brothers, but monkeys could not have done this.

So they worked the field that day, and departed as they had before. But they came quietly back at dusk, and hid themselves, and watched.

At midnight the animals of the field and forest came: the

puma and the jaguar, the deer, the coyote, the wild boar, the rabbit, and the various birds. "Rise up, trees," the animals said in their own tongues. "Rise up, vines!"

So they spoke, and the trees and vines responded, being magically restored.

Furious, the two youths jumped out and grabbed for the animals. But the animals fled, and could not be caught. Hunter got hold of the tail of the deer, and Little Jaguar caught the tail of the rabbit, but the tails came off in their hands and the animals escaped. Ever after, the tails of these animals were short. The others escaped entirely.

Then the rat passed, and they both pounced on it. They squeezed its head and tried to choke it, and they burned its tail in the fire. Ever since, the rat's tail has had no hair.

"I must not die at your hands," the rat protested. "I helped your mother to harvest the corn, the first time, and thereby helped secure her place here, and yours. Neither is it your business to plant the cornfield. You have something better to do."

"How can you say that?" Hunter demanded, not letting it go.

"Loosen me a little, and I will explain," the rat said. "But first give me something to eat, for I am very hungry."

"First tell us; then we will give you food," Little Jaguar said.

The rat agreed. "Did you know that the property of your father, One-Hunter, and his brother, Seven-Hunter, has remained in your grandmother's lodge? I refer to the gear for playing ball, which they left behind, for they suspected treachery and were not disappointed. That gear is hanging from the roof of the lodge: the ring, the gloves, and the ball. But your grandmother does not want you to know of this, because of what her sons did."

Now, the boys knew of the ball game, but had never been able to play it because they had been working all the time, and had no gear. This interested them very much, for tlaxtli was the greatest game known on earth. Of course they wanted to get that gear and start practicing the game, so as to become great players and win fame.

"This shall be your food," Hunter told the rat. "Corn, chili seeds, beans, and cacao drink. All this belongs to you, and if there should be anything stored away and forgotten, that, too, will be yours. All these things are at our grandmother's lodge."

"That's wonderful," the rat said. "But I don't think your grandmother likes me. What should I tell her if she sees me coming into the lodge?"

"Don't worry," Little Jaguar said. "We shall distract her long enough for you to get in unobserved."

They did this, sneaking the rat into the lodge when they returned in the morning, so it could forage in the dark corners. Then they asked Xmucane for a meal of tortillas, chili sauce, and broth, and she made it for them.

"But we need water too," Hunter said.

"It is in that jar," Xmucane said. But it wasn't, for he had magically dried it up. She shook her head, perplexed, and took the jar, and went with Xquic to the river to fetch more.

Then the boys saw by looking in the red chili sauce the reflection of the game ball, which was suspended from the roof. They wanted to get it, but knew they needed more time. So they used their magic again, and sent an insect like a mosquito to puncture the side of their grandmother's water jar so that it could not be filled.

Then they told the rat to bite through the cord that held the ball, and it fell down to them, together with the gloves and the leather pads. The boys seized them and quickly hid them by the road which led to the ball court.

Then they went to the river, where their mother and grandmother were trying vainly to plug the hole in the jar. So the boys plugged it, and all was well, and Xmucane never realized that they had found and taken the ball gear. Or that the rat had been admitted to her lodge, and would be in the lodges of all human folk thereafter, taking whatever was spilled or accessible. Rats were not popular with human folk, but they had earned their place and could not be driven out.

After that Hunter and Little Jaguar played ball all the time, and quickly became proficient. In this game, no one was allowed to touch the ball with his hands, head, or feet; it had to be bounced from the knees, hips, back, or shoulders from teammate to teammate until a score was made. The protective gear was essential to protect their bodies from harm, for the ball was solid, about the size and heft of a human head. The greatest honor could be achieved by bouncing the ball through one of the vertical stone rings set high on the walls of the court. This required enormous skill, and few players could do it even when there weren't opposing players to interfere, but Hunter and Little Jaguar learned to do it.

They were not just amusing themselves. They knew that the only way they could reach the underworld and achieve vengeance for their father was to be invited to play ball there. They knew that the lords of death would try to deceive them and kill them, as they had One-Hunter and Seven-Hunter. But the four owls had told them of these tricks, and about all the rest of the underworld of Xibalba, and they were ready to deal with it.

As they matured and assumed their full growth, Hunter and Little Jaguar's notoriety spread all across the land, and even to the underworld. That was the way they wanted it.

Then the lords of death sent messengers. "The boys must come to play ball in Xibalba," the messengers told Xmucane. "They must be there within seven days. We will show them the way."

Actually, the young men already knew the way, for the four owls had told them this too. Those owls had served the sons of Xquic well!

But their grandmother did not know this. Indeed, she was horrified to learn that they had been playing the ball game, for she feared that they would be brought to the underworld and betrayed and killed, just as her sons had. But it was too late to stop that; all she could do now was send the message to the young men, though she grieved to do it.

"But whom shall I send?" she asked, for the court was too far for her to go to, and too far for Xquic.

A louse fell into her lap. She seized it and held it in the palm of her hand. "I will send you," she said. So she gave the message to the louse.

At once the louse walked off, but it was small and did not move quickly. A toad spied it.

"Where are you going?" the toad asked.

"I go to the ball court to give a message to the boys."

"I will help you move faster," the toad said, and snapped up the louse. Then the toad hopped down the road toward the ball court.

A snake saw him. The snake concluded that the toad was too slow, so the snake swallowed the toad and slithered on down the road. Always after that, toads were the food of snakes.

A hawk spied the snake, and instantly swallowed it. After that, hawks always ate snakes. Then the hawk flew rapidly to the ball court, and perched on the cornice, where Hunter and Little Jaguar were playing ball. "Here is the hawk! Here is the hawk!" it cried.

"Bring our blowguns!" Hunter exclaimed. In a moment he fired a pellet that hit the hawk in the eye and brought it down. "What are you doing here?" Hunter asked the bird.

"I bring a message in my stomach," the hawk replied. "First cure my eye, and then I will tell you."

So they took a bit of rubber from the ball, and squeezed juice from it onto the hawk's eye. Immediately the eye healed.

Then the hawk vomited out the snake. "Speak!" they said to the snake.

The snake vomited out the toad. "What is the message that you bring?" they asked the toad.

The toad tried to vomit out the louse, but could not; it did not come out.

"Liar!" Little Jaguar cried, kicking the toad in the rump, and the bone of the toad's haunches gave way. It tried again, but its mouth only filled with spittle.

Then the boys opened the toad's mouth and looked inside. The louse was stuck to the toad's teeth; it had not been swallowed. Thus the toad had been tricked, and the kind of food it ate was not known. It could not run, because of its crushed haunch bone, and was the food of snakes.

"Speak," Hunter said to the louse.

The louse, noting what had happened to the toad, did not delay. "The messengers of the lords of death have come to your grandmother. You have seven days to go to Xibalba with your playing gear. Your grandmother grieves already for your loss, for she remembers what happened to your father."

The boys exchanged a significant glance. This was the invitation they had been waiting for!

But they pretended to be sad, so that no one would know how well prepared they were for this occasion. They wanted the lords of death to be surprised.

They hurried back to the lodge. "We are going, mother and grandmother," they said. "But do not fear, for we shall return."

"That's what your father said," the old woman grumped.

"But you shall know how we fare," they assured her. They planted two reeds in the lodge, which grew magically there. "If these dry, it is a sign of our death. But if they sprout again, we are alive." Then they took their gear and departed.

Hunter and Little Jaguar followed the messengers down the long steps and across to the river that ran between the ravines. They passed the river of corruption, and did not drink from it. They passed the river of blood, but did not touch it even with their feet; instead they stretched their blowguns across it and crossed on them.

They came to the intersection of the four roads: black, white, red, and green. Here they paused, as if undecided, though they knew better than to take the black one. There was information they needed, so they took advantage of this pause to get it.

Hunter touched his leg. From it appeared a mosquito, the same one who had magically punctured the water jug. "Go sting the lords, one by one," he murmured to it.

"I shall," it replied, and flew away.

The magic mosquito flew to the ceremonial chamber of the lords of death. They were all there, awaiting with grim relish the arrival of the ball players from the realm of the living, and conjecturing on the terrible things they would do to these innocents.

The mosquito stung the first, but it was one of the wooden figures, and it made no response. The insect flew on and stung the second, but this one also was wood.

Then it stung the third, who was One-Death. "Ah!" he exclaimed, swatting at the mosquito, but the insect had jumped away before it was caught.

"What is the matter, One-Death?" the next lord asked.

"Something stung me, Seven-Death," he replied.

In this manner the mosquito stung all the lords, making each exclaim, and each was identified by the queries of the others.

When this was done, Hunter pulled out a hair of his leg, where he had touched it before. The hair was the magical mosquito he had sent. Now it told him all their names, according to where they stood, so he would not be fooled.

They followed the green road on to Xibalba, where the lords awaited them. "Greet the one who is seated," they were told, and the lords waited, ready to burst out laughing when the visitors fell for the trick.

"Why should we speak to that one?" Hunter asked. "It is only a wooden figure."

The lords stifled their laughter and their annoyance, disgruntled at the manner in which the youths had seen through their ruse. But they did not yet understand how well prepared Hunter and Little Jaguar were. These two had the magic of their father, and the cunning of their mother, and the information of the four great owls, and they knew what they were doing.

"Hail, One-Death!" Hunter said to that lord. "Hail, Seven-Death!" He continued, naming every lord as he faced him, making no error, for his magic mosquito had told him true. The lords nodded graciously, but they were really most annoyed and somewhat mystified. How had the visitors come to know them so well?

Then One-Death indicated the stone seat. "Sit here, and we shall confer," he said.

Little Jaguar walked to the stone and made as if to sit on it. But he paused, then seemed to change his mind. "This is not a fitting seat for a guest," he said. "It is only a hot stone. Is it the best you have to offer?"

The lords of death could scarcely conceal their ire at the failure of this ploy. But they thought that Little Jaguar had merely felt the heat when he paused, so had discovered the trick by chance.

"Very well, go to that lodge," One-Death said, pointing to the Lodge of Gloom. This was the first real test of the underworld; the wooden figure and the hot stone seat were merely jokes. The lords believed that the youths would suffer the beginning of their downfall here, as all visitors had before them.

The youths entered the lodge without protest. One-Death immediately gave them sticks of fat pine and cigars, warning them to return them whole in the morning.

"Very well," the youths agreed. But when they were shut inside, they put out the flames and put red-colored feathers on the torches; these feathers were so bright they looked like flames. They put fireflies on the ends of the cigars, making them glow. In this manner they fooled anyone who watched, and the lords rejoiced, thinking that they had prevailed.

In the morning the door was opened, and the youths emerged. Their torches and cigars were intact.

"How's this?" the lords of death demanded. "Who are these clever folk? Who gave birth to them? Their conduct is disturbingly strange." But still they did not make the connection to One-Hunter's skull and Little Blood, whom they thought long dead.

They summoned the youths. "Let's play ball," they said, though they had not intended it to get this far.

Hunter and Little Jaguar agreed. This was, after all, what they had come for, supposedly.

"We shall use our ball," Seven-Death said.

"By no means; we shall use *our* ball," Hunter said.

"I insist that we use ours," Seven-Death said, glowering.

Hunter shrugged. It didn't matter; he had argued merely to deceive the lords of death about what the youths knew. If they anticipated every trick, the lords of death would know that they had information that made them dangerous.

They continued to argue about the terms of the game, yielding when the lords of death became insistent.

Then they went to the ball court, donning their gear.

But the ball of the lords of death was enchanted, and the youths could not make it behave as it should. Soon they lost control of it, unable to score. The lords of Xibalba seized the ball and threw it directly at the ring on the side of the court; if it went through that ring, they would win. Meanwhile some of them grasped the handle of the flint knife that was used for sacrifice. They were eager to cut out two beating hearts and roast them.

The shot was not good, because the ball still misbehaved.

The lords of death really did not care, as they lacked the necessary skill anyway. They just wanted to kill the youths. All their reputed skill as players was mere sham; it required diligent practice to be good at the ball game, and the lords of death practiced only deceit and betrayal.

"What is this?" Little Jaguar demanded, indicating the knife. "The game is hardly started, yet you wish to kill us as if we are losers? Can it be that we misunderstood, and that you did not call us here to play ball with you? In that case we shall leave at once, being unwelcome."

That shamed the lords of death in their own eyes. Indeed, they could not honorably kill the youths without first beating them in the game or causing them to violate one of the devious rules of the underworld. They certainly wanted to kill Hunter and Little Jaguar, but they would be a laughingstock if they did it dishonorably. That was to say, in a manner that showed their dishonor, for in truth they had no honor, only the pretense of it. Their pride was based on the appearance of honor, not on the reality, but that meant that they could not cheat openly. This the young men knew.

"Do not leave, boys," One-Death said as he put away the knife. "We shall continue the game, and now we shall use your ball." For the ploy with the ball had become evident when the lords themselves could not score with it.

"Very well," the youths said. They took their own ball, which was firm and true, and bounced it from one to the other on their bodies and buttocks, and the lords of death were unable to interfere with them or to take the ball away. Soon Hunter bounced it off his hip straight through the ring on the opponents' wall. The game was over, and the youths had won.

"We shall play again tomorrow," Seven-Death said, offended by the defeat of the lords of the underworld.

Now, the youths did not have to agree to this, for they had won, and would have been sacrificed had they lost. But they had more in mind than merely humiliating the lords of Xibalba. To accomplish what they wanted, they had to play along with their enemies for a while longer.

"Go and gather four gourds of flowers for us, early tomorrow morning," One-Death said.

The youths knew that this was another cunning trick, intended to deceive them and make them forfeit their victory, but they pretended not to know. "What kind of flowers?" Little Jaguar asked.

"A red one, and a white one, and a yellow one, and a blue one," One-Death said.

"Certainly," Little Jaguar said. "We shall go immediately to cut them. Where is the path there?"

"Through that lodge," One-Death said, indicating the Lodge of Knives. This was the second place of torture in Xibalba, where the terrible knives cut any intruders to pieces. He believed that the youths would never get to the field of flowers beyond.

"We shall fetch the flowers, and play ball again with you in the morning," Hunter said.

Then they entered the lodge, and the lords of death rejoiced, expecting mayhem.

But the youths had been warned of all the tortures of the underworld, and had prepared for each of them. As they entered, Little Jaguar spoke to the knives, and his words were a spell that caused them to settle down. "Yours shall be the flesh of all the animals," he said.

The knives were quiescent, and made no move against the youths. Since that time, knives have cut the flesh of all animals they encounter, and the flesh of men too, but not that of those who master them.

Meanwhile Hunter addressed the red ants of the region. "Go, all of you, and bring the four kinds of flowers we must have," he said. "Thereafter, the flowers of the night shall be yours."

"We agree," the ants said, and they marched off in a mass.

Now, the lords of the underworld had put guards at the field of flowers, warning them to let no one approach the plants. These guards were owls with long tails. So even if the youths survived the Lodge of Knives, they would still fail the mission, being unable to get the fowers.

But the ants crept in and cut the flowers in the darkness, needing no light to distinguish the colors, and carried them away. The guards never noticed, for they were alert for men, not for insects. The ants filled the four gourds with flowers of each color, and returned before dawn to the Lodge of Knives. But before they returned, they crept up behind the owls and cut away their tails, so quietly and cleverly that the guards never were aware of this either.

When the youths emerged unscathed, with the four colors of flowers, the lords of death were livid. They sent for the guards. "Why did you allow them to steal our flowers?" they demanded.

"We noticed nothing," the guards protested. Then they discovered the loss of their tails, and were further dismayed.

"Idiots!" the lords exclaimed, and tore at the mouths of the owls. Since then the owls have had short tails and cleft mouths, though they really had tried to do their job.

Hunter and Little Jaguar played ball with One-Death and Seven-Death. But the lords had improved their technique using special magic that gave them more speed and power than any living man could muster, and neither side was able to score. They played several tie matches, and agreed to play again the next day. But in truth the youths could have won, had they been minded to. They preferred to remain longer in Xibalba, so as to complete their mission of vengeance.

This time they were sent to the Lodge of Cold, the third great torture of the underworld. It was full of hail, with a terrible wind, and so cold that it seemed that no one could survive within it. But they dug out old logs and made a fire and were warm. The lords of death smoldered.

So it went, from day to day and night to night. The youths entered the Lodge of Jaguars, and Little Jaguar threw them bones, and the animals were satisfied, thinking they were eating flesh, because of the enchantment. The boys entered the Lodge of Fire, but their magic made them impervious. They entered the Lodge of Bats, where huge vampires with teeth as sharp as fire-hardened stakes lurked, but the youths made themselves small and slept inside their blowguns, where the bats could not reach them.

But here was disaster, because they could not see the light of dawn. Hunter went out to see, and it was too early, and the terrible Death Bat who was a god pounced on him and cut off his head.

"We are completely undone!" Little Jaguar cried, discovering the fate of his brother. One moment of carelessness had cost Hunter his head!

The lords of death rejoiced. They hung the severed head up in the ball court, where all could see it. Half of their intention had been fulfilled.

But though Hunter had been the better ball player, Little Jaguar was the better sorcerer. Now he was suffering the death of his brother, and he was angry. He was like a wounded jaguar, and that is the most dangerous kind. He resolved that he would restore his brother, but he could not do so unless he had the head back, to place on the body.

He called all the animals, large and small, during the night. "What does each of you eat?" he inquired. "I have called you so that you may choose your food." Actually, he needed to find the one that was right for his purpose.

All the animals went out to find their types of food. But slow behind them was the turtle. Little Jaguar worked a spell on it as it passed his brother's body, and it became compressed in its shell and assumed the form of Hunter's head. Little Jaguar worked to make the likeness perfect, and indeed, it seemed that Hunter was alive again. But really it was just his body, made to move by Little Jaguar's magic, with the turtle for its head.

"Now we shall play ball," Little Jaguar said grimly. "You, turtle, must only pretend to play, for you cannot do it truly; I will do everything alone. And you, rabbit, go wait in the grove beside the ball court. When the ball comes to you, run out and away, and I will do something to make them follow you."

Soon day broke, and the two youths emerged, seemingly both healthy. The lords of death were amazed, but did not know what to make of it. They suspected that it was pretense, so they tried to make Little Jaguar give himself away. After all, the true head of Hunter was hanging over the ball court.

"Hit that head with the ball!" they cried, trying to get Little Jaguar flustered about the indignity. But Little Jaguar ignored them, and went straight out to play, so that they had to concentrate on the game.

The lords of death threw out the ball. Little Jaguar went for it, sending it straight toward the ring. But his aim was deliberately bad. The ball stopped, bounced, and passed out of the ball court and rolled toward the oak grove, where the rabbit was.

Instantly the rabbit ran out, hopping madly. Little Jaguar's sorcery made the rabbit look like the ball. The lords of death chased after it, shouting, but it veered and dodged so crazily that they could not catch it. More of them joined in, determined to trap the ball, and soon no one remained at the court except Little Jaguar.

That was what he wanted. He ran up and took possession of his brother's head. He took the turtle and hung it where the head had been, so that it looked the same. Then he set the real head firmly on the body, and that enabled Hunter to recover, because of the magic the two of them had. They were very happy to be restored to each other. In their arrogance and certainty of victory the lords of death had failed to cut out Hunter's heart and burn it, or to destroy his body, so that his death had not been irrevocable. Now the evil lords faced both youths again, and did not know it.

The lords of Xibalba finally found the ball, when the rabbit led them to it and dodged aside. They brought it back, and play resumed.

The game was tied. Then Little Jaguar hurled a stone at the turtle, which seemed to be his brother's head, and it fell to the ground and to the stone ball court, breaking into a thousand pieces that resembled seeds. The lords were amazed to see the head shatter like that, and understood that it wasn't the head, but something else. They realized that they had been deceived, and they thought that Hunter had never died. They resolved not to be fooled like that again.

Meanwhile, Little Jaguar knew that the time of his own death was approaching. But this was part of his plan, and he was ready to die—in the right way. He had prepared for this by approaching two notable soothsayers who were also known as diviners, called Xulu and Pacam. "You shall be questioned by the lords of Xibalba about our deaths," he had told them. "For they are planning to kill us, as they killed our father and uncle. When they find how much trouble it is to overcome us, they will seek advice about how best to do it. We believe they will burn us. When they come to you about how to dispose of our bodies, tell them that the only way to be sure we will not be restored is to grind up our bones into powder and throw them into the river."

The soothsayers agreed to do this, though they found it an odd request.

Now, as the youths had anticipated, the lords of death tired of trying to torture them and of trying to beat them in the ball game, and resolved to cast aside the pretense of honor and kill them directly. So they made a great bonfire in a kind of oven, filling it with thick branches so that it would burn long and well.

Then the lords sent messengers to fetch the youths. "Tell them to come here so that we may burn them," they said. For they wanted the boys to suffer the torment of expectation.

The youths came readily, and the lords thought to play a mocking game with them. "Let's drink, while you fly over the fire!" One-Death said, preparing a rope with which to swing them through the flames.

"Whom do you think you're fooling?" Little Jaguar asked. "You cannot burn us! We shall burn ourselves!" Then he clasped his brother, and both of them jumped into the fire. Soon their bodies were roasted in the terrible heat.

At this the lords of Xibalba were joyful. They shouted and whistled. "Now at last we have overcome them!" Seven-Death said. "They knew they could not escape, so they gave up rather than be tortured anymore!"

But the lords had learned caution, after seeing how Hunter had returned to life, and how much trouble the two had been to kill. So they summoned the two soothsayers, Xulu and Pacam, exactly as Little Jaguar had anticipated. "What should we do with the bones?" they inquired. When the soothsayers answered, it seemed good to the lords. They ground up the bones between stones, as if they were grinding corn, and cast them into the river. "Now we are truly rid of them," they said, satisfied.

But this was the death for which Little Jaguar had prepared. If the lords had done something else, his magic would not have been effective, and he and his brother would have been truly dead. The powder of the bones settled down to the bottom of

the river, where they coalesced, and the spell shaped them and
absorbed water, and they were restored to handsome youths,
as they had been before.

But they took care to conceal their identities, and gave themselves the appearance of old men, so that the lords of Xibalba
would not recognize them. Then they went about as miracle-
workers, doing many strange tricks. They did the dance of the
owl, and the dance of the weasel, and of the armadillo, and
the centipede, and the dance on tall stilts. They burned lodges,
then restored them, showing that the fire had been but illusion.
They cut each other into bits, and brought each other back to
life. This was of course more illusion, but no one could discover
the trick of it, or fathom how they did it. Soon they became
quite famous.

Then the lords of death heard about them, and were curious.
They sent messengers to summon the dancers so that the lords
might be entertained. It was really pretty dull in the land of
death, and the lords were always alert for something that might
amuse them.

"But we don't want to go there!" the youths protested with
mock reluctance. "We are ashamed of our ugly faces and our
poor clothing. We are not worthy to perform before such high
lords."

Of course the lords of death insisted, and in due course, with
much seeming reluctance, the two came before One-Death and
Seven-Death and the other lords of Xibalba, where they waited
in the court of their lodge.

"Now do your dances," One-Death said. "We will pay you
for your effort. Do the trick where you kill yourselves and burn
your lodge, yet all is undone." For this really intrigued the
lords, who had an interest in all things relating to death.

So Hunter and Little Jaguar began to sing and dance, and
they were so entertaining that all the folk of the underworld
came to watch.

"Cut my dog into pieces," One-Death said. "And bring him
back to life."

"Very well," Little Jaguar said, and cut the dog into bits,
then restored him. The dog wagged his tail, for his death had
been illusion and he had never been hurt.

"Now burn my lodge," One-Death said.

So they set fire to the lodge in which all them were, and the flames roared high, yet no one was hurt. The lodge burned into ashes around them, but it was all illusion, and after it was done it was restored, and it was clear that it had never been touched.

All the lords were amazed, for they had never before seen such effective illusion. They pondered as they watched the dances, and then asked for more.

"Now kill a man," One-Death said. "Not an animal, but a man, so we can see how you do it."

"Very well," Little Jaguar answered. They seized one of the spectators, who was somewhat reluctant but unable to protest. Hunter bent him back on the altar and Little Jaguar used his knife to cut out the man's heart. He raised the beating heart high, showing it to everyone. Then he put the heart back into the man's chest, and closed up the wound, and suddenly the blood was gone and the man was alive again. This, too, had been illusion, and even the man had not seen how it was done. He was much relieved to find himself alive and unharmed.

The lords of death were amazed, for they still could not penetrate the illusion. "Now kill yourselves," One-Death said, thinking that they would not be able to perform the illusion successfully then. They were excruciatingly curious about this technique.

So Little Jaguar sacrificed Hunter. He laid him on the altar and cut off his arms one by one, and then his legs, and then his head. Finally Little Jaguar cut out Hunter's heart and threw it onto the grass of the court. Then Little Jaguar stabbed himself through the chest, and cut out his own heart, and fell back on the floor, holding the beating heart aloft.

Everyone stared, believing that the dancers could never recover from such dismemberment. But it was really the dance of only one man, Little Jaguar, and the illusion of his brother, and the illusion of his own beating heart.

Then Little Jaguar seemed to set his heart back into his chest, so that he was whole again. "Get up!" he said to the dismembered remains of his brother, and the illusion faded, and the real Hunter stepped out from the shadow to take its place. He was as healthy as if he had never died, which was of course the truth.

One-Death and Seven-Death were caught up in the excitement of this realistic show, and determined to find out how the illusion was made. "Do the same with us!" One-Death cried. "Sacrifice us the same way! Cut us both into pieces, and hold up our beating hearts!" For they were sure that they could not be deceived once they participated directly.

"If you insist," Little Jaguar said, as if reluctant to let them in on it.

Then he took One-Death, and cut off his head, and cut off his limbs, and cut out his heart most realistically, and all the spectators were impressed with the seeming realism.

"Now bring him back to life," Seven-Death said.

"But you didn't say that," Little Jaguar protested.

"But—"

That was all Seven-Death was able to say before Hunter plunged his knife into his chest and cut out his heart. He fell, and Hunter held up the heart. "No, we did not agree to bring either of you back to life!" he cried. "We shall have no mercy on you. No more than you had on us."

Then the two youths cast aside their disguises and revealed their true identities. The other lords of death recognized them and were appalled. They knew that the vengeance of their victims was at hand.

The other lords fled, and Hunter and Little Jaguar chased them. The lords tried to hide in a great ravine, but the ants came in hordes and stung them and drove them out. Then they prostrated themselves before the two youths, knowing that they had no chance to prevail against those who had slain One-Death and Seven-Death.

Now the youths told them also the names of their father and uncle, who had been betrayed and killed here, so that they would understand the full measure of this vengeance. The boys did not kill the folk of Xibalba, but they reduced them to common level. No more were there any lords among them, only lowly laborers. Thus was the vengeance complete.

Then Hunter and Little Jaguar returned to their own realm, where their mother and grandmother had been watching the two reeds in the lodge. The reeds had dried up when the youths were consumed in the bonfire, but later had turned green and sprouted again. Then the two women's hearts had filled with joy.

In this manner Xquic, Little Blood, had helped wreak the downfall of those who had killed One-Hunter and Seven-Hunter, by providing sons whose great magic and courage destroyed the power of the lords of death.

Of course, living folk still do die, but only in their turn, in battle or from malignant spirits or because of the weakness of old age. They are never taken when their time has not come, because the lords of death are dead. Little Blood did this great favor for all who followed her in life.

CHAPTER 5

⟨❧⟩

CALUSA

O Spirit of the Mound, I have told you the tale of Tzec's people, the mighty Maya, and her ancestor Little Blood, who deceived and defeated the lords of death. Truly, her heritage was phenomenal! Now I will tell you how we traveled through the waters of the Calusa, the Powerful Men, and the reception we had there, for this, too, is never to be forgotten. But one thing I must clarify lest it seem wrong: Tzec's memory of her approach to Throat Shot about her purchase differed from his memory of it. When I told you her tale, I told it her way; now I tell it his way. One of them must be right.

Throat Shot was stunned by the story of Little Blood. It made the Maya heritage come to life. The girl had been Wren, the half-mute slave child; now she was Tzec, the descendant of godlike creatures. Such magic! Such great deeds! Such treachery, and such vengeance! Such a wonderful realm, seen through the mouth of a little girl!

He had heard the tales of the evening fire as a child and thrilled to them. But as he grew, he had grown away from them; they had become too familiar, and he had not wanted to appear childish by listening with the children. Now that old fascination had returned, for this was a new tale, and strange. He had not realized that other tribes *had* tales, or that they could be as awesome as this.

He was hardly aware of the huge expanses of water they passed, or of the channels between long islands. He paddled mechanically, listening to the Tale, and translating it for the Trader as they went along.

As the Tale and its translation ended, Throat Shot realized that several days had passed, and they had traveled far down the coast, beyond any region he had visited overland. They had stopped several times at places on the shore that the Trader knew of, to eat and camp for the night, for it was not safe to remain on the water when not alert. The hungry alligators normally left the canoe alone, but they watched it, and they were larger here than they were inland. The poisonous snakes hunted here, and some of them would swim if they saw something worth biting. So time had been spent in necessary chores, and he had done his share—but somehow it had all faded out beyond the compelling other reality of the Tale.

Now they were coming into the territory of the Calusa. He asked Tzec if she was afraid of the Calusa, for she was looking increasingly nervous. She demurred, pretending not to understand his question. That did not relieve him.

That evening, as they made camp, Throat Shot spoke briefly to the Trader while the girl was handling a natural function a bit apart. "She was captive of the Calusa. Maybe she fears they will harm her."

"It was the Toco who harmed her, by killing her mother," the Trader reminded him. "She speaks Calusan. See that she does not run away."

Throat Shot was appalled at his own naiveté. Of course this would be the tribe to which she would flee: the one she knew best. But how could he stop her from fleeing, if that was her intent?

Soon he was with her, gathering wood for the evening fire, while the Trader used a bamboo pole and bone hook to fish for their supper. "You did not answer me before," he said. "I have told the Trader you will not flee. It will be my blame if you do."

Tzec paused, staring at him. "I will not flee!" she protested indignantly. "You have been good to me."

"Then are you afraid of the Calusa? You seem to hate this region."

"No, I am not afraid. I understand the Calusa well enough.

I can get along, and I may even meet some I know."

"Then what is the matter? I cannot trust you if I do not know."

She hesitated a moment, then shrugged. "I will tell you. I am afraid he will sell me to them."

"But if you get along with them, it would be better to be sold here than to some other tribe where you don't know what will happen." He did not want to be more specific, but probably she understood: she was a child, but soon would not be, and the man who bought her might not have the scruples of the Toco or Calusa. Most men preferred nubile women, but youth was attractive, and opinions differed about how young a woman was best. It was said that a girl matured faster when taken early by a man. Some girls even sought that type of enhancement, being eager to leave childhood behind.

"I wish *you* would buy me."

That stopped him in his tracks. "I can't buy you! I am only one step from being a slave myself! I serve the Trader, until he reaches his home. This is how I pay for traveling with him."

"I know," she said. "So I hope he doesn't sell me."

She wanted to stay with him! This possibility had not occurred to him before. Now, flattered, he realized that it was mutual. The Tale of Little Blood still colored his thoughts, and in a way he saw Tzec as that young woman, trying to save herself and her culture from the onslaught of evil.

"I would be glad if he did not sell you," he said. "But it is his business to buy and sell, and if someone offers more than three feather cloaks, or something of equivalent value, he will do it. It is not my place to tell him no. In fact, if I learn of anyone who will pay more, I must tell him, because I serve him."

"I know," she said forlornly.

They continued to gather wood, not speaking again.

The Calusa did not wait for them to enter their domain; three swift canoes approached, with four men each, one of whom carried a drawn bow. "Who are you?" the man demanded.

Throat Shot knew that this was his job, for he spoke their language. "We are a Trader and his goods and translator," he called in Calusan, tapping his chest as he mentioned the last. "We come in peace, to trade with you."

One canoe drew close so that the man could peer into the Trader's vessel. He saw the goods there. "Then come; the Cacique will be glad to see you."

The warlike party became an honor guard, as the Calusa showed the way to their town. As they approached it, Throat Shot saw many boats, of many kinds. Some were so strange that he stared.

"You have never seen a sail before?" the leader of the Calusa party inquired, smiling. "How can this be, when you speak our tongue?"

"I traveled inland, carrying messages to your people, but I never saw the big sea. I knew you went on it, but it meant little, until now."

The man laughed. "I would not like to be trapped always in the jungle! That is a sail, which catches the wind and pulls the boat along without paddles—when there is wind, instead of calm."

"But suppose you don't want to go the way the wind blows?"

The man glanced at him as if finding something funny. "Oh, we manage," he said.

Throat Shot wasn't satisfied with that answer, but let the matter drop. Tzec had been with the Calusa; she would know, and she would tell him, when there was a chance. Indeed, later he did learn that they had a way to slide across the wind, and travel in a different direction from it. They could even travel *into* it, by going back and forth across it. There was surely some potent magic in operation there!

Then he saw two canoes lashed together, and that was another surprise. Not only did they seem to work, they seemed more stable than the single ones. What a curious craft!

Then they came to the island town, and his amazement grew. Here were mounds like that near the river, where the spirit had told him to seek the Tale of Little Blood. But they were not rounded and weathered; these were sharp and new. They seemed to be formed of shell, and towered above the island; it would be dizzying to stand at the summit of one of them. Some were round and some were square, with sharp edges at each corner, rising to a flat terrace at the top. Those were ceremonial, but there were also burial mounds; he could feel their spirits sleeping within them. He wanted to go and talk with those spirits, but that would have to wait on the Trader's business. He had not imagined that there would be so many in one place! It reminded him of the great pyramids of the Maya, which Tzec had not quite seen, and Dzibilchaltún with its Temple of the Seven Dolls. Oh, to go and commune with the spirits of that fantastic city!

They entered a canal that led to the interior of the island. The banks were graded, rising to the level of the houses, which seemed to be square hard mud roofed with palm thatch. He had not seen that kind before, either. Near the water they were on stilts, and he could see right under them. It was one oddity after another. In fact, this whole region seemed almost as strange as the homeland of the Maya that Tzec had described. He wondered whether the Calusa were related to the Maya.

They landed near the Chief's house, which was huge. They walked up a ramp that spiraled to the top of one of the highest mounds. Here the houses were larger than any he had seen, and their walls were plastered smooth, like the surface of a mud flat after a rain.

The Cacique came out to meet them, with his retinue of wives and warriors. He wore an ornate deerskin cape tied over his shoulder, artfully showing his elaborate tattooing. His hair was tied up in a knot on the top of his head so neatly that it must have taken the labor of a skilled woman to do it. He was impressive not so much for his body, though he stood half a head taller than the other men, as for his clothing and jewelry and manner, and the way others deferred to him. On his forehead was an ornament of brightly painted shell, and there were beaded bands on his legs. Two of the women with him were beautiful, their breasts full and well formed, and their faces smooth and large-eyed. He had his pick, of course, and was not limited to one. "Wait for him to speak to you," Tzec murmured. "Answer only when he asks you a question. And do what I do."

Throat Shot appreciated the warning, for he had no idea of the proper protocol here. The Trader evidently knew, but was keeping silent.

As the Cacique drew near, Tzec dropped to her knees and lifted her hands, palms up. Throat Shot did the same with his right hand, unable to lift the left that high. After a moment, so did the Trader.

"Ah, the Trader!" the Cacique exclaimed, smiling. "You were here last year!" He placed his hands on the Trader's upturned palms, acknowledging his humbling.

The Trader nodded, not using his hands for sign language. He got up, not speaking.

"We bargained by each bringing out our goods for trade," the Cacique said. "We thought you were stupid, but you got the best of us." He scowled, and Throat Shot's heart sank.

"But this year we'll get the best of you!" the Cacique continued, smiling. "After we feed you and your son and daughter."

Throat Shot's pulse jumped, but he kept his mouth shut. Tzec remained as she was, so he did too. However, the Trader indicated him, shaking his head in negation.

The Cacique turned to Throat Shot. "You are not of his family?"

"I am traveling with him and translating," Throat Shot said. He indicated his left arm. "I cannot be a warrior, so I must use my mouth."

"Ah, this will facilitate our business," the Cacique said, seeming well satisfied. He put his hand on Throat Shot's palm, releasing him. "And the girl—your sister?"

"No, she is a slave taken in trade. She speaks your language also." Throat Shot would have preferred to let Tzec remain mute, but that would not have been in the Trader's interest.

The Cacique faced the girl. "True?"

"I lived among your people, with my mother," Tzec said.

"Who was she?"

"The Lady Zox, from across the sea. She married the priest of the town to the north, but he was killed in a Toco raid, and I was taken by the Toco."

"The one who tamed the tigress!" the Cacique exclaimed. "He tamed her for my father, but my father gave her back. My father was cautious. Do you know what she did?"

"A man abused her, and she cut out his heart," Tzec replied evenly.

"And she cut out the heart of the Toco who took her!" the Cacique cried. "We laughed until we fell on the ground when we learned of that! But we thought her child dead."

"No, I lived," Tzec said. She peeked up at him. "But my mother—oh illustrious one, may I ask?"

The Cacique finally touched her hands, allowing her to rise. "They killed her, of course," he said. "But later we raided, and killed many of them. She was avenged."

"Thank you," Tzec said, bowing her head. Her eyes were squeezed tightly closed. Throat Shot knew she had expected this answer, but still the confirmation hurt. She would never see her mother again, never hear more of the tales of the marvelous Maya tribe.

"You will eat with the women." The Cacique turned back to the Trader as Tzec was led away by the wives. "The Toco tricked you; that child will be dangerous." His gaze flicked to Throat Shot. "Tell him."

"He says the Toco tricked you about the value of the girl, because her mother cut out the heart of the man who used her."

"Then I will sell her to someone who doesn't know," the Trader said, smiling. "Yes, tell him."

Throat Shot translated, and the Cacique smiled without further comment. It was evident that he enjoyed the prospect of bargaining with someone who was good at it, and understood the ethics of trading well enough.

They entered the most impressive building. There was a larger room than Throat Shot had ever seen before, and he did not bother to conceal his awe, knowing that this pleased the Cacique. There were brightly painted shields hung on the walls, and ornate masks, and wooden carvings of animals. There were great spears, and bows, and fine arrows. Throat Shot had enough of an eye for weapons to see that these were of the finest quality. This was a most impressive collection.

The meal was of strange meat, served by children who were slaves or whose families owed service to the Cacique. The meat was good, but from what animal had it come? Certainly no deer or bear! The Cacique noticed Throat Shot's perplexity. "From the deep sea," he said. "The finned killer. He came into our net, eating our fish, and we speared him." He was obviously pleased. He seemed quite comfortable on his low stool; Throat Shot and the Trader and the other warriors present sat cross-legged on the floor.

Water was in fancy cups made of conch shells. But when Throat Shot sipped from his, he discovered that it wasn't water, but some other drink that burned against the tongue. Since he was thirsty, he drank it anyway, but he noticed that the Trader barely touched his. Soon his head was feeling light, and he realized that it was the drink: it was an intoxicant! It was possible to ferment berries and make a drink that made the head float, quite different from the ceremonial White Drink. As a child he had not been given any such at home, and he had been too briefly a man to have encountered it in the interim.

After the meal the Cacique snapped his fingers, and his wives entered the chamber. "My sister and first wife will lead the dance for us," the Cacique said. He gestured, and a single woman stood and came forward.

Throat Shot almost choked on his last mouthful. The Cacique had married his own sister? He had heard of this sort of thing when he learned the tongue, that the caciques did what no lesser personages did, but it had not occurred to him when he first saw the women.

The Cacique's sister was an older but still comely woman. She stood in the center of the chamber, spread her arms, and began to move. Her breasts bounced, and the beads of the necklace that lay across her bosom rattled. She spun around, and her moss skirt flared out, showing her thighs in a way that made them far more interesting than otherwise.

The two younger women joined in, with similar motions. Throat Shot was fascinated. He had seen dancing before, of course, but always for a purpose: to make the corn grow, or to bring rain when it was dry, or to appease an evil spirit. Men and women and often children participated in these dances, every person doing his part to help the tribe. But the dance of the Cacique's wives was evidently not for any of these purposes. It was to make men wish to indulge sexually. Throat Shot thought of Deer Eyes, who had approached him at the time of his manhood. What a fool he had been to turn her down!

The dance ended, and the women departed. "It is time to

trade," the Cacique said briskly, rising from his stool.

The Trader unkinked his legs and stood. Throat Shot started to do the same, but his crotch was uncomfortably tight under his breechcloth because of the effect the dance had on his penis, and his head seemed to be floating some distance from his body because of the drink. He lurched up and almost fell down again, his cloth extended before him.

The Trader caught him on one side, and the Cacique on the other. It was evident that his condition surprised neither of them. "You are young," the Cacique said, chuckling.

Mortified, Throat Shot managed to steady himself and follow them outside. He would be far more careful of that drink next time!

They proceeded down to the canoe, which was undisturbed. The honor of the Calusa, as elsewhere, permitted hard and even deceptive bargaining, but not theft. No more traders would come if news spread that such protocol had been violated.

The wives came out, bringing Tzec, who looked improved. Her hair had been combed and her body washed, and she had been fed. The Calusa were good hosts.

"Oh, you drank that stuff!" she muttered as she came close. "Didn't you know better?"

"Not this time," he said, pleasantly dizzy.

"Did the Trader drink it?"

"Hardly any."

She nodded. "He's smart. They wanted to make him bargain badly."

Now it came clear! The Cacique certainly intended to gain an advantage this time.

"And the women danced for you," Tzec added, glancing at his breechcloth. "You must have liked them."

"Yes," he said shortly.

"Someday I will dance for you."

His irritation faded. She really did want to be with him, despite his arm and her youth. It was a compliment of a kind he had had only once before. But as before, the situation was wrong.

The Trader brought out his bright feather cloaks. The Cacique's men brought out cleverly wrought palm and shell masks. The Trader made Tzec stand beside the cloaks. The Calusa brought out good bows and arrows. It was clear that each side knew what the other was interested in.

They bargained, and Throat Shot did not need to translate. Each representative simply pointed to what he wanted, and indicated what he proposed to trade for it. Each then made elaborate signals of protestation about the inadequacy of the other's offering. But in due course the deals were struck, and the rest of the Trader's feather cloaks were traded for a number of excellent masks.

By this time a fair crowd had gathered. The Calusa, named for their own word for "powerful men," were deceptively friendly. Throat Shot, however, had no doubt of their ferocity in war; there were stories among the Toco, and he had seen their weapons and skill on the water. The Trader had been in every way polite and respectful, and this seemed to be an excellent policy.

The Trader made a signal to Throat Shot: time to finish. Throat Shot faced the Cacique. "If I may speak, illustrious one?"

"I saw his signal," the Cacique said jovially. "It is time for you to stop so you can trade our fine masks at enormous profit to the ignorant inland tribes. But I warn you: folk all the way to the Mayaimi, the wide lake, are subservient to me. Where do you think we got those masks? You won't sell them their own goods!"

Throat Shot translated for the Trader. "But those beyond the wide lake covet the masks," the Trader replied. "We shall make a swift trip up the river to reach them."

Throat Shot translated, and the Cacique nodded. "They are his own people, the Ais, there. He can deal with them as he chooses." He lifted his hand, about to signal the end of the dealing. "My sister will show you to your house for the night. Women will come to you."

But before he made the signal, a man approached. He dropped to his knees before the Cacique, lifting his hands.

"You come to bargain with the Trader?" the Cacique inquired, touching that man's palms. "You are too late; we have bought all his wares."

"The girl," the man said, rising. "She is not sold?"

The Trader took an interest. "He wants to bargain for the

girl," Throat Shot said, translating so that the Calusa would
not realize how much of their language the Trader understood.
But he felt dread; he had thought this hazard was safely past.

Tzec seemed to shrink into herself. She, too, had hoped not
to be sold.

"What does he offer?" the Trader inquired.

Throat Shot turned to the new man, who smelled of fish.
"The girl is for sale. What do you have to trade?"

The fisherman opened his fish-hide bag and brought out a
large, lovely conch. Its spiral was perfect, and there was an
iridescent sheen on the surface. The Toco valued such shells
enormously.

The Trader made a sign of negation. "Not enough for this
fine young woman."

Throat Shot translated. The fisherman brought out a second
conch, as lovely as the first.

The Trader considered, while both Throat Shot and Tzec
grew tight with apprehension. "What does he want with her?"

"I need a small, clever-handed person to help handle my
net," the fisherman explained after Throat Shot relayed the
question. "One who does not take up space better used for a
good catch of fish."

"He wants her for more than that," the Trader said when
he heard the translation. "Tell him this is no fish wench; she
is fit to serve in a chief's house."

In response, the fisherman brought out a third conch. Throat
Shot's dread grew; among his people, such an offering would
readily purchase a slave.

"How do you feel about this?" the Trader inquired in his
own tongue.

"I think it's a good offer," Throat Shot said reluctantly.
"Those conchs—"

"I know it's a good offer. I know my business. I asked about
your feeling."

"I would not like to see her go there."

"You like her."

"Yes."

"And she likes you. I saw her smiles. She will work hard to
please you."

"But I cannot buy her. I have nothing."

"Ask him if he has pearls," the Trader said.

Alas, the fisherman had no pearls. The exchange fell through, and Tzec was not sold. She seemed about to faint with relief. Throat Shot was similarly relieved—but also privately amazed. The Trader had thwarted a good sale because his assistant liked the girl? That was suspiciously generous.

The day was getting late. They went with the Cacique's sister-wife to a small house near the canal. "The women will bring blankets," she said. "Also food in the morning." She departed.

The house was square and dark inside, and smelled of fish and shell. There were no furnishings, just bare daub walls and a floor of packed shell fragments. Throat Shot didn't like it, but had slept in worse situations. There were two chambers, separated by a curtain of palm fronds.

"You spoke to save me," Tzec murmured in her tongue.

"He asked me. I told him it was a good price, but he wanted to know how I felt, so I told him. He was the one who saved you."

"How *do* you feel?"

"I like you. You're useful, and your story of your people—"

"I will make it up to you," she said, obviously gratified.

By this time Throat Shot was in need of a place to relieve himself, for the meal had gotten his system working. But this was an essentially private matter, and there were houses and people all around.

"Find a pot," the Trader said, noting his discomfort. But Tzec was already bringing one from a corner. It was a large clay vase whose odor plainly indicated its function.

He didn't argue: this was not a thing he had done before. To him, pots were for cooking and storage. He took it into the other chamber and did his business in a hurry. Then he covered it with the large shell provided.

Just in time, for the women were arriving. There were two, both young and pretty, and one was the Cacique's wife!

To Throat Shot's chagrin, this was the one who came to him. "I saw you watching me," she told him. She was the loveliest creature he could imagine, with the shell beads across her breasts. "I saw how you wanted me. I am Heron Feather."

"But—" he protested, appalled.

"Take her in the other room," the Trader said. "I will keep this one here." He put his arm around the other woman, who was younger.

Throat Shot stood frozen. "I thought—only to bring a blanket—" But he had known better; his own tribe had similar hospitality. There was the smell of honey about her, which meant she had dosed herself with the honey-flavored grease that served to stop her from getting with child. Every priest knew the key herb that made this work; the grease and honey were only to make it easy to use, for the herb itself was bitter. No, there had never been doubt about her purpose here. It was her identity as the Cacique's wife that bothered him. That, and his complete inexperience.

"My husband said you needed good instruction," she told him, guiding him to the other chamber. "I am extremely good. I will make you float like a cloud. After me, all other women will seem inadequate."

"She surely will," Tzec said, settling down in a corner with a separate blanket. "It's a lot better than spittle from a skull."

She was going to witness this? Throat Shot was bothered again. Such things were usually done privately in Atafi. Children knew, but normally did not watch, unless they were part of the family. He knew this was a different culture, but that did not help much. "All I want is to see the largest burial mound!" he blurted.

The woman paused. "You have something to bury?" she inquired, glancing at his breechcloth. "This is what I shall help you do."

"No, I mean—out there," he said, gesturing wildly. "Where your elders repose."

"Oh, you mean the place of honor for our dead," she said, her lovely eyes widening a bit in surprise.

"Yes! I must go there." He realized that he sounded crazy, but he had not yet thrown off the effect of the intoxicating drink, and he could not organize his thoughts well.

"You must have a high opinion of your prowess," she remarked. "I think it would be better to do it in here, at least the first time."

She still misunderstood! "No! I mean, I must go and talk to

your spirits, to ask whether they will help me in my quest. This is why I am traveling."

"It is true," Tzec said. "He can talk to the dead."

"This I must see," the woman said. "Come, then, Toco priest; I will take you to the mound."

"I am not a—" he started to protest, but the touch of her sweet fingers on his lips cut him off. She knew what he was and was not.

She guided him out and along the paths between the houses. Others going about their business glanced at them curiously, but did not intrude; they evidently knew that she was the Cacique's wife, and he a visitor.

They came to the mound, outlined by the setting sun. It was a magnificent structure, with a charnel platform at the top, where the bodies of the ordinary dead were prepared for later burial. The smell was not sweet, which was why no one lived nearby. "Is this close enough?" she asked, wrinkling her pert nose.

"Yes." He stepped off the path, to the base of the mound, and abased himself before it. He felt the spirits within, many of them, and powerful. There were caciques here going back to the dawn of the world! Surely they would be able to help him.

O spirits of this mound, I beg you to help me find the Ulunsuti, he thought, knowing they could hear. *I must have it, to save my people from disaster.*

But these spirits did not answer. He had sensed their presence, but now there was only silence. They had turned their backs on him. They were angry with him.

Then he knew that he had erred badly. He must not have shown proper honor to the dead, coming here like this. They surely had reason to reject him.

I am dust, he thought to them.

You are garbage! Had he imagined that? He could not be sure. The stuff he had drunk still interfered with his thoughts.

I am garbage, he agreed. *I apologize for intruding on you like this.* He got up and backed away, chagrined. He had brought their rebuke on himself. He was not sure just how he had erred, but he had forfeited any help this mound might have given him.

"What did they say?" the woman asked as they walked away from the mound.

"They would not speak to me."

She laughed. "And what did they say of me?"

"They said nothing of you," he said, surprised.

She nodded. "The dead have no use for the likes of me. But the living are another matter."

Throat Shot felt guilty, but he was among the living. She was a beautiful woman, and her body and her manner tempted him strongly. The honey smell made him desire her, and his penis rose again. He had to resist that temptation, but he felt guilty for even feeling it.

"Do you have a problem with me?" she asked, perceptively enough.

"You are the Cacique's wife!" he said.

"His secondary wife," she said. "His concubine, really. His true wife is his sister. You are an honored guest, so he extends to you the privilege of family. Is it not true in your tribe, as in ours, that a man's brothers may share his wife, just as a woman's sisters may share her husband?"

"No," he said. "I mean, they are allowed, but it seldom happens. In our tribe, if a man and woman are unmarried, they may do what they want, but when they marry, they are only with each other."

"How quaint! But you are not with your tribe now."

To that he had no answer. They returned to the lodge as darkness closed, and inside it was completely black. But that was no relief: she went to the other side and fetched a lighted fish-oil torch. It was smoky and dim, but illuminated the chamber well enough.

The woman spread out the blanket, which was padded so as to make the floor comfortable. "Shall I undress you?" she inquired solicitously. "Or will you leave that to your slave girl?"

"No, I—" What was he to do?

"I will be happy to help," Tzec remarked mischievously, well understanding his problem. She had evidently recovered from the shock of learning of her mother's death, or perhaps was satisfied to be distracted from it. "Do you need more honey?"

"Go to sleep!" he snapped at her in her own language.

She decided she had teased him enough. She closed her eyes.

"Perhaps I should dance for you," Heron Feather said. "While you undress."

"Yes," he agreed quickly. With luck, by the time she completed her dance, it would be too dark for any of them to see anything. It wasn't that it was in any way complicated to remove a breechcloth, or that there was anything wrong with a man showing his erection before a willing woman. It was just that he had a deep uncertainty that this was real. Perhaps she was teasing him, setting him up for laughter when she succeeded in making him strip for action with a woman who never intended to complete a sexual engagement. After all, a man with one arm crippled—what could she see in him? So he only played at undressing, believing this to be the safer course, though he desired her ferociously.

She went into her dance. If it had seemed suggestive before, it was compelling now. Her hips swayed as if detached from her upper torso, the flesh of her thighs quivered invitingly, and her breasts bounced with abandon under the tinkling beads. Her hair swung out and around, echoing the motions of her fine moss skirt. She was Heron Feather, and surely no heron moved more evocatively than she!

Then she dropped the skirt, and stepped out of it. "You have not undressed," she told him reprovingly. "I shall have to do it for you after all."

Before he could make another ineffective protest, she came up to him, and her hands went to his breechcloth. In a moment she had him naked. "Yes, I think you are ready," she said, her hands caressing his standing penis. "Lie down."

"I can not," he muttered.

"I mean your body," she said. "I don't mean this." She stroked his rigid member.

"I am propped against the wall," he explained, embarrassed again. She was nudging his right side, and he could not use his left arm effectively, so he was caught.

She nodded. Then she put her hands firmly on his two upper thighs and pulled, so that his legs and body slid down, and he was able to get his shoulders and head away from the wall.

It was easier to go with her than to oppose her. He lay on his back on the blanket. She came down on him, her hands still busy, and suddenly she was embracing him with arms and legs and touching his lips with hers, her breasts pressing against him. The herb honey caused his hard penis to slide right into her, as if it had always sought this lodging, and the sensation was like nothing he had experienced before.

"So fast!" she murmured appreciatively. He was perplexed, then realized that she had known his state before he did. She was truly experienced and wonderful.

He gouted within her, again and again, caught by the exquisite storm. Then as he relaxed, it did indeed seem that he was floating on a cloud, held in place by her contact. The torch burned out, but it didn't matter; touch was better than sight. Her body remained in contact with his, warm and exciting and inviting even after he cooled, and her hands played about him, smoothing here, rubbing there, and her breasts slid across his body and into his hand as her lips kissed him and her tongue licked him in wonderfully odd ways. Very soon he was clasping her again, his member tasting the honey and adding to it, though with less force than before.

She stayed with him the night, and every time he woke and realized where and with whom he was, she moved against him and put him inside her and carried him into the sweet storm that faded into a cloud. He lost track of the times after three, and hardly cared. Nothing in his prior life had been anything like this, and he suspected that nothing in his future life would match it, just as she had said.

As dawn came, she got up. "Has the storm passed?" she inquired with a lurking smile.

"Yes," he breathed blissfully. His head felt bad from the drink of the night before, but this was more than compensated for by the delight his body had experienced.

"Let me see." She began to dance again, provocatively, and he could not help but watch. As he watched, his penis reacted, slowly but definitely.

"No, some rain remains; I see the wind rising," she said. She came to him, and once more took him in to the honey and caressed him into performance. It took some time, for it was the last that was in him, but it was almost excruciatingly intense when it finally came. Then she disengaged, and danced again, and this time he could not react. Only at this point was she satisfied. She had wrung out all the water of the storm. It would be many days before it could rain again.

She brought a damp sponge and cleaned him up, wherever he was soiled, for there was honey spread on him and on the blanket. He no longer protested her familiarity; he had had a lifetime of experience with her in a single night, and seemed to have no secrets from her. It was gentle pleasure feeling her touch, and he wished it could be forever like this. But he knew better; she had played with him one night, and her interest was not in him but in the quality of her performance. Certainly he could attest to that! He would be happy to tell the world of her competence, which was surely what she wanted him to do.

Heron Feather helped him don his breechcloth, her hands caressing his thighs and buttocks even during this routine act. Nothing was routine with her! Then she kissed him once more, smiled, and went to fetch fruit for him to eat.

"Your arm may be weak," Tzec remarked. "But something else isn't."

She had been in the room throughout. In the darkness, close to Heron Feather, he had forgotten. It no longer seemed to matter. Tzec had slept through most of it anyway.

The Trader appeared. "I thought you would do better with the experienced one," he said. "Next time you can have an inexperienced one, if you wish. How many times?"

"Times?" Throat Shot asked, confused.

"Five," Tzec said, making the five-finger signal. "No, once more just now. She wanted to be sure he was done."

She had been listening! "I should have let you be sold to that fisherman," he said, chagrined.

"No, you are right," the Trader said. "That girl will be worth far more than conchs. Keep teaching her, and keep learning from her."

Teaching and learning what? But Tzec was smiling mischievously, and he had to smile too.

The young women returned with baskets of fresh fruits. There were berries and pieces of Palm heart. "Now we shall leave you," Heron Feather said. "May we tell my husband that you are satisfied?"

The Trader frowned as if in doubt, teasingly. "Yes!" Throat

Shot said, so quickly that both Tzec and the Trader laughed. Heron Feather smiled knowingly, and then the less experienced woman did too, reassured. Throat Shot understood her feeling.

"Perhaps I shall see you again, if you pass this way, mighty hunter," Heron Feather said to Throat Shot with an almost motherly smile. Then the two women turned away and were gone, carrying their soiled blankets.

"The Cacique is a good host," the Trader remarked. "It is good that you did not dishonor his hospitality. You will be a legend by the time she is done exaggerating your prowess in the honey field."

Throat Shot ate his fruit, not able to think of any appropriate response. Both the Trader and Tzec were smirking.

"How was your trip to the mound?" the Trader inquired.

"Her mound is like none other." Then Throat Shot saw Tzec's smirk and realized that he had mistaken the question. "The spirits would not talk to me."

"I'm not surprised."

Throat Shot glanced at the man, surprised. "You knew I would fail?"

"I thought it likely. Consider this: if you were a spirit, and a man approached you by day without proper reverence, what would you say?"

Throat Shot shook his head. "I don't understand."

"Pretend I am a spirit," the Trader said, standing with his head bowed and his arms close to his body, as if covered by sand. "You came and said what?"

"O spirits of this mound, I beg you to help me find the Ulunsuti," Throat Shot said. "Because—"

The Trader lifted his head, glaring. "You come to us, intoxicated, with the Cacique's whore, to ask our help?" he demanded. "Get away from here, Toco cripple! You foul us by your presence!"

Throat Shot's mouth dropped open. Of course that was the way it was! How could he have been such a fool?

This time Tzec did not laugh. "I am sorry," she said.

But behind his chagrin, a new appreciation of the Trader's insight was dawning. The man understood things better than he normally let on.

From there they proceeded up the great Calusa river, returning inland. Here the glades were so extensive that it could be hard to tell where the river left off. Grass grew in broad plains, interspersed by islands of pine. But near the river there was often cypress, with its immensely swollen trunks, and mangrove. Black vultures sailed above, watching for anything ailing or dead. Grasshoppers clustered on the leaves of those bushes they favored. Green lizards watched for the careless approach of any of the buzzing flies. In some regions storks waded, and there was a heron. Ah, the feather of the heron!

But there was nervousness too. Alligators drifted in numbers greater than Throat Shot had seen before, and some of them were huge. They remained clear of the canoe, but he was concerned. If the canoe went down, he would not even be able to swim effectively, and would be unable to help Tzec. He had no fear for himself, but the thought of her being taken by the reptiles was uncomfortable.

She seemed to be aware of his thoughts. "Teach me the sign tongue," she said.

"Child, it's all he can do to paddle upstream," the Trader objected. "He can't use his hands for anything else." He spoke in his own language, and Throat Shot had to translate, but the girl already knew the essence. She was picking up the Trader's tongue herself.

"You can tell me now, and show me later," she said. She turned back to face the Trader. "You didn't sell me because you think I can be useful to you. I can be more useful if I learn this." Her words were halting, in his tongue, but close enough.

"Teach her," the Trader agreed gruffly.

So Throat Shot told her the signs as they moved slowly up the river. When a water bird flew up from the slough, she asked for its sign.

"Hold your hands at shoulder height in front of your body, flat, your fingers pointing out," he said. "Flap them: slow for big birds, fast for little ones."

"Oh, that's nice!" She practiced, and when he glanced back he saw that she was doing whole flocks of birds, ranging from the tiny hummingbird to the giant eagle. She was expressive with her hands.

"Tree," she said, looking at an oak that had ventured close to the river. A gray and white mockingbird perched in its foliage, staring curiously at them.

"Put your left hand up near your shoulder, in front, palm toward you," he said. "Spread your fingers wide. Move it up a little, to show how the tree grows."

"Yes!" she said, excited. "That's just like a tree!" She practiced growing.

There were assorted fish visible in the water under the canoe. "Fish," she said.

"First you must know Water: cup your right hand, as if holding water in it, and tilt it to your mouth as if drinking." He paused. "Have you drunk yet?"

"Yes; I am no longer thirsty," she said brightly.

"Then hold that hand, thumb up, flat, near your waist, fingers pointing away from you. Move it forward sinuously, in the manner of a fish swimming."

"Oh, yes!" she exclaimed, making the gesture with glee.

Then they went through the basics: Man, the right index finger pointing up before the face, emulating a penis. "That is the same to indicate any male," he explained. "Do it with an animal, to show it is male." That took them, of course, to Woman or Female: the curved spread fingers combing downward through the hair, and then the hand indicating her height with the fingers together and pointing up. Girl was the same, but with a lower height, and Child lower yet, after the sign for Male or Female. The sign for Yes, starting with the right index finger pointing up, as with Male, but at shoulder height, then moving down and closing the finger, as if tapping on something. The sign for No, with the right hand held flat, palm down, then moving briskly to the right while turning over and back, as if shoving something out of the way.

Then they got into counting: the right hand in an outward-facing loose fist at shoulder height, the little finger lifted, then the two smallest, three, four, and five. Then the thumb of the closed left hand touching the right thumb for Six, and on through the fingers starting from the thumb, up to ten. Tens could be counted by showing the doubled open hands twice or more, or by showing ten, then counting off the fingers of the left hand: the thumb was one ten, two fingers were two, and so on through five tens, and again to go higher. The Ten sign swung in a downward left circle showed ten tens, and if that sign was followed by counting off on the fingers of the left hand, each finger was ten tens.

"The Maya can count higher," Tzec said smugly.

"This is not Maya territory," the Trader put in.

"Laugh," she said.

"Hold both five-hands up by your chest, palms up," Throat Shot said. "Move them up and down."

Tzec made a violent laughing signal back at the Trader. He made a sign back at her. "What is that?" she asked.

Throat Shot hadn't seen it. "Describe it," he said.

"Left hand in front of the body," she said. "Right hand wiped across it. No, wait—that's like brushing off dirt!"

"Wiped out," Throat Shot agreed. "He exterminated you."

"Just so long as he doesn't sell me!" But then she wanted to know Sell, so she could see it coming.

"That's the Trade sign," Throat Shot said. "Both hands up in the One posture, index finger up. Then swing them down past each other, in part of a circle."

She practiced that, but evidently her mind was still working. "Apologize," she said.

"That would be Ashamed or Embarrassed," Throat Shot said. "Draw a blanket over your face: both hands up flat before your cheeks, then crossing."

Tzec practiced the gesture, then turned to face the Trader and made what must have been a most apologetic sign. He responded with his flat right hand held at the level of his chest on the left side, then swung it out to the front and right side.

"That means Good," Throat Shot translated in due course. "He forgives you for your impertinence. But don't make him talk anymore; I can't paddle this canoe by myself."

They continued up the river. But in the afternoon the heat increased, and the clouds piled up, and a great storm loomed from the horizon. The soaring birds disappeared, and so did many of the insects.

"We must get out of that!" the Trader exclaimed, alarmed. "Find a safe landing place."

But there was no landing place. The flat swamp stretched

out all around them, the river winding through it like a great lazy snake.

"See if your Spirit of the Mound will help," the Trader said, cynically. "Because if we sink here, the alligators will feed on us all. We cannot remain afloat in a bad storm."

Throat Shot closed his eyes. *O Spirit of the Mound,* he thought. *We need your guidance, if I am to complete my quest. Where can we go to survive the storm?* He was not intoxicated now, and not with Heron Feather. Most important, he was addressing a familiar spirit, though the mound was far away.

There. The Spirit guided his eyes as he opened them, and he focused on a distant stalk. It was south of the river, in the heart of the worst of the swamp.

"There," he said, pointing.

"There's nothing there!" the Trader protested.

"The Spirit answered," Throat Shot said.

"Then that is where we go," the Trader said grimly. "It is as good a place to die as any." He turned the canoe and paddled vigorously. Throat Shot paddled too, extending his weak arm to its utmost, despite the pain.

The canoe fairly leaped along, disturbing snoozing alligators. The distant stalk came rapidly closer, but so did the looming storm from the west.

"Look at that!" Tzec exclaimed, her sharp eyes peering ahead. "That's a splinter of a tree!"

So it was. The stalk was the sole remaining part of a giant cypress whose widely spreading roots had snagged brush and moss to form a tiny island. The tree had been struck by lightning, or perhaps had been blown over, so that only a single sliver of wood projected up like a long finger. From a distance it looked like no more than a weed shorn of its foliage, but it signaled a small but truly solid anchorage.

They drew the canoe up to it just before the storm struck. Grackles flew up, spooked from their hiding place, upset about having to find other shelter. An alligator was lying astride the most solid part. "Move out, brother of the river," Throat Shot said, poking it with his paddle. The creature, startled, scrambled into the water and swam away. Then Throat Shot climbed out of the canoe, helped Tzec out, and drew its end up.

The Trader joined them. As the winds buffeted them, they quickly unloaded the canoe, turned it over, propped it on high roots and projections, shoved the Trader's goods under it, scrambled under it themselves, and caught hold of the seats and edges to hold it firmly in place. Now they had shelter, and the trading goods were protected, but their freedom was limited.

There was a nearby crack of lightning, followed immediately by a terrible boom of thunder. Tzec screamed in terror. Throat Shot, lying beside her, let go of the canoe for a moment and put his good arm around her shuddering body. "I have no fear," he said. "I will share that lack with you."

Her shuddering eased. "It is true," she murmured. "With you I feel no fear."

The rain came down, pelting the canoe. The wind tried to lift it away, but they clung, keeping it in place. They were dry, because the water could neither strike them nor flow into them. They were on the high part of the cypress isle, and the old roots were quite solid. The Spirit of the Mound had directed him truly!

"Can you get a stick?" the Trader asked. He was at the other end, his head pointing away from them, his hands locked on the sides.

Throat Shot let go of his end of the canoe again and reached outside as the rain beat down. He dropped a stick beside him and grabbed the canoe as another gust of wind tried to take advantage of his neglect. "I have one. Why do you want it?"

"Cottonmouth."

Throat Shot craned his neck around. There was the snake, crawling under the canoe to avoid the storm. He knew how dangerous such snakes were; they were aggressive, and could strike with very little provocation, but they had bad aim and often missed. This was not welcome company.

"I have the stick, but can't reach the snake," Throat Shot said. "Maybe it will come up here."

"I am going to play dead," the Trader said, as another blast of wind tried to lift the canoe. It was evident that he could not let go without risking calamity.

"I can get it," Tzec said. "If you hold my hand so I don't get terrified."

Throat Shot felt no fear himself, but was concerned for her and the Trader. He was not sure how well his lack of fear could be transmitted. But if she believed, then maybe it would work. He propped one foot up inside the canoe to hold it along with his bad hand, and gave her the stick. "I will touch you. You will use the stick to block the snake's mouth so it can't bite, and to push it away. I will tell you how."

She took the stick and wriggled her way around. She was small and agile, and could do what he, with his greater size and bad arm, could not. In a moment her slender legs and feet were by his head. He transferred his grip to her ankle so that she could go farther.

She approached the snake, who was now watching her, as the one person who was moving. It started to coil.

"Poke the stick into its mouth," Throat Shot said quickly. "Before it strikes."

She poked the end of the stick forward, and at the same time the snake struck. Its aim was bad, and it snapped on air. The stick caught it on the side of the head and shoved it out. The snake, surprised and confused, splashed into the water and swam for another projecting root.

"You may have saved my life, girl," the Trader said. "I could not have done that."

"Throat Shot took away my fear," she said. "I'm terrified of bad snakes, otherwise."

"Still, I am glad I did not sell you."

There was a silence among them, but not around them. The rain beat down incessantly, and the winds buffeted the canoe and tried to catch at them beneath it; both Throat Shot and the Trader had to hold on firmly.

"We must keep watch until the storm passes," the Trader said. "Let the girl be alert for snakes, and we can tell stories while we wait."

"Do you know stories?" Tzec asked the Trader.

"I hear them in the course of my travels, from other traders and sometimes from the women I am with. There is nothing quite as good as a full belly, an affectionate woman, and a lively tale."

"I told a tale," she said. "Will you tell one? Throat Shot can tell me any of your words I don't know."

"If you keep the snakes off me, I will tell you a fine tale from far away," he said.

So it was that while they waited for the storm to pass, the Trader told a marvelous tale of a far distant tribe. Again Throat Shot's awareness of his situation faded as he listened. There was magic indeed in a good tale.

CHAPTER 6

⚜

SWEET MEDICINE

O Spirit of the Mound, I have told you how Throat Shot, the Trader, and young Tzec came to huddle under a canoe in the middle of the great swamp during a storm. Now I will tell you the strange tale the Trader told, from the far tribe of Tis-Tsis-Tas, in their tongue the People, who dwell near huge lakes like seas and have many strange things in their land. In this story are huge hoofed creatures like buffalo and elk, never seen among the Toco or the Calusa, and a kind of lodge called a tipi which is pointed at the top. I mention these, O Spirit, to let you know that later I was to encounter them, so I know they are real despite what I thought then.

A long time ago a baby was born to a family of the People. From the start he was a strange one, not in his appearance, which was normal, but in his activities. They would wrap him in his blanket and leave him to sleep, but when his mother checked during the night, only the blanket would be there. The first time this happened, she was terrified, and roused her husband, and they searched all around the house but could not find him. They feared that some wild creature had taken him, though there was no sign of violence. They could not search outside for him at night, so with heavy hearts they slept until dawn. But when they woke, there he was in his blanket, as if he had never been gone.

They did not tell anyone else, thinking they had been confused or had a bad dream. But when it happened again, they knew that he was no ordinary baby. They named him Sweet Medicine, and hoped that no evil would come of his unusual nature.

The baby grew rapidly, and soon was so large and strong that he could run and walk, at an age when other babies were still crawling. They pretended he was older than he was so that others would not be suspicious.

But when Sweet Medicine was still little, his parents had the misfortune to eat bad food and died. This was no fault of his, but it put him in trouble, since there were no other relatives. A poor old woman took him in because she could not suffer a child to die, and cared for him as well as she could. When he learned to speak he called her grandmother, though he knew she was not, because he knew he owed her his life.

Sweet Medicine was very poor in childhood: because the old woman had been poor before she took him in and was poorer when she had to share what little she had with him. He had only a small piece of buffalo-robe to wear. A buffalo was a huge strange animal that roamed the plains of that far region, and had horns, so that even a bear would fear to attack it.

He had no good place to sleep, so did so most of the time out in the brush. But his sleeping was so odd that often this didn't matter. He would lie down and sleep anywhere when he was tired, and no one could wake him. It seemed as if he were dead. But later he would wake, surprising the others. So they said, "Let him alone. Do not try to wake him. Let him wake by himself." And that was the way it was. They did not know how much stranger his sleeping could be, for he had learned not to disappear when others could see.

As Sweet Medicine grew older, he was often mischievous, and this aggravated some people. Once a woman was using her dog to drag a travois, which was a frame on two poles that carried her belongings, and he kept putting his foot on one of the poles to hold it back. The poor dog strained to no avail, and the woman was angry. "What are you doing?" she demanded. "Who are you, anyway? You have no father, you little piece of filth!"

Sweet Medicine was surprised to be called such a bad name, and not pleased. He realized that others did not like him when he did bad things to them. After that he behaved better, but he did not forget that he was different from the others, and not just because his father was dead.

Another time there was to be a dance. "Grandmother, may I dance too?" he asked.

"No, you had better wait. You are too young."

But Sweet Medicine was determined to go, and he begged and cried until she relented. So she helped him get ready for it by donning a little animal-skin robe painted white, and painting his body in yellow stripes. He wore a yellow feather in his hair, and a yellow bowstring around his neck.

"But why do you want to wear a bowstring around your neck?" she asked.

"I will use it to take my head off my body."

She thought he was joking, and she agreed to put his head back with his body, facing the rising sun, after it was done. She also agreed to pick up his robe and shake it four times, and then to put it on his body. She was a good woman, and she preferred to humor the boy rather than criticize him.

Then they went to the dance. It was in a lodge, and there was a great crowd around the lodge. The medicine man in charge of it welcomed Sweet Medicine. "Come and sit by me!" he said, so Sweet Medicine sat by his right side and watched the dance, his robe lying close beside him.

From time to time the people stopped dancing and rested and talked, but they did not talk to Sweet Medicine, because they regarded him as a troublemaker who had no father. Near the end of the dance he got up and danced, holding the bowstring around his neck with both hands. At the end, just before they were going to stop and eat, he pulled the bowstring tight. It passed through his neck and cut off his head. The head fell to the ground, but his body kept on dancing.

Now the others took notice of him. "Sweet Medicine has cut off his head!" they exclaimed, amazed. They had not seen anything like this before. For one thing, there was no blood.

The body continued to dance, and the head rolled about on the ground. Every so often it looked up at the people, which they found disconcerting. They stopped dancing. Then the body stopped dancing too, and fell down, and seemed to be dead.

Then the old woman did what she had agreed to do, realizing that his instructions had been no joke. She put the head together with the body, and placed the bowstring by the boy's side, and picked up the animal-skin robe and shook it four times. Then she put it over Sweet Medicine's body, and took the bowstring and wiped it off four times, and returned it to the ground beside him.

Then Sweet Medicine got up, and his head was connected to his body again as if it had never been severed. He smiled, and adjusted the eagle's feather he wore in his hair. He had done this so that the people would know what kind of power he had, and would not treat him like an outcast. He might not have a father, but he had power. He was only partly successful: he made the others wary of him.

Sweet Medicine grew to be a young man, but still was not held in high regard by others. He was a good hunter, but had never killed a buffalo by himself. A boy's first kill was important; it signaled his onset of manhood, and his father would hold a feast for him and give him a man's name. There was no feast for Sweet Medicine when he made his first kill, because he had no father, but it showed how good a hunter he was. He skinned the buffalo himself, and laid out the hide to dry.

Then the Chief came. "That is exactly the kind of hide I have been looking for," the Chief said. "I will take it and make a robe for myself."

"But this is my first kill, and I am entitled to the hide," Sweet Medicine said. "It is not right to take a boy's first hide. But you are welcome to half the meat, because of your age and status."

"No, I want the hide," the Chief said. He picked it up and started to carry it away.

Now this was not right, but the Chief knew that Sweet Medicine was only a boy, and had no father to stand up for him. He had forgotten the special power this boy had.

Sweet Medicine grabbed the other end of the hide, and would not let go. "How dare a poor nothing boy defy a chief?" the Chief demanded, outraged. He brought out a whip and whipped the boy across the face, trying to make him let go. But the boy would not let go, and the Chief saw that he could not get the hide.

Then the Chief, furious, drew his knife and slashed the hide to pieces. "Now you can have it," he said.

Sweet Medicine had only been trying to hold on to what belonged to him. He had not struck back at the Chief. But now he was enraged. He picked up the bone of the buffalo's hind leg and struck the man on the head. The blow was so strong it killed him.

Now the boy was in real trouble, for no one killed a chief with impunity. He ran home, but by the time he got there, everyone knew what he had done. They were organizing to kill him, for they would not tolerate such an outlaw among them. They did not know how the Chief had treated him, only that he had killed the man.

"Run, run!" the old woman cried. "The warriors are coming! They say you are an evil person who must be killed."

"But all I did was stand up for myself," he protested. "The Chief was trying to take what was mine, and then he destroyed it when I would not let him have it."

"I believe you," she said. "But no one else will. They don't like you anyway. This is their excuse to be rid of you. You must flee for your life!"

"But what will happen to you, grandmother, if I leave?" he asked, for she was very old and frail, and he had been doing the work for her. Even the woman's work, which of course was degrading for a man to do. That was one of the odd things about him.

"I do not matter," she said. "My life is near its end anyway. But you have a great future! You must save yourself."

As they talked, the warriors came up and surrounded the house. But they were wary of Sweet Medicine, knowing his prowess, and did not challenge him directly. Instead they drew their bows and aimed them at the house, ready to shoot him down as he came out. This was a problem for him, because he believed he could escape them, but he did not want to leave his dear grandmother unprotected.

"My life is worthless," she told him again. "Save yourself!" Sweet Medicine realized that she spoke the truth, for she would soon die no matter what happened to him. He was sorry for her, but he could not help her. All he could do was give her an honorable death.

Unless he could use his magic to rescue her, as he rescued

himself. He wasn't sure it would work, but he decided to try it, for there was no alternative. "Grandmother, do not be afraid," he said. Then he put a torch to the house, so that it blazed up.

"Oh!" the woman cried as the fire destroyed all that she had. She fell down, and was dead even before the fire touched her. That was not what he had intended; he had hoped she would trust him better.

Sweet Medicine was struck by grief and anger for her needless death. She had been good to him, and was a good old woman, and he had intended to take care of her in her dotage. Now she was dead, because of him. But there were too many warriors for him to fight; the moment he went out, they would riddle him with arrows, and he would die. Yet he couldn't remain in the fire, either.

Now he used his magic. He upset a pot of water on the fire. It did not put it out, but it made a great cloud of steam and smoke and floated up out of the smokehole. He stepped into it, and floated out with the smoke, invisible to the others.

The house burned down to ashes, but there was no sign of Sweet Medicine. The warriors poked through the remains, and when they did not find his bones, they knew that he had escaped. They remembered his magic, and were alarmed; they knew they had to catch him and kill him, or he would kill them. So they spread out, searching for him.

Soon one of them spied him sitting on a little hill not far distant, dressed like a Fox warrior. "There he is!"

They chased after him, but when they got to the hill, he was some distance beyond it. They ran after him again, but he was standing in the forest. They pursued him, but somehow he was always just out of their reach, though they never saw him actually running. By the end of the day they were exhausted from chasing him, but he remained untouched.

The next morning he appeared outside the village, garbed like an Elk warrior. Again they gave chase, but somehow he was never quite where they thought he was, when they got there. They sought him all day, but only wore themselves out.

On the third day he wore the red face paint and feathers of a Red Shield warrior, and was as evasive as ever. Long before the day was done, they gave up, seeing the futility of the chase.

On the fourth day he appeared dressed like a Dog warrior, shaking a small red rattle tied with buffalo hair at his pursuers. They had to chase him, but soon gave it up.

On the fifth day he was in the full regalia of a Tis-Tsis-Tas chief. That made the village warriors angrier than ever, and they swore they would not rest until they killed him, but they could not do it.

So it continued. On another day a man saw a little smoke near a great cut bluff. Looking down, he saw Sweet Medicine among the thick bushes at the foot of the bluff, roasting meat over a little fire. He reported this, and the warriors gathered to surround and catch Sweet Medicine. But as they closed in, a coyote ran out of the bushes, past them. They could not find Sweet Medicine, only his meat on a stick, still roasting. Then they knew that the coyote must have been their quarry.

Another time they thought they had him, but a magpie flew out and lighted on a hill, chattering at them, and Sweet Medicine was gone. Yet another time they thought they had him trapped in a canyon with high bluffs all around. A crow flew out as they advanced, and they had lost him. Another day it was a blackbird watching them search fruitlessly. And finally an owl.

Day after day it went, and at last the warriors realized that they were unable to catch Sweet Medicine. They resolved not to chase him anymore, as it only wasted time and left them tired, while their hunting did not get done and they went hungry.

One day they heard a great rumbling beyond a hill. They saw an animal coming toward them. They thought it was a buffalo, but when it got closer it seemed more like a bear, and closer yet it seemed like a wildcat, and then like a wolf. Finally it turned out to be Sweet Medicine, dancing close to their camp, as if tempting them to chase him. But they had suffered much fatigue and misery trying to catch him before, and were hungry, and knew it was useless, though they still bore him malice. So they did not chase him. He moved on past them, and disappeared over a hill. The rumbling grew fainter as he departed. His steps were so heavy they made the ground rumble, because of his magic. This was a warning to them not to interfere with him anymore.

When they thought about it, they realized that Sweet Medicine was now strong, while they were weak. If they had tried to chase him, he might have turned on them and killed them. They were afraid of him, because they had been responsible for the death of the old woman he called his grandmother. They were afraid he meant to see them all dead, without touching them himself, just as they had seen his grandmother dead without touching her. The pattern of his harassment was coming clear, and they wished they had never started this war with him. But they did not know how to end it, for they could not get close enough to Sweet Medicine even to talk to him.

Finally they went to his brother, who was really the son of the old woman, who had helped take care of Sweet Medicine when he was young. This man had gone out on his own when Sweet Medicine grew old enough to get along by himself, and had not been there when the old woman died.

"Tell Sweet Medicine he may come back now," they told the brother. "We will not hurt him. We are tired of fighting him; he has beaten us and we only want peace."

"Why should I help you?" the brother demanded. "You killed my mother!"

"And we will kill you, too, if you do not do this!" they told him. "You must cooperate with us so that there will be an end to this trouble, and we all benefit."

The brother was not wholly at ease with this, but he agreed that there should be an end to the strife, for the good of the tribe. "He may not want to talk with you."

"You must take him out hunting," they told him. "You must kill a buffalo, and pile up the meat, and leave Sweet Medicine there to keep the flies off it while you return to camp to get dogs and a travois to haul it back. Then we can all come, and make our peace with him, and fill our bellies."

That seemed reasonable. So the brother went out alone to a place only he and Sweet Medicine knew, and made a whistle that was a signal between them. Then he went home and waited.

That night Sweet Medicine came to his brother's lodge. He checked around, but found none of the warriors near. He trusted his brother, but thought the others might be watching without his brother's knowledge. Then he made a signal, and his brother heard him.

"Is that you, little brother? Come in and sit down." So Sweet Medicine entered, and his brother's wife gave him food to eat. Then he lay down and slept, glad to be with what remained of his family.

The next morning his brother asked him to go hunting. Sweet Medicine agreed, and they went out. They killed a buffalo, cut up the meat nicely, and heaped it together in a pile. But the flies clustered, eager to feast on it and foul it. "You stay here and keep the flies off while I go back home for the dogs and travois so we can haul it all."

"I will wait here until you return," Sweet Medicine agreed. He started walking around the meat in a circle, keeping the flies away from it.

The brother went back home. The warriors were there, but they told him they had to move their camp and needed his help. He helped them, but when he wanted to return to Sweet Medicine they made other excuses, and he could not get away.

The truth was, this was their plot. They couldn't fight Sweet Medicine, but they intended to get rid of him by leaving him distracted. He had told his brother he would guard the meat, and he would do it, and while he was doing it, he would not be bothering them, and so they would be rid of him. His brother did not know this; they fooled him.

So it was that the brother did not return, though he expected to. They took him to a new camp, far away, always finding other pretexts to keep him from returning to Sweet Medicine. So the hours became days, and the days became moons, and he remained too busy to go back.

But what the tribe had done harmed it more than it harmed Sweet Medicine, because the region to which it moved had poor hunting. They found no game of any size, and could forage for no good fruits or grains or berries. They were obliged to eat whatever they could: bitter roots, the bark of trees, and even mushrooms. They did not like to do that, because they knew that some mushrooms had evil spirits that could kill, and sometimes the evil ones looked very much like the good ones. It was a hard time. Everyone was hungry.

After they had struggled through the winter, they realized

what a mistake they had made. Surely nothing Sweet Medicine had done to them was as bad as this starvation! Maybe it would be better to return to their old hunting grounds and take their chances.

So they trekked back. Now at last the brother was able to return to Sweet Medicine. He hurried out to the place he had left him, and Sweet Medicine was there. He was still walking around the pile of bones where the meat had been, and he had worn a trail so deep that only the top of his head could be seen above the ground.

His brother felt very sorry about this, blaming himself for leaving Sweet Medicine for so long. "My brother, I have returned! I was delayed and could not come, but now I am here. Speak to me!"

But Sweet Medicine did not respond directly. He was still marching around, and talking to himself. "Surely by this time my brother has become a great chief!"

The brother realized that Sweet Medicine's mind was clouded. It was possible that one or more of his souls had been lost. He would have to fetch help, to make the man well again. "I shall return soon," he promised as he left.

This time he did return soon, with help—but Sweet Medicine was no longer there. Only the bones of the buffalo meat and the deep track remained. They searched all around the area, but could not find him. "It must be my fault," his brother lamented. "I told him I would return soon, before, but I was gone all winter. So when I told him that again, he didn't believe me, and didn't wait."

Sweet Medicine was gone for four years, and in that time there was famine in the land. The buffalo and other animals disappeared, and the people were starving. They had hoped to eat something better than roots and berries and grass, but all they could find was worse. They scavenged for the dread mushrooms, despite the risk, and even then found only little clumps of them, which were soon gone. They ate rosebuds and the inner bark of trees and insects and they chewed on old bones, and these too were running out. They became too weak to travel; they were mere skin and bones, and their children were dying.

Now, too late, they understood that it had been Sweet Medicine's presence that made the hunting good. When they had left him behind, they had encountered poor hunting, and then when he left them behind, there was worse hunting. They were sorry they had ever wronged him. All the time they had treated him with contempt, he had been the source of their good fortune. He had not sought any quarrel with them, and had never hurt any of them directly. But now, with his absence, he was wreaking a terrible punishment on them all. They could only struggle through, hoping for his return.

Meanwhile, what had happened to Sweet Medicine? He had heard his brother's words, and thought they were false, so when his brother left, he had climbed out of his pitlike path and wandered away, sad at heart. It had been only for the sake of his brother that he had returned, and now he had no reason to stay.

He walked disconsolately across the prairie, not caring where he went, for life was no longer of great value to him. Then he heard a voice calling to him. He could not see who it was, but the voice sounded friendly, and he needed a friend, so he went in that direction.

He found himself walking through a land of many hills, beautifully forested. Standing apart from the others was a single mountain shaped like a huge tipi, the pointed house of the people of that region. This was the sacred medicine mountain called Bear Butte. The voice led him to a secret opening that no other person or creature could see, and he entered the mountain. It was hollow inside, like a tipi, forming a sacred lodge. Therein were people who looked like ordinary men and women, but they were really powerful spirits.

"Come in, grandson," these people said. "We have been expecting you."

He came in and took the seat they provided for him. Then they began teaching him the Tis-Tsis-Tas way to live, so that he could return to his people and give them this knowledge.

First the spirits gave him four sacred arrows. "With these arrows, your tribe will prosper. Two are for war and two are for hunting. But that is only a small part of their mystery. They have great powers. They contain the rules by which men ought to live."

Sweet Medicine was interested. He had seen how men ought

not to live, but had not known how they should change.

The spirit folk taught him how to pray to these arrows, how to keep them, and how to renew them. They taught him the wise laws of the forty-four great chiefs whose spirits they were. They taught him how to set up rules for warriors. They taught him how to honor women. They taught him many useful things to enable people to live, survive, and prosper, which had not been generally known before that time. Finally they taught him how to make the special tipi in which the sacred arrows were to be kept.

Sweet Medicine listened most respectfully, and learned well. Finally the oldest spirit man burned incense of sweet grass, to purify Sweet Medicine and the bundle of sacred arrows. Then he put the bundle on his back and began the long journey home. He did not realize that four years had passed, for time was different inside the mountain, and he had not eaten or slept there. It had seemed like one afternoon.

One day seven little boys were out searching for food. They were lucky; they found a clump of large white mushrooms. While they were sitting there eating them, a strange man approached. He was tall and handsome, with long hair hanging loose well down his back. "You look very hungry," he said. Indeed, they were listless, with their ribs sticking out, their bodies gaunt.

"Throw away what you have," he told them. "We shall find you better food."

The boys were reluctant to throw away the only food they had, but the man spoke with such authority that they did it.

"Now each of you go find one buffalo chip, and bring it to me," the man said.

The boys scattered, searching the ground for the old bits of dung left by the buffalo long before. While they were gone, the man took a stick in his hand and broke it in two. He set it on the ground, and it burst into flame, forming a good fire.

The boys returned with seven chips. The man took off his robe and spread it on the ground, and placed the chips there in a special pattern. The five chips brought by the larger boys he formed into a square, with one in the center. The two brought by the smallest boys he set on the east and west corners of the square. The four corner chips represented the four directions, and the middle one stood for the sun at noon. The two at the east and west represented the rising and setting sun.

Then he took the four corners of his robe, and folded them over so that the chips were in the middle, and covered them up. He broke them up with his hand, crumbling them into powder. He opened the robe, and there within it was good solid meat. They boys were amazed by this magic.

"Now eat as much as you want," he told them. They did so immediately, until they were full.

"Now grease yourselves all over with the fat," he told them. "Grease your faces, your hands, and your whole bodies. You look all dried up, as if you have been baked in the sun."

They did so, and their bodies began to fill out, so that they were normal children again. They became lively and happy, as boys should be.

"Now take the rest of this food back to your camp, to share with the others. Tell them to put their lodges in a circle with an opening toward the rising sun. In the middle of this circle they must pitch a big lodge. Tell them to have all the headmen come together in that lodge, with their pipes filled for smoking. Tell them that I am he who has returned to them."

The boys went to the camp, happy and full. But they were young, and were tired, so they went to sleep without telling the people what Sweet Medicine had said. But in the morning the smallest of the boys woke and remembered. "O father!" he cried. "Sweet Medicine has come back, and he gave us plenty to eat yesterday, and we brought more home with us."

His father did not believe him. But the boy showed him the food, and woke the other boys, who confirmed it, and delivered the message.

The people sent for the chiefs and told them what the boys had said. The chiefs went to the lodge of Sweet Medicine's brother to ask if he had known about this. "No, I have not seen him," he said. "I fear that he blamed me for not returning with the travois, though I had really intended to, so he thought that my word was no good. Indeed, I am sorry I was unable to return for so long, and I cannot blame him for being angry."

At the head of the brother's bed a man was lying. He was covered over with robes, so that they could not see who he was. "Who is that person?" a chief asked.

"I don't know. He came in during the night. But he is welcome, for I know how hard it can be to find good shelter, and I will share with him what I have."

"If Sweet Medicine has truly returned, and with him the wealth of our forest and field, we will all have much to share," the chief said. "We treated him with great disrespect, and have repented that long since."

Then the man on the ground rolled over, sat up, and drew the robe away from his head. It was Sweet Medicine! He had overheard their conversation, and knew that they were ready to accept him.

"Is it true, what the boys said?" his brother asked after welcoming him.

"Yes, that is what I said. Now put up a big double lodge and level the ground nicely inside. When it is ready, send for me."

They hastened to set things up as he directed. When it was done, Sweet Medicine went there. The news of how he had fed the little boys had spread throughout the tribe, and the remaining food had quickly disappeared. "O Sweet Medicine!" the people cried. "Take pity on us and help us get food, as you did for the children!"

Sweet Medicine sat down in the big lodge and said, "Go fetch an old buffalo skull and put it in the opening in the circle." They did this. Then he began to sing. As he sang, the head moved toward them. It filled out, becoming a buffalo head, but without any body. Then it grunted, as if it were alive, but still it was only the head.

"Take it into the back of the lodge," Sweet Medicine said. "Put it near the fire."

Then he spoke to the others. "I have been gone four years, though it seemed like only an afternoon to me. I know that you are starving because there are no buffalo. I want you all to remain in this lodge for four days and four nights. Whatever happens, remain here, for if the magic is interrupted it will end, and you will not achieve what you desire."

They promised to do this. Then Sweet Medicine sang again, and they sang with him, to help him do what he had to do. They sang for two days, and every so often the buffalo head near the fire would grunt as if calling someone.

On the third morning there was a shaking of the ground, and the grunts of the buffalo head were echoed in the distance beyond the camp. They looked out, and there was a great herd of buffalo ranging toward the camp, blowing and grunting in the manner of their kind. The people wanted to go out and kill some buffalo, but they knew they must not. Instead they remained inside and helped Sweet Medicine sing.

On the fourth morning the buffalo were all through the camp and surrounded the lodge. They were grunting back and forth to the head inside, which they could not see. It was as though he were the chief of the buffalo, calling them to him.

Then Sweet Medicine said to the people, "Now go out and kill as many buffalo as you need for food for yourselves, but no more than that. I will remain here and sing, and they will not go away."

They went out, and it was true: the buffalo did not flee, and they were able to kill a number quickly. But they heeded Sweet Medicine's warning, and killed only the number they needed. The remaining animals walked out through the gap in the formations of lodges, and disappeared into the forest.

So it was that the people lived better and had more to eat than before. Because they had killed only what they needed, more buffalo remained in the area, and could be hunted after the first were used up. The people marveled at this, and were grateful to Sweet Medicine for what he had done.

Sweet Medicine told them the whole story of how he had listened to the spirits in the mountain, and learned from them. He showed them the arrow bundle. "You have not yet learned how to live in the right way," he told them. "That is why the spirits were angry, and took away your buffalo. Now you must live as they tell you, and you will prosper."

They agreed to do this, and Sweet Medicine taught them all he had learned from the spirits of the mountain. When he had done this, the Chief of the tribe gave him his daughter to be his wife. She was a very pretty girl, and she was very grateful for what Sweet Medicine had done for the tribe. She had been a child of twelve winters when he left, but now she was quite another person.

"But I cannot marry yet," Sweet Medicine said. "I have to return to the mountain, to report to the spirits there, and tell them that I have done their bidding." This was true, but it was also true that he had little experience with women and was alarmed at the prospect of being bound to one. It had been said that he had no father; it was also true that he had no mother. The old woman who had cared for him as a child was the only one he had known well, and though she had been a good woman, he could not imagine being married to one like her.

"Then I will go with you," the girl said.

"But it will be a hard trip!"

"I will make it easier." She smiled at him, and her beauty caught hold of him and would not let him go, and he could not deny her. He felt a desire rising, and did not know what it was, except that only she could satisfy it. Indeed, he had much to learn about ordinary life and the ways of love!

So it was that Sweet Medicine set out for the mountain, accompanied by the girl. The people gave him a good dog with a travois, to haul supplies, and they started walking.

The journey took several days, and when he rested at night the girl rubbed his tired feet and kneaded his muscles and covered him with a blanket and lay down beside him, and she was quite warm and soft and pliable. It occurred to him that it might not be a bad thing to be married.

They reached the great lodge within the mountain. They entered by the secret way, and the spirits there said, "Ah! Here is our grandson, returned with his wife!"

"No, I have not married," Sweet Medicine protested.

They glanced at each other, knowing better than he. "Let her sit aside while we converse with you," they told him. "She must not speak or gesture."

The girl agreed, not knowing what they intended.

The spirits in this lodge were not ordinary spirits. They were all the beings that belong in the world. There were human people and buffalo and antelopes and birds and trees and grass and rocks. All the things that grow or exist on earth were there, each represented by its spirit. But they all looked like people, for they could assume any forms they wished, for their convenience, and speak in any tongue.

Four of them seemed to be the principal men. To the right of the door as he entered sat a black man, and to the left was a brown man. At the back was a white man, and near the front was another brown man. All of them were as handsome and well made as he had seen, being perfect men except for their odd colors. They neither spoke nor did anything; they just sat there.

"Choose one of these four to be yourself," the chief spirit said. Sweet Medicine looked at each man, and he liked them all; he would be glad to resemble any of them. The chief seemed to be making signs with his lips that he should choose the black or the white one. But Sweet Medicine did not know why he should do that, and he was wary of the strange colors of those men. He chose the brown man to the left of the door instead. "I will be like that one," he said.

There was a moment's pause. Then the girl made a sad exclamation, and all in the lodge made low groans. They were sorry for Sweet Medicine, for he had made a mistake.

He looked around again, but the men were not there. Where the white man had been was only a great white, smooth stone; the black man was a smooth black stone. The brown man near the center was a tall, slender weed-stalk, while the one he had chosen was a pretty weed as high as a man's knee, with green leaves and pretty flowers.

The chief spirit pointed to one of the stones, and then to the other. "You should have chosen one of those. Then you would have lived to old age, and after you grew old, you would have become young again. It would always have happened; you would never have died. The man you chose is a mere fish-bladder in comparison. You could have lived forever with the black or the white stone. I placed both where you would see them first, hoping you would choose one."

One of the spirits got up and left, saying, "That man is a fool."

Sweet Medicine did not like that remark, but the chief spirit said to him, "Follow him; he has great power."

This time Sweet Medicine took his advice. He and the girl went out of the mountain and followed the spirit man for a long time. It seemed as if they went all over the world, till at last they came back to the same place. He was afraid they had made a fool of him, but the chief spirit smiled. "You succeeded in staying with him; we shall reward you." For the man they had followed was the wind, and few people could keep him in sight for very long. They told him of many of the things that were to come to pass in the world, so that they would not catch him by surprise, and he could warn his tribe.

They gave him a feather, from the same eagle whose feathers had completed the sacred arrows. He put this feather in his hair, and he was to wear it ever after, as his token of honor.

Then he departed, with the girl and the dog, and made the long journey back to the tribe. By the time they got there, Sweet Medicine understood that he was married, and was to be a father, for the girl had led him into pleasurable things which had that effect, and he was satisfied.

But another four years had passed since their departure from the tribe. Sweet Medicine was not surprised, but his wife was, for she had not experienced this before. Her little sister now seemed as old as she, for neither she nor Sweet Medicine had aged in that time.

They settled down near Sweet Medicine's brother, who now had children who seemed as old as they were, and made a family. But Sweet Medicine's pattern of life was odd, because of his choice of men in the mountain. All through the summer he was young, but when fall came he looked older, and by the middle of the winter he seemed old, and walked bent over. But in spring he became young again, like a stripling. His wife did not change that way; she aged in the normal fashion. She indulged his changing needs as the seasons shifted, being like his mother in the spring, and his lover in summer, and his daughter in winter. If she preferred one role over another, she was too smart to say so.

But Sweet Medicine could not live forever, because he had chosen wrongly. His several phases of life all became older, until he was a middle-aged man in spring, and a gaunt skeleton of a man in winter. When he knew he would not survive another winter, he summoned the people and spoke to them.

"I shall not be with you much longer," he said. "I chose wrongly, in my youth, preferring appearance over reality, and so I paid the price for my folly and now must die. I have endured as long as I care to, and I do not wish to be a burden to my good wife and sons, and so I shall depart. But do not forget what I am telling you this day, lest the tribe suffer again as it did before, and come to nothing. You must guard the sacred arrows, and honor their precepts always. You must come together often and talk over the principles I have taught you. A time is coming when you will meet other people, and fight them, and your two tribes will kill each other because each wants the land of the other. This is folly, for there will be a much greater threat coming from far away across the great sea, and you will need all your strength to stand up against this. Keep the peace with other tribes, and do not fight each other foolishly, or everyone will suffer grievously."

Sweet Medicine died, and his wife and brother mourned him, and the people respected his memory. But in time they did resume their quarreling with their neighbors, and weakened themselves. Whether they will pay the penalty Sweet Medicine foresaw remains to be seen.

CHAPTER 7

⚓

WIDE WATER

O Spirit of the Mound, I have told you the Trader's Tale of Sweet Medicine, and how he brought the four sacred arrows to his tribe, which was far distant from here. I wonder if you knew him? Surely you were a leader like that, when you lived! Now I will tell you how we came to the enormous inner lake called the Mayaimi, the Wide Water, and what the spirit of the mound there told me.

The rain had at last abated, and they were ready to resume their journey. Throat Shot, absorbed in the story, was a bit surprised to return to the swamp. He had not been as deeply moved by this one as he had by Tzec's, yet there was magic in it, and things to think about.

They turned over the canoe and loaded the goods back into it. They were damp, but had survived the storm well enough. What could have been a disaster had become an interesting session.

They made their way back to the main channel of the river, and forged on east. They did not speak. As night closed, the Trader directed them to a place he knew, and they found a ridge of land solid enough for them to camp on. Tzec gathered brush and dry moss and sticks, and Throat Shot brought out his punk pot, fed its slowly smoldering belly, and made a fire. That was something he didn't want wet down! It was possible to make a fire by twirling a stick against a hole in a piece of dry wood, but with his limited arm this was difficult and even painful; far better to save the fire he already had. The Trader shot a fat turkey, and cooked it over the fire, and the heat and food were very good. Then they damped the fire down, making it smudge and smoke, to keep the mosquitoes and other creatures of the swamp away, and slept. There was no need to be alert, for only the Calusa would pass this way, and they were friendly, while the fire would keep the dangerous animals away.

In the morning they went on, following the continual winding of the diminishing river. Grapevines hung on the trees, so close they could have been harvested from the canoe, had there been anything ripe on them. The curtains of moss were so thick they gave the trees an almost ghostly quality. Throat Shot almost fancied he saw faces of spirits in the deep shadows under that thick foliage, but when he peered more closely he realized they were only great spiderwebs. This was like a land apart, beautiful in its richness. Tzec was staring too, fascinated by this region of the birth of the great river.

In due course they came to the final narrowing, and then to a series of shallow grassy lakes that had water only because of the recent rain. Throat Shot was afraid they would have to portage, but the Trader knew where the channels were, and they were able to get out and slog through the sharp-edged grass beside the canoe and haul it along through the muck. Finally they slid it over a low bank and came to the huge lake that was not quite its source: the Wide Water.

Both Throat Shot and Tzec stared at this. It seemed to be quite shallow, with reeds and water plants growing up through it in many places, but it extended as far as they could see. It was indeed an inland sea. Birds floated on it, and flew above it, questing for their food. Dragonflies of several colors darted busily, pursuing insects. Fish swam close beneath the surface. Otters played, but moved out of bowshot range as the canoe approached. Turkeys took flight from its bank. Only the alligators refused to give way to the canoe, until the Trader splashed violently with his paddle, causing them to back off for now. Bubbles rose from the water's depths, popping as they touched the light. This was the Mayaimi, the greatest of lakes.

"That way flows the River of Grass," the Trader said, pointing to the southeast. "There are folk there, but I have nothing left that they might want in trade, and it is a treacherous region because of the storms. But if you ever have a chance to go there with someone who knows his way, it is a great experience."

"It was enough of an experience just getting here," Tzec remarked. Then, as an afterthought: "I liked your story."

"I liked yours," the Trader said.

Throat Shot did not comment, knowing that the Trader would not let storytelling interfere with business. When he found a suitable price for the girl, he would sell her.

The canoe turned north, following the nebulous fringe of the lake, finding channels through the reeds and shallows. Not far along there was another river, this one flowing into the lake instead of away from it, and this one was navigable. They followed this toward the setting sun, and came to a landing where there was a solid dugout canoe similar to their own. They glided in to dock beside it.

"I was here two seasons ago," the Trader said. "Speckled Turtle was young then, twelve winters, but she should be a fine woman now, if she's not married."

Throat Shot didn't comment. The Trader liked his women, but they did have to be nubile. Throat Shot was glad of that, for Tzec's sake.

There was a path leading generally southward through palmetto and marsh vegetation. They followed it until they reached an east-west ridge overgrown by slender plants.

"Corn," the Trader said approvingly.

Corn! Throat Shot went to the ridge and examined one of the plants. Sure enough, there were green ears on it. He had seen corn so seldom that he hadn't recognized it. On its edge grew squash, its vines reaching down toward the marshy area.

"Maybe they're civilized," Tzec murmured. She knew about corn; her ancestors were indeed civilized.

At the end of the long ridge was a lodge, at about the same height. It occurred to Throat Shot that there might be periodic floods here, as there were along the Little Big River of his home, so that they had raised their house and garden to protect them. It took only one flood to command respect, and the Toco watched the level of the river when it rose, and moved their belongings away.

The members of the family came out. There was a solid adult man, his similarly solid wife, two grown sons, and Speckled

Turtle: not the fairest of girls, but young and healthy and not yet running to the fat of her parents. She was bare to the waist in the common Toco and Calusa mode, and if her breasts lacked heft, they had good form. That was the advantage of youth.

"Speak to them," the Trader said. "I have trinkets for each, and hope they have room for us this night."

Throat Shot did so. "The Trader was here two years ago, and remembers you with pleasure," he said. "I am translating for him as I travel with him, and the girl was taken in trade. The Trader has gifts for you, and hopes you will welcome us this night."

The man smiled broadly. "He spoke in signs before," he said, waving his hands illustratively. "He was a good guest, but we could learn only a little of his news. Now we can hear it all! You are welcome!"

It was a good start. This was Corn Husk and his wife, Corn Tassel, who lived on the corn they grew and traded it for other items. Once this had been a larger community, Corn Husk explained, but now they were the only family remaining, except for a few others up Fish Eater River. They were hungry for contact with others. For one thing, they had a daughter to marry off.

Speckled Turtle flushed demurely. The gesture became her. Surely the Trader would have her for the night.

They fed on corn fritters and squash, excellently prepared, with fermented palm drink. Throat Shot had the wit to take it slowly so that it would not have a full effect on his mind. Throughout the meal the Trader told of the events of the distant regions to which he had traveled, encouraging Throat Shot to augment the descriptions liberally. When he spoke of the Cacique and his fine lodge and several wives, Corn Husk nodded knowingly; he had been there. But Speckled Turtle listened eagerly, evidently wishing she could visit.

As evening came, Speckled Turtle showed them to an outlying chamber of the lodge. It had no pot, but there was a path to the nearby waste trench. Throat Shot was glad of that; he was not comfortable urinating into crockery. There were blankets for each. The girl evidently expected to share the night with the Trader, but he demurred. "I remember you as you were," he told her, as Throat Shot translated. "You are a fine woman now, but my memory stays me. Go with Throat Shot instead."

Throat Shot jumped, finding himself abruptly referring to himself. The girl looked at him, seeming not pleased, but determined not to shame her family. His feelings were mixed, on more than one level. Speckled Turtle was not as attractive and surely not as experienced as Heron Feather, but of course that was not to be expected; *no one* could match that standard.

What was a problem was her evident diffidence. She averted her gaze from his hooked left arm, and seemed to wish she were elsewhere. There was the odor of herb honey about her, so she knew what to do, but he knew it had been intended for the Trader.

Throat Shot had been interested in having the experience with another woman, and that honey smell excited him, but this put him off. Heron Feather had led the way throughout, carrying the action to him, knowing exactly what to do and how to do it, and that had made it easy. It was evident that he would have to do the carrying with Speckled Turtle, who would neither resist nor encourage, and would probably depart as soon as it was done. The notion of doing such a thing with an unwilling woman was foreign to him. But he knew he could not simply tell her to forget it; she would be in trouble with her family if she did not perform as expected. It would also be necessary for him to give a good report of her, regardless of the truth, lest he shame her.

He was tempted to offer a deal with her: they would not do it, and each would give a good report of the other. But he had to know her better before he dared broach such a delicate matter. It might be easier to struggle through the sex.

"Let's talk a bit," he said. "I would like to know something about you."

"I am of no consequence," she said immediately. "I have never been to another village, or done anything unusual. Not like you."

Throat Shot laughed. "The most unusual thing I have done is get myself shot in the shoulder!" He touched where the scar was, uncertain whether this would alleviate her distaste for his injury or make it worse. "So I couldn't be a warrior, and am traveling instead." That was an oversimplification, but seemed sufficient.

But she seemed interested. Now she glanced at his arm, as if given leave, and perhaps saw that it was neither withered nor scarred; it simply was not properly mobile. "You are marked. Is it true you talk with the dead?" she asked.

News had not only spread, it had been most specific! This family seemed isolated, but evidently did have contacts. "It is true," he said. "Do you have mounds here I can visit?"

"Certainly they do!" the Trader said from across the dark chamber. "Why do you think I brought you here?"

"Our own burials are of no significance," the girl said. "But up the river a little way are many mounds of our ancient ancestors, who were greater people than we are."

"I must visit them!" Throat Shot exclaimed, excited.

"What, now?" she asked.

He hadn't thought of that, but suddenly realized that the night might be a better time to commune with the spirits than the day. His failures had been when he visited mounds by day, and his successes, such as they were, had been by night or in special circumstances. "Can we go now?" he asked, afraid she would laugh.

"I will show you the path," she said. "But I would not go there at night. Don't you know that the spirits wake at night, and they do not like intrusions?"

Were Calusa spirits different from Toco spirits? Each Calusa person had three souls, instead of one, but did that make a difference after death? It was possible. Now he knew he had to go at night! "Show me the path," he said.

"I'll go with you," Tzec said. "With a light."

That was a good idea. They lit a torch and started out as a party of three.

The path wound west away from the village, and curved around the stands of cypress and pine and occasional large oaks. Speckled Turtle's torch shook as she showed the way, though the evening was not cold. She was obviously nervous about this business.

They came to a split in the path. "That way," Speckled Turtle said, indicating the left path. "There are many mounds, not just ours. It is a place of fright by day, and terror by night. Don't you feel the fear of it?"

"I feel no fear," Throat Shot said.

She glanced back at him in the darkness. "No fear?"

"The Spirit of the Mound—my local mound—took my fear," he explained. "Other emotions I have, but not fear. Not till my quest is done."

She gazed at him a moment more. "I don't know how to believe that."

"Come the rest of the way to the mounds," Tzec told her. "You will see that it is true. When I am afraid, I touch him, and then my fear is gone."

The girl shook her head in disbelief. Throat Shot, uncertain whether it would work, extended his right hand. Speckled Turtle took it with her left. Her right held the torch.

"See—the fear is gone," Tzec said. "Now you can lead us all the way to the mounds."

The girl looked uncertain, but then tried it. She led Throat Shot down the path beside the long corn-mound, her hand clutching his tightly, as if she were dragging him along. She did seem to be less frightened, but he wasn't sure it was because of any power of his. He never doubted the power of the Spirit of the Mound to take away his own fear, but he had no certainty that this was a thing that could be extended to others. It might be that Tzec, and now Speckled Turtle, imagined it. But he didn't argue, as it was more convenient to have the girl lead them all the way.

The corn-ridge ended, but the path continued west, narrower, indicating that it was not used as much here. There was some moonlight, helping somewhat.

Soon enough they came to the region of the mounds. In the darkness under the starry sky it was not possible to see much, but he felt the presence of many spirits. "They are all around us," he said. "But they wish us no ill."

"If you go on one of the mounds, they will be angry," Speckled Turtle said.

"I think not. Not if I approach with proper humility. But I must go alone; they might not like the two of you there."

"Yet if I let go of your hand, the fear will come!" Speckled Turtle protested.

"Then maybe you should return to your lodge. You have shown me the mounds, and I thank you; I will find my own way back later." He disengaged his hand.

Speckled Turtle neither went nor spoke. She was rigid.

"That's like taking someone out into a storm in the swamp and dumping her out of the canoe," Tzec said reprovingly. "She's terrified!"

Throat Shot considered. He knew better than to take the girl onto the mound; the spirits would turn their backs on him immediately. But it would be a tedious waste of time to conduct her all the way back to the lodge, then come out here again by himself. Tzec seemed less frightened; she tended to be wary of physical threats, like poisonous snakes, rather than spiritual ones. That might be the key here.

He took Tzec's hand. "I take from you your fear," he said. "Now take Speckled Turtle's hand, and stop her fear." He wasn't sure how much of this Tzec believed, but she had lost her fear in the canoe, and perhaps could do this, or pretend to do it.

Tzec took the girl's hand. "He takes from you your fear," she said. "Through me." She was playing it out, knowing it was best, whatever her true state of emotion. His respect for her increased a bit more.

Speckled Turtle lost her rigidity. "My fear is gone."

"Do not move, and no spirit will bother you," Throat Shot said. He let go of Tzec's hand. "I will return." He thought of Sweet Medicine's brother, who had made a similar promise, before taking most of a year to honor it. But he would not allow that to happen!

The two girls stood, hands linked. Somehow the small one seemed more mature than the big one. If either was terrified now, she did not show it.

He walked to the nearest mound, which was low, less than half his height. It was level, and there were no spirits in it. Beyond it was a pond, and beyond that another mound that seemed to rise to about three times his height: much larger than his original mound, but much smaller than those along the coast. The size really did not matter; a great spirit could be in a small mound as readily as a large one.

He skirted the pond and stepped onto the base of the larger

mound. He felt something strange, but could not place it. It was not a threat, just an oddity.

O spirits of the mound, he thought. *I come to ask a favor of you. Who among you will talk to me?*

The whispering of the spirits ceased. None of them would talk with him. It was as if they were angry, not specifically with him, but with any living person. What could account for this?

He turned back toward the pool. The oddity was there.

What is it, O spirits? he thought. *What angers you?*

Then a vision formed. Above the scummy surface of the dark water he saw a platform, fastened on stout posts projecting from the pond. Atop a number of posts were lifelike carvings of eagles, their wings extended upward as if at the top of the wingbeat. Surely no accident had brought him here, for he was of the Eagle Clan! On some posts were carvings of turkeys, ducks, herons, kingfishers, owls, and other birds, or of panthers, foxes, and bears. On the main part of the platform were carefully wrapped bundles.

Throat Shot stared. He had never seen a more impressive display! He knew what it was: a charnel structure, where the bones of the dead were laid to rest. In his culture, and in the current Calusa tribe, the dead could be exposed for months or years before someone of sufficient stature for formal burial died. Then they would be buried along with the chief, their spirits to serve him in the other realm as the living ones had served him in life. But here, Throat Shot saw, the bones were never interred; they were laid to rest above the water, for spirits could not cross deep water. Thus this mode of honor for the dead protected them from the intrusion of hostile spirits from elsewhere, and protected the living folk of this region from molestation by the spirits here. The animal spirits, represented by the elaborate carvings, were honor guardians. It was not the same as a mound, but now he understood that it was as good. Indeed, here where flooding could occur, it was probably better; the spirits of the dead did not like the touch of seeping water.

Then he saw flames rising at one end of the platform. Fire was eating at it, burning out the wood of both platform and support posts, and consuming the guardian animal carvings. No living person was there to put it out. The desecration continued, eating out the platform until it collapsed, and the bones

slid into the water. Many tens of tens of spirits were thus
delivered into a hideously profane burial in the charnel pond.

The vision ended. Only the awful water remained.

Now he understood the rage of the spirits. How could the
living have so neglected their duty as to let this atrocity happen?
There was supposed to be always a priest, and helpers, as well
as carvers of the figurines. The charnel site was never unguarded! Yet it had happened, and a greater dishonor had been
done to these spirits in death than any in their lives.

He looked back at the mound. He felt the spirits stirring
restlessly. Many of them had been rescued, he understood
now, and given a belated burial. This was not what they preferred, but in the absence of the charnel platform, it was the
best that offered. But the stain on their bones had never been
cleansed—and half of those in the water had never been rescued even to that extent. They had been left to the eternal horror
of the water.

He knew what should be done. The pond should be drained
and the remaining bones taken out and buried properly. Or a
new charnel platform should be built for them, with new carvings to honor them. Only then would the spirits be able to rest.

A question came from the massed bones. *You?*

Throat Shot shook his head. *I cannot. I have only one good arm,
and I am on a mission elsewhere.*

The spirits went silent again. He was among the living; they
had expected no better of him. He felt guilty.

Throat Shot turned away from that mound. He knew that
his mission here was hopeless; no spirit of this region would
answer him, because of their rage against all his kind. Their
justified rage.

He returned to the girls. "They will not talk to me," he said
glumly.

"I'm sorry," Tzec said. "I wish they would talk to me."

He was surprised. "You? Why?"

"I have no one but you, and when I am sold I will have
nothing. Could they tell me what to do?"

Throat Shot was touched. "Maybe they will talk to you. You
are a child from afar, and innocent. I will take you to them."

"Don't leave me!" Speckled Turtle protested.

What was there to lose? "You may come too," he said. "But

keep your mind clean; think no thoughts of offense to spirits, for they will know." He took Tzec's hand, and the three of them walked linked to the mound by the pool.

"Think your thought to the spirits," he told Tzec. "They do not hear our voices, or answer in voices, but in thoughts. Be respectful. One will answer if he chooses."

Tzec stood there, concentrating. Throat Shot felt her hand stiffen in his, then loosen. Her face turned to him. "I think— I think it said I must go alone. To—that way." She moved her hand in his, indicating the direction.

They were talking to the child! The spirits knew she had not done this thing. "Then do it. We will wait here."

She slipped her hand free, shivered as if she had stepped into cold water, and walked away, north. There was enough light to enable him to see her form, vaguely.

Speckled Turtle grabbed for his hand. She was shivering, though the night was not cold.

Tzec walked almost to the shore of the river. There was a small, low mound, hardly noticeable under the overgrowth, but she had known where to find it. The spirits had told her. She got down on her knees, and put forward her hands, and finally lay on the ground, facedown. She remained that way for what seemed like a long time, but the stars hardly changed their positions.

Something swooped down, silhouetted against the stars, and away again. "An owl," Throat Shot whispered. "An omen!"

"With you I feel no fear," Speckled Turtle murmured, awed.

Tzec got to her feet, brushed herself off, and walked back. "The spirit of the solitary grave answered me," she said. "I know what to do."

"What did it tell you?" Throat Shot asked, unable to hold back his curiosity.

"It said the others had been dishonored, and are angry."

He had not told her that. Truly, she had talked with the spirit of the small mound! "It spoke truly. They were supposed to lie over water, with totems in their honor, but their platform burned. If your spirit was of another time, more recent—"

"Yes, more recent," she agreed. "It never knew the other spirits until it was buried. It was never defiled."

That was good. "Did it answer your question?"

"I must go to the Trader and tell him to do with me as he wishes," she said.

"But you're too young," Speckled Turtle protested.

"And you will go far away, Throat Shot, for a long time, but you will come back," Tzec continued. "I must wait for your return."

Had the spirit given her the answer for him? "Did—?"

"Far north," she said. "The biggest mound. There the spirit will tell you."

The spirit *had* told her! Throat Shot nodded. "I thank you, Tzec. The spirit preferred to speak to you, not me, for it knew you were blameless."

"Maybe because I'm related," she said. "It didn't say, but I felt it. My ancestors, the Maya, knew his ancestors."

They walked back toward the village, hands linked.

"But she's too young," Speckled Turtle repeated, evidently fixed on what a man would want of a girl. "The Trader must not do it with her."

"It is something else he wants," Tzec said.

That was a relief. The Trader had shown no sign of desiring her in that manner, but there was something obscure about the relation between them. First the Trader had declined to sell her; then he had told Throat Shot to teach her the signs; finally he had spoken of owing his life to her. What was on the man's mind?

"He understands more than he speaks," Throat Shot said.

"He *feels* more than he speaks," she responded.

True. But what was the nature of his feeling? It seemed that the spirit had indicated that Tzec would be staying with the Trader until Throat Shot returned. What kind of an association were they to have?

They reached the village, and their lodge, as the torch guttered out. The structure was silent; the Trader was evidently asleep.

Tzec found her blanket in the corner. Speckled Turtle remained with Throat Shot. When he settled down, she paused, then joined him, her skirt gone. She touched herself, and the odor of honey became stronger. Her mouth found his in the darkness for a passionate kiss. It was evident that her attitude toward him had changed; now she was eager to do what before had seemed a chore.

He did not argue. After some awkwardness, because she did not quite understand about his arm, and tended to bang into it, they achieved a comfortable union. She clung to him, seeking more than the sexual culmination; it was as if she wanted a spiritual merging too.

"With you I felt no fear," she whispered again.

That seemed to be it: she had gone with him to the mounds at night, and had seen that what he had said was true, and he had enabled her to feel no fear too. Now she wanted more of him, perhaps to take in some of that quality about him that stopped the fear. He doubted that the effect would last beyond this night, but he hardly cared to argue. Speckled Turtle in her eagerness was much more of a delight than she would have been otherwise, and his penis was almost as comfortable in her as it might have been in Heron Feather.

In due course they slept. Speckled Turtle did not seek to make him perform again each time he shifted position, but she cooperated when he woke and got interested. He penetrated her sleepy body a second time, and spouted his seed again, glad to verify that he could do this successfully on his own initiative. He was well satisfied.

In the morning Speckled Turtle went to report to her family. The Trader stretched and eyed Throat Shot. "You went to the mounds. Did you get an answer?"

Throat Shot looked at Tzec. "I will be going north. She—also got an answer."

The Trader gazed at Tzec. "I am interested in that answer."

She gulped, evidently uncertain now of her reassurance of the night. "It told me to—to tell you to—to do with me as you wish."

The Trader considered. "Do you know what I wish?"

"I thought it was to sell me for a good price. Now I think it is something else." She remained tight.

The Trader looked at Throat Shot. "You must go north, without her? You cannot buy her? I would accept a promise for payment in another season."

Throat Shot spread his hands. "You know I cannot. I have nothing to trade for her except my continued service, and I cannot offer that. I must go north alone."

The Trader nodded. "It will be several days before we reach my tribe. You must teach her the rest of the signs so she can talk with those of other tongues."

"I will do that."

The Trader turned to Tzec. "I am unmarried. My sister keeps my house." He smiled briefly. "The Ais are not like the Cacique of the Calusa. My house is *all* she keeps. That is good, for she takes excellent care of my goods while I am away, and a wife would be impatient with my long absences. I have never had a family, and have been satisfied. Now I am unsatisfied, having seen what a child might be like. A son to travel with me, who would listen to my stories, and help me trade. It is never lonely, with company."

He took a deep breath. "I feared to broach this matter, for it is more personal than business, and is not a thing I would do purely for business. Tzec, you are a fine girl, and clever and useful. You have made me see that I thought too narrowly. It is not a son I wish, but a daughter. One who knows and accepts my ways and is not eager to prove herself as a hunter. I want to adopt you, to be my child until you are of age to marry, and give me grandchildren to carry on my business, and to remember me when I am old and infirm, and see that I am buried with proper respect."

Tzec's mouth had slowly gone slack as she listened. This was different from any expectation she might have had, and better. "You will not sell me?"

The Trader made a mock grimace. "The Ais do not sell their children, however valuable they may be."

"Yes!" she exclaimed. "Yes, I will be your daughter! The spirit knew! I will do all that you wish, the best I can. Oh, thank you, thank you, Trader!" There were tears on her face, happy ones.

"Then it is done," the Trader said. Then, covering his evident pleasure at this ready resolution, he became brisk. "We must be on our way. There is a long river to paddle."

They thanked the family for the hospitality, and the Trader gave them trinkets that pleased them, and the three returned to their canoe. It had been a significant night.

They followed the Fish Eater River back to the Wide Water, then turned north. They moved well, because there was no perceptible current to fight, and because they were rested and strong. Throat Shot had been gaining proficiency with his paddle, so that his restricted arm inhibited him less; he could stroke only on one side, with limited range, but he was strong within that range.

He worked with Tzec on the sign language, as they had before. Now there was joy in it, for she would not be sold, and she wanted to prove how good she could be in this universal tongue.

"Daughter," she said.

"It is the same as for Woman, Female, or Girl," he said. "Then bring your hand down to show her height."

Tzec quickly brushed her hair with her hooked fingers on the side, showing how well she remembered. "But how can you show whose girl it is? It could be any girl!"

"You will know by the pride of the gesture," the Trader said. "Some other girl is just anyone." He made a negligent gesture of height. "*My* girl is special." He gestured again, this time as if touching something precious.

Tzec considered that a moment, and was satisfied. She got back to work. "Color."

"Rub the tips of your right fingers on the back of your left hand, in a circle. Then look around and find the color you mean, and point to it."

"But if there is no such color in sight—"

"Choose another color," Throat Shot said, laughing.

"Skirt," she said, beginning on clothing.

"Make two four-hands," he said, letting go of his paddle long enough to show the figure when it wasn't actual counting, with the thumb and forefinger spread, and the three other fingers closed. "Put them on your body to show what clothing you mean."

She put her four-hands on her hips. "Move them down a bit," the Trader said. "To show you're not just resting your hands. Form the skirt with them."

So the instruction continued, as they crossed the edge of the Wide Water and came to the mouth of the Winding Water River.

Now there was a perceptible current, and the paddling was harder, but still not difficult. With the distraction of the instruction, Throat Shot was hardly aware of the passage of time.

But he was also interested in the region. He saw raccoons frequently near the water, with their black eye masks. When he peered down through the water he saw fish and crabs, and knew that every one of them was fighting for its life and food. The region seemed peaceful, but it was not; the little hidden creatures were constantly struggling and killing each other. He wondered whether they apologized to the spirits of those they killed, the way men did, to be sure the spirits would not seek vengeance. It seemed likely, as it was the sensible thing to do.

They came to the Winding Water Lake, and on north to the river again, camping where the Trader knew good people. It was evident that the Trader had many long-standing friends through here, for he had been by often with his goods, and it was not far from his home. Throat Shot realized that the Trader probably made shorter trading trips by foot to this region when he wasn't making his long canoe route.

Then, before the river ended, the Trader drew up to a lodge by the right bank. "This is where the canoe lives," he said. "I cannot carry it overland to my tribe, but when I make my next circuit, I'll go north to the end of the river. Two portages take me to the source of your Big Little River, and from there it is easy going." He glanced at Tzec. "How well can you portage, daughter?"

Tzec looked down at the solid log of the dugout canoe. She quailed. The thing was obviously far too heavy for her tiny body to carry. "I will try, father."

The Trader laughed. "It is swampy there, and there are channels. We will not have to carry it. We will tie vines to it and drag it along from either side, loaded. It will be slow and wearing, but it can be done by two because I have done it with one. It is a great relief to reach deeper water again, and float!"

Indeed, she looked relieved.

There was another family here, who evidently lived mostly on fish and mussels, for the bones and shells were piled near. As it turned out, they kept and guarded the Trader's canoe during his off-season, and had the use of it then. In the spring he would return for his next trading loop, having gathered more goods.

Now they faced an overland trip to reach the Trader's tribe. The Trader made packs for each of them, filling the packs with the conchs and other items he had acquired. Because he had taken an assistant and a slave (now daughter) in trade, the hands were more and the burdens less; they would carry in one trip what would otherwise have taken him two.

They made the trek, following the winding paths the Trader knew. Here the ground was firmer, and they spooked deer and watched them bound gracefully away, and once even saw a bear. Another time they almost blundered into a nest of wasps, and had to retreat in a hurry and circle around it. Their repellent grease stopped the flies, but aroused wasps didn't bite, they stung, which was another matter. In two more days they reached the Trader's home village in the Ais tribe, by the bank of a river flowing north. By this time Throat Shot had learned enough of the language to get by with the help of some signs, and Tzec was making progress. The life-style of this tribe was close enough to those of their own tribes to be no problem.

The Trader's sister was Three Scales, with fish scales sewn into her shawl, and she looked stout and grim. But when the Trader introduced Tzec as his daughter, she smiled. "That is one way to do it," she said. "But you will not mistreat her in this house." It was a joke, for the Trader was not a violent man. Then they knew it would be all right.

Throat Shot would travel with another trader, when one passed through who would take him. Meanwhile he shared the Trader's lodge, and continued to teach Tzec tongues and signs. It was a good time.

CHAPTER 8

SIGNS

O Spirit of the Mound, I have told you of the rage of the spirits of the mound near the Wide Water, and how Tzec came to be adopted by the Trader, and Throat Shot's decision to go far north. Now I will tell you of his stay with the Yufera tribe on the way north, and of his mixed feelings there.

A moon later, another trader came, canoeing up the Fresh Water River. He was Half Eye, so named because of his perpetual squint after some past injury. He was a powerful, gruff man who preferred to work alone, but when he met Throat Shot and saw his half arm, he relented. He understood about such a liability. He agreed to take him to the mouth of the river, for one fine conch.

"But I have no—" Throat Shot began, abruptly remembering that a trader's company was not free. The Ais Trader had paid two fine feather cloaks to take him as a translator and assistant, but the man had been looking for someone like that. This man was not.

"Done," the Trader said, producing a conch. Then, to Throat Shot: "You delivered more than I expected. You found me a daughter. That is worth a pretty shell."

Throat Shot could only nod with appreciation. It was unusual generosity.

He bade parting to Tzec. The tears came freely to her eyes, and fought to reach his own. "You will return," she said bravely. "The spirit said."

"When I find the Ulunsúti," he agreed. But that seemed

166

impossibly far away at the moment. The local mound had been silent to him; he had only Tzec's word to go on, that he would go far north to the biggest mound. He still could not be quite sure the spirit had truly spoken to her; she might have imagined it, hoping to help him. But he would not say that to her, or to himself; he had to believe in her.

Constrained by manhood, he showed no emotion. But she, under no such restraint, leaped and hugged him tightly before turning away. For that he was glad.

Paddling downstream was easy, and progress was good. Half Eye talked to him, ascertaining his situation. "I wouldn't have taken you if it weren't for that arm," he admitted. "You lost half the use of it, just as I lost half the use of my eye, so I knew what you suffered. But see that you do not interfere with my business."

Throat Shot understood that this man's temperament was different, and he agreed to stay out of the way. "I wish only to visit any mounds I may along the river, if the people let me."

"Do you really talk to the spirits?"

"I try to, but often they do not talk to me."

"Aren't you frightened by them?"

"I have no fear."

Half Eye was openly skeptical. "Then you would swim this river, heedless of the alligators?"

"That would be foolish. I have no fear, but I am not crazy."

The man was evidently unconvinced, but let it drop. They moved on, until they reached the region of the Acuera. There was a fair-sized village by the bank, set on a solid mass of old shells. Throat Shot could understand them, because their main hunting grounds were not far from those of the Toco, beyond the Cale, but they were regarded as a hostile tribe and he did not care to identify himself as a Toco. He looked more like an Ais now, after his moon with them. It was easier to use the signs, where his origin didn't show; every tribe used the same signs, with only minor variants.

Throat Shot was a complete stranger here, and his arm made him ugly. The people were polite, and they provided excellent deer meat for a feast, but they sought no close contact with

him. There was a lodge to spend the night in, but no maidens
came; either this was not part of Acuera hospitality, or the
travelers were not regarded as guests. There seemed to be no
significant mound in the region, and in any event the villagers
seemed unlikely to want any stranger there.

Next day they moved on north, following the serpentine
winds of the growing river. There appeared to be few residents
here, and canoes were scarce, in contrast to the number farther
upriver. They passed a lake which would have seemed large
but for the memory of the Wide Water; in an afternoon they
traversed it and were back on the river.

In due course they reached a settlement of the Fresh Water
tribe. These people migrated seasonally between the sea to the
east and the river, and were preparing to return to the sea as
the land cooled. Here things were better, from both Half Eye's
and Throat Shot's views. The natives were eager to trade for
goods from afar, such as the special Calusa masks, and they
had a substantial mound. They were amazed that Throat Shot
wanted to go there at dusk, but showed him the path, which
was well kept.

As he approached the mound, he reflected on his prior failures. What had he been doing wrong on the other mounds?
He had been intoxicated once, and had encountered antipathy
to the living another time. But neither had been the case at the
Ais mound, yet it had been silent. What could he do this time
that would be better, so that the spirits would speak to him?
He didn't know.

Still troubled, he came to stand at the base of the mound.
He felt the spirits stirring within it, and most were ancient. He
decided to be open with them.

*O spirits, I am from afar, sent by Dead Eagle to seek the Ulunsuti.
He told me to ask of the spirits of other mounds where it might be.
Will you answer me?*

There was a hesitation. Then a spirit answered. *I knew Dead
Eagle. Let me into your mind.*

Throat Shot opened his mind to the Spirit. He felt an odd-
ness. Then the Spirit spoke again. *Yes, he had touched you. He
has taken your fear. You must go north, far north. But there is some-*

thing for you to do on the way. Go to the Yufera, stay the winter with the Chief's woman. Guard her.

But the Chief will not let me be with his wife! Throat Shot protested. Yet he remembered Heron Feather, the Cacique's wife. Conventions differed. So he amended his protest. *Who may I say is sending me?*

Frog Effigy.

I will tell the Chief, Throat Shot promised. *If he lets me stay with his wife, I will guard her as well as I am able.*

The Spirit was silent. Throat Shot backed away, then turned to find the darkened path.

He was elated as he moved slowly back to the village. The spirits had spoken to him! Because Frog Effigy had known Dead Eagle! He had confirmation of Tzec's message.

But to stay with a foreign chief's wife, and guard her? That seemed laughable, considering his inability to use a bow. Yet he would have to seek that tribe, and that chief, and state his case, and see what happened.

The river became huge, almost lakelike in its breadth. There were extensive marshes and flatlands covered by pine trees. Here they encountered a number of canoes carrying warriors, but when the tribesmen recognized the trader they relaxed. This was of course one reason Throat Shot preferred to travel with a trader; not only did it facilitate progress, because the trader had a canoe and knew the route, it protected him from possible hostilities. No one harmed a trader!

These were the Saturiwa, the folk of the river's mouth. They were evidently populous and active.

Throat Shot and Half Eye were conducted to the large town where the river poured into the monstrous eastern sea. It was guarded by a wall of stakes set into the ground, each stake pointed at the top. This was more impressive than the Toco defenses. The lodges were circular, with thatched roofs and small doors.

The hospitality was more impressive too. The head Chief, the *Holata Ico*, welcomed them. They dined on corn cakes and alligator meat, with drink made from corn. Throat Shot was extremely careful with this, aware of its potency at the first sip.

Then Half Eye brought out his wares and did his business, bargaining with the Chief and other well-set people, disposing of the masks and other items he had obtained from the Ais Trader. In return he gained beautiful feather cloaks of the type so valued by the Toco and Calusa. The pattern of trading was coming clear. Throat Shot listened carefully, picking up the tongue; it was another variant of the larger tongue of this region, spoken by the neighbors of the Toco, the Cale, and by the Fresh Water tribe. Thus what had at first seemed entirely foreign was gradually becoming intelligible as his facility with language took hold.

Throat Shot was not a trader, but the Chief was interested in him. He had to tell all about himself and his tribe and his quest. He used the hand signs liberally to clarify his limited spoken vocabulary. There was a fair group listening by the time he finished; the Saturiwa liked to know about far places.

"And you talk to the spirits of the dead?" the Chief asked.

"Sometimes. When they will talk to me."

"And you have no fear?"

Throat Shot was becoming wary of this question. "I have caution, not fear."

"The spirits will not hurt you?"

"They have no reason to."

The Chief smiled. "Then I will put a fair maiden in the lodge atop our eldest ceremonial mound, and bar the direct path. If you will go alone in darkness by the path that passes the burial mounds, to reach that lodge, that maiden is yours for the night. You should have no trouble going there. You can talk to the spirits on your way."

Throat Shot saw that the Chief expected to have some cruel fun with him. The Chief would be disappointed. "No trouble," he agreed.

They showed him the path by the afternoon light. It was clear enough, but it did pass through a swampy region where wild creatures probably ranged at night. Still, such creatures seldom came near men. He should be safe enough.

When darkness was complete, they brought him to the path. "May I have a torch, to see my way?" he asked.

"You said nothing about a torch before!"

Throat Shot shrugged. He set off down the path, able to find it by its firmness, and by the faint ambient light. He made noise with his feet as he walked, so that any creatures on the path would hear him and get out of the way. When he was beyond the range of the torches of the tribesmen, he felt by the side, plucking a tall weed with a brittle stem, which he used to feel ahead for obstructions. Progress was slow, but he knew he would get there. He could have used his punk pot to light a makeshift torch of his own, but knew the warriors would be watching for that light. He preferred to prove himself this way.

In due course he reached the burial mound. He stopped there and addressed the spirits, but they would not speak to him. He wasn't surprised; this tribe was not as friendly as it had seemed. "I apologize for intruding on you," he said, and turned away.

Beware.

Throat Shot jumped. That had been a spirit warning! He turned to face the mound again, but it was silent. It was almost as if the spirits were of two minds about him: seeing him as a potential enemy, but also as one who did not deserve to be punished without warning. So they had given him only the hint; he would have to do the rest himself.

He went on, and found the ceremonial mound with its circular lodge. He was about to enter, but paused, considering. The mischief of the Chief might not yet be finished. Could the spirits' warning relate to this? Was there an ambush in the lodge? He would have to be extremely cautious about entering it; the darkness outside might be his best friend.

He stood for a time, listening. Then he called out: "I am Throat Shot, the traveler from the Toco. Is anyone there?" He moved to the side immediately after speaking, so that an arrow shot there would not catch him.

In a moment there was an answer. The voice sounded like that of a child or a young woman, but the words were foreign. He had barely communicated with the Saturiwa people, and could not have done it without copious use of signs, and that had been one-way: they had been the listeners. It would have been hard enough to talk with this girl in the darkness if she used the Saturiwa tongue, but this seemed to be another dialect, which at this stage might as well have been a completely new tongue.

At any rate, this indicated that there were no warriors here. He could tell by the trace echo of her voice that she was alone. Whatever the danger, it was not a direct physical attack.

If he did not understand her, did she understand him? He thought not; her words seemed frightened. Why should that be, if she had been left here for him?

"Friend," he said, using one of the Saturiwa terms he had picked up.

She replied with an unfamiliar term, still frightened. Now he was sure she spoke a different tongue. Why had they left him a girl who did not speak their dialect?

He could not even communicate with her in signs, because of the darkness. Of course, neither speaking nor signs were necessary, to be with a woman for the night. Still, there was something wrong here. For one thing, there was no smell of honey about her.

Then he had an idea. He could use signs.

"Touch me," he told her, stepping forward.

She retreated so quickly that she stumbled and fell with a little shriek.

He knelt, finding her foot in the dark. "Touch me," he repeated, feeling upward until he found her arm and hand.

She lay as if stunned, whimpering.

He lifted her hand with his own, and made the sign for Friend: his right hand palm out, first and second fingers straight, the thumb and small fingers closed, his hand lifted to his face. He actually touched his face so she would know it in the dark. "Friend." He repeated it, making sure she felt the position of his hand and fingers.

She sat up, seeming reassured by the warmth of his hand and his gentle approach. Then she made a signal of her own: her left hand out before her body, flat, and her right hand coming out to move down and out to the left. Because he could touch her hands only with his right, it took him several trials before he understood the positions and motions of her two hands. When he did, he was dismayed.

She had made the sign for Die.

"No!" he said. He found her right hand, let her clasp his lightly, then extended it flat, palm down. After a pause, he swung it right, turning it over.

She caught his hand again so it would touch hers in the Listening pose, then held it up closed with the index finger extended. Then she moved it to her left and down, closing the finger somewhat: Yes.

"No," he repeated. Then: "No Die." He was catching on: the Chief was playing a game with him, but also with her. He had told her she was to be killed. What a joke that was, to send a stranger in the dark with a promise of love, and tell the maiden that the man was coming to kill her!

They settled down to further dialogue. It was halting and slow, and he had a problem because of the incapacity of his left arm, but it improved as they became more familiar with each other. Sometimes he had to arrange her two hands in the appropriate positions to indicate how his should be. She was Colored Stone—he could not tell what color, but read the sign for Hard, which meant Rock or Stone—and was twelve winters old. She was the daughter of a chief of a tribe to the north, here against her will, as far as he could tell.

It seemed that her tribe, the Tacatacuru, was allied with the Saturiwa against the Utina, who lived farther inland. The alliance was not always easy, and the more powerful Saturiwa had chosen to buttress it by making a guest of the Tacatacuru Chief's young daughter. It was done politely, but the truth was she was a hostage against possible reluctance by her father to engage in any direct combat with the Utina. She wanted only to return home, because here she was not only treated like an outcast, she was subject to various subtle unkindnesses, reminders of what her fate would be if her father became too independent. The present case was an example: she had been left here in the place of fear at night, and told that a priest might come to sacrifice her if her thoughts were evil. So her fear was that either an evil spirit would come to steal her sanity or a priest would come with the sacrificial knife.

Throat Shot knew of the Utina, but the Toco had not had any direct interaction with them. The fact that the Saturiwa were the Utina's enemies meant nothing to a Toco, who had no preference either way. But the Toco's tongue, he understood, was more closely related to that of the Utina than that of the Saturiwa, so it was possible that the Saturiwa Chief had seen him as a potential enemy. Constrained by hospitality and courtesy to the trader, the Chief had not been able to take any action against Throat Shot directly, but had arranged to make it easy for Throat Shot to get into trouble on his own. If he had indulged himself sexually with the barely-of-age hostage daughter of a foreign chief, he could have been identified with the Utina: the enemy had ravaged her. Not only would that humiliate her, it would guarantee the cooperation of the Tacatacuru.

I (right thumb touching chest) No (flat hand turned back) Love (hands closed, wrists crossed over heart) Chief (right index finger pointed up, moved in an arch forward and at head height, as if looking down on others), he remarked. His memory of little Tzec was fresh; this girl was older, but not so much so as to defuse his feeling.

She laughed agreement, her first expression of humor.

After that their conspiracy developed naturally. They left the lodge and followed the path out to the burial mound. She clutched his hand tightly, able to follow because of his lack of fear. There they took another path she knew of, and proceeded to the bank of the river where there was a cove at the verge of the sea. Several canoes were beached there, and one, she indicated, was hers, or supposed to be.

They took this canoe. Colored Stone was in the front, guiding it, while he provided power paddling on the left rear. They slid silently into the dark expanse of water and into the choppy surface of the sea. They did not dare go too close to land, lest a Saturiwa sentry spy them.

But after they had gone north for about the time the sun would have taken to move one finger in a ten-finger sky, they cut back close to shore, feeling more secure there. They kept paddling, not hard, because Colored Stone had indicated that it was a full day's distance to her home. As it was, they would both be very tired by the time they got there. Throat Shot had experience canoeing, but the girl had never paddled for any distance. After a while he had her simply use her paddle to keep the canoe straight, while he continued to move it forward.

Dawn came, and they were not there. But they were getting close, she indicated. All they needed was to encounter one of her tribesmen, and then it would be all right. He hoped so, because it would be impossible for him to defend against a warrior's attack.

He saw her now by day. She was definitely a child, not yet progressed to womanhood. He was angry again at what he had been told, knowing that she had been set up to be unable to explain her situation in the darkness. Misunderstanding would have been easy, as the Chief had intended. Only Throat Shot's caution had enabled them to avoid a highly negative encounter.

Colored Stone made an exclamation. He looked, having been intent on his fatigued paddling. There was a canoe ahead. If it was one of her tribe's—

It was. Colored Stone hailed it, and soon two warriors were beside them. She spoke a torrent in her tongue, while the warriors stared at Throat Shot. But as she spoke, their expressions relaxed. Now they knew he was no enemy.

The girl leaned forward over the end of the canoe and grasped the back of the other canoe. Then the warriors paddled briskly, hauling them along behind. What a relief it was to lay his own paddle down and rest!

If Throat Shot thought he had been welcomed before, it was nothing compared with what happened when Blue Stone (now he had her color) was reunited with her father the Chief, and her mother. The longer the girl talked, the more positive they became. But all Throat Shot wanted at this point was to eat a little and sleep a lot.

Soon enough he found himself on a feather mattress, the softest thing he had encountered. He sank into sleep.

When he woke in the late afternoon, there was a maiden with him. She was beautiful, and she smelled of honey.

Next morning, his every possible need more than adequately sated, Throat Shot had a more formal meeting with the Chief. They conversed in signs, and soon the Chief understood where the visitor was going.

We Friend Saturiwa, the Chief signed. Yufera No Friend Saturiwa. Night Day Sun East (tomorrow) Perhaps Friend Yufera. Take You There.

What more could he ask?

He remained several more days with the Tacatacuru, enjoying their hospitality and learning something of their tongue. They were based on a marshy island with oak hammocks. Their villages were roughly square, with circular lodges; he had not seen that layout before. They lived on shellfish and the animals of the hammocks. It wasn't fancy, and they were evidently not a powerful tribe, but he liked them and they liked him. Probably Blue Stone had something to do with that.

When the time came for him to go, the girl approached him. She was rested and happy now, and he saw that she would soon enough become a pretty woman. But she reminded him of Tzec, not from any similarity of appearance, but because she was young and friendly and had been through bad times. He realized that from the moment he had understood her situation, in the lodge on the mound, he had been determined to save her. That was the legacy of Tzec.

She touched the center of her chest with her thumb: I. She compressed her fingers and brought them down across her heart: Heart. Then, immediately, she closed her hand, leaving only thumb and forefinger extended, and moved it back and turned it over: Know. Together the signs meant "I remember."

Her father the Chief, standing a little apart, echoed the motions with his hand. They were thanking him for what he had done.

Throat Shot, touched, extended his two hands flat with their palms down, then made a sweeping gesture toward Blue Stone with his right: Thank You. He should have done it with both hands, but could not move his left that far. He knew they understood. He repeated it toward the Chief, who nodded.

There was no more to be said or signed. With surprisingly sweet sadness he turned toward the waiting canoe, where two husky warriors had their paddles poised. He stepped into the center and sat. Immediately the warriors stroked the water, synchronized, and the canoe leaped forward.

They quickly left the island, moved north, and crossed to the mouth of the Enemy Boundary River. Throat Shot hoped it hadn't been recently named, but feared that there could still be warfare along it. They drove upstream, and before long reached a settlement.

The Yufera canoes quickly came out to intercept them. The

lead warrior signed Peace: his two hands clasped before his body, the right palm down, the left palm up. He also spoke the word.

The Yufera accepted this. They might not be friendly with the Tacatacuru, but they were evidently willing to negotiate.

The canoe came to the shore, and Throat Shot got out and made his case as well as he could with signs. The subchief cut him off with smile, making the sign for Woman, Small: the news of his rescue of Blue Stone had spread. It seemed that even an unfriendly tribe appreciated the gesture. They would accept him.

The two Tacatacuru warriors paddled their canoe back out into the river. The Yufera let them go without further challenge; they had done their job. Now it was up to Throat Shot to make the rest of his case, to the Chief.

The Chief resided in another village, inland from the river. A boy guided him there. Throat Shot saw that the vegetation was different here from what he had seen throughout the southern swamps; the palms were gone, and the oaks and pines dominated. There were many new trees and shrubs of types he didn't recognize.

They reached the interior village. A woman came out to meet him. She was beautiful, perhaps twenty winters old, and garbed in cloths that covered her breasts as well as her hips. Behind her were several warriors who stood relaxed, but were evidently ready to move into action at any moment if the need arose. This was evidently the Chief's wife.

She lifted her open right hand, palm up, before her mouth. She drew it toward her lips sharply. This was the sign for Tell Me.

Throat Shot used his own signs to explain that he was talking with spirits, who would direct him to the Ulunsuti. One spirit had told him to stay the winter with the Chief's wife and guard her.

The watching warriors gradually lost their impassivity as he progressed. When he came to the part about the wife, one laughed.

The woman glanced at him, and he became immediately serious again. Then she addressed Throat Shot. Dead Question? She signed.

She wanted to know which spirit had told him this. He made the sign for Frog, which was that for Water followed by jumping motions; then he made the sign for Stone, which was as close as he could get to Effigy in signs. Frog Effigy was the one who had told him.

Now was the critical point. Would she believe him? He was not at all certain that she would, yet he had been obliged to do the Spirit's bidding.

She considered. She glanced again at the warriors behind her, who remained expressionless. Then she decided. I Called Beautiful Moon, she signed. I Chief Wife No. I Chief.

Throat Shot stared. Beautiful she was, certainly; she had been well named. She was the Chief? He had heard of female chiefs, but had never thought of that here. How could he guard the Chief's wife when there was no Chief's wife, and could be none?

His chagrin evidently amused her, for her mouth quirked the tiniest bit. Then she glanced again at the warriors. She lifted her hand toward Throat Shot, forefinger raised. She brought it toward her: Come.

Dazed, he followed her to her lodge, while it was the turn of the warriors to stare. Apparently Beautiful Moon liked a good joke as well as anyone.

She indicated a niche within the round lodge. She closed her fist and moved it down: Remain.

It seemed that this was where he was to stay. Throat Shot sat there. His mind was in a turmoil: how could the Spirit have sent him here? But now that he focused on the contact at the mound, he remembered: the Spirit had said "Chief's woman," not "wife." Perhaps "chief woman." Throat Shot had misunderstood.

Now the woman spoke verbally to him. The Yufera tongue was part of a large complex of tongues, one of which was the Cale, the Toco neighbor across the Little Big River. Because he knew that tongue, he could follow hers when she spoke slowly and augmented her words with signs. He could have followed the speech of other tribes similarly, but they had spoken rapidly, losing him. This dialect was a bit easier than the others he had encountered, fortunately.

Before long they had a basic vocabulary, and it was broad-
ening as he inquired about new words. Beautiful Moon seemed
pleased with his facility. She made it plain that she did not take
his message from the Spirit too seriously, though there was
indeed a long-lost ancestor named Dried Frog. The chiefs were
usually women here, selected by the council, and normally they
were young and beautiful. They seldom married, being regarded as brides of the original male chief. So in that sense,
she explained, she could be regarded as a wife, and perhaps
the Spirit was thinking of that.

But he could also have made up his story, having picked up
Frog Effigy's name somewhere. It would be easy to verify the
validity of that contact: if his message was real, by the time the
winter was done, he would save her life. If he had no occasion
to do so, then he would be exposed as a fraud. In that case he
would be executed when the Green Corn Ceremony came.

With that she departed to see to other business, leaving
him to ponder. Now he understood that the Yufera did not
appreciate being fooled, and had their own ways to discourage
it. Beautiful Moon had treated him well, and had told him
the truth, but she would see him dead if she judged it warranted.

Throat Shot's life was easy, physically; he was given food
and shelter and was not bothered. But there was always a sly
glance, not quite of mockery but of expectation. The members
of the tribe regarded him as a clever impostor who would pay
the price for it next year. He was free to go where he chose,
but discouraged from crossing the river or ranging too far out
from the main village. They kept an eye on him, nominally to
be sure he was near when the lady Chief needed protection,
actually to be sure he did not slip away after enjoying their
hospitality on false premises. He was in fact captive, in somewhat the way Blue Stone had been.

After the novelty of his presence wore off, and he learned
enough of their tongue to have no trouble communicating, they
put him to some simple tasks during the day while Beautiful
Moon was engaged in other business. He had to help the
women gather roots and herbs, and to grind corn into flour,
and to fetch wood for the fire. It was woman's work. He pre-

tended to be unaware of the insult, for how could he protest? He was unable to do man's work.

Actually, some of it was interesting in its own right. Some of the women were young and pretty, and they appreciated having the help on communal tasks. He helped them carry the baskets of hickory nuts they gathered; his left arm was bent, but he could brace his hand against his hip and hold one side of the basket, while his good right arm functioned freely. He was soon drafted to carry all the baskets back to the village as they filled them; this entailed much walking, and he was good at that. In truth, it became very like a man's task, and the work went faster for all of them.

When the nuts were in, the women had to pound them to pieces, then cast them into boiling water. Again, Throat Shot was good at this, bracing the club-hammer with his left hand and smashing it down with his right. He was stronger than the women; indeed, his right arm was stronger than that of most men, because he used it where others would use two. The pounding went faster than usual.

They strained the water through fine sieves which held on to the oily part of the liquid. This was the hickory milk, sweet and rich, used in most of their cooking. For the first time he understood exactly how it was prepared; he had never, as a male child, deigned to observe the process among the Toco. He would remember.

Only once did his situation make him angry. That was when a warrior used the term for a special type of man in his presence. There were some men in each tribe who chose to dress in skirts, and to wear their hair loose in the fashion of women, and to do woman's work. Such a man would also play the part of a woman sexually, when asked. They were generally held in contempt by both men and women, but tolerated. The implication was that Throat Shot was such a man, though it was obvious he was not. It was the kind of teasing done to an enemy. An ordinary warrior would have challenged the teaser to a contest of honor, and perhaps killed him. But Throat Shot did not have that luxury. He would only have gotten himself killed.

The season changed, becoming colder than he had known before. He had to don heavier clothing, which they provided.

Part of it was new to him: moccasins for his feet. The Toco always went barefoot, but here more was needed. He understood now that it was no intent to tease or conceal that caused the maidens to cover their bodies; the weather often required it. Perhaps that was just as well, for the women of this tribe seemed unusually lovely, and none of them cared to share his nights. They were friendly, and he knew them well now, but they saw him as less than a man, and seemed to have no more interest in him sexually than they did in other women. Had he been able to see their bodies better, he would only have been more frustrated.

Beautiful Moon was a different matter, not in the way she saw him, but in what he saw of her. She had taken him as guard, which meant he had to be close to her when she slept. By day she was generally with the warriors and needed no other protection, but at night those warriors were with their wives and she was alone. Throat Shot saw her in full clothing, and in partial dress, and naked when she washed; she treated him like some pot, present in her lodge but of no account. He pretended not to notice, or to react to her presence, but she knew he did. She did no woman's work; he did. He desired her intensely, and could neither say so nor avoid her tantalizing proximity. That was part of his punishment for imposing.

He guarded her. He slept when she slept, but roused himself periodically to check around the lodge. He slept lightly, and was alert when there was any sound he couldn't immediately classify. He did not know what threat might come, but he intended to intercept it, or he would surely be killed long before the Green Corn Ceremony!

Once a snake slithered into the lodge. He heard it and caught it. It was a harmless variety; he carried it out and let it go unharmed. But another time a rattlesnake entered the village, and the women screamed. Then Throat Shot caught it in his hand and carried it safely away. After that there was a subtle change in the attitude of the others. They were coming to understand that what he said was true: he felt no fear.

Overtures were made to the Tacatacuru, and one day Blue Stone arrived with her father, who smoked the pipe of peace with Beautiful Moon. The alliance of the tribe had shifted; Tacatacuru and Yufera were no longer hostile to each other. Blue

Stone smiled at Throat Shot; it seemed that she had had something to do with this.

That night Beautiful Moon questioned Throat Shot about Blue Stone, and he explained how he had rescued her from the Saturiwa. He knew the Chief had heard the story before, but now she was doing him the honor of hearing it openly, and she gave it more credence. "Perhaps it is your business to save women," she remarked.

"It is my business to find the Ulunsuti," he replied.

"That, too, perhaps," she agreed, and went to her bed to sleep.

The agreement with the Tacatacuru signaled the onset of hostile relations with the Saturiwa. There were no raids across the river, for this was the winter. But as spring came, and with it the proper combat season, it was obvious that there was likely to be trouble.

The warriors ranged out constantly, alert for any hostile traffic on the water. The two rivers were their bastion; the tribe was nestled between them, and their territory was plainly defined. They were ready to riddle any approaching hostile parties with arrows before the canoes landed.

But they could not guard the rivers well at night, as Throat Shot knew. He remained especially alert, but feared it wasn't enough; suppose a party of warriors raided the village, setting fire to the lodges?

The Yufera burial mound was not far from the central village. Throat Shot visited it, but its spirits would not talk to him. He was not sure whether they were offended with him or just not interested.

Could Frog Effigy have told him wrong? As time passed, his doubt increased. Yet if the spirits misled him, then his quest was futile, so this was as good a place to end it as any. He had to believe in what they told him!

In the long nights he pondered things, coming to no certain conclusions. For example, the matter of combat: he had given it up, yet was this final? His curiosity would not let go.

He put his hand on the bow that was in the lodge. Beautiful Moon, as Chief, was entitled to a chief's weapons, but as a woman, she did not use them. He, unable to extend his left hand, could not use the bow, but knife and spear were feasible.

He wore his own knife, always, and kept the spear close.

But the bow: now he wondered whether he truly could not use it. Suppose, instead of his left arm, he used his foot?

In the darkness he tried it. He had to put the bow sideways, and his right foot mainly got in the way, but his left foot was able to brace the bow in such a way that his right hand could draw back the string. It was clumsy, and he had to jam one end of the bow against the ground to steady it, but his leg had more power than even a healthy arm. His aim might not be much, but he could probably shoot an arrow.

He smiled. What point? It wasn't as if he could go out to battle, hopping on one foot, or that the enemy warriors would wait for him to sit down and aim his bow! Even if he could, why should he do it? He didn't like to kill or even harm a human being. So this was an idle exercise.

Meanwhile Beautiful Moon slept. He would not see her in the darkness, and in any event she was covered by her blanket, but he could hear her breathing. Even that sound seemed beautiful; he pictured her fine breasts gently heaving. She trusted him, but this was not from any genuine respect for him as a man, but because she saw him as no possible threat to her. He wished he could prove himself to her in some way, and had no assurance that he ever could. He was the one-armed joke, a source of muted amusement to the tribe.

He did make some limited use of that amusement. In the afternoons now, he told stories to the children. They enjoyed it, and it kept them out of mischief, and it helped them learn the lore of their tribe and of neighboring tribes. Their mothers approved. They, like the Chief, knew he was harmless. Who could fear a prisoner who was going to die or be seriously humiliated at the next Green Corn Ceremony?

In the spring came warmth. Soon it would be summer, and they would have to be on guard against raids. But right now was the time to enjoy life. Throat Shot wished he could enjoy it with a woman, as the warriors both married and single did, but he could not. He had to guard the Chief.

One night when the forest was quieter than usual, Throat Shot became alert. He had learned to recognize the calls of individual night birds, and he was accustomed to the chirping of the little frogs and insects. Tonight they were muted, and

that gave him notice. Something was out there. It could be a
panther laying for a deer, or it could be something else. A
panther would not come close to the village, so was not to be
feared. But something else—

He got up and stepped outside, listening. He detected nothing. He went back inside the lodge. Still it was too quiet. The
frogs had started, but not the particular bird he had come to
know. That suggested that whatever was out there was not
moving, but was not gone. The bird was smarter than the frogs;
it would not speak until it knew it was safe.

Probably it was nothing. Just the same, he set the spear near
him, and made sure of his sheathed knife, and put the great
bow by his left foot. The thought of fighting and possibly killing
a man appalled him, but he was here to guard the Chief, and
how could he guard her except with weapons? If someone were
to attack her, yes, Throat Shot would do his best to protect her.
That was his trust, and what the Spirit had told him to do.
Most likely it would simply be a matter of waking her if something worthy of her attention came up; when the harmless
snake had come, he had been uncertain of its nature, and had
called to her in a low warning voice, and she had come instantly
awake. A false alarm, as it turned out, but she had not reproved
him; they both had known that it could have been a genuine
threat.

Suddenly there was a battle scream from the far side of the
village. There was no mistaking it; it was distinctive, and not
of the Yufera tribe. Immediately there was a flare of light from
that direction: someone had torched a lodge!

Throat Shot knew now why the night bird had been silent.
An enemy attack had been in the making. The warriors had
lain in ambush until full night, silent and hidden, but the bird
could not be fooled.

Throat Shot did not lurch out to run to the torched lodge,
though it needed immediate attention. Others would do that.
Instead he turned quietly, braced the bow on his left foot, and
set and drew the arrow. He faced back toward Beautiful Moon,
who was sitting up, startled. He had a notion of what to expect.

Sure enough, a figure wedged into the back of the lodge.
The torching of the distant lodge was a distraction to enable
the enemy to attack the Chief without being opposed. The

enemy had not known she was guarded. Only the Spirit had known that she needed to be. Frog Effigy had spoken true.

That told him what he had to do. His aversion to killing left him, as if taken by the Spirit. Throat Shot lifted the bow with his foot, braced one end against the ground, and loosed the arrow without hesitation. It passed Beautiful Moon and struck the man, who fell back with no more than a groan.

But now two more were coming in, and his arrow had been expended. In this clumsy position he had no time to loose another. One charged Throat Shot, knowing where he was by the twang of the bowstring. Throat Shot scrambled up, dodging out of the way, then crashed his right shoulder into the man.

The warrior fell back, surprised and pushed off-balance. His knife-hand flailed wildly. Throat Shot tried to grab for it, but caught only the arm. The man braced against him, trying to orient the knife. Throat Shot knew he had blundered; he should have let the man fall, and then attacked him when he was down. Now he was locked into a struggle in which he was at a disadvantage, for the other had two arms to his one, and knew his location, since they were in contact.

But Throat Shot's arm was stronger, because of the way he had been using it alone, and it was more powerful than it would ever have been otherwise. He forced the man's knife-hand back.

Then the enemy warrior caught a leg behind Throat Shot's and threw him backwards to the ground. Throat Shot landed and rolled immediately, knowing the man's knife would be plunging toward his heart. He couldn't get his hand on his own knife! Why hadn't he drawn his own, before engaging the attacker?

Then his hand slapped against the spear. He snatched it up and shoved it upward at the sound of the man's panting. The position was bad and the thrust was clumsy, but he put all the power of his arm into it. The spear struck, and the other dropped. Lucky move!

Throat Shot scrambled to his feet again and lurched toward Beautiful Moon. But she was not there; the third man had hauled her away while Throat Shot had been fighting the second. He had not protected her after all!

He found the place where they had wedged between the

reeds of the back wall. Why hadn't he thought to put some stiffer material there? He had assumed any attackers would enter by the front, and he now knew that this had been foolish. The front opened into the central court of the village, where anyone could see; no enemy would use that approach!

He paused to listen. There was a commotion at the other end of the village, but he was able to distinguish some noise in the brush. He set out after it.

They were using the path that wound back to the burial mound. They must have come in on that one, knowing that it would not be used at night. Brave men, to risk such a near approach to the spirits of the dead at night! But the spirits had been ready for them, assigning Throat Shot as guard, and he intended to fulfill their assignment. He was well familiar with this path and was able to run along it in the darkness. The enemy warrior, in contrast, was moving clumsily, hauling along the reluctant woman.

Throat Shot caught up to them at the mound. The moon shone down brightly in the clearing here, and he confirmed what his ears had told him: it was just one man.

"Die, enemy!" he cried, hoping to startle the man into releasing Beautiful Moon. Throat Shot couldn't risk attacking with her in the middle!

It worked. The man threw her aside and brought his bow around from his shoulder. His motion was practiced and swift; he was an experienced warrior, wasting no effort. He could see Throat Shot as readily as Throat Shot saw him; his arrow would not miss.

The distance between them was too great. Throat Shot could not charge the man and close the gap before that arrow was loosed. He had blundered again, by pausing as he made his challenge.

The knife was in his hand. He had only one chance. *Help me, O spirits!* he prayed as he hurled the knife at the silhouette of the warrior.

The knife struck. The man did not even grunt; he went down at the edge of the mound, silently. The spirits had guided the knife true.

Then the man moved. He started to get up. There was no

knife in his body. Throat Shot realized that it had not struck true; the handle had hit the man in the head and stunned him, but only momentarily. It was almost impossible to strike with the blade of a thrown knife, because it was constantly turning in the air. Even as Throat Shot ran toward the man, he knew the issue was in doubt. If he did not finish the warrior immediately, the warrior would finish him. And Beautiful Moon.

He saw the knife on the ground. He swept it up and leaped at the man, thrusting the stone point at the man's face as he stood. He misjudged, and caught him in the throat instead. The blade sank in, and the man dropped again, carrying the knife with him.

Throat Shot walked to Beautiful Moon, who was getting to her feet. She stepped into the circle of his arm, sobbing.

He held her there, looking around to be sure there were no other enemy warriors. He had no weapon now. But all was quiet.

In a moment she straightened. "Do not tell them I was woman-weak," she said. Then she marched back toward the village.

Throat Shot followed. Woman-weak? How else could she have been, so suddenly attacked by three men in the night? It was evident now that she had been the true object of the attack; they had intended to abduct her, so as to torture her later or keep her hostage, or both. Her captivity would have hurt the tribe worse than her death, for they would not have been able to select a new chief while she lived. They would have had either to mount an impossible rescue effort against the enemy stronghold or to bow to the enemy's terms to get her back. Meanwhile the enemy chief could have a delightful time with her. Ordinarily, no woman was forced, but an enemy captive could be another matter.

The spirits had known. They had saved her—and redeemed him. How could he have doubted?

But now, his battle ardor cooling, he realized what he had done. He had fought and perhaps grievously injured three men. He, who had renounced combat! He had thought that when the crisis came, he might sound the alert for the Yufera warriors, saving her that way. Instead he had done the job himself. Now there was more blood on his hands.

Warriors were coming down the path—but they were Yufera.
Throat Shot recognized their voices.

So did Beautiful Moon. "Here," she called, knowing they
were searching for her. "I am safe."

In a moment the warriors were there. "There are two dead
men in your lodge!" one exclaimed.

Beautiful Moon turned to Throat Shot. But before she could
speak, he did. "No! It cannot be!"

She put her hand on his bad arm, understanding perhaps
too well. "We will settle this in the morning." Then, to the
others: "Throat Shot got me away safe. He guarded me well."

They understood her as she intended: that Throat Shot had
alerted her in time to escape, and had guided her to the relatively safe region of the mound. They believed that he could
not actually have fought on her behalf.

The bodies were hauled out of the lodge. It seemed that there
had been only four warriors in the raiding party: one to torch
the far lodge, the other three to abduct the Chief. They were
Saturiwa, starting the combat season early. The one who had
torched the lodge had gotten away. That was just as well: he
would carry the news that the raid had failed.

Men with torches went out to fetch the body at the mound.
By the time the lodge fire had been doused and the family in
that lodge had found other places to sleep, that body was back
in the village. The tribe gathered to stare at it in the torchlight.

Throat Shot's knife was still wedged in the neck. It had sliced
through the great front vein and penetrated to the back of the
neck, killing the man instantly. The truest throat shot.

The Chief's leading guard, the one who had been most con-
temptuous of the visiting one-armed "guard," turned his head
slowly toward Throat Shot. It was evident that his doubt about
the two bodies in the lodge had been resolved. What he said
would guide the attitude of the others.

Throat Shot started to protest that the strikes had been
lucky, and the last had been a desperation thrust which had
lodged in the throat almost by accident. But the woman forestalled him.

"Say nothing," Beautiful Moon said, speaking to them all.

Then she took Throat Shot's arm and guided him toward her lodge.

In the darkness of the lodge, she questioned him. "The spear I understand, and the knife. But how did you use the bow?"

"I braced it on my foot," he said. "My aim might not be good, but he was so close I could not miss."

"He was beyond me. The arrow passed me. It was through his heart," she said. "And the spear was through the other's eye. And the knife through the throat. All perfect, all with force enough to make no other blow necessary. Three of the cleanest kills we have seen—by one man, with one arm, in the night. We must honor you for this feat at the Green Corn Ceremony. You spoke true, though we doubted. We are shamed."

"No!" Throat Shot protested in anguish.

"How is it that you, having proved yourself a warrior more than worthy of your name, are not eager for this recognition?"

"I prefer not to speak of this."

She reached out and caught his hand. "You must tell me. I will decide what to do. I am the Chief."

She was right. She had taken him on faith before, and he had to trust her now.

"Last summer, when I was fifteen winters, I went on my first raid," he said. "To establish my manhood, with two others. We did not do well, and were pursued. I put an arrow through a warrior's neck and killed him. But it was done from ambush, at point-blank range. I take no pride in it. I learned then that I hate to kill a man, and am no warrior. Before we returned to our village, I was struck in the shoulder by an arrow. I was punished by the dead man's spirit for my unmanly attack, or for my cowardice. I hid by a burial mound, and the Spirit of the Mound told me of a terrible danger to my tribe. He would not let me die, for he told me I had to find the Uktena and get from it the Ulunsuti, for only with the Ulunsuti could I see the danger, and warn my tribe, and devise some way to avert it. He marked me, and took from me my fear, but not my shame. Since then I have sought the great diamond crystal, asking the spirits at every mound I find for guidance. That is all that my life is for. I am no warrior, and must not take credit for the guidance of the spirits. Without them I would have had neither the courage nor the strength to act as I did."

"And it was a spirit who sent you here," she murmured.

"Yes. I admit sometimes I doubted, but the Spirit spoke true. It knew what I did not. It helped me stop the warriors. The spirits of your mound must have guided my weapons, for I could not have done it alone."

She sat in silence for a time. Then she got up. "This tribe will not speak of this, as you desire. You will have no recognition at the Green Corn Ceremony. We will facilitate your journey north. You will be relieved of woman's work."

"I prefer to travel now, for my business here is done."

"No. You must remain here until the Green Corn Ceremony, when there will be contacts with others. We can send you with a good trader then."

Throat Shot nodded in the darkness. "I will wait." It was a good four moons until the Ceremony, but he was obliged to do as she decided. Certainly it would be better to go with another trader. "I thank you."   ·

"And in the interim, you will remain here with me," she said from the far side of the lodge. "With one change."

"Of course I will do as you wish," he said, relieved to have this business settled.

"You will sleep on my bed."

This surprised him. "But—"

"Come to it now, secret warrior."

She couldn't mean—

He got up, keeping his emotion reined. She might plan to sleep elsewhere. Perhaps she had some token she wished to give him in private reward. He came to stand beside her feather mat.

"I have had a narrow escape from abduction, defilement, or death," she said. "I do not wish to be alone."

Oh, of course. In his concern over his own horror, he had forgotten hers.

"Take off your clothes," she told him.

Silently he did so.

"Lie down here with me."

He got down. She reached over to embrace him. Her hair was unbound, indicating that she was now to be viewed as

woman rather than as Chief, and her perfect body was bare.
There was the smell of honey.

Now he knew what she had in mind for him until the Green
Corn Ceremony. No one would speak of this, any more than
they would of what else he had done this night. But all would
know.

"You spoke truly about the spirits," she murmured as she
fitted herself to him in a manner that demonstrated her competence. "But you did not speak of the Calusa Cacique's wife.
Is it true what she said of you?"

How could she have learned of that? How much did she
know of him?

"You do not answer?" Beautiful Moon asked with mock se-
verity. "Well, then I must make the proof of it myself."

Six times? He doubted it.

She kissed him, and his long-suppressed longing burst free,
and by morning she had made that proof.

Only later, when he finally had time to reflect, did he begin
to understand what she had done. Perhaps she had been in
horror of being alone after her narrow escape, as she had said.
But more likely she understood his own horror of bloodshed,
and had chosen to override it with something even more compelling. She had hardly let him rest, until he had no thought
of anything but sleep. By the time he had leisure to feel the
horror, it was barricaded beyond the endless rapture she had
given him. The horror remained, but muted.

He was never under any delusion that Beautiful Moon loved
him or wanted to spend the rest of her life with him. She had
chosen a way to reward him that she deemed appropriate, no
more. But once she had made the decision to do what she did,
she seemed to enjoy it. That pleased him in another way, as
perhaps she intended.

Thus it was that the Green Corn Ceremony seemed to come
in two days, rather than in four moons. Beautiful Moon had
made her namesake irrelevant.

CHAPTER 9

⚜

MOUND

O Spirit of the Mound, I have told you how Throat Shot helped
Blue Stone return to her people, and how Beautiful Moon rewarded him for doing the bidding of the Spirit of the Fresh
Water Mound, who knew you. Now I will tell you how he came
to the big mound to the north, and what he learned there.

After the Green Corn Ceremony, Throat Shot went north
with a trader from a tribe well to the north, the Oconee. This
was Huge Oyster, who seemed well named, being very large
and taciturn. He spoke the Yufera tongue, which was a relief,
but his own tongue was of a different nature, not a mere dialect.
He was part of the great group of related tribes of the north,
the People of One Fire. He had not wanted to take a man, and
certainly not a one-armed one, but the Yufera proffered trade
goods that changed his mind. Beautiful Moon's favor counted
for a lot, and the fact that she had taken no other lover during
Throat Shot's stay encouraged the other warriors to cooperate
in making his departure easy. So they said, at any rate; the
respect with which they now treated Throat Shot showed how
much they appreciated the thing that no one claimed he had
done. He had no enemies here now. The trader was bemused
by this, but he accepted the goods and promised to see Throat
Shot to the end of his tribe's river.

That, as it turned out, was a long way. First they paddled
to the coast, and north, and then into the Oconee River. The
Guale tribe who lived at its base might have another name for

it, he said, but it was the tribe at the source who had the spirit of it.

The first night was at a Guale village. Here they had two types of lodge: a long, large communal structure for ceremonial use, and many small oblong homes made from posts. The large one was impressive: it was circular, fashioned of the limbed and barked trunks of entire pine trees, their bases sunk into the ground and their tops meeting far above. It was the biggest man-made structure Throat Shot had seen, and he could hardly keep from staring. But the people did not live in here; they used the little lodges. These were not well made, because the Guale traveled a lot, going where the hunting and fishing were best from season to season. They made their shelters for only two or three moons, then deserted them.

A small lodge was provided, but little more: some food and no maidens. It was not that the Guale were inhospitable, but that they had little to offer.

In the morning they met with the Guale mico, the village headman who had the authority of a chief. He wanted news about the Yufera and the Tacacaturu and the Saturiwa: were any on the warpath? Throat Shot had trouble following the dialogue, for this was a completely new tongue, with few words the same as any he knew; only the mico's gestures gave him the essence. Huge Oyster spoke rapidly, imparting his news.

Then the mico addressed Throat Shot. Now Throat Shot supplemented the news with what he knew of events to the south, using the signs. The mico nodded; it was as he had heard elsewhere. Like any smart chief, he gathered information from different sources. As it was said: it was best for the rabbit to watch the eagle when it first crossed the horizon, not when it was close.

But he had a question: did they know anything of the white men?

Huge Oyster looked blank. Throat Shot had heard of such a thing from the Ais, and he relayed what he knew. Signs were inadequate for this, so he told Huge Oyster, who told the mico in his own tongue. There was a story about a big canoe with men of pale skin who made slaves of people. The Ais claimed that they had encountered white men on land three winters before, and driven them back into the sea, and they had not been seen since. The Trader had been away at the time, so could not verify it. It was so strange that Throat Shot had taken it for a fable. Was that what the mico was asking?

It was. The mico had heard from another trader that such pale-fleshed men had been seen, and that they even had pale-fleshed women, and were always in huge craft on the sea. They were evil, and had to be avoided or fought. But no one had seen any such man in this vicinity, so perhaps it was mere bravado by some imaginative young warrior.

The journey resumed. They paddled on up the Oconee River, stopping at the villages. At some the hospitality was better than at others. At one there was a maiden who was glad to teach Throat Shot some words of the Guale tongue in exchange for his stories of the folk to the far south. They spent half the night conversing in signs, and almost forgot to make use of the honey. It was a good night.

In due course they passed beyond the Guale territory and came to that of the Oconee. Its dialect differed, but was close enough to that of the Guale that Throat Shot was able to pick it up.

Here their reception was better, because these were Huge Oyster's own people. But the river was narrower and the current swifter, so progress was slow. Throat Shot had to paddle till he was worn out, and Huge Oyster seemed no better off. How did the man manage when he traveled alone?

He learned that from the girl who came to him, at the village they finally reached. As she kneaded his stiff shoulders and arms with marvelous gentleness, she explained that normally a young warrior would join the trader and help him handle the strong current. He would pay something of value for this service. This time he had not had to.

Throat Shot nodded. The Yufera had paid to send him with the trader, and the trader had cleverly used him for service. Huge Oyster was making a double profit.

Then the girl removed her skirt and demonstrated what else she could do. She seemed unaware of his bad arm, yet she managed to get quite close without aggravating it. He concluded that he had no complaint.

Huge Oyster's village was beside a lake amidst mountains. Throat Shot stared at the steep slopes, amazed. There was nothing like this in the lands he had seen before.

"You think these are mountains?" Huge Oyster inquired derisively. "Wait till you see the ones in the land of the Ani-Yunwiya."

"The Ani-Yunwiya?" Throat Shot was not familiar with that tribe.

"In their tongue, it means the Principal People. You are going north. They are our neighbors north. They live in the true mountains."

Throat Shot didn't believe that these were not the true mountains, but he was satisfied to find out. He got directions and a good fish line for his hook, and set off on foot, because the river north from the lake was too swift for a canoe. Once he reached the source, he would be close to the next lake, and that lake was in Principal People territory. They had a different tongue, he had been warned, so he would have to use the signs, but they would surely help him on his way. They were friendly folk who freely adopted strangers.

It turned out to be a five-day walk. He had always had strong legs, and he moved well, but Huge Oyster was right: these were mountains such as he had never imagined. Their slopes seemed almost vertical in places, and they towered into the sky, each one smaller than the one beyond it. They were clothed in trees of types he hadn't seen before, as well as oaks and pines of new dialects. It was cooler here, though this was summer; he understood why the people of this region tended to wear more clothing than he was used to. It was not any shame of their bodies, but because the night could be chill. He had thought it might get warmer beyond the territory of the Yufera, but this was not the case.

The animals and birds remained familiar, however. He saw squirrels and woodpeckers in the trees, and crows and hawks in the sky, and the prints of bears and wildcats where they came down to drink in the stream. There were white deer, of course, bounding away as he approached, their white tails flashing. Had he been able to use a bow when standing, he could have taken one. But he was satisfied to let them go; butchering a deer would have taken time, and there would have been more meat than he could eat or carry far. No man would kill more than he could use, if he were not starving.

The river became a creek, and the creek a brook. He found that he did not need to use his fishhook. Each evening he stood absolutely still, with his knife poised, until a fat trout relaxed and swam into range; then he struck swiftly. He skewered it, glad to verify that he had not lost his touch, and lifted it out of the water. He made a small fire to cook the fish, and to discourage bears and mosquitoes when he slept. He did not like traveling alone, but discovered that he could handle it, both physically and emotionally. That was a good thing to know.

Maybe, he realized, the Spirit of the Mound was watching over him. Possibly his lack of fear applied to being alone too: he just hadn't realized it until he tried it. He preferred company but would not again be unduly governed by that preference.

A detail Huge Oyster had neglected to mention was that the source of the river was *high*. Throat Shot had to scramble up over a lofty ridge, then make his way down the other side. But this brought the next lake into view. What a beautiful sight!

He camped one more night alone, preferring to approach the Principal People by morning. Then he walked down to the lake, and found a path, and followed it until he came to a village.

Soon enough he encountered a woman who had been gathering acorns. She stopped still when she saw him, knowing he was no villager. He signed to her that he was a traveler, a friend. She signed to him to wait, and she ran back to her village.

Soon warriors came to escort him to the Chief. They were a war party, for their bodies were painted blood-red and their faces half black. He had not seen the pattern before, but the significance of red paint was universal. He stood quite still, making no move that could possibly be interpreted as hostile. Only when they had inspected him thoroughly did he move, and then only to make the sign for Friend.

They held an extended signs dialogue. The Chief nodded: they would help him. There was a man who wanted to travel to that mound, needing a companion. The spirits had evidently sent Throat Shot. The man was in another village, but they would guide Throat Shot there.

Throat Shot was wary. This seemed too good to be true. He remembered how the Saturiwa Chief had set him up for trouble. This Chief did seem to be in good humor, as if he was aware of something slightly funny. Yet what motive could there be to do that here? He agreed to go to the other village and meet the man.

A child guided him. The boy stepped fleetly along the path, and Throat Shot followed, going north. They left the lake behind and followed a new river through the mountains.

They reached another village before nightfall. The boy explained about Throat Shot. The village Chief nodded. This one, too, seemed to take a bit more pleasure in the matter than was warranted. Yet there was no sign of hostility or deceit. He would spend the night here, and have another guide tomorrow.

Were they simply leading him to some distant place so they wouldn't have to bother with him? Again Throat Shot suppressed his suspicion as unworthy. The Principal People were evidently just being helpful.

After several days of such travel, he reached the village where the man who wished to travel lived. They brought out the man. Then the reason for the Chiefs' humor was apparent.

He was different from the Principal People. Throat Shot realized immediately that he was of another tribe, probably one far away. A traveler far from his home. He was lame; his right knee was a mass of scar tissue, and his leg evidently would not readily bend.

Throat Shot understood: the two injured strangers to this region could help each other. The Principal People were doing both a favor by introducing them. Injuries were not subjects for levity, so nothing was said about them, but the coincidence of both men being handicapped had evidently caused the chiefs some reflection.

The other man was large and muscular, especially in the arms. He seemed to speak the Principal People tongue, but since Throat Shot could not, this was no help. The Principal People withdrew and let the two converse in signs.

Question You Called, the other man signed, his hands moving rapidly through the signs: right hand lifted, fingers spread, palm out, and twisted slightly several times. Right finger pointed to Throat Shot. The loosely closed hand poking forward, index finger extending.

Throat Shot responded by pointing his right thumb to his chest, then making the Called sign, then touching his throat, then moving his closed hand down and to the left in the Shoot gesture. Then he queried the other similarly.

The man rubbed the tips of his right fingers in a circle on the back of his left hand: Color. Then he looked around, spied a gray spot on a nearby tree trunk, and pointed directly to it. Gray. After that he pointed upward. There was nothing there but a passing cloud. Gray Cloud.

Then they established that Throat Shot came from the Toco tribe far to the south, while Gray Cloud came from the Peoria tribe of the Illini folk to the northwest. No wonder they shared no tongue!

They indicated where each was traveling: Throat Shot to the biggest mound, and Gray Cloud home. Gray Cloud smiled: Mound Near Home, he signed.

Finally they exchanged information on their injuries: the one had taken an arrow in the left shoulder, in warfare, while the other had been clubbed in the knee, in captivity.

Gray Cloud produced a strip of dried deer meat, offering it. Throat Shot took it and chewed off an end. He handed it back. Gray Cloud chewed off another section.

They had shared food. They were friends, by the oath that constituted. They would travel together.

Gray Cloud had a good canoe. It was so strange that Throat Shot was amazed. Instead of being formed of a burned-out tree trunk, it was fashioned of thin, white, stiff, clothlike stuff anchored on a sturdy frame. It was much lighter than a dugout, so that it was even possible for Gray Cloud alone to heave it up and carry it on his shoulders and head. Had his legs both been good, he could have walked with it from lake to lake.

It turned out that the Principal People fashioned such canoes from the thin bark of a certain kind of tree that grew well up in the mountains: the mountain birch. It was said that such trees were far more common farther north, where the air was cooler; they did not like the heat of the southern forests. But it was cool up here, in fact often quite chill, as Throat Shot had discovered during his journey here. It seemed that the heights were cooler than the lower ground, odd as that might be. It should have been otherwise, since the heights were closer to the hot sun.

Gray Cloud knew the route to his home, which was beyond the big mound and on the same river. It seemed that he had been a prisoner of the savage Mexica, and had escaped with two companions. They were of the Principal People, residing in this region, and so their canoe had come here. Now he needed a companion paddler to retrace the river route and take the other fork to his own tribe, the Peoria. The Peoria were to the Illini as the Oconee were to the People of One Fire: one of a number of tribes with similar customs and tongues. He had been here since before the last winter, and had begun to despair of being able to return before winter made the journey too dangerous. Throat Shot's arrival was like a gift from a beneficent spirit.

Throat Shot explained about how directly that related, for he had indeed been sent by a spirit. Gray Cloud nodded, not surprised. The spirits worked in strange ways, but usually did know what they were doing.

They set out, Gray Cloud in the rear, his bad leg stretched out before him, and Throat Shot in front, paddling only on the left side. But they both knew how to handle a canoe, and the lightness of this one was an almost unmitigated pleasure for Throat Shot. It made him feel half again as strong, and when they both bent to it, synchronized, the little craft fairly leaped forward. They were going downstream, which also helped.

As they traveled, they conversed. Gray Cloud taught him some terms of the tongue of the Principal People, as it seemed more likely that he would be returning this way than that he would continue on beyond the mound. If the spirits of the mound had the information he needed, and he was able to get the Ulunsuti, then he would want to hurry home by the most familiar route. The Principal People were on that route, and the other tribes whose tongues he had begun to pick up.

The river flowed southwest, but Gray Cloud assured him that it changed direction in due course and would take them to the mound. It soon opened out into a lakelike expanse, and was pleasant to follow. They passed other birch-bark canoes, and Gray Cloud called greetings to their occupants. "Yes, I am going home!" he agreed when they inquired. "So I can see pretty women again!" They made gestures of friendly insult, indicating what they thought his tribe's women might look like, their gestures most resembling swollen gourds.

"It is a tradition," Gray Cloud explained. "When warriors pass on the river, never to meet again, they can insult each other and never have to settle accounts. But it is done only when they know they are not enemies, in fun. The Principal People have interesting notions of fun."

So it seemed. Throat Shot decided not to risk any such fun himself, as he was not generally known to the Principal People.

When they passed near the bank, he asked about the strange varieties of trees he saw. "That one is an ash," Gray Cloud said obligingly. "Very straight, strong wood for arrows. That one is beech; the nuts are excellent. That one is chestnut, and its nuts are very good too. That one is maple; they say it has sweet sap, but I have not tasted it." The terms he used were unfamiliar, but Throat Shot made careful mental note. Trees with edible fruit or nuts were always valuable. There were no palm trees here of any variety, which reduced his ability to forage unless he learned the new ones.

They camped for the night on the south bank, because Gray Cloud knew the Principal People better than he knew the Yuchi on the north bank. Actually, they called themselves the Tsoyaha, the Children of the Sun, Gray Cloud explained; Yuchi meant simply, in their tongue, "from far away." But other tribes did not care to accept such a claim of divine ancestry, so left it at Yuchi. Indeed, their claim was odd, because they lived low: their lodges were half dug into the ground. This was not a time of warfare, but still it was best to stay with known folk, with understandable customs. So the south side was best, as well as being most familiar. Gray Cloud used his bow to put an arrow through a turkey, and they stripped and roasted it and had a wonderful meal.

They made a shelter of branches and leaves, trying to overlap the larger leaves so that water would flow across them instead of through. That was just as well, because it rained during the night, putting out their smoldering fire, but they remained dry except for some splashing from the front.

Next day they navigated a swampy region where cypress stood tall. Throat Shot felt nostalgia as he viewed their swollen bases; he had been long away from home, and this reminded him of it.

The next night they used Throat Shot's fishhook with a fat bug for bait, and caught what Gray Cloud said was a bass: a big solid fish with a big mouth.

As they proceeded, the great river did curve, going first west, then north. Now the canoes they saw on it contained strange warriors, but they made no hostile challenges. "They recognize the bark canoe we use," Gray Cloud said. "They think we are Principal People, and that is well."

Yet the man seemed pensive. Throat Shot was now acquiring a small collection of words of the Principal People tongue, and was happy to use it, gaining further proficiency. Signs remained important, however. "You regret that?"

"No, it is well. But now that we are fairly on our way, and have left the Principal People behind, I remember Red Leaf."

"A woman?"

"We have kept some company. But I long for my own people, and she is not of them. I gave her little encouragement. Yet now that I have left her behind, I remember her good qualities. Before I noticed that she was two winters older than I, but now I know she is lovelier than those two winters younger than I am, and considerably more competent."

Throat Shot remembered Beautiful Moon. He had appreciated her qualities throughout, knowing it was never more than a temporary liaison for her, yet the parting had been hard. She still came to his dreams, as beautiful and accommodating and temporary as ever.

"But did you have a woman in your own tribe?"

Gray Cloud smiled. "That, too. The Illini are not great warriors, though we have our foolish pretensions. We generally lose our big battles. But our women are loyal, and Glow Fungus was loyal to me. Now I am loyal to her, and that perhaps is half my reason to return home."

Throat Shot nodded. He wanted to return to the Toco, but

if Beautiful Moon had asked him to remain forever with the Yufera, he would have remained.

"How is it you left her?"

That turned out to be a long story. Throat Shot listened to every detail, fascinated. He had known little of the dread distant Mexica tribe; now he learned much, noting the ways it complemented little Tzec's tale of the Maya.

Tzec. He had not thought of her in some time, for her traces had been to an extent obliterated by those of real women, but now her memory returned. He hoped she was doing well with the Trader. Were they out on a trading circuit now?

When Gray Cloud's story was done, Throat Shot told him that of Little Blood. After that Gray Cloud told one of the legends of his people, and Throat Shot told the tale of Sweet Medicine. Thus they entertained each other, as they made the moon-long journey down the great river.

They shared the work as well as the entertainment. Gray Cloud was good with his bow, but could not move rapidly; Throat Shot was the opposite. So Throat Shot would run fleetly and circle around behind prospective prey and drive it toward Gray Cloud, whether it was bird or animal, and Gray Cloud would put an arrow through what seemed best.

But usually they simply drew up fish from the river. It was easy prey, and good enough to eat. Sometimes they would just drift with the current, dangling the hook on the line, and have a good fish before they camped. This was certainly the way to travel!

Then they saw a number of great shaggy beasts at the bank, small in the hind part but huge in the forepart, with low-set, heavy horned heads. Throat Shot stared. "What is that?"

"Buffalo. I think that's more meat than we need at the moment."

Throat Shot was at a loss for words, until he realized that Gray Cloud was joking. The animals must have massed as much as any ten men, and looked unconscionably fierce. It seemed unlikely that one could be killed with an arrow, and any other weapon would require too close an approach for any safety. As for the meat—yes, they would have to camp for a moon to be able to consume any great portion of it.

Then the name sank in. Buffalo. "Sweet Medicine—"

"True," Gray Cloud said. "That is the animal there. You told the tale without knowing it?"

Throat Shot had to admit it was true. "I knew it was of a far place, but I did not know that *this* was the place."

"It may not be. Buffalo are everywhere, except where your tribe is, it seems. They are the mainstay of our lives—the Illini and the tribes of our region. The Principal People live too high in the mountains for the buffalo, so they have to trade for the hides. We use buffalo hides to make clothing and tents, we eat their meat, we make weapons of their bones, we make fires with their dung."

"Fires with their dung!"

"I will show you, next time we camp, if we can find some good dung."

So it happened: the dried chunks made a good and well-behaved fire. Throat Shot was impressed. He put a little dung in his punk pot to see how well it would sustain his slow fire. This could simplify the care of the pot.

They intersected another great river, and followed the doubled water on down. Then they came to another juncture, and this time they followed the new river up. They were now entering the territory of the Illini, though Gray Cloud's tribe was still some distance upstream.

By the time they reached the vicinity of the great mound, they were firm friends.

They followed a small offshoot creek to the east, and before it gave out they were there. The tremendous mound could be seen rising to the south.

The region was desolate; only scrub and small trees grew, though elsewhere there had been dense forests.

They landed the canoe and drew it well clear of the water. Then they walked to the mound. The distance was so short that Gray Cloud could handle it; they did not need to hurry.

There was a small village nearby. The two approached and made signs of peace. The people were of the Illini tribes; Gray Cloud spoke a dialect, and was able to converse with them.

No, they had not made the big mound. It had always been there. The spirits must have made it long ago.

Indeed, the inhabitants seemed little interested in any of the mounds. They were too busy scratching out their survival from the meager offerings of the land.

Throat Shot was surprised by their lodges. Instead of being round or square structures of wood or mud, they were tall pointed cones of sewn animal skins. On occasion as they traveled the tremendous river he had seen the points of similar objects in the distance, but he had not thought that they could be for people. How strange!

Gray Cloud saw his glance. "Our tribes live in tipis instead of lodges. We sew cured skins around a framework of poles, with a flap for entry and a hole at the top to let out the smoke of our fires. They are durable and comfortable and easier to move than lodges, as we can simply take down and fold the skins. I will show you one when we are done here."

Throat Shot nodded. That should be interesting. It had never occurred to him that a lodge could be made movable, but it made sense, as it was always a nuisance to have to build new lodges. A light lodge—or tipi—serving much the way the light bark-of-birch canoe did. Such things did make sense. It would be nice to take one of each home, if that turned out to be possible.

He glanced again at the working people. There was evidently no hospitality being offered here.

But Throat Shot remembered the massive mounds near the mouth of the Little Big River, whose spirits had recognized the child Tzec and told him to learn the story of Little Blood. The people didn't matter, only the spirits within the mounds. For there were many mounds here, perhaps ten tens of mounds, most of them relatively small, dominated by the huge one. The amount of work that must have gone into forming them was beyond his imagination. All the people of the villages of Atafi and Ibi Hica could have dug and carried sand for a summer and a winter, and not made this! The spirit of the Wide Water mound had surely spoken true: this was where he would find his answer.

They gazed at the mound. It loomed as high as the tallest trees, though there were no trees near it. It had four great terraces, and the ruins of a massive building at the top. "I think this is more than I care to attempt," Gray Cloud said. "I will wait at the base."

"Yes." Throat Shot was so impressed by the mound that his friend's problem with climbing hardly mattered to him. "I will go up to that building."

Gray Cloud glanced at him. "What building do you mean?"

"The one at the top of the mound. It is in ruins, but that is surely where the spirits reside."

"There is no building there."

This made Throat Shot pause. "You do not see it?"

"You *do* see it?"

Throat Shot knew how keen Gray Cloud's eyes were. They had to be, to enable him to shoot an arrow through a flying bird. "Perhaps it is a spirit building, which appears only to me, for my quest."

"It must be," Gray Cloud agreed.

This was a positive sign.

He walked to the south side of the mound. It was a rough square in outline, with the corners sharp. It rose into a crude pyramid. Throat Shot thought of the great stone temple structures Tzec had described among the Maya. Was this one of those, fashioned from dirt instead of stone?

There was an old overgrown set of steps at the south side, leading up to the first terrace. *I come, O spirits of this mound*, he thought, and started up them.

He reached the first platform. He listened, but no spirits spoke to him. He felt a sudden chill: suppose the spirits refused to give him the answer he sought? Because this was day instead of night, or because he was from too far away, or because he was not a proper warrior?

No, they had to answer! This was the mound where the spirits knew where to find the Ulunsuti, and if they did not tell him, he had nowhere else to go. He could not leave here until he had that answer.

He walked across the platform to the next set of steps. He mounted them to the third level, which was to the east of the second level and higher. Then he made the short additional climb to the fourth terrace and stood before the ancient building.

It was constructed of stones and wood, and even in its ruin
it was monstrous. Its half-fallen walls reached up three times
the height of a man, and its length was much greater than that.
What a magnificent edifice it must have been in its heyday!
Now it was gone, its stones stolen, its wood rotted away.

Just to be sure, he reached out and touched the wall of the
building. His hand felt nothing. This was indeed a spirit structure, remaining after the physical one had been killed. However, if he entered it, he would be in the realm of the spirits,
and they could kill him if they wished.

He turned and gazed south, across the numerous smaller
mounds, and the paths and bushes stretching out to the horizon. Had there ever been people living there? It was hard to
imagine, for the region seemed desolate.

Where should he address the spirits? The collapsing building
did not seem safe, for any further collapse could kill his own
spirit, yet this had surely been their temple. That seemed the
most likely place to find the most important spirit.

He checked the entrance warily. It seemed firm enough, in
its image. Probably whatever was going to collapse had already
done so, so he could enter if he did not touch anything. He
remembered that Gray Cloud had not been able to see this
structure. That indicated that it was visible only to those who
had business here. Why should the spirits give him so clear a
signal, only to kill him in it? They surely wanted him to enter.

He stepped in. Light filtered through the interior, and he
could see the various chambers. Dirt shrouded everything, but
he could see decorations on the walls. A recurring figure was
part bird, part man, evidently one of their deities.

He came to a broad central chamber and stopped. This
seemed to be the center; it should be the place.

O spirits of this mound, who will answer me?

There was no answer. Yet he felt spirits stirring below. They
were aware of him; they just did not deign to speak with him.
He had encountered this attitude before.

*O spirits, I was sent to you by Dead Eagle and Frog Effigy. I am
Throat Shot, of the Toco tribe, and I must find the Ulunsuti to save
my people. Only you can help me. I beg of you, speak to me!*

But they would not.

This could not be. He had to have their help. Otherwise his

mission was lost, and his tribe would suffer grievously. What could he do to change their minds?

Do you want your lodge repaired? he asked. *I am not good at such work, but I can try.* Yet he feared this was an empty promise, because he could do very little physically, and perhaps nothing at all in the spirit realm.

Still no response. They weren't interested in him or in anything he might do for them.

But he had come here to find the Ulunsuti, and this was the mound that contained the spirits who would know where it was. If he left here without that knowledge, his mission would be lost.

O spirits, I wait on your answer, he thought. Then he waited, standing where he was, immobile, as if about to spear a cautious fish.

The day passed. The spirits did not respond. Yet he knew they were there, aware of him, watching him. Perhaps they felt he was unworthy, because of his arm. That was understandable. But he had to have their answer. So he remained as he was.

Night came. Throat Shot was hungry and thirsty, and he needed to urinate, but he could not pause for any of these things without showing weakness, and the spirits would judge him thereby. So he held firm, unmoving.

Mosquitoes came, and he had not smeared grease to make his flesh resistant, and had no smoky fire to discourage them. He had to tolerate their bites, for he dared not flinch.

A snake came, slithering through the ragged wall. Throat Shot could not see it in the darkness, but he heard it, and knew the sound. He could not tell what kind it was, but was not concerned. He had no fear, and knew that no serpent short of the Uktena could consume a man, and no snake would bite a man who made no motion.

His legs were tired, and now they felt as if they were swelling. He was not used to standing so long, so still. No fish required so much time! But he remained as he was, waiting for the spirits to answer.

Toward dawn he was feeling faint. That was another threatened weakness: if he fainted, and fell, he would be discredited before the spirits. He clung resolutely to his consciousness.

Then at last, as the wan light of false dawn came, Throat Shot felt a stirring. A spirit was touching his mind, ready to talk with him! Yet it did not. He would have to find a way to address it, or it would lose interest.

He looked again at the walls, and around the chamber. He saw a fallen figure. He went to it and lifted it out of the dirt. It was a smudged clay statuette of the bird-man.

Their sacred figure?

He brushed it off, then held it up. It seemed physical rather than spiritual, though he could not be certain. *By this figure I conjure you: speak to me. I respect your gods, if only you will tell me who they are.*

I will speak to you, a spirit answered. *But first you must know us. Go outside.*

Throat Shot did not argue. He carried the figurine carefully outside the building, retracing his footprints in the dirt. He blinked as he emerged into the dazzling sunlight. Then, as his sight cleared, he stared south, amazed.

The desolate landscape was there no more. Now it was filled with lodges. Directly before him was a huge plaza with two small ceremonial mounds. All around that were the lodges, so thickly placed that he could not count them. Beyond them, enclosing the whole, was a wall of stout pointed posts, a palisade, more formidable than any he had seen before. Throughout were people—tens of tens of them, tens of tens of tens.

It was no village, no town. It was a city, such as the Mayans used. A vast city, teeming with activity, fortified, with warriors at the palisade. The stockade walls projected at regular intervals, where archers stood guard. The gateways were screened so that no mass of men could storm them head-on. Beyond the enclosed compound were fields where corn grew, and there were lodges out there too, as there were too many people for the stockade to include. To the west was a great Calendar Circle that priests used to tell the exact times of the ceremonial occasions. Captives were enslaved to carry dirt to build more mounds, and buffalo were hunted in great numbers to supplement the food. Trade routes extended out in every direction, and levies were made on subject peoples, the barbarians of the outer reaches.

And in the center of this empire was the Pyramid of the Sun, with its bird-man totem, supreme over all. This was the height to which all eyes turned. Travelers came from far away to see this mighty complex and to lay their offerings at the bird-man's feet, and to participate in the Corn Harvest Ceremony. This was the trading capital of the region.

But at the moment a special ceremony was going on. The priests were approaching with torches. They came to the great lodge behind Throat Shot, walking past him as if he was not there—and indeed he was not, for he was seeing into the past. They set fire to the steeply pitched thatch roof. It blazed up, the timbers catching, and became an inferno.

Within it was the body of the Chief of these people. He had died, and had been buried beneath his house, and the house was being burned so that no one else could use it. It would go with him into the spirit world. Only its stones would survive for the next building, and they would remember.

After the fire was done, the laborers brought baskets of dirt, carrying it from the distant borrow pit, each load a quarter the weight of a man, and dumped it over the ashes. The pit was turning into a lake because so much dirt had been taken from it in the past. A new terrace was formed over the old one, entombing the old Chief with the ashes of his lodge.

Then, more rapidly than could ever be done in life, they built the new lodge for the new Chief. Throat Shot realized that he was seeing many days passing by as if they were moments, in the vision.

Then it was done, and the vision faded. He was looking at the fallen building, which had not been burned. That suggested that the last Chief had not died—yet had not remained, either. What had happened?

He reentered the lodge, and came to stand where he had before. *O Spirit, I have seen you buried and your lodge burned. I have seen the great empire you governed. Now will you answer me?*

Are you truly from Dead Eagle?

I truly am. I open my mind to you, O Spirit, that you may see. And he did so.

It is true. I knew Dead Eagle. I am Sun Eagle, also of the Eagle Clan, and you hold my totem. I will deal with you.

I thank you, Sun Eagle. I must find the Ulunsuti.

But at a price.

He wasn't surprised. Spirits had their own imperatives. *What is your price, O Sun Eagle?*

You must warn the tribes of the danger that threatens them.

But this is what I mean to do!

No. This is a different danger, threatening other tribes than yours.

This was a surprise. *What different danger?*

The one that destroyed this city.

But this city is here! Throat Shot protested. *Only the people are gone.*

There was a ghostly laugh. *The people* are *the city! Without them it is merely a husk.*

Obviously true. *What happened to them?*

See. The vision resumed. The lodge faded out, and he seemed to be flying up like an eagle, looking down on the complex of all the mounds, until he saw not only them but the creek leading to the region of the mound, and then the great river it flowed to. It was an amazing scene.

Then he realized that this was what a true eagle would see. Sun Eagle was carrying his spirit up to the level of the clouds so he could see everything at once.

He saw the tiny individual lodges, which were of the type he was familiar with, rather than the strange tipis of the folk who were here now. He saw the palisade, forming an outline like a great spearpoint pointing south, and the square plazas, and the many squared-off mounds within and without the protected compound, like so many neatly carved blocks of wood. Some were circular, either with flat tops or points. He saw the lakes where the earth had been taken to make the mounds. There seemed to be a pattern to it, orienting on the great central mound of the chief. The whole thing was fascinating, for he had never imagined such an assembly of mounds, as if they were a conclave of greater and lesser chiefs.

The region nearest the largest mound was clear of vegetation. Farther out were fields of corn, and still farther out was the edge of the forest. But that edge was moving away. The forest was retreating, like a blanket being drawn back, leaving the ground bare. Why was this?

Then he realized that it was because the trees were being cut. The people here had good stone axes, and good tree-felling skill, and there were many of them, and they were taking down the trees and using their wood to renew the palisade and the calendar circles and for timbers in their temples, and the fragments were being used for their fires. They had lines of men carrying wood on their shoulders from the forest to the compound. Other lines of men used ropes to haul larger logs. Still others used levers to roll the greatest trunks. The forest was being eaten by the city.

The lines grew longer as the forest drew back, hurting. Now it required a day for a man to carry his load of wood to the city. Now two days. Now three. There was wood, but it was too far away; it was reaching the point where all the men of the city would have to haul wood, doing nothing else. Most of the haulers were slaves, who had no choice in the matter, but still it was getting difficult, for they had to be fed while they carried, and their food had to be carried by other men. And the food was running out.

Now he oriented on the cornfields. They too were retreating. The ones closest to the city, which had been producing the longest, were not as green and strong as they had been; somehow they were turning yellow, and their ears were smaller and infested by bugs. The fields farther out were verdant. Then those too faded as if tired. So the corn was retreating in much the way the forest had, and the people had to go farther to tend it and harvest it and fetch it into the city. The same thing was happening to the berry bushes and edible roots; they were disappearing near the city. That was why it was getting harder to feed their wood-carriers, or themselves.

He oriented on the buffalo and deer and other animals who ranged near the city. But these also retreated as they were hunted, until finally there were none close enough to be worthwhile.

Yet this was a powerful city, with trade routes extending everywhere. The people traded for corn and meat and the other things they needed, and had enough for a time. Still, it was getting harder.

Finally it became too difficult to manage. The people were hungry and unhealthy, and unable to work as well as before. But other cities were developing, and the people moved to them and did better. In the end all of them were gone, including the last Son of the Sun. His lodge was not burned because he was not in the city when he died; he had deserted it. The City of the Sun no longer existed, except as a grouping of mounds which were slowly losing their form and being overgrown by weeds and bushes and finally trees. It was a horrendous affront to the Chiefs buried here, but there was no one to maintain the premises.

Now there was wood, and animals, even buffalo, though not in the abundance they had been before. Only the people were gone. New people came, but they knew nothing of the heritage of this great city, and didn't care; they were primitives intent only on scratching their living from the returning wild things. They stole the great stones for their own use, destroying what remained of the building. They thought the largest mound was just a hill. The spirits suffered this indignity in silence; it wasn't even worth afflicting the intruders with illness, because they would not understand its source, or realize that they were being punished. The grandeur of the past was forgotten.

And lo—it was the present.

Throat Shot floated back to the collapsing lodge. He had seen the vision, but still he did not understand. *O Sun Eagle, I saw what happened to the trees and buffalo. But why did the corn wither?*

I did not understand this while I lived, but I think I do now that I have watched it these tens of tens of winters. The land lives, like a man; it grows tired with labor, like a man. Finally it dies, like a man, and its spirit departs. It must rest before it can be strong again.

The land has a spirit? Throat Shot asked, surprised. He knew that all animals and trees had spirits, but the land itself seemed dead.

I have not seen it, but I believe it does. It may be that the spirit of the land can be seen only by other land. But it is there, and we must let it rest, or it fails.

Throat Shot was dazzled by the revelation. *Then it is wrong to make too big a city, and to tire the land. And it is wrong to take all the trees, and all the buffalo. For then the people cannot live, and all they have made must be deserted and lost.*

That is the danger you must warn the people of, Sun Eagle agreed. *It is too late for my people; they are scattered among other cities, which have also been cruel to the land and made it die. They have lost their great mounds and now live like the primitives who never knew better.*

But the primitives do not do this, Throat Shot thought.

That is true. You must warn the people of the danger of being cruel to the land.

But they will laugh at me!

You must find a way.

Throat Shot nodded. *I will search for a way to tell them, O Sun Eagle. Will you now tell me where to find the Ulunsuti?*

I cannot, for it went with my successor, and to his successor, and finally to the one who did not remain. But I will look for it, and will signal you when I find it.

How will I know your signal?

You will know it. Go with your friend until I send that signal.

But how long—?

I do not know. You must be patient.

Throat Shot tried to question the Spirit further, but Sun Eagle had had enough, and refused to answer. Realizing this, Throat Shot made his way out of the lodge and faced the blinding light of day. He staggered across the terrace, then down the steps, across the next, and down the other steps. Then he reeled and fell.

But Gray Cloud was there, waiting for him, and caught him, and let him down gently. Throat Shot let his consciousness fade. His quest was over—for now.

CHAPTER 10

SACRIFICE

O Spirit of the Mound, I have told you how I came to the Pyramid of the Sun and talked with Sun Eagle. Now I will tell you the Tale of Gray Cloud, as he told it to me while we traveled, and if I have some details wrong I regret it, but it is only because I have had no experience with his culture and his adventure. But he was my friend, and I retain the gift he gave me, and he is part of what I am, and I feel his story is worthy of your attention.

Gray Cloud was strong with the spear and bow, and had more buffalo kills to his credit than any other warrior his age. He was handsome and quick-witted. The women liked him, and he seldom slept alone. But he was cursed by bad luck. This caused some women to marry others, though they liked Gray Cloud. One thought that his luck would turn, so she let him know that she was interested in a more lasting relationship. He was interested too. Then she caught her foot in a bramble, and an evil spirit got into her leg, and she turned dark and died. After that no women wanted to marry him.

Then he encountered Glow Fungus. She was pretty, and competent, and she was not afraid of bad luck. She had already had enough of that, she said, to last her, and doubted that he could bring her any more. But a vestige of her own luck prevented her from marrying him: her mother was dead and her father was ill and near death. She was the only one who could take care of him properly and ease his passing, while her brother provided food for them both. The end was inevitable,

214

and when her father had gone to the realm of the spirits, she would be free to marry. Her brother, Bear Penis, agreed. In fact everyone agreed. The other maidens preferred to see Gray Cloud married, so that they did not have to feel guilty for passing him by.

Then bad luck struck again. A party was ranging down across the river, looking for buffalo, which had been mysteriously absent from their usual grazing range this season. They discovered Osage with bright cloths, and skin drums, making displays and noises to herd the buffalo away from the river and into their own territory. Now it was clear what had happened: the Osage were taking the buffalo!

The Osage were formidable fighters, but this could not be tolerated. The Peoria allied with the Moingwena and the Tamaroa across the river, and made war on the Osage. But if there was one thing the tribes of the Illini had in common, it was that they were not very good at winning battles. They tried hard enough, but somehow they generally had the worst of it. This occasion was no exception; though they had more warriors on the field, they became isolated, and some fell back while others lunged forward, and Gray Cloud found his band cut off by the enemy.

The Osage closed in, and now their numbers were superior. The Illini fought, but it was soon apparent that they could not prevail. They tried to cut through the ring that was forming around them, and almost made it, but an arrow caught Bear Penis in the chest. He grasped the shaft with his hand and wrenched the arrow out, making no sound. He staggered forward, determined not to fall, and Gray Cloud put an arm around him and helped him. But together they were too slow, and the Osage swarmed in to close with them, their spears ready.

Gray Cloud paused. He could not fight while supporting his friend, and even if he had been able to, it would have been hopeless at this point. He was out of arrows.

The Osage Chief approached. He was a large man, taller than Gray Cloud, with no hair on his face: even his eyebrows had been removed. His head was partially shaved, with only two long braids beginning on the top of his head and two strips of hair running from the same region to the nape of his neck, in the Osage fashion. Blue tattoos covered his neck and much of his torso. He wore an armband of buffalo hair. He was quite handsome. He made a throwaway sign.

Gray Cloud considered. Should he throw down his weapons, or die fighting? If he tried to fight, both of them would be killed, and Glow Fungus would lose both lover and brother, and things would go hard with her without a protector or provider. If he surrendered, they might be spared, and traded back for Osage captives the Illini had taken. It galled him to surrender, and alone he might not have done it, but it did seem to be the best course. There was no chance to bluff his way out; the Osage were the fiercest warriors of the region, often at war with *all* their neighbors; they would kill him and Bear Penis immediately if there was not a prompt capitulation.

He eased Bear Penis to the ground. The man was losing consciousness; too much blood was flowing. Then Gray Cloud unslung his bow and dropped it to the ground. He drew his good stone knife and dropped it beside the bow.

The Osage Chief put his foot on the weapons, claiming them. He had accepted Gray Cloud's surrender.

Now Gray Cloud squatted to tend to his friend. He removed his own breechcloth, having nothing else suitable, and tied it around Bear Penis's chest to stop the flow of blood. The wound was small, and this was effective; the material slowly stained red, but the blood no longer dripped. The fact that Gray Cloud was now naked did not matter; he was a prisoner, and this merely emphasized that status. He had found a use for his clothing before they took it away from him.

At the Chief's order, an Osage warrior came to take Bear Penis's left arm. Gray Cloud took his right arm. They hauled him up and half carried him forward, following the Chief.

Gray Cloud knew why the Osage had chosen to take them captive instead of killing them. All warriors respected valor, and they had seen Bear Penis yank out the arrow and keep his feet. They had seen Gray Cloud sacrifice his own escape to help the other.

They walked to the Osage camp, where Bear Penis was allowed to rest. They put him in a tipi. He recovered somewhat, and took some water. But his breathing was rasping, and when he coughed, painfully, red froth showed at his mouth. The arrow had penetrated his lung.

A priest came and saw to Bear Penis, applying a poultice of herbs, giving him a bitter brew to sip, and performing a brief ritual of healing. Bear Penis's color improved, and he sank into sleep.

Gray Cloud made the sign for Thanks, extending his two hands, palms down, in a sweeping curve outward and downward toward the priest. The Osage were being generous; they could have let the man die without touching him, and been held blameless by the conventions of war.

Now Gray Cloud slept. The fact that this camp consisted of tipis meant that it was temporary; the Osage used this type of residence only when traveling. There would be a long way to go the next day.

In the morning the march resumed, Bear Penis supported by two warriors. The travel was hard for him; without the priest's treatment he probably would not have been able to survive it. As it was, he was a gaunt shadow of himself by the time they reached the Osage village several days later.

The site for this village had evidently been chosen with great care. It was on a ridge which overlooked low ground, and a river was near. The lodges were made of wooden posts sunk into the ground, with saplings bent to form a curved roof. The walls were sealed with reed mats and bark.

Now there were women. Osage men were handsome, but the ugliness of Osage women was well known. Their ear decorations did not help; they were made of clay or shell or bone, and were so heavy that they stretched the earlobes down. Not even their pretty decorations of porcupine quills or snake skin were enough to compensate.

Another priest treated Bear Penis, and a maiden was assigned to keep him warm, for now he was alternately feverish and shivering. Gray Cloud was given an Osage breechcloth and a collar of black beads: the mark of his captivity. He was bound by honor not to remove that collar, and not to try to escape while he wore it. By accepting it, he had given his oath again. He was a prisoner until the Osage freed him.

But it seemed there were no Osage held captive by the Illini, so there was nothing to trade. Days passed, then a moon, and the two remained at the camp. Gray Cloud was given woman's work to do, as another signal of his status. He did it without protest. Actually, this was one occasion when the women almost became attractive, for they sang as they hoed out the weeds of the corn patches, making a festive occasion of the chore.

Bear Penis improved, but the ravage of his injury remained on him, and he was woman-weak. They set him to woman's work, and promoted Gray Cloud to man's work. They trusted him not only because he wore the collar and would not try to escape, but because they knew that he knew that his friend would be tortured to death if Gray Cloud fled. A smart chief never depended unduly on honor.

He learned the Osage tongue, well enough to give up his reliance on signs for communication. He came to know the people. He had seen them as despicable enemies; now he knew that they were merely other people, with conventions differing from those of the Illini only in detail. There was no doubt about their valor in battle. He gained respect for them even as he gained their respect.

Gray Cloud was a good hunter. He could bring down a hawk in flight with a single arrow. He could put a spear through a deer's heart from farther than any other man. He was an asset to the Osage hunting parties, and they gave him increasing freedom to go out armed. But never alone. He understood that limit, and did not contest it.

A young woman came to his lodge one night. This was another signal of favor; no woman would have done it had the Osage Chief not allowed it. It was legitimate for Gray Cloud to accept such favors, as it was for the maidens to offer them: as an unmarried male, he was expected to be virile, and Glow Fungus would understand. The fact that he found the woman attractive showed how far he had acclimatized; the features that had seemed homely before seemed intriguing now.

But there was another aspect. "I am glad for your company," he told the woman. "I hope that if you come again, you will bring a friend for my friend."

Two nights later another maiden came. She had a friend. The Chief had allowed it. This gave Bear Penis status, and he was no longer given woman's work, but allowed to carry a bow and join the hunt. He lacked endurance, as his breathing had never properly recovered, but he could handle bow and knife well enough.

Then the Osage had trouble with the Wichita to their southwest. It was late in the season, but there was still time to mount a war mission. The Osage had two groups: the people of the sky, who governed during peace, and the people of the land, who governed during war. Suddenly the power shifted.

The war Chief summoned Gray Cloud for a conference. "You are an honorable man and a good hunter," the Chief told him. "You have found favor in our tribe. You have Wakonda." That was the Osage concept of the central essence which permeated all things. It could assume any aspect, but normally enhanced what was already worthwhile. This was a significant compliment.

"I am warmed by your favor," Gray Cloud replied.

"Will you join us and marry our women and fight against our enemies?"

He was being offered adoption into the Osage. This was a singular mark of favor. If he agreed, he could marry any amenable Osage maiden, and wear the Osage paints, be tattooed in the Osage manner, and be accepted without reservation. There would be no bars to his freedom, and his sons would be honored as Osage.

But he remembered Glow Fungus, and he was concerned for Bear Penis. "Is my friend offered similar favor?"

The chief frowned. "Bear Penis has an injury." They had given the man ample time to recover, and he had not. Not sufficiently. That indicated a lack of Wakonda.

Which meant he would be a liability to the tribe. Perhaps they had other reasons not to want the two of them, but that was the one that could be stated openly without implying dishonor.

"Bear Penis is brother to the Illini woman I would marry," Gray Cloud said carefully. "I would not take such a step if he did not join me." For Gray Cloud still wanted to marry Glow Fungus, and could not do so if he deserted his tribe or her brother, or married a woman of a foreign tribe. In this manner he informed the Chief of his continuing commitment to the

Illini, without impugning the Osage or implying that he would break his oath of captivity.

The Chief accepted it. Perhaps he had not really wanted to make the offer of tribal status, but the elders of the council had urged it. Gray Cloud would remain a captive.

The war party departed without him, for a captive could not partake in such activity. Gray Cloud and Bear Penis hunted for the tribe during the war party's absence, and now they were allowed to do it alone. Had dishonor been intended, Gray Cloud could have agreed to join the Osage, then fled when alone. So both of them now had much of the freedom that tribal status brought, though still technically captives.

The war party returned victorious, but it had taken losses. Three warriors had been killed, and two taken captive. They had taken one Wichita captive, whom they would ordinarily have tortured, for there was bad blood between the two peoples. But one of the captives lost to the Osage was the son of the Chief. They had to negotiate.

While the bargaining session was being arranged, the honors were done for the dead warriors. They were buried under the ground, as they were not important enough to rate a sitting interment with stones and logs to protect them. They had food, clothing, weapons, and personal belongings to assist them in their journey to the setting sun. After three days of mourning, parties of the kinsmen of the dead set out from the villages. They would march in straight lines until they encountered some stranger. They would kill that man and hang his scalp on a pole by the grave, letting each of the dead men know that vengeance had been accomplished, as well as giving them company on their journey.

The Wichita bargained fiercely, knowing their advantage. In the end they won three for two: the return of their man, and two others. Why they wanted such captives was not clear, but in this manner Gray Cloud and Bear Penis were exchanged. "We are sorry to do this," the Chief told Gray Cloud. "We had hoped to trade you back to your own people. But we have no choice. My son thanks you."

Gray Cloud understood. The Chief had to recover his son, who would be chief after him. Gray Cloud could have avoided this by joining the Osage; he had known when he declined that this was the risk he faced. "I am glad to do it for your son," he replied courteously. "What is to be our status with the Wichita?"

"Tied captive," the Chief said with regret. "No honor."

"Then we will not be on oath," Gray Cloud said.

"Once you are at their camp," the Chief agreed. "We will know nothing of you."

In this manner it became understood that Gray Cloud and Bear Penis could flee the Wichita if they had the chance; their oath not to flee the Osage would no longer apply. But they would suffer the risks of doing so. If they did escape, and made it to Osage territory, the people would pretend not to see them, so as not to be required to help recapture them. But they would be on their own. If they made it back to Illini territory, they would be safe; if not, the Osage would not help them.

The two of them were ritually bound by the hands, as was the Wichita captive, and turned over to the Wichita contingent. The Wichita warrior was immediately released, but Gray Cloud and Bear Penis were not. Yet neither were they reviled; they were simply guarded, so that there was no chance to escape. What was it the Wichita wanted of them?

They were marched rapidly back to Wichita territory. Bear Penis tired, and Gray Cloud helped him as well as he could. Observing this, the Wichita warriors were angry. They stopped and looked at Bear Penis's chest, discovering the scar. They seemed to feel they had been cheated, but were resigned to it.

What did they intend to do with their acquired captives? Gray Cloud had not been easy about this to begin with, and he trusted it less now. But he knew better than to try to ask.

In time they reached the Wichita main camp, where they joined several other captives from other tribes. They were untied, as they would have no chance to escape from here. With signs Gray Cloud learned from the others what they were here for—and was appalled.

There was a levy on the Wichita by the major tribe to their southwest, the Coahuiltec. Every month they had to deliver ten men. It did not matter whether these were Wichita or captives, as long as they were in good health. Now there were five here, half the levy; there were probably more in another camp. All of them would be delivered when the time came.

And why did the Coahuiltec want them? Because they had to fill a levy by the Mexica to the south. The Mexica had a great need for blood sacrifice to their spirits, and constantly gathered more men for this. The Mexica gods were extremely thirsty for blood.

Gray Cloud had not known of this, and neither had the Osage. The Wichita had kept it secret, knowing that they would have much more trouble gaining suitable captives if the tribes to the north knew.

Gray Cloud shook his head. It would have been better to be adopted into the Osage tribe!

All of them were desperate to escape, but there was no opportunity. They were kept under constant guard. When the time came, they were turned over to a trader who specialized in slaves and marched south, a walk of many days. It was fall now, and the land was cooling, but not as much as it would have cooled in Gray Cloud's homeland. Did it matter, considering where they were headed?

The Coahuiltec did not keep them either. They were delivered to the Mexica along with a throng of other captives, as tribute, along with many other staples of food and clothing and things of value. There were large bundles of cotton, the white or yellow stuff of cloth. The feathers of birds, of many colors. Caged wildcats. Turtle shells. Pearls. Bows. Maidens.

It was a long and arduous walk, for captives had to carry some of the parcels of tribute items. Gray Cloud quietly arranged to take some of Bear Penis's burden, and the captors, noting this, allowed it. It was evident that they wanted to deliver healthy men, and not lose any on the journey, so they were lenient. But it was also evident that any attempt to resist or escape them would be effectively dealt with.

By the time Gray Cloud and Bear Penis completed the long trek, it was spring. They had marched so far they had lost all notion of their location, knowing only that it was far south of the world as they had known it. They had passed high mountains and great valleys. They had not encountered many people; as captives, they were regarded as the lowest sort, and shunned. Even their own company changed: groups of captives were detached and taken elsewhere, and other groups of captives brought in. Thus they had no real chance to get to know others well. Only the need for Gray Cloud to help Bear Penis carry and walk enabled them to remain together.

"The Mexica are experienced," Bear Penis remarked. "They let no one associate for too long, lest we form friendships and consider rebellion and escape."

So it seemed. That made their prospect for survival dim. But Gray Cloud was no longer bound by oath, and he intended to escape—when he could take Bear Penis with him.

They came at last to the great city of Tenochtitlán, or the Place of the Fruit of the Prickly Pear Cactus. It was an amazing sight. It was on an island in a lake, reached by causeways. In its center were phenomenal squares and temples of stone and stucco, brightly painted. Beyond the enormous buildings were smaller residences, square and solid, quite unlike the tipis and lodges of his homeland. The city extended on and on, so that he could see no end to it. Several canals crossed it, so that canoes could come almost to the center.

There were more people thronging the broad streets than Gray Cloud had known existed in all the world. They were of small stature, the men half a head shorter than he, and the women even less, but beautiful. Their clothing indicated their social status. All of them wore lengths of cotton cloth, yet the manner and quality of it varied widely. Men wore the loincloth, but the capes differed according to the importance of each man. No two designs seemed the same. The warriors wore feather-covered tunics with bright designs. Only the highest ranks wore sandals; the rest were barefoot. The women wore ankle-length underskirts and sometimes an overdress. Gray Cloud knew that every detail of every person's clothing signaled his profession and status, but he could make sense of almost none of it.

Not that it mattered. He would have no chance to wear any such clothing anyway. His tattered, soiled breechcloth and cape were good enough, until he was killed.

At last the group of them was taken to a cell in a building some distance behind the ceremonial center of the city. Here they joined other captives, some of whom seemed to have been there for a long time. The cell was dank and unpleasant, but at least it was a place where they could rest.

Gray Cloud was tired, but he wanted to learn more of his

situation. "Is there anyone here who speaks a tongue of the Illini?" he asked.

He was met with dull stares. Obviously a number of the captives were from far away, but none from the Illini.

"They mix up the captives," Bear Penis said. "So the tongues don't match, and we can't conspire to escape."

A guard came to the cell entrance. "Silence!" he shouted. That was one of the few Mexica words they had learned to understand, because blows followed swiftly when the command was ignored. So their captors didn't depend on the confusion of tongues; even if others spoke Illini, they would not be allowed to talk to each other.

Gray Cloud went to signs. I   All   Sleep, he signed to Bear Penis. The I and All signs indicated "we," so he was suggesting that they rest.

Now another man perked up. His hands moved. Question   You   Sit? they signed, the final word shown by the closed fist moving down. It meant "Where do you live?" and, by extension, What was his tribe?

Gray Cloud glanced at the door. The guards couldn't hear the signs, and probably wouldn't know their meaning anyway! They could talk this way!

We   Illini, he signed. That identified both culture and location.

We   Ani-Yunwiya, the other signed back, indicating the man beside him. Gray Cloud was not sure of the particular tribal designation, but that was all right; any man from his region of the world was a friend, here.

An extended dialogue followed. It seemed that these were two Principal People, who came from far up a great river. One was called White Bark, because he was good at working with the papery bark of that tree, and the other was Black Bone. The three of them traced the river by assorted signed comparisons, and concluded that the Principal People lived in mountains some distance southeast of the Illini, but that their rivers connected. The Principal People wanted to escape too, but it seemed hopeless. The Mexica city was so big, and there were so many people, and none of them would help a captive. All were loyal to the great Chief, Moctezuma. The city was surrounded by a great wall that was constantly guarded. If they reached a canal, and stole a canoe, it still was no good, because there was a tremendous amount of traffic on the lake, and lodges all around its shore, so that no one could get away from it without being spotted. In any event, there was no escape by water, for all local rivers flowed into the lake.

But suppose it was possible to get away from the city and the lake? Gray Cloud inquired. Could an escape be made overland? Maybe, White Bark agreed. But that was not for him. Then, at Gray Cloud's query, he indicated his right knee: it was a mass of scar tissue. He could stand and walk, but he could not run. He had tried to run away once, seeking to escape to the nearby hostile tribe of Tlaxcala, and the guards had clubbed his knee to prevent it from happening again. That had been effective. Tlaxcala remained, unconquered by the Mexica, but White Bark would never get there.

So escape remained unlikely. But now there was someone to talk with, and to hope with. The Mexica were often at war, Gray Cloud learned; in fact, they liked to fight, so as to gain honor through capturing men, and the captives were then sacrificed to the Mexica gods. If an enemy should prevail, maybe the captives would be freed. But this seemed doubtful, because the Mexica were the strongest of tribes, and almost always won their battles, and when they lost, they sent warriors in greater number so as to win the next time. Still, it was worth pondering.

The next day the captives were put to work. There was construction going on in the city, and a tremendous amount of earth had to be moved. It was carried in from beyond the lake, across a causeway, and dumped in a pile. The group of captives Gray Cloud was with had to take that earth and spread it evenly across the site where something was to be built, and tramp it down. The day was hot, and the sun beat down, but the guards did not care; the captives worked all day, with reprieves only for drinks of water. The guards were indifferent to their suffering, but had to let them have water lest they die and be lost as sacrifices.

That was the way of it, for many days. The captives were fed well, and the guards watched their health. In fact, in some ways they seemed better off than the poor peasants who worked their poor fields, growing corn and gourds to sell to the nobles. Gray Cloud learned that, indeed, slaves had a better

standard of living than the peasants, and that the poorest folk
often sold themselves into slavery. All a man had to do was
appear before four or more witnesses and state his desire to
become a slave. He would be given twenty capes and food to
survive, and did not have to actually begin serving until a
winter had passed. Even as a slave he could own land and
marry, and his children would be free. If later he was able to
ransom himself, he would be free again. Meanwhile he worked
for his owner, and if he was competent he might attain considerable authority in that capacity. But most slaves worked as
porters, carrying the loads of tribute that were constantly being
brought in. Such people were able to walk tremendous dis-
tances with their burdens. Gray Cloud had seen them on his
own march in, and been amazed that these small, quiet men
could work so tirelessly.

Then the entire roomful—ten men—was organized for a
march. There was to be a ceremony at Tula, the ancient Toltec
capital two days' march to the north. The Mexica claimed to
have inherited the mantle of the Toltec, and still honored the
memory, though Tula was no longer a major city. There were
to be a number of sacrifices for the honor of the gods, who
were sustained by human blood. It was time for this group to
receive the honor of sustaining the gods.

Gray Cloud realized that if he was going to escape at all, it
had to be soon. Once they reached Tula, it would probably be
too late.

He consulted with White Bark and Black Bone, who agreed.
Any attempt to escape would probably mean death, but they
preferred to risk getting cut down in battle to having their hearts
cut out of their bodies on an altar.

But there was no chance to flee from Tenochtitlán; they
would have to wait until they were fairly well between cities.
So they walked dutifully down the street and across the causeway, flanked by five guards. The guards were slaves, but ranking ones; they could hardly be distinguished from citizens in
their attitude, though their insignias clearly indicated their status. They were well armed and alert; they intended to see that
nothing happened to their charges on the march.

The group moved up into the mountains that surrounded
the great city, and the population thinned out. The lodges be-

came smaller and poorer, until they resembled the kind that Gray Cloud knew at home. The farmers tilled small plots of corn on the contour, their narrow leveled fields forming a series of terraces up the slope. No one paid any attention to the traveling party; evidently such marches were commonplace.

They stopped at a way station in a high valley. The ten were put in a tight cell evidently made for this purpose; its only window was too small for a man to get through. There was a ditch for natural functions behind; a guard took each prisoner out separately for that, always alert. They certainly knew how to ensure that no captive escaped!

In the morning the march resumed. They crossed a high pass, then began the long descent into the valley of the city of Tula. There had been no good opportunity to escape.

Bear Penis had borne up well on the first day, but the march had debilitated him. He started out weaker this morning; his breathing was harsh. Gray Cloud helped him on the uphill path, but when the downhill part came, the guards forbade it. So he walked alone, and continued to fade.

At midday, in the heat, Bear Penis fell, gasping. The fatigue and heat were too much for him.

One of the guards had lost patience. He screamed at Bear Penis in the Mexica tongue and beat him about the shoulders with his light club.

Gray Cloud reacted without thinking. His right hand lashed out and struck the guard on the side of the head. The guard, furious, lunged at him with his spear. Gray Cloud dodged the spear, caught the man, and hurled him to the side. The guard fell, and his head cracked into a stone.

It had happened so swiftly that no one else had reacted. Gray Cloud turned away from the guard and helped Bear Penis to stand. By the time he had done that, the four other guards were close. Two were tending to the fallen guard, and two were covering Gray Cloud with their spears. If he made any further resistance, he would be dead.

He put his arm around Bear Penis and helped him walk. The guards let him be. He knew why: if they killed him, their group would be short one captive for the sacrifice. They would wait until they reached the city, and report what he had done, and let an official decide what to do.

They resumed the march, but without the fifth guard. Gray Cloud didn't know whether the man was dead, but it was possible; his head had hit hard. It was an interesting situation, he thought: he had done something surely punishable by death, but he could not be killed for it, because he was already slated for death. They couldn't even torture him, because their blood-thirsty god accepted only healthy offerings. In fact, it seemed that many Mexica went willingly to the sacrifice, proud to support their gods with their blood and hearts.

Belatedly he realized that he had lost his best chance to escape. If he had grabbed the fallen guard's spear and attacked the other guards, instead of helping his friend up, then the two Principal People could have joined in, and they could have made their break. He hadn't even thought of it—and if the others had, they had not been able to act in time. He should have seized the moment!

Yet what would have happened to Bear Penis, then? The man could have died just trying to make the effort to escape, for they would have had to flee across the mountain without protection against the chill night. The Mexica would soon have been after them, and no peasants would have helped them. Perhaps he had, after all, done what was best.

By night they reached Tula. The cell here was larger, but no less secure. There was no chance to break out, even if it had been unguarded. There was nothing to do but take their rations of corn bread, and sleep.

In the morning the guards took Gray Cloud out, held him in place, and expertly clubbed his right knee.

Pain exploded. He did not cry out, because his discipline as a man and a warrior gave him strength, but this abrupt injury, coming when he was not in the throes of battle, was a horrendous experience. When he became aware of his surroundings, he was back in the cell, and White Bark was tending to his knee. White Bark had suffered this injury himself; he knew how to ease it.

They now had the Mexica answer to Gray Cloud's attack on the guard. He had been crippled so that he would have no hope of escape, even if there should be some opportunity. The six "civilized" captives nodded; they had known it would be this way. They at least were at peace with their situation, con-

sidering it an honor. The primitives were fools to try to fight
it, and were only bringing more discomfort on themselves. Now
perhaps they would learn some grace.

But White Bark signed a message of hope: he thought escape
remained possible. If Gray Cloud could handle the pain, he
could still walk, and carry weight. Indeed, he had to, for the
guards made the captives work while they were waiting for the
ceremony. They had to go out and sweep the streets of Tula
with special brooms. Gray Cloud learned to walk with his right
knee stiff, so that it did not send excruciating jolts with every
step. White Bark showed him how to point his foot out so that
he did not automatically roll off his foot and bend his knee.
Now the pain was continuous, but bearable. But there was no
doubt at all: he could not run. So what was White Bark thinking
of? Surely only a fleet and durable runner could ever hope to
win free.

The next evening White Bark signed his plan. The Tototepec
were a hostile tribe that the Mexica had not conquered. One
part of the Tototepec territory was near this city. They needed
to make their break by night, and flee to that territory, and
then Mexica would not be able to pursue them. Of course, then
they would be at the mercy of the Tototepec, but surely those
folk would be glad to help enemies of the Mexica.

But Gray Cloud could only hobble along! he protested, touching his knee. He could never get away from any pursuit.

Yet there might not be any pursuit, White Bark replied. The
concept was hard to convey by signs, but gradually Gray Cloud
came to understand how. He doubted it could work, but it was
certainly worth a try, considering the alternative.

Bear Penis and Black Bone could read the signs. They made
no comment. They were aware that one of the other prisoners
could be a spy for the Mexica, so it had to seem that this was
merely a foolish dialogue between two.

Then, sooner than they expected, it was time for the sacrifices. They had delayed too long!

The ten of them were marched out to the ceremonial site.
Their hands were bound behind them, and wooden collars
linked them together. No, there was no chance to escape.

Gray Cloud made what peace he could with his aspirations
and memories, and knew that Bear Penis was doing the same.

There was nothing to do now but die bravely.

They came to the sacrificial plaza where the great temple pyramid stood. It was impressive, as was all the Mexica construction—only this predated them, being a Toltec structure, and honored by the Mexica, who claimed descent from the Toltecs. This sacrifice was in honor of the ancient builders.

Here a group of priests met them, garbed in their black cotton Xicolli open jackets and breechcloths, their hair bound back under tight hoods. Their hair was quite long, as it was never cut; the braid of one reached down to his knees. Their bodies were blackened with soot, and streaks of caked blood were on their temples from self-inflicted cuts: they offered their own blood to their gods, as well as that of others.

The guards retreated, having delivered the captives to the priests. But the end was not yet. The ceremony was in progress, and at the moment a group of dancers was in the square, moving eloquently as several others sang sacred hymns. Gray Cloud was impressed despite the peril of his situation; this was a formidable and even beautiful ritual, every aspect accomplished with precision.

But soon enough it was time for the sacrifices. The priests approached the group of captives. They took the first captive, who was one of the Mexica, and stripped him to his breechcloth. They painted him with red and white stripes, reddened his mouth, and painted a black circle around it. Then they glued white down on his head, making him look vaguely like a giant bird. He offered no resistance; indeed, he cooperated, standing proudly for the decoration.

They took the second captive and decorated him similarly. They continued until they had done six. All of them stood with their heads held high, pleased to have been recognized as the best of this sacrificial group.

Gray Cloud was the next. Denied his chance to escape, he was uncertain whether to stand as proudly as the others, trying to shame them, or to spit in a priest's face. It was not that he lacked the courage to face his end unflinchingly, but that he did not regard this as an honorable death.

He decided to spit, then to offer no further resistance. That would show both his courage and his contempt for the proceedings.

The head priest gazed at him, then made a negative motion with his hand.

He was being rejected? That was too much to hope for!

Gray Cloud and the three other primitives were taken to a spot not far from the steps and made to stand facing the altar. When any one of them tried to look away, the guards quickly became threatening. They were being required to watch the sacrifice of their companions!

Was it coincidence that only these four were being treated this way? Gray Cloud doubted it. But what was the point? Had the priests anticipated the gesture of contempt and acted to prevent it? If so, they were smarter than he had thought.

The sacrificial altar was on a high terrace. The priests escorted the first captive up to the higher level. He walked up the steps unassisted, still demonstrating how proud he was to do this. He went to the altar, where six hefty priests stood in their white robes. They took him by the arms and legs, one to each limb, and laid him backwards across the altar. A fifth caught hold of his head, pulling it back so that his body arched.

Then the high priest lifted his fine obsidian knife, the tecpatl, and plunged it into the victim's bared chest. He lifted it and brought it down again, and again. He was carving a hole in the chest!

In a moment he put his hand into the cavity he had opened, and brought out the man's dripping heart. Even from here, Gray Cloud could see that *it was still beating*! The priest held it high, as an offering to the sun, then put it reverently in a special bowl.

Meanwhile the other priests lifted the body, which was still quivering, and sent it tumbling down the steps. Two men grabbed it at the base and dragged it away. They looked excited and eager, as if they had gained a great prize.

Gray Cloud had seen death before, but never anything like this. The Mexica were traders of death; they joyed in killing those who did not resist, in the name of their great spirit. It wasn't any spirit Gray Cloud cared to honor!

He knew the symbolism here, for White Bark had explained it. The sacrificial captive was the rising sun; the rolling body was the setting sun. They were reenacting the natural order of the day, and giving the heart and blood to the sun. Perhaps it was sincere, but he wondered how willingly the priests themselves would go to a similar sacrifice.

The second painted victim was escorted up the steps. He was bent back across the altar, and his heart was cut out, exactly as the first had been served. The priests were obviously well practiced in this technique.

All six of the prepared captives were sacrificed similarly. Then the four remaining ones were marched back to their cell. "Next sun—you!" a guard told them, smiling.

Whether this was torture or guidance Gray Cloud couldn't tell. The six done this day had all seemed more than willing and proud; none had resisted in any way. In contrast, the four remaining had made clear their aversion to the business. Had they been done first, the others would not have been bothered; as it was, the prospect was that much worse. But perhaps it was just a matter of privilege: the civilized captives had the right to go first.

Gray Cloud glanced at White Bark, who nodded very slightly. They had to make their break tonight.

The four ate their evening meal, performed their natural functions, and returned to their cell. They wrapped themselves in their blankets and lay still. For a time. Then Black Bone rolled over so that his head and arms were near the barred door. Quietly he scraped under the bedding straw with his hands. The dirt was loose there. He had been working at it for several nights while feigning sleep, scraping with a small stone he had found and hidden in his mouth. He had loosened the soil of the packed floor some way down. Now he scraped it more vigorously, drawing out the dirt into a pile to the side.

Bear Penis lay with his head facing the door. He was watching and listening, ready to warn Black Bone of the approach of any guard. But the guards were evidently celebrating this night, not paying close attention. Tomorrow they would be able to go home, their duty done. They were by the sound of it playing a gambling game with hard grains of corn as counters and dice; their explanations could be heard irregularly. "Three!" "Five!" "One!" "Ha! I eat you!" "Two!" "One more and you would have killed me!" In another circumstance Gray Cloud would have been more curious about the details of the game; now he was glad for the distraction it provided.

Black Bone put his head down. The hole was deep enough: his head fitted under the door! But not quite wide enough to let his shoulders pass. He was a thin man, but he needed more room.

Gray Cloud joined him and scraped at the dirt with his fingernails. Progress was painstakingly slow, but only a little more clearance was needed.

Black Bone tried again, and this time managed to get his shoulders under. He scraped through on his back, like a sacrificial victim, wedging himself under the door. Soon he was out.

He stood before the door. It was barred by a heavy plank that could not be reached from inside, or jogged loose, but was no problem for a man outside. He did not touch it. He only put his face to the tiny window in the door, so that they could see that he had made it. Stupid captives might have unbarred the door and charged out—and quickly found themselves surrounded by enemies alerted to the commotion.

Then the others quickly filled in the dirt where it had been, tamped it down, and covered it again with straw. It looked undisturbed. Black Bone smoothed it similarly from outside. Then he went to a niche and flattened himself within it, out of sight of the main entry hall. He held his breechcloth between his hands, stretched out to make it as long as possible. In that form it was most of the length of a man.

Now Gray Cloud, lying farthest from the door, began to groan. "Oh, my knee, my knee!" he exclaimed in his own tongue. "Oh, how it hurts!" Indeed it did hurt; the pain had never stopped, but it was relatively slight now. Had he banged the knee in his sleep, it would hurt worse, however. Of course, he would never have expressed his pain had it not been for the need of this ruse, for he was a warrior.

After a while there was a yell from one of the guards, who were in a chamber down the hall. "Be quiet!" Even if Gray Cloud had not picked up the words from recent association, the tone would have been intelligible enough.

He moaned louder. "Oh, my knee! My knee!"

The guard uttered an expletive and came down the hall. He had evidently had to leave his gambling game, and was annoyed. "Be quiet, you primitive whiner!" Or words to that effect. The ruse was working: the Mexica in their arrogance chose to believe that primitives had no courage, despite abundant evidence to the contrary. Thus they sent only one guard to deal with this nuisance.

Gray Cloud was moaning and writhing with increasing vigor. The guard came to stand before the door, his torch casting a flickering light into the cell. "Quiet, or I'll give you reason—"

He did not finish, for Black Bone's breechcloth dropped over his head and tightened around his neck, cutting off his breath. Black Bone might be thin, but this task required only brief exertion, and he was quite competent to handle it. There was only silence, and the wild wavering of the torch.

After a pause of about the length required for a man to stop breathing permanently, they heard the bar being lifted. The door opened, slowly so as not to squeak.

Outside was Black Bone, holding the torch, and the body. Bear Penis stepped out to pick up the forepart, and Black Bone took the legs. They carried the body inside and laid it in Black Bone's place. Quickly they stripped off the guard's clothing, and Bear Penis, who was the one of the four of them who most resembled the guard in body type, exchanged clothing with him. Gray Cloud helped, adjusting his friend's hairstyle to match as closely as possible, and advising him on posture. White Bark arranged the guard under Black Bone's blanket so that he seemed to be sleeping, his face away from the door. With the torchlight, this should be enough.

Bear Penis took the guard's club and joined Black Bone in the hall. Black Bone hid, while Bear Penis pretended to be the guard. He closed the door and set the plank in place. The whole thing had been done rapidly, for they had rehearsed it carefully, knowing that any faltering could cost them everything. If the other guards grew impatient with the man's failure to return promptly—

Gray Cloud resumed his moaning, louder than before. "What are you going to do, kill me?" he demanded of the supposed guard outside. "Then you will have no sacrifice!" For they had learned that the four of them, as lesser sacrifices, were to be awarded after death to lesser folk, and the four guards would get to share one of the bodies for their ceremonial meal. But if any prisoner were lost, the guards would be in trouble. Trouble, among the Mexica, was likely to wind up on the sacrificial altar. There were different types of death, and a person slated for a shameful one could make it honorable by volunteering for the sacrifice, and carrying through in a courageous manner. The bloodthirsty spirits of the Mexica did not like the taste of the blood of cowards.

Then there was a call in the Mexica tongue. Bear Penis had picked up enough of it to speak the basic commands they heard so often, and he was good at imitating voices. Now he sounded a lot like the guard. "Come! He needs discipline!"

The three remaining guards came out, one of them with another torch, two brandishing the light disciplinary clubs. They too were annoyed about the interruption of their game. They barged down toward the cell; Gray Cloud heard their heavy footsteps and muttered curses.

Even as they came, Bear Penis was heaving up the plank, evidently determined to go in there and beat the obnoxious captive into silence. As they arrived, he dropped the plank and pulled the door open so that he was concealed behind it, only his torch showing at the edge of the door.

Two guards charged directly in. The third, more cautious, or perhaps simply not wanting to crowd the small cell too much, stayed back.

Bear Penis swung the door back, almost banging it into the third guard. The guard made an angry exclamation—which was cut off by Black Bone's garrote. The guard's torch wavered as he struggled silently.

But already Gray Cloud and White Bark were moving. Neither could get up readily because of his stiff right leg, but they grabbed the legs of the guards and shoved them off-balance.

Bear Penis charged into the cell, swinging the club. He caught one guard on the head, hard, and the man went down. The other turned to face him, but was entangled in White Bark's legs and could not get his own club into action. Bear Penis clubbed him in the face once, twice, and he went down.

Now they got busy, for though they had taken out all the guards, they could not be sure when some higher official would pass. Black Bone used his garrote to strangle the two Bear Penis had clubbed, to be sure they were dead, while the others stripped the guard who most resembled Black Bone of his clothing, taking turns holding the torches. Black Bone donned it and arranged his hair appropriately.

It seemed like a long time, but no one came. Evidently the captives were not of much interest until they were bent across the altar.

They left the four guards seemingly sleeping in the cell, emulating the prisoners, and barred the door. They went to the guards' chamber and found food there, beside the scattered kernels of corn the guards had used in their game. They ate as much as they could on the spot, and wrapped the rest in skins for Gray Cloud and White Bark to carry. Black Bark and Bear Penis slung the guards' bows across their backs, and donned quivers of arrows.

Then they set out, marching openly down the street in a formation. Gray Cloud and White Bark walked awkwardly, carrying their burdens, in their own clothing, while the two others carried the torches and held their clubs menacingly. It looked as if two prisoners were being moved to other quarters for the night.

As it happened, there were few Mexica out this evening, and these were peasants. They paid no attention to the party. The four marched down the long streets to the east—and did not stop at the edge of the ceremonial section. There was no cry of alarm behind, and no pursuit. They seemed to have made a clean escape.

Then they came to the wall that surrounded the city. They stopped at the last corner before the road led to the gate, and took turns peering ahead at the gate. They had hoped that the gate guards would be asleep, but this was not the case. There would be no chance to march out unchallenged; they were going the wrong way at the wrong time.

"We gambled and won before," Bear Penis said. "This time we have gambled and lost. I lack the stamina to make the long walk home, or even to paddle a canoe there. I knew I would never see my sister again. I will distract the guard. You three go quietly through, and never look back."

The others consulted quietly, using signs as needed. What Bear Penis had said was true, and Gray Cloud had known it but chosen not to think of it. Even with the bad legs, he and

White Bark had a better chance to win free, because they could paddle a canoe for an extended period. Bear Penis was choosing to sacrifice himself, to enable them to escape.

"We will speak well of you," Gray Cloud said, and the two Principal People nodded. Each of them touched Bear Penis on the shoulder, briefly, in the mark of respect accorded to a warrior about to set off on a dangerous mission.

Then Bear Penis lifted his torch, held his chin high, and marched out alone to the gate. This was merely a narrow gap in the wall, angled so that it was necessary for those who passed it to walk single file under the eye of the guard, who stood in an alcove beside it. There was only one guard, as there was no immediate threat to the city.

Bear Penis waved his torch, calling out something indistinguishable. The guard looked, perplexed.

Then Bear Penis stumbled. He almost fell, staggered a few more steps, and called out something to the guard.

"Get away from here!" the man exclaimed, evidently afraid that a bad spirit would afflict him. But Bear Penis struggled on, reaching for the guard as he made choking sounds. He seemed either badly injured or inhabited by an evil spirit. The guard shoved him away, cursing.

Meanwhile the other three, their torch doused, walked quietly behind the guard and through the unwatched gate. In a moment it was done. They emerged outside the city and hurried on, never looking back.

But when they got a suitable distance from the wall, they paused and waited, hoping to see one more figure come out. It did not happen. Bear Penis probably had not even tried to leave, but had recovered and returned to the city streets after he knew they had passed. Maybe he could hide in the city, disguised as a peasant.

Unable to speak the Mexica tongue, other than a few words? Gray Cloud knew better. His friend was lost, and they could not wait. Grimly, they resumed their walk in the darkness.

But this was only the first stage. Once they were well clear of the city, they took the guards' knives from the two bags, so that each of them was armed. The two "guards" had bows slung across their backs, and arrows, but it had not seemed wise to have the captives carry bows. One bow had been lost with Bear Penis. If they were discovered at this point, they would have to fight with what they had.

They continued walking east, toward the Tototemec territory. It was wearing for Gray Cloud, swinging his stiff leg out and around, but he kept a good pace. They had to get far from Tula by dawn!

"How is it there is no pursuit?" White Bark asked in his tongue.

Gray Cloud had been pondering the same thing. They had now been walking for what seemed like half the night, and there should have been a change of guards by now, or a routine check by a more important person. The authorities had to know of the escape. "They may be afraid that there will be terrible punishment if it is known that the captives escaped," he said. "Rather than that, they are hiding it, and rounding up other people for sacrifice. Peasants, perhaps."

"But if that is so, then there will be no pursuit!" Black Bone exclaimed, amazed.

"That may be the case," Gray Cloud agreed. "But I think we had better keep moving anyway."

But Gray Cloud and White Bark were tiring, because of their bad legs. They slowed the pace, but didn't like it. If day caught them marching like this, the farmers would know something was wrong, for they should be marching toward the city, not away from it. In any event, two of them could not walk much farther.

Then they spied a stream. They had reached water! They scooped it up to drink. "A canoe!" Gray Cloud exclaimed. "If we can find a canoe—!" For that was the rest of their plan: to paddle out to the great sea, and along the shore to the great river, and home.

They walked along the bank of the stream, and soon they did find a canoe. Gray Cloud did not like stealing it, even from an enemy, but they had to have it.

In this manner, without any commotion, they escaped the empire of the Mexica. The stream took them through the territory of the Tototemec, but the peasants there took them for traders and let them pass unchallenged. Two paddled and one rested, taking turns. They followed the river all the way down to the great sea, and then they followed the coast for many days, staying clear of others as much as possible. In the shallows they were able to kill fish by shooting them with arrows, and they ate them raw. They came to the great river on whose tails all three of them lived, and forged up it.

Because the season was late, they did not take the branch of the river that led to Gray Cloud's tribe, for that would strand the two Principal People for the winter. They went directly to the Ani-Yunwiya territory, with the understanding that Gray Cloud would be treated well there and would be given a good canoe to return when a companion could be found for him.

Thus it was that Gray Cloud came to stay with the Principal People—waiting, as it turned out, for Throat Shot to appear. But now Throat Shot would have a similar problem getting back to his own tribe.

If that was what he was supposed to do.

CHAPTER 11

⚜

TALE TELLER

O Spirit of the Mound, I have told you Gray Cloud's tale of
the dread civilized Mexica. I am glad I am primitive! Now I will
tell you how Throat Shot became the Tale Teller among the
Principal People.

They decided to paddle up the river to Gray Cloud's tribe of
the Illini, the Peoria. There Throat Shot could decide where to
go next, since he had no instructions other than to go with his
friend and wait for Sun Eagle's signal. He hoped it would come
soon, but he had no certainty of that. The spirits took little heed
of time.

They reached the tipis of the Peoria ten days later. Gray
Cloud was greeted like a dead man returned to life: with limited
enthusiasm. Soon it was apparent why: things had changed in
the tribe during the past two winters, and there really was no
place for a returned, ranking, disabled warrior. Glow Fungus,
deprived of both brother and lover, had married another and
now was great with child. Gray Cloud's presence was awkward.

"Now I think that I should not have left Red Leaf," Gray
Cloud said, speaking of his Principal People maiden. He
seemed neither completely surprised nor completely disappointed. "Will you go with me back to the Principal People?"

That seemed to be as good a prospect as any. Throat Shot
had been told to go with his friend, and Gray Cloud was his
friend. So Gray Cloud informed Glow Fungus of the heroic fate
of her brother, Bear Penis, and wished her well. Then they set

off on the return trip, paddling down the river, and to the junction of rivers, and the next junction, and up the final river to the land of the Principal People. Winter was pressing close as they completed it, and they paddled hard and long, making good distance each day. They worked well as a team, and it was good.

The Principal People welcomed them back, for Gray Cloud was good with the bow and was an asset to their hunts. Throat Shot knew how that was; if any animal or bird passed the man, that creature was dead. All that was required was to drive the creatures toward Gray Cloud. Gray Cloud had been learning the art of birch-bark canoe making from White Bark, and showed excellent promise in that, and such craftsmen were valued. It also seemed that Red Leaf had been quite down-hearted at Gray Cloud's absence, and not subject to cheer by any other man. Now she was happy again.

In fact, Red Leaf turned out to be an attractive woman, older than Gray Cloud but quite deferential to him. Perhaps it had been her knowledge of his loyalty to the brother of his former woman that charmed her. Gray Cloud had made it clear that first commitments came first, and that he had a commitment to Glow Fungus in his own tribe and had to return to her. Were that not the case, he would have been willing to marry Red Leaf—if she were willing to join him among the Illini. She had not been, so for two reasons their liaison had been temporary. Now both reasons had changed, and Gray Cloud's first loyalty was to Red Leaf and her village. Red Leaf had gambled and won, as she saw it—and she welcomed Throat Shot as one who had benefited her by bringing her man back, though he tried to demur.

But what of Throat Shot himself? He could be no asset to the hunt, and he had no woman waiting here. Yet Gray Cloud spoke well of him, and so he was treated as a welcome guest. He felt out of place.

He tried to help Gray Cloud with his chosen work, making birch-bark canoes. The man was now doing it alone, with the understanding that White Bark would assist if needed; but Gray Cloud hoped to demonstrate his ability to get through without that. It was somewhat like a boy's initiation into manhood: he had to prove himself without the help of the instructor. All stages of the work required great care and patience, and Throat Shot was able to be useful. First they had to locate a good birch tree, and it was pleasant exploring the high slopes for them. When they found one, they had to fell it carefully, so as not to damage the precious bark. They built a fire around its base and charred a ring, keeping the bark above it wet so that it would not burn. They pounded out the charred region and renewed the fire several times, until the trunk narrowed and the tree was ready to fall. They burned it unevenly, so that it would fall uphill and in a spot where there was nothing to bruise the trunk. When it finally came down, Gray Cloud inspected it carefully, then marked off a section three times a man's length. He cut a circle around the trunk at each end, and then cut the bark lengthwise and used wood wedges to help peel it off in one great piece.

After that they flattened the great curved section of birch bark by toasting it with a carefully applied torch. They used split sticks to hold burning pieces of waste bark to the moist inner side of the canoe strip. Throat Shot was amazed to see it slowly flatten until it lay like a blanket on the ground. Then they rolled it very carefully, again like a blanket, the bark side in, and carried it to Gray Cloud's place of canoe making.

Here he had stakes set out in a rough canoe pattern on level ground. He used these as a frame to hold the bark in place and in the proper shape while he fitted lengths of cedarwood to form the ribs of the canoe. This task was so delicate that he allowed no one else to do it, and it was not proper for anyone to assist, and so Throat Shot's usefulness here was at an end. He thanked Gray Cloud for allowing him to participate this far, and departed; it was all he could do.

A thin man with scars all over his body approached him with a signed question: You Walk Fast (Run) Good? When Throat Shot agreed that he could run well, the man made an offer: run with him to the various villages of the Principal People, and learn their tongue and dialects, and perhaps he would find some way to make himself useful among them.

Throat Shot realized that Gray Cloud must have set this up. He agreed to do it. Question You Called? he signed.

The man rubbed the back of his hand in the sign for Color, then pointed to a black section of bark on a nearby tree. Then he signed Die, Long Time, touched one leg, and pointed to a white flower. That meant Bone.

Black Bone! This was Gray Cloud's Principal People friend who had escaped captivity with him! Suddenly Throat Shot felt he knew the man well.

They set out on what turned out to be a long series of runs, visiting every village of the immediate region. There appeared to be quite a number; the villages here were set closer than those of the Toco, and many had more people. They ranged in size from hardly more than ten lodges to two tens of tens of lodges, each with its family, which could be extensive. In the center of each village was an open square for dancing and ceremonies. Many were surrounded by walls of stakes set in the ground, and these walls were guarded, so that no one could enter unchallenged. The fortifications were not nearly as formidable as the palisade around the city of the ancient Pyramid of the Sun, but were sufficient.

They spent the nights with families who had room for them. Each house was four-sided, longer than wide, made from impressively solid logs, with a roof that sloped up to a high ridge. In the center was a scooped-out fireplace with a large flat hearthstone used for baking bread or cakes made of corn. Possessions were stored on one side, and the people slept on the other side. The houses were amazingly large, up to six manlengths long, and some even had a second level for storage or for special meetings.

The beds were strange, too, for they were on platforms raised well above the floor, instead of close to the ground. It took Throat Shot a while to get used to it, but he discovered that there were fewer biting fleas at that level, because they could not jump that high, and he got to like it.

On occasion they stayed at a winter house, which was smaller and circular and made partly under the level of the ground, like those of the tribe across the river, the Faraway People, who called themselves the Children of the Sun.

They usually fed themselves between villages by killing birds or small animals. Black Bone preferred to employ a weapon with which the Principal People were more skilled than any others of this region, the blowgun. He showed Throat Shot how to use it. It was a tube longer than the height or reach of a man, fashioned of a type of cane that the Principal People knew how to find and cure and polish inside. It used a tiny wood dart, feathered with thistledown and dipped in a special poison only the priest knew how to make. At first Throat Shot found it hard to appreciate how such a delicate thing could be of use in hunting, but he learned that it was more effective in many cases than the bow and arrow. When Black Bone put in the dart, put his mouth to the end, aimed the blowgun, and blew hard, the dart flew out the other end so fast that it was difficult even to see it, and scored on its prey instantly. The dart did not really hurt the animal, but the poison soon brought it down, and then they could pick it up and kill it. Throat Shot resolved to obtain one of these hunting weapons for himself when he was able to, for it was something he could use one-handed, when he propped it appropriately.

Black Bone usually met the village Chief in the local council hall, which was a seven-sided building which could be of enormous size, depending on the village. Seven was the Principal People's sacred number, and it showed often in their ways of doing things or describing things. Sometimes a man would say "seven sevens," and it took Throat Shot a moment to realize that he meant a number close to five tens.

It seemed that the Principal People had a big ball game coming, the seventh of the season before winter shut things down, and Black Bone was alerting seven villages to the time and place. Five villages were not participating; only two were doing that. They were Gray Cloud's home village of Five Birches and the neighboring village of Shallow Stream. But their interest was high because this was also a betting event, and huge value might change hands as a result of individual wagers. At each village he introduced Throat Shot as a visitor, which meant that each village Chief would recognize him if he came again, and treat him well. This was a very nice gesture, for otherwise his bad arm could have caused a cold reception. Villages were not partial to extra mouths to feed in winter, if the visitor could not do a man's work.

Black Bone was a good runner. He was thin, as runners tended to be, and had endurance. He set an easy pace, which was just as well, because even though Throat Shot could run indefinitely on the level ground, he was not used to the constant slopes of these mountains, and had to acclimatize. Still, he did not slow the other man's pace very much, and of course he never objected to it. He knew he was making a good impression.

At each village he listened carefully, picking up the words. He had already learned many from Gray Cloud, but since Gray Cloud spoke this tongue imperfectly, there was much relearning to do; now it was mostly a matter of attuning to the dialect of the region. He did this quickly and well, and knew he was making a good impression in this, too. By the time they had completed the circuit of villages, he was able to speak well enough to be understood by any tribesman.

That was to his advantage, for now the other villagers were coming to the game site, and Black Bone had to help organize the teams and the attendant festivities. This was evidently to be a considerable occasion. Throat Shot was on his own.

But as it happened, many people now knew him from the tour of the villages, and some asked him for information about the arrangements. He answered as accurately as he could, and became more competent, because more people were constantly arriving and were in need of similar information.

Anetsa, he learned, was a ball game, called "the little brother of war." It was played only by young men of the greatest physical prowess, and a good player had much prestige. Black Bone had been a good player, and so he remained respected though he no longer played. Each village had its team, and the players on that team suffered rigorous training. They did not eat rabbit, because the rabbit was readily confused and frightened; its reaction to danger was to bound away and hide, its body quivering nervously. They did not eat frog meat, because the bones of the frog were easily broken. They did not eat the sluggish sucker fish, or the young of any animal, for the young were weak and prone to error. Neither did they eat hot food, for the fierce wolves and wildcats did not, nor flavor their food with salt, for truly strong creatures did not require anything to make their food more tasty. They did not touch a woman for a number of days before the game, because women were soft and weak. If a woman even touched a ball stick, it became unfit for use in the game; that softness was contagious. In fact, if a man's wife was with child, he could not play, because it was obvious that some of his strength had gone into the making of that child. It was said that there had been a time when men who broke these rules were put to death, but this seemed unlikely, since they would be punished enough by losing because of their weakness.

The rivalry between villages might be friendly, or it might become bitter. Sometimes players would consult priests, in an effort to weaken or even kill rival players. Thus it became rivalry between priests too, and this could be as important a factor as the skill and preparation of the players. It was Black Bone's suspicion that he had been taken captive, and almost sacrificed by the Mexica, because of a hostile spell put on him by the priest of a rival village. Gray Cloud had helped him overcome this, which was one reason his village welcomed Gray Cloud.

Throat Shot saw that he owed much to Gray Cloud, though he had not understood this until spending time with the Principal People. Gray Cloud had a bad knee, but he had had a friend who had given his freedom and probably his life to help two Principal People tribesmen escape horrible death, and he had seen them all the way home. He was also a good man and a good hunter in his own right, and therefore an asset to the tribe. The Principal People had not barred him from leaving them, but had hoped he would remain. When Throat Shot had come, they had brought him to Gray Cloud, seeing that the spirits wished this. But when Throat Shot had brought Gray Cloud back, in much the way Gray Cloud had brought White Bark and Black Bone back, Throat Shot had been met with similar favor. Of course, he was on trial until they could judge just what kind of man he was, but they were giving him the winter to establish his credits as a man.

Yet like Gray Cloud, Throat Shot was not in a position to commit. He was on a mission of his own, and could be called away by the Spirit of the Mound, Sun Eagle, at any time. He appreciated the Principal People's generosity to him, but he wanted to earn his own keep, and was searching for some way to do that. If he did not find it by spring, he would seek some other region, so as not to be a burden to this tribe. But he hoped that a way would manifest, because already he liked these people, and he liked Gray Cloud and Red Leaf and Black Bone.

He did not want to go among strangers again, where he would face similar problems.

Men continued to arrive. Some came by canoe—and one had a bad knee. Throat Shot knew him instantly: White Bark. Gray Cloud's instructor. The one who made the excellent light canoes, so was valued despite his bad knee.

But Throat Shot's bad arm made it doubtful that he could learn such a trade, for there was much armwork in the harvesting and preparation of the bark, and much skill in the crafting of a canoe. By the time he could become competent, even were his arm no problem, he would probably have to go, because of the signal of the Spirit. He needed to find something to do that required no long apprenticeship, and that would not leave another person without help if he abruptly left.

On the night before the big game, Five Birches staged a dance. Its location had been secret, to prevent magical sabotage by a rival village, and was announced only just before the start. If a rival knew the spot, its priest could spread a potion on the ground, made from rabbits, so that any players who danced there would become timid and readily confused. The players fasted from supper of the night before the game through the game itself, but that would go for nothing if they were polluted by the region of the dance.

Throat Shot hurried to notify the folk of the location. The other village had its own dance elsewhere, taking similar precautions. Actually, this was more show than substance, for the two villages were friendly. Still, the games with other villages were not necessarily friendly, so it behooved the players to honor the conventions. Indeed, the local priest had been trying hard to locate the site of the other village's dance, so as to do something to it, but without success.

The dance began after dark, so that those who weren't near one of the small fires could be recognized only by their voices. It was by the bank of a stream, where the ground was almost level under stately beech and maple trees and the underbrush had been cleared away. The folk of the village came: men, women, and children. The little ones were wrapped in blankets and laid under bushes to sleep. Others leaned against trees or sat on the ground, watching.

The dance itself was done by groups of men and women.
The men were the players of the game, who were with their
ball sticks and moved around a larger fire, wearing only their
breechcloths. The women were seven, specially selected, one
for each clan, near two upright posts that were connected by
a crosspiece.

The drumming started, and the figures began to move. The
men danced in a circle around their fire, while a performer
shook a rattle as he circled outside them.

The women formed into a straight line not far from the men.
They were in full dresses, with their hair garlanded with the
pretty colored leaves of fall, and individually and as a group
they were so lovely that it was a delight to watch them.

Now the women began to move and sing, advancing toward
the men provocatively. But before they got there, they wheeled
and danced away again. They re-formed their line and advanced again, keeping time to the drum, but again did not go
all the way. They were taunting the men, pretending to approach them but declining their favors, in accordance with the
pattern of the dance.

The men, in response, continued their dance, and called
upon the spirits to make them strong against such temptations,
and to enhance their prowess in the coming game. They asked
the spirits for swiftness and endurance as runners, and to be
made elusive and quick-witted. They waved their ball sticks
threateningly. Each stick was about as long as a man's arm,
fashioned from hickory or pecan wood, bent into a loop at the
end. The loop was laced with animal skin or strong vegetable
fiber, and might also incorporate bat whiskers or colorful bird
feathers, to make the sticks' motions as swift and accurate as
these flying creatures. The sticks were not clubs, but looked as
if they could be used as such.

The women sang of loss of strength and the onset of weakness and confusion. Their songs were directed at the opposing
players, because their weakness was as important as the home
team's strength. There was a large flat rock to one side of the
dance arena, on which were black beads representing the players of the other team. Every so often the women would get up
on this stone, close to those beads. In this manner they hoped
to weaken the other players by exposing them to the heaviness

and sluggishness of women. Throat Shot had to smile at this
gesture, for though he understood the symbolism, the women
were not at all as represented. They were light on their feet
and lively, and any man who got close to any of them would
have been inspired to rise to new heights of performance. Perhaps not in the game, however, which might be the point.

Actually, the women addressed two groups. When they sang
of the players of the home village, they called for victory. To
this they added another kind of inducement, promising that
tomorrow the players would get to sleep with their wives and
be well rewarded for their efforts. When they sang of the opposing players, they suggested that they had slept with their
wives too recently and weakened themselves, or that they had
touched pregnant women in public, or done other debilitating
things. They also sang of the opposing priest's probable incompetence, using the wrong magic and weakening his own team.
Some of the details were funny, and there was a rumble of
laughter from the watching people.

The male and female dancers were separate, never directly
interacting. But both danced to the same drumbeat, and they
did not interfere with each other's songs. Thus their dances
made a harmonious whole, showing both the opposition of the
two sexes and the nature of their larger interaction.

After a while the women were relieved by other women, for
endurance was not supposed to be their nature. But the same
men danced throughout the night, periodically shouting war
whoops in the direction of the rival village. At the end of each
interval of dancing the men ran toward the women, frightening
them, and the spectators would shout "Hu-u!" This was the
ritual greeting to the Great Sun.

The only other break for the men was when they paused to
go to the river, to purify themselves by splashing the cold water
on their bodies. They were indefatigable, as was proper for a
winning team.

In due course a man called the Woodpecker and garbed as
a bird left the dance and walked toward the rival village. He
stood facing it, raised his hand to his mouth, and made four
great yells. The players answered with choruses of yips. The
fourth yell was prolonged and quavering, like the cry of the
largest woodpecker who ever existed, resounding through

the night forest and echoing weirdly from the surrounding hills.

Throat Shot remembered his friend called Woodpecker, with whom he had gone on his first hunt. Now that man was called Striker of Warriors. Was it only a winter and a summer ago? How long it seemed!

The Woodpecker ran back to the dance ground. "They are already beaten!" he cried. It was a hope rather than a fact, but it carried such conviction that it was easy to believe.

The dance continued through the night. When dawn approached, the players took boughs from the sacred tree, the pine, and threw them on the fire. The flames blazed up hungrily, and thick clouds of smoke roiled out, enveloping the dancers. No men coughed or showed discomfort, though their eyes and lungs must have been stinging. This was the smoke that would protect them from the other village's head priest and make it difficult for the opposing players to see them during the game.

Sunrise came, and the dance was over. The players got no rest. They set out immediately for the assigned site of the game. The priests and priests' assistants went with them. Black Bone and Throat Shot went too, for it was their job to report on the progress of the game to the villagers who were unable to see it directly.

The route was circuitous, because the other village's priests might have planted magical traps to weaken them. The players were pure and strong, but could never be quite safe until they were there. As it was, they stopped four times for additional purification by water, in case they had inadvertently been fouled by hostile magic. Each time, the priest performed a rite for each individual player. Nothing was taken for granted.

Because of this necessary care, progress was slow. It was noon before they actually reached the game site. The players were forbidden to sit on a stone or log or anything other than the ground itself, if they sat at all, and were not allowed to lean against anything except the back of another player. They all knew what could happen to a player who violated these rules: he could be defeated in the game, or if he was lucky, only bitten by a rattlesnake. This was very much like war, and the rules of war were honored.

While the priest was administering rites to one player, the

others had to wait, but they did not rest. They twisted extra strings for their ball sticks, adjusted their clothing or their decorations, and talked about the coming contest. After the fourth water purification, the head priest gave an inspirational speech to the players. All the omens were favorable, he told them; they should play to their utmost ability, and their victory would be applauded by all who knew them and bring great honor to their village. It was a dramatic speech, and the players interrupted it several times with their exultant yells.

They came in sight of the playing ground. The Woodpecker advanced again and gave four whoops similar to those of the dance. The players answered with a shout and charged off the path to make their final preparations.

The priest marked off a small area of the forest floor: a symbolic representation of the playing ground. He took a small bundle of sharpened stakes, each about as long as a man's foot. As he stuck each stake in the ground, he told the players what positions they would assume when the game began. Each stake stood for a player, and the pattern was clear enough.

Then the players stood for the ordeal of scratching. This was done by one of the priest's assistants with a kanuga, a special comb made of seven sharp splinters of turkey-leg bone tied to a frame made from a turkey feather. The turkey was a fierce, warlike bird, so this sharp comb would impart these qualities to those whom it scratched. The splinters were tied so that only their tips projected from the body of the comb; the instrument was useless as a weapon, but capable of giving great pain.

Every player was scratched four times on each upper arm, the scratches covering about half the length between the shoulder and the elbow. Another four scratches were done on both forearms, and four more for each upper and lower leg. Each scratch was shallow but painful, and every set of seven was excruciating, but no player even winced. Then the kanuga comb was used to scratch the chest in the form of an X, which was then crossed from shoulder to shoulder, with a similar pattern across the back.

When it was done, the players had blood welling from an overlapping network of scratches all across their bodies. But they knew that this ordeal was necessary for the game, and they were glad to endure it. Now Throat Shot understood how

Black Bone had come by the scars on his body. This was like the Toco preparation for the rite of manhood, but much more extensive.

The priest gave each player a piece of medicinal root to chew. They spit the juice on the scratches and rubbed it in. It evidently helped, for the skin became less inflamed. Then they went to the river and washed off the blood. The ritual preparation was almost done.

Now they smeared their bodies with bear grease to make them slippery, so that opposing players could not get hold of them. They put eagle feathers in their hair for keenness of sight, and a deer's tail for swiftness in running, and a snake's rattle to make them terrible to their opponents. In this manner they invoked spiritual help from the air, the forest, and the ground. They marked their bodies with red and black paint, and the black was charcoal from the dance fire that had been made of the wood of a honey locust tree that had been struck by lightning but not killed. Everything had to be exactly right, to invoke the most powerful spirits.

Dressed and purified and ready, they went to the water one last time. The priest chose a bend in the river that enabled them to face east while looking upstream. The men stood side by side, gazing down into the water, with their ball sticks clasped across their breasts. The priest stood behind, while an assistant spread red and black pieces of cloth on the ground, with red and black beads set on them. There was one red bead for each player on the team, and one black bead for each opposing player.

The first player approached the priest. He was a tall young man no older than Throat Shot, with an intense expression. This was obviously no game for him; it was a spiritual mission.

"Tell me your name," the priest said formally. He obviously knew the names of all of them, but the ritual had to be followed exactly.

"I am Split Spear, of the Deer Clan," the man said.

The priest took a red bead in his right hand and a black bead in his left hand. He held them high and spoke to the river. "O Long Man, we exult in your power, which can toss great trunks about in white foam. We beg you to lend your strength to this fine young man, Split Spear, so that he will be able to toss his opponents about." The priest invoked the powers of birds and animals to enhance the player's abilities. He spoke of the seventh level of the world, which the player sought for ultimate success.

Then the priest addressed the player. "Split Spear, who is your most hated opponent?"

Split Spear whispered the name to him. The priest now spoke that name. "Fox Foot, of the Wolf Clan, I lay this curse on you! I invoke the Black Fog to smother you, and the Black Rattlesnake to poison you, and the Black Spider to drop down his black thread from above you to wrap up your soul and drag it to the darkening land in the west, and there to bury it in a black coffin under black clay so that you will be unable to prevail against the mighty Split Spear of the Deer Clan, and you will fall ignobly and be humiliated before everyone."

That was a curse such as only a favored priest could give! Split Spear looked well satisfied.

The priest performed similarly for each of the players, raising each to the seventh level of the world and damning the worst opponent of each in splendidly potent terms. At the end the players shouted once more, with the vigor of those who expected to forge to victory with all the power of the relentless current of a flooded river.

Now the players walked in single file to the ball ground. Their opponents came from the other side. The ground was completely surrounded by spectators from the two villages and from other villages, including those who were betting on the result, relatives, and many who were fascinated by the game, regardless of who was playing it.

The challenging team from the local village furnished the ball, but before it was used, the other team examined it carefully. They wanted to be sure that nothing was wrong with it. For example, it might be made so small that it would slip through the netting of their ball sticks, while the challenging team would be prepared with tighter netting. Or it might be the wrong color, so that it matched the sticks of the challengers and could not be seen, while it would show up clearly on the sticks of the other team. There were any number of tricks that might be associated with the ball. But this one passed inspection; if there was anything wrong with it, it was magical, and that was hard to detect by a physical inspection.

Already the betting was starting. Bettors could get so involved that they even removed their clothing to offer it as stakes. The players waited until the bets had been established, for each team wanted those who bet on it to be sure of their winnings.

Now the teams shouted as they lined up opposite each other, each player with his two ball sticks lying on the ground before him, pointing toward the sticks of his opposite number. In this way they made sure that the teams were evenly matched. The number of players might vary, but the teams always had to be even.

Throat Shot asked Black Bone about the names of the other team's players, so that he could get them straight. He learned that Split Spear's nemesis, Fox Foot, was the chief player, a short but broad and powerful young man who moved swiftly and silently, like a fox. Throat Shot did not like him, affected by the priest's curse on him.

An old man walked out, holding the ball. He made the final speech to the players. "Remember, the Sun is looking down on you. You must observe the rules and show good sportsmanship. After the game each of you must go along a white trail to your white lodge." What he meant was that the game should end in peace. Then he shouted, "Now for the twelve!" and threw the ball high into the air, and hurried out of the way. The game had begun.

The players dived for their sticks and then for the ball. Split Spear got it, perhaps because the priest's blessing on him and curse on his opposite number had been first and most potent. He scooped it up in his right ball stick and ran for his goal.

But two players from the other team converged on him. Fox Foot tripped him while the other knocked his stick, jarring the ball out. It bounced on the ground. Three more players dived for it, tripping one another. In a moment there was a pile of players of both teams—while the ball scooted out to the side.

The pile had formed near Split Spear, but he was not in it, because the ball had been knocked away from him. He now scrambled down and got it again, and this time was able to dodge around the pile and run for the goal. An opposing player pursued him, but one of his teammates stuck out a foot and tripped the pursuer, and Split Spear got away. He charged the goal and hurled the ball between the standing poles before another player could stop him.

There was a cheer from the local villagers. The home team had scored the first point! The first team to make twelve goals would be the winner.

The ball was brought back to the center, and play resumed. The game got rougher as players collided and sometimes wrestled with each other even after the ball was gone. Players were not supposed to try to injure those on the other team deliberately, but some of the accidents were suspicious. The ball traveled up and down the field, changing sticks often, before the next goal was scored. When one player found himself trapped, he would try to throw the ball to a teammate, who would then resume the advance on the goal. The sticks were well suited for throwing, being like extensions of the players' arms. The young men had evidently spent much time practicing; Throat Shot knew that he could not have handled such sticks well.

Meanwhile, in a secluded place, the team priests were taking ritual measures to bring their teams to victory. It was possible to tell when one priest was doing well, because the ball seemed unable to get out of the section of the field nearest that goal, giving that team the advantage. Each priest was kept informed of the progress of the game by an assistant—in this case, Black Bone—who was in turn advised by seven counselors who had been appointed to watch the game. Throat Shot went along with Black Bone, intrigued by the whole thing. This was a better celebration than the Toco had!

The game continued fiercely. The score changed sides almost as often as the ball did, seemingly. The players could not drink water during it, only a beverage concocted from wild crabapples, green grapes, and similarly sour ingredients. The injuries mounted. This had started as a friendly, or at least not a grudge, match, but it was becoming uglier. It was indeed like a small war.

As dusk approached, not a man was unscarred, and several were limping badly. The teams were almost evenly matched, and neither could get far ahead. But finally Split Spear emerged from a pileup to knock Fox Foot back, stagger to the goal, and put the twelfth ball through. The home village of Five Birches had won.

There was a great cheer from the winning villagers, and silence from the losers. The spectators and players settled their bets, and the players went once more to the river, where the priest protected them from the curses of their defeated rivals. They washed off the dirt and blood, tended to their injuries as well as they could without showing unmanly discomfort, and dressed. Now at last they were allowed to eat and drink, though exhaustion diminished their hunger.

On the following days Black Bone and Throat Shot went to the neighboring villages and told about the details of the game. The women and children who had not been able to attend were hungry for news of it, and when Throat Shot realized this, his descriptions, augmented by signs when he needed words he had not yet learned, became fancier. He had always had a good memory for detail, which had served him when he had been a messenger among the Toco, and the game was fresh in his mind. Soon he found himself the center of an avid circle of youngsters wherever he went, for news of his narrative powers was spreading.

"... and when the score was six goals to six, the men of Shallow Stream forged ahead with the ball, knocking all others out of the way as they charged the goal. Their priest had invoked one of his three most powerful spells, and it seemed that nothing could stand against it.

"But as Fox Foot was about to hurl the ball through the goal, his archenemy, Split Spear, leaped for him, and caught him about the waist, and threw him around so hard that he rolled to the edge of the field, his two sticks clattering. But the ball remained in the web of his right stick, held there by the spell.

"Then Split Spear called upon the foaming power of the great river to lend him strength, and the river answered, and he struggled with Fox Foot's arm and wrested the ball from him. He put it in the webbing of his own right stick, and scrambled to his feet, and charged toward his goal. But three players of Shallow Stream converged on him, crying that the true power of the water was theirs. One tackled him, another grabbed his arm, and the third took away the ball.

"But by this time the other players of Five Birches were there, and they caught the third man and bore him to the ground. The ball popped loose and rolled off the field and into the water. Now there was a pileup *in the water*, as they fought for the ball, and it was fortunate that no one drowned.

"It was Split Spear who came up with it again. This time he dodged behind one of his own players, so that the men of Shallow Stream could not get at him, and looped around until within range of the goal, and he hurled it through for the score just before being tackled again. The folk of Five Birches gave a mighty cheer!"

So it went. The more he embellished, the more closely the audience listened, and the larger it grew. He was careful never to deviate from the facts, and to remain impartial in the telling, for there were partisans of both villages in many of his audiences. But his memory was good, and there was much to tell.

"Do you know," Black Bone remarked, "you have a talent for tale-telling. This is something we value. Do you know stories of other tribes?"

"Many," Throat Shot agreed. "But—"

"Tell them."

Throat Shot tried it—and found his audience growing. The villagers liked to listen to him, despite his imperfect command of their tongue, because of the clarity of his vision and the novelty of the far episodes he related. To them, the Toco childhood stories were new and intriguing, and his adventures and misadventures with women were hilarious. He had to explain what palm trees were, but even that was interesting and even magical to these people who had seen none. He told only the truth, but it seemed that he had art in telling.

He tried telling a more general tale about the origin of tobacco, with similar success, especially among the children. They had already heard it, of course, but they liked the way he told it. So did some of the older people.

There was once a young warrior who was required to guide a maiden to another village for a special ceremony by her clan. She was pretty, but many men of her village had been killed in warfare, and she had found no husband. On the other hand, there were too many men in his village, and he had found no

wife. The farther they walked together, the more intrigued they
became with each other, for they had many interests in common
and knew some of the same people. She was a member of the
Bird Clan, which perhaps accounted for her birdlike prettiness,
and he belonged to the Twister Clan, also called the Longhair
Clan, which might have accounted for his ability to find his
way accurately to any place he sought no matter how long,
twisted, and devious the paths that went there. It occurred to
them that there had been no recent marriage between these
two great clans.

"But it is said that the members of these clans are not sexually
compatible," she remarked. "That the penises of the men of
one clan point in a different direction from the clefts of the
women of the other, so they cannot merge."

"I have heard this," he agreed. "But not everything that is
said is true."

"It is better to test a thing before challenging it as untrue."

"I agree. Let us find a suitable place to test it."

So they left the path and found a glade where nothing grew.
They laid down their cloaks and he removed his breechcloth
and she removed her skirt. "I do not think your penis is pointing the wrong way," she remarked. "It is aimed straight up at
the sky."

"Perhaps it is your cleft that points the wrong way."

"I am sure that is not the case."

So they lay on the cloaks and tested the alignments, and
there did not seem to be any problem. They then proceeded
to an episode of sexual expression so sweet that the honey
seemed sour.

"It is certainly false," she breathed as they embraced.

"It is an awful forked tongue," he agreed.

But to be quite certain, they decided to try it again after a
little while. He stroked her full round breasts, and she kissed
his muscular neck, and they merged again, and it was sweeter
than before.

"Whoever said that must never have tried it," he said. "The
alignment is as perfect as your great beauty."

There was something about his mode of expression that
pleased her. "Maybe he did not want anyone else to know,"

she suggested. "For I agree that the alignment is as wonderful as your strength and virility."

He was almost as impressed with her insight as he was with her body. "That must be it! All this time everyone has been fooled into believing what was not true!"

But it occurred to them that it would be best to test it once more, to be absolutely sure there was no mistake, for it was a serious matter to challenge the wisdom of the ages. So in a little while they indulged a third time, and she wrapped her firm legs around his hips, and he thrust so deeply into her that there was scarcely any room remaining for the honey. The alignment remained perfect.

"Oh!" she cried. "I wish we could do this forever!"

"We must marry," he decided. "Just in case we are the only two members of our clans who are compatible."

"Yes, we would not want to look foolish if it did not work for others," she said.

So they married, and the two clans were pleased to discover that the old saying was not true. The warrior and the maiden were held in high regard for this discovery, and became important in the tribe, and had many children, all of whom were in perfect alignment.

Later, on a hunting trip, the man passed the place where he had come to know his wife. There in the glade he found a pretty plant growing, with broad hairy leaves and three funnel-shaped flowers on the end of its tallest stalk. When he came close, he discovered that the leaves were scented. Because he had three fond memories of this place, and thought the flower might be imbued with the magic of the experience, he dug it up carefully and took it back to his people. "Surely this is the plant of harmony between clans," he said.

"We shall dry the sweet leaves and smoke them," the clansmen said.

"And we shall name it 'Where We Came Together,'" his wife said.

They did this, and when the dried leaves of the tobacco plant were smoked, the people felt at peace and contented. They knew it was because the plant had originated where the warrior and the woman had such harmony, and that everyone who smoked this plant would experience similar harmony.

For this reason, tobacco is always smoked at council meetings, and it has helped promote peace and friendship between the tribes. Wherever people come together from different backgrounds, there is tobacco to help them. This is why it is an honored tradition not only with the Principal People, but with all the other tribes.

"I think you have found your occupation," Black Bone said. "You will be the Tale Teller."

Surprised, Throat Shot agreed. So it was that the village of Five Birches had a minor ceremony and bestowed that new name on him. Henceforth he would go from village to village, and entertain and educate them with his stories, and the people would give him hospitality and gifts for the pleasure he brought them, and in this manner he would earn his keep.

As it turned out, he did more than that. As the Principal People learned that they could trust him with messages, they used him to send greetings or insults to acquaintances in other villages. He established a regular route, going to each village where invited, remaining for several days, then running to the next. The children turned out for his arrival, and there was always a lodge waiting for him, sometimes empty, sometimes with a family. They gave him gifts, and in time he received the one he most desired: a good blowgun. He practiced with it, in private, at first with unpoisoned darts, then with real ones, until he was able to bring down squirrels and rabbits at will. It was not good for larger game, but he was satisfied. Now he could bring his own game to the fire. He was to this extent a man again.

But one thing was missing. The Principal People were more open about the sport their maidens indulged in, and a woman could do exactly as she pleased. But maidens did keep a clear eye on prospects, and a young woman generally bestowed her favors freely only if she was considering a man for a serious association. Tale Teller had three marks against him in this respect: he was not of the Principal People, he had only one useful arm, and he could not commit himself to remaining here. At any time the spirits of the mounds might summon him away.

Occasionally a woman did come to him, as a matter of courtesy, but she made it plain that this constituted appreciation for the service he rendered the village, rather than any direct interest in him as a man. He accepted what was offered, but it distinctly lessened his pleasure in the experience. This was a far cry from what Beautiful Moon had given him, though she too had made no pretense of permanence.

Yet he could not fault the women. Their attitude made sense, and was consistent with their culture. Were he ready to join the Principal People tribe, and agree to remain here, he would be a better prospect. But that he could not do.

So he told his tales, and was at the same time the most popular and least popular visitor among them. He continued to learn the tongue and ways of the Principal People, never speaking of his private dissatisfaction.

In the beginning, water covered everything. Living creatures existed, but their home was up in the sky, above the rainbow, and it was crowded. "We need more room," the animals said. "We are tired of being all jammed together." So they sent Water Beetle to look around to see if he could find something better.

Water Beetle skimmed over the surface, but he could not find any solid footing, so he dived down to the bottom and brought up a little dab of soft mud. When it came to the surface it spread out in four directions and became a huge island. To prevent it from sinking, Someone Powerful took rawhide ropes and tied them to the four corners: north, east, south, and west. The ropes were anchored to the ceiling of the sky, which is made of hard rock crystal. If those ropes ever break, this world will come tumbling down, and sink under the water, and all living things on it will drown. Then it will be as it was before, as if the land never existed.

But the new land was soft, moist, and flat, which was not much good for living on. The animals were eager to live on it, so they kept sending down birds to see if the mud had dried and hardened enough to hold their weight. The birds reported that there was no spot they could perch on. But they did not fly across the whole of it, for the mud flat was quite large; indeed, it was hard to see from one side of it to the other.

"I will look into this," Grandfather Buzzard said. He was the biggest bird and the strongest flier of them all. He flew down quite close, and saw that the ground was still soft. But he continued to look, and when he passed what was to be the country of the Principal People, he glided low and found that the mud was getting harder.

But by this time even this great bird was getting tired, and he was too low. When he flapped his wings down, they touched the earth and dented it, making valleys. When he swept them up, they dragged earth with them and made mountains. He tried to gain elevation, flapping harder, but it only made the valleys and mountains deeper and higher.

The animals watching from above the rainbow saw this, and were worried. "If he keeps on, there will be only mountainous country!" So they called to Grandfather Buzzard to come back. He turned around, and managed to get far enough above the earth so that his wings no longer touched, and he returned to the rainbow. This is why there are so many mountains in the land of the Principal People, and not so many elsewhere.

At last the earth was dry enough and hard enough, and the animals came down to inhabit it. But it was dark, and they could not see well, because the Sun and Moon remained up beyond the rainbow. "Let's grab the Sun and bring her down too!" they exclaimed. Many tribes are too ignorant to know that the Sun is female and the Moon male; they get it backwards, and only the Principal People remember it correctly.

So they pulled down the Sun, and told her, "Here is a road for you!" Indeed, they had prepared a path, so that the Sun could travel all the way across the land, from east to west. The Sun was happy to do this, for she too preferred not to be crowded.

Now they had light, but it was too hot, because the Sun was too close to the earth. The crawfish had his back sticking out of a stream, and the Sun burned it red. His meat was spoiled, and the people would not eat it.

The people went to the priests. "The Sun is too close and hot!" they said. "You must put her higher!" So the priests pushed the Sun up as high as a man, but it remained too hot and parts of the earth were getting burned. They pushed her higher yet, but it was still too close. They kept trying, and stood upon each other's shoulders so as to push the Sun as high as they could. After the fourth time, they finally had her high enough, and the heat was just right. Everyone was satisfied, and the Sun remained at that level, and she is there today.

Someone Powerful first created plants and animals, and told them to stay awake for seven days and seven nights. But most of them couldn't manage it. Some fell asleep after one day, some after two, and others after three. Only the owl and the mountain lion remained awake after seven days and nights. So they were given the gift of seeing in the dark, and now they hunt in the night. Among the plants, only the cedar, pine, holly, and laurel were still awake at the end of the allotted time. To them was given the gift of not losing their foliage in the winter, and now they remain green all the time.

Then Someone Powerful made a man and his sister. The man thought there should be more than just the two of them, so he poked her with a fish and told her to give birth. After seven days she had a baby. Seven days later she had another. She kept having more every seven days. The human people were increasing so rapidly that Someone Powerful was concerned that they would soon squeeze all the other animals and the plants off the earth and ruin it for everyone. So he changed the woman, so that it would require more than a fish to make her have a baby, and she could have only one child a year. After that it was possible for the human people to live together in harmony with the animals and plants, and it was good.

The Principal People came to the mountains, and remain here, and this, too, is good.

CHAPTER 12

·⚬·

MAD QUEEN

O Spirit of the Mound, I have told you about the great ball game of the Principal People and how Throat Shot became Tale Teller and told the tales of the game and the tobacco and the origin of the land. Now I will tell you how the child Tzec fared, for later I was to meet her again and learn her story of the Castile Woman and the Mad Queen of the strange, distant Tribe of Castile.

Tzec was sad when Throat Shot left, for he was the man she intended to marry. By the time he returned, she would be old enough. The spirit of the little mound at the Wide Water had told her that. But he had to marry elsewhere first: the Spirit had told her that too. She was fiercely jealous of his first wife, but she intended to make him forget her when he returned.

Meanwhile, she had what turned out to be a good life here with the Trader. His sister, Three Scales, was a forbidding but good woman who asked only that men and children stay out of her way. Tzec found herself in league with the Trader to do that, avoiding the woman's cutting tongue. It was evident that the unmarried state made women sour. But the lodge was well kept, the food was good, and the tongue was the only weapon the woman used.

The Trader was held in respect among the Ais, and so was his family. Tzec was allowed to associate with others her age, and she soon enough picked up their tongue. She learned the things of the Ais, and they were like the things of the Calusa and Toco, but different in detail. It didn't matter to her, as she

regarded herself as a civilized Maya on an extended visit to the
primitive world. If she ever had the chance to return, and if
she could be sure her father the Trader would not suffer by her
absence— But her thought always ended there, because she
did not want to leave the Trader. Also, she had to be here when
Throat Shot returned, so she could marry him.

In the spring it was time to make the trading circuit. The
Trader gathered his wares, some of which he had gotten from
other traders who came from the north or the south, and she
helped him haul them to his canoe on the inland river. This
was the hardest part of it, because the loads were heavy, but
she was resolved to show that a daughter could be as strong
as a son, and she carried her share. What a relief it was to get
into the canoe!

She took the front seat and plied her paddle vigorously. She
had practiced this over the winter, knowing that what the
Trader needed most was a strong supplementary paddle. He
had paddled himself before, but as his age advanced, his muscles tired, and a canoe was much easier to handle with two.
That was why he had been willing to pick up Throat Shot, in
part, and Throat Shot, though one-armed, had done a good
job. Tzec was an apt learner, and she intended to do as good
a job.

They moved up through the lakes, and into a stream, northwest. At times the water seemed about to expire in a mudhole,
but they pushed on through. In one place it became no more
than a muddy channel the Trader must have made by hauling
his canoe along it in past years. Had there not been a good rain
recently, they would have had to portage here. But that was
not an accident; the Trader had been alert for the weather, and
had been glad when it rained. Now she understood why.

But soon enough they had to portage anyway, in a fashion.
They did not unload and carry the canoe; they got out and
hauled it with ropes, loaded, so at least they did not have to
carry the stuff on their backs. The ground was mucky, and
there were snakes; she wished fearless Throat Shot were here
to banish her fear, as he had before. There really was something
magical about him; he associated with the spirits, and it
showed, especially when there were bad snakes around.

Both Tzec and the Trader were covered with sweat and grime

by the time they reached a north-flowing river that he said
would hold. But they would have to wash before they reached
the first village along it, he said. She didn't know why, but
knew he knew best. So they took turns watching for snakes
and alligators as the other washed both body and clothes. In
due course they were wet but clean.

"You are young and small," the Trader remarked. "But you
are nearly a woman. One more winter, I think."

She thought so too. Her smallness came from her mother; it
did not mean she was not maturing. She wanted to achieve
her maturity so as to be ready in case Throat Shot returned
early.

They dried in the sun, then resumed paddling. It was still
slow, as the water was shallow, but they did not have to get
out of the canoe.

They reached the village. The people shook their heads as
they signed greetings, recognizing the Trader. Where was his
river through the swamp? they wanted to know. They could
not pass it without getting all muddy, yet he and his child had
evidently never left their canoe.

It was a trade secret, the Trader signed good-naturedly. Now
Tzec understood why they had had to wash: it was to mystify
the villagers and give themselves an advantage. It was easier
to strike an advantageous bargain with people who did not
understand your ways well enough.

They were provided a small lodge, so that Tzec was jammed
right next to the Trader and the woman who came to him,
honey-laden. It was dark, but Tzec took advantage of the proximity to study in detail exactly what went on. She wanted no
mistakes when it was her turn to entertain some young man.
She had never been able to see quite enough when Throat Shot
did it, and in any event he was new at it, and was limited by
his bad arm. The Trader was thoroughly experienced, as was
this woman, and they made a fair game of it, teasing each other
before concluding it with abandon.

So it went, from village to village, trading goods and news
at each. Tzec helped by modeling the fine feather cloaks so that
every feather showed off to full advantage. Because she was
small, they looked larger on her, and even more valuable. The
Trader was pleased; he was doing well. "It was a good day

when the spirits brought me a daughter," he murmured in Ais, and it was all she could do to mask her pleasure, lest the villagers think she was laughing at them.

In due course they came to the village where Throat Shot had lived, Toco Atafi. She inspected it carefully, for one day she hoped to live here with him. The villagers were surprised to see the Trader with a daughter, when they had not known he had one; they assumed she had been too young to travel before.

Then they reached the village where she had lived among the Toco for a winter, pretending to be mute rather than speak their barbaric tongue. Her attitude on that had changed when Throat Shot came! He had been the first to respect her as a person, and to make a genuine effort to communicate with her. She had been wary, distrusting any friendly overture, but soon knew that despite his bad arm he was a good man, with a fine and ready mind. His arm would distract most women, who saw things only superficially, but Tzec had already had enough experience to know how to look deeper. She had wanted this man to buy her, but he lacked the wealth. Then, as they traveled together, she had come to understand her real desire, and that was to marry him. When she was ready. It had all started here in the village of Ibi Hica, one year ago.

Here they recognized her. "You have not sold your slave?" the Chief inquired of the Trader. He used signs, not realizing that Tzec had learned enough of the Toco tongue to translate. She elected not to clarify that, and the Trader kept a similar silence. They both knew why: there was advantage to be gained when the other party did not know you could understand his private consultations.

"She is my daughter," the Trader signed in return.

The Chief and the others were amazed. Why should a man waste a good prospect for trade by adopting a slave? For they knew that if the Trader had a secret hankering for the sexual use of children, he would have indulged it without adoption. Such use of his daughter would be shameful. The adoption had to be genuine.

The Trader let them ponder for a moment, then added in signs: "She saved my life."

Their amazement faded. So it was gratitude! Traders were

not known for that sentiment, but it was possible.

They proceeded to the trading, and Tzec modeled the feather cloaks of the type that had constituted her purchase price before. The women gazed at her, and saw how lovely she became in the feathers, and believed that the cloaks were responsible, and their desire for these items increased. The men saw the same, and it occurred to them how much better any man or woman would look in one of these, and how much status such a possession would confer.

The bargaining became brisk.

After it was done, Tzec knew she had earned back her purchase price by her enhancement of the cloaks, because the villagers had paid more for them than they would have. She had also murmured to the Trader when anything was said that he should be aware of, helping him keep track. The Trader had made a good bargain when he adopted her, and that pleased her, for she preferred to be truly beholden to no one.

She was invited to share the night with the children she had known. She glanced at the Trader. "Do it," he murmured in Ais. "It will give me more room with my woman."

She smiled. It was the first indication he had given that her presence bothered him, and she knew it was false. He liked to have her near him, even when he clasped a woman. He knew her, and he trusted her, and it was a bond between them that had strengthened over the year. But he wanted to give her some freedom. She was truly his daughter.

So she joined her erstwhile companions, who were eager to know where she had been and what she had done. She surprised them by speaking Toco; now that the trading was done, it didn't matter. Her vocabulary was not large in this tongue, because she had not been long enough with Throat Shot to learn it all, but she had the basic terms. Also, she had picked up some on her own while here, making it easier.

She told them of her canoe journey down the river and out to the sea, and of the Calusa people with their island village and odd double canoes, and of the great Wide Water that was not the sea but the biggest lake anyone could imagine. She told them of the mounds she had visited with Throat Shot, and how he talked with the dead. She did not mention her own experience in that regard, not being quite sure of it. Finally, she told how Throat Shot had helped her have the courage to handle a bad snake so it did not bite the Trader, and how the Trader had then adopted her as his daughter.

They were awed, but they believed. They all remembered how the one-armed man had picked up the rattlesnake without being bitten. "He has no fear!" they said in wonder.

"He has no fear," she agreed. That was perhaps the thing that had truly quickened her interest in Throat Shot. She had liked him from the start, but the sight of him with that dire snake had affected her profoundly. Many claimed to have had experience with the spirits, but he had proved it, because the Spirit had truly taken his fear. Surely there was no other man like that in all the world of the living.

She enjoyed her visit much more than she had liked her stay here before. She was now not a possession waiting to be traded, but the Trader's daughter, and that made all the difference. She had the respect accorded a person with a family.

They continued on the trading route, exchanging wares for others more valuable where they were going. Tzec loved it. She was caught up in the spirit of striking bargains, of outwitting opposite numbers so as to come out ahead despite seeming not to. It was as if the Trader's spirit had entered her and made her similar, as if she had always been his daughter.

The Cacique of the Calusa was as hospitable as before. He, too, recognized Tzec. "So you adopted him as your father?" he inquired, smiling. His eyes narrowed appraisingly. "Next year you will come to me with the honey, eh?"

Tzec, astonished, was unable to respond. It had never occurred to her that so prominent a chief could desire so insignificant a child.

The Trader laughed, covering her confusion. "My daughter is innocent in the ways of men. She has no notion that she is beautiful."

"She will learn," the Cacique said, joining the laugh.

Actually, Tzec did expect to be beautiful, because her mother had been. But the Cacique had access to the loveliest grown women of his tribe, which was a different matter.

They proceeded to the trading, and Tzec assisted, and it was good. But her mind remained on the Cacique's remark. She well understood it; what had surprised her was that he should bother to make it, for he knew her origin. She was too small, and she had no true culture other than that of her mother, and her mother was dead. Probably it was just his way of complimenting her, in order to please the Trader and perhaps gain an advantage in bargaining.

That night Heron Feather, the Cacique's beautiful young wife, came to the Trader. Tzec remembered her well; she had initiated Throat Shot into the mysteries of sex. Tzec had learned a tantalizing amount, being unable to see the detail. This time she watched even more carefully, studying what it was that made a man react most directly. She saw that it was not just the woman's good body, but the way she moved it, accentuating the parts of it that drew a man's eye. There was art to this, and it had to be done just right, or the effect was weakened or lost.

And when the Trader was done with her, Heron Feather was not done with him. She continued to stroke him and speak to him, whispering what a fine man he was and how happy he had made her, though she had been the one working to make him happy. She made it seem as if she had never before encountered as skillful a lover as he. The Trader was not for a moment deceived, yet he evidently enjoyed hearing it. That was another lesson: the man was willingly deceived.

They slept, and Tzec slept too. In the morning Heron Feather teased him awake and into action again, twining around him like a serpent, forcing him to respond while making it seem that it was his initiative. It was as if she were doing a dance, with every aspect just right. "You wear me out with your power!" she breathed without the slightest indication of humor.

When they were back in the canoe and alone on the river that traveled inland, the Trader spoke. "You noted what we did, as you did last year?"

"Only twice, for you," Tzec replied.

"Twice is enough, for an old man. Heron Feather is the best I have encountered. If you learn from her, you will learn well."

"The Cacique," she asked hesitantly. "Did he really mean . . . ?"

"He has an eye for beauty, and you will be beautiful," the Trader said seriously. "He was complimenting you, but it was not empty. He thought to make you react as you did, most fetchingly."

"But the honey—"

"You will still be young, next year, but I think not too young. It would be a great compliment to him if you asked him to teach you the way of honey, that you might learn first from the best."

"Is he the best?"

"Of course not! But you must never let a man know that. Did not you see how Heron Feather flattered me?"

"You liked it, though you knew she pretended."

"That is the folly of men. Do that with the Cacique, and he will be generous, though you will fool him no more than Heron Feather fooled me."

And future trading would be good. She saw the rationale. Yet she doubted. "What if I am not good with him?"

"A girl need not be good her first time. A man values it anyway, for there can never be another first time. The Cacique especially, for he counts the number of firsts to his credit."

"But suppose he wanted to keep me? I do not want to leave you, my father."

"He has no need to keep any who do not wish to stay, for there are many who do wish to stay. I will, if you wish, make clear that I cannot do without your help on my rounds."

She considered that, and it seemed good. Here would be an excellent way to learn, without commitment. The fact that it might also improve the Trader's reception by the powerful Calusa made it that much better.

The Trader mistook her silence. "I do not urge this course on you, my daughter. Only if you are ready, and wish it. This matter must always be the woman's choice, until she marries. I merely advise you what is good."

"It seems good to me, my father," she said. And it did.

They completed the circuit, having made an excellent season of it. Tzec had helped the trading, and even the Trader's sour sister, Three Scales, was hard put to it to conceal her pleasure at this success.

During the winter Tzec's body began its development, and so at ten and one winters she was nubile, though her breasts were as yet small. She asked Three Scales about honey, and the woman, acting in the capacity of mother, got a pouch of it from the priest. "Use it sparingly," Three Scales warned. "This much at a time, no more, lest it be wasted." She demonstrated by dipping a fingerful. "Every spring, get new; it does not keep longer than a summer and winter. Do not use it when you see no need; the men smell it." So it was that Tzec's sexual education was completed; she was now ready to be a woman, when she chose.

On the Trader's next circuit, Tzec did as he had suggested. When she saw the Cacique, she knelt and lifted her hands in the prescribed manner. When he touched her hands, she murmured with unfeigned hesitancy, "Illustrious one, you spoke of honey last year. I have saved my first honey for you because I wish to learn from the best. Will you teach me?"

The Cacique had evidently forgotten his remark of the prior year, but now he looked closely at her, becoming interested. He glanced at the Trader. "Your daughter—"

"I must have her help on my rounds," the Trader signed, approximately. "I am getting older, and she makes it easier. But I can spare her for one night."

The Cacique turned to Heron Feather. Without a word, the woman took Tzec by the arm and guided her to the women's chambers. There they ate, and after that Heron Feather took her to a special room to get ready. "You must be in a better outfit," she said, and brought out a fine, almost translucent cloak. "We will keep your moss skirt for you." She made Tzec stand naked, and washed her body with a sponge. "He will like you; you are young but pretty."

"But what do I say? What do I do?" Tzec asked, worried. "I have seen it many times, but never done it, and I fear—"

"Say yes, always, unless he asks whether you are uncomfortable. Do whatever he says. Do not sleep until he sleeps, and wake when he wakes. If you bleed, apologize. He will treat you well, for he likes you."

"I am frightened," Tzec confessed.

"So was I, the first time," Heron Feather said. "He expects it. He will try to be gentle. He is very pleased that you came to him, and his pleasure is a good thing."

"So my father said."

"And ever after, until you marry, you must say that the Cacique was best."

Tzec nodded tensely. She understood the protocol.

As evening came, Heron Feather saw to her application of honey and brought her to the Cacique's chamber. "May the spirits be kind to you," she murmured.

Tzec stepped inside. The Cacique was waiting for her. He had an elevated bed that looked very soft. "Come to me, lovely little woman," he said.

After that her memory fuzzed. She remembered the feel of his hands on her small breasts, and of his mouth on her mouth, and of his great hard penis deep inside her body, but the rest was vague, except that she had been tense at the start and was less so at the end. She hoped he had had good pleasure with her body, but she had had none with his.

"Have you enjoyed it, little woman?" he inquired.

"Yes, illustrious one," she replied.

"It is not true, but I thank you. I think you are just a little too young, but you will not be too young for the next man. I will make you glad you came to me."

She was afraid he was going to do it again, but instead he slept. Relieved, she let herself join him.

He stirred several times during the night, and each time she woke, tense again, ready to do what he asked, but he did not ask. When morning came he smiled at her. "You did not cut out my heart, little woman."

Tzec's mouth dropped open. "Oh illustrious one, I never—"

He laughed, and kissed her on the forehead. "Go to the women's room, and then to your father. You have done well."

Somewhat tired and somewhat sore, she donned her cloak and went. Heron Feather wasn't there, but another woman was and she knew what to do. "You have pleased the Cacique, and he will please you," the woman said as she cleaned Tzec up and put her regular skirt on her. "Now eat, and I will take you to your father."

Tzec was hardly hungry, but she did take some fruit. Then Heron Feather returned, looking as if she had had a far better night's sleep than Tzec. "He is pleased," she said.

Everyone seemed to know that, but Tzec wasn't sure. She

knew she had not performed at all the way she should have; she had been tense no matter how hard she had tried to prevent it, and the Cacique had known. She had seen Heron Feather in action, and knew that the Cacique would have been much, much better off with her.

Then at last she was taken out to rejoin the Trader. Only now could she truly relax. He saw her and smiled. "You pleased him," he said in Ais.

As they went to their canoe, they paused, for it was different. There was a pile of beautiful shells in it, any one of which was an excellent trading item. Their trading venture had abruptly become much better than before.

Now at last Tzec understood just what the Cacique's pleasure was worth.

When they were well away from the Calusa island and paddling up the river, they talked about it. "My daughter, I know the first time is hard," the Trader said. "I see you are tired. We will find a place to camp, and you can rest for a day."

"No, I can paddle!" she protested. But his offer had opened the subject, and she continued. "I know I did not do well. Why was he so pleased?"

"He did not hurt you?"

"He did only what a man does, but I was so tense I am ashamed. He treated me well, but I was afraid."

"My daughter, that is the difference between the first time and the other times. No matter how often she has seen it done, and how well she is prepared, a girl cannot do it well at first. At best she is tense, and at worst she hurts and bleeds. He expected that. I have done it with first-time girls, and I know."

"Then why did he want me? Heron Feather would have been so much better!"

"Three reasons. First, because you are beautiful."

She paused in her paddling, turning around to face him. "It is true, my father?" Somehow she always needed to be reassured on this, though she knew she was being foolish.

"It is true. You are small, and your breasts are slight and your hips narrow, but that is because you are young. Next year you will attract the eye of every man who encounters you. But already your face is one to make men dream. I know that when the Cacique's wives cleaned you and garbed you in fine clothing, you were lovelier than any of them."

"Not Heron Feather!" she protested.

"Heron Feather has a body like none other, and her face is pretty," he agreed. "But she is two tens and two or three winters old, and so has lost the perfection of youth. You are prettier than she now."

She suspected he was flattering her to make her forget her ignominy of the night. He was succeeding. "What are the other reasons he wanted me?"

"Because it *was* the first time for you. It is special mettle for a man to be the first to do it with a woman. There is only one first time, so it is important. When you came to him and asked him to be your first, it magnified him in the eyes of all his people."

"But he must have had many firsts!"

"Certainly—and he values each one. It shows that he retains his appeal and his prowess. You are not his subject; you did not have to seek him. You flattered him in the best way he could be flattered. Others will speak of this for a long time: how the girl from afar sought him because he is the best."

"But how could he be sure that it *was* my first? I mean—"

"He is experienced. He knows. There are things a woman cannot pretend. What you thought made you poor actually confirmed your inexperience. That pleased him."

It made sense now. The Cacique had not wanted mere sex, he had wanted to be the first—and she had given him that. "What is the third reason?"

"It is who you are."

"Your daughter!" she said immediately, pleased.

He smiled. "That, in part. But more, it is that you are your mother's daughter. Your mother had a certain notoriety."

"She was a Maya!"

"She cut out the heart of any man who took her by force."

Suddenly the Cacique's remark of the morning fell into place. "He said I did not cut out his heart! But I never intended—"

"He knew that. But the notion added spice. Others will say he is a special man, because the daughter of the Maya did not cut out his heart, after he possessed her and slept in her presence. No other Chief can make that claim."

Tzec shook her head. "And you have a fine collection of shells! I am glad I chose him to be my first."

"He knew you would be. He is a fair man, and you gave him much. Those shells are yours."

"Oh, no, my father, they are yours!" she protested. "You are the Trader."

"They are yours," he repeated firmly. "When you marry, your husband will be wealthy."

"I thank you, my father," she said, near tears in gratitude.

"You have given me more than shells," he said.

"You have given me more than anything," she responded.

They continued paddling, and her body remained tired and sore, but her heart was high.

When they returned to the Ais village, and Tzec's time was free, she considered the matter, and then went to the lodge of a young man she knew had not much experience. His face was scarred from a childhood accident, and because the scar had not been acquired in battle, it shamed him rather than being handsome. Thus he was called Scar Nose. The girls were fickle, and avoided him. Tzec went to him because she knew he would be grateful.

He was unbelieving. "You—the most beautiful girl of the village?" he asked. "Do you come to tease me?"

"I come to you only this night," she said. "But it is not to tease you. I know you are a better man than others think." She kissed him, knowing that he smelled her honey and was aroused by it.

He found that easy to accept, in the fashion of men. He was relatively clumsy in the sexual act, and she had to help him, and it was not any genuine pleasure for her. But she complimented him on his performance, and indeed she was pleased that she had done this. She had proved that she could handle it, and that she was competent even when the man was not. She also knew that she had enhanced Scar Nose's status in the village, especially among the men. That gave her a feeling of power.

She did not go often to young men's lodges, but did it enough to gain the experience she needed. Now she felt competent to make a man happy, when she chose.

The third trading circuit went well. Tzec was conscious of the eyes of young men on her at each village, and sometimes she chose to go with one of them for the night, especially when this enhanced the prospects of trade. When they reached the Calusa island, she sought the Cacique, and this time she gave him much more pleasure of the body and less of reputation, for she was obviously experienced. "I have had men," she told him, "but none to match you, my first."

"I have had women," he replied. "But none to match you, my loveliest."

"Really?" she asked, thrilled, forgetting herself.

He laughed. "My tongue can be as forked as yours! Never question a compliment."

She knew then that she was not fooling him at all. But as long as she said the same thing to others, insisting that the Cacique was the best—and she was careful to do so—he would never object.

"As it happens, what I said was true," she said. She did not add that he was the only truly experienced man she had been with.

"What I said was true also," he said. He did not add that she was his youngest, and therefore freshest, woman, making her the most attractive regardless of her body.

They slept, understanding each other well enough. In the morning he indulged with her again, languorously, stroking her with exquisite feeling, and she knew she truly appealed to him. For the first time she felt the deeper pleasure of the act, and cried out in rapture during the embrace, surprised at its power.

"You have been the first, again, illustrious one," she breathed, amazed.

That surprised him. "No man ever took time with you?"

"They were young." That said it all.

"When you marry, lovely Maya, you must teach your husband."

"Men can be taught?" she asked, surprised in her turn.

"Carefully," he said. "Have you not observed Heron Feather? She teaches without seeming to."

She nodded, understanding another aspect.

This time he gave her a lovely shining bead, to wear on a string around her neck. She loved it.

"The man you marry will be lucky," Heron Feather told her later. "No one has pleased the Cacique twice in the way you have. That is his finest bead." She had a number of beads about her own neck.

"He pleased me twice," Tzec said. "I did not know how it could be."

"And you did not know enough to pretend," Heron Feather said. "No wonder you pleased him!"

"You pretend about that too?" But of course it was true. No woman could have as much pleasure of a man as Heron Feather seemed to. Tzec resolved to be the same.

The fourth summer, when Tzec was ten and three winters old, the trading was good but the Trader's sister, Three Scales, was not. She became more bitter, and moved more slowly. The Trader hesitated to leave her, but she told him to get gone so she would have less to do.

When they returned at the end of the circuit, they learned that Three Scales was dead. A bad spirit had taken her, despite all that the priest could do.

The Trader was appalled. "I should not have left!" he exclaimed. "I did not need to go; my trading has been good, and I could have missed this summer."

Tzec consoled him. "If the priest could not fight the evil spirit, my father, how could you? You are a trader, not a priest. Three Scales wanted you to go because she knew you could not help her."

"Who will take care of my lodge?" he asked, looking around at it.

"I will, my father." She knew well enough the nature of woman's work, though it did not appeal to her. She much preferred being out on the circuit, bargaining with villagers and spending the night with those men she chose. But now it had to be done.

She did it, and the Trader recovered from his grief. Tzec was glad to support him in this way, but she wished Three Scales had not died. She felt old before her time.

* * *

In the spring they closed up the lodge, and she went with the Trader as usual. It was a great relief.

This time there was something new at the Calusa island. "There was a great canoe, larger than any we have seen," the Cacique told them, for he regarded them both as old friends now. "It wrecked in a storm, and fell apart, but we went out and found many wonderful beads and a woman."

"No men?" the Trader asked.

"We killed them, of course. They tried to stop us from taking the beads. But the woman did not fight; she just wept. I thought to marry her, but she is too old and she does not speak our tongue, so I will trade her to you."

The Trader's expression did not change, but Tzec knew he had no desire to take a strange old woman. He could hardly refuse the Cacique, however.

Tzec, on the other hand, was quite interested. Her mother had been such a woman, to these people. Could this be another Maya?

That was not the case. The woman was pale-skinned and wore strange clothing. She did not speak, but responded to the Cacique's brief peremptory utterances. She seemed to understand the gestures better than the words. Tzec felt sympathy; she had been like that, as a child among the Toco.

"May I talk to her?" she asked.

"For you, anything," the Cacique said expansively. This was one of the advantages of being on his good side.

Tzec took the woman to a separate chamber. She spoke to her in Calusan, but the woman understood only the simplest bwords, such as "come," "stand," and "be quiet." She addressed her with signs, but the woman looked blank except for the most obvious, such as pointing a direction.

Tzec remembered how Throat Shot had worked with her, showing human sympathy as well as an alert mind. She tried to do the same, for there was something she wanted to know that she did not care to speak.

She closed her right hand and tapped her chest with her thumb, then spoke: "Tzec." Then she pointed to the woman.

The woman made the same gesture, indicating herself. "Doña Margarita."

"Doña Margarita," Tzec repeated, smiling, matching the odd inflections.

The woman returned the smile. It was probably the first time anyone had shown direct personal interest in her. Tzec remembered the feeling.

But the barrier of tongues was too great for anything else. She could not ask the woman where she was from or whether she wished to be traded. She doubted the woman even understood the concept. She was a captive from a strange canoe, helpless amidst those she could not talk with. Just as the Lady Zox, her mother, had been. This woman was the age of her mother.

Tzec decided. She embraced Doña Margarita and kissed her on the cheek. The woman was surprised, but evidently appreciated this gesture, for she hugged Tzec back.

"Come," Tzec said, gesturing. She led the woman back to the main chamber.

The trading was about to begin. Tzec brought the woman to the Trader. "I want to buy her," she told him in Ais.

The Cacique did not understand the tongue, but he knew what she was saying. "It was a joke, lovely little woman! She is not worth trading for. She is of no use. She can't cook or dance, and she's too old to give a man pleasure. I will not make you take her."

Tzec turned to him. "Illustrious one, I want her."

"I give her to you, then!" he exclaimed, making a grand gesture. "I will be glad to be rid of her. All she does is weep and sleep."

The Trader was as perplexed as the Cacique, but did not challenge his daughter in public. He merely nodded, agreeing, and then proceeded to the trading.

When the bargaining was done and goods had changed hands, they settled down to dinner. Tzec brought Doña Margarita with her to the women's section.

"What are you up to, Tzec?" Heron Feather asked.

"We have taken this woman in trade. Will you make her beautiful?"

Heron Feather shook her head. "We have tried, but she will not have it."

Tzec considered. "Make us both beautiful." She stood beside Doña Margarita and spread her arms.

Heron Feather approached Tzec and removed her clothing, so that she stood naked. Then she approached the strange woman. Doña Margarita drew away, not wanting to be touched. Tzec reached out and caught her hand. She tapped herself between the breasts, then pointed to the woman.

Doña Margarita hesitated, then sighed. She spread her arms in the signal of nonresistance. Heron Feather removed her torn and dirty clothes.

After that the Cacique's wives sponged the two of them off, marveling at the paleness of Doña Margarita's skin. The woman's body was not broken down; the clothes had made it seem worse than it was.

The wives put light cloaks on the two. Then they worked on their hair, brushing it out and setting shell combs in it. Doña Margarita's hair, when unbound and unknotted and untangled, was as long and fine as that of any ordinary woman. They set necklaces of beads about each neck.

Finally the wives led the two to a clear pool so they could gaze at their second souls, their reflections. Both of them were beautiful in their ways, Tzec a radiant girl, Doña Margarita a stately woman.

The woman turned to the girl, surprised. Tzec smiled. "We are like mother and daughter," she said, making the signs for Woman and Girl, her hand indicating the different heights.

Then they ate, and then Tzec led Doña Margarita out to meet the Trader and the Cacique.

Both were amazed. Tzec let them look for a moment, then led the woman away again. She had made her point: she could work with this woman.

But now they had to separate. "Stay," Tzec said, using a word the woman understood. "I will return in the morning." She made the sign for Sleep, her two hands posed as if about to cradle her reclining head.

Heron Feather guided the woman to the sleeping chamber, while Tzec went to the Cacique's room. She no longer had to express her intent; everyone knew she would be with him when she came here.

When he saw her, the Cacique shook his head. "You surprise me anew," he said. "What will you do with that woman?"

"Adopt her, perhaps," Tzec replied. "I have been without a mother too long."

"Marry me, and I will let you keep her in style."

That brought Tzec up short. He had spoken lightly, but it was not the type of thing he joked about. She knew better than to refuse him directly. "Oh illustrious one, I could never live here! I must take care of my father."

"Yes, you must," he said with regret. He liked her too well to cross her, though he knew she would not try to cut out his heart.

"But for this night only, let me believe I am your wife," she said, making it seem as if he had refused her, instead of she him.

"Truly, you are worthy," he said, and embraced her with a passion that was more than sexual. They had been together only one night each year, but they were now close friends.

Doña Margarita rode in the center of the canoe, with the shells. She was back in her original clothing, as Tzec was in hers, but the Cacique had given them the cloaks and beads they had worn together. Tzec worked with her as she paddled, pointing to things and speaking their Ais names, and Doña Margarita repeated those names. In this manner they made rapid progress, for the woman was now interested in learning.

"What are you doing, daughter?" the Trader asked when they camped for the night. "You are teaching her Ais!"

Tzec tried to avoid answering, but he knew her too well, and she had to tell the truth. "We need a woman for our lodge."

He nodded. "You do not like woman's work."

"I like to be with you, my father. But the lodge cannot travel with us in the summer."

"The Cacique said she could not do woman's work."

"I think she does not know how. If we teach her—"

He shrugged. "I leave it to you, my daughter."

When they stopped at the edge of the Wide Water, and the Trader was joined by Speckled Turtle, who was now married but free to be with this special man, Doña Margarita recoiled. Tzec took her aside and explained, using the few words they now shared. "My father—man—with woman. Our way." Then she spread a blanket for them both, and ignored the Trader. Doña Margarita could only do the same.

By the time they reached their home village, Doña Margarita had a fair notion of how things were. She was willing to learn woman's work, and shared the chores with Tzec.

While they did this, they talked. The limited vocabulary broadened, and the signs diminished. Doña Margarita adopted the Ais costume and manner and became more like a normal person. As winter came, they got beyond the routine of gathering and cooking and working with material for clothing and blankets, and Tzec learned in detail where the woman had come from and what her tribe was like. Indeed, it was not the Maya, but it was as strange and intricate in its fashion. Many of the terms it required did not make sense, but Tzec was able to understand them by substituting the closest terms that did make sense.

The Trader let Tzec and the woman be. By day he was out with other men of the tribe, or working with his trading goods, polishing shells or repairing feather cloaks. By night he slept in his corner as always. Tzec had her own corner, and Doña Margarita had Three Scales' corner. At first the woman had seemed nervous, but when she saw that Tzec's assurances were accurate, and that no more was expected of her than this, she settled down without objection.

When winter's cold made the Trader's bones grow stiff, and he had to rest in the lodge instead of going out with the men, Tzec fetched the healing salve the priest provided and prepared to rub his limbs as Three Scales had done in prior winters. But Doña Margarita took the jar from her hand and knelt to do it herself, surprising both Tzec and the Trader.

The woman's hands were sure and gentle, and she quickly made the Trader feel better. She had evidently had prior experience with this sort of thing.

Thereafter, Doña Margarita did this for the Trader. Tzec was glad, for though she had been willing to do it, it was an aspect of woman's work that she did not relish. Doña Margarita was alleviating the burden made by Three Scales' death.

Now the Trader took more of an interest in the woman than he had shown before. "I have heard you talking with my daughter," he said to her. "Tell me of your distant tribe across the water, and how you came here."

Doña Margarita immediately became reticent and was silent. Tzec, now aware of some of the differences between this woman and an ordinary one, quickly explained. "In her tribe a woman does not talk to a man who is not her husband. But I will tell you her story and that of her tribe, if you wish."

"Yes, tell me," he replied, disconcerted.

So while Doña Margarita worked elsewhere in the lodge, listening but not intruding, Tzec told him the tale of the Mad Queen.

Many generations ago, far across the great sea to the east, where the sun rises, there were three great tribes called the Castiles, the Aragons, and the Portugals. They had been small tribes, but their warriors were strong and fierce, and they succeeded in driving back the demons called the Moors, who had occupied their lands. But these tribes were always fighting each other. They realized that they might all be raided by the Moors if they weakened themselves too much, so they tried to make peace with each other. The way they did this was to plan a marriage between the Chief of the Portugals and the sister of the Chief of the Castiles. But the sister didn't like the Chief of the Portugals, who was a conniving man, so she sneaked away to marry the son of the Chief of the Aragons instead. Her brother, Chief Henry, was furious, but the deed was done and he had to make the best of it.

The son was called Ferdinand, and the sister was called Isabella. Their marriage was based on convenience and not love. Isabella was a plump country woman who placed great faith in the priests, while Ferdinand sought all the power he could get. He was a brilliant schemer. When the Chiefs of the Castiles and the Aragons died, Isabella and Ferdinand became the chiefs of their tribes, but the people would not let the tribes be joined together. Ferdinand governed the Aragons, and Isabella governed the Castiles as Queen, which is that tribe's name for a female Chief. They got along together about as well as might be expected.

Then a man named Cristóbal Colón from the far tribe of the

Italies came to the Chief of the Portugals and asked him for some big canoes with sails so he could go to a distant island by sailing in the wrong direction. He thought the world was round like a ball. The Chief did not think much of this idea, understandably, so five winters later Colon came to Ferdinand and Isabella and asked them. They also hesitated, for he did not seem to be making much sense, but he was persistent, so seven winters after that they let him have three canoes. He sailed toward the setting sun. He found land, but not the land he was looking for: it was an island of *our* land, or at least of tribes near us, but he did not know that. He left some of his warriors here and went home.

After that other canoes came across and settlements were started, and the people of the Castiles and the Aragons fought with the people of the tribes here.

Meanwhile, Ferdinand and Isabella had a daughter named Juana. She grew up and married a lesser chief named Philip. He was not supposed to have more than one wife, but he was a handsome man and many different women came to his lodge. This bothered Juana, and she began to lose her soul and act strangely. She and Philip visited Ferdinand and Isabella, but then Philip had to return to his home village to settle something. She wanted to go with him, for she knew what he would be doing with other women otherwise, but her mother made her stay at the lodge.

As time passed, Juana became increasingly upset. She really wanted to get back to her husband. But Isabella told her that the weather was too harsh for that difficult journey. One evening Juana left the lodge wearing only her sleeping clothes and got ready to leave the village. The people tried to persuade her not to do this, but she paid them no heed, and because she was the daughter of the Queen, they could not prevent her. But the weather was very bad, and she would surely die if she went out of the village like that. Finally the priest closed the gate of the palisade around the village, and Juana could not get out.

Each day thereafter Juana would stand forlornly at the palisade, wanting to get out. She was the daughter of the Queen, but she was a prisoner. Each night she slept near the cookfire

the servants used, until Isabella came and talked her into returning to their good lodge. That was when she began to be
called "The Mad."

At last Juana got to return to her home village, to be with
Philip again. She attacked the first woman she saw who had
been coming to Philip's lodge. This woman had long yellow
hair, unlike any seen among Juana's people, so she was surely
possessed by a strange spirit, and this was what had attracted
Philip. So Juana made her servants cut off the hair. In this manner she got back at her husband and the woman he liked.

In later winters Juana refused to talk with the priest, and this
made the people sure she was mad, for in that land the priests
are very powerful and important and know the secrets of every
person.

When Isabella died, the people of the Tribe of Castile made
Juana's husband, Philip, their Chief instead of Ferdinand. Ferdinand was not pleased. Perhaps this was because Ferdinand
had wanted to remain Chief of the Castiles as well as the Aragons after his wife died, and had even gone to the trouble of
marrying the niece of Chief Louis of the northern tribe of the
Frances in order to stop Chief Philip from getting the support
of the Frances. But Chief Philip marched through the land of
the Castiles and they supported him, and soon there were tens
of tens of warriors in his army. He met Chief Ferdinand, who
had only a few warriors with him, and Chief Ferdinand was
obliged to agree that Chief Philip and Queen Juana should rule.
But he also had to agree that Juana was mad, so that left just
Philip.

However, Chief Ferdinand was not a man to be forced. Not
long after Chief Philip assumed power, he died of chills. It was
suspected that Chief Ferdinand had arranged to send an evil
spirit or perhaps bad food to make Philip sicken and die, but
this could not be proved. So Chief Ferdinand resumed power.
Juana didn't care; she was grieving for her husband. She never
again shed a tear, after losing him.

Three moons after Chief Philip died, Juana decided to move
his body to its final resting place in a mound at a holy site called
Granada. She insisted on personally inspecting the body before
making the journey, to be sure the evil spirits had not molested
it. The Castiles, though marvelously advanced in some ways,

were primitive in others: they did not expose the bodies of their dead on a charnel platform, but sealed them immediately into great boxes. Thus the rotting flesh remained on the bones, and the smell was awful. This made the people more certain she was mad, for they did not like bad smells.

Juana insisted on traveling only during the winter nights, because she said that a widow who had lost the sun of her own soul should never expose herself to the light of day. It seemed that she now considered herself to be one with the spirits of the night, to which the sun would of course be hostile. But the people did not understand her reasonable position, and thought her madder than ever.

They came to a large lodge which Juana had understood to be a monastery, which was the home of male priests. She was horrified when it turned out to be a nunnery, which was the home of female priests. She immediately ordered her party out into the open fields, and would not camp until she had opened Chief Philip's burial box and inspected the body for possible damage or contamination. She knew that even in death, her husband would seek the company of other women, and though female priests were not supposed to indulge sexually with men, Philip had had such a way with women in life that he would surely seduce one or two of these females if he got the chance in death. But the body's penis was not stiff, so it seemed she had gotten him away in time. Despite this, the people continued to think she was mad.

After the body was in the mound at Granada, Juana talked with a priest who told her that it might be possible for Chief Philip to return to life. The priest said this had happened to an earlier chief after he had been dead for ten and four winters. This prospect appealed to her. Unfortunately, the priest was not skilled enough, and Chief Philip remained dead. This pleased her father, Chief Ferdinand, who resumed power, and kept it for ten winters, until he died in the year of the Castiles' Great Spirit 1516.

The next Chief, Charles, was only ten and six winters old, which they felt was too young. So they had another man do it for a winter, and then Charles took over.

He did not make a good impression. He did not speak the Castile tongue, and he gave honors to friends of his who were not Castiles. He had to travel around the region to visit each village and convince it that he was a good Chief.

Then his foreign grandfather, a great Chief named Maximilian, died, and Chief Charles went to try to be Chief of that tribe too. He decided to use Castile supplies to help him, and this made the Castiles angry. There were ten and six villages that were supposed to decide, and only three of them supported him. So he used tricky methods to get the support of another eight villages, and then said that the Castiles supported him, and sent their messengers home.

Meanwhile, the news of the great lands across the sea to the west had spread, and many people of the lands of the Portugals and Castiles and Aragons were interested in going there and perhaps obtaining wealth. One of these was Doña Margarita's husband, Don•Pedro. He was very influential in his village, and when Charles told him that he could keep anything he found in what they called the New World, he caused his village to support Charles, becoming one of the eight. He got a great canoe and a willing crew and sailed there, taking Doña Margarita along. He wasn't satisfied with the settlement at Santiago, so went beyond, seeking workers to bring in to replace those who had died. But a storm carried his canoe far off course, and then wrecked it near land.

The canoe lay half submerged, with many of its crew washed overboard. Doña Margarita, in the inner chamber, had been thrown violently about, but had survived. Then the people of this land came out in their little canoes and swarmed over the wreck. These were the Calusa. The remaining crewmen tried to hold them off, but the warriors struck them with arrows and spears, and soon all were dead, including Don Pedro. Doña Margarita alone was spared, because she was a woman. She was roughly taken to the village of the local Chief, who was the Cacique, where she gave herself up for lost among the savages, expecting to be killed at any moment.

"Until we came," Tzec concluded. "By that time she had realized that it was not yet time for her to die, and perhaps she could be useful somewhere. She knew that she would never return to her tribe across the sea."

The Trader glanced at the woman, who was keeping herself

busy with her cooking. He stared at Tzec. "Why did you take her?"

She knew he would not settle for her prior answer: that they needed a woman to keep the lodge. They could have gotten one from the village. "I am without my mother," she said. "I am older now, but I thought of my mother, from a far tribe in a far land, and I could not leave Doña Margarita there."

"You want to adopt her as your mother?" he asked sharply.

Tzec looked down. "Yes."

"How can you have a father and a mother, and they are not married?"

Tzec did not answer. It was impossible, she knew. Unless he did what she hoped.

The Trader sighed. "Very well. I will marry her. She has good hands."

"Thank you, my father." Tzec got up and went to Doña Margarita. "My father wishes to marry you. Will you do that?"

"It is better than living in sin." The term she used was one that Tzec had been unable to fathom; it seemed to mean that the spirits objected to something about a man and a woman being together without marriage. There were many aspects of Doña Margarita's tribal beliefs that did not seem to make much sense; she was like the Mad Queen here. But despite this she was a good woman.

So it was that they went through the rituals, and Doña Margarita moved her bed across the lodge to join the Trader's bed. Tzec spent the night with a young warrior, knowing that her new mother had odd notions about company on such a night.

There were, as it turned out, other peculiar ideas Doña Margarita had about marriage. Both Tzec and the Trader learned to keep silent about their activities away from the lodge. It was a relief when summer came and it was time to go on the trading tour.

The oddest thing was that Doña Margarita, who was to remain behind to keep the lodge, seemed similarly relieved.

CHAPTER 13

TWICE CURSED

O Spirit of the Mound, I have told you how Tzec met the woman of the Tribe of Castile and how she helped that woman and herself. Now I will tell you more of my life among the Principal People, and of the joys I had in it, and of my marriage to two fine women, and of the dread boogers, while I waited for the call by Sun Eagle when he finally located the Ulunsuti crystal.

Spring came, and with it the war- and ball-game season. Tale Teller was kept busy attending the various games between villages, and reporting on them to the other villages.

At the village of Five Birches, Tale Teller stayed with Gray Cloud and his wife, Red Leaf. He lay down alone, but she came to him in the night. "I have a favor to ask of you, warrior," she murmured, sitting by his blanket.

Tale Teller knew that women among the Principal People, whether single or married, had the same sexual freedom the men had. They could do as they wished, and it was problematical for men to make any issue of this. But among the Toco marriage was sacred: only a husband could allow his wife to indulge with another man, and he seldom did.

"I sleep alone in the house of my friend," he said carefully. "You are a beautiful woman, but in my tribe—"

Her soft laughter interrupted him. "You misunderstand!" she exclaimed, and he felt the blood coming to his face. "I want you to marry a woman of my clan."

"But I am not of the Principal People, and no woman—"

She put her delicate hand on his, silencing him. "Hear me

290

out, warrior, for this is a serious favor that may not please you, yet there may be compensation. If you do not wish to do it, I will return to my husband and it shall be as if we never talked."

So this was her way of broaching the matter privately, so that other parties would not need to suffer embarrassment if he chose not to do her favor. "I listen, wife of my friend."

"My clan is the Wild Potato," she said. "In many ways, a person's clan is more important than his village or his friends—or his mate. We look out for our own. When I became interested in Gray Cloud, I could not marry him because he was not of our tribe, and had no clan of ours. But when you brought him back, he was adopted by the Blue Clan, and so he could not marry any woman of that clan, but could marry me. I was fortunate, for if he had not returned, I might have had to marry some other man approved by my clan, and I did not want to do that. Now, I have a clan friend, a woman who was like a mother to me and guided me well when others did not approve. She was cursed because her husband died in war, leaving her with her young daughter to mourn. She remarried, for she was still beautiful, but last summer her second husband also died in war. Now she is Twice Cursed: that is the name the clan has given her. She is old, thirty winters, and the men are not interested in marrying her when she has her daughter to care for. But if you—"

"But I am only seventeen winters!" Tale Teller protested. "And I cannot do the things a man—my arm—I cannot build a lodge for her, or—"

"Your mouth has become your arm," Red Leaf told him. "You are becoming a wealthy man, because of the gifts the villagers give you for entertaining them so well, and for carrying the news to all who otherwise would have it late or never. You have good baskets, and finely crafted soapstone pipes, and carvings of birds and animals in stone and wood. Our people are excellent craftsmen, and they give you their best. And you can do what a man can do, for you know the use of a blowgun, and you have many excellent ones. We who appreciate the arts of carving and weaving and dancing recognize the art of talking in you, and honor you for it. You are worthy of marriage. You need a competent woman, and Twice Cursed is among the most competent; indeed, I learned much from her, and know she will be good for you in more ways than you may suppose. She is skilled in gathering and cooking, and she can weave expertly, and she knows well the art of pleasing a man, and she already has her lodge. You will not have to build one."

"But a woman of thirty winters! And a daughter! I know nothing about fatherhood, and in any event, that daughter would not want a one-armed father!"

"Twice Cursed has heard you talk," Red Leaf continued as if his objections were of no consequence. "As has her daughter. They are agreed: they are willing to marry you."

They had already discussed this! He had never suspected such a thing. He found it both flattering and astonishing that a woman should be willing to marry such a man as he, without ever meeting him formally. She had to be desperate, which was not the best sign. "The child does not mind a crippled father?"

"Not a crippled man; a talented husband," Red Leaf said firmly. "Do not be concerned; though you may have seen Twice Cursed in her bereavement, with her hair matted, she is not that ugly when unbereaved, and her daughter, Laurel, is not ugly at all. You will have great pleasure in her." She spoke as if it was already decided.

Tale Teller was for a moment at a loss. He did remember seeing a woman with matted hair and disreputable clothing. A widow was supposed to be unattractive, and a man was not supposed to stand upstream of her or even upwind of her, lest his presence touch her and be considered adulterous. But if it was the daughter rather than the mother who was to be married, that was more appealing. "I thought you said—the mother was the one—"

"You would marry them both. Laurel is of age, and does not want to leave her mother, so this is best."

Both? Tale Teller had to take stock again. Of course, he knew that men sometimes married sisters, or even mothers and daughters. It happened on rare occasion among the Toco, when there was need to protect a daughter who was not yet ready to leave her mother and was nubile. But he had never imagined doing it himself! "I—how old—?"

"Laurel is thirteen winters. She is ready to do woman's work, and whatever she does not know, her mother will show her. You need have no fear of a cold bed."

He remained overwhelmed by mixed feelings. "I am subject to the call of the spirits. I must leave when I receive their signal. No woman would want the uncertainty of—"

"A marriage is only till the first Green Corn Ceremony, if it is not satisfactory," she reminded him. "If you married them now, you could leave them in only three moons if your spirits called. That does not seem too great a risk. They are willing to take it; after all, it allows them to change their minds too."

"But why would they want—even for three moons—an outsider, with no—"

"Twice Cursed cannot get another husband now. She is too old, and no man wants to be the third of that curse. I must warn you that there may be a reason for it, and that this curse may indeed be a danger to any husband she takes. But you are alien; it probably does not apply to you. For one thing, you will not be going to war."

"A reason?" He did not like the sound of this either.

"There may be a curse invoked because of something her first husband did. But she knows how to abate it, if she chooses. In any event, it seems to take longer than three moons to take effect. If you do not like the marriage, you can say the curse frightens you, and everyone will understand."

"I have no fear," he said. "I cannot plead fright."

"Then you have merely to say you are unsatisfied with the marriage. You have very little risk, Tale Teller, and perhaps a great deal to gain. I ask you to accept my judgment that this marriage will be the best thing for you, and it will make you a satisfied man." She squeezed his hand suggestively. "There are stories about you. I would not believe them, of course, but it may be that two wives are what you need."

Her logic and insight were impeccable. He did need a woman, and he understood the condition of being virtually unmarriageable. Red Leaf proposed to put the leftover folk together, and perhaps she was right. Still, it was no easy thing to contemplate. "I have no clan here—"

"The Blue Clan will adopt you, as it did Gray Cloud."

She had obviously been talking to others. "Though the Blue Clan knows I may not stay?"

"How can any person know what will happen tomorrow?"

she asked rhetorically. "Perhaps you will remain longer than you suppose."

He was running out of objections. "When was she last widowed?" For there was something about this that nagged at him.

"Last summer, as I said."

"But then she cannot remarry for four years!"

"Not so. We do not have so long a period of misery as some tribes do. In any event, that limit does not hold if she remarries a man of her dead husband's clan."

"And his clan was—"

"Blue," she said.

Now it fell into place. Red Leaf was of the clan of Twice Cursed, which was the Wild Potato, and had married a man of Clan Blue, so had influence there through her husband. But no man of Clan Blue was interested. Yet if the clan adopted a suitable person, it could settle this problem with honor, and not leave a clansman's widow without support.

"My business is to travel between the villages," he said. "I would be away from the lodge most of the time."

"Twice Cursed understands. She does not require the constant presence of a man. But she prefers the prestige of being married, with a man to represent her interests and those of her daughter, and to bring in goods which can be traded for the things she needs. You will have to give her some of the gifts you have received, for her to trade for deer flesh and hides. She keeps a good lodge; her husbands grew fat. You would have a good place to return to."

All things considered, it seemed a reasonable offer. "If Clan Blue wishes to adopt me—"

"Leave it to me." Red Leaf leaned over in the darkness and kissed him on the mouth. Then she got up and returned to her husband, leaving Tale Teller's thoughts in turmoil. What had he agreed to?

The adoption ceremony proceeded the next day. The men of Clan Blue stood with Tale Teller and declared before the spirits that they were adopting him into the clan, and they set a blue feather in his hair which he would wear henceforth. He agreed to honor the conventions of Clan Blue, and to defend its interests with his life if need be. That was it; some tribes had arduous adoption ceremonies, but the Principal People preferred simplicity where it was appropriate. Also, they wanted this adoption, so made things considerably easier than they might have been. He now belonged.

Next, he walked to the village where Twice Cursed and her daughter lived. Black Bone, also of the Blue Clan, went with him. This time Black Bone carried his bow rather than his blowgun. They went quietly, hoping for a good omen, and there was one: on the way they spied a deer. It might have been the case that other men were deeper in the forest, herding the deer toward the path, but no one would ever admit to that. Black Bone brought it down with a single arrow, after apologizing to the deer's spirit for having to take its life, and they gutted and cleaned it there. They made a rig of poles and hauled it on to the village, arriving the following day. By this time, of course, other men of Clan Blue had had time to get there by other routes. They were standing near the lodge, pretending not to be paying attention to it. Nobody was supposed to be fooled; they were there to see that the marriage occurred as planned.

Tale Teller and Black Bone brought the deer to the lodge of Twice Cursed. Black Bone backed silently away at the end, letting Tale Teller haul it the last bit, so that it might appear that he had done it all himself. An older woman and her bare-breasted daughter came out, wearing deerskin skirts and moccasins—the moment Tale Teller stood alone, as if they had just discovered his presence. Of course, they had been watching, waiting for the appropriate time. The woman's face was lined and severe, but her hair was now combed and her sleeveless shirt was clean, making her not nearly as unattractive as Tale Teller had feared. The girl was indeed rather pretty.

"I—I come from Clan Blue," Tale Teller said awkwardly. "I bring this deer for Twice Cursed and Laurel." He took an uneasy breath and continued the ritual. "To show my willingness to provide for both of you, and my ability to do so, in the manner of a man." He was embarrassed, for it was obvious that the only weapon he could use to bring down prey was his blowgun, and that would never be enough for a deer.

Twice Cursed and her daughter did not laugh, as his wild fancy had threatened. They nodded together, turned, and went into their lodge. In a moment they emerged. Twice Cursed had a bowl of salad, and Laurel carried an ear of corn. "We of the Wild Potato Clan accept your meat," Twice Cursed said with equal formality. "We present you with these tokens of our willingness and ability to gather and cook for you, in the manner of women."

"I accept your vegetables," Tale Teller said.

"Welcome into our lodge," Twice Cursed said, showing the way for him to precede them.

Tale Teller walked inside. It was done. He was a married man. If there was a satisfied chuckle from among the men who stood incidentally near, none of them admitted to overhearing it.

Twice Cursed was indeed qualified in lodgekeeping. Tale Teller had a wonderful meal of deer meat, beans, pumpkin, corn cakes, mushrooms, grubs, and sunflower seed bread, which the older woman prepared and her daughter served. The tastiest was the wild potato stew; naturally the folk of the Wild Potato Clan knew best how to grow and cook this special root. Rather than making large portions of a few things, they had small portions of many things, the better to demonstrate their competence. Indeed, he was to eat well from then on, for on other days they were to bring in and prepare edible roots, small crayfish (the large ones were not suitable to eat), birds' eggs, frogs, cicadas, gourds, nuts, and assorted fruits. But the main staple was corn, of course; they grew three kinds, and the kernels could be red, blue, yellow, or white, so that any number of combinations and preparations were possible. The Spirit of Corn, as he soon learned to tell the villagers, was named "Old Woman," because corn had been created from the body of a woman killed by her two sons. He was never to be hungry while he remained in this lodge, despite his inadequacy as a hunter of larger game.

But what made Tale Teller nervous this first day was the approaching night. Which one of them would he be expected to stay with, and what was he expected to do with her? Was he supposed to go from one to the other, or remain after sex to sleep with that one? No one had clarified this aspect for him. Marriage he thought he could handle; he had seen how well it suited Gray Cloud and Red Leaf. But two wives—what was the protocol here?

Dusk came. The two women, old and young, said nothing. They only gazed at him, waiting. He had to decide. Yet he feared that whatever he decided to do would turn out to be wrong. They would do what he decided, and neither would reproach him, but they would judge him for it, and that judgment might remain for the duration of their marriage.

He glanced at Twice Cursed, named for her misfortune. She no longer looked so grim, in the deepening shadows of the lodge. She had removed her shawl, showing her full breasts, which hardly sagged. He might almost forget how old she was. But could he ever forget how experienced she was, having outlived two husbands and raised her daughter?

He looked at Laurel, named after the shrub that grew on the mountain slopes. He might almost forget how young she was. She was, after all, old enough, though surely inexperienced. Who was he to teach her?

The question, unanswered, returned: did they expect him to indulge sexually with both, the first night? Or was this a marriage of mutual convenience, so that the clans needed to have no further concern for uncommitted people, and sex was not intended as part of it?

No, sex was always part of marriage, as it was part of life. But he had before indulged in it only with women who had come to him, knowing his disability with the arm, and who had been experienced enough to accommodate him despite it. These two—the one might not care to make it easy for him, and the other might not know how.

He did not know what to do—but also knew that the worst error of all would be to do nothing.

Then he remembered how to get good advice. He closed his eyes and turned his thoughts inward, visualizing the mound of the Toco where the spirit of Dead Eagle governed. This lodge was far away from that mound, but perhaps not too far for communication. His need was desperate, giving his thought power.

O Spirit of the Mound, help me now! Tell me what to do, that I may not shame myself before these women.

The Spirit had always answered when the need was pressing,

and it did so now. *The old one without honey tonight. The young one with honey tomorrow night.*

Without honey? Why? The Spirit did not say.

But the Spirit had to know. Tale Teller pondered intensely for a moment, working out a rationale for what he now knew he had to do. Then he spoke.

"Twice Cursed, I am young, and ignorant in the way of marriage. I have been with women before, but my arm makes it difficult, and I require the understanding of experience. I know that this is not a marriage you would have chosen had your prospects been better, and that I may not be any great joy to you. Your husbands were better men than I am. But I ask that you share my bed this night, and if anything I do displeases you in any way, you will tell me before you tell any other, so that we share no shame with others."

Twice Cursed nodded without speaking.

He turned to the girl. "Laurel, you are younger than I, and perhaps soon you will find a better prospect for marriage. I ask you to share my bed tomorrow night, and use the honey, so that you will remain free to choose your course when the Green Corn Ceremony comes."

"You will divorce me?" Laurel asked, upset. "How have I offended you?"

"No, no!" he protested. "You are beautiful, and you are young, and I think you can find a better man than I when you choose. But not if you are with child."

Still upset, Laurel looked at her mother. Twice Cursed nodded affirmatively, and the girl relaxed. She was not being cast off, only saved.

He turned again to Twice Cursed. "But you—if you are willing—no honey."

Her face remained impassive, but she jumped and her eyes widened. He had truly surprised her. "You understand—I am not yet beyond the age."

"If we are to be married, let it be real—if the spirits choose," he said. "I think they would not give me a child, only to call me away while that child was too young. It is not good for a child to have no father." This was emphatically true; it was part of what had made Laurel's situation unkind.

Twice Cursed nodded again. Tale Teller got up, went outside

to urinate and prepare his mind for the ordeal ahead, and returned after a suitable interval. There was just enough light from the coals of the central fire to show him how things were.

Sure enough, Laurel was supposedly asleep in her part of the lodge, and Twice Cursed was lying naked by the bed of covered pine needles that had been set up for him. She could have hidden herself with the blanket, but she was showing him that she was ready. In the dim glow of the banked cookfire she looked surprisingly well formed. Whether she liked or disliked him he might never know, but she intended to do her duty by him. Probably neither of them would enjoy this, but each would have to pretend that it was wonderful.

He stripped off his clothing and lay beside her. He reached across to stroke her flesh with his right hand, as if eager to do what he was supposed to be eager to do. Her body was warm, and if it was old, he would never have known this by touch. Her breasts were large and fine, and her thighs were firmly fleshed.

"If you will," she murmured in his ear, "I will be passive for your pleasure, asking no more. If you will, I will be otherwise."

"I would have you otherwise." For it was always best for him when the woman was active, making up for his arm. Also, it gave her more control, so that she had a better chance to enjoy it too, or at least to avoid what displeased her. He remembered Heron Feather, who knew so well what she was doing. But most important, it would relieve him of the need to take the initiative. If it wasn't good, the blame would not be his.

She got up and sat astride him, leaning forward. Her inner thighs pressed against his hips. She took his good arm and brought his hand to her left breast, which now reached down toward him. She made his hand stroke her breasts a good deal more competently than before, and her belly and between her thighs. She moved on him with such expertise that not only did he become interested, he was soon at a pitch of excitement. Then she put his rigid penis inside her, lay down on him, and embraced him tightly while he thrust with a vigor and desire he had not anticipated for this night.

He had been some time without a woman, and longer without a truly responsive one, and he had experienced nothing like this since Beautiful Moon. He had underestimated how much experience counted. Twice Cursed was expert at pleasing a man, and somehow she did not seem old now. Again he remembered Heron Feather, the older woman who had been so completely good for him. Had he married her, it would have been like this. How well Red Leaf had known what he had not!

As he relaxed, transported, she kissed him, lingeringly. He brought up his good hand to stroke her hair. She was as much of a woman as he would ever need!

But still his thoughts nagged him. It was evident that Twice Cursed knew much more about satisfying a man than he knew about satisfying a woman, yet why had she bothered? She had surely given him better than he deserved.

"Have I pleased you in some way?" he asked.

She did not pretend to misunderstand. She knew how well she had pleased him, and knew that he knew this was artifice rather than true passion. "You do not intend to divorce me at the Green Corn Ceremony. You would not take the risk of no honey otherwise."

"I need a woman," he said. "You need a man. I would not make a promise and break it."

"And you will let Laurel go if she wishes. You would not otherwise ask her to use the honey in marriage."

"That seems only fair."

"I had expected the opposite."

Suddenly he saw the wisdom of the Spirit's advice. The average man might indeed marry the mother in order to have first access to her daughter, then keep only the daughter. That had never been his intention. This might be an odd marriage, but he intended to do his best to make it work. If it ended at the Green Corn Ceremony, it would not be because he had not done what he could for it. The Spirit had enabled him to show his commitment in a way that could not be doubted.

What he had not anticipated was the force of Twice Cursed's gratitude. This marriage of convenience had abruptly become a marriage of pleasure. He had done the best possible thing.

The next night it was Laurel's turn. Twice Cursed arranged to fall asleep early; this was an artifice that fooled no one, but it signaled clearly that Tale Teller and Laurel were on their own.

He had been surprised by the passion of the first night. He was surprised the opposite way this night. Not only was Laurel inexperienced, she was terrified. She had the honey, but she was rigid. He would have let her go, but knew that an unconsummated marriage was suspect; he had to do it.

He tried to take his time, stroking her and murmuring encouragement to her, but it was no good. Women varied in age and nature and experience, and Laurel was at the extreme edge of each, afraid of pain, of error, and of making a bad impression. Thus she was inviting all three. He wished he could be with her mother instead, leaving Laurel untouched.

He knew it was possible for a woman to receive as much pleasure from the sexual act as a man, if she cared to. He decided that it would be kindest not to try for that in this case, but just to get it done as gently and swiftly as possible. But swift might hurt her. So he set himself on her as well as he could with the partial support of one arm, and sought the honey, and slowly pushed into it. She was so tense that it was immediately a choice between force and failure. But he jogged a bit at that point, and managed to finish with that partial entry. It would have to do.

"It is done," he said, relaxing—and at that point she too relaxed. He realized that if he had told her it was finished before it was, it would have been possible to finish it better thereafter. But all that mattered was that the ordeal was over, for them both.

They slept. He woke in the night, feeling her beside him. She grew tense again, sensing his waking. The first night of marriage was traditionally a busy one. "It is done," he repeated sleepily, and she relaxed. In such manner they made it to the morning.

Thereafter he slept with Twice Cursed by preference, leaving Laurel alone. The woman surely knew why, but said nothing. She merely fed him so well that in time he could indeed get fat, and gave him what he wanted at night so perfectly that he seldom had to speak. Sometimes he wanted only to sleep, and she let him do that too. It was as if her spirit could feel his spirit, needing no words.

Until it was time for him to travel again. His grace period of early marriage was over. He had tales to tell and gifts to get, so that his wives would have goods and status.

He prepared to go. He saw Twice Cursed getting Laurel ready for travel too. "Where is she going?" he asked.

"With you, husband," Twice Cursed said.

"But I must travel to all the fifteen villages before I return!" he protested. "She will tire and be bored."

Laurel sent him a grateful glance. She agreed, and did not want to go.

But this was the first time Twice Cursed opposed his will. "Would you have the women of those villages think you were not married? Your wife goes with you."

Now he understood. It was to see that he did not entertain any village maidens, who might find him more interesting now that he was a clansman of the Principal People. Twice Cursed could not tell him no, but she could see that he behaved. There would be no visiting maidens as long as Laurel was with him. The fact that there were no actual sexual relations between him and Laurel didn't matter; she was his wife, and had the rights of a wife.

He looked apologetically at Laurel, letting her know that this was not his wish. Then he set off, and she walked with him.

But it was slow, because he normally ran much of the distance between villages, in this manner refreshing his strength. He would be late to the first one, and the children there would be sad.

"I am delaying you, my husband," Laurel said, accurately enough.

"I thought I would be alone when I planned my route," he said. "It is not your fault."

"I can run," she said. "Not as fast or as far as you, but maybe fast and far enough."

"You can? Then follow me, and I will slow when you tire." This was an interesting prospect. Youths of either sex did like to run, and some girls were quite fleet. He had not known this about her.

He set off, running slowly, and she followed. He picked up the pace, and she matched it. He achieved what was for him a comfortable rate, and she seemed to be able to hold it. She had good legs. His displeasure at having her along diminished.

After a time they came to a mountain stream. He stopped for water, but waited a little, because it was not good to drink too much when hot. Laurel sat beside him, breathing hard, sweating. Her hair was disheveled and her face streaked with a line of dust, but her heaving small breasts were pretty. At this moment, she had considerable sex appeal.

"Laurel—" he said.

Her face turned to him. "Now?" Even the youngest of women knew that look in a man.

Immediately he was contrite. "It is daytime, and you are not ready."

"You are my husband." She brought out her package of honey, lifted her skirt, and applied it. He had not seen this act before, and it made him instantly ardent.

But he had the caution not to proceed immediately. He did not want a repetition of the tension of the night. It might be unavoidable, but perhaps he could diminish it. So he spoke the spell to fix the affections of the loved one. This was normally done alone, with the loved person absent but held firmly in mind, yet could be done at any time by either party.

Laurel!
I am victorious! I am as beautiful in your eyes as the rainbow!
I have just captured your heart.
I have taken your blood.
I have taken your flesh.
I have taken your eyes.
I have taken your saliva.
Your flesh and mine are one forever.
I have magic! You must love me!

The formula required that the spell be repeated four times. But with the second, Laurel spoke it with him, with so much feeling that he realized that she was not merely acquiescing to his desire; she wanted this to work. She wanted his love, as he wanted hers. This surprised him and gratified him.

"Your flesh and mine are one forever," they said together. "I have magic! You must love me!"

They never finished the other repetitions. In a moment they were together, still mostly clothed, embracing, still breathing heavily. He penetrated her without difficulty, and she kissed him as he climaxed.

Thus suddenly it was done, there in the forest by the stream. "But before—" he protested belatedly.

"That is true!" she agreed, surprised. "I never had time to be afraid!"

But perhaps it was more than that, for there *had* been time. Laurel could have developed her fear during the recitation of the spell. Instead she had become warmer, and as ardent as he. Why? Before, it had been the first act of marriage, with a man who was relatively strange to her. Now it was with one she knew, and they had done it before, however imperfectly, so the fear was less. Then it had been dark, in the lodge; now it was light, in the open forest. But even more important was the fact that she was hot and breathless from running, and this state was like that of passion. Maybe she had just needed to be properly warmed up. It was not that he doubted the efficacy of the spell, but it had worked so much better than expected! He knew that the reliability of such spells was imperfect; if the spirits helped, then the spells worked, but often the spirits did not care. Whatever the reason, this experience had been immeasurably better than the last with her. He wanted to understand why, so that it would be so in the future.

"Maybe your mother knew," he said, thinking of the story of the discovery of tobacco. They had reenacted it!

"She knows much," she agreed.

They drank from the stream, then resumed traveling at a walking pace. Now they talked. "How is it that you agreed to this marriage when you could have saved yourself for some other man?" he asked.

"I was afraid," she confessed.

"Of other men? You mean it wasn't just me?"

"Yes. I thought maybe with my mother there—" She shrugged.

That had not been effective. Yet now she had done it with him, away from her mother, without being afraid. He liked her much better, with this success.

They ran again, and reached the village on schedule: well before darkness, so that the children had time to gather. Before he could start, they were clamoring for the news. "How is it to be married, Tale Teller? How is your wife?"

"This is my wife," he replied, indicating Laurel, who was sitting demurely behind him.

They were taken aback, seeing a girl who was no older than some of them. "How is she with the honey?" a bold one asked.

"She is so good that I could not wait until we reached a lodge," he said. "I had sex with her halfway here, by the crossing of the stream. Perhaps a tobacco plant will grow there." There was scattered laughter, for they all knew his version of the origin of tobacco.

The older girls looked at Laurel appraisingly, seeing by her flush and downcast eyes that it was true. It was not a woman's place to boast of such an accomplishment, but she could acknowledge when the man did the boasting. Laurel had just achieved real status as a woman. The villagers did not realize, of course, that the two of them had not been doing it nightly. That made his eagerness more impressive.

"We heard that you had married an old woman," a boy said.

"I married Twice Cursed, Laurel's mother," he explained. "And Laurel too."

"And you satisfy them both?" a woman asked.

"They have not complained," he replied with a smile.

There was general laughter. No worthy woman complained about such a thing, nor would any husband admit it if she did.

He went into the first tale, which was familiar to them, but the children liked to hear them over and over, especially when they were well told.

". . . and the other wives of the Chief were resentful of the new one, and decided to embarrass her by demonstrating that she was not the most beautiful in all ways. They conspired to have a beauty contest of a special kind. Each of them would step out of her skirt before the Chief, and the one with the loveliest pubic hair would be the winner. They were sure that a woman with perfect face and breasts would be defective where it did not show.

"But the new wife suspected that there was some trick, so she consulted with her friend the hummingbird. 'They are going to show off their pubic hair,' the bird told her. 'But do not fear, for I will help you defeat their scheme and be in even better grace with the Chief.'

"Then the hummingbird took some of his own feathers and

the down of his breast, and wove it into her hair, so that the region shone iridescently. The maiden put her skirt back on and went to join the other wives.

"When the Chief's first wife proposed the contest, the Chief was pleased, and agreed to judge it. He was always interested in seeing more of his lovely women. Then, one by one, his wives stepped out of their skirts, and each had her pubic hair combed and greased and painted to be impressive. The last was the maiden, the least senior wife. She pretended reluctance, but the Chief directed her to take down her skirt, and so she did.

"Then her pubic region shone forth in many colors, by far the most beautiful. The Chief was so impressed that he sent the other wives away and took her immediately to his bed. Once again, with the help of her friends the animals, she had triumphed."

A young girl looked perplexed. Tale Teller interrupted his continuing tale to question her. "You do not believe, little lady?"

"It is not that," she said, abashed. "But was it that way with your wives?"

Everyone laughed at her naiveté. Not everything spoken of in a tale reflected reality. But he had mercy on her embarrassment. "Of course it was not," he told her. "Laurel needed no hummingbird feathers. Her hair was already more beautiful than that. Shall I have her take down her skirt and show you?"

"You shall not!" Laurel exclaimed, flushing furiously, and everyone laughed again. It was not the notion of nakedness that bothered her, for that was common enough; it was the suggestion that she should show off, which no maiden ever did openly.

"You will have to take my word," he said, smiling, and went on with the tale.

So went the evening, until they were invited to the village Chief's table for a meal. Laurel, hesitant at first, came to enjoy herself when she discovered that due courtesy was extended to her as the wife of the Tale Teller.

When at last they were alone in a lodge, he touched her— and found her tense. "No, no!" he said. "It was done this noon!

I want only to hold you and kiss you, for you have been a good wife this day."

She relaxed, and he did just that. But he wondered: she now knew from experience that the sexual act was not to be feared, yet her fear was back. How could that be?

By the time the circuit of villages was completed, Tale Teller was deeply in love with Laurel. They indulged in sex always in the day, on the paths between villages, when both were hot from running. This novelty was wonderfully satisfying for him, and he thought for her also. Yet at night she could not be touched.

But at home there was Twice Cursed, and though he had been delighted with the quick, hot acts by day with Laurel, he was also delighted with the slow, perfect acts with Twice Cursed by night. They were two different creatures, these women, and he was well satisfied with each.

The first night back, after treating him to her type of joy, Twice Cursed inquired in the oblique way of her gender. "I see my daughter happy."

"You see me happy," he replied. "I love her."

"I feared there was a problem between you."

"There is none now." Yet that was not quite true. "My wife, may I ask what perhaps should not be asked?"

"She must tell you that herself."

So she did know about her daughter's fear of intimacy at night—and probably also the reason for it. But he would have to wait until Laurel herself was ready to tell him. Meanwhile, he was satisfied to have her travel to the villages with him. He was happy just with her company at night.

Twice Cursed seemed satisfied too. It was evident that though she knew well how to please a man, and was ready to do so, she was also content to remain alone, knowing that her daughter was secure. She made no pretense of loving him, and he made none of loving her, but they had a solid respect for each other. This had turned out to be a much better marriage than he had expected.

The Green Corn Ceremony came. Folk gathered from all over. Actually, the Principal People called it the Great New

Moon Ceremony, but it was equivalent to what others called
the Green Corn Ceremony, and Tale Teller thought of it that
way. This was the celebration of the ending of the old year and
the beginning of the new year. The world had been created in
this time, so each renewal dated from it. Each family brought
in food from its fields, and the products of its hunts. Part of
this food would be used for the great feast, and part of it would
be taken by the Chief and given to those families in need,
for not all had good fortune. The Principal People took care of
their own.

On the night of the appearance of the full moon no one slept
except tiny babies. The women performed a special dance. Before dawn everyone assembled at the riverbank, and the head
priest placed the sacred crystal on a wooden platform by the
edge of the water. It was a tiny thing, no longer than the breadth
of a man's thumb, but it was clear and sharply edged and full
of the wonder and power of the spirit realm. At sunrise he
signaled, and every person submerged seven times in the river.
Each emerged and passed the sacred crystal, gazing into it, and
if he saw himself lying down within it, he would know that he
would die before spring. This was the only time that the people
saw the crystal, because only those trained from childhood
could handle such magic without suffering harm. Everyone was
relieved when the gazing was done; no one had seen the death
image.

Now came the time of clearing animosities and settling re-
lationships. Tale Teller was required to stand before the tribesmen and declare his intentions: was he satisfied with his
marriage, or was he dissolving it?

He had no hesitancy. "I have found in Twice Cursed and
her daughter two fine women, and I am content to remain with
them for the rest of my life," he said. "If not called away by
the spirits."

Then the challenge came to the two women. "I have found
in Tale Teller a good man, and I wish to remain with him,"
Twice Cursed said formally. "Especially since I am now with
child by him."

Tale Teller's jaw dropped. The men laughed to see it, then
applauded, despite the seriousness of the occasion.

Then Laurel stepped out. Suddenly abashed at the cynosure

of so many eyes, she turned and flung herself into Tale Teller's limited embrace.

The marriage was now permanent.

But Twice Cursed was not quite finished with him here. She approached him again. "In recognition of the esteem in which I hold this man, and my desire never again to be cursed by the loss of a husband, I give him my most prized possession: the lesser magic crystal." She lifted from her neck a cord he had not seen her wear before. From it hung a little rabbit-pelt pouch. She opened the bag and brought out an object which brought a murmur of awe from those who watched, and astonished Tale Teller: a translucent stone crystal, like the priest's, with several flat sides, roughly pointed at the base. It was smaller than the other, and less perfectly faceted, but definitely magic. It was an emulation of the Ulunsuti he sought, of far lesser power, but of great significance in its own right. Such a crystal could bring a man success in warfare, hunting, rainmaking, and even love, as well as enabling him on occasion to see into the future. Usually only a priest possessed such a stone, or a highly respected woman. Later he was to learn that Twice Cursed's first husband had killed an enemy priest and taken this stone from him, but had been afraid to keep it himself. He had given it to his wife—and then been killed, while she had survived. The council elders had decided that she should keep it until she chose to whom to give it, because it could be as dangerous to dispose of such a stone as to keep it, and now she had decided. It was a phenomenal gift, and it showed that he had not come here by any accident. Sun Eagle had to have known, and by this means signaled him that in time he would have the Ulunsuti itself.

Twice Cursed returned the magic crystal to its pouch, for it certainly was not safe to show it openly for more than a moment. She pulled the closure tight, then put the cord over Tale Teller's head and around his neck, while he stood as if stunned. The pouch with its precious content came to rest against his chest, warm from her bosom and perhaps from its own animation. He realized only sometime later that he had not even thanked her for it. But the elders of the tribe had understood; the gift was overwhelming. It was also not quite a gift; it was a transfer of responsibility. It was evident that the tribal elders approved; perhaps they had been consulted. Perhaps this was what Red Leaf had referred to, obliquely, when she told him how much better his marriage would be than he supposed. She had had the welfare of the tribe in mind, as well as his own. Tale Teller communed with the spirits; he should be able to keep the crystal safely, if anyone could.

When the Ceremony was over and they returned to their lodge, he sought to put the magic crystal away in a hidden place. "No, you must wear it always," Twice Cursed told him. "My husbands did not wear it, and they died. It will protect you only if it is close to you."

"But such a stone—I cannot wear it for all to see, during common occasions!" he protested. For there were sacred dimensions to this crystal, as everyone knew.

"True. I will make you a pocket for it, so you can wear it where it does not show." She did so, and he wore that pouch strapped to his left arm, in the hollow of his shoulder, where it could not be seen. Only on special occasions would he bring it out.

"My wife," he said to Twice Cursed, after sorting out his thoughts for several days. "I have not said I loved you, nor expected you to say it to me. We know that each of us needed a mate. I have said only that I love your daughter. But now I know that I do love you as well as Laurel. You are all I have ever needed in a woman, and my fortune is doubled because I have her too."

"You are impetuous," she said, turning aside the question of her feeling for him. "You say more than you mean." But she was pleased, and she had ways of showing it that could not be mistaken or forgotten. He suspected that she did love him, to the extent that her prior tragedies allowed. She was afraid that whatever man she loved she would lose, so she did not speak of love.

Twice Cursed had not been joking about the state of her body. In the spring she birthed a son, whom they named No Spirit, because his birth was the signal that the spirits were not going to call Tale Teller away soon. The boy was big and healthy, and found favor with the priests.

Laurel became troubled. When they were on the route around the villages, Tale Teller asked her why. They were at their first and favorite stop, at the stream that crossed the path, and he was excited at the prospect of her honey, but he did not like to see her in distress.

She was forthright. "Why will you not let me bear you a son? Am I not also your wife?"

He was taken aback. "But if you bear a child, you cannot divorce me, because—"

"I never wanted to divorce you!" she exclaimed. "I have loved you from the first!"

That was a bit of an exaggeration, he knew, but it would not be prudent to challenge it. Certainly it had been evident that she loved him as he loved her, dating perhaps from their first successful liaison at this spot. He had spoken without thought, and regretted it. "Of course you may bear my child," he said. "If that is what you want."

She opened her arms and her legs to him, without the honey. Somehow it was sweeter than ever.

Then she told him why she feared him in the night. "My father—my second father—he hurt me. In the way that does not show. I dared not tell my shame, but every night I lay in fear that he would come again, and often he did. Now the thought of a man, in the dark, in the lodge—"

Tale Teller was chagrined. "Had I known, I would never have—"

"You had to. I knew that. But I could not make my body know."

"Our love will be always in the day," he promised. Now at last he understood not only why she feared the night, but why it had been best for mother and daughter to marry together. There could then be no shame of wrongful attentions. But how glad he was that they had discovered the secret of love in the day!

In the spring of the following year Laurel's son was born, and they named him Halfway Stream. It was not certain that he had been conceived exactly there, for they had joined in rapture all through the forest, but they agreed that the dawn of their love had been there, so it was proper.

* * *

When the boys were five and four winters old, they had their
first experience with the boogers. This was a Principal People
tradition that Tale Teller had learned, but it had not been
convenient for his sons to participate before, because the occasion had not come up while he was at home with them. Laurel
still traveled with him to the villages, leaving the boys in the
more-than-competent care of Twice Cursed, but the boys could
not go.

This night the villagers were assembled in the central square
by a great fire, dancing. Then Tale Teller and several other men
quietly departed. The Chief raised his hands for silence, and
made a serious face. "Do not be alarmed," he said. "We are to
have strange visitors. We hope they will be well behaved, but
they are from far away and do not know our ways, so we must
be especially courteous to them." He glanced at the children seated at the edge of the dance ground. "Do not be afraid,"
he said grimly. "Our priests will protect us." But he looked
doubtful.

At this the women made muted exclamations of alarm, and
the older children, who had attended such a dance before,
contrived to look worried. "I thought we were safe from them!"
one whispered loudly. The smaller children picked up the tension and clung close to their mothers, No Spirit and Halfway
Stream among them.

When the suspense was at its height, the boogers arrived.
They were seven men with blankets wrapped around their
bodies, wearing grotesque masks. Tale Teller was among them,
unrecognizable behind his mask with a grossly phallic nose.
Other men had masks formed into crude likenesses of bears,
wildcats, or horrendously distorted human beings. Most were
fashioned of wood, dyed glaringly bright green or red or yellow.
One had been made from a huge hornet's nest hollowed out
so that the man's head fitted inside it and his eyes peered out
from slits in it. Tale Teller's was from a hollow gourd. There
was opossum hair around the base of the pendulous nose,
making it uncomfortably realistic as a penis.

The Chief approached them. "If you are to receive our hospitality, you must give your names," he said firmly, and the
children were encouraged by this show of authority.

At this the boogers seemed confused. One even made the Question sign, as if not understanding the Chief. Two of them walked around the Chief, hunched over like animals, growling, evincing perplexity. The watching children were amazed at this audacity; no one treated the Chief with such disrespect!

Finally the boogers seemed to get the message. Tale Teller stepped forward, hooking his nose in a manner that made several children giggle. "I am Giant Stiff Penis," he announced in a changed voice. He had a mock left arm hooked to the outside of his blanket, so there could not be much doubt about his identity. He had developed a certain quiet reputation, because both wives had let it be known that he had congress with them every day, and others had verified enough of his daytime activity with Laurel to believe it. The truth was that it was not feasible to do it with Twice Cursed every night he was home, or with Laurel every day he was on the path. But the lost power of his left arm did seem to have gone to his penis, and his sexual life was a joy to him and a source of muted pride to his wives. When they exaggerated his prowess in that respect, it diminished any suggestion that they had settled for less than a fully physical man, or that he had settled for any unattractive women. Thus it was a pleasant conspiracy from which they all benefited, and a giant stiff penis was an acceptable symbol of it.

Now the small children were catching on, and there was open laughter. Even the women, normally quite sedate, allowed themselves to smile.

The other boogers introduced themselves, with appropriate gestures and signs to clarify their meaning, though at this point it was already overly clear. They were Sooty Buttocks, Rotten Rectum, Her Slit Is Too Hairy, Beaver Snot, Three Small Testicles, and the last one bent far over, pointed his rear at the audience, and made the sound of the most monstrous possible flatulence. Up until now the women, at least, had been silent, but at this point everyone broke into uproarious laughter.

"And what have you come to do?" the Chief asked with a straight face.

"We have come to shove our penises up every woman here!" Tale Teller exclaimed. Then every booger lifted aside a flap of his blanket, exposing a phenomenal fake penis made of a gourd, and charged the audience. The women and girls screamed and fell over each other in their effort to get away, while the boys fell rolling on the ground in their laughter.

The society of the Principal People was ordinarily well mannered, and even men were cautious about giving offense unless they intended to fight. But it was evident that the boogers honored no rules at all. The children knew that such behavior would never be tolerated in them, yet here were these men, whom they now recognized as some of their fathers and uncles, behaving in the worst possible manner and getting away with it. This made it twice as funny as it otherwise would have been.

Now the boogers put on their show. They formed a circle and danced, but not in any ordinary way. They stumbled about, taking pratfalls and making threatening gestures at each other when they bumped, while the children and even some of the older girls laughed so hard their sides were hurting. But soon the dance fell apart, and the boogers began to wander into the audience. One normal man stood with his wife; a booger shoved him aside, grabbed her, and planted an obvious kiss on her face, though his mask could not make it quite real. In real life this could have led to a death-challenge, but the husband merely spread his hands in a gesture of incapacity. Boogers could not be punished, for they were strangers who did not know the civilized rules. Indeed, some of them seemed totally mad; one of them was foaming at the mouth. At least bubbles were squeezing from the mouth-slit of his mask. Another grabbed an ordinary man and tried to dance with him, evidently supposing him to be a woman, while the man tried to escape without being impolite or violent.

The Chief did his best to restore order. He shoved the boogers into some sort of line while the priest silenced them for a moment with hex signs. "What do you want here?" the Chief asked when the boogers were quiet.

"Girls!" Tale Teller cried, hooking up his phallic gourd nose again, and once more the women and girls screamed and giggled as they crowded back. But this time the magic of the priest stopped the boogers from charging. The priest had drawn a line along the ground, and the boogers were comical as they crashed into the invisible barrier above it and bounced off. Now the women and children laughed and teased the boogers, feeling themselves safe for the moment.

"If you will not be serious, I will have the line extended to surround you and make you prisoners," the Chief said grimly. "I conjure you by the Great Spirit: what is your purpose here?"

"We have come to fight!" Tale Teller cried in his artificial voice, and leaped for the Chief—only to be felled by the barrier and take an ignominious roll on the ground. The laughter was overwhelming, tinged with amazement, for they knew his identity now, and wondered how he could do it with his bad arm. The truth was that he had practiced it assiduously, until able to made a dive to the side that was broken by a rolling motion over his good arm. Thus his seeming fall was actually the beginning of a controlled partial somersault guided by his arm.

There was another laugh, tinged with embarrassment, for though war was integral to the culture of the Principal People, as it was to all peoples, overt aggressiveness in a community gathering was so rare as to be shocking.

Indeed, it became more shocking, for now the boogers proceeded to brawl among themselves. They struck each other clumsily, and shot mock arrows at targets which they invariably missed, and did dreadfully complicated pantomimes of dying. Two had blowguns, which they tended to get caught between their legs and to misuse horrendously; one tried to blow from the center of the tube instead of the end. When he finally got it right, he scored on another booger, who happened to be bending over; that man leaped up, angrily clapping his hands to his rear. He gestured as if pulling the dart out of his rectum; then he jammed it in the face of the one who had fired it at him. That one in turn pantomimed dying in disgust, crying, "Help! I am poisoned by booger dung!" Even some of the other boogers laughed at that, as it was an extemporaneous improvement.

"We can't have this!" the Chief protested when the laughter died down enough for him to be heard. "You must behave in a proper manner. See if you can dance decently with our women."

At this the boogers lost interest in combat. They threw away their weapons, which was yet another affront, for no good weapon was to be treated with disrespect. The dead ones came to life, and they stepped across the former barrier and selected women to dance with. By an odd coincidence, each booger chose his own wife, who pretended to be much frightened and reticent, but compelled by courtesy to accept. Tale Teller chose Laurel, who was a better foil for this sort of thing than the more serious Twice Cursed.

The boogers made a large circle around the fire, and their women made a smaller circle inside, in the customary manner. The women were nicely dressed, having prepared carefully for this event. Laurel, now nineteen winters old and a mother, had flowered into a spectacularly lovely woman who could indeed have found another husband had she chosen to dissolve her marriage at the first Green Corn Ceremony. But she would have stayed with Tale Teller even had she not had a child by him, because he kept her secret and never forced her. Indeed, he now realized that his one-armed status had been an encouragement for her, because it was evident that he could never hold her if she did not wish it.

The women danced in their normal manner, decorously, their feet shuffling with their knees relaxed, making dainty steps. The balls of their feet slid across the ground, with only their heels lifting and dropping. They moved rhythmically, circling in the direction the sun did, opposite to that of the men. Each one held up a fan with her left hand to shield her eyes from the fire, letting her right arm hang limp. The dance was not the place for gestures.

But the boogers seemed never to have heard of the set forms for dances. Instead of doing the eagle or bear dance, they seemed to be attempting a fish or frog dance, making the children laugh. They made obscene gestures at their women and did vigorous emulations of copulation, which the women pretended not to notice. But Laurel could not suppress the flush that spread across her fair features, however composed her face remained. In that moment she was breathtakingly beautiful, and Tale Teller was not the only man who noticed it. What a prize he had married!

Then, suddenly, the boogers charged away, pausing only to grab at a pretty girl of twelve winters, who screamed piercingly as they tried to haul her away from her laughing companions.

Foiled in taking this prisoner, they disappeared into the night, leaving behind only one final blasting sound of enormous flatulence.

The boogers went to their hiding place in a lodge at the edge of the village. The men removed their costumes and laid them aside. They checked each other to be sure that no evidence of their booger activity remained, then returned quietly to the dance as quite ordinary, well-behaved men.

The women, deserted by the boogers, had ended their dance and returned to the side. Laurel shot Tale Teller a reproving glance as he rejoined her, but he pretended not to understand her meaning. He moved on to join Twice Cursed and the two boys. Twice Cursed seldom smiled in public, but even her mouth quirked when No Spirit exclaimed, "I want to grow up to be a booger!"

"But boogers are terrible folk, with no manners at all, and insatiable sexual appetites," Twice Cursed reminded him. "Not at all like your father."

"Oh." The boy pondered that, disgruntled. Finally he sorted it out. "But—"

"Like your father in only one way," she amended her statement.

Someone else laughed. It seemed their dialogue had been overheard.

CHAPTER 14

RENUNCIATION

O Spirit of the Mound, I have told you how happy I was in marriage to Twice Cursed and Laurel, and how they bore me two fine sons. Now I will tell you how I thought you betrayed me, and how in my arrogant folly I renounced you and thus blinded myself to the danger you knew was coming.

When No Spirit was eleven winters, Tale Teller took him along on his tour. The boy was bright and interested in things, and had an aptitude for repeating stories, so it was time to give him further exposure. Ordinarily he would not have traveled with his father, but with his uncle of the Wild Potato Clan, because his closest relatives were those of his mother's side. But Twice Cursed had no surviving brother, and other clansmen were otherwise occupied at the moment, so they had agreed to let the boy's Blue Clan father substitute. Tale Teller suspected that a clansman could have served, but that they had seen the boy's aptitude and concluded that this trip with Tale Teller would be a good thing. The Principal People were in general nice to guests and women and adoptees, and were being nice now.

For years Laurel had kept him company on these trips, and this had always been his delight. After bearing Halfway Stream, she had returned to the honey, because she had found that she preferred the company of her husband to that of her child. This was not a negative thing, but rather that Twice Cursed was so competent to handle both boys and run the lodge that it had been easiest from the start to let her do it. But on the trail,

Laurel had charge of all female things, and had her husband all to herself, and this pleased her. So she remained slender, and ran with him, and satisfied his every interest.

Twice Cursed, too, was content with this arrangement. She was absolute chief of the lodge during Tale Teller's absence, and the two boys snapped to when she spoke. They were treated as brothers, though it was possible to figure a more complicated relation between them, and they were normal. It seemed that there had been a third curse that Twice Cursed had not seen fit to mention, and that was that she had not been blessed with a son. Now she really had two. But she too had gone to the honey, not caring to risk bearing another girl. The spirits had been good to her, late in her life, though they could become impatient if a person pushed them too far.

But it seemed that some of Laurel's honey had not been properly ensorcelled, or the herb in it had been cursed, so that it had not worked. Now, as a mature woman of twenty-five winters, she was with child again, and not wholly pleased. So she had to remain home, and this had made it even more convenient for Tale Teller to take No Spirit along.

Unfortunately, the spirits were angry with one of the villages on the route. The people there were suffering and sickening, and this was no occasion for the telling of tales. There was nothing that Tale Teller could do, so he and his son spent the night there and moved immediately on to the next village in the morning.

"Why are the spirits punishing that village?" No Spirit inquired, his curiosity piqued by the sight of the misery of the people. He knew that it was the work of hostile spirits, but he knew also that spirits usually had a reason for what they did, if it could be fathomed.

Tale Teller, raised in a different tribe, had had occasion to ponder such things himself. He was glad to share his conjectures with the boy, who would be a better tale teller for it, if that happened to be the way his life went. Tale Teller had seen how the understanding of the spirits differed from tribe to tribe, and how the attitudes of the spirits of the mounds were distinct according to their cultures. It had made him wonder whether there was any single truth about the spirits, or whether what the living folk knew was subject to interpretation.

"You know that there are several categories of spiritual beings," he began, reminding the boy of the larger framework. "That there are the great spirits of the Upper World, such as the Sun, the Moon, the Great Thunder—"

"And the Corn!" the boy exclaimed, happy to show how well he remembered.

"And the Corn," Tale Teller agreed, smiling. "Without these we would not be able to live through the winter, for they bring us light and rain and food, and measure the seasons. These great spirits seldom intervene in ordinary affairs, which are beneath their notice. However, the lesser spirits take a greater interest in lesser things—"

"Such as us!" No Spirit said.

"Such as mortal people," Tale Teller agreed. "For example, the Immortals are invisible spirits, unless they choose to be seen. Then they look like ordinary people, and we cannot know them from strangers from other villages. This is why it is best to be cautious when encountering strangers; you can never be sure what they are. But they seldom bother to be among the living folk for long, so if you know a man for more than a day, you can be almost sure he is mortal."

"Where do they live?" the boy asked eagerly.

"We cannot be sure, because they tell us only what they want us to know, and they may not tell us true. But we believe that many live atop the bald mountains, where no trees grow, and some live under the great mounds, and a few even live underwater."

"But how do they breathe there?"

"They don't need to breathe," Tale Teller explained. "They cannot die, so they breathe only when they want to, such as when they want to talk to mortal folk. Actually, we don't have to worry much about them, because they are friendly and will even help lost children." He glanced at his son. "But don't get lost; that would be embarrassing. They would think that neither I nor your uncles of the Wild Potato Clan had taught you well."

The boy nodded, having no intention of shaming his teachers by such incompetence. Every male child learned early how to find his way in the forest, noting the small details of his travels. "Then there's the Little Folk, no higher than a man's knee, with hair reaching to the ground, like Trolls," No Spirit said. "They help children too!"

"Yes, but they are mischievous, and if you disturb them they can make you magically ill. They may even curse you if you tell others you have seen them. So if you ever do see them, treat them with great care. If you find something on the ground that you think may have belonged to one of them, don't just pick it up; say, 'Little Folk, I mean no offense when I take this, and will return it if you ask.' Then you may keep it, if they do not ask." He took a breath. "In fact, it is best to be highly considerate of all the spiritual beings, because they are as resentful as anyone else when slighted, and may strike you with fever and weakness."

"Is that what happened to that village?"

"It may be. It might also be ghosts. Each person has a soul that lives on as a ghost after he dies, and these can make much mischief to the living if they are angry. That's why we shout and make noise when a person dies, to frighten his ghost up into the western sky. It is safest to be rid of ghosts, though they are by no means always harmful. I have talked to many spirits in the mounds, and they have never hurt me, and indeed, they sent me to the Principal People so I could marry your mother. I owe my life to the spirits of the mounds, and when they call I must answer."

"Is that why our mothers ask you not to visit the mounds?" No Spirit asked. He and his brother tended to refer to Tale Teller's two wives as mothers to both of them; it was the convenient way. "So you won't leave?"

"That is true. But their call cannot be escaped that way. When I receive the signal, I will have to go, however much it saddens me."

"May I go with you to a mound? Maybe I can talk with a spirit too!"

Tale Teller grimaced. "Do you know what your mothers would give me if I did that?"

The boy laughed. "Nothing—night and day!"

"Nothing except food and shelter," Tale Teller agreed. "And when you are grown, you will know how effective a threat that is."

"How did the villagers anger the ghosts?" No Spirit asked. "They looked very sick!"

"Very sick," Tale Teller agreed grimly. "But we do not know that ghosts are responsible for this."

"Animals, then. Maybe they killed a lot of animals and made them angry."

"It is true that animals also have souls, and that if a hunter does not apologize to an animal for slaying it, and take proper precautions, the ghost of that animal can wreak fearsome vengeance on the man. The man's limbs may stiffen and hurt, his digestion may become painful, and his head can ache. Even slain insects can curse with blisters and swellings. Their ghosts intrude themselves into a person and cause the illness. This can take some time, so the priest must inquire into the man's behavior for several moons or even seasons. Still, I doubt that the ghosts of animals are responsible for this, for those villagers honored the rules when they hunted, and indeed, they were careful of all spiritual beings."

"Then what is doing it?"

"In my travels I listen to all the tales others tell," Tale Teller said. "In this manner I learn new things, and can tell them thereafter. I have heard that a winter ago there were villages among the Catawba, who live to the east of us, that were stricken with bad illness, and many of the people died, yet they seemed to have done nothing to deserve this. As far as they could tell, there were evil spirits, coming from their east, who had been ravaging other villages. It is my fear that these are rogue spirits who are striking down the living folk without proper reason, or with no reason we know."

The boy was awed. "But suppose they attack our own village?"

"When we return there, I will talk to the priest and tell him what I fear, and then he will act to protect us from that. He will invoke stronger spirits to keep the rogue spirits away."

No Spirit nodded. "That is good."

Tale Teller had spoken reassuringly to the boy, but doubt remained in his own heart. He had no fear of evil spirits himself, because he lacked any fear and got along well with the dead. Also, he had the magic crystal Twice Cursed had given him, strapped always to his arm, which would guard him from personal harm. But others were not protected by this. Suppose the spirits did come to their home village of Bald Peak and attack his wives?

He put that ugly thought from his mind. His wives were such good people that he felt guilty even worrying about any harm coming to them. He knew they had never antagonized any spirits. Except for their insistence that he remain away from burial mounds. But anyone could understand that; they did not want to lose him as their husband. Women were like that. The spirits surely understood.

But when he and his son reached the next village, it too was under siege by the spirits, and they had to move on to a third. That one was all right, and their stay there was a success. No Spirit enjoyed listening to the familiar tales, because now he was seeing how important his father was to these people. Everyone loved the teller of funny and romantic and educational stories, and the village Chief presented him with a little wood flute that could be played one-handed.

As they traveled to the next village, they spied a great eagle in a tree near the path. It spread its wings and flew away, a giant among birds.

"Is that an omen?" No Spirit asked.

"It might be," Tale Teller agreed. "But it might also merely be looking for prey. I have seen such birds on occasion in these mountains. It is hard to be certain, because I was a member of the Eagle Clan of my tribe, before I became one of the Principal People, and they might be keeping an eye on me."

"Are they angry because you left them?"

"I don't think so, because it was the Eagle Spirits of the Toco mound and the Pyramid of the Sun who led me here to marry your mothers, and got for me the magic crystal to hold until the Ulunsuti is ready. I think they merely watch, to be sure I am ready when they call me."

"I hope they do not call you soon!" No Spirit said.

"I am sure they will wait until the time is appropriate. They have given me so many years with your mothers and with you and Halfway Stream that they must be able to spare a few more." He spoke with confidence, not wishing to alarm the boy. He hated the notion of leaving his family.

But when Tale Teller slept that night, he dreamed that the

spirit of Sun Eagle came to him in the form of that eagle they had seen. "The curse is coming!" he cried in the voice of the bird, but Tale Teller understood the words.

"Have you found the Ulunsuti?" Tale Teller asked.

"Not yet, but the search grows close. Soon I will tell you where it is."

Tale Teller hoped again it would not be too soon, for though he had left his home tribe in quest of it, he had found an excellent life here among the Principal People. At first he had expected at any moment to be called away, but when Twice Cursed got his child, he thought it would not come for a while. Somehow the ensuing years had caused the urgency of that quest to fade, and his doubt had grown that there really was a terrible danger.

Now, however, his belief strengthened. He had seen the spirits afflicting the two villages. Still, he could not leave without the Ulunsuti, so it was not yet time.

Yet if Sun Eagle was close to locating it, Tale Teller could not be certain how long he would be able to remain with his wives. He woke determined to return immediately to them, for every moment now seemed precious. He explained this to his son, for this was not a thing to be concealed from any member of his family.

"Let me go with you to fetch the Ulunsuti!" No Spirit exclaimed, excited by the prospect.

Take his son with him? The notion appealed. For that would mean that he would have to return to his wives, to bring the boy back, even after he got the great crystal. "We must see what the spirits say," he said.

They ran directly back to Bald Peak Village, the boy keeping the pace well. Even so, it took three days, for they had been far along on the circuit.

The women were well. "Why have you returned so soon, my husband?" Laurel inquired as she came to meet him, great with her child.

"I dreamed of Sun Eagle, and he told me a curse was coming. He may soon call me back to my quest. I want to have every moment I can with you, my wives and children, before that happens."

Both wives greeted this news with dismay. "We thought you

had forgotten that quest," Twice Cursed said gruffly. "Do you want to make me Thrice Cursed by taking my third and best husband from me?"

"When I need you to support me and my child?" Laurel added, patting her belly.

"No! I do not want to go!" he cried in anguish. "I want to stay with you both! But I cannot deny the spirits who sent me here."

Their two heads bowed as one. They knew it was so.

That night Twice Cursed treated him to a phenomenal demonstration of her prowess as a lover. She was old, four tens and two winters, but she knew him well, and she pleased him well. She was reminding him of what he stood to lose if he departed their lodge. It was a potent reminder, and he felt both guilty and sad at the thought of losing this fine family.

For he knew that he would not be able to take his family with him. Even if No Spirit came with him to fetch the magic crystal, that would be only the first stage. If he found the Ulunsuti, he would have to take it back to the Toco, to abate the terrible danger there, and that was surely no place for any member of his family.

This awareness bothered him by day and night. "No!" he cried aloud. "I do not want to do this! I want to remain with my family, who needs me. I have another baby to care for!" The others, overhearing, offered no argument.

The following night No Spirit came down with a fever.

Then Tale Teller feared indeed, for he remembered the fevers of the afflicted villages. Were the spirits warning him how quickly they could deny him the family he cherished?

No, that couldn't be! He had been ready to go to the spirits when they called. That was why he had returned, fearing that the eagle and the dream had been warnings of the approaching call. He didn't want to go, true, for he had had thirteen years with the Principal People, twelve with his wives, and all he wanted now was to remain with them. He made no secret of his desire to stay, but he had not *refused* to go.

He watched Twice Cursed stroking her son's hair back. Halfway Stream had been sent to fetch the priest, who would surely banish the vengeful spirits who had brought this illness to the boy.

The priest arrived. "An animal spirit has entered him because he traveled too far, without being prepared."

But Tale Teller feared worse. "The spirits have been devastating villages to the east of us. We were in two of them. Could one of those rogue spirits have entered him?"

The priest did not like to have his diagnosis questioned, but he had known Tale Teller a long time, and knew that he had deep respect for the spirits. "Have you asked the spirits of the mound?"

Tale Teller spread his hands. "My wives won't allow it."

"If you will not consult the spirits you know, you risk their anger."

How true! Tale Teller went to his wives. "I must consult with the spirits of the mound, to learn the nature of our son's affliction."

"No!" Laurel cried.

But Twice Cursed gazed at her fevered son. "If this is how they summon you, we can not oppose them. Go learn what they want, but ask them to spare your innocent son."

"Yes, go," Laurel agreed then. But there were tears in her eyes. She feared the power of the spirits, now being demonstrated. "Tomorrow."

"I should go now!" he protested.

"Can you not speak to the spirits from here?" she asked.

"A supplicant does not seek his own convenience. They are more likely to answer if I go to the mound."

"Tomorrow!" she repeated. "I want to be with you!"

She was afraid that he would not return. That the spirits would have a mission for him, and that she would never see him again. He could not deny that possibility. Laurel was great with child, and she feared being with a man in the lodge, but she was offering herself to him this night. That showed how great was her concern.

"Tomorrow," he agreed, ill at ease.

He intended only to sleep beside her, not to require the awkwardness of sex with her, but she insisted. She assumed a position that made it seem that she had no baby, as any woman could do when she chose. Because she faced away from him, he could not tell whether she feared, but somehow it seemed that she did not, and it was good. He was deeply

touched by her eagerness to please him and keep him close.
Perhaps she feared the loss of him more than she feared his
closeness in this circumstance. He preferred to believe that she
had finally put her old horror to rest.

But by morning he knew how badly he had erred by that
delay—for the fever came upon him too. His wives had prevailed upon him, but the spirits were now punishing him for
his weakness in yielding to the wishes of women.

Tale Teller wanted to go to the mound anyway, to plead with
the spirits for his son and for himself, but the fever rose and
took away his strength and made him first burn as with fire,
then shiver with seeming cold, and weakness made his body
collapse on the bed. His head hurt as if it had been smashed
with a club, and his heart was beating as if he were running
at his utmost speed.

Twice Cursed took the magic crystal out of its pocket on his
arm, and lifted it from its pouch, and hung it around his neck
on its original chain. Now its power was unfettered and it could
help him fight the evil spirits. This enabled him to sleep, irregularly, and gave him confidence that he could defeat the
invasion of spirits. They had to be ferocious ones, because even
the concealed, muted magic crystal would have stopped any
lesser spirits from attacking him.

No Spirit started vomiting, and then Tale Teller did too. The
priest gave them purifying water with the essence of redroot,
but they only threw it up again. He gave them snakeroot, and
wormseed, and a tonic of red cedar, but none seemed to have
effect. He invoked the most powerful spirits of the Sun and
Moon and Corn, but the hostile spirits inhabiting No Spirit and
Tale Teller were too strong.

"I must go to the mound!" Tale Teller cried. But he was too
weak to walk alone, and too sick to attempt it, even with the
help of the magic crystal. His back was sore, his muscles hurt,
and his nausea continued. He could remain on his feet only
with the support of both women, and they had to see to No
Spirit also.

As his fever raged, he suffered visions. In his mind he flew
to the mound and begged the spirits for help, but they only
laughed at him. "You ignored us for ten winters," one said,

holding up both hands with the fingers spread. "Now we are ignoring you. Fight your own battle with the hostile ghost!"

"But I would have come if you had called!" he protested. "I was waiting for Sun Eagle's call!"

"Sun Eagle!" they retorted, laughing.

"Why do you laugh, O spirits?"

"Who do you think sent this affliction to torment you and your son?"

"It could not be Sun Eagle! He was to send me a signal when he had the Ulunsuti!"

"Precisely."

"But he did not need to afflict me with this terrible illness to tell me that! I was ready to answer any other signal!"

"Did you answer the signal of the eagle?"

"That was just a bird!"

"Did you answer the dream of the eagle?"

He remembered how in the dream the eagle had been Sun Eagle, telling him that he had not yet found the Ulunsuti, but expected to soon. "But he did not tell me to come to him!"

"He told you," the spirit said. "You chose not to hear."

Tale Teller came out of his vision, wondering whether it had been a true one. *Had* he deliberately misunderstood the dream-signal? Because he did not want to leave his good family? "No!" he cried, but he feared he lied.

For a time he lay helpless but quiet, the vomiting stopped because there was nothing remaining to bring out. Then he heard his son groaning and thrashing, while the women tried to calm him. "Give him the magic crystal!" he gasped. "He needs it more than I do!"

Twice Cursed considered. "I fear it is a device of the spirits to strip your protection so they can kill you," she said. "I love my son, but I must not let them do this."

He had to accede to her logic. It was exactly the devious way evil spirits could act. He was doing better than his son was, because of the magic crystal—but that could quickly change if he gave up that protection. Still, he hated to let No Spirit suffer, and guilt lay with him.

The boy's exertions became more hectic. Tale Teller tried to cry out some reassurance, but could not. He heard No Spirit choking, and then the sounds stopped. The boy had settled into sleep at last, and now Tale Teller did also.

Only next day did he learn that No Spirit was gone. It had not been sleep for the boy, but death. The women had not told him.

Tale Teller had lied, and Sun Eagle had known it.

It was dangerous to attempt to deceive the spirits.

O Spirit, he thought, grief-stricken. *You did not need to kill my son to punish me! He had no guilt in this!*

But Sun Eagle did not relent. Small red spots appeared on Tale Teller's forearms, the palms of his hands, and the soles of his feet. The women informed him that they were on his face too. They formed into pimples, which became blisters. They itched, and he had to scratch them, but it did little good. He looked awful, but he did not feel as bad as before. Perhaps the evil spirit sent to torment him was being driven out through the skin. He was getting better!

But his son had been killed. Tale Teller had much time to ponder that as he lay resting in the lodge, and the longer he thought about it, the less he liked it. He had been ready to do what the Spirit had asked; it just hadn't been clear. He was sure Sun Eagle, in his first dream, had not told him to come; he had said that the time was near. That meant either that this illness was not a punishment for transgression, or that it derived from some other source. Which meant that it would be wrong for him to leave his family because of this; it could even be that the evil spirit was trying to harm him beyond its capacity by fooling him into thinking it was from Sun Eagle. The magic crystal had fought the evil spirit off, and it could not kill him, so it was trying to deceive him.

He began eating again, and some strength returned. He considered how he might get back at the evil spirits who had made him deathly ill and killed his son. Could he go to the mound, once he recovered, and get help from those good spirits against the evil spirits? That was the best way: to set a spirit against a spirit.

Then the blisters turned pussy, and his fever returned. Again he ached all over, and delirium carried him through the endless night.

"You still refuse to answer the signal?" the spirits of the mound demanded as his spirit floated from his body. "You wish to invoke further punishment?"

"What punishment can there be?" he retorted. "My son is dead, and if I too die, who will do your bidding?"

"Foolish mortal," they said, fading out.

It was a dream, a frivolous fancy, he thought as he woke. Sun Eagle had never appeared, and he could not trust what other spirits claimed. He doubted the ones who had spoken to him were even from the local mound. Once he recovered, he would go there and ask them.

His sores solidified and crusted over. The scabs smelled foul. But Tale Teller was feeling better, and he knew he was going to recover. He had defied the evil spirit, and it was rotting as it was pushed out of his body, and it had not succeeded in fooling him into leaving his family.

If only No Spirit had not died! Twice Cursed had been thrice cursed, losing two husbands and a son, and she was too old to have another. But at least Laurel's son remained, and he was very much like a son to Twice Cursed too.

Then Halfway Stream turned feverish.

"Why doesn't the priest come?" Tale Teller demanded.

"The priest has the fever," Twice Cursed replied.

Tale Teller was recovering, but still weak. "I must go to the mound!" he said. "I must ask the spirits there to drive out these evil spirits who are attacking us!"

But the women, worn from tending him and from carrying No Spirit to the charnel platform, and from their grief, and from the care of Halfway Stream, would not help him walk there, and he could not do it alone. He was recovering, but he remained lean and weak; when he tried to walk out of the lodge, he grew faint and had to lie down wherever he was. He had to wait.

Laurel got the fever.

"I must go!" Tale Teller cried. "This evil spirit is trying to take us all! I must go to the mound and get the spirits there to stop him!"

"I will get help for you to do that," Twice Cursed said, and left the lodge. Soon she returned, having given a message in the village. She did what she could to care for Halfway Stream and Laurel.

Hurting in his heart, Tale Teller sat down by Laurel and repeated the spell they had spoken together when their love first bloomed, in the forest by the stream. But he could not say it correctly; it changed in his mouth.

> Laurel!
> You are victorious! You are as beautiful in my eyes as the rainbow!
> You have captured my heart.
> You have taken my blood.
> You have taken my flesh.
> You have taken my eyes.
> You have taken my saliva.
> Your flesh and mine are one forever.
> You have magic! I must love you!

She smiled at him, briefly, remembering. But her fever did not abate. The evil spirits refused to release her.

When he looked up, he saw Twice Cursed watching them. There were tears on her face—the first time he had seen them there.

He got up and went to her and embraced her and kissed her, and they pretended that the tears were only hers, for it was known that no man wept.

Time passed. Days and nights seemed to be of little account, in the face of the terrible siege by the spirits. Slowly Tale Teller regained the strength of his body, but he was losing the strength of his heart.

Gray Cloud and Black Bone came to the lodge, all the way from their village of Five Birches, with their wives. Tale Teller was enormously glad to see them, for by this time Twice Cursed, too, had the fever, and Halfway Stream had red sores.

They did their best, but Halfway Stream died. Then Laurel faded. Tale Teller clung to her hand, and pressed the magic crystal against it, but its power was diminished by the effort it had made to save him, and she sank into a deep sleep, and then she died. Finally Twice Cursed died, seeming to have no further reason to live. All of them were taken to the charnel platform, for there could be no burials yet: too many others in the village were sick.

Black Bone and his wife went to help elsewhere in the village, where the need was now greater. Gray Cloud's wife, Red Leaf, remained with Tale Teller and Gray Cloud, taking over the woman's work for this lodge which now had no women of its own. She had always been the best of women.

Tale Teller was numb. He kept sleeping, and in his dreams his family was alive and well and happy. When he woke he tried to persuade himself that those he loved were simply outside, doing chores, and that they would return soon. For a little while he was able to believe it.

Tale Teller's scabs fell off and he was well again, but with depleted strength. Now at last he went to the mound, with Gray Cloud helping him.

As he walked, he went over things in his mind. He remained stunned by the deaths of all whom he loved, and now could function only by focusing on a single thing: why. Why had the spirits done this to him, when he had been ready to heed their call? He might have doubted, he might have hesitated, he might have balked, but he had known from the moment No Spirit got the fever that the spirits would compel him, and he would have gone right then had they told him to. They had not. Instead they had attacked every member of his family. Why? Only when he had the answer to that question could he think about anything else.

Gray Cloud did not speak. He knew what loss was like. His slow limping pace matched Tale Teller's weak one.

They came in sight of the mound, and Gray Cloud stood back. He understood about the private nature of this communion, too.

Panting and tired from the walk, because his recovery was not complete, Tale Teller stood before the mound. *O spirits, I come to you to ask your intercession against the evil spirits who are killing the people of this village. They have killed my family and attacked me, but others remain to be saved.*

That was not what he had planned to say to the good spirits, but it made sense. He did want to help others, and to stop the rampage of the malignant spirits.

He waited, but there was no response.

O spirits, did you speak to me in my dreams when I was fevered? I thought it was the evil spirits pretending to be you, saying bad things about Sun Eagle, but I am not sure. I could not believe that you would let such evil come to me and my family when I was ready to do your bidding.

Still the spirits of the mound did not answer.

He was becoming faint, for he was not used to standing this long, and the walk had tired him. He had to go while he had enough strength left to get back to the lodge with Gray Cloud's help.

O spirits, why did you not intercede when the evil spirits attacked? Even if I deserved punishment, my family did not!

Then at last he got an answer. *Arrogant man, you did not come to us from the time you took up with those women! They made you stay away, and you agreed! Why should we have helped you when you paid us no honor? Go away! We want nothing to do with you!*

Now at last he understood. He had alienated the spirits by not coming regularly to commune with them, and they had therefore cut him off. Their anger must have been building for ten winters—and was directed at his wives as much as at himself. Sometimes he had almost suspected this, but he had been unwilling even to think it, because he loved his wives. Now the stark reality of their deaths left him no alternative.

He made his way back to the village, increasingly leaning on Gray Cloud as his weakness manifested. By the time he reached his lodge, all he could do was lie down and sleep.

Now he dreamed of Dead Eagle, and the dream was so intense that he knew it was a true communion. *You have had the signal, Hotfoot/Throat Shot/Tale Teller. Go to Sun Eagle and fetch the Ulunsuti.*

Yet he was in doubt. *O Spirit of the Mound, I have had no signal. I saw an eagle, and dreamed of it, but I was not yet called.*

Foolish living man, you were called! You did not choose to hear. You were to go immediately to Sun Eagle to fetch the Ulunsuti.

O Spirit, but my son—

*You were to go with him, not stopping at any village. Only when
you held the Ulunsuti in your hand could you have rested. Now you
must go for it without your son.*

It was easy to accept strange things in a dream, but he remained confused. *But my wives—*

*You disobeyed, so you were stricken and your wives and sons were
taken into the spirit world. Do not again disobey.*

Tale Teller was appalled. *My innocent family—because I did not
understand?*

*Your family was merely an interim. When Sun Eagle found the
Ulunsuti, there was no further need to keep you entertained. When
you chose not to leave it, Sun Eagle took it from you. Now you can
proceed on your mission.*

Again he was appalled. *Good Twice Cursed and lovely Laurel—
dead because of me?*

*Your duty was to the spirits, not the living. Now your wives are
spirits.*

At this point Tale Teller woke with a cry. Gray Cloud was
there. "The spirits?" he inquired.

"Dead Eagle came to me in my dream, and told me that the
spirits took my family because I did not go immediately to fetch
the Ulunsuti. But I had not understood the call!"

Gray Cloud shook his head. "The spirits care little for excuses. You understand now."

"I understand now," Tale Teller agreed grimly. "But I'm not
sure that this is truly what the spirits want. Maybe it was only
a dream." He spoke as if he still had doubt, but it was something
other than that.

"You did see the eagle. Your family did die."

"But so did the people of the other villages we saw—and of
the villages of the Catawba last year. How can I tell that this
was truly a punishment directed at me?"

Gray Cloud had been with him at the Pyramid of the Sun.
He knew how important the quest for the Ulunsuti was to Tale
Teller. "Could it be that all those deaths in other villages were
warnings to you so that you would know it was time?"

"But my dream did not say that!"

"And you are unsure of the validity of your dream. Maybe
the spirits knew you would be reluctant to believe a dream, so
they showed you their power over the living people so that

you would know your dream was a valid signal."

He was making sense. "But how can I go to the Pyramid of the Sun alone? I can hardly walk to the local mound without collapsing!"

"I will go with you so that you can fetch the Ulunsuti," Gray Cloud said. "Then you can take it to your home tribe and use it to avert the danger there."

Tale Teller was amazed at his friend's generosity. "But your wife, Red Leaf, your family—"

"We have discussed this among ourselves," Gray Cloud said. "We decided that if the spirits are punishing you, they are punishing us also, for many others have died. It is better to help you, so that they will stop."

Tale Teller was grateful, for he knew that Gray Cloud had decided to help him regardless of the spirits. They had traveled to the great mound before, so now it was feasible.

Still, to have had the family he loved so well killed, merely because Sun Eagle's message had not been clear—Tale Teller could not accept that. He would do what he had to do, but he had lost any love he might have had for the spirits.

They prepared for the journey, setting up the good birch-bark canoe and loading it with supplies. Each day Tale Teller grew stronger; in just a few more days he would be able to travel, though Gray Cloud would be doing most of the paddling. They hoped that by the time they had to forge upstream, Tale Teller would have recovered enough to do his part with the paddle. Only in this way, leaning on his friend far more than he cared to, could Tale Teller do it at all.

Gray Cloud made an overnight trip to the high forest to gather more birch bark to repair a weakness in his canoe. Red Leaf remained, not concerned about staying there without her husband, and quite competent to keep the lodge in order. Tale Teller was relieved; he had seldom been alone since his marriage, and had grown used to company. Laurel had been with him on his tours—

A man did not show weak emotion, of course, but Red Leaf knew. She paused in her work and put her arms around him. "I will be your wife, this night," she said.

She was now a more solid woman than she had been when

he had first met her, but the beauty of her youth was echoed in her lined face. He realized now that this, too, was part of Gray Cloud's generosity; the man had arranged to leave his wife here for this, and she had agreed.

There was nothing to do with a gift of this nature except to accept it. Again he held a woman with his arm, and loved her, and in the darkness he could pretend it was Twice Cursed or Laurel. He even forget himself so far as to speak their names, and Red Leaf answered to them. How well she knew!

But on the day before they were to set off, Gray Cloud had the fever. The three of them stared at each other in horror. They all knew what it meant.

"But we are going for the Ulunsuti!" Tale Teller cried. "How can the spirits do this?"

They had to cancel the journey. Gray Cloud's fever raged, and he spoke in unearthly tongues as he thrashed his limbs about. Now Tale Teller saw how bad it looked to those who watched, and how it had been for his wives while he and his sons were possessed. He had faded in and out of awareness at the time, beset by his own discomfort, and had not appreciated how bad it was. He did what he could to help his friend, knowing it was hopeless. If the power of his magic crystal had not been exhausted, or if they had been able to fetch the Ulunsuti before the evil spirits struck again—But the good spirits had betrayed him. The spirits had betrayed them all.

Gray Cloud's skin developed red spots. These developed in the unfortunately familiar manner, and Tale Teller knew that the worst was coming. "If the spirits take me," Gray Cloud said in a moment of peace, "I give you my canoe, my friend, for you helped me build it."

"I would rather have your friendship than your canoe," Tale Teller replied fervently. The canoe was valuable, but Gray Cloud had been his first friend among the Principal People, though he had not originated with them any more than Tale Teller had. It was a phenomenal gift, but he did not want to receive it.

"So you can complete your quest," Gray Cloud said. Then he lapsed into troubled sleep. Red Leaf stroked his head, grieving for him, and Tale Teller saw the great love she bore her husband. She had been wife for a night to Tale Teller, but it was impossible to doubt where her love was.

Then Red Leaf got the fever.

Tale Teller ran out into the village. "All those I love are dying!" he cried. "Black Bone, where are you? Where is your wife?" All he could think of was a woman for the lodge.

A woman emerged from her own lodge. "They are ill with the fever," she said. "Someone is caring for them, as they cared for others."

"Who is there to help me or the friends in my lodge?" Tale Teller asked, appalled anew.

"I will help you, Tale Teller," she said.

She was Rat Fur, whose man had also come down with the malady of the spirits. "But you need to tend your own family!" he protested.

"My family is dead," she said. "The spirits came for me too, but I lived—as you did. I will do what has to be done."

So it was in the village. The horror of the savagery of the spirits continued day by day and night by night, unrelenting. By the time the last evil spirit had departed, three of every four people in Bald Peak had died, and those who lived were scabbed and gaunt. It was all they could do to take their lost family members to the charnel place.

Gray Cloud and Red Leaf were dead. Black Bone and his wife had also come to help, and they too were dead. Rat Fur was now going from lodge to lodge, helping those who were recovering. Tale Teller helped a surviving man haul the last body to the charnel place.

The charnel platform was too small. The extra bodies were lying on the ground beside it. No one had been buried, for there was not yet strength in the village to do it.

Tale Teller gazed at the bodies. All whom he had respected and loved were there. His terrible grief was replaced by a terrible anger. He had suppressed it before, hoping the spirits would finally relent, but now there was no need. "O spirits!" he cried in anguish and rage. "Your fury is meaningless! You punished me for nothing! You killed even him who was to bring me to you! I renounce you! I serve you no more! I curse you for this great wrong you have done! May the Sun burn you to foul smoke and the wind dissipate you across the land! May you suffer as you have made me suffer! I will never speak to you again!"

Then he turned away from the hideous sight and walked to the river where the canoe was ready. He got in and pushed away from the bank.

He was going to make a journey, but not to anywhere the spirits wanted him to go.

It wasn't easy, but he was able to handle the canoe from the rear position, paddling and sculling to keep it in the current. He moved down the long river, remembering his first journey with Gray Cloud and all that had happened later. But the one he remembered most poignantly was Laurel, so young at first, so frightened of a man at night, yet so wonderful when he came to know her better. He cursed the spirits for all the mischief they had done, but for her most of all.

The canoe had supplies for two, so he had enough to eat despite his inability to hunt with bow or spear. His blowgun was ready for any rabbit or squirrel he might spy. He dangled his line over the side and caught fish, which he cooked and ate when he camped.

He did not know where he was going, only that it was to his death. He would follow the canoe, and die where it took him to die. Then, perhaps, his spirit would return to wreak vengeance on the spirits who had killed all those he loved. That alone gave him comfort.

On occasion he passed other canoes. To those men who inquired, he replied that the spirits had killed his family and his friends and many of his clan, and now he hoped to die and settle accounts with them. They nodded with understanding; it was a good thing to do.

He wanted to die, but the canoe had not completed its journey, so he continued fishing and eating. At night he lay in the canoe and just let it float. Sometimes he woke to find it snagged in brush at the bank; then he disengaged it and set it drifting again.

The days passed. He did not keep count. He floated and ate and slept and paddled at need, continuing his journey. All he cared about was the torment of his loss, and the vengeance he hoped to take once he reached the place of the dead spirits. For now he knew that this was where the canoe was going.

In fact, as the endless hours and days faded behind, he realized that when he reached that place, the spirits of those he loved would be there waiting for him. Gray Cloud and Red Leaf, and Black Bone and his wife, and Twice Cursed and Laurel and No Spirit and Halfway Stream. He would be happy with them again, reunited. His separation from them was only temporary. He had been the one unlucky enough to have survived the onslaught of the spirits. Because they had arranged for him to have the magic crystal, now hidden again on his arm. Because they wanted him to complete his mission. He would have done it, if they had spoken more clearly. Punishing all those he loved, because of his misunderstanding—no, he would not do what the spirits wanted! Not now!

He knew that much time was passing as he slowly followed the river, because he saw the cycle of the moon. One moon, and another moon was passing—and he was in the enormous sea Gray Cloud had described, at the mouth of the monstrous river.

He paddled back toward the shore, for the immensity of the open water was daunting. He was not afraid of it, for the spirits had never returned his fear to him, but he did not see how he could make a fire to cook fish, or urinate or defecate conveniently, if he could not touch land. So he followed the shore, keeping it on his left, paddling into the rising sun.

Had he made a mistake? It was the setting sun where the spirits dwelt! Yet he had turned this way, and this was the way he was going. So he shrugged and continued. He would get where he was going, sometime.

There seemed to be no end to this journey into the sun. The second moon was gone, and he was observing the third—when a storm came up and caught him before he could get to land and drag the canoe to safety. All he could do was throw himself down inside the canoe and hang on.

The storm caught the canoe and turned it about and filled it with water. Tale Teller clung, gasping as the waves tried to wash over his head and drown him. Now that the time had come, he discovered that he was not eager to die. He had somehow pictured it as a more gentle thing. Suppose his body was carried into the sea and hidden there? How would his spirit find its way to the place of souls? He might never be reunited with his family!

The storm went on and on, the wind driving the canoe where it wished. Tale Teller managed to rouse himself enough to splash out some of the water with his good arm. The birch-bark canoe was so light that it could not sink, but it was no fun to lie in water. His paddle had been ripped away by the spirits of the water, and all he could do was go where the spirits of the wind were taking him.

He had no food, for his fishhook and line were gone, and everything else, even his wonderful blowgun. Only his magic crystal remained, strapped in its pouch to his arm. Perhaps had he had the full use of both arms, he could have hung on to more. Now he was at the mercy of the sea.

Gradually the storm faded. Each day the winds became less, until finally he was drifting in the still sea, with no idea where the land was. The sun beat down, and he was thirsty, but he would not drink the salt water. He remembered the Trader's warning, so long ago, that the water of the great sea was not fit to drink; the salt in it would kill a person faster than not drinking at all. So he did not drink, despite his knowledge that he had come here to die. Why he clung to life he did not know, but he did. Perhaps it had been that same reluctance to go that had prevented the evil spirits from taking him when all his family had died. That and the magic crystal, which his illness had so depleted that it could not save the others.

His family. How long ago and far away that was now! His love for them remained, but the intensity of his anguish had been somewhat purged by his journey toward death. He would never forget them, but he could live—now that he was truly going to die.

He realized that he would have renounced death itself, at this point, had he had the power. But he did not; death was going to take his spirit regardless. This, perhaps, was the meaning of the canoe's long journey: it had known that he would change his mind when the time came, so it had taken him to a place where he had no choice.

Slowly he sank down in the canoe, and the things beyond it had less meaning. Facedown, he waited for his arrival at the place of the spirits. At least he was not completely lost; his body was still in the canoe, instead of in the depths of the sea. He had been able to save that much.

A woman was holding him, putting water to his lips. He gagged on it. She tried again, and this time he managed to swallow some the right way.

"Is this the land of the spirits?" he rasped.

The woman seemed not to understand him. He had spoken in the tongue of the Principal People, so he repeated the question in Toco, and then in other tongues, trying all he remembered. When he tried Calusan, at last she seemed to understand.

"No, Throat Shot," she replied, calling him by a name he had discarded long ago. How could that be?

"Who are you?" he asked, realizing that this was strange, even for dying.

"I am Heron Feather."

"You cannot be!" he protested. "Heron Feather is the Cacique's wife, beautiful and loving!"

"That was ten and five winters ago," she said. "Now I am old, and he long ago set me aside for younger wives."

He stared at her, his tortured vision clearing, and the recognition came. She looked as Heron Feather's mother might, her beauty a memory. "You are still lovely to me," he said, grateful for her care, and fell asleep.

Something about their exchange must have pleased her, for Heron Feather was extremely attentive to his needs, always there with more water and food when he woke, and holding him when he slept. His waking periods became longer and his exhausted sleeps shorter; he was recovering. He discovered that his armband was missing, and was alarmed, but Heron Feather immediately brought it back to him, clean, with the magic crystal still in it. She had not stolen it from him.

He learned from her that his beautiful strange canoe had been found adrift, far out in the sea. Thinking it empty, fishermen had checked it, and found him inside. So they had brought him in, and the Cacique had recognized him because of the bad arm, and assigned Heron Feather to revive him. She had been glad to do this, remembering their prior liaison.

Tale Teller nodded. He was glad she was the one, for the same reason. He explained about his current name, and how he had come to be in the sea. "I thought I would die, but when the time came I wanted to live, though I still hurt for my wives and sons and friends."

"One of your wives was older than I, yet you loved her?"

"Yes. Twice Cursed was a good woman and a good wife."

She nodded as if that meant something to her, but did not comment. He slept again.

He dreamed he was indulging in sex with Heron Feather, and woke to discover it was true. He remained weak, and she had to help him, and it was as it had been ten and five winters before, for different reasons. She seemed very pleased to do this for him, and it did give him solace, for he had seen in the reflection of the water how ugly he was now, with scars on his face where the evil spirits had emerged as sores.

But when it was done, she was sad. "Now you are well enough to meet the Cacique," she said.

"How do you know that?"

She touched his penis. "When a man is well enough for this, he is well enough to travel."

That seemed to make sense. "But where am I to go? I had no destination in the living realm."

"The Cacique will tell you." She, as a woman, was not privy to man's business.

The Cacique was older and fatter, but recognizable. "You are too weak to paddle yourself home," he said. "My men will take you there, in exchange for your valuable possession."

"My possession?" he asked, thinking of the magic crystal. He had hoped that Heron Feather had not told the Cacique of that, for it was all that remained of his association with Twice Cursed, and he did not want to give it up.

"Your magic canoe."

Now it came clear! Seldom if ever was a birch-bark canoe seen here. Even battered as it was, this one was a novelty. Yet it was Gray Cloud's gift, and he could not wholly give it up. "Let me keep one little piece of it, and I give it to you in return for saving my life from the sea."

The Cacique smiled. "Done!"

They went to the canoe, which was not in good condition,

but remained riverworthy, for Gray Cloud had been good at
his craft. Tale Teller stripped off a loose curl of white bark the
length of his finger, and bound it into his hair. He had lost the
blue feather of his membership in the Blue Clan of the Principal
People, and by this token knew that he was no longer one of
them. The spirits had taken even that from him. But they could
not take away his memories of friendship and love. "He who
made this was my friend. I keep this to remember him."

The Cacique smiled. "If ever you have another friend like
him, bring him here to make canoes like this for us!"

Tale Teller returned to Heron Feather. "I thank you for leaving me my—" he began, touching his arm.

"Do not speak of it," she said quickly. That could have been
from generosity, or from fear of the power of the crystal, or
from concern about what the Cacique would do if he learned
she had concealed something of such value.

"Then how may I thank you?" he asked.

"Perhaps you will think of a way," she said, opening her
robe. Then he realized how much she valued his sexual interest
in her, for it seemed that no one else had such interest since
her casting off by the Cacique.

He had three more days with Heron Feather, which he enjoyed, for he saw within the larger casing of her flesh the beautiful woman who had taught him sexual love, and she was
flatteringly eager to please him. She also now reminded him
somewhat of Twice Cursed. In that time they managed to complete the sexual act five times, making the total the same as
that on their first night, when they both were young. This
seemed fitting to each of them.

"You have been as generous to me as you were when we
first met," he said sincerely. "I would like to take you with me
to the Toco."

She shook her head. "I cannot go among the primitives. But
you have given me much cause for joy." By that she meant
that her joy had been in having him desire and possess her,
rather than any inherent pleasure of the act. She lived to be
desired, and perhaps the act had no other meaning for her.

Then it was time for him to leave, according to the Cacique,
and Tale Teller was in no position to question this. He rode in
a double dugout canoe with four strong paddlers, and they set

off north. Heron Feather waved to him, and he felt sad to leave her, as if they had had a longer association. In a way it had been ten days, much like man and wife; in another way it had been ten and five winters, much like lost lovers. It was also as though some of his futile remaining love for his two fine wives had detached and joined Heron Feather, easing his loss. He knew now that he needed a woman, and always had, and she was the woman he needed at the moment.

So rapidly as to amaze him, the Calusa paddlers reached the mouth of the Little Big River, and forged up it. In another day they reached the village of Atafi.

The people were surprised to see Calusa here, in their strange craft. But Tale Teller got out and spoke to them in Toco: "I am of your tribe. I have returned after ten and five winters. The Calusa brought me."

Soon the chief had verified his identity and welcomed him back. The four Calusa were treated as guests, with the company of four beautiful and attentive young women, and in the morning they set off for their own territory, well pleased. Relations between the Toco and the Calusa had not always been good, but they seemed likely to be better in the future.

For Tale Teller things were not as good. The Toco accepted him, for he was a member of their Eagle Clan, but his parents had died of natural causes in the interim and few people really knew him after his long absence. He was a relative stranger.

Then Striker of Warriors approached him: the man he had known as a boy as Woodpecker. Deceiver of Enemies also came, the one he had known as Alligator. They were now prominent warriors of the tribe, and their recognition caused a significant mellowing of local attitude. It was good to have friends again!

He settled into his role as Tale Teller, telling of his strange adventures, and the other tales he had learned. He traveled to the other Toco villages and did the same. Now he became known and liked here, because of his skill in entertaining and teaching. His life became as it had been among the Principal People, except that he had no family. He tried not to think about that, preferring to seal it off as some other life. That way it did not hurt as much. There were ways in which his present situation reminded him of his first travels among the Principal People, before he was married. How he wished the evil spirits had never come, and that he was still with Twice Cursed and Laurel!

Three moons later the Trader came in his canoe. He too was older, and looked as if he would not be making many more such strenuous circuits. With him was a woman who saw to his comfort and handled the details of his trading.

Tale Teller approached to introduce himself to the Trader, for the man was a valued part of his past experience. Indeed, each such person he met helped strengthen his ties to this region, and make him stronger here. It seemed that his roots, at one time cut off, were growing back, while the roots he had developed among the Principal People were healing over, remaining severed.

The Trader recognized him. "You have suffered much!" he remarked in his own tongue. "But I think your suffering is done." Then he turned to the woman, who was mature but small, and actually quite pretty. "The spirits told you true, my daughter. He has returned."

She was the Trader's daughter? Then what had happened to little—?

The woman faced Tale Teller squarely. "Do you not know me?" she inquired. "I have loved you since I was nine winters old."

"Tzec!" he exclaimed, amazed.

CHAPTER 15

WREN

O Spirit of the Mound, I had renounced you at this time, because I did not understand the nature of the warning I had received. Now, too late, I understand, and I know also that I cannot hope for your favor after what I did. But these others buried here did not renounce you, and they are blameless, so I tell you their stories and beg you to listen. All are dead because I renounced the mission you gave me, but at least their spirits will be safe with you. Now I will tell you of my life with Tzec, and of our daughter, Wren.

The grief of Tale Teller's past fell away as he gazed at her. So this was Tzec, the little girl the Trader had bought and then adopted. Somehow she had remained nine winters old in his mind, though fifteen winters had passed since he left her. She was now a fully grown woman of ten and ten and four winters. Two winters younger than Laurel.

Laurel. The horror of her death surged up, clouding his vision. The deaths of all his friends returned in a rush, because he had in his surprise let down his guard, and they tried to overwhelm him. Such sieges came less often now than they had at first, but he knew they would never entirely fade. He did not want them to; there was pain in the memories, but also joy. They were much of what he was.

"Am I so ugly in your sight?" Tzec asked.

He returned to the present. He saw her exquisitely formed body, like that of Beautiful Moon, but smaller. Her two breasts

346

were so full and perfect and her face was so lovely that he knew her to be the equal of her Maya mother. "No, Tzec. You are beautiful. You reminded me of one I loved." Actually, she had reminded him physically of Heron Feather in her vibrant youth, and Beautiful Moon, but most of all of Laurel in her entirety. He had truly loved only Laurel.

"She is dead?"

"Yes." There was so much more to say, but that had been a different world, best left alone.

She smiled tentatively. "I would do for you what she did."

Her import began to register. "You are not married?"

"Little Blood did not marry."

He looked at her with a new appraisal. She was not merely beautiful, she was ardent. She looked as if she were a maiden of ten and six winters, full and fresh, in the sight of the warrior for whom she longed. She was small; that was part of it. But increasingly he recognized the features of that long-ago child he had traveled with, as if her present face and form were a lovely mask which concealed her nature only imperfectly. The one who had told him the Tale of Little Blood and introduced him to the wonders of the ways of the Maya. The one who had been there for his initiation with Heron Feather—and who was now as lovely as the Cacique's wife had ever been. The one who the spirit of the huge mound where the Little Big River ended had said would change his life.

She had done that, he realized, for she had with her story of Little Blood introduced him to the marvel of serious tale-telling. Thereafter he had collected tales, and now they were his livelihood. Without the tales, his life among the Principal People would have been otherwise, and he might never have married. But now—could the spirit have meant more than tales? For Tzec was speaking as plainly as a woman could of marriage.

"I have only one arm," he said.

"I noted that some time ago."

Of course she had; he had been foolish to mention it. But it was hard to believe that this desirable woman could desire him. He was now thirty winters and aged by grief.

"I have to travel, to tell my tales."

"I like to travel." Of course she did; she traveled with the Trader. She surely took good care of her father, and would take even better care of a husband.

"I have no wealth, and I cannot hunt." Actually, he could gain wealth through the gifts he received for his tales, and he could hunt if he got another blowgun, so he knew he was not being forthright. Yet he was reluctant to accept her interest directly; he wanted her to persuade him that she was sincere.

Tzec smiled, sensing her victory. "I have shells to make you wealthy."

He looked at the Trader somewhat desperately. "What would you do without a traveling companion?"

"I have a good wife at home," the Trader said. "I am old; I want to stay home now and get to know her. I have been waiting nine winters for you to take this daughter off my hands." There was a quirk at his mouth, for it was obvious how satisfied he was with Tzec. But a father's duty was not complete until his daughters were married.

No help there! Yet, though this was completely unexpected, Tale Teller discovered that his feeling was rapidly conforming to their expectations. He had thought there could be no woman for him after the two he had married, no family for him after the one he had lost. But Tzec—she had known him so well, so early. She could be under no illusions about his nature. If she truly wanted him, she could have him, despite his lingering image of her childhood.

The woman had approached him, and her father had approved. The Toco tribesmen were witnesses. Tale Teller's silence constituted agreement. This was not the way a marriage was normally made among the Toco, because the relatives and clansmen had not been involved, but none of the three was truly Toco now. It was close enough.

Tzec took him by the hand and led him away from the Trader and the standing group of villagers. No one had moved or spoken except the three of them since Tale Teller had encountered Tzec and the Trader. Suddenly he realized that they all had known that he was to be married on this day.

They walked out of the village, to a clearing in the forest. There, secure from the eyes of others, Tzec held his arm, brought him to a stop, turned in to him, and embraced him.

She kissed him with a hunger that amazed him. Ten and five winters of desire—and he had never known! He had thought of her only passingly in that interval. Yet now he realized that all his encounters with women had been echoes of her, of a desire for her he had never allowed himself to recognize. A nine-year-old child!

"The spirit told me you would have to marry another before you returned to me," she said, inviting him to clarify the matter.

"I married two. A mother and her daughter." Now he found he had to tell her. "Both good women. I loved them. They bore me sons. But the evil spirits came and killed them. I thought to die myself, but the river bore me here."

"The spirits of the mounds—"

"I have renounced them because they did not protect my family or my friends."

"But they were so much to you!" she protested. "And you are marked, showing your affinity. When I saw that mark, I knew I would marry you. How can you renounce them?"

"They killed Gray Cloud and Black Bone," he said. "They killed Twice Cursed and Laurel. They—"

"Laurel," she said, attuned to his greatest feeling. "Tell me of her."

"She was Twice Cursed's daughter, only ten and three winters when I married them, but pretty. Later she became beautiful, as lovely in my sight as you are now. Twice Cursed knew all the ways of a man, but Laurel was afraid. Even with the honey, it was—" He shrugged.

"I know how it was," she said.

He glanced at her, wondering how that could be true. "But in the daytime, she was—we were running together, and I had a sudden passion for her, and then she—" Again he had to shrug. Why was he telling this woman that?

"In the day she could do it," Tzec said. "Because she loved you, and you loved her."

"Yes. She took my heart, she took my blood, she took my flesh, she took my saliva, and I took hers. We joined forever."

"I would do for you what she did," Tzec repeated.

"But to me you are still little Tzec, nine winters old!" he protested.

"And as lovely in your sight as Laurel was when you loved

her," she reminded him. "Girls do mature, in time."

Had he said that? It didn't matter, for it was true. Yet that image of her childhood restrained him. How could he take little Tzec as a woman? He did want to, but he could not. He felt desire and guilt.

Then he remembered something else.

"When I was with her mother, Twice Cursed, my other wife, the first time, I did not know what to do," he said somewhat falteringly. "She asked me whether I would have her passive for my pleasure, or otherwise. I told her—"

Tzec took his hand and set it on her left breast. It was as full and firm and soft as that of Beautiful Moon. Answer enough! In a moment in his mind's eye the child became clothed in the body of the woman. He had protested because he did not want to seem to have a sexual hunger for a child, but now he knew it was for the woman that child was to become, and had become. Yet the child remained, seeming to mock him in that lingering familiarity of feature.

Then they were in the throes of it. He was not conscious of removing his breechcloth or of her getting out of her skirt or of finding a place on the ground. She must have done what needed to be done. He found her on him, embracing him, fitting herself to him in the manner he had first learned with Heron Feather, her hands kneading the flesh of his shoulders as her legs squeezed his own. This was as experienced a woman as he had ever been with! The remaining part of his image of nine winters dissipated like smoke, yet his memory of their prior time together became sharper. He was having both: that girl he had not known he loved, and this woman who had such passion. Ten and five years of buried longing were flowering, for both of them.

Yet also it was Laurel, who had now become the one he had longed for in Tzec. Her heart, her blood, her flesh, her saliva. "Oh my love!" he whispered. "It was always you I desired!"

"I know," she said, and lifted her face to kiss him.

"But I did not know!"

"I know that too." Satisfied that she had wrung out his passion for the moment, she relaxed. "But you had to learn the way of love with others, and so did I, before we were right for each other."

"But they were good people!" he said, not wishing to wrong his prior wives. "I cannot give up my memories of them!"

"I know they were. I know you cannot. I have been with good people too. But now we are together."

So it seemed. He remained amazed, yet his grief had been mitigated by joy. He knew the others had been worthwhile in their own right, but for him they had been only temporary. Tzec was the one he should have been with all along.

Then he realized something else. "The honey! You used no honey!"

"Yes, I did," she said. "Always. Until now."

Somehow that made sense.

That day was not their marriage formally, for it was necessary first for Tzec to be adopted into the Toco tribe and the Panther Clan. Thereafter her new relatives of the Panther Clan consulted with his relatives of the Eagle Clan, and they concluded that it was a suitable union, and an Eagle warrior approached Tale Teller while a Panther woman approached Tzec, and notified them quietly of that conclusion. Then Tzec approached Tale Teller and formally proposed marriage to him, as was the custom at this stage, and he accepted. A time for the ceremony was set.

There was a dance around a big outdoor fire. Then Tale Teller sat on one side of it, and Tzec sat on the other. Beside each of them was a clan sponsor, for this was more than a liaison between two people, it was a union of the two clans.

Tzec's sponsor stood. She was an elder matron of the Panther Clan. "I have known this woman since she was a child at River Village," she said. "Then she was quiet, for she was new, and orphaned. But she was adopted by the Trader of the Tribe of Ais." Here she glanced at the Trader, who nodded graciously. "She was with him many winters, and helped him trade, and though we saw her only once each summer season, we came to respect her well. We know her to be a good woman, and we of the Panther Clan are honored to have adopted her. We know she will be an excellent member of our tribe."

Then Tale Teller's Eagle Clan sponsor stood and spoke of him, as Hotfoot and then Throat Shot and finally Tale Teller, whose stories they so liked to hear. "He has been long away from us, but now he has returned, and we know him to be of good character and a credit to the Eagle Clan.''

The Panther matron addressed Tzec. ''Now you, oh our fair daughter: you are about to take upon yourself the duties of a wife and the care of a lodge. You must give the son of the Eagles your talents, even when you find him tired or angry. You must be patient, and treat him well at all times, for this is the responsibility of a wife. I have spoken.''

The Eagle elder warrior addressed Tale Teller. ''Oh our good son, you are to be a husband. Be true, be kind, be patient with her, though there may be times when you wish to speak harsh words. Hold back those words, and speak pleasantly, so that your wife will be glad to see you. By your thoughtfulness you will prove yourself as a husband and a father. I have spoken.''

The Panther matron took Tzec's arm and brought her around the fire, and the Eagle warrior did the same with Tale Teller. They came to stand beside each other. Then Tale Teller gave her his most prized possession: the magic crystal. There was a gasp of awe from the tribespeople as he opened the pouch and let the crystal flash in the firelight before concealing it again and putting its cord around her neck. They had known he would give her something of great personal value, but this was far beyond their expectations. Tzec herself was so surprised that for a moment she forgot her role, and just stared down at the pouch which lay between her breasts. Then the matron nudged her, and she remembered the ritual. She lifted up her long hair and flung it over Tale Teller's head like a cape.

The priest came forward. ''These two are one,'' he said, seeming somewhat daunted himself by the appearance of the magic crystal. Tale Teller was a far more important person than they had realized, to have carried such a thing! Now Tzec was important too, for the crystal had not struck her down. ''Let them go with our good wishes.''

Tale Teller and Tzec linked hands and walked to the lodge they had set up in the River Village. Behind them, the dancing resumed, with shouts and music and noise, to cover any sounds that might be made in the lodge. There was great good humor; weddings were always happy occasions.

As soon as they were alone, Tzec faced him, her eyes round. ''Where did you get it?'' she demanded.

"Twice Cursed gave it to me, to keep me safe. It kept me safe, though everyone else died. Now I want to keep you safe, for I love you as I loved my two former wives. Its power was depleted, saving me from the evil spirits, but perhaps it has recovered now."

"But with this I can be a seer and a healer!"

"You surely are already," he said. "All the tribe knows how you have helped those who are in distress."

She nodded. "I will use it only for good purpose."

Only then did they get down to the business of love. It was savagely sweet.

Thereafter they traveled together. Another woman went with the Trader: a young widow who was satisfied to do what she could for him if he delivered her to a place where she might find a new husband. The Trader suggested that she check the prospects at each of his trading stops, and remain at the one that seemed best. Tzec advised the woman on the Trader's tastes and on the villages with the most interesting males. Tale Teller was surprised and a bit dismayed at her evident competence in this regard. But Tzec showed no resentment of his prior love for other women, and he could afford none for her knowledge of other men. All that had ended now, for both of them. Or so he thought, at first.

They made a journey up the river, following a route Tzec well knew. They had to drag their canoe through the mud in several places, but there was always a channel ahead. The people they encountered were friendly; they knew Tzec, though they were surprised to see her with a man other than the Trader. They reached the tribe of the Ais, and met the Trader's wife, Tzec's adopted mother. The Trader had not yet completed his long circuit, so she was alone, and seemed satisfied that way. She was old, and somewhat sour, but Tale Teller saw that there was genuine understanding and affection between the two of them. Tzec had explained on the way that her mother's name was Doña Margarita and that she was from far across the eastern sea.

Intrigued, Tale Teller talked with the woman, studying her native tongue. He had not worked on a new tongue for several winters, and the challenge appealed to him. In a few days he had enough of it so that he could hold a limited dialogue with Doña Margarita, and she warmed to him considerably then. She asked him to visit again when he could.

"She has never said that before," Tzec confided. "I am her only friend."

"Not the Trader?"

"My father is her husband." Answer enough; a husband was no friend to a wife, ordinarily.

Tale Teller plied his trade in the Ais village, entertaining young folk who had not been alive when he was last there. They were impressed; they had never heard such excellent stories of such far places. They, too, asked him to visit again, and they gave him a fine feather cloak.

Tzec collected her shells, and they carried them to their distant canoe. The trip might have been tedious, but she made sure that it wasn't. She seemed to have an appetite for sexual expression that matched his, and she was always thrilled with his performance. Not since Heron Feather and Beautiful Moon had he been coaxed to such repeated exercises. Whether they were in a lodge at night, or paddling in the canoe, or walking through marsh, Tzec always made him feel like a man ten winters younger. Not for some time did he catch on that much of it was artifice—and then he was smart enough not to let her know he had caught on.

Next spring Tzec birthed a girl, and they named her Wren, for a reason no one else but the Trader would know. Wren had an irregular purple mark on her spine, just above the swell of the buttocks. "She has my mother's mark!" Tzec exclaimed when she saw it, thrilled. Thereafter she used the honey, and though she always welcomed his interest, she no longer encouraged him to multiple demonstrations. She now had another thing to take her attention.

Tale Teller remembered how it had been with Laurel, and let it be. He realized that while Tzec loved him, her sexual fervor had been driven by her desire to get her child. Now that had been satisfied. Her birthing had been difficult, for she was small and the baby was large, and at ten and ten and five winters she felt the strain of it worse. He still thought of Tzec as young, but in truth she was not, any more than he was. So he did not object to the honey. He had, after all, many fond memories of it.

During the later stages of the child within her, and the early stages after the birthing, Tzec did not travel with him on his tale-telling circuit. "You have had the monotony of one woman for a while," she said. "Now you will have some variety again."

This was a more liberal view than most Toco wives had. But he knew from his experience with the Principal People that attitudes differed, and Tzec was not Toco in origin or experience. She had traveled widely with the Trader, and the Trader took his women where he found them, even after he married. So it was not surprising that she accepted this in her traveling husband.

"I thank you for your understanding," he said, a bit disgruntled.

"And of course I shall use the honey when any man I desire comes to me," she said.

Then he realized the full nature of her understanding. She had taken her men where she found them too, when she traveled. He had learned of her continuing relations with the Cacique of the Calusa, for she kept nothing from him. His feelings about the Cacique were mixed: he was glad the man had taught Tzec so well about sex, but he was not eager for Tzec to visit him again.

But now she had her child, and was disinclined to travel, and the Cacique was far away. There was no problem.

Women did come to his lodge now, in other villages, for he had become a person of stature. They were young and pretty and obliging. Yet somehow none of them came close to Tzec in his estimation, though she was ten winters older than some. There were other things than youth to recommend a woman, as he had learned with Twice Cursed. He would rather have had her traveling with him.

Tzec was pleased when he returned and told her that. "You would not mind having Wren along?"

"She is my daughter. I want her with me."

So when they deemed it safe for the baby to travel, they went as a family. Sometimes Wren was nursing at the same time as he was in Tzec. His penis felt her cleft squeeze as the baby sucked. It was a wonderful closeness.

But when Tzec saw a young warrior who had been injured in the foot and was spurned by the local women, she gave Tale Teller the baby to care for and went to that man's lodge with her honey. Tale Teller reminded himself forcefully that if Tzec had not had a concern for those who had suffered injury, she would not have cared about him. He had to let her do what she wished. He knew her motive was generous, and that this in no way disparaged her relationship with him.

She returned later in the night, having, as she described it, put the young man to sleep. She embraced Tale Teller ardently, before she went to nurse, though her breasts were now swollen with milk. "I was a woman to a youth," she said. "Now let me be a woman to a man."

If he had had any resentment about her action, it became of little consequence. It was quickly apparent that however much she had satisfied the youth, the youth had not satisfied her. Tale Teller did that. He knew her well enough now to distinguish her pretense from her genuine feeling, and what she had with him was genuine. Now he better appreciated Heron Feather's need to be desired, for he was having his own need to be desired satisfied. The sexual experience was phenomenal, because his heart was beating against her full breasts as strongly as his penis was thrusting into her cleft. His whole mind and body loved her, burning like a fire.

"Yes," she gasped. "That is what I need, my love!"

There were other cases, but never again did he suffer the mixed feelings he had that first time. Sometimes Tzec even asked a neglected maiden to come to his lodge, so that she could discover what real sexual experience was. Deeply flattered, he did his best to please such maidens, and in that effort found a special type of pleasure himself. It was not simply sexual; there was a reputation spreading that the best night a maiden could have was with a one-armed old man. For that reputation he would have given up more of the sexual pleasure than he did. Tzec's way was providing him unanticipated benefits.

The news of Tale Teller's skill as a storyteller spread more widely, and he was invited to more villages. His circuits became longer, and his stays at River Village briefer. Since Tzec now traveled with him, he did not feel the need to hurry home. In fact, she had started using the magic crystal to heal those who were hurting, when she deemed it appropriate, or to enhance the sexual prowess of those in doubt of it, and was now in demand in her own right. When they could use a canoe they did, but some villages were inaccessible by water, except by their making an extremely long trip to the mouth of the Little Big River and back up a new river. Often it was easier simply to walk, carrying Wren. Had he been alone he would have run, but Tzec was not a runner, so he learned to walk. It was worth it.

When Wren was two winters old, an old warrior came to ask Tale Teller to visit the village of Chief Mocozo to the south. This was a considerable distance by foot, and Tale Teller was uncertain, but the warrior spoke of the Chief's eagerness to have him, and of his generosity. "Also," he said, "there is one we think you would find interesting to meet."

"I am interested in all I meet," Tale Teller said. "But not so much so that I care to make such a long walk."

"This man is from across a great sea."

Suddenly Tale Teller was indeed interested. Tzec had told him of her adopted mother, Doña Margarita, and he had met the woman and learned part of her tongue. Could this be another like that? Still, such a long walk for Tzec was daunting, and he did not want to go alone.

"He is with me," the warrior said. "His name is strange: Juan Ortiz. Chief Mocozo thought you might come if you could talk with this man while you walked."

Tale Teller talked with the man, and indeed, he was from the same far land as Doña Margarita, but he did not know her. He was short, and there were the scars of burns on his body. He was happy to tell his story in detail, but that would take time, and Chief Mocozo had instructed him not to do so unless he brought the Tale Teller to the village.

So it was that Tale Teller agreed to go, and they made the long trek. On the way the strange warrior, Juan Ortiz, told his story, and Tale Teller learned more words of what he called the Castile tongue from him. He had started with Doña Margarita, and now added considerably to his knowledge of this strange type of speech, because its oddity intrigued him. Tzec, listening, picked up a few words, and even littie Wren seemed interested.

Chief Mocozo was indeed gracious and generous, and they remained in his village for half a moon. Only when Tale Teller had told every tale he knew was the Chief willing to let him go, and then it was with some fine gifts of beads that gladdened Tzec's heart. He even sent Juan Ortiz with them so that Tale Teller could continue studying his tongue. By the time they reached Toco Atafi, where Juan Ortiz spent the night and turned back for his home village, Tale Teller had learned much, and he was glad he had made the trip. So was Tzec. She had surprised Juan Ortiz with her knowledge of the activities of his home tribe of Castiles and the Mad Queen Juana. They might never meet again, but they had become friends.

As Wren grew older, Tzec taught her the ways of women. She learned to gather sticks for the evening fire, and her sharp little eyes were able to spot some excellent pieces. She learned to harvest berries and tubers and the fruits from trees, for these were the main things people ate, to supplement the mussels from the river, and it was the woman's job to provide them. Tzec, of an independent nature, did not enjoy doing these things as other women did, and preferred to trade for food when she could. She expended her precious shells to get corn from traders to the north, and showed Wren how to grind the kernels between flat stones to crack them and crack them again, so that they could be cooked or baked for eating. The child was fascinated by the way the corn swelled up in hot water and became mush, and how it hardened when baked, becoming bread. Wren was bound to be a better wife in this respect than Tzec was, when her time came.

Tale Teller took Wren out when the tribe burned the forest. They did this every few years, to get rid of the thick jungle and clear the ground, so that new growth would develop, and the deer would come to graze on it, and hunting would be good. Deer meat was prized, and they made it last as long as they could, and of course tanning the skins was important. The child was awed by the rearing flames as the spirits of the fire consumed the ground. But after it burned out, black ashes lay everywhere on the ground, and the trees were not damaged. Then soon new green shoots appeared, and the forest became fresher than before.

Both of them taught Wren the significance of her mark. Not only did it show that she was of the blood of the Chiefs of the Maya, it showed that she had an affinity for the spirit realm, as did Tale Teller. She might be able to talk with the spirits of the dead, if she chose. She did not have to do this, but if she were ever in extreme distress, the spirits might help her, as they had once helped him.

Wren also learned how to use fire for the moss, so that it could make skirts. When the moss hanging on the trees was fresh, it was infested with tiny mites that dug into the skin and made welts. But there was a lodge made to hold in the smoke of its fire, so that it became chokingly thick. The priest supervised this, adding herbs to the fire so that the smoke became bitter. No one could go in there without extreme discomfort, and neither could the mites. After a day of such smoking, they were gone from the moss, and it could be used for clothing. Then Wren learned to weave it together so that it covered exactly as much of a woman's torso and legs as she wished, when she wished. This was important.

Tzec demonstrated this in a practical manner. She put some of her special honey into her cleft, and worked it deep into her body. Then she donned a moss skirt, and stood in it when Tale Teller returned to the lodge. She sat, and moved her legs, and the moss fell away in places so that the deep shadow of the crevice between her legs showed. The smell of the honey spread out. She shifted position again, and her breasts quivered. She glanced sidelong at him, and smiled. Tale Teller suddenly decided that the time was right for sexual experience. His male member got large and lifted up, and sought the honey in her cleft, and worked to add its own honey to it.

Wren watched in silence, seeing how the magic worked. Honey, the parting of the skirt, the motion of the legs, the shaking of the breasts, and the right look and smile. These lured the man in, like a bee to a flower; he could not prevent it. She would remember, when she had breasts and honey of her own. Such magic was important to a woman; she needed to know how to do it right, and how to avoid doing it when she did not want the man's penis in her cleft. There were surely times when it would be inconvenient, though it did look like fun.

Wren also learned about pottery. Cups were very important, and it required skill to fashion them from clay, and they could use them for drinking water or soup. But it was more than that. Each cup or bowl had to be finished and painted its own special way, which only the Toco people used. She could instantly tell a foreign bowl, and would not use it, because it might have hostile foreign spirits in it waiting to poison the food.

So it was that she went with her aunt of the Panther Clan to the bank of the river, the special place where the clay was good. When the woman took her big basket of pure clay, Wren took her little basket of it. They carried it to the workshop where they kneaded it by pounding it against a flat rock. Wren loved this part: she picked up her double handful of clay and threw it down again and again, and it always made a satisfying thunk. "Take *that*, bad spirit!" she cried as she bashed it. She knew *her* clay would be pure, because no spirit could take such a pounding.

Then they added fine sand to the clay, because it was said that the pot would crack when it dried, otherwise. The sand did not want to mix, so they had to add it a little at a time, by sprinkling it on the surface and then folding the clay over and pounding it some more. They kept adding sand until the clay was as big as three of the pieces they had started with.

Then they rolled it into snakelike lengths. "The Rattlesnake Clan must be good at this!" Wren exclaimed, and her aunt smiled. Then they coiled their snakes into the base of open gourds, forming the bottom of each cup. They used their fingers to smooth the inside and outside flat, so that no snakes or coils could be seen. Then they let them sit for a day to harden, because otherwise the cups would squish down with the weight of their upper portions.

Later the cups were baked in a fire. Wren did not see that part of it, but she recognized her cup when she got it back because it was the smallest and least regularly shaped. But it was hers, and she treasured it. She painted it spotted brown, because that was as close as she could get to panther color. She used it whenever she could. It was her personal involvement in the four elements: the water of the river, the earth of the clay and sand, the air in which it dried, and the fire that finally hardened it. There were other cups and pots of much fancier design, with the patterns that showed which tribe had made them, and some of these were beautiful, but her little brown cup was *hers*.

When Wren was five winters old, her Grandfather Trader visited. He had visited before, but she had been too young to remember. Now she remembered, because he brought her a fine feather cloak. He was an old, old man, fifty winters at least, and the spirits were pulling on him to join them. She could tell by the wrinkles in his skin; already some of his spirit was gone, so that his body was shrinking, leaving his skin too big. But she liked him, because of the feather cloak, and because her mother, Tzec, liked him.

"You are marked," he remarked, gazing approvingly at her naked body.

"Like my grandmother of the Maya," she agreed.

"The spirits will favor you. I will tell your grandmother of the Castiles."

After he had given Wren the cloak, he gave Tzec some nice beads. Then he got back into his canoe, and the strong young warrior who had come with him paddled him back the way they had come, up the Little Big River.

He never came again. That was how Wren knew the spirits had taken him. She hoped he was happy in his other life. If she ever went there, she would see if she could talk to his spirit in the mound. She knew that death was only a stage of life, and she had no fear of the spirits of the dead.

Tale Teller told his daughter tales, of course; she had a special right to them. She liked to hear them over and over. So one day when she was supposed to rest because of an injury she had taken in a fall, and bad weather kept him inside the lodge, he winked at Tzec and told Wren a special version of one of the most compelling native Toco stories. It was the Tale of the Rolling Heads. It was set in a village of the south, down beyond Mocozo's region, where interesting trees grew.

Two brothers lived together, for neither had found a woman

to his liking. The truth was that each was shy about approaching a maiden, but afraid to admit it lest he be laughed at.

One day a young woman of the village decided that it was time to do something about this. She took her honey and went to the brothers' lodge. "I am Strange Woman," she said. "I have come to live with you. Will you allow me this?"

Startled, they looked at her and then at each other. She was beautiful, and each realized how much he had been missing by living without a woman. "But you cannot live with us unmarried!" Elder Brother protested.

"Then choose which one of you will marry me," she replied. For though a man could have two wives, a woman could not have two husbands. That was the natural order of things.

They both desired her, but Elder Brother was the more generous of the two, so he suggested that since she was closer to the age of Younger Brother, he should be the one to marry her. Younger Brother, who was the more selfish of the two, agreed. They went out fishing so that Younger Brother could present her with a fine fat fish in token of their marriage, and she could cook it for him in response.

They had extraordinary luck, for a giant fish came close and got stranded in the shallows. It would not take their bait, but just thrashed around, seeking a way out. "It would break our line anyway," Elder Brother said, for he was the more reasonable one. "I fear it is too much for us to handle."

"No, we must have it," Younger Brother replied, being the more stag-headed one. "We can wade in and grab it and carry it out."

"But the fish is too big!" Elder Brother, who was more cautious, protested. "It would knock us down with its thrashing and we might drown in the mud."

"Tie a hickory-bark rope around my waist, to pull me out, and I will go in and grab the fish," Younger Brother said, being more impetuous. "Then you can haul me out together with the fish, and I will truly have caught it. Then I can marry Strange Woman and be happy." He said nothing about Elder Brother's happiness.

Elder Brother tried to demur, fearing for the other man's safety, but Younger Brother insisted, so as usual they did it his way. Younger Brother waded in and tried to grab the fish in his arms, but the fish was even bigger than they had thought, and it turned and swallowed the man.

Appalled, Elder Brother hauled on the rope, hoping either to draw his brother out or to bring the fish to the shore, where he could cut it open and rescue Younger Brother. But the fish closed its mouth and snapped through the rope with its teeth. It was impossible to haul it in.

Elder Brother ran along the bank, crying out to the animals there. "My brother has been swallowed by the fish! He is supposed to get married, and this is most awkward! Who will help me rescue him?" But all of them were terrified of the monster fish, and ran away.

Then Kingfisher flew in. "I will help you, if you give me the entrails," he cried.

"Gladly!"

So Kingfisher flew to the fish, perched on its head, and hammered with his long bill on the side of the head until the fish died and drifted to the bank.

Elder Brother immediately took his knife and cut open the belly of the fish, and the entrails came out for Kingfisher. But the fish had a very fast digestion, and all except Younger Brother's head had been dissolved. The situation looked very bad.

Then the head spoke. "Wash me off and set me on a log," it said imperatively.

Elder Brother was surprised, for he had thought Younger Brother was dead, but did as it asked. Soon the head was clean and perched upright on the log. "I fear your marriage to Strange Woman will be difficult to manage," Elder Brother remarked.

"Take some of the fish home," the head said. "Explain to her that I am indisposed and will not be able to marry her. She will be extremely upset. I will come in the morning when she has calmed down, and I will sing to her, and then she will be consoled."

Elder Brother was not sure of that, but he cut some excellent portions of the fish and carried them back to the lodge. "We caught a great fish, but it ate all of my brother except his head, so he cannot marry you, but here is the fish," he told her circumspectly.

"That is unfortunate," Strange Woman said. "Is there no chance he will recover?"

"None for his nether portions," he said sadly.

"Then it is decided," she replied, seeming not unduly disturbed. "I will marry you instead." She took the fish and began to cook it.

"But—" he said after a moment.

"You are more of a man than he was, anyway," she said, serving him the fish.

Elder Brother did not want to be impolite, so he ate it, and then she ate some of it too. "Now we are married," she said, and removed her skirt. It seemed that she did not require a completely formal ceremony.

"But—"

She glanced sharply at him. "You find me unattractive?"

"Not at all!" he said with feeling, for she was excellently proportioned. "But—"

"Your penis is weak?"

"Not at all! But—"

"Good, for now I have no need of honey." And she kissed him and embraced him and bore him down on the bed. Sure enough, his penis turned out to be so strong that it would not stay down long, and they had a strenuous night. By morning he had forgotten the word "but" and much else, and was quite satisfied to be married.

They woke to the sound of singing. It seemed to be coming from the roof of the lodge. "What is that?" Strange Woman asked, alarmed.

Now Elder Brother remembered some of what he had forgotten in the night. "It is Younger Brother. He has come to console you for your loss of him as a husband."

"You consoled me well enough," she replied. Then she got up, put on her skirt, combed her hair, and went outside to talk to the head. "I married your brother instead," she told it diplomatically. "Now go away."

The head of Younger Brother considered this. It was very angry that this had happened, for it had assumed that no one could get along without it. But it realized that it would do no good to speak harshly to them, and besides, it still admired the woman's appearance. It decided to kill Elder Brother and recover Strange Woman for itself. It was sure she would be reasonable once there was no one else.

"Congratulations," it told her. "I will help you pick fruit. Both of you come with me." It rolled off the roof and across the ground, away from the lodge.

Relieved that the head was taking it so well, they followed it to the nearby grove of coconut trees. It rolled up a tall palm and bit through the stem of a coconut. The coconut fell to the ground, right toward Elder Brother's head.

But Strange Woman saw what was happening and pushed her husband out of the way. "That head is trying to kill you!" she exclaimed indignantly.

"You stole my wife!" the head cried from above.

"You must kill the head," Strange Woman told Elder Brother. "Otherwise it will kill you!"

"But I can't harm my brother!" he protested. He had always been protective of his brother.

She was disgusted. "Then I will have to do it." She picked up a solid stick.

"No, you must not!" he said. "He is my brother, and I will not have him harmed."

She sighed. "Then we had better get away from here, because it is coming down."

Indeed, the head was rolling down the tree, and it looked determined. Younger Brother had always been one to carry a grudge.

They fled. But the head rolled after them. They came to the bank of the river, where Strange Woman slipped in the mud and sat down.

Elder Brother saw a mud wasp. "Oh Mud Wasp!" he cried. "You must hide us from the head!"

"Why should I do that?" Mud Wasp asked.

"We will always treat you well and respect your rights."

"Take off your skirt and lie down beside the river," Mud Wasp said to the woman. She did so, and he packed mud around her genital region so that she seemed to have a dirty penis and testicles, and more around her torso so that instead of breasts she seemed to have an enormously fat belly, and he tied her hair back in the fashion of a man. Meanwhile, Elder Brother used some mud to make himself look different too.

The head rolled up. "Hand over the woman!" it demanded.

"There is no woman here, just this thin man and this fat

man," Mud Wasp replied, indicating the other two.

The head looked at them, and was almost fooled. It was about to roll on, but then it saw the imprint of Strange Woman's buttocks where she had fallen in the mud. "She is here!" it exclaimed. "That is no man's posterior!"

Indeed it was not. The imprint was about as full and fetching as it could be.

"She was here, but she crossed the river and went on," Mud Wasp said.

The head was not convinced. "Then cross the river with me and help me find her."

They agreed, for they wanted the head as far away from the lodge as possible. Strange Woman picked up the head and waded in, while Elder Brother swam beside her.

But the water dissolved away the mud and revealed them as they were. "Ha!" cried the head. "You are the ones I seek!"

Then Strange Woman dived under the water with the head. She found a tangle of cypress roots and put the head under it, so that the head was trapped under the water. Then she swam to the surface.

"Where is my brother's head?" Elder Brother asked.

"I persuaded it that the river is its home, and it will stay here," she said. "It no longer objects to our marriage."

Elder Brother was relieved that the matter had been so amicably resolved. He thanked Mud Wasp for his help and pledged always to remember it. Then he returned to the lodge with Strange Woman, pausing only to pick up the coconut, for it was good food.

They lived in the lodge for a number of years, and Strange Woman bore Elder Brother two fine children. The first was a pretty girl, and the second a boy. They named the girl Kingfisher, after the first creature who had helped Elder Brother, and the boy Mud Wasp, after the one who had helped Strange Woman. Elder Brother taught his son to respect the creature who was his namesake, and always to show it due honor, and the boy did that, and the original mud wasp was pleased that it had helped the human folk. Strange Woman taught Kingfisher the ways of women, and she learned them well, and always respected the pretty bird who was her namesake.

Every day Elder Brother went hunting, while Strange Woman

took care of the lodge and children. One day he caught a rabbit early and came home before he usually did. He was surprised to find the children there, but his wife absent. "Where is your mother?" he inquired.

"She is out fetching water, as she does every day," Kingfisher replied.

"Why doesn't she fetch it first thing in the morning? This is noon!"

"She does," the girl replied. "It takes her a long time to get it, and she is usually wet."

"Then who feeds you during the day?"

"I have learned how to cook and keep the lodge," Kingfisher said. Indeed, he saw that she was a competent girl, despite being only seven winters old, and she took good care of her little brother.

"This is good," he said. "I will go out and complete my hunting." He departed, and returned at the usual time with another rabbit.

Strange Woman was there, and sure enough, her hair was slightly wet, though her dress was dry. This was very curious. Elder Brother resolved to find out just what she was doing during the day. He wasn't worried, but the little mystery intrigued him, and he meant to get the answer.

Next morning he went out as usual. But instead of going far afield to hunt, he went down the path to the river, found a sandy place, dug a hole, and buried himself. He left only a little hole so that he could look out and see what was happening on this section of the river.

Soon Strange Woman came down the path, carrying the large water jar. When she got near the river she stopped, set down her jar, unbraided her hair, and stepped out of her skirt. She was not quite as pretty as she had been eight winters before, but she remained an enticing figure.

She walked to the water's edge and waded in. She swam out into the center, then dived below. In a moment she reappeared, carrying an object. She came back to the shore, and Elder Brother saw to his amazement that it was Younger Brother's head she carried. She held it up to her face and kissed it on the mouth, then lay down on the bank.

"When are you going to kill your husband and bring me to

the lodge?" the head asked as it rolled down her body and licked her breasts.

"You ask that every day, and I tell you every day," she said impatiently. "When your son is old enough to hunt and provide food for the family, then I will not need my husband."

"If you had not had his daughter first, we would not have had to wait so long," the head complained.

"I couldn't help it," she said. "His penis was faster than your tongue."

"Well, maybe two sons will be better than one," the head said, and rolled down across her body and stuck its tongue deep into her cleft. She put her hands down and held the head close to her, enjoying its attention.

Now Elder Brother understood that Strange Woman had never given up Younger Brother. She had saved the head, and visited it every day, while Elder Brother supported her. She had fooled him completely, and it was just his luck that one of the children was his.

Elder Brother was very angry. Whatever had been human and decent in him faded away, and he became a creature of vengeance. He climbed out of his hole, took up his bow, and fired an arrow right through Younger Brother's head, from ear to ear. The head was swept into the river and borne away by the current, where a big fish chased after it. He was sure he would never see it again.

Strange Woman, realizing that her lover was finally all the way dead, turned to Elder Brother. "Oh my husband!" she exclaimed. "I am so glad to see you! That horrible head—"

But Elder Brother was no longer a fool. He had seen and heard more than enough. He shot an arrow through her heart, cutting short her lies. Then he cut off her head and threw it into the river. He did the same with her arms at the elbows and her legs at the knees. "Go join your lover!" he cried. But in his cruelty, he did not toss into the water those parts of her his brother's head most desired.

Then he cut open her torso and took out a side of her ribs. He skinned it and carried it back to the lodge, after hanging the rest in a tree for future use.

"Ah, my children," he said. "I have killed a deer and brought back some meat. Where is your mother?"

"She has gone to bring water," Kingfisher said.

Elder Brother looked at her. She was his child, but she looked too much like her mother. He looked at Mud Wasp. He looked like Younger Brother. Elder Brother decided to be rid of them both. But he didn't want to be blamed for killing them. "Well, you cook up this good meat while I return to fetch the rest of it. If your mother does not return before it is ready, eat it yourselves."

Kingfisher took the meat and put it in the pot, while Mud Wasp put sticks on the fire. Elder Brother got his moccasins and other things together and left the lodge, intending never to come back. He would go down to the village and prepare things there.

After he had gone, Kingfisher cooked and served the meat. Mud Wasp took a bite. "Sister, this tastes like Mother," he said, remembering the last time he had suckled.

"Oh keep still," she replied. "Father said it was deer meat."

They ate it, and Kingfisher saved a portion for their mother to eat when she returned. Then she settled down to make moccasins, decorating them with tiny shells, for she was a practical girl.

Then they heard something rolling outside. A voice exclaimed: "I love my children, but they do not love me. They have eaten me."

The girl was startled, for it sounded like their mother's voice. "Look out the door and see who is coming," she said.

The boy looked out. "Kingfisher, here comes our mother's head!"

"Shut the door!" she cried, realizing that something was seriously amiss. Their mother had always been strange, but this was frighteningly strange. "Fetch your things," she told him. She had decided that it would be best to go and find their father, and tell him about this development.

Kingfisher picked up her moccasins, root digger, and other belongings and rolled them up in a bundle. Mud Wasp did the same. Meanwhile, the head rolled against the door, striking it. It rolled partway up the sloping side of the lodge, and fell back again. "My children, open the door!"

The two ran to the door, pushed it open, and stood to the side. The head rolled into the lodge and all the way across to the back. The girl and boy sprang outside and closed the door. Then they ran away as fast as they could. They heard their mother's voice calling to them from the lodge, but they were so afraid of the severed head that they only ran faster.

"Kingfisher, I am tired!" Mud Wasp gasped. "I can't run any longer!"

"I will help you," she said, and took·his package of things and carried it for him. They ran on as far as they could.

Finally they had to stop. They looked back. There was the head rolling along behind them. Somehow it had gotten out of the lodge.

Horrified, they found strength to run again. But the little boy was tired out, and could not go fast, and the girl would not leave him behind. The head was gaining on them, and would soon catch them.

Kingfisher knew that her brother could not run much more. She looked around, and saw prickly vines and thorny blackberry plants. She grabbed these and stretched them out on the ground, making a barrier. Then the two walked on.

When the head reached this place, it got caught up in the prickly vines and thorns and had a terrible time getting through. It had to roll around that region instead. By the time it was past, the children had gone a long way.

They caught up to their father, who was resting beside the river. "You fed our mother's meat to us!" Kingfisher cried accusingly at him. "You killed her!" For she had done some thinking while they ran, and had figured out some of what had happened.

"She was going to kill me!" he retorted. "And Mud Wasp is not even my son." Then he grabbed them and tied them up, because he did not want them talking to others about this. It was a bad thing for people to know that a man's wife had been unfaithful to him, especially with something as odd as a separated head. They might get the notion that the man had not been able to satisfy her sexually. He was sitting on the ground, trying to decide what to do with them, so that he would not get in trouble for killing them, when the head of Strange Woman arrived.

"You cut off my head!" the head screamed at him, with a

certain justice. "I was lucky to float out of the river before being carried to the sea!" Then, before he could move, it rolled up the slope of his back and bit him on the neck.

Elder Brother lurched up, trying to claw off the head, but it clung fast. He fell into the river, and both of them were carried away by the current. The big fish took notice and swarmed after them.

Now the children were left tied, unable to help themselves. They could not get free, and would die of thirst and hunger if no one helped them.

An old dog came by. She had been a good hunting dog, but now her teeth were tired and she had been cast out to fend for herself. She had pups nearby, and was afraid they would starve. She saw the children, and realized that they had been badly treated. She knew how they felt.

She came over to them. "I will help you if you will help me," she said to them.

"How can we help you?" Kingfisher asked.

"You can provide a safe, dry lodge for my pups, and cut up the meat that is too tough for my tired old teeth."

"If you get us free, we will do that," the girl said.

So the dog tried to gnaw on the ropes that bound them, but her old teeth were too weak. However, her slobber got Kingfisher's hands so wet and slippery that she was able to work them free. Then she untied her feet, and freed her brother.

The dog fetched her three little pups, and they walked back to the lodge. It was dry, and the fire warmed it. Kingfisher cut up the last of the ribs so that they were small enough for the dog and her pups. She did not want to waste them, but did not care to eat them herself. Then she went out with her root digger and found some tubers to cook, while her brother gathered more sticks for the fire.

Next day they went down to the river and found some mussels. They brought them back and shared them with the dogs. They also fetched fruit and berries for themselves.

In this manner they survived, and soon the pups grew big enough to hunt, and started bringing in rabbits and quail. They had become a successful new family.

* * *

"Except for one thing," Tale Teller concluded somberly.

"What was that?" Wren asked, for always before, the tale had ended there.

"The head came back!" Tzec cried from across the lodge. There was her head, sitting on a pile of cloaks.

Wren screamed. Then she saw that her mother was sitting under the cloaks, and began to laugh. It was a good joke, and Wren knew that her father would never cut off her mother's head. It would be too difficult to manage, with his one arm.

So they were never able to fool her that way again.

CHAPTER 16

⚜️

CASTILE

O Spirit of the Mound, I have told you much, yet there is more to tell. This is the tale I learned from the Castile called Juan Ortiz, whom we met as a guide. The end of it I learned later, but I include it here so as not to confuse you, O Spirit.

Juan Ortiz was a young warrior of seventeen winters when he joined the war party of Chief Narvaez and crossed the endless sea in a huge canoe to come and plunder the land of the tribe they called India. It was not India, it was our land, but even after they realized this they still called it that, and called us Indians. He was the son of a lesser chief, and joined the party so that he might gain honor for himself and his family.

The huge boats stopped at a big island they called Cuba, and then came north to our land. His boat returned to the island to report to the Chief's wife; then she sent it back to rejoin Narvaez. But the Chief had sailed north, and they could not find him. So they came in to the shore, looking for him, and saw the town of Chief Hirrihigua, where Narvaez had been. There on the beach was a cane sticking upright in the ground, split at the top, and wedged in the split was a piece of thin bark they called paper.

"That must be a message from Chief Narvaez!" the Captain (for so the subchief who commands a big canoe is titled among the Castiles) exclaimed, excited. "We must fetch it and read it, for surely it will inform us where he has gone!"

Several Indians were walking on the beach, gazing at the strange craft. They signed to the Castiles to come to land, but most of them were afraid to do this, unsure whether the Indians were friendly. Then four Castile warriors entered a smaller canoe and paddled to shore, and Juan Ortiz was one of these. He was excited by this adventure, and wanted to be the one to get the paper and bring the Captain news of Chief Narvaez.

Two Castiles remained with the small canoe, cautious. Juan Ortiz and a companion jumped out and ran toward the paper. Juan Ortiz was a good runner, and he was faster than his friend, and was the first to reach the pole.

Then the Indians on the beach closed in and took hold of both Castiles. Juan Ortiz, surprised, did not resist. "I only want the paper!" he protested. "I mean no harm to you!"

But the other Castile tried to fight. He wrenched away and started to run toward the canoe. But, provoked by this action, a warrior swung his club and brained him on the spot. He fell to the sand, surely dead already, and the victor set about scalping him. This was a technique sometimes used against enemies, in which the hair and skin of the top of the head was cut off and saved as a memento of the encounter. This was standard practice in warfare, and not anything to be concerned about.

But inexperienced Juan Ortiz was appalled. He had known that adventure was dangerous, but had never truly believed it until this moment. He realized that if he tried to run, or even struggled, he would be killed as quickly as his friend. So, like a child, he let himself be led, while behind him the two remaining Castile warriors paddled desperately back toward their boat. Now the Indians were shooting arrows at them. Juan Ortiz wanted to watch, though horrified, to see whether they escaped, but he was hustled to the village. He thought they did, though, because he never saw their scalps brought into the village.

He became aware of the odor of his captors, of oil and fish and pungent unfamiliar herbs, as if they were alien creatures risen from the deep ocean to prowl the land. Their skins were darker than his own, their muscles harder, and they were big. He was afraid of them, and of their intentions.

They took him into the village, which was some distance inland. There was a well-trodden path through the palmettos and jungle, suitable for the Indians' bare feet. One moment they were amidst thick wilderness; the next they reached a glade and a waterway, and there were the native houses. The stench was awful, by his reckoning, though the Indians did not notice it. In a moment he realized what it was: there were piles of clam shells and the bones of animals. The guts were surely thrown among them, to rot in the heat. He thought that this was not a good thing to do.

Their arrival was like jogging a wasp's nest. Other Indians swarmed out, old men, women, and children, the adults with very little apparel and the children completely naked. To Juan Ortiz this was strange, for the people of his tribe always wore much clothing, even in the warmest weather, as if they were ashamed of their bodies. Perhaps this was because of the light color of their skin, certainly a source of embarrassment. The Indians were staring and screaming with open hostility. "But I have not done anything to you!" Juan Ortiz protested. "Why do you hate me?"

It was no use; they spoke a tongue that was foreign to his ears, and could understand his words no more than he understood theirs. The Indians formed a throng and followed him, gesticulating excitedly. It couldn't be because they hadn't seen a Castile before, because Narvaez had visited this village or one like it. Juan Ortiz had not been along, but he knew that his Chief had landed here and made contact with the Indians; indeed, that was why the Captain had sailed here, thinking that Narvaez remained in this vicinity. The paper on the cane was proof of that. Evidently Chief Narvaez had traveled elsewhere, but the Indians surely remembered him.

The fact that they were so evidently angry made Juan Ortiz increasingly nervous. What had happened between Chief Narvaez and these Indians?

They passed through the town and came to a square cleared area, where several men sat on logs under a thatched shelter. These were evidently the rulers, for the others immediately quieted and gave them glances of respect. Juan Ortiz's captors brought him to stand before a man whose face was like carved mahogany, with an eagle's beak for a nose. Blue tattoos formed patterns all over his body. His skin glistened with oil. There was a hush, so deep that for the first time the buzzing of the flies was audible.

Juan Ortiz found himself sweating. It was hot here, and he

was overdressed for this climate, but that was only part of it. This was obviously the Chief of this hostile tribe, and the tense expectation with which the others waited for his decision was alarming.

Chief Hirrihigua grunted and gestured, hardly more than a turn of one hand. That was all, but immediately the captors hauled Juan Ortiz roughly away, back into the village, past the gawking natives. Now he saw that a number of the young women wore nothing above the waist except their long black hair, and despite his present straits he could not help glancing at them with admiration. One girl was exceptionally well formed, her breasts erect and full, her waist slender, her skin without blemish and almost as fair as that of a Castile. For a moment his eyes met hers, and he was dazzled by her beauty. Then he was cuffed and shoved into a hut, and the vision of her remained only in his fancy.

They tied his hands roughly behind his back with crude cord and left him there alone. So he remained the night, frightened and bruised, working his wrists as well as he could to restore the blood in his hands, listening to the sounds of some kind of celebration in the village. Periodically a warrior would check on him, to make sure he had not escaped, but that was all. He was offered neither food nor water, and his thirst became painful.

He suffered and listened and slept; there was nothing else to do. He gave himself up for lost, realizing that the Indians would never treat a prisoner so callously if they intended him to live, but still he somehow hoped it was not the end. The processes of his body brought him to the point where he had to relieve himself; he had no choice but to urinate in his trousers, which were the lower part of his costume, similar in form to a breechcloth connected to very long leggings. Now he stank as much as the natives!

Yet that terrible night had a single joy that made up for much of its discomfort. It was the face and body of that lovely Indian girl he had seen so fleetingly. The vision of her sustained him, foolish though he knew this to be; it was almost worth the torment he was enduring. To him, the sight of a woman's breasts was a novelty, and he found them just as interesting as a normal man does. Why the Castiles insisted on covering up the breasts of even their loveliest young women we cannot explain; it seems to have been some kind of punishment directed by their Great Spirit, causing all their men to suffer.

At dawn they rousted him out, hauled him to his feet, and marched him to a place where low posts were set among ashes. A great crowd had gathered, most of the inhabitants of the village, and all were eagerly watching. Juan Ortiz knew that this was the finale; they were going to execute him.

Now the men tore at his clothes, ripping at his shirt and his trousers, using stone knives to cut what would not tear. In a moment they had stripped him naked, while all the villagers stared and exclaimed over his humiliation. For it seemed that even his penis was pale, and he was especially disturbed that this should show.

Then they brought poles, and lashed them to the tops of the low posts, forming a grid over the ashes. They brought brush and piled it beneath the grid. Now Juan Ortiz realized what manner of thing this was, and cried out in horror. His expression needed no translation; there was laughter among the men, who appreciated his understanding.

Juan Ortiz tried to run, but they caught him easily and tripped him and threw him down on the grid, spread-eagled, and tied his hands and feet so that he could not move. He stared into the morning sky, hoping that this ordeal would soon be over, and that he would die quickly.

A man brought a blazing torch, and touched it to the tinder below. Immediately the fire caught and spread, its smoke billowing up. Then the heat touched Juan Ortiz's skin, and he screamed and screamed, unable to die with dignity; the agony would not be denied. He was being roasted alive on the side the fire burned. "Mother of the Great Spirit!" he cried, believing this to be the last exclamation he would make in this life. "Mercy on me!"

Then several figures were there, with poles, and they poked and scraped at the burning brush, shoving it out of the pit so that the heat abated. They were women—one old one and three young ones, taking the fire away. The old one screamed a torrent at Chief Hirrihigua, who stood stoically, neither helping nor interfering, and his warriors beside him behaving similarly. She was not Mary, mother of Jesus, who was the Castiles' Great

Spirit, but an Indian woman. These were, Juan Ortiz later
learned, the Chief's wife and daughters, who condemned this
barbarism and acted to stop it. The warriors would have made
short shrift of anyone else, but the Chief could not deny the
women of his own family, so he abided their decision. In truth,
it is not the way of our people to torture captives; we prefer to
adopt them. But Chief Hirrihigua had a special reason.

Now one of the daughters leaned over Juan Ortiz and worked
at his bonds, loosening and untying them. Lo, it was the beauty
he had seen the day before! The child of the Chief had come
to his rescue! She got him loose and put her arms around him,
her bare breasts touching him, lifting him up. The others
helped, and soon they had him standing, but his pain and
disorientation were such that he could not keep his balance
alone.

The lovely woman set herself under his shoulder and put
her arm close around his waist, and called to one of her sisters
to do the same from the other side. Together they supported
him and walked him across to face Chief Hirrihigua. Then the
three girls and the old woman glared at the Chief, as if daring
him to make an issue. At length the Chief sighed, and made a
tiny gesture with both hands, as if to say, "Women—what can
you do with them?"

That was it. They took Juan Ortiz back to the hut in which
he had spent the night, but this time he was not bound. The
Chief's wife rubbed oil on his back and side where the blisters
were rising, and the lovely girls brought him cups of water.
He gulped these desperately, his thirst assuaged at last, and
ate the breadcakes they also provided. He remained in severe
discomfort, but he gave thanks to the Virgin, which was another
name for the Castiles' revered Spirit, that his life had indeed
been spared. He had invoked her name, and she had interceded
for him.

So it was that Juan Ortiz spent the day recuperating, and the
night. Yet his travails were far from done. His blisters formed
into great swellings that burst and bled, making him horrible
to behold, and he feared he would, after all, die. But the Chief's
eldest daughter, Mouse Pelt, bathed him and applied poultices
of herbs, and the pain eased. He could not get dressed again:
not only was his own clothing torn and gone, his sores were

such that any clothing would only have aggravated them. He had to remain naked, and this bothered him almost as much as the physical pain. Yet even in this his feelings were mixed, because the presence of the young woman was not only his greatest embarrassment, it was also his greatest pleasure.

Indeed, the sight of Mouse Pelt as she bent to her ministrations might have been as soothing as the herbs, for she was as lovely a creature as he could have imagined. She wore a necklace of small shells about her neck that lay upon the upper swell of her breasts, and each day she had a new flower in her hair. Her skirt was of that moss which dangled from the trees, and it hardly concealed her private parts when she stood, and did not even make the effort when she sat. As she squatted to tend to a blister, and his gaze fell on her taut thighs, his penis stirred. He tried to look away, but could not; she was holding him, so as to complete her medication despite his flinching from the pain. She treated the sores on his side, then moved toward those on his leg.

In a moment she glanced down and saw the situation. He felt the flush spreading across his face. She could not speak Juan Ortiz's language, but she hardly needed to; the language of the body was universal. Yet, oddly, she did not seem alarmed or disgusted, merely curious. She touched her finger between her breasts, near her heart, and spread her knees somewhat, silently inquiring his interest. Juan Ortiz flushed worse, terribly embarrassed, but his penis stood boldly up and made answer for him.

She left the lodge, to his mixed relief and chagrin, but soon returned. Now she smelled of honey, which he found odd. But odder yet was her attitude, for she touched his penis, which had slackened somewhat during her absence, causing it to stand up again. It was as if it were a familiar friend to her. She seemed intrigued rather than repelled, but he remained embarrassed.

This was the daughter of the Chief! Juan Ortiz feared she would hurry to her father and demand that the prisoner be returned to the fire. But she only smiled, and leaned forward, so that her breasts touched him again, and embraced him. Her face was close to his, and he did what he could not help: he kissed her lips.

She remained in contact for a moment, then drew away. She stood, and again he thought she was about to leave, but instead she stepped out of her skirt. Then she got down beside him, carefully so as not to touch his blisters, and set herself for that most intimate contact. She knew that his ability to move was limited, and that he must remain lying on his good side. She made the connection for him, taking his penis in her hand squeezing it gently, and putting it to her cleft. Then she spread herself against him, thighs and breasts and lips, becoming one with him in a surprisingly facile manner. No Castile maiden was like this!

Juan Ortiz no longer questioned it. He embraced her, and in an instant his penis was as deep within her as it could be, and jettisoning all that it contained. The pain of his blisters seemed only to heighten the effect. But though his ecstasy of body was spent in a moment, his joy of Mouse Pelt was not. He realized already that she was the one who had saved him from her father's wrath; her mother and sisters had joined in only at her request. She had seen him that first day, as he had seen her, and she had found him handsome even as he had found her beautiful. She was a creature of action; when she had seen that her father the Chief could not be dissuaded otherwise, she had stepped in and defied him. Such was her hold on her father as on any man she might deal with, that Chief Hirrihigua could not deny her. She had saved Juan Ortiz for herself, to be her lover, and this was the culmination of that decision. He was hers now, in every sense.

So it was thereafter. Mouse Pelt tended to Juan Ortiz's burns until he was well, and tended to his desire too, and his love for her knew no bounds. She taught him the ways of the Indian and brought him a loincloth and showed him how to wear it. She rubbed fish oil into his skin so that the mosquitoes would not suck his blood. And, most important, she taught him the key words of her language, so that he could make his need known.

But he was to discover two sobering things as his captivity continued. First, he was not yet free of Hirrihigua; the Chief maintained an implacable hate, and though Mouse Pelt had saved Juan Ortiz's life, she could not save him from abuse. Second, her love for him was intense but not exclusive. Sh had done for him what she did for any man who took her fancy, and thought no more of it than she did of taking a pleasant swim in the river. What he deemed to be the ultimate act of commitment was for her merely the joy of the moment, which she could as readily share with another man—and, indeed, frequently did.

Fortunately, it took him some time to realize this second thing, for he had first to learn the Toco tongue. She taught him this, between and during their labors of love, and he was an apt learner. Soon he was learning also from others in the tribe, in the process assimilating the elements of culture that differed so much from his own. He came to understand that Indian maidens, before marriage, could share their favors with any man they chose, and were expected to do so freely. It was the business of a man to be a warrior; it was the business of a woman to please a man. Each learned the appropriate art well. Thus it had been no accident that Mouse Pelt had been able to please him so early and so aptly; she had done it many times with other men before him. He had to accept the fact that she would please others after him, and that he was free to accept the attentions of any other maiden who fancied him. Thus his jealousy had hardly developed before it was dissipated: Mouse Pelt's next younger sister, almost as lovely and experienced, came to spend the night with him while Mouse Pelt went to another warrior. Juan Ortiz's emotions were mixed, but he accepted what had to be accepted, and indeed, the girl was nice enough.

Thereafter he had the favors of many maidens, some quite young. In the Castile tribe a girl was not supposed to indulge in sexual activity until she was married, which could be some winters after she was fully developed. Here she was free to do it the moment her breasts formed, or even somewhat before, if she felt inclined. Already he had learned enough to know that age was not the criterion; the will of the maiden was. A man could not force a woman, unless he was married to her; he could only do what she wished. Among them was one who seemed to be hardly ten winters old, and her body was not yet developed. She had no prior experience. But she desired the favor of the handsome visitor, and he was obliged to render it. She alone came to him purely for love; she was smitten with

him, and afraid he would depart before she grew old enough
to attract him, so she came now. It was his first conquest of a
genuinely inexperienced girl, and he had the wit to proceed
with caution, so that she would not be hurt. In fact, he moved
so slowly that she grabbed his penis impatiently and crammed
it into her cleft, which was overflowing with honey. In her
naiveté she had used too much. Honey squeezed out and got
all over everything, but it did make the penetration easier. He
was afraid that it was hurting her even so, but she seemed not
to care. Everything was clumsy. Evidently he succeeded in
initiating her appropriately, despite his misgivings, for the following evening Mouse Pelt returned, and expressed her pleasure with him in a most thoroughgoing manner. What a
difference experience made!

Juan Ortiz would have been satisfied to marry Mouse Pelt,
and be true to her thereafter, and she to him. But she was the
daughter of the Chief, and so was beyond his aspiration. She
had been promised to Mocozo, the Chief of a village to the
north, and in due course would marry him and go to his village.
She did not know Mocozo well, or love him, but marriage to
a chief was too important a prospect to be affected by details
like that. Mocozo was reported to be quite taken with her
beauty, and eager to consummate the marriage as soon as
Mouse Pelt had sufficient experience. That was something Juan
Ortiz could understand; a man had only to see her to feel that
way. He could also have spoken quite well of her experience.

His problem with Chief Hirrihigua was not so readily ame-
liorated. As he learned the tongue, Juan Ortiz came to understand the reason for the Chief's enmity. Narvaez had indeed
landed here. He had at first professed friendship, but soon
demanded food and women and something called gold. The
food Chief Hirrihigua had provided as a gesture of hospitality—
but the greedy Castiles had taken not a proper share, but all
of it, leaving the village supplies impoverished. The gold was
a mystery; Hirrihigua finally ascertained that it was a yellow
stone, like the copper they sometimes traded for, but more rare
and useful. There was none here, but the Castiles seemed reluctant to understand that, so the Indians had told them there
was plenty of it far away to the north.

The women, by this time, had hidden themselves away beyond the Castiles' reach. It was not that they were reluctant to indulge, if they had a chance to get to know the men, and to choose which ones they preferred to be with. But the Castiles' idea of love was akin to the Indians' idea of force, and that was another matter. Also, they wanted to take the women away to their big closed-in canoes, and that was nervous business. So Hirrihigua's initial goodwill had hardened into distrust.

Then the Castiles had made a sudden raid into the village and taken all the women they could find. These were only the old wives, thought to be of no interest to them. Indeed it was so—but one of them had been Chief Hirrihigua's mother.

Hirrihigua knew then that he had to attack, for he could not allow his mother to be savaged by the Castiles. But many of his warriors were out on a hunt, to replenish the stock of food taken by the intruders; he had to get them back in order to have a sufficient force. Still, he dared not wait. So he approached the camp of the Castiles, which was in his village— the remaining Indians had fled, of course—and challenged Chief Narvaez to single combat for the freedom of the women.

Instead, the Castiles seized him. They had absolutely no sense of honor! Even though they did not speak his tongue, they could not have mistaken the nature of his challenge.

"Women!" Chief Narvaez demanded, using one of the few Castile words the Indians now recognized. Of course Hirrihigua could not bring them in, and would not have if he could; the Castiles had proved themselves to be barbarians whom no maiden would now touch. So he did not answer.

The Castile barked unintelligibly to a subordinate. Immediately the man drew a monstrous metal knife, one of the weapons that were the envy of the Indians, and brought it to Hirrihigua's nose. The message was plain: bring the women, or the nose would be cut off.

But Hirrihigua was a warrior, and a Chief; no torture could make him yield. So he kept silent while the terrible knife sliced off his nose. Then, the blood streaming down his chin, he simply stared at the Castile.

This only enraged the man further. He had ascertained the identity of Hirrihigua's mother. Now he brought her out and put her in the first pit and brought out five huge vicious dogs. "Women!" he repeated, and when Hirrihigua did not reply, the dogs were loosed. They leaped upon the old woman, heed-less of her screams, biting her until she collapsed, then tearing out her throat and killing her. They continued, consuming her flesh before Hirrihigua's eyes, for the Castiles held him so that he had to watch.

But by this time the day was ending, and the tribe had had time to gather its warriors. Now they attacked. The Castiles, caught by surprise, fled to their boats and their ship. They got away, but the damage was done: Chief Hirrihigua had lost his nose and his mother, most cruelly.

That was the source of his abiding anger, the Indians told Juan Ortiz. "But Narvaez would not do that!" he protested. "He was a good man!" But they were adamant, and, indeed, the Chief's nose was gone, and his mother. The other Indians had not seen either thing happen, but they believed what their Chief told them. Juan Ortiz had to admit it made sense, and that there was some justice in the Chief's attitude. If Indians had done something similar to his own mother, he would have hated them similarly.

While Juan Ortiz healed, he was put to woman's work. He realized that this was intended by the Chief as a mark of hu-miliation, for Juan Ortiz was now a slave. But he was satisfied, for in his weakened state he was not capable of more. It also put him in the constant company of the girls, and this acquain-tance was perhaps responsible for the number of them who came to his hut in the evenings to give him "speaking" lessons. Indeed, they taught him well!

So Juan Ortiz labored to fetch wood and carry water, the servant of any who commanded, and he dared not protest, knowing that death would be the penalty. He grubbed in the soil for edible roots, and he scraped the surfaces of fresh animal skins without complaint.

He even learned to weave baskets. The women collected the leaves of palm trees, which were very broad and ribbed, and cut them into long narrow strips. These they passed back and forth, over and under each other, in special patterns, to make flat sheets. Baskets were made by tying many strips together at the centers, their ends pointing outward like the rays of the sun, and then working strands between them in increasing circles. Slowly the shape of the basket formed: perfect for the

women, so lumpy and irregular for him that the women had
to laugh and come to help him straighten it out. Fashioning
the rim was the worst of all. This required special skill, and his
fingers were so clumsy that finally a woman would do it for
him, gesturing to him not to tell, lest he be punished. He understood that aspect well enough, and was happy to keep the
secret. In time he was to fashion better baskets, but each new
type was another challenge, and he despaired of ever doing
any as well as the least of the women. Even little girls could
do it better than he could, as they delighted in demonstrating.
But it was friendly; when the young women bested him in this,
and he acknowledged their superiority, they smiled, and sometimes one would bring her basket to his hut to show him again.
Then the basket lesson was very like a speaking lesson, and
his night was quite pleasant. There were ways in which he was
even coming to enjoy his captivity.

Even so, he was subject to harassment. Every time Chief
Hirrihigua saw him, the man was moved to renewed rage. He
had, it seemed, promised his daughter that he would not touch
the slave or do him direct injury, but he found other ways.
One day he ordered Juan Ortiz to run back and forth across
the cleared plaza, barefoot, in the manner of the Indians, while
the warriors watched. Whenever Juan Ortiz slowed, one of
them would shoot an arrow at him, not scoring, but close
enough so that it was obvious the next one would score if he
did not speed up. The Indians did not miss so easy a target
except by design; they were playing a game of seeing how close
they could come without actually hitting him. For hours he had
to run, his breath laboring, his legs knotting with fatigue, his
bare feet bleeding. When at last he fell, exhausted, in a faint,
Mouse Pelt came in from the forest where she had been gathering nuts and knelt by him, and was angry that this had happened. She set her shell necklace on his back as a mark of
protection. Then she walked about the plaza and gathered up
every arrow, knowing each by its special markings, and made
a bundle of them. She kept the arrows; in the following days,
each warrior had to come to her to request his arrow back, and
he got it back only on condition that never again would he use
it in this manner. Mouse Pelt was beautiful, and the daughter
of the Chief, and most favored of the Chief despite her defiance

of him; had these warriors refused to deal with her on her terms, they would have lost not only her favor, but her father's favor too. Thus it was apparent how strong her hold on her father was; Hirrihigua had to support her even in her defiance of him, lest she be shamed. So it was that she protected Juan Ortiz from further molestation of this nature, after allowing the first.

But in this war of wits between father and daughter, the resolution took time. Hirrihigua found another way to humiliate Juan Ortiz. He assigned him to watch the temple mound. A baby had died, the son of a subchief; the small body had to be left out for four days so that its second spirit would have time to depart in peace. No Indian cared to undertake this duty for fear of the evil spirits that abounded there, and Juan Ortiz felt no better about it than they. But he was a slave, and had to obey.

He was given a good stone knife and four spears and a fire, and some food. He would maintain this vigil for the full period, protecting the baby's body from the predators of the wilderness. If he failed, not even Mouse Pelt would be able to help him, for the sanctity of the dead was paramount.

Juan Ortiz gathered wood by day so that he could keep the fire high by night, frightening away the wild creatures. All night he remained alert, nervous about the exposure, the darkness, and the malignant spirits. He was a Christian, but in this his belief aligned with that of his captors: he believed in ghosts. Every sound of the night sent a shiver through him.

In the morning, when the danger of predators was reduced, he slept, but not for long. Fatigued, he resumed his vigil. Two warriors stopped by to check on him; they had participated in the mock game-stalking, but had their arrows back, and offered him no further discourtesy. They had given their word, and honored it; they would report to Hirrihigua that all was well. They even left him a fresh rabbit; he could roast it over his fire and eat well. The courtesy was in order, but the rabbit was a favor; he would let Mouse Pelt know, and she would see that they did not regret it. No one would tell the Chief. This was a thing his own honor required, as they knew.

He was less worried the second night, though the howls of the predators were closer; they winded the roast rabbit and were hungry. He slept fitfully the third day, aware of encroachments from the wilderness, but the blazing fire kept them at bay.

But in the night at last he lost vigilance, and slept, and the fire sank low. Suddenly he woke, hearing something at the mound; an animal was raiding for the body! Juan Ortiz leaped up with a spear, and charged, but the shape was already retreating. He hurled the spear after it, desperation giving him strength. There was a commotion, and the thing was gone. No chance to catch it now!

He lurched to the fire and threw on more wood. It blazed up, and in the renewed glare he saw the mound, and the log structure on it, and saw that the body of the child was gone. The creature had gotten away with it, and Juan Ortiz had not been able to stop it.

What could he do? He could only hope to set out in pursuit at dawn, and try to track down the creature, and drive it off, and salvage the remains of the child. Otherwise he would be lost, having fallen into the very trap Hirrihigua had laid for him.

But at dawn, as if to prevent this very thing, two Indians arrived. There was no help for it; Juan Ortiz told them what had happened. He pointed to the region where he had thrown the spear, though he had not been able to find it in the dark. That was a further blemish on his record: the losing of a good spear.

Quickly they went there, and searched. They were two more of those who had bought back their arrows from Mouse Pelt, but they were here by Hirrihigua's directive. If they found anything that was bad for Juan Ortiz, they would have to tell the Chief.

"Blood!" one exclaimed. "You struck it, and it dragged the spear away with it!" Then, in a moment: "Here is the child, untouched!"

Juan Ortiz's heart leaped. His throw had scored after all, and caused the animal to drop the body. Quickly he fetched the body back to the mound, and put it back in its crude box, hardly the worse for wear.

"And here is the panther!" the warrior cried from a farther distance. "Come look at this!"

Juan Ortiz and the other warrior hurried to join him. There

lay the panther, dead, with the point of the spear still lodged in its throat.

The two warriors exchanged a private smile. Now they could report honestly, and not be in trouble with Mouse Pelt.

Soon Hirrihigua himself was there, and the father of the dead child. There was no question what had happened. The panther had come in and taken the child, and Juan Ortiz had thrown his spear at it and killed it in the dark. Juan Ortiz had done his job. Moreover, he had with a single stroke slain a panther, a thing seldom accomplished by even the most proficient warrior. It was obvious that the evil ghosts had put him to the most severe test, and that he had prevailed. Actually, he had been, as he put it, "extremely lucky." That was his way of acknowledging what the spirits had done for him.

Hirrihigua was a fair man. He honored heroism where he found it. "This man has acted as a warrior should. Henceforth he shall be treated as a warrior." That was the end of his enmity toward Juan Ortiz. Possibly his daughter had given him an ultimatum, and this was a pretext to change his attitude. Perhaps he had come to recognize that Juan Ortiz was in no way like Narvaez, and also served as a kind of honor: a Castile captive. No other tribe had that.

Juan Ortiz undertook training in the skills of the warrior, and was given complete freedom. He was accepted by the members of the tribe as an equal. He was not able to develop the proficiency of the Indians, and indeed, his throw with the spear which saved the body of the baby must have been guided by some power other than his own arm, but he was useful as a beater. He would walk openly into the region of the hunt, startling the deer into flight—and they would bound right past the spot where the other warriors waited, spears and arrows poised.

For the next three winters his life was good. Not the least of it was the continued attentions of the unmarried maidens, who found him remarkably handsome and intriguing. Each season several of them got married to warriors of the tribe, but each season new girls ripened, with attitudes similar to those they replaced. He was initiated into a clan, and tattooed. Not all Toco villages used the painful tattooing; most preferred paint. But this was one of the better regions. He became very much an Indian warrior. Now he could marry a maiden of the village, if he chose. The young one who had overused the honey had hinted several times, and she had grown into a far more sophisticated creature both physically and mentally. All he had to do was give her a sign, and she would make a formal public proposal. But two things prevented him: he still had some hope of returning one day to his original Tribe of Castile, and he privately longed for Mouse Pelt. He knew she would not ask him to marry her; she was promised to Chief Mocozo, and only her attachment to her father delayed her departure. Even so, as long as she remained unmarried, he had a foolish hope.

Then his luck turned again.

Mocozo, Chief of the region to the north, growing impatient of the delay in his marriage to Mouse Pelt, made a raid. His warriors descended on the village while most of the warriors and Juan Ortiz were away on an extended hunt, and killed several of the old folk, carried away several maidens, and burned the houses. Hirrihigua was enraged; he had to take up residence in a farther village and plan revenge. But Mocozo was too strong; a raid against him could not succeed at this time.

Hirrihigua considered the auguries, and concluded that it was necessary to gain the favor of the spirits by making a blood sacrifice. The subject of such an offering was normally a human captive. As it happened, one was available. True, he had become a warrior, but this was more important.

Mouse Pelt came at night to Juan Ortiz, but not this time for delight. "My father means to sacrifice you tomorrow," she whispered. "You must flee tonight to Mocozo's village!"

Hastily he rose and went with her, taking only his weapons and a little food. She showed him the path to Mocozo's village, then turned back, for she could not allow her father to learn of her part in this. Juan Ortiz marched on through the night, following the path, startled by every sound for fear of pursuit. But there was none; his flight was completely unexpected. Hirrihigua thought he did not know about the coming sacrifice, so would not flee.

In the morning he reached the river that marked the boundary between Hirrihigua's territory and Mocozo's. As he made his way along it, looking for a suitable place to cross, he came upon two Indians fishing. He called out to them, but they were young and inexperienced and did not understand him. They fled, shouting. Soon several warriors came, making ready to shoot him with their arrows, and he had to take refuge behind a tree. "I am the Christian captive from Hirrihigua's tribe!" he cried, but still they seemed not to understand.

Then an Indian came up who spoke the dialect of Hirrihigua's village. He understood Juan Ortiz's words, and told the others, and they ran to tell their Chief. Mocozo came immediately and talked to Juan Ortiz; he understood the tongue, for it was merely a variant of his own. He accepted Juan Ortiz's pledge of allegiance, and promised to show him much honor, for he was happy to have such a rare visitor. If the Castiles should ever come again, Mocozo said Juan Ortiz would be free to return to them. He even accepted the fact that this cost him his prospective marriage to Mouse Pelt, for now Hirrihigua's anger was directed at him, and he would never allow his daughter to join him. Fortunately, Mocozo had other wives to console him.

So it was that Juan Ortiz's new life was even more satisfying than his prior one. The young maidens of this region found him as handsome as the others had, and came often for the joys of the night. For eight more winters he remained here. Yet he never forgot that he was a Castile and a Christian, and he longed to return to his own kind.

Then another Castile conqueror named Hernando de Soto sailed several of the huge canoes to this land and came to the harbor. This time the Castiles had not only big fierce dogs, but even larger animals of a type the Indians had never seen before. Mocozo told Juan Ortiz this news, and gave him leave to go, as he had promised. At first Juan Ortiz doubted, fearing either that the Chief was joking or that he had tired of Juan Ortiz's company and wanted to rid himself of him. But he went to see, and it was true: there were Castiles there!

He went with a party of Indians to meet Chief de Soto. But when they encountered a party of Castiles, the Castiles immediately attacked, and the Indians fled. Only Juan Ortiz and one other remained. Juan Ortiz cried out in the Castile tongue, giving his place of birth—but he had been so long among the Indians that he had forgotten how to speak it well, and it came out garbled. The Castiles turned on the two, wounding the Indian, and one of their warriors thrust at Juan Ortiz with his long spear.

Juan Ortiz used his bow to beat aside the lance, and leaped aside, so that the Castile's huge animal called a horse did not run him down. Then he made the Sign of the Cross with his bow.

Now at last the Castile realized that this was no ordinary Indian. "Are you Juan Ortiz?" he demanded in his own tongue.

Juan Ortiz quickly nodded, repeating his name. At least he could still say that clearly!

"We have been looking for you!" the cavalier exclaimed. "We were told that you had been captured and not killed. Get up behind me on my horse! How glad I am I did not kill you! You look just like an Indian!"

And so it was that Juan Ortiz's long captivity was over, and he joined Chief de Soto's party as an interpreter. He enabled de Soto to establish friendly relations with Chief Mocozo, and thereby greatly helped the Castile effort while sparing Mocozo's people the problems of those who tried to oppose the Castiles. For indeed the Castiles were warriors like none other, as we all were to learn to our cost.

CHAPTER 17

⚜

DE SOTO

O Spirit of the Mound, I had deserted you, yet you did not desert me. You sent me one more signal of the terrible danger threatening my people, and still I did not understand it. I could have resumed my mission, and fetched the Ulunsuti even then, and saved them, but I did not. I was too absorbed with the immediate threat to my family. I have told you of my joy in my second family and my first daughter. Now I will tell you how the savages from the Tribe of Castile stole her from me, and what I did to recover her. I tell it not as Juan Ortiz saw it, but as I saw it, and as my daughter saw it.

Wren was eight winters old when the war party of the Castiles invaded the land. Runners spread the news ahead: monstrous canoes had come from the sea, and tens of tens of strange men had come from them and taken over the nearest villages. They had driven away the men, captured many of the women, and stolen all the food. Chief Mocozo's village was one of them. Juan Ortiz was of the same tribe as the invaders, and he had persuaded them not to burn the village, but even so, it had been an evil experience. The Castiles were formidable warriors whom it seemed none could stand against. They had with them ferocious dogs, and huge animals on which they rode, like nothing seen before.

Now this terrible war party was marching north, forcing warriors from the despoiled villages to guide them. They were looking for something, but it was hard to tell exactly what they wanted. They were ready to torture people to make them tell where this thing was, but since no one knew *what* it was, no one could tell. It seemed to be some kind of stone, the kind that could be melted in fire: perhaps the rare copper used to make special beads or plates.

But the Castiles already had many beads, for they gave them out in trade. They were excellent beads, hard and shiny and of many colors, better than the ones the people had. So how could they want stone for beads? It did not seem to make sense.

Our people sent warriors out to keep watch for the approaching army. The Castiles were mired in the swamp; the captive guides had directed them into the worst of it, hoping they would get lost and die. But it wasn't working perfectly; the Castiles caught on, killed a guide, and made another guide put them back on the northern course. They might be ignorant of our land, but they knew how to find their way.

We hoped that the Castiles would turn aside or pass some distance from Atafi and Ibi Hica. In any event, there was not much the villagers could do about it. It was still necessary to eat, so Tale Teller and Tzec went out on the Little Big River to fish, while Wren scouted for mussels by the shore. Tzec and I drifted out of sight, floating with the current so as not to alarm the fish, but Wren knew we would return soon. She drew up her moss cloak so that it would not drag in the water, and felt with her toes for a suitable mussel in the muck.

There was a pounding noise, as of many people dancing in step, but with the wrong beat. It grew rapidly louder. Wren peered in that direction in alarm: what could be causing this? She got up on a rock that was just under the surface of the water, trying to see better.

Then the strangest creature she had ever seen burst into view. It seemed to have six legs, two of which did not reach the ground, and two heads: one in front, and one rising from its back. It was followed by another like it. It was their feet that made the pounding noise; they seemed to be hard in the manner of rocks.

Wren stood frozen on the rock, staring at the monsters. Indeed, there was nowhere she could go, because the water was behind her and the monsters were in front. She hoped that if she was absolutely quiet, in the manner of a rabbit, the monsters would not see her. If they were evil spirits, they might not be able to cross the water to catch her.

But the monsters halted directly before her. One of them separated, and she saw that it was a strange man on the back of the strange creature. His body was thick and shiny, and his face was half covered by fur. He called something to her, but she couldn't understand it.

Then he strode forward. His feet were encased in leather. He reached out and put his arm around her. He lifted her from the rock, carried her from the water, and threw her to the monster. She landed on top of it, across its back, her head dangling down one side and her legs down the other, her cloak bunched somewhere between. Then the shiny man climbed back on it, sitting upright, and the monster started moving again.

She flopped painfully, for the monster bounced as it walked. The man muttered something, then put his hands on her hips, heaved her up into the air, and set her down so that her legs were on either side of the monster, just as his were, and she could see forward over its head. Its ears were like those of deer, making it slightly less frightening, but she was still terrified.

The monster moved on, and she bounced just as painfully on her bare bottom, but the shiny man put one arm around her and held her in place. They forged on through the forest at a rate that would have had her soon out of breath, but the monster was able to maintain the pace.

They came at last to a camp where there were a number of monsters and even more men. Wren realized that these must be the Castiles, the fearsome tribe from across the sea. They had come here much faster than seemed possible—but now that she saw their monsters, she realized how it had happened. The monsters moved like demons.

The man who had taken her lifted her off his monster. The others looked at her. One of them laughed. Now Wren was able to make out some of his words, for she had learned a few in the Castile tongue. ". . . child, Alvaro!"

Her captor turned her roughly around. He ripped off her moss cloak, leaving her naked. She was indeed a child; she had no breasts. He uttered an exclamation of disgust.

Wren could guess what had happened. He had seen her in the water, but hadn't seen the rock she was standing on, so he thought she was taller. He had taken her for a woman, because the cloak concealed her lack of breasts. Castiles, like all men, evidently raided other tribes for women. Now he knew her for what she was, and knew he had wasted his effort.

He put his hand to his side and pulled out a huge long knife made from some very smooth, shiny stone. He pointed this at Wren. He was going to kill her!

She stared around, looking for some way to flee. But she was ringed by the shiny fur-faced men, who seemed glad to see her die.

Then she saw one coming up on foot. She recognized him! He had shiny clothing like the rest, but his head was bare. "Juan Ortiz!" she screamed.

The man was startled. So were the others. They wondered how it was that she knew one of them. Juan Ortiz passed through the circle of men and stared at her. "Who are you?" he demanded in the Toco tongue.

"I am Wren, daughter of the Tale Teller!" she cried. "I saw you when you walked with us to Chief Mocozo's village."

"The Tale Teller's child!" he exclaimed. "You have grown! Why are you here?"

"This shiny man put me on his monster," she babbled. "My father and mother were fishing, but I was alone, and he picked me up and I didn't know what to do. Don't let them kill me, Juan Ortiz!"

Juan Ortiz turned to the man holding the big shiny knife. He spoke rapidly in the tongue of the Castiles. The one who had captured her, Alvaro, seemed uncertain; he still gripped the knife. But Juan Ortiz kept talking, and finally Alvaro put away his knife. Wren relaxed, slightly.

Now Juan Ortiz spoke to her in the Toco tongue again. "Alvaro has taken you captive, and you remain his captive," he said. "I saved your life only by telling him that your father would be useful as a guide and translator. I did not like to do this, but it was the only way. You must remain with us and not try to escape."

"But I must return to my family!" she protested, frightened again.

"Your father the Tale Teller must come to us," he said. "Wren, these are hard men. I tell you what is best. None of your people can fight them. If you try to run, they will set the dogs after you."

She had once seen a dog when a trader had passed with it; it had been a friendly little animal. She smiled.

"You do not understand," he said. "Come with me." He led her to another part of the camp, where there was a stake in the ground, and a rope was tied to the stake, and at the end of this rope was a huge snarling animal, not as big as the monsters they rode on, but as massive as a deer. It saw her and lunged at her, its teeth snapping viciously. Only the rope stopped it from reaching her.

Out of range, she studied the dog. It had a band around its neck from which great long thorns extended, and its body turned to stone, so that only its legs and head were furry. She thought that an arrow would probably bounce off that stone hide. She knew she did not want that demon dog pursuing her!

"There are others of your people at the main camp," Juan Ortiz told her. "You can be with them. But you must stay. I cannot protect you if you run."

She understood. Juan Ortiz knew her people, and did not want them to be hurt, but he was not the Chief.

"What are the big monsters?" she asked as they left the presence of the awful dog. "The ones they ride on?"

"Those are *horses*," he said, using an unfamiliar word. "They are from Castile. They do not attack people. They may even be friendly, if you feed them something they like."

"I don't want them to eat me!" she protested.

He smiled. "They do not eat flesh. They are like deer. They eat grass and leaves and corn. Here, I will show you mine." He led her up to one of the horses, though she hung back. He got a branch with some succulent leaves and held it out before the animal's nose. The horse opened its mouth and bit into the leaves, and chewed them.

After a bit Wren got up the courage to offer the animal a branch of leaves she had fetched. It chewed on them. It did not growl at her the way the dog had. It was big, but not hostile. She was relieved. "This one is with you?"

"My leader the Governor gave me this armor and this horse, and I interpret for him, because I know your tongue," he said.

"But I do not know the way through the swamp. I thought I did, but I lost the path. So I am with this scouting party, seeking a better route north. I am glad you recognized me, for I would have been grieved by your death. Your father is a good man, and your mother a good woman."

"But you say I can not return to them," she reminded him, her fear returning.

"This you must understand," Juan Ortiz said grimly. "I told them that your father can interpret because he knows some of the tongue of the Castiles as well as other tongues. I did this so they would not kill you. But if the Tale Teller does not come in and do this, they will hurt you and kill you, and I can not stop them. You must ask your father to come and serve my Chief, Hernando de Soto."

"My father will not want to do that," she said.

"He must do it. There is no other way."

"Maybe if my mother came too? She knows some of the Castile tongue."

He shook his head. "Do not let your mother come!"

When the war party of Castiles moved on, Wren rode with Juan Ortiz on his horse. This time she was much less frightened, for she knew that neither the horse nor the man wished to hurt her. She knew that Alvaro, the one who had captured her, now was her master, but he did not care where she was as long as what she did brought him some benefit.

By nightfall they reached the Castiles' main camp. Wren was amazed. It was bigger than Atafi, the main village of this area! There were so many tens of tens of men she could not hope to count them on her fingers, and there were many dogs and horses too. There were also many Toco, mostly men but some women. She did not recognize any of them, but they wore Toco clothing and spoke the Toco tongue. They were from villages to the south.

"Go with them," Juan Ortiz told her. "But if any Castile calls, go to him and do what he tells you." He lifted her down from the horse.

So it was that she joined her people again, yet she was not free. They had some food, but not enough, and they had to provide food for the Castiles by gathering anything they could. The men were made to walk, linked together by the hard stone

ropes she learned were called iron chains, carrying burdens for
the Castiles; and not only did the women cook, they had to go
to the lodges of the Castiles, where several of those men would
do sex with each woman even if she lacked honey. If any
woman tried to protest, two men would hold her while a third
pushed her legs apart and shoved in his pale penis, and soon
she did not protest anymore. It was not at all the way it was
supposed to be.

They came to Atafi. The Castiles had sent out several captives
to whom Juan Ortiz had talked, and they told the Chief that
Chief de Soto wanted only to be friendly, and take their stones
called *gold* and *silver*. The Chief replied that Atafi had none,
but that farther north among the Ocale there were many of
these stones. Wren had never heard of this, but of course she
was not the Chief.

Then Chief de Soto had Juan Ortiz tell the Chief to give the
Castiles all their food. The Chief did not want to do it, but there
were so many Castiles with their fierce dogs that he did not
want them to become unfriendly, and he gave them the food
that was stored in the main lodge.

Then Juan Ortiz asked that his friend Tale Teller join the
Castiles, for he was good with tongues. Tale Teller was there
but did not want to come. Then Juan Ortiz explained about
Wren, and showed how she was with the Castiles, and Tale
Teller realized that he had to do it.

But when he came forward, the Castiles protested. They did
not want a man with only one good arm! Juan Ortiz explained
that two arms were not needed for interpretation, and that this
man had the best tongue among all the Toco. He asked Tale
Teller to speak in Castile, and he said a few words, and then
the Castiles decided to take him. But they did not let Wren go.

So it was that Wren was reunited with her father, but not
her mother. Tzec might have come, to be with Tale Teller, but
Wren signed to her No! No! because now she understood Juan
Ortiz's warning against this. She knew her mother would not
want to be held down by two men while a third shoved his
pale penis into her cleft. In fact, Wren doubted that Tale Teller
would be very pleased to see that happen, either. Tzec looked
uncertain, but she remained in the village, and only Tale Teller
came. She saw that he was wearing the cloth band on his ba

arm: Tzec must have given him back the magic crystal, to keep him safe.

Tale Teller was allowed to be with his daughter only briefly, to verify that she was in good health. Then he had to go with Juan Ortiz, who joined a party with three tens of the huge strange animals called horses, with the men riding them. The armored Castiles sought to tie Tale Teller with their hard chains so that he would have no freedom and could not escape, but Juan Ortiz interceded, protesting that this Indian was an interpreter, not a captive. That saved him from the chains, and it was a great relief, because he was not sure he could have survived such treatment. A number of the men already in the chains seemed extremely uncomfortable, and it was evident that the Castiles did not care about their welfare. Any who paused or stumbled were promptly beaten.

So Tale Teller walked with his friend. There was a similar number of men on foot, and a number of the ferocious armored dogs. Juan Ortiz had a horse, but he decided to go afoot because his animal needed rest and he wanted to talk with Tale Teller. The horses could run faster than the men, especially since the men wore their heavy stone armor. But the thickness of the jungle and the marshiness of the ground slowed the horses to the men's pace, and they tended to get in each other's way. Tale Teller was better off on foot. Not that he wanted to be up on one of those strange animals. He had no fear of it, but he knew that he would quickly fall off when the animal moved.

Wren, however, was put on the horse of the man who had captured her, Alvaro. She rode in front of the armored man, and it was evident that any arrow shot at him was likely to strike her. She was really more armor for him!

Tale Teller did not like this. He wished she had been left with the women captives at the Castiles' main camp.

"You must understand, Governor Hernando de Soto is a fine man," Juan Ortiz said as they walked. "But he is impatient with our slow progress, and he does not tolerate obstruction well. We must do our best to please him."

"I just want to get my daughter away from captivity!" Tale Teller told him, glancing at Wren. "She has nothing to do with this."

Juan Ortiz shook his head. "She became part of this when Alvaro picked her up. He thought she was a young woman, and was going to kill her when he learned that she was a child; I saved her only by promising that you, her father, would translate for the Governor. I would have freed her if I could, but I could not. So you must serve the Governor as an interpreter, to ensure her safety. I do not like this, but it is the way it is."

Tale Teller saw that Juan Ortiz believed what he was saying, and wanted to make things easy for his friend. But he could not accept this situation. "I have no loyalty to this Chief who stole all the food of our main village," he said. "I have no loyalty to this Chief who holds my daughter hostage. When I have a chance to take her away from here, I will. You know that is the way it is."

"I know," Juan Ortiz said sadly. "But I serve the Governor, and I must do his will. In this case, his welfare and yours are the same; he needs interpreters and you need to keep Wren unharmed. You speak the local dialect, and so will be much better here than I; I can hardly understand the Atafi villagers when they speak rapidly, though it is the same tongue. Serve the Governor in this way, which is not a bad way, and all will be well. If you do not, I will not be able to protect you or your daughter. It would grieve me to see either of you come to harm, and I tell you this so that you will know how to avoid it. Do not try to oppose or escape the Governor! He is a fair man but a hard man. He cannot be balked; you can only be hurt."

Tale Teller did not argue further. He believed his friend's warning; he knew how any chief could be when balked. He remembered Juan Ortiz's own references to the Castile Narvaez, who had cut off Chief Hirrihigua's nose and thrown the Chief's mother to the vicious dogs. He would have to cooperate, until he had his chance to escape with Wren. The threat to her bound him more surely than any chain.

The Castiles moved north, following the guides. Juan Orti directed the guides to show the Castiles the best route through the swamp and across the river. But some of them were from villages to the south and did not know the local land, and the ones from Atafi, here under duress and angry because of the way the supplies of their village had been taken, had devious intentions.

Tale Teller knew this, because he was as familiar with this region as anyone, having lived here as a child and then having traveled all through it to tell his tales. He saw that the guides, whether from ignorance or from intent, were leading the Castiles into the very worst thickets and marshes, where alligators lurked and flies swarmed and thorns and prickles abounded. But he did not feel obliged to call attention to this. He might have to interpret for the foreign Chief, but he did not have to do the man any special favors.

The Castiles cursed in their brute tongue as they hacked through the vegetation with their impressive hard knives and slapped at the biting flies. One spooked a water moccasin and stepped back, nervous despite his armored legs. Tale Teller stepped toward him. "Wait!" he cried in Castile. Then, as the man stared, he tossed a twig at the snake, causing it to strike, and swooped his good hand down to catch it behind the neck when it was stretched out and unable to strike again. He tossed it into the water to the side, where it landed with a splash and slithered immediately out of sight.

The Castile continued to stare, until Juan Ortiz came up and spoke to him rapidly in his tongue, explaining that this native had a special way with snakes. Then the man shrugged and moved on.

"Maybe you should not be so free to show your fearlessness," Juan Ortiz murmured in Toco. "If they thought you were dangerous to them, they would chain you or kill you. Remember, I cannot go against the Governor's orders."

"I did it for the snake," Tale Teller explained. "It could not have hurt that Castile, but the Castile could have hurt it. We must not harm our brothers unnecessarily."

"The Castiles do not understand about animals as brothers," Juan Ortiz said. "Neither do they understand about the spirits. I understand only because of my time among your people. I beg you, for your own safety, do not draw attention to yourself in this manner."

Tale Teller had interceded with the snake automatically. It was bad to kill any animal without need, but especially bad to kill poisonous snakes, for their spirits could be worse than their living bodies. But he realized that Juan Ortiz was correct. Castiles did not understand, and might think him to be a crazy man. Also, if they understood that he was without fear, they would know that no threat against him would bind him to their tribe. It was only his concern for Wren that kept him here.

There was a scream ahead. Two villagers charged toward the column of Castiles, shouting to frighten them. They each fired an arrow, then ran back to the cover of trees before the Castiles could respond. But a Castile pointed some kind of stone tube, like a hollowed-out sapling, at one man before he reached his tree. From the tube burst black smoke like that from a stifled fire, and a noise like thunder.

The Toco who was running dropped to the ground. The terrible noise must have felled him! But now Tale Teller saw blood on the man's back. It was as if he had been speared, but there was no spear.

"You see, arrows can't penetrate the armor," Juan Ortiz said. "But our guns can bring men down from a distance. That's why it is useless to oppose the Governor."

"Tell me about guns," Tale Teller said, realizing that this was a strange and effective weapon.

"They are iron tubes with gunpowder and lead balls," the man said. That led into a number of marvelous new concepts. It seemed that *iron* was the shiny stone that was used for the Castiles' armor and the chains and big long knives. It was very hard, and could be melted under great heat and formed into anything desired. There was also gunpowder, which was like dust, but it caught fire when there was a spark and hurled the lead ball out the tube and through the air until it struck someone. The ball was like a tiny arrow, but it moved so fast it could not be seen, and hit so hard that it killed the man it had struck. Indeed, the weapons of the Castile tribe were terrible!

He was glad he had learned of this. He would make sure when he rescued Wren that there were none of those guns near.

More Toco attacked, and this time a Castile made his horse run behind and cut them off so they could not retreat into the jungle. Three were herded in among the Castiles, and their arrows did them no good. The Castiles swarmed over them

and soon disarmed them, striking them about their bodies until
they realized that they would be beaten to death if they continued fighting.

The Chief rode back and spied Juan Ortiz. "Get me a guide
who knows this swamp!" he snapped in Castile. Tale Teller
picked up the meaning as much by the context and need as by
the foreign words.

"This man will do it," Juan Ortiz replied, indicating Tale
Teller. "He speaks their tongue best."

The Chief's gaze fell on Tale Teller from the lofty height of
his horse. He did not speak again, but Tale Teller had the
disturbing impression that the Chief understood him and his
motives perfectly, and would not hesitate to do whatever he
thought necessary to compel cooperation. The man was a true
leader, who knew how to make others do what he wanted.

Tale Teller quickly went to the new captives. "You must
guide the Castiles out of the swamp," he told them in Toco.
"So they won't kill you immediately."

"We will do it!" the men cried eagerly.

But before the sun had traveled far across the sky, they were
in worse trouble than ever. The new guides had shown them
a way to higher ground, where one of the regular trails went,
and the Chief was pleased. But then there was an ambush,
with many Tocos firing arrows from cover, and the Castiles
had to fire their guns many times before the ambushers were
driven off.

Night came, and the Castiles ate what they called *cheese* and
biscuits and made camp for the night. The cheese was a food
made from the curdled milk of deerlike animals, and the biscuits
were a form of bread. Tale Teller and Wren had some, and it
was strange, but was far better than going hungry.

Some Castiles kept guard during the night, in several shifts,
so there was no chance to escape. Tale Teller hardly dared talk
with Wren, lest this be taken as plotting to flee and bring the
wrath of the Castiles down on them. At least they were together, and Tale Teller reassured his daughter as well as he
could that once they got their chance they would run away and
be free of captivity.

They slept uncomfortably on the ground, allowed no cover
by the captors. Tale Teller had a little of the grease that kept

the mosquitoes off, which he shared with Wren; otherwise it would have been worse. The Castiles did not seem to have anything similar; they tried to cover their heads and arms to keep the insects out, but their intermittent curses suggested that this was not wholly effective.

Next day the war party was led even deeper into the least penetrable regions. Tale Teller knew what the Toco guides were doing, but kept silent; he hoped they would bring the Castiles into such an ambush that all except Juan Ortiz would be killed, and this horror would be over.

Indeed there was an ambush, but it wasn't successful; the Castiles were alert and broke it up without taking any losses. Their gun-tubes were too effective at a distance.

But Chief de Soto had had enough. He knew his Toco guides were deliberately leading him into trouble. Now he acted. "Loose the dogs," he said.

The Castiles herded the Toco into the center of a circle. Then they separated one from the others. They brought up the huge vicious dogs and let four of them go.

The dogs charged the lone man in a pack. Horrified, he tried to run, but one bit into his leg, another bit into his arm, and the other two crashed their bodies into him so that he fell. Then one dived for his crotch while another bit at his throat. He hardly had time to scream before his penis and seed sac were ripped away and gulped down. Then the dog at his throat tore it open, and his blood spouted red and rich, and he was dead.

Wren turned away, hiding her face. She was young and female; she could show her horror. Tale Teller was an old man; he had to watch impassively.

The dogs' trainer shouted a word, and the four dogs abruptly stopped their attack. They were spattered with blood, but their tails wagged when they faced their trainer. They knew they had done well.

The Castiles shoved another Toco out toward the dogs. He tried to back away, but they only shoved him out again. The dogs merely stood and watched him alertly. He began to hope. He circled around them, then bolted for the far side of the circle, nearest the protective jungle.

The trainer spoke a word. As one, the dogs were in motion. They swarmed over the Toco, first hauling him down, then going for his crotch and throat as before and ripping them out. This time the trainer did not call them off, and they chewed into his belly and pulled out his guts.

Meanwhile four more dogs were brought up. A third Toco was shoved into the circle, and the new dogs went after him. This time the trainer spoke before they tore out his throat, and they halted and stood over him as he writhed and moaned, his penis and seeds gone.

"I will guide you to the right path!" the fourth Toco cried. Tale Teller called out the translation in the Castile tongue, for this was now his duty.

"You led us into an ambush," Chief de Soto replied. He made a gesture with his hand, and the trainer spoke, and the four dogs charged the Toco. He tried to hide among the Castiles at the edge of the circle, but the dogs knew their target, and caught him and brought him down and killed him.

The Chief gazed at the sight. "It seems we are without a reliable guide," he said. "Where shall we find one?" He looked around as if baffled. But in a moment, by no accident, his eyes fell on Tale Teller.

"I am an interpreter!" Tale Teller protested. "I know nothing about—" He was trying to speak in Castile, but in his distress he lapsed into Toco.

"Bring out the girl," de Soto said grimly.

Wren screamed as Alvaro put his hand on her shoulder and shoved her forward. The heads of all eight dogs lifted, orienting on her.

Tale Teller threw himself down before the Chief. "I will guide you!" he cried, mostly in Castile. "As well as I can, as far as I can!"

The Chief of the Castile war party gazed down at him for a terrible moment. "Yes, I think you will," de Soto said, and walked away. It was obvious that this was what he had had in mind from the moment he had the dogs brought up. He had known that Tale Teller could do it, and had known how to make him cooperate. It was no bluff: the Chief cared nothing for the girl, and would have given her to the dogs if Tale Teller had tried to defy him. He would do it tomorrow, if Tale Teller failed to cooperate tomorrow, or led them into a swamp or an ambush.

Juan Ortiz had been correct: it was not possible to oppose the Castiles. Not while they had a leader like Chief de Soto.

Tale Teller led them directly to the best Little Big River crossing, by the best path. When they came to the dead end of a blind path, he explained that this was deliberate, to deceive enemies, and guided them to the spot nearby where the path quietly resumed. By the end of the day they were there. Chief de Soto was evidently pleased. He even gave Wren a piece of his own cheese to eat. This was generous, as they were running out of it. It was also a reminder which Tale Teller understood all too well. The Chief knew perfectly the love Tale Teller bore his daughter, and that his lack of fear for himself had no meaning when the threat was to her. There would never have to be another demonstration.

The water was shallow at the edge of the river, but there was a deep channel in the center, with a fast current. Here the Toco had made a bridge for a hundred paces, fashioned from two great tree trunks tied in place. They had allowed it to deteriorate because relations with the Cale tribe on the far side were bad. It would have been smarter, Tale Teller knew, for the original guides to have brought the Castiles directly to this, so that they would leave Toco territory promptly and start harassing the Cale. But when the food of the village of Atafi was stolen, the Toco had been so angry that they had done anything they could to punish the invaders.

In the morning the Castiles started the crossing. The men could use the trunks-bridge, which they shored up with other branches, but the horses could not. They were led out to the edge of the deep center channel, where they were tied by ropes anchored at the far side, and the men pulled on these ropes and helped haul the horses the rest of the way across.

There was delay here, as the horses had to be moved across one by one, and the crossing took all day. Tale Teller talked to Juan Ortiz. "I do not know the land or the tongues well across the river. I will not be able to serve as the Chief wants, there."

"But you know both better than I do," Juan Ortiz said.

"When there is a problem, the Governor may tell me in Castile, and I will tell you in my Toco dialect, and you can tell a Cale warrior in a dialect he understands."

"He will not let me go home?"

"Not as long as he has use for you. It is his way."

And as long as de Soto had use for him, Wren would be hostage. The Castiles seemed not even to worry about the one-armed native, but they watched Wren, knowing she was the key. They treated her well enough, and normally one or another would have her ride with him on his horse. But their very kindness made clear how readily it could change, and how difficult it would be for her ever to leave the Castile camp unobserved. Chief de Soto even introduced her to his personal dog, called Bruto, who sniffed her frightened hand without biting. But Tale Teller had seen how the dogs obeyed their masters, and knew that if Wren disappeared into the forest, Bruto would know how to find her. The Chief had made sure Tale Teller saw his daughter with the big dog. It was as if an invisible chain were being forged, link by link, and it was firmly in place around his heart.

The ground was less swampy beyond the river, and Tale Teller had no trouble guiding them along a clear path. But the Cale tried to stop them as the Toco had, by attacking from ambush. One Cale sprang up and attacked a Castile with a knife, while others shot arrows. But the Cale had not realized how strong the Castile armor was, and were not able to kill anyone. They ran away.

The Castiles pursued them on their horses, and because this was better ground for the big animals, they were catching up. But the first Cale plunged into a nearby river, and his companions did the same. The horses could not follow them well there, so it seemed they would escape.

Then Chief de Soto's dog, Bruto, broke away from the servant who was holding him on a short rope. Bruto plunged into the river after the Cale, and pressed forward until he caught up to the first warrior. Then the dog struck the man with his great paw, and bit at him, and tore shreds from him in the water, so that the man died. He returned to his master, tail wagging, and de Soto smiled in a way he never did for a man, and rewarded him with a tidbit.

They came to the Cale village nearest the river, but it was deserted. The villagers had been there, but had fled at the approach of the Castile war party, leaving their food behind. There was a good supply of corn, enough to feed the war party and many more. The Chief sent loads of corn back on horses called *mules* so that the main part of his army could have it.

The Castiles camped here for half a moon, while the rest of the Castiles came to join their Chief here. They went out into the fields where the Cale grew corn and harvested it all. The Cale who had deserted their village were angry, and attacked the Castiles, but with no better luck than the Toco had had. They did succeed in killing three Castiles, but two of the Cale warriors were captured.

Chief de Soto also tried to negotiate with the Chief of the local Cale, as he had with the Toco Chiefs, sending messengers, but the local Cale Chief would not come. Instead he sent a message, which Tale Teller had to relay to Juan Ortiz: "I know who you Castiles are, for you are not the first to come here. You are nomads who go from place to place, robbing and murdering people who have given you no offense. I want nothing to do with you, and promise to wage war against you as long as you are here. Every few days I will cut off the head of one of your warriors, and since you have no women to breed more of you, in time you will all be gone. I and my people are ready to die ten tens of deaths to maintain the freedom of our land. This is my answer to you, now and forever."

Tale Teller had not liked the Cale, but his respect for them was growing. A Toco Chief could not have sent a better challenge.

Indeed, the Cale did as their Chief had promised. Any Castile who strayed alone a hundred paces from the camp found himself under attack, and that was how the three Castiles were killed, and many others wounded. When the Castiles were able to recover a body before the Cale cut off its head, the Cale would dig it up in the night and take the head anyway. Sometimes they hacked the bodies apart and hung the pieces from the branches of trees, taunting the Castiles with this deliberate desecration. Chief de Soto was not pleased, but bided his time. Tale Teller knew that the Cale might suffer terribly in due course. When it served de Soto's purpose.

* * *

The weather was hot, and the Castiles suffered from flies by day and mosquitoes by night. Juan Ortiz knew the Toco and other tribes had ways to protect themselves from these, but he did not know the particular herbs used to make the preparations. He asked Tale Teller, but he did not know either. As a result, soon everyone was suffering, but the native folk less, because their bodies retained some of the oils they had used, and their clothing was lighter. The chiggers especially sought those places where clothing was tight against the skin, and there they burrowed into the flesh, and their welts lasted for many days. The Castiles were covered with sores wherever their armor pressed in, in the very worst places. The captives did not dare express their delight with this situation openly, but they were of better cheer than before.

Chief de Soto decided that it would be better to relieve the party of some of its burdens. The Castiles took the extra armor that was not needed, and extra stores of beads used to trade for food and favors, and buried them in a secret place in the village. They concealed it carefully, and thereafter had fewer burdens to carry. This was a relief to them. Later they would return and fetch these things, knowing where they were. It seemed to be a good strategy.

Tale Teller said nothing. He knew that what the Castiles thought was hidden would be obvious to little Wren, who had been taken along with Alvaro. Her memory for location was as sharp as any. If she ever got free, she would be able to lead the Toco right to the spot.

If she ever got free. There was the problem.

Chief de Soto set off again, this time with five tens of horsemen and six tens of foot-men. He left the main part of the army behind again, where it had food and the wounded could recover. He took a few of the Toco women, to help prepare food and entertain the men. The women were resigned, knowing what to expect. At least they weren't chained in the way the warriors were. Juan Ortiz and Tale Teller and Wren went with the advance party, for that was where the need for interpreters was. This meant that they were proceeding ever farther from Toco territory, and escape became more difficult, for Tale Teller had never been here before.

However, he served well as an interpreter, because he had
learned more than one dialect of the Timucua tribes, and though
the dialects of this region were new to him, he was able fairly
readily to establish their affinities to those he remembered from
his first great journey north. They were now going through
Potano territory.

The Potano attacked, of course, but like the Cale and the
Toco before them, they underestimated the power of the Castiles' weapons and tactics, and lost a number of warriors to
death and capture. Tale Teller was required to interview the
captives promptly, and to select a few as interpreters. There
were three tens of them, so this took him some time. He had
to do it well, because Chief de Soto made clear that if the men
Tale Teller selected performed inadequately, Tale Teller's
daughter would be held responsible. He might as well have
had an arrow touching Tale Teller's back, the bow drawn and
ready to be loosed.

Several of the captives spoke Utina, the tongue of the tribe
to the north. One also spoke Yustaga, the tongue to the west.
That one was potentially the most valuable, but he was
wounded in the leg and was losing blood. Tale Teller first
thought that was a liability, but then he realized it was the
opposite, and he selected him as well as another injured man,
who spoke Utina.

"But those will be a burden to care for!" Juan Ortiz protested.
"We need healthy ones who can travel well!"

"Healthy ones can run away the moment they have a
chance," Tale Teller pointed out. "These ones will sicken and
perhaps die unless you give them special treatment, so are more
likely to cooperate if you treat them well, and they will not be
able to flee as readily. None of these captives is a friend to the
Castiles, no matter what they may say to escape torture or
death. Only the injured can be trusted even partially, because
of their situation. Promise them good treatment and food, and
release after their usefulness is done—and immediate and humiliating death if they do not serve. They will agree more readily than the others."

Juan Ortiz went to Chief de Soto and talked with him. The
Chief looked at Tale Teller, and even from a distance that ruth-
less calculation was chilling. Tale Teller's reasoning in this case

was much like de Soto's own, and the man evidently recognized that. Then Juan Ortiz returned. "He approves. Recruit those two."

Tale Teller talked again to the two. Both spit at him in response; they would not help the invader.

"Heed me, warriors," Tale Teller said as persuasively as he could in his bad Potano. "Chief de Soto is a man without compassion. I am a captive like you; I cannot fight, and my daughter there is hostage to my cooperation. He will throw her to the dogs if I fail him. He will throw the two of you to the dogs if you do not serve him, for he does not want the trouble of keeping you alive when you are sickly. But if you do serve him, he will be generous, and you will be cared for, and later allowed to return to your tribe when he is done with you. You do not have to fight for him; only guide him to the Utina territory, and interpret to any Utina we encounter."

Still they rejected the offer. Tale Teller was about to report to Juan Ortiz, but Chief de Soto had been watching. He rode up on his impressive horse, with his dog, Bruto, held by a rope. He pointed to one of the Potano warriors Tale Teller had not selected. "Serve me as interpreter," he shouted.

Tale Teller did not dare tell the Chief he had the wrong man. How could de Soto have made such a mistake? Tale Teller had to translate for the man addressed. "Chief de Soto demands that you interpret for him to the Utina, or he will punish you," he called to the man.

The man spit his defiance in true warrior fashion.

The Chief loosed Bruto. The dog sprang at the warrior, knocking him down. Bruto paused, looking back at his master. De Soto rapped a brief command to the dog, causing him to wait, and one to Tale Teller. "Ask!"

"Will you serve him?" Tale Teller asked the man.

The warrior did not answer. The Chief spoke again to the dog, and the dog's head plunged for the warrior's neck. In a moment the teeth had laid open the throat, and the blood gushed out. While the other captives watched, horrified, the dog lapped up this blood.

"Ask them!" de Soto cried to Tale Teller.

Tale Teller turned again to the two selected warriors. Now he understood: the Chief had made a demonstration on a captive he didn't need, to impress the ones he did need. He had not been confused.

"Will you serve?" Tale Teller asked them.

They hesitated. Bruto's head lifted from the body of the slain warrior, and his eyes oriented on the standing two. He growled.

It was the mark of a warrior to face torture or death without flinching. But these warriors had never seen such a dog. Bruto was like a demon, a malignant spirit from the underworld. He terrified them. First one man nodded, then the other.

Chief de Soto called Bruto to him and rode away. Juan Ortiz called to the Toco women captives. "Two of you see to these warriors," he said. "Bind their wounds, feed them, make them comfortable."

After a moment two women came out from the group. They attended to the two selected warriors. There was no more defiance. The job had been done.

Juan Ortiz approached Tale Teller. "The Governor is pleased with you," he said.

Tale Teller did not reply. He was not pleased with himself. He had learned all too well from Chief de Soto. He had done what he had to do, to protect himself and his daughter.

Next day a Potano warrior garbed in a Chief's robes met them near a town. He stood in the center of the path, making no move, so that they could see he was neither fighting nor fleeing. Chief de Soto sent Tale Teller to talk with him.

"I am the Chief of the Potano, for whom you have been looking," the warrior said. "I will yield myself as captive, if you will free my people you have taken."

"All but the interpreters," de Soto said when Tale Teller translated the offer.

It was done. The captives were allowed to go ahead to the village, but the two injured ones remained with the women who were caring for them. De Soto had never wanted to keep those captives, for it would have been a burden to feed them; he used them only as convenient, and at the moment he had as many bearers as he needed.

They marched on toward the village. "Let me speak with my people," the Potano Chief said. "I will reassure them and have them prepare a welcome for you."

Increasingly de Soto was speaking directly with Tale Teller, letting Juan Ortiz stand by to verify the dialogue. "Is this man really their Chief?" he asked.

"I doubt it," Tale Teller answered. "He is not to be trusted."

"Tell him yes."

Startled, Tale Teller did so. The ways of the Castile Chief were sometimes strange!

As soon as the claimed Potano Chief approached his people, he took off running, his betrayal now manifest. But de Soto's dog, Bruto, took off after him, and ran him down and held him until he could be recaptured. Again de Soto had known what he was doing. He had caused the captive to reveal himself as an enemy who had betrayed his captors at the first opportunity.

Now, using this episode as justification, the Castiles sacked the village, taking all its food and some of its women. If the Potano Chief was genuine, he now had reason to regret what he had done. The man had been no match for Chief de Soto in cunning; de Soto had *wanted* this betrayal to happen.

The party marched on. It reached a river that was swollen by recent rains. There were banks rising high on either side, so that the Castiles could not readily cross it. It would be necessary to build a bridge.

Chief de Soto had Tale Teller tell the Potano Chief to have his warriors build the bridge, under the direction of the Castiles. They went out to see where the best place was for this bridge.

Suddenly there was an ambush. Warriors rose up on the far side and fired arrows at Chief De Soto. This distance was too far, and the arrows did not strike, but the ambush annoyed de Soto. "How can you permit this shameful behavior when you agreed to help us?" Tale Teller asked, translating de Soto's words.

"I am not to blame," the Chief of the Potano replied. "My warriors no longer obey me, because they see I am serving the wrong side."

Chief de Soto did not react, as he evidently expected no better. But Bruto tore himself free from the man who was holding him by the collar, and plunged into the water. De Soto called him back, but the dog was so intent on his prey that he did not respond. He swam toward the Potano. They aimed their bows at him, and riddled him with arrows, but the dog kept swimming. He finally reached the far shore and climbed out, arrows sticking from every side of him. Then he fell dead.

This was the only time Tale Teller saw Chief de Soto grieve openly: for the death of Bruto. The Potano, in contrast, treated it as a major victory, for they considered the dog their worst enemy.

The Castiles named this the River of Discord, because of what had happened there. They made the bridge, and the war party crossed over.

In this manner they proceeded on into the territory of the Utina. In due course de Soto had the remainder of the army rejoin him. Then he proceeded ahead again, to the Utina town of Napetuca.

Tale Teller, in constant touch with the Utina because of his duty as interpreter, learned that an attack was planned to free the Potano Chief. They were going to deceive the Castiles with promises of friendship, them ambush them in Napetuca. He struggled with himself, wanting the Utina to succeed, but was afraid that de Soto would win anyway, and de Soto would know that Tale Teller had known. He could not risk that! He told Juan Ortiz, who told de Soto.

De Soto took it in stride. He continued his advance to the town, which was deserted. He and his men settled in, but instead of resting, they made preparations for battle. Each man checked his gun and crossbow and knives and armor, and they consulted about strategy. Now it was virtually certain that the Castiles would win. Tale Teller wished he could have kept silent, but as long as Wren was hostage, he had to serve the Castiles loyally.

Suppose the Utina succeeded anyway? If they did, they would surely kill all the Castiles—for the Castiles would die fighting—and not know Tale Teller's part in this. Then he could take Wren and go home. What he had done seemed to be the safest course, though his mouth tasted bad from it.

On the day before the attack, the Castiles confined the interpreters and servants and women to certain lodges, while the Castiles hid themselves in other lodges, ready for battle. Wren went with Alvaro; that ensured that Tale Teller would remain where he was supposed to be. Thus he remained confined, though he could have escaped alone.

He learned of the battle secondhand. Four tens of tens of Utina warriors advanced on the town: what they felt was an overwhelming force, considering that de Soto had only his leading war party with him: five tens of horse-men and six tens of foot-men. His force seemed even smaller because the foot-men were hidden in the lodges. Two warriors came forward to demand the surrender of the captive Potano Chief. De Soto met them with six of his horse-men, on their feet with their horses back with the others. The Utina warriors thought this was easy prey, and made ready to attack, but de Soto signaled his forces to attack first. The horse-men charged forward, using their lances to strike the warriors, who were taken by surprise. Three or four tens of them were killed immediately, and the rest, dismayed, fled to the forest and to two marshy lakes nearby. Thus the first part of the battle was won by the Castiles because of the power of their horses and their sudden charge. The Utina feared the horses, and directed their arrows first at them. They succeeded in killing de Soto's horse, but he took the horse of one of his horse-men and continued the battle. While the Utina were trying to kill the horses, the horse-men were killing the Utina.

The Castiles hidden in the lodges swarmed out and joined the pursuit, firing crossbows and guns at the Utina. They stood at the edge of the lakes and continued firing, but the warriors were beyond effective range. The Utina helped each other to fire their arrows, because of the difficulty of doing this in deep water: one would be lifted up by several others, shoot his arrow, and then drop back into the water. But this, too, lacked effect.

At night the Castiles surrounded one of the lakes, so that no Utina could escape. They demanded surrender, and by morning the warriors were so chilled and exhausted that all but ten and two of them had done so. Then de Soto ordered the Toco servants to go in and drag the remaining warriors from the lake, and they had to do so. This much Tale Teller saw directly, for he had been brought out with one of the interpreters to relay the Castile's demands to the Utina.

The battle was over, and the Utina Chief had been taken

captive, and more than two tens of tens of his warriors had been taken prisoner. Most of the rest were dead. It had happened as Tale Teller had expected; probably the Castiles would have won anyway, because of the terrible power of their weapons and armor. That was why Tale Teller had betrayed the secret. What was the point in risking his daughter unless he was sure the Castiles would lose?

They rested and recovered for several days, waiting for the main part of the Castile army to catch up. Tale Teller was further in de Soto's favor because he had discovered the plot, and now he was allowed to be with Wren all the time, except when there was fighting. In fact, de Soto treated him well, seeking to win him over with kindness. The man was quite charming when he chose to be. But Tale Teller wanted to rescue his daughter, and be home with his wife, so while he did not reject the man's courtesies, he never gave his oath not to escape. De Soto understood this, and did not force the issue, knowing that true loyalty could not be compelled.

Tale Teller was eating when the Utina captives rebelled. This time the Utina made sure Tale Teller knew nothing of their plot; in fact, they intended to kill him after they killed the Castiles. One of the recent captives who served as a new interpreter attacked de Soto while he sat eating, striking him a terrible blow in the face with his fist. The Castile Chief was knocked unconscious, his nose bleeding. But nearby Castiles quickly closed in and killed the Utina warrior before he could finish the job.

This attack signaled the others, who still outnumbered the Castiles. They rose up and attacked the Castiles with whatever they could lay their hands on. They used rocks and captured weapons and burning brands and even their bare hands. They were brave and strong, and they fought with determination and imagination and ferocity. For a time it seemed that they would succeed in their rebellion.

But even when caught by surprise, the Castiles were formidable fighters, and they knew how to use their weapons with a skill the Utina could not, for they had been long trained in them. The crossbows were especially effective, for the Utina still did not understand that such a weapon could fire properly when it was not held up and drawn by hand. They also were slow to appreciate how securely the Castiles' armor defended them against blows, and tried to strike it with their fists. The guns completely amazed them; they could not believe that a little ball of iron-stone could fly so fast they could not see it, yet bring them down.

The fight was savage, but the Castiles subdued the Utina. Now came the reckoning. The young Utina were bound with the iron-stone chains, and the older ones were killed. But the Castiles did not kill them themselves; they required the Toco servants to do it. Even Tale Teller: Juan Ortiz gave him one of the big iron knives called a *sword* and told him to slay a bound Utina warrior with it. Tale Teller was appalled, and did not want to do it, but Chief de Soto himself, his face bruised and bandaged, looked meaningfully toward Wren where Alvaro held her, and Tale Teller knew he had no choice. Wren had always been treated well, and now served as a servant to Chief de Soto himself; she was learning the Castile tongue. But none of them ever forgot what she was, or how she would fare if she failed in that.

The Utina warrior gazed at him with contempt. The man was bruised and bloodied from a number of strikes, but his will was unbroken. "A one-armed coward!" he sneered.

"It is not fear but regret," Tale Teller said. "I do not like killing men who are not attacking me." That was not the whole truth; he did not like killing men at all, but he could do it when he had to.

"It is fear!" the warrior taunted him. "When did you ever kill a man?"

"Have you ever fought with the Saturiwa?" Tale Teller asked. "I have." He was remembering the three he had killed defending Beautiful Moon. He remembered, too, how it had been necessary. It was necessary now, to save Wren.

The man spit insultingly.

"You do not need to believe," Tale Teller said. "I will kill you cleanly."

The man stared into his eyes, trying to make him flinch, but Tale Teller met his gaze. He held the sword with his good right hand and shoved it through the Utina's heart so that he died immediately: as honorable a death as was possible. Only when the point touched his heart did the man begin to believe, and he was dead before that belief was complete.

Then Tale Teller set down the sword and walked away, his own heart hurting as if stabbed. No one stopped him.

In this manner Chief de Soto had his vengeance for the rebellion, and ensured that the Toco captives would never find comfort with the tribes of this region.

The Castiles resumed their march. One day beyond Napetaca they reached another great river, which they had to cross after making a bridge. They entered the territory of the Yustaga. Two parties were sent out in opposite directions to capture more natives, because there were not enough remaining after the slaughter of the Utina to do the labor of servants. The parties brought in ten tens of men and women. Now the Potano who knew the Yustaga tongue was useful; Tale Teller had him speak to the captives, and translate for Tale Teller, who relayed it to Juan Ortiz. The men were put in chains attached to collars around their necks and used to carry burdens and grind corn. The women were always useful in their way. Actually, the Toco women who remained had become resigned to their lot, and were learning to speak the tongue of the Castiles, just as Wren was. Seeing this, the Yustaga women served more readily.

The army came to a deserted village where they found corn, beans, pumpkins, and dried plums. There was plenty to eat. They continued until they reached the chief town of the region, called Apalache. There de Soto decided to camp for the winter. The army was to remain there for five moons, and the rigors of the winter were such that most of the captives died. But de Soto took good care of his most competent interpreters, Tale Teller chief among them.

CHAPTER 18

·ᒣᔑ·

SEARCH

O Spirit of the Mound, I have told you how the Castiles captured my daughter, and therefore me also, and prevented us from escaping. Now I will tell you how we traveled with the Castiles to the land of my two wives, and beyond, and how trouble occurred. Of course, trouble was continuous with the Castiles, who may have been related to demons.

It was a terrible winter. The Toco were accustomed to a warmer climate, and lacked proper clothing, and the Castiles hoarded their own clothing, not sharing it. Tale Teller, having lived in the far colder climate of the Principal People, tried to warn them, but they did not believe him in time. At least he was able to take care of himself and Wren. When the Castiles killed deer for food, he prevailed on them to let him have some of the hides, and he cured these in the sun as well as he could, which was not very well, and he and Wren fashioned them into cloaks which were largely proof against the wind and chill of the bad nights. In this manner they survived, while many did not.

The Yustaga knew about the climate, but they were in chains and could not help themselves. Tale Teller pleaded with Juan Ortiz to intercede with Chief de Soto on their behalf, but it became apparent that the Chief did not much care about their welfare, and was more concerned that they would use any freedom they got to attack the Castiles. Neither would he let them go, for similar reason. The rebellion at Napetaca had made him more cynical.

Tale Teller had reason to believe that he and Wren would not have survived had they not been free of chains and had the friendship of Juan Ortiz. One of the scourges of that winter was the presence of marauding evil spirits. Wren got sick, along with several of the other captives and some of the Castiles.

It started gently. Wren's nose began to run, as if she had been crying or sneezing, but it was from another source. The same happened to the others. Their eyes burned red, a sure sign of infestation by spirits, but there was no priest to banish the malign presences. The light seemed to be too bright, and they had to hide their eyes, preferring the gloom of the interior of their lodges.

Then they started coughing, and it got worse, becoming harsh and hacking. They became tired, even when they were not working hard, and their bodies got hot, showing that the spirits were trying to get out, but without the proper ceremonies this could not happen. Tale Teller was afraid that his daughter would die, for the spirits had come after him again, to finish what they had started when they killed all of his prior family except himself. He took the magic crystal and showed it to her, and put it on her, to help fight the spirits, and she smiled and thanked him.

White spots appeared inside Wren's mouth, surrounded by red. Then her forehead developed brownish-pink spots, which advanced upward into her scalp beneath her hair, and downward to her neck and across her body. The same thing happened to the others. The spirits were definitely moving out, but in their own ugly fashion, disfiguring the people they possessed.

The Castiles were not as concerned. They called it *measles*, and said it was a natural illness. They did not seem to appreciate the nature of the spirits or know how to deal with them. Yet they did not suffer as much, so perhaps their foreign nature was less attractive to the spirits, and they were not as badly infested. Perhaps their priests were more effective in interceding against the spirits. But the priests would not do it for the natives unless they renounced their *pagan* beliefs and swore fealty to the Castiles' Great Spirit, Jesus Christ. The natives would have been glad to do this, but it turned out that it was not enough to honor this spirit in addition to their own; the

Castile priests insisted that the regular spirits be cursed and forgotten. That was such manifest nonsense that there was no point in considering it.

Wren became so hot she sweated profusely, soaking her clothing. Then she turned cold, shivering uncontrollably. Tale Teller remembered suffering similarly when the Principal People had been attacked, and knew what to do. He used his dry cloak to wrap her and warm her, and hugged her, sharing his own body heat. Then she got hot again. This time he quickly removed the cloak, so as to prevent it from getting soaked, and let her sit naked on the chill air. She soon chilled, and he wrapped her again.

She slept, and woke with a terrible thirst. He gave her water, and she slept again. She woke again, thirsty, and he gave her more water. This continued through the night; whenever he heard her stir, he fetched water for her. He lost sleep, but at least she seemed to be surviving.

Finally she sank into a lethargy, seeming too weak to sit up or even turn her head. Tale Teller wished he could pray to the Spirit of the Mound, but he had renounced all spirits and knew there would be no help there. All he could do was watch her and keep the magic crystal with her and help her in whatever way she needed help. When she urinated, he cleaned her up. He wiped off her face, and spoke to her, telling her how he loved her and would always be with her. It seemed so little, but what else was there to do?

It was enough. The magic crystal outlasted the evil spirit, and Wren tided through. Her spots faded and her body resumed its normal heat. She slept in greater comfort, and when she woke he was able to feed her small amounts of dried fruit.

At last she looked up at him and smiled, and he knew she was getting better. With the help of the magic crystal she had conquered the evil spirits! *Twice Cursed, I thank you*, he thought, remembering when his wife had given him the crystal. He would have used it to save his first two wives and sons if he could have; at least it had saved his daughter.

From that day Wren got stronger, and ate better, and her cheer returned. She remained weak, but it was evident that she would be normal again soon. The evil spirits had not succeeded in killing her.

But most of the other people who were affected died. They had not had the magic crystal, and many of them had been in chains, and they lacked sufficient clothing and water. Only the Castiles were sure of recovery.

Then the evil spirits attacked Tale Teller, and most of the native folk who had not suffered before. He knew what had happened: the spirits had been banished from their first victims, but they thought they would have better success with the others.

Now Wren took care of him, as he had taken care of her. She was young, now in her ninth winter, but she understood exactly how these spirits worked because of her recent experience, and she loved her father as he loved her. She put the magic crystal back on him. When the terrible fever came, she took away his dry cloak, and when the chill came, she restored it. When he woke with thirst, she was there with water. When he sank onto the ground, too weak to get up to urinate, she cleaned him up.

At last he woke feeling better, though weak. He smiled at her. She smiled back. She brought him food, and he ate. Then he slept, and she did too; she had lost sleep while caring for him.

But by the time he recovered, there were few native folk remaining. The Castiles were tending their own chores, and not happy about it. The winter passed, day by day.

The horses, however, did well. They were larger, and able to handle the cold, and they were fed before the captives were. Wren, at first afraid of these huge animals, lost her fear as they became more familiar, and then became friendly with them. She learned how to brush their hides and how to tell when they caught stones in their feet. She enjoyed riding on them, and knew the commands that made them go where the rider wished. She would go with them sometimes when they were let out to graze. But Tale Teller did not learn how to do these things, and did not care to, and the Castiles did not care to have him learn. They knew that Wren would not ride away on a horse without her father, and they watched him when Wren was away from the camp. He was not in chains, but he could not escape. Neither would they let him go; he was part of the chain of interpreters, and so remained useful.

On the third day of March, in the strange calendar of the
Castiles, in their year after the birth of their god-on-earth 1540,
they resumed their march. They were guided by a captive taken
at Napetuca, who was not of any of the local tribes. Tale Teller
had talked with the boy at length, and the Castiles had named
him Pedro. Pedro said that he was from a tribe far to the east
and north, where they had much of the gold-stone and silver-
stone the Castiles sought. He had been traveling with a trader
when he was captured and the trader killed. Tale Teller knew
enough of such things to know that this could be true, so he
had told Juan Ortiz that this was a person worth interviewing
further, and the boy's life had been spared. As it turned out,
he was good company for Wren, who until then had been the
only other child with the army.

Pedro described how this gold was taken from the earth,
mixed in with other stone, and melted so that it flowed out
while the other stones remained hard. He said it was used for
ornaments by the Chief, who was a woman. She governed a
very large town, and many other tribes paid tribute to her. The
Castiles talked with this boy, and were impressed, for to them
his nonsense about melting stone seemed to make sense. This
was how they got gold, and they wanted more of it. So when
Tale Teller thought the boy was inventing something impossible, it seemed he was making his case best. The Castiles referred to these special melting stones as *metals*. Among them
were Gold and Silver and Copper and even Iron.

The journey was arduous. First they went north, following
a river. Then they reached the mountains. The country was
beautiful, and Tale Teller remembered when he had passed
through similar terrain on his way to the Principal People. Some
of the tribes were friendly, but when the Castiles took their
food and their women by force, they became less so, and the
army proceeded under intermittent siege to the northeast. It
also seemed that some of these tribes were enemies of each
other, and were trying to inflict pain on their enemies by sending the Castiles into their midst. They ran low on food, and
finally had to kill and eat many of their pigs, which were strange
hoofed animals with flattened snouts.

The guide lost his way and pretended madness, so they had
to explore for themselves. Chief de Soto was annoyed by this,

and would have thrown the boy to the dogs, but Pedro was the only one with any hope of serving as interpreter at this stage. Neither Juan Ortiz nor Tale Teller knew anything of the local tongues, while Pedro had at least some familiarity with them.

But at last they reached the territory the boy had spoken of, and indeed he was able to speak the local tongue with competence, so this confirmed what he had said. They hoped to find at last the valuable gold they had been seeking.

Chief de Soto rode forth with a hundred men on horses and a hundred more on foot, and came to the bank of a river where the path ended. On the other side was a large village. Pedro shouted to the people there to come and receive a message for the Chief of that land. The people were amazed to see the men on horses, and soon several canoes came across. They bowed first to the Sun, and then to the Moon, and then to Chief de Soto. Their leader spoke in their tongue, and Pedro translated this into the Ucita tongue, and Tale Teller translated that into the Toco tongue, giving Juan Ortiz the chance to make the final translation for the benefit of de Soto. Tale Teller could have done it more directly, but protocol was important, and it was best that his Castile friend have the honor.

"My lord, do you seek peace or war?" was the question.

"I seek only peace," de Soto replied formally. "I ask no more of you than passage across the river and food to enable my party to continue on its way to certain provinces for which I am searching. I hope you will grant us your friendship while we pass through your lands."

This message was relayed through the three translators to the people from the village. Tale Teller performed as he was supposed to, though it bothered him, as it always did, that what he relayed was at best a half-truth. Chief de Soto wanted gold and women as well as food, and he would take them regardless of the wishes of the people. His polite address was only to lull the people into friendliness, so that the fighting could be postponed at least until after the army got across the river. Certainly de Soto preferred peace to war, but neither mattered as much as the wealth he sought.

But these people were evidently not fools, or perhaps they had heard about the ways of the Castiles. "We are glad to have peace between us," they replied. "But we have little food, for evil spirits have ravaged our people in recent seasons, and only our own town escaped them. The people of the other villages fled to the forests without sowing their fields. Now the bad spirits have passed, but the people have not yet returned to their homes or gathered much food."

Tale Teller found this most interesting. He had assumed that the spokesmen were merely making excuses for the other villages which were even now being vacated, their food hauled to safety. But the mention of evil spirits was another matter. Tale Teller had crossed his own long-ago trail; he had recognized the river when they crossed it, and the dialects of the people of the villages there. He could have found his way home from there, going down the river, but Wren had been on one of the horses with a Castile, and besides, he had no canoe. So he knew that there had been evil spirits here; how well he knew! It seemed they were still rampaging, a ten of winters after they had destroyed his family. That gave him a chill. He had departed the region, renouncing the spirits; had that made them so angry that they continued hurting any people they could find?

"But our village Chief is a beautiful young maiden, the niece of our tribal Chief, and she recently came to power when her mother died," they continued. "She will soon marry, if she can find a warrior of appropriate stature. We will return to her and tell her what you have said. We are sure that she will do everything she can to assist you, as she is a woman of discretion and great heart."

Tale Teller remembered Beautiful Moon, of a tribe farther south of this one. How the past winters were coming back to him now! He relayed the message, with his own addition that it was quite possible that it was true.

Chief de Soto, guided by this, was gracious in his response. The people went in peace, crossing the river, while the Castiles waited. Soon two large canoes returned, the second towed by the first. In the first were warriors, but in the second were nine pretty women wearing fine clothing and many beads, their canoe covered by a pleasant canopy. It was the most impressive sight Tale Teller or the Castiles had seen in all their travels. Again Tale Teller remembered Beautiful Moon, who could be

absolutely charming when she chose. He suspected that the
Castiles were about to be treated to a similar demonstration.
Was it to be trusted?

The Lady of Cofitachequi came to meet Chief de Soto, flanked
by her women. She was indeed beautiful, with a nice face and
nice proportions. She greeted de Soto, who stood to meet her,
as an equal; then she took her seat in a chair which had been
brought for her. No warrior and no woman spoke or made any
sound, only the Lady.

"My subjects inform me that you have need of food for your
party, Chief de Soto," she said, and her voice was dulcet. "I
regret that the scourge of the evil spirits has robbed us of the
supplies we require to minister to your needs more adequately,
but we shall do all we can."

Pedro, Tale Teller, and Juan Ortiz translated this, while the
Lady waited patiently. Then she resumed. "We have two stores
of corn of similar size, which we have gathered to help our
people in other villages who are hungry. But we shall make
one of these available to you, and save only the other for ourselves. I will make my own house available for you, and my
village shall provide pleasant bowers for your warriors. If these
are not enough, I will clear the entire village for your use, and
my people will go to one nearby. We shall quickly provide
canoes and rafts for you to cross the river; in the morning they
will all be here."

Chief de Soto was evidently touched, for this was a most
generous offer, delivered in a most attractive form. De Soto
was a cruel and cynical man, but the presence and courtesy of
these lovely women moved him in a way that the threat of force
could not. He replied that he and his men would try to use as
little corn as possible, so as not to inconvenience her people,
and that her plans for their lodging were certainly good enough.
He said that he considered her generosity to be a favor never
to be forgotten.

The Lady of Cofitachequi then had her women bring from
her canoe some very nice shawls and cured animal skins and
present them to de Soto. Then the Lady lifted from her body
a large necklace of pearls, which circled her neck three times,
crossed her decorous bosom, and fell all the way to her shapely

thighs. Some pearls were small, but others were large, and all were perfectly formed: in their fashion, images of herself. "Please give these to your Chief, as a token of our friendship," she told the interpreters.

But Juan Ortiz, as smitten by the Lady as the others were, protested. "You should make the presentation yourself, as it is your gift." Tale Teller and Pedro relayed this.

"But I must not do such a thing," the Lady protested in turn, "lest your Chief feel that I am violating the modesty which must be observed by those of my gender." Her way of speaking was as pretty as her person.

At this point de Soto inquired what was going on, since there was an interchange but no final translation. Juan Ortiz explained it to him.

De Soto, suspicious of some devious ploy but also intrigued by the Lady's beauty, decided to play it out. "Inform her that I shall esteem the honor of receiving such a gracious gift directly from her hands more than I would the pearls themselves. I will not regard this as any breach of decorum, because this is a matter of peace and friendship, signifying the amity between us and our people." When it came to charm, he was as cunning as any demon spirit before it showed its true nature.

The Lady then rose and walked directly to Chief de Soto, who stood to meet her. She reached up to set the great necklace about his neck, brushing against him by seeming accident and smiling as she did so. Oh, yes, she was conversant with the art of women!

Chief de Soto was highly impressed with the gesture and perhaps also with the nearness of the Lady's delightful body as she reached her arms around his neck, her breasts only partly covered by the thin cloth of her dress. Any man would have considered sacrificing all his wealth to be in the Chief's place at this moment. On impulse de Soto put his hand on his finger and twisted free a fine gold ring set with a bright red stone of great value. He gave this to her, and she accepted it graciously and put it on one of her own fingers.

Then the Lady of Cofitachequi withdrew with her companions, and crossed the river to her village. The Castiles stood and watched in rapt silence, all of them impressed with her beauty and poise. Not one of them had thought to inquire her name. She was just the Lady at that moment, and perhaps always, in their fancy.

Tale Teller found his daughter staring after the Lady similarly. "I think my mother must have been like that when she was young," she murmured.

"And her mother too, surely," he replied. "And you, when you are grown." He remembered Heron Feather in her youth, and Beautiful Moon, and Laurel, but most of all Tzec: the Lady of Cofitachequi was the perfect essence of them all.

"I hope so!" Wren breathed.

Next day the rafts and canoes were there, and the army crossed without incident, except that the carelessness of some of the Castiles allowed several horses to drown. They were mourned more than would have been the case had it been men who had died. They camped in the half of the village which had been cleared for them. There were a number of fine mulberry trees there, shading the region, and it was very nice.

Now de Soto asked the Lady to show him the metals she had, for he had come here to find gold and silver. She had her people bring samples of other metals which were colored like the ones the Castiles desired but which were not the same. Instead they were what the Castiles called copper and *iron pyrite*, which it seemed were of less value. The Castiles were disappointed, but could appreciate how the boy Pedro had been mistaken, as he was not in a position to know the distinction between similarly colored metals.

But the Castile's fortune was better with the valuable stone crystals the Castiles also sought. The Lady showed them a lodge which was a house for the spirits of their dead. Tale Teller avoided going there, because he had renounced the spirits and did not want to encounter them again. He tried to warn Juan Ortiz that the spirits might be angry if the Castiles took anything from their house, but Juan Ortiz did not believe this. Day by day he was reverting to the Castile attitudes he had had before he became a captive, and Tale Teller was grieved to see it.

In the lodge were the decaying bodies of the dead tribesmen, and so many fine pearls that it was not possible for the Castiles to carry them all away. Each took as many as he could carry, and left the rest, somewhat frustrated.

The Lady received word that there were other types of metals beyond the mountains, and promptly relayed this to de Soto. This was the type of news that most tribes discovered soon after the Castiles arrived, because it encouraged the army to move on more rapidly. De Soto was getting cynical, but his lust for gold caused him to believe what he should not. He organized for a march northwest to the mountains.

Meanwhile some of the Castiles were taking what the Lady had not offered, which was the young women of the Cofitachequi tribe. The men forced them to have sexual relations in the manner they had done with the Toco women, and the Lady, learning of this, was not pleased. She approached de Soto and asked that he leave immediately with his men, as they were doing harm in her village. Tale Teller tried to caution her, knowing that de Soto could be harsh when criticized, but she insisted, so he translated.

Chief de Soto frowned. "Place her under guard," he snapped. "She will come with us."

The Castiles laid hands on the Lady, who was appalled. "But what of our friendship?" she cried, thinking there must be some mistake. "What of the gifts we exchanged?"

De Soto turned away. He intended to keep her hostage against any reprisals by her people, as was his way. How well Tale Teller knew!

The men brought the chains. Tale Teller, appalled at the thought of the Lady being treated this way, took a risk. "No chains!" he cried. "If her people see her prisoner, they will attack immediately! It must seem that she comes of her own choice!"

"But the Governor—" they protested.

"I will explain to Chief de Soto!" And to the Lady, he said: "You must smile and go with them as if happy to do so, or they will put chains on you. That must not be."

She glanced at him, knowing his own situation. She had been deceived by de Soto, but she retained her poise. She recognized the truth of the warning, and this time she heeded it. She smiled and set about making herself and her attending ladies at home in the Castile camp.

Tale Teller went immediately to de Soto and explained about his intercession to prevent the chaining of the Lady. De Soto ignored him. That was his way of expressing approval of a presumptuous action. He knew Tale Teller was right, but also knew his motive. So he pretended that it had always been his intention to do it this way.

They resumed their march, taking a number of the Cofitachequi warriors to carry burdens, and a number of their women to serve their purpose. The Lady, their Chief, set her jaw and showed no fear, only regret. She knew she had been betrayed, despite all her efforts to treat the visitors well. She also knew that resistance would bring disaster. The only way to avoid bloodshed was to cooperate. For now.

Meanwhile it served de Soto's purpose to have the Lady cooperative, so he treated her like a guest. Neither was fooling the other, but it was pleasant enough on the surface. No one molested the Lady or her attendants, and there were no attacks on the Castiles. But Tale Teller knew that things could change suddenly and drastically if anything went wrong, for warriors were stalking the army.

This was the province of Xuala, the northernmost of the territory where the Lady of Cofitachequi had any authority. Indeed, the people here seemed to treat her more as a visiting foreign dignitary. They spoke a dialect of the Ani-Yunwiya, the Principal People. The villagers here were helpful, but they had little to offer. The Lady had spoken truly: the region had been ravaged by spirits of the type the Castiles called *small pox*, and they had not been able to grow their corn, and had used up most of what they had stored.

The Castiles camped in a village here for two days, allowing time for the sick and wounded to be brought up from the south. The scarcity of supplies prevented them from waiting any longer.

They came to the high mountains, part of the great range through which Tale Teller had passed alone so many winters ago. Their progress slowed, for it was an arduous climb. But they had been told that there were more riches on the other side, and Tale Teller chose not to correct that impression, though he knew that the Principal People had no such metals. His only regret was that this Castile menace would be inflicted on a tribe he knew and loved. But he hoped that the rigors of the mountains would weaken the Castiles, and perhaps divert them from the territory of the Principal People. This seemed to be the case, for the Castiles became tired and careless.

Tale Teller called Wren aside when the Castiles were busy with other things. "I want you to learn a few words in the tongue of the Ani-Yunwiya," he told her quietly. "When you are riding one of the horses, pass by the Lady of Cofitachequi and call these out to her."

"But what do they mean?" she asked, perplexed. She was good with tongues, but this one was new to her.

"It is a warning to her that she may be degraded and killed when her presence no longer enhances respect for the Castiles," he explained. "She is not a lady Chief among the Principal People, but she will remain a beautiful woman."

"She knows that already."

"I know the nature of this country. There are some very dense thickets. The mountain passes are very high, and the Castiles and their horses will be panting and tired and inattentive. She must escape before her value diminishes and they put her and her women in chains and abuse them."

"I will speak the words," Wren agreed. "But why not in her own tongue, which I understand a little bit?"

"Because the boy of their tribe who brought us here has joined the Castiles. They have removed his chain and now call him Pedro with respect rather than derision. He has forsaken our spirits and honors their one spirit. He cannot be trusted, and he will hear and know if you give her warning in that tongue. But I think she or one of her women will know the tongue of the Principal People, having had trade relations with them, while the boy does not."

Wren worked on the words he taught her. "The last words are 'If you understand, pretend to be insulted, so as not to betray me,'" he concluded.

His daughter stared at him for a moment, comprehending the danger all too well. Then she repeated the last words in the foreign tongue.

A day later Wren reported that she had spoken the words, and one of the Lady's women had cursed her and thrown a stick at her, which missed widely. The Castile guards, spying this from their horses, had laughed at both the supposed insult and the woman's inability to throw accurately. They liked Wren, and thought she liked them.

Nothing happened for two days. Then, when Tale Teller and Wren were near the front of the column, and the lady captives were near the rear, it happened. He learned about it only later, glad it was obvious that he and Wren had no involvement.

The Lady of Cofitachequi paused to go into a thicket to defecate, as she did every so often. As long as she remained pleasant and cooperative, she was allowed this privacy. She never emerged from it. The Castiles searched desperately, but could find neither her nor the box of most valuable pearls one of her female attendants carried.

Chief de Soto was furious. "That ungrateful woman!" he exclaimed, using a term for woman that Tale Teller could not render in any ordinary tongue. It signified one who accepted gifts from many men in exchange for her sexual favors. The Castiles believed that there was something wrong with that, perhaps because they did not proffer gifts, but simply forced the women they captured to do it. The Lady of Cofitachequi had not been treated this way, thanks to Tale Teller's intercession; had she been put in chains and degraded in the normal manner, her people would have renounced her and she would have lost her authority. She had not chosen to indulge with any man on any other basis, either. So the epithet hardly seemed to apply.

"He wanted to use her himself," Wren confided. "His penis got hard every time he was near her." She was an observant girl. "Also, she took with her the very best pearls."

But they were now over the cold ridge of the mountains, and it was pointless to go back. The horses were lean from hunger and fatigue, and the cold of the mountains had weakened them; they needed warmth and rest and feed, and that seemed more likely to be ahead than behind.

They arrived at the village of Guasili, where the best the people could do was give them a large number of small dogs for food. The Castiles were glad for this, for they had come to enjoy the taste of dog meat and always scrambled to get more of it.

They proceeded on to the village of Chiaha, which was of

the Principal People. This was not the region where Tale Teller had lived, being north of it, but he had been here on occasion and knew the general lay of the land. The village was on an island in the great Ani-Yunwiya river which flowed all the way to the sea. It was surrounded by a circle of stakes set into the ground, with guard platforms at regular intervals. This was the first such defense the Castiles had encountered in this land, and they studied it with interest.

The people did not have any gold. But one tribesman spoke of a place to the north, called Chisca, where metal like this was worked. De Soto sent two men north to check on this, but when they returned they reported that it was copper of the type they had seen in the town of Cofitachequi.

The Chief of the village claimed to be happy to host the Castiles, and he had plenty of food for both men and animals. In fact he even sent a gift of a honeycomb, which was the first the Castiles had seen in this region.

Tale Teller looked at the honeycomb, and his penis swelled. He had been long without a woman, on this terrible journey! He knew Tzec would not mind if he indulged with one of the captives, but he did not like to do that after they had been forced by the Castiles. Such women no longer valued the plea-sure of men.

Tale Teller told the Chief the good news about the food, supposing he would be pleased. Oddly, he was not. "The gold," de Soto said. "Where is the gold?"

"I know of none here," Tale Teller said. "To these people it has no value." The Chief of the village said the same, being baffled by the request.

"Go downstream and ask," de Soto said. "We shall be camp-ing here for some time, to put strength back into the horses, but I will send two men with good horses with you."

So Tale Teller went with two Castiles, showing them the way. Wren remained at the camp, of course; she was under close guard now that Tale Teller was among folk who might help him escape. De Soto was always courteous in speech to Tale Teller, and treated him well, but never forgot this detail. Especially after the way the Lady of Cofitachequi had escaped.

The Castiles were on their horses, while Tale Teller was on foot. This was satisfactory for him, for he liked to run, and it allowed him to proceed at his own pace without wearing out the Castiles. He could readily have given them the slip and disappeared as the Lady of Cofitachequi had; Castiles were quite clumsy about getting through brush. But if he did, Wren would be thrown to the dogs; there was no question about that. So he led them, and when he got out of sight ahead, he waited for them, and sometimes he explored to find a route their horses could handle while the two men rested. They could trust him, though he was their enemy.

They came to the village of Five Birches, where Gray Cloud and Red Leaf had lived. It was smaller than it had been, for the evil spirits had killed more than half its people, and the surviving children were not enough to maintain its population. Yet here he was recognized, for those who had been children were now men and women. "Tell us the tales!" they cried, making him welcome.

"But I am here as a captive of the Castiles," he explained. "They are looking for a yellow kind of stone called gold."

"We will kill them for you," they said.

"No, these two are only scouts for tens of tens of them," he said. "You cannot fight them. You must avoid them if you can. You must treat these two as honored guests, and send them women at night, so they will not be displeased, and then they will go away and you will be safe. But tell me if you know of any gold or other valuable things, for I must find them."

"We have heard of valuable things far away down the river," they said. "But we have not seen them."

Tale Teller nodded. "I will tell them that."

They spent the night in the village, and five of their prettiest young women joined the visitors and made much of the two Castiles. No translations were needed. The women fed fruit to the Castiles and brought pillows to make them comfortable. They sat by the big central fire while Tale Teller told stories as he had in the old days. The Castiles could not understand the tongue, but it didn't matter because the women were sitting in their laps and stroking their heads and giggling as the Castiles put their hands on their breasts. Then the women took the Castiles away to their lodges, two girls to each man, and Tale Teller retired to his.

But one young woman came to him there. "I do not demand this of you," he told her. "The Castiles are enemies who must be pacified, but I am not your enemy."

"I was five winters old when I first heard your tales," she said. "And six when the evil spirits came. Now I am ten and seven winters, and I have given my favors to many men, but always I longed for you. Now you are here, and I wish to give you back some of the joy you gave me, when times were better. As you told me it was with the warrior and maiden who first found tobacco, let it be with us, for this night."

He could not decline such an offer. Indeed, she had proved she remembered, for that had been one of his favorite tales. He clasped her, and her body was lush and her honey was sweet. He thought of Laurel, and was sad, yet it was good to hold a woman of her tribe. "I thank you for doing this," he told the woman. "I loved your people, and I loved my two good wives here."

"We know," she said. "Now give me your seed again, for we are not yet sure our clans are compatible." Thus she took him through the stages of that tale, cajoling his repeated performance, until the frustration of his long abstinence faded and he was satisfied. Surely this was a fitting place for a tobacco plant to grow!

Next day he went alone to visit the village of Bald Peak. He knew it was deserted, for the people of Five Birches had told him, but he had to see it for himself. The two Castiles were happy to remain where they were. Even their horses were happy, for the grazing was good, and after Tale Teller's tale of the wonder of horses, the children and some adults found them fascinating, and some were even bold enough to fetch the animals sprigs to eat.

Not only was Bald Peak deserted, it was overgrown. There was little remaining to show where it had been. Brush grew up in the center circle, and young trees were closing on the fringes. He tried to find where his lodge with Twice Cursed and Laurel had been, and could not be sure of it. Then he found a little bit of pottery with a design, and knew it for one Twice Cursed had made. This was the place.

He stood there for a time, hurting. *O spirits, you took from me all that I loved here. Why did you do it?*

There was no answer, for he had renounced the spirits. Yet now he wondered, and felt the beginning of doubt. Had he done right in giving up his quest for the Ulunsuti?

"Farewell, my loves," he said at last. "I know your spirits will never harm me. To you alone would I speak, if you came to me."

Then he felt them, mother and daughter. *We love you, our husband. You still wear the magic crystal, so we know you despite your age.*

They knew him! *Oh my wives! My heart warms to your presence.* He had not quite dared to hope for this wonderful contact.

We saw you enjoying the hospitality of Five Birches. There was no jealousy in the thought, only gladness.

She was a delight, he agreed. *If I am with her again, will you join us?*

They considered, and thought they might. But they had something more serious to say to him. *The spirits who killed us were rogues. Your Spirit of the Mound did not betray you. We learned this after we died.*

Surprised by this revelation, and gratified that they had spoken to him, he felt again his great experience with them. *I love you, my wives. I married again, and I love her, but my love for you remains. I will never forget you.*

We know. She is our sister-wife. Guard your daughter, for we love her too.

Then he left, but he felt the faint touch of Twice Cursed and Laurel. They had been thirty winters and thirteen winters when he married them, and forty-two and twenty-five when he lost them. Now he was forty winters, and Tzec was thirty-four. His prior wives no longer seemed old or young; they were companions. He was glad to have their company, for it healed some of the hurt of their loss.

What they had told him also healed some of the hurt of the betrayal of the spirits. Dead Eagle was innocent! That was wonderful news indeed. But it was too late to resume his quest for the Ulunsuti. Ten winters had passed, and he still wasn't sure whether to trust Sun Eagle. He would have to return and talk with Dead Eagle, and see what it was best to do at this stage.

The two Castiles were sorry to leave Five Birches and the

attention of the maidens. The villagers smiled warmly, but were glad to see the men depart. Tale Teller's advice had been good, for no harm had come to any of the villagers, and now they had been warned about avoiding the main party of Castiles. He had repaid them with his tales, and had in turn been repaid himself with the favor of a maiden who was sincere, and it had been good.

"You lived there, One-Arm?" a Castile inquired as they departed.

"In a neighboring village, now gone," Tale Teller replied. "I had two wives."

"That is the life!" the man agreed. Two young women had catered to him for a night and a day and a night, and if he had ever had a better time, it was surely long ago. The Castiles did prefer to have their women like them and enjoy the sex, but seldom was this the case. It had not been the case this time, either, had they but known.

They returned with their report, just in time for an event which caused Chief de Soto to be fearsomely annoyed. He had Tale Teller ask the Chief for three tens of young women as slaves to take along on the journey, as the men always had a passion for them. The women had immediately fled the village and could not be found. The Chief was most apologetic, explaining that their women were precious to them, and would not obey him if it meant they had to leave their home. De Soto had to change his mind and let the women go. He hated that.

Nor was that the only thing to make him angry. Wren told Tale Teller how a Castile had been walking near the river and had seen a dog. Hungry for the meat, he had hurled his spear at it. He missed the dog, and the spear fell over the bluff to the river below. When the Castile went after it, he discovered that his spear had gone through the head of another Castile who was fishing, and the man was dead. A sheer, stupid accident of carelessness, and the army was that much weaker. Wren admitted that she would have found the matter funny, but the dead man had been one of the decent ones.

After two tens and three days the army left Chiaha and marched south along the river, seeking the gold that seemed somehow always just a few days farther ahead. De Soto was satisfied that there was none in the region. He had sent scouts north as well as south, and their reports had been consistent. The southern scouts had added that the people were very friendly and open, and represented no threat.

But the Castiles' greed and arrogance tended to alienate people who had started out friendly. A good example was the town of Coste. The Castiles were met by the Chief and escorted to the town. But the men stole corn, and the Chief protested, and de Soto reacted in typical fashion by trying to make him prisoner. The Chief escaped. The Castiles ransacked the lodges, looking for corn. The people beat the Castiles with clubs.

De Soto, seeing that he did not have enough men to overcome the tribesmen, sent for reinforcements, then pretended sympathy for the natives by yelling at his troops and even beating at them with a staff. This persuaded the Chief that the Castiles had not been acting with de Soto's consent, and the Chief and his leading warriors came out to talk with de Soto. De Soto then made them captive and put them in chains. Then he forced the Chief to provide the supplies he wanted.

The people of the neighboring villages sent their women and children into hiding so that they would not fall into the hands of the Castiles. What could have been a friendly passage had become hostile. Tale Teller made no comment, knowing it would be pointless and dangerous. He had seen it before, and expected to see it again, unless the tribes ahead learned more of the Castiles before the army arrived.

They came to the town of Coça, where they were well received. Indeed, their entire journey south had been relatively pleasant, for the villages of the Principal People took care to be extremely courteous and helpful, making it easy for the Castiles to move on out of their territory. Tale Teller's advice had been heeded, and the word had been spread. In this manner he had managed in most cases to spare these people he loved so well the disaster that could have befallen them.

Coça was beyond Ani-Yunwiya territory, however, and Tale Teller was not sure these folk had received the word. However, the Chief of that tribe spoke with the interpreter brought from the Principal People, and said that he welcomed the visit of the Castiles and would do all he could to make them comfortable.

Tale Teller contented himself with translating from the tongue of the Principal People to that of the Toco, so that Juan Ortiz could make the final rendition to Chief de Soto. He was not surprised when de Soto took the village Chief prisoner, in that way compelling his people to obey the Castiles and to provide slaves to serve as bearers and women for the nights. How well he knew that system! All he could do was play his part, and watch for the time when he could escape with his daughter. There had to come a day when the Castiles would forget to guard one of them when the other was free.

It did not become entirely negative. Sometimes the Castiles traded fairly for what they wanted, when it suited their convenience to do so. The people valued the superior metal knives of the Castiles, and they were amazed by the shiny *looking glasses* that enabled them to see themselves as if gazing into calm dark water. These items could be traded for women, and everyone was satisfied.

After more than a moon at Coça, the army moved on to the village of Talisi, where it remained another half moon. Here they met Chief Tascaluza of the neighboring tribe, who was so tall his head was above the heads of every other person. The Castiles tried to have him ride a horse, but he was too big for the horse. That was just as well, because these people feared the unfamiliar animals and did not want to ride them.

Things were amicable on the surface, but there were hints that the people of this Tuskegee tribe were not as eager to help the Castiles along as the Principal People had been. Tale Teller was aware of a veiled hostility toward him and all the Castiles. But it was never expressed openly. He told Juan Ortiz, who told de Soto, who nodded; he had felt it too. All the tribes resented the Castiles, once they came to know them, but this seemed more serious.

One of the Castiles went in search of a female slave who had escaped him. He went out into the forest and did not return. Another Castile simply liked to explore, and was always ranging well out. He also disappeared.

Now Chief de Soto became nervous, because he well understood what this could mean. He suspected that Chief Tas-

caluza was not as good a friend as he indicated, and had had
the men waylaid when they were ranging away from the main
army. Tale Teller participated in the questioning of Chief
Tascaluza, and the man inquired whether it was his responsibility to guard those men. This bordered on insolence, and
de Soto reacted typically. "You have had these men killed,
and I will tie you to a stake and pile brush around it and
burn you to death if you do not have the assassins brought
to me for punishment!"

"This is not wise," Tale Teller told Juan Ortiz. "We should
not threaten the Chief like this. He is tough-minded, and he
has a lot of power."

Juan Ortiz agreed; his own experience had shown the folly
of challenging any chief in such a manner as to shame him.
But de Soto was adamant, and so Tale Teller translated the
message into the tongue of the Principal People, and their interpreter translated it into the Tuskegee tongue.

Chief Tascaluza masked his anger. "I did not realize that the
matter was so important to you," he replied. "I cannot immediately find out who did this, but when we reach my town
of Mabila, I will see to it immediately. Meanwhile I will send
a message there to prepare the town for your stay; they will
gather provisions and clear lodges for the members of your
party."

"You see, I know how to deal with this savage," de Soto
muttered as he turned away. Tale Teller understood him, but
kept silent until Juan Ortiz, with a slight smile, translated:
"Chief de Soto is glad for the clarification of this misunderstanding, and thanks you for your gracious offer to hospitality
at Mabila." That was the version Tale Teller translated.

But they all knew that the Castiles would have to proceed
carefully and be on constant guard. Tale Teller remembered
how the Principal People had spoken of the tribes of this region;
they could be fierce indeed, and now de Soto had given them
reason.

De Soto set out with five tens of horse-men and the same
number of foot-men, traveling with great caution. He left an
order for the rest of the army to follow as soon as possible. But
the members of the main army, accustomed to the peaceful
progress they had been making, set out late and spread out

across the countryside, hunting and relaxing. Tale Teller
learned this later from Wren, who was with this portion of it
and could readily have escaped because they did not guard her
at all. But she could not flee without her father. This easy
progress was folly, as they were to discover.

CHAPTER 19

🔖

BATTLE

O Spirit of the Mound, I have told you of the Lady of Cofi-tachequi and my meeting with the spirits of my lost wives, and how the arrogance of the Castiles angered the people. Now I will tell you of the terrible battles that occurred, and how that helped my daughter and me.

On the morning of their lord October 18, by the Castiles' calendar, the two groups of men arrived at the town of Mabila. An advance scout reported that the townsmen were busy making preparations, with many coming to the town bearing weapons, and they were working to strengthen the palisade that surrounded it.

There were signs of a recent fire outside the town. The vicinity had been cleared of brush, and several burned structures were in sight. Were the townsmen preparing for a special celebration in honor of the visitors, or was something more sinister being arranged? Tale Teller was not at all easy about this, but he was only the interpreter. He wished he could get well away from here, but he could not. Not while his daughter remained captive.

De Soto's leading advisers suggested that it would be better to camp in the woods outside Mabila, because they did not trust the temper of the tribesmen. But de Soto replied that he was tired of sleeping out, and that he intended to lodge in the town. He was so accustomed to having his way that he despised sensible caution.

They left the foot-men camped outside, waiting for the arrival

442

of the rest of the army. De Soto himself, with his interpreters and forty picked horse-men, proceeded to the town.

Mabila was impressive. The wall of stakes that protected it was twice the height of a man, and they were braced by cross-beams and plastered with hard dry mud. It would be easy to defend this town from siege, and de Soto decided that he would be prepared to do that.

The people of Mabila came out to receive the Castiles, dancing and singing and playing on their flutes, making a nice welcome. They presented de Soto with three fine cloaks of the skins of martins.

The Castiles left their horses under guard just outside and entered the town and went to an open square in its center. Tale Teller saw that there were several tens of tens of people of the tribe there, and he distrusted this; the scout had reported many more. Where were they?

The bearers with the supplies caught up and entered the town, setting down their burdens with relief just inside the wall. They had not been allowed to rest; de Soto wanted his supplies safely inside, rather than exposed outside. His remaining horse-men and foot-men would be approaching at a more leisurely pace, expecting to arrive at Mabila by nightfall.

They began to move the goods into a lodge which had been set aside for storage. The most important things were moved first: the supplies for de Soto himself and those for his principal subchiefs and the Castile priests.

"Why are those people carrying bundles of arrows?" Juan Ortiz muttered in Toco. Tale Teller saw what he meant; not only were they doing this, they were moving toward particular lodges and disappearing within them.

Now the lovely young women of the town danced for the visitors, most winsomely. The Castiles normally were not much interested in native dances, and remained ignorant of their symbolism, but they were intrigued by this one. It was a welcoming dance, but its costume and form had been modified, evidently to appeal to barbarian tastes. The maidens smiled, which was unusual, and their breasts bounced, which was not. Every Castile eye remained fixed on the faces and torsos of the two tens of dancers. Perhaps only Tale Teller saw the continued movements of the people of Mabila, carrying their arrows and spears. The warriors were getting ready, either for a dramatic dance of their own or for something else.

Chief Tascaluza spoke. The local interpreter had disappeared, but Tale Teller was able to make out the gist. He rendered it into Castile for de Soto, as he had learned this tongue well enough sometime back, though always deferring to Juan Ortiz for the final translation. He did not want to wait for Juan Ortiz to conclude his business elsewhere; he wanted to get out of Mabila, and he wanted a pretext to encourage de Soto to do that.

"He asks you to release him, because we are near the boundary of his territory," Tale Teller said.

"Not until we are *at* the boundary," de Soto said. "You know my policy."

"I know it," Tale Teller agreed. "But my lord Chief, it might be better to—"

"No." The man turned away, refusing to yield.

Tale Teller spoke in limited Tuskegee to the Chief, augmenting his words with signs. "Chief de Soto says no."

Chief Tascaluza got up and went into one of the lodges where his son was. De Soto called to him to come back out, and Tale Teller helped translate in case there was any doubt, but the Chief refused. "I will not be forced to leave my lands!" he called. "If your Chief wishes, he may depart my lands in peace, but I will not go with him."

How nice it would be if de Soto agreed to do just that! But the man would not yield one step on anything, unless he had some cunning plan, and in this case he was simply impatient. Chief Tascaluza's intransigence was interfering with de Soto's pleasure in the dance.

De Soto sent a man to bring the Chief out, but the man discovered that the lodge was full of armed tribesmen, prepared for battle. Nevertheless he tried to go in after the Chief, but a warrior barred his way and shoved him roughly back.

The Castile drew his sword and struck the warrior so hard it almost severed his arm. The warrior cried out—and the other warriors surged from the lodge, their weapons ready.

The dancing maidens, seeing this, quickly fled to other lodges. In a moment there was nothing in the square except a few Castiles and many warriors.

It was an ambush—and de Soto had walked blithely into it, despite the clear warnings. The problem was that Tale Teller was caught in the same trap; the tribesmen knew him for his association with the Castiles and considered him an enemy.

"Fetch the horses!" de Soto cried when he saw this. He never lost his poise when in trouble. Tale Teller responded to this immediately, though the order had not been directed at him, and ran quickly for the gate, eluding the warriors coming from other lodges. He dodged here and there, noting where the converging warriors were, and using his speed of foot to be where they were not. He reached the gate, yelling as he passed it: "Fetch the horses! Ambush!"

Then he glanced back, to be sure no one was about to strike him from behind. The center circle was still filling with warriors, massing for battle. There was no longer any mystery where they had been; all the lodges had been packed with warriors, waiting for the signal to converge.

Now the tribesmen attacked. They surrounded the small party of Castiles, and some shot arrows from the cover of the lodges. They intended to kill everyone.

The Castiles grouped themselves around Chief de Soto and drew their swords. They struck at any tribesman who came close, and cleared a way back out of the town. But they had to leave their possessions behind, and hurry to the point of running, while the tribesmen harassed them.

Such escape seemed impossible, for the warriors greatly outnumbered the Castiles. But the Castiles were horse-men on foot, and their armor was heavier than that of the foot-men, and could withstand attack well. Meanwhile the horse-men outside were charging in, their lance-spears lowered, and others were leading the riderless horses in.

Tale Teller ran backwards from the town, alert for any spear that might be thrown at him, knowing that the horse-men would not strike him. The warriors were intent on the Castiles within, throwing spears at them and shooting arrows. Some of the arrows missed the Castiles and struck other warriors, because they were on all sides. But many weapons were striking the Castiles, and one by one they fell as they retreated. The armor was strong, and the warriors did not understand how effective it was against all but the most direct attacks, but there were so many warriors attacking that some were bound to score. Thus many arrows bounced off, and many others lodged but did not do serious damage, while a few were deadly. Five Castiles died before the party got out the gate, and the rest were staggering. De Soto himself fell several times, and was helped up and forward by his companions.

Meanwhile, Tale Teller learned later, there were several members of de Soto's party caught in the lodge where the important supplies had been taken. One was a priest, another was a *friar*, another a servant, another a cook, and the last was a female slave of de Soto's who had agreed to serve the Castile spirit Jesus Christ and no other, so was not in chains. These people closed the entrance to the door and guarded it as valiantly as they could. The servant picked up a sword from the supplies and stood at one side of the door, while the priest and friar took clubs and stood at the other side. They struck at any warrior who tried to come in.

The warriors, discovering that they could not safely enter by the door, began to pull the roof from the lodge so that they could climb in that way. It was evident that soon the people inside would be overwhelmed and slaughtered if rescue did not come.

The warriors climbed up and looked down into the lodge from an opening in the roof, but now one of the defenders took up a crossbow and aimed it and loosed its shaft, and the first warrior fell back with the bolt through his body. So as it turned out, the party trapped in the lodge was able to defend itself better than the warriors had expected, and had some reprieve. But the outlook remained bleak as time passed, for they knew that if they survived the day, they would not survive the night.

Meanwhile de Soto got on a horse, and the surviving horsemen got on their horses and rode away from the town. The warriors, seeing the Castiles escaping, charged out after them, determined to kill them all. But they did not venture far from the stockade, while other warriors were shooting arrows from cover. So the Castiles used a maneuver that should not have fooled the warriors: they retreated. They retreated until they joined the horse-men coming up from the rear, while the warriors followed. Tale Teller made his way to the cover of a tree, and saw it all.

The Castiles turned their horses, lowered their lances, and charged back at the warriors. The warriors, caught out in the open, were unable to withstand the charge; many were pierced by the lances and died there. Others shot their arrows at the horses, but the armor of the horses protected them. The Castiles charged again and again, cutting down the warriors who tried to flee, and few made it back to the safety of the palisade. They had thought the open space around the town would benefit them in their slaughter of the Castiles, but instead it was the other way around. The Castiles were matchless in the open, and the warriors had been foolish ever to venture from their protected town.

Seeing this turn of the battle, the warriors urged Chief Tascaluza to leave Mabila, because they were no longer certain of winning and did not want him to be lost to the entire tribe if the Castiles prevailed. He did not want to go, but as the lookouts reported how the Castiles were organizing their horsemen and foot-men to attack the town, he was finally convinced. He took a scarlet cloak and other items of value from the supplies of the Castiles that were in the town, and left with ten and five of his warriors.

The Castiles saw that a party of warriors was departing, but did not know that Chief Tascaluza was among them. He was hunching down to conceal his unusual height. They gave chase, but the warriors reached the forest and hid among the trees, shooting arrows at anyone who followed. Because the warriors had left by a gate opposite the one where the horse-men fought, and the Castiles were surprised by this, there were only a few foot-men there, and they were unable to stop the warriors.

When this was reported to Chief de Soto, he reorganized his army so as to prevent any more warriors from escaping. He had been betrayed and ambushed, and he intended to have his vengeance in full measure. He divided his forces into four groups, each with horse-men and foot-men. These groups surrounded the town, so that no more people could escape from it. Then they charged each of the gates, heedless of the arrows, the foot-men following the horse-men so they could get close without being struck by those arrows.

When they got close, men with axes chopped at the gates, bursting them open. Then the horse-men charged through, and

behind them came men with burning torches, one torch-man
in each of the four parties. They set fire to the straw of the
lodges in the town. The straw blazed up, terrifying the women
and children in the lodges and driving them out into the streets
along with the warriors.

Now the horse-men charged down the length of the streets,
using their lances to strike through any people they found
there, and their horses shoved down people and trampled on
them with their hard hooves. The horse-men went back and
forth along the streets, killing everyone caught there. Those
who remained in the lodges were burned by the spreading fire,
and those who fled the town were killed by the Castiles surrounding it. The slaughter was terrible.

In this manner the Castiles rescued the party caught in the
lodge, and brought them out of the burning town. Because any
who came into the streets were killed, the natives were not able
to put out the fires, and they spread throughout the town. The
Castiles withdrew, and waited outside to kill all those who were
driven out.

Even so, there were many warriors, and they fought with
great courage. The struggle lasted the full day. Chief de Soto
rose in his stirrups to strike a blow at one townsman with his
lance, and a warrior behind him shot an arrow into his left
buttock where the overlapping armor was not quite strong
enough. De Soto continued to fight, with the arrow sticking in
his flesh, but he was unable to sit down in his saddle and had
to remain standing. Another Castile was struck in the chest
with an arrow while charging the wall. He got down off his
horse to pull out the arrow with both hands, leaning over—
and received another arrow in his exposed neck, which killed
him. Another Castile was surprised when an arrow pierced his
lance near its base, and neither the lance nor the arrow broke.
"I have a cross!" he exclaimed. "A holy cross!" The cross was
sacred to the Castiles, as it is to many folk, but they had an
ugly rationale for it: they thought of it as the framework on
which their Jesus Christ was tortured to death. Perhaps he had
died with much courage, so they honored him above all others.
At any rate, the Castile took it as a good omen, and perhaps
it was, for he survived the battle.

But in the end it was the people of Mabila who suffered the

most. Once the Castiles were on their horses and in battle formation, they were a more effective fighting force than any warrior band, and the ruthlessness with which they set fire to the town and killed all the warriors and many of the women and children showed what made them such a terror. Tale Teller had seen it at Napetaca, and he saw it again here. The warriors simply were not able to fight the Castiles well. When they were forced from the town, outside the walls, even the Tuskegee women and children took up weapons and fought, but the Castiles had no mercy on them. It was a dreadful slaughter, and the blood flowed so freely that when some Castiles grew thirsty with the work of killing natives, and went down to a pond to drink, the water was tinged with the blood of their countrymen.

Tale Teller, even as he watched the battle, tried to understand how it was that such a well-prepared ambush, with such a great superiority of numbers, could be destroyed so completely by the Castiles. He knew he could never be sure, but he thought that the warriors had made several subtle but grievous errors. They had sought at first to drive the Castiles from their town and shut them out, supposing that once they were defeated they would never turn back to fight. They had thought themselves successful in this, and had gone immediately to the supplies. So they divided their forces, many of them ransacking the baggage before the battle was done, while others chased after the fleeing Castiles, thinking to win further honor for themselves. Thus the Castiles had surprised the warriors when they turned and fought again, and had killed many before the warriors understood how the battle had changed. When the Castiles charged back into the town, and torched it, the ones inside were caught similarly unprepared, and had fought poorly. Both groups had given up their advantage, but when the Castiles seized the initiative, they never relented, pausing neither for spoils nor for rest. They had made sure their enemy was done.

The Tuskegee had been too confident of victory, and had been careless. Had they set their ambush in the forest, maintaining the cover of the trees, the horse-men would have had trouble catching them, and they could have brought the Castiles down one by one with their arrows. It might have taken several days, but with the numbers of warriors they had, they could have done it. Even if they had not been able to win, they would have been able to flee readily, saving themselves. But they had allowed the Castiles to fight on their own terms, and the Castiles could not be conquered that way.

By nightfall it was done. Every warrior of Mabila was dead, and most of the women and children too. Only those attractive young women who surrendered themselves to the mercy of the Castiles were allowed to live. A number of them had been the dancers; now they would have other uses.

Tale Teller went with Juan Ortiz to talk with these women, and learned that many of the warriors had been from other villages, summoned by Chief Tascaluza for the ambush. The number of people dead was reckoned at three tens of tens of tens.

But the Castiles had suffered grievously too. More than two tens of them were dead, and ten tens and five tens were wounded, with about five arrows each. Many others had lesser injuries from knives or bruises. As many as three tens of horses had been killed, for though these big creatures with tough armor were hard to kill, the warriors had concentrated on them as the most feared aspect of the army. Many more horses were injured and needed attention.

Also, all the supplies had been burned in the fire, including the *wine* and *wheat bread* used by their priests in their veneration of their Great Spirit. These could not be replaced, for nothing similar existed here. Their medicines were also burned. They had to tear up any spare clothing they had to make bandages for their wounds, and when that was not enough, they used the clothing of the dead.

There was no food, other than what was with that part of the army that had never entered the town. Everything inside Mabila, belonging to the Castiles and the natives alike, had been burned.

The Castiles needed fat to make healing salve, but there was none. So they cut open the bodies of the dead warriors and used the fat in them to make their salve.

The Castiles buried their own dead in the ground on the day following the battle. They did not make a mound, but simply put them under level soil, marked with crosses. This was their custom, odd as it was, so their spirits were probably used to it.

The Castiles remained for most of a moon in that vicinity, using makeshift shelters and recovering from their wounds. Those who were fit among them ranged out to hunt deer, and others fished. They captured some natives and made them fetch corn. Gradually they got more stores of food, and the health of the wounded improved.

A messenger from another tribe arrived. He talked to the Tuskegee interpreter, who talked to Tale Teller. He was from the south, by the sea, and he said that the Castiles with the big canoes on the sea had found a place for them to come to shore. Because the canoes were so large, with space enough for many tens of tens of men, they floated deep in the water, and could not come to land unless the water was deep beside it. The canoes had found such a place, and it was only six days' march away. The Castiles could go south, and soon be back on their canoes, and go away from here.

Tale Teller thought Chief de Soto would be pleased, for it was evident that he was not doing well at the moment. He told Juan Ortiz, who told de Soto.

But instead of reacting with joy, de Soto told them to be quiet, and not to tell any other person. They were astonished, but finally came to some understanding of his attitude. He was afraid that if his men learned that escape was so easy, they would desert him and go to the canoes, seeking better success elsewhere. That would leave de Soto as a failure, for he had lost the pearls and never found the gold. The man had the pride of a Chief, and could not abide shame, and he was determined not to return to the canoes until he had discovered the great wealth he sought.

So they kept their silence, and the Castiles never knew. Tale Teller had mixed feelings about the matter. He still wanted only to escape with his daughter, and if the Castiles returned to their canoes now, he might be able to do that. But they might take him and Wren with them, so as to interpret for the remaining captives, and once they were taken on those big canoes, they would never be able to escape. So he concluded that the secret was best kept for him also.

* * *

On the ten and fourth day of November by the Castile calendar, they resumed their march. They went north, following the river, entering the territory of the Choctaw tribe. The province was called Long Hairs, because the tribesmen did not shave their heads. In that respect they resembled the Castiles.

They passed a village they called the "place where the fire has gone out," because the villagers had moved all its corn and people across the river, where the Castiles could not get them. The people shouted insults from the far side, baring their buttocks in the direction of the intruders and threatening to kill any Castile who tried to cross. It seemed that the time of friendly introductions was past, since the battle of Mabila.

Chief de Soto ordered the Castiles to build a raft to cross the river. But they did this in secret, in the course of four days, so that the people on the far side would not know. It was a big raft, made to support horses. Tale Teller knew that the natives were going to have a very nasty surprise. Chief de Soto did not care about their insults, only about the supplies, bearers, and women he needed for his journey, and about the gold he sought. So he was annoyed because the villagers had placed the barrier of the river in his way, and he would make them feel his ire.

The Castiles put two tens of horses with their men already on them on the huge raft, and four tens of foot-men were also there. They launched the raft a distance upstream so that the natives would not realize that it was coming. But the warriors saw it in the river, and massed at the shore where it would come, firing arrows at it. The Castiles suffered some wounds, but soon the craft landed. The horse-men charged into the warriors and drove them away.

Tale Teller watched, and assessed the tactics. As usual, the warriors had not known how to fight the Castiles. Had they concentrated their arrows on those who were rowing and poling the raft across, so as to kill them or make it impossible for them to do their work, the raft would have floated on downstream. The warriors could have kept it there in the current, and would not have had to face the terrible horse-men. If any tribe were to fight the Castiles by attacking their weaknesses, that tribe could wipe them out. But by the time a tribe learned anything significant about the Castiles, that tribe had been van-

quished. The Tuskegee alone had come close to victory, and
that only because de Soto had been careless. The Tuskegee had
paid a terrible price for their own carelessness.

It was similar with this village. The warriors had wasted their
effort trying to insult the Castiles, instead of studying them
and preparing an effective defense. The Castiles had routed
the warriors defending the river. After that there was little
trouble bringing the rest of the army across, and they captured
the supplies. At least it meant that there would be enough for
Tale Teller and Wren and the slaves.

They captured several of the warriors. Chief de Soto, annoyed by recent events, was in no mood to be balked any
further. "We have spent two summers and a winter on this
quest," he declared. "The gold is always somewhere else! Make
these savages give us a direct answer."

Juan Ortiz relayed this command to Tale Teller, who translated it into the tongue of the Tuskegee as well as he could
manage, using signs freely. He knew there was no gold here,
but also knew that there was no point in trying to tell de Soto
that. The Tuskegee interpreter translated it into the Choctaw
tongue.

The warriors expressed bafflement. "We have no stone like
that," they protested.

The word went back through the chain of interpreters. Chief
de Soto, of course, would not accept it. "I will have no more
of this! If they will not talk, I will make them talk! Warn them!"

The warning proceeded through the chain. It brought only
further confusion. "We expect to be tortured to death," the
warriors said. "If it makes our enemy angry to know that we
have no yellow stone, then we tell him ten times more: we
have no yellow stone."

De Soto grimaced. "Cut off their noses," he said.

The Castiles held one of the warriors, put one of their iron
knives to his face, and sliced off his nose. Blood flowed down
his face and spattered his chest. He did not even cry out in
pain. He was a warrior; it was honor to withstand the worst
his enemies could do.

But Juan Ortiz was evidently disgusted. He had suffered
torture himself, because of the way the Castile Chief Narvaez
had cut off the nose of Chief Hirrihigua and thrown his mother

to the dogs. He knew that the Choctaw would not react any more kindly to such treatment. They would only be even more determined to kill all the Castiles.

None of the captives told of any gold. When all their noses were off, the Castiles cut off their ears. They still would not talk. Finally the Castiles cut off their lips, so that their teeth showed bare and bloodstained. They remained defiant.

De Soto, in a fury, threw two of them to the dogs while the third watched. Then he let the third go. "Tell him that this will happen to everyone else in his tribe if I don't find that gold!" he shouted.

The message was relayed. The Choctaw warrior seemed surprised that he was being let go, but soon he disappeared into the forest. He would surely deliver the message, though he would have to use signs, because he would not be able to talk without his lips.

Later an old woman came. "The gold is far away, in the direction you are going," she said. "Across a big, big river." It was the standard response, but de Soto was as foolish about gold, which could be neither worn nor eaten, as he was practical about warfare.

"How far? How big?" de Soto wanted to know.

"A moon to walk there," she said. "Two moons, perhaps. So big it is hard to see across."

That sounded like the river Tale Teller had traveled with Gray Cloud. "She may be telling the truth," he told Juan Ortiz. "There is a very big river. I don't know about the gold."

Juan Ortiz nodded, and relayed the news. Chief de Soto made a grim smile. "The savages are learning," he said.

It seemed more likely to Tale Teller that the Choctaw just wanted to encourage the Castiles to get on out of their territory. But again it did not seem expedient to say it. The one who did that might forfeit his own lips.

In this manner they proceeded through Choctaw territory and into Chicaza territory, traveling for a moon. Tale Teller was allowed to walk with Wren; there was nowhere for them to go except where the army was going. It seemed that de Soto had forgotten that they were enemy captives, but Tale Teller knew better than to test it. He remained loyal to the Castiles in all

things except his underlying nature. Only when he was sure
of a clean escape with his daughter would he act.

They came to the Chicaza river, which was swollen with rains
and overflowing its banks. Again there were hostile warriors
on the far side, arrayed for war. Again the Castiles made a
barge, but also crossed the river afoot where the warriors did
not see, and soon drove them away. They occupied the town
of Chicaza, where there were good supplies of corn as well as
nuts from groves of walnut trees.

Tale Teller and Wren went out to gather walnuts, and no
one objected. But the Chicaza warriors were hostile, and no
one dared go far from the security of the town. If they escaped
now they could die of hunger and cold, without the assistance
of the people of the local tribe. It was obvious there would be
no help there; torture and death were more likely.

Now it was winter, and snow fell, so this was where the
Castiles made their camp. De Soto continued his policy of lull-
ing the tribesmen when possible, and finally this was effective.
The Chief of the Chicaza arrived, borne on a litter by his sub-
jects, bringing deer skins and some small dogs to eat. Later the
Chicaza brought many rabbits, so that the Castiles ate well.

In return de Soto served the Chief and his warriors meat
from the pigs, and the warriors liked this meat very well. In
fact they sought more of it, and kept trying to steal pigs from
the corral.

Three natives were caught stealing pigs. The Castiles killed
two of them and cut off the hands of the third. They returned
this one to the Chicaza Chief, and Tale Teller explained as well
as he was able what had happened. The Chief considered, then
said: "We do not tolerate stealing any more than the Castiles
do. As long as Chief de Soto holds his own warriors to the
same standard, it is good."

Tale Teller relayed that to Juan Ortiz, who nodded. They
departed.

"He was surprisingly nice about it," Tale Teller remarked.

"I think our men do more stealing than the natives do," Juan
Ortiz replied. "He surely knows that."

Suddenly the Chief's attitude made sense. Now the Castiles
would have to pay for their stealing, too. The Chicaza would
be better off if the rules were enforced impartially.

Juan Ortiz reported to de Soto, and he spoke at some length.
Tale Teller was not present, but he knew that Juan Ortiz was
a good man who had more sympathy with the natives than he
usually showed.

Then four Castiles raided the Chicaza camp and stole some
shawls and skins. One was a horse-man named Osorio, and
three were servants. They were seen and identified, and de
Soto ordered them taken in and the two leaders killed. He was
a harsh man but a just one, and Juan Ortiz had made an impression on him.

Meanwhile the Chief sent a party to complain, not realizing
that action was already being taken. De Soto was satisfied; they
could witness the execution and report it.

But other Castiles were appalled. "These are good men! We
must not lose a horse-man when we are already shorthanded!"
They knew it would be useless to approach de Soto, once his
chin was set. Instead they pleaded with Juan Ortiz, who was
persuaded.

"I must do what I must do," he told Tale Teller grimly. "Do
not give me away."

Tale Teller did not like the sound of this, but Juan Ortiz was
his friend.

When the native party came, de Soto met them with a smile,
not waiting to hear their complaint. "I have put the offenders
in chains, and shall execute them now," he said. "I am returning the things they stole. It is as your Chief said: one law for
all." He handed over the items.

Juan Ortiz turned to Tale Teller. "Tell them he has the offenders, and will make an example of them that will be a lesson
to the rest. He thanks them for calling this to his attention, and
here are the stolen things."

That was close enough, and Tale Teller had no problem with
it. He relayed the news.

The Chicaza were gratified, as they accepted the shawls and
skins. "We feared that might not be the case," they said. "We
shall tell our Chief."

Tale Teller relayed that. Juan Ortiz nodded and turned to de
Soto. "They bring word from the Chief that Chief de Soto has
misunderstood their purpose. They heard that the Castiles had
been charged, but that they are innocent of any offense against

his people. The Chief had thought that the items had been stolen, but they had been lost, and the Castiles found them and did not know to whom they belonged. The Chief asks Chief de Soto the favor of letting these men go free, so that there is no wrong done."

Tale Teller's mouth dropped. He covered up his amazement with a cough.

De Soto seemed surprised too. "If that is the way they feel, I am glad," he said. "I wish only justice."

Juan Ortiz turned to Tale Teller. "He thanks them again. They have no need to remain longer."

The native party departed, satisfied. So it was that Osorio the horse-man was saved from death.

Tale Teller kept his mouth shut, but he saw the consequence. When it became apparent that the guilty Castiles had not been executed, the Chief of the Chicaza was grim, and he did not bring any more such complaints to de Soto. That did not mean he had forgotten the matter.

As the winter began to ease, Chief de Soto decided it was time to resume travel. He asked the Chief of the Chicaza for several tens of tens of men to serve as bearers for the supplies. The Chief said he would provide them the next morning. He realized that the Castiles were about to move on, and he was privately angry with them. It would have been best for him to encourage the army to depart peacefully, but he was as proud a man as was de Soto, and was determined to have revenge for what he believed was de Soto's betrayal of their agreement for justice. Juan Ortiz was Tale Teller's friend, and had saved Wren from death, but the terrible mischief resulting from Juan Ortiz's deception was about to manifest. As the Castiles put it: the path to the land of the demons was fashioned from good intentions.

On the morning of the Castile calendar of the fourth day of March, 1541, in the darkness before dawn, the Chicaza attacked. They had learned from the manner in which the Castiles had destroyed Mabila, and used similar strategy against the Castiles themselves. It was a perfectly organized raid, and only confusion in the darkness prevented it from being completely successful.

First several warriors crept into the village with burning brands hidden in clay pots, like Tale Teller's traveling punk pot, but burning more fiercely. When the sentries discovered them, they were already among the houses. They gave fearsome war cries and torched the lodges. There was a stiff wind, and this made the blazes spread rapidly. The Castiles were caught sleeping, for their sentries had been lax, and instead of catching the intruders early and driving them away, they merely fled and gave the alarm—too late.

When the war cries sounded and the smoke went up from the lodges, war drums began beating in the darkness. These were joined by the playing of flutes and shells, not as music but making a terrific amount of noise intended to panic the defenders. This seemed to be successful, for the Castiles woke in dismay and confusion, bewildered by the sound and blinded by the smoke. Few were able to climb into their armor, let alone get to their horses. Indeed, some emerged scrambling on their hands and knees, trying to get under the smoke.

The Chicaza attacked from four directions, as the Castiles had at Mabila, and when the Castiles blundered out of their lodges the warriors fired arrows at them. The Castiles were unable to regroup, and the horses panicked. Only Chief de Soto himself and one other horse-man were able to mount before their horses were lost. But when de Soto charged the warriors and struck the first with his lance, he discovered that his servant had not fastened the saddle properly on the animal, and he was dumped from his horse. Had any warrior seen that, he would have laughed so hard he might have forgotten to use his weapons.

Tale Teller learned such details later. At the time he was intent only on saving his own skin and that of his daughter. They wrapped cloaks around their bodies and fled the village. The warriors thought they were Castiles, and attacked them, but in the confusion the two were able to duck into the mass of fleeing Castiles and get away. Several arrows struck them, but the many layers of cloaks stopped these from making any bad injuries.

This would have been the perfect time to escape, Tale Teller realized. But not with the warriors after them! Once again he had to remain with his enemies, trusting to their protection for him and his daughter. As it happened, the fires caused some of the horses to break their tethers and escape their stalls, and these animals charged madly around, seeking their own escape. The warriors thought that there were horse-men on the horses, and tried to avoid them, and so did not properly pursue the real Castiles. Had the warriors realized, they could have killed all of the Castiles, just as the Castiles had killed all the warriors at Mabila.

The Castiles ran to a sloping hillside covered by a thicket, and there they gathered together to make a defense. Some were partially clothed and some were naked, so that their only hope was to make fires for warmth. But they were tough men, and already they were doing what was necessary. Some formed a defensive circle so that the group could not be attacked, while others gathered wood and made the fire, and others ranged out to catch the horses and pigs and lead them in. They found materials to put together a few crude lodges, and they buttressed these with branches and dirt.

Even so, they could have been overwhelmed by the Chicaza warriors, had the warriors concentrated and attacked them directly. They did not. They should have realized that the horses were by themselves and harmless, as they had come to know the nature of the horses in the course of the winter. They should also have realized that they greatly outnumbered the Castiles. But it was their nature to strike swiftly, win their objective, and return home with their spoils of war, and that was what they did. They took up the burned bodies of the pigs, and whatever pieces of Castile equipment remained, and went home, well contented. Even in victory, the warriors suffered their folly. So it was that they won the battle but not the war. Here was the most significant difference between this encounter and the one at Mabila: the Castiles had not relaxed until they had exterminated their enemy.

Yet it was impressive enough. It was the first time that any of the people had defeated the Castiles in direct combat. It proved that it was possible to prevail against these demons.

Tale Teller, secure with Wren by the Castiles' fire, marveled even then at the escape of the group. When the totals were tallied, they would find that ten and several more Castiles were dead, and most of the rest wounded. Five to six tens of horses had been lost, and three of every four pigs. In contrast, they knew of only one dead warrior: the one de Soto had lanced when he fell so ignominiously off his horse. Surely that warrior's spirit was laughing!

The Castiles, having been caught napping, took pains to see that it did not happen again. They made new saddles so that they could ride their surviving horses, and new round shields and lances, because all these things had been lost in the fire. The Castiles looked odd, because each was clothed with whatever he had been able to patch together. They used the parts of their big guns to handle the hot fires needed to melt metal and forge new weapons. They needed a thing called a *bellows* to blow much air through the fire, and they made this from two bear skins. They were clever enough in their adaptations, which was part of what made them so formidable in combat. The only safe Castile was a dead Castile.

But this work took time, and until it was done they remained vulnerable. The Chicaza warriors massed to raid again on the third morning after their victory, but it rained heavily, and wet their bowstrings, making them useless, and they did not attack. Tale Teller learned this from a captive the Castiles took later, and it was verified by the tracks that were close to the camp. It had been another narrow escape for the Castiles, and another foolish squandering of opportunity for the warriors. Had they raided on the first or second morning, they would have succeeded.

Warned by this, the Castiles maintained guard, and every morning sent out groups of horse-men to scour the countryside and kill any warriors found there. In this manner they prevented the warriors from gathering close by. Here was another difference between the two forces: the Castiles did not repeat their mistakes.

But on the ten and fifth day of March the warriors did attack, at the same time before dawn, and this time the rains did not interfere. They came from three directions, carrying their torches to set fire to the camp as before. But this time the Castiles were ready. De Soto drew up his men in three groups to meet them, and their weapons were in their hands, and the horse-men were on their horses. The warriors thought it would be the same as before, but they did not know how well the Castiles could fight when prepared.

"Stay with me," Tale Teller told Wren. "I do not want any Castile to mistake you for a fleeing captive." She nodded, knowing the danger. They both understood that this was to be another slaughter like that at Mabila, for the Castiles were angry about the humiliation of their first defeat, and intended to take their vengeance.

Indeed, the warriors charged in, and were met by such a devastating countercharge that they were rapidly routed. For the first time the Chicaza felt the full power of the Castiles' battle fury. They fled, and the Castiles pursued them—but maintained their formations, wary against any trap.

"To the camp! To the camp!" a friar cried. Startled, Tale Teller looked at the man. There was no cause for the Castiles to retreat! The man seemed mad or badly confused.

But the Castiles heard, and left off their pursuit of the foe to return. Tale Teller went out to reassure them. "There is no reason!" he cried. "It's only a crazy friar with a bad dream!"

Chief de Soto heard him. "The idiot!" he exclaimed in a fury, and galloped his horse back to silence the friar. But the damage was already done, for the warriors were disappearing, scattered, and it would be impossible to regroup in time to catch any significant number of them.

Tale Teller and Wren were left standing beyond the camp, down near the river. The warriors were fleeing and the Castiles were milling around, trying to get reorganized. Wren tugged at his hand. "Look," she whispered.

He looked. There at the bank of the river were several canoes that the warriors of one party had used to come close to the Castile camp in the darkness. A canoe was the most silent of things when properly used. Now they were deserted.

Tale Teller and Wren walked toward the canoes, not swiftly but not slowly either, as if to inspect them. They did inspect them—and picked out one with two good paddles and some supplies inside. Quietly they got in and took up the paddles, Tale Teller in the front and his daughter in the rear, because she could paddle on either side. They pushed the canoe off into the river.

A Castile horse-man came toward them. Tale Teller froze,

fearing discovery of their intent. If the man saw them, he could poke his lance through the canoe and stop them immediately, and then Chief de Soto would throw Wren to the dogs and cut off Tale Teller's nose and ears and perhaps also his hands, to prevent him from ever using a paddle again.

The Castile came to the bank and peered at them. He was Osorio, whose life had been saved by Juan Ortiz's ruse. Tale Teller had never revealed that, because Juan Ortiz was his friend, though he often wondered how much that act had cost the Castiles. This present battle was surely one that would never have occurred had de Soto's order for Osorio's execution been followed.

Osorio pondered briefly, then shrugged as if he had seen nothing of interest. In a moment his horse was moving in to join the others of the formation. Tale Teller and Wren resumed paddling. Soon they had slipped out of sight of the camp, down the river.

"Why didn't he cry the alarm or attack us?" Wren asked, her tone showing how frightened she had been.

"He was returning a favor," Tale Teller replied. It had not been his favor, and he had not even liked Osorio. But he had kept his tongue quiet, and it seemed the Castile had remembered. Like de Soto himself, the man had shown his decision by turning away without comment. In this manner he repaid everything he might have owed to Tale Teller, if not to Chief Hernando de Soto.

CHAPTER 20

☙

RETURN

O Spirit of the Mound, I have told you how we at last escaped from the terrible Castiles, seizing our opportunity and benefiting from the return of an inadvertent favor. Now I will tell you of our life thereafter, and how we raised the boy you gave us. You never forsook me, O Spirit, though I had forsaken you.

There was no cry of alarm. They moved down the river, helped by the current, paddling as rapidly as they could. Wren was a good paddler, because she had done it often when they went in the canoe to other Toco villages for him to tell his tales. She had not been able to practice in the past two seasons, so she tired soon, but she did her best. She knew how to guide the canoe, and kept it from snagging in brush at the banks.

No people challenged them, for there seemed to be no reason for any part of the Castiles' party to go alone away from the camp, and these were obviously travelers on their own mission. But they did not risk camping on the bank at night. They continued to float with the current, taking turns watching and sleeping. The supplies in the canoe turned out not to be food but cloaks, and in the cold nights these were better than food. Tale Teller caught a bug in his hand and used it to bait his fishhook, and in due course caught a fish. He cut it open and they shared it, chewing on the raw meat of it. Later they passed a walnut tree, and paused to gather in the fallen nuts and two stones with which to crack them open. They dipped water in their hands when they were thirsty. They did not eat well, but they traveled well.

Tale Teller realized that his daughter was now ten winters old, and would soon enough be a woman. Tzec had been nine winters when he had first known her. Now, in Wren, he would have the chance to see how Tzec had grown up in the years he had been away from her. It was a pleasant realization. Wren was different, and larger for her age than Tzec had been, but she was Tzec's daughter and could be recognized as such.

"I am glad I rescued you, my daughter," he said. There was irony in that, for she had been the one to spy the canoes and realize their significance. But his entire captivity by the Castiles had been for her sake.

"I always knew you would, my father," she replied. And indeed, she had maintained her faith throughout, knowing the constraints on him.

That was all they said on that subject, but his heart beat strongly with love for her, and he knew that she was crying, finally free after two winters. She had been well treated throughout by the Castiles, but she had never forgotten how close she had come to being killed at the outset, or how Chief de Soto had brought her before the terrible dogs, and would have set them on her if Tale Teller had not done his bidding. She had also seen what had happened to the other captives, especially the Toco, few of whom still survived.

They came in due course to the great sea, and he knew it was the same one he had circled before, when the spirits had sent him out to die but delivered him instead to the Calusa and then to his original home. He knew that if they just turned east and followed the shore, they would get there in time.

They did that, landing when they had to, sometimes gathering nuts or making a fire to cook fish. When a storm came they went to shore and hid under the canoe, as he had done with the Trader and Tzec so long ago. It was warmer here, but not too warm, and they moved well each day as they paddled. It was pleasant, traveling with his daughter, getting used to the feeling of being free. He was glad that they had this time together, for in the rigors of the Castile army they had often been separated and never had the chance to know each other without tension. They had been closest during the first winter camp, when each of them had suffered the siege of the evil spirits, but that had been a time of misery rather than pleasure.

Within a moon they reached the Little Big River, and paddled up it. At last they returned to Ibi Hica.

There, standing by the bank, was Tzec, seeming unchanged. "I have been waiting for you, my husband, my daughter," she said. Both of them were amazed at her aplomb.

"I have something to return to you," Tale Teller said, bringing out the magic crystal. Tzec accepted it, putting the cord around her neck and letting the pouch dangle between her breasts, as before.

But it was not, after all, that casual. Tzec had believed the spirits, who had told her that her time with them was not done, but she cried as she hugged them, and he knew that her belief had been severely tested, these two winters.

Once they were settled in, Wren remembered how the Castiles had buried things of value near the village in Cale territory. She went there with Tale Teller and Tzec and a party of warriors and showed them the exact spot. They dug there, and found the cache: some useless bits of Castile armor, but also a package of beautiful beads, a rare treasure. They brought these back and shared them with those who were worthy in the village, and used the rest to trade with the nearby villages. Wren herself had a fine necklace of them, for she had made this wonderful discovery possible. Ibi Hica was now the richest village of the region, because of that treasure, and its people lived very well by trading the beads for food and cloaks.

Tzec disdained the Castile beads. Instead she took a piece of the iron armor. "It is evil but it is strong," she explained. "With the magic crystal I may be able to turn it to good." Later she was to do just that, and that seemingly ugly and useless and evil metal became one of the most potent forces in the area.

They traveled together from village to village, the three of them, for they all knew how tenuous life could be and how readily separation could come. Wren, who had borne up so well during the time with the Castiles, now suffered agony in her spirit, and feared that if either her mother or her father left her sight for more than a moment, they would not return.

Tzec, too, feared for her husband and daughter. She had, by other accounts, proceeded bravely when her family was taken, maintaining her lodge and helping others. She was independent, having learned it as a trader, and refused to take another husband. "I have a husband," she had said. "I have a daughter. They will return." She had seldom shared her honey with other men, either, giving the impression that she did it only to be sure she retained the ability for the time when her true man returned. Others had pitied her, but she had held firm, and had finally been vindicated. But now all the desolation she had suppressed was finding its way out, and she clung to him. Indeed, she demanded much of him, and did not use the honey, as if determined to have as much of his seed as possible, storing it within her, lest the lean seasons come again.

Tale Teller had lost two wives and two sons, and he did not want to lose a wife and a daughter. He, too, had held up well during the time of separation, never doubting that Tzec waited for him at home—but now he, too, discovered the terrible doubt that had lurked beneath. So it was that he lay beneath Tzec, and kissed her sweet mouth as her warm breasts pressed down on him and her soft, loose hair stroked his neck, and he sank into her cleft with his hard penis, seeming never to get deep enough or close enough, and gave of his seed as often as he could, and joyed to feel her heart beating near to his heart as they shared their love and their passion—without ever letting go the hand of his daughter beside them.

They told the folk of the villages the tales of the Castiles, for all three of them had had experience with them in one way or another. Tzec had known the Mad Queen, and Wren had been with the Castiles, and the stories of these strange folk were endlessly fascinating to the villagers. When Wren told how Chief de Soto had lanced a warrior and fallen off the back of his horse, everyone laughed uproariously. This helped Wren, and Tale Teller too, for it made the captivity by the Castiles seem more like an adventure and less like a time of horror.

Later they learned through traders that the Castiles had marched on until they reached the great river Tale Teller had followed down to the sea, the same one Gray Cloud had followed up to the land of the Principal People. They had gone beyond it, looking for their gold, and come back to the river to spend the winter. The interpreter Juan Ortiz died there; Tale Teller and Wren were grieved to hear that. Chief de Soto died not long after, and that made Tale Teller feel somewhat better

The remaining Castiles had gone far to the west, still looking for gold, then returned for another winter at the river. They had built big rafts and floated down the river, chased by many warriors, until at last they reached the sea and went down toward the region of the Mexica. Beyond that, nothing was known of them.

Meanwhile, though Tzec was now an old woman of ten and ten and ten and six winters, she got a child in her belly again. She had been seeking it desperately. But it was born dead, and they realized that the effort had been a foolish one. She had helped save the babies of many others with her magic crystal, but somehow it did not save her own. Wren, now twelve winters but still lean in the fashion of childhood, consoled her mother as well as she could. Tale Teller took the dead baby boy out to the charnel platform beside the old mound. For this short trip he was able to paddle the canoe alone; there was no hurry.

As he came into sight of the mound he realized that though he had learned that Dead Eagle had not betrayed him, he had not returned to apologize to the Spirit of the Mound. Somehow the years of his alienation had not let go, and he had continued to live isolated from the spirits. Perhaps it was because he was not sure how to make up for the wrong he had done Dead Eagle.

The dead baby—was this their way of reminding him of his error? For this was what had brought him here at last. This mound had not been used for a long time, but now the priest had decided that it was time, and they had made the charnel structure. It was the invasion of the Castiles that had done it; if such evil could come, it was because the spirits were angry at the tribe, and that could be because they had been using the other mound too long. So they were returning to the ancient mound of their ancestors, and that should protect the tribe against further invasions. But Tale Teller had been with the Castiles, and had not come back to the mound, though now there was a path to it from the river. So he had been brought here.

He laid the baby on the platform above the mound, beside the other bodies. There were not many, because the change had been made only a winter ago. Then he walked to the base of the mound and stood there, uncertain what to do.

You must apologize to him, Laurel told him. She remained with
him, still ten and ten and five winters old, as she had been at
death, but she never manifested when he was with Tzec, out
of courtesy. Since he was with Tzec all the time he could be,
Laurel seldom spoke to him. But the spirit realm was now her
business, and she knew best. *You must tell him why you renounced
him, and beg him to forgive you.*

That made so much sense that he wondered why he had not
thought of it himself. He bent his head and spoke in his mind.
O Spirit of the Mound, I apologize for renouncing you. I thought—

Something stirred on the far side of the mound, distracting
him. He looked, and saw a child, a small boy, walking there.
He was perhaps three winters old.

What was a live boy doing here? This was a place forbidden
to any except the spirits and those who had business with the
spirits. Tale Teller walked around the mound, approaching the
boy. "Why are you here?" he demanded.

The boy stared up at him, unspeaking. He did not seem to
be afraid, only uncomprehending.

"Come here," Tale Teller said, squatting. When the boy did
not respond, he used the sign, extending his forefinger and
sweeping it toward his own face: Come.

The boy approached. He was scrawny and dirty; indeed, his
limbs were emaciated. His bare feet were scabbed and oozing.
His hair was wild. But that odd lack of fear remained; he was
simply waiting for Tale Teller to do whatever he chose to do.

Tale Teller questioned him in all the tongues he could think
of, and the boy simply stared at him. But when he used signs,
there seemed to be some understanding.

He cannot hear! Laurel thought, understanding.

A starving deaf boy? Where was his family? There seemed
to be no way he could have come here.

In a canoe, she thought. *Put off here to die, because they did not
want him.*

That made sense. The boy would have come to the mound,
and the Spirit of the Mound, Dead Eagle, could have given him
back his life and taken his fear. Tale Teller understood about
that. But the boy could not live long this way.

He looked back at the mound. He had started to apologize

to the Spirit of the Mound, and this boy had appeared. Dead
Eagle required something of him before accepting his apology.

"Come with me," he told the boy. Then, when the child
simply stared at him, he made the Come sign, and walked back
toward his canoe. The boy followed.

The old woman and the young one looked up as he returned,
reminding him of Twice Cursed and Laurel. He showed them
the boy. "The Spirit of the Mound gave him to me," he said.
"He has no fear, and he cannot hear."

They stared at the boy without a seeming reaction. Then the
two looked at each other. Then Wren got up and took the boy's
hand. She led him outside.

"The spirits promised me another child by you, a son," Tzec
said. "I thought they took him away in anger."

"I started to apologize, and the Spirit of the Mound gave me
back a boy," he said. "But not a whole one."

"The spirits do not forgive readily or completely," she said.
"We must take what they give."

In a while Wren returned with the boy. Now he was clean
and his hair was combed. The extreme thinness of his limbs
was more evident.

Tzec signed to the child: Come.

He went to her, and she made him lie by her. Then she put
her newly filling breast to his mouth.

So it was that they became a family of four. They named the
boy Death Gift, and if others wondered at the name, they explained. Their son had died, and the spirits had given half a
boy back. When they made the boy whole, the Spirit of the
Mound might accept Tale Teller's apology.

Death Gift filled out, for Tzec's milk was good. The magic
crystal helped him mend, but not to hear. He learned to make
the signs so that he could speak freely with others. He went
with his new family from village to village, and he helped gather
wood for the fire, and he did whatever he was told. The other
children learned to accept him as he was, and when they did
not, his big sister, Wren, took him away, shaming them.

Wren meanwhile was maturing into a beautiful young
woman, as her mother had been in the years when Tale Teller
had not known her. At ten and four winters, which was late

for Toco girls, she changed, and instead of being a big child, she became the prettiest young woman of the region. Tale Teller thought that the rough years with the Castiles had set her back, and so she had been longer about getting her breasts and hips. But once she did, they were good enough to command the attention of any man in the vicinity, and not only when she danced.

Tzec instructed her daughter in the way of honey, and indeed, Wren was familiar with it, having grown up with the love between Tale Teller and Tzec. But though every man was interested, Wren hesitated to spend a night away from her family. So when she was ten and five winters she still had not been with a man. Tzec was getting worried. "Maybe we should send her to an elder man, one well experienced," she said, evidently remembering the Cacique of the Calusa.

"If she will not go to another lodge in the village, she will not go to the Cacique," Tale Teller responded dryly. "It is not knowledge she lacks, but confidence to spend a night away from us. We must accept this, and give her time."

But even he got worried when Wren, ten and six winters and so lovely that there was a hush when she entered a village, still could not leave them for a night. People were beginning to wonder what it was that kept her so interested in her home lodge, and they glanced sidelong at him.

Finally Tzec consulted with her daughter, then had him invite a young man with a reputation for virility to their lodge. "My daughter worries about her brother, who cannot hear," Tale Teller told the warrior. "She will not leave him untended. But she would like your company this night, to test her honey."

The man looked hesitant, for this was not normal procedure. But Wren smiled at him and led him to her corner of the lodge and he was not able to object. To be approached by this beautiful young woman—that was the dream of every young man of the tribe, and not a few older men too.

Tale Teller and Tzec lay in the darkness, listening. Soon she squeezed his hand, one time, and turned in to him, and placed his hand on her breast, which remained firm despite her age. Then she climbed on him, her legs falling outside his own, and his penis quickly found its natural lodging in the depths of her cleft. She kissed him as she felt him pulse within her, and closed

er legs so as to hold him there longer. He was old and she
vas old, but it remained surprisingly good.

As he was falling asleep, Tzec squeezed his hand again, two
imes. She had heard another action across the lodge. But Tale
Teller was old; he had no intention of trying to keep the pace.
Nor did she want him to; she was just interested in the progress
f her daughter.

Later yet she woke him with three squeezes. He squeezed
er bottom and went back to sleep.

When she woke him with four, and stretched out against
im, he had to comply. She lay on top of him again and took
im into her and moved her hips, and he rested his hand on
er thigh and let her do it, and it was peaceful and delightful,
nd he lapsed back into sleep while she was still on him. It was
delightful way to do it.

By morning she was squeezing him seven times. "You just
weren't trying, with Heron Feather," she whispered reproach-
ally.

"If I had been with you, it would have been eight times,"
e replied. That silenced her. She did not see fit to remind him
nat she had been nine winters old then.

When the young man departed in the morning, he looked
red and Wren looked smug. If there had been stories about
er honey being weak, they had been given the lie. But the
uth was, she was somewhat sore; she had set out to make a
ase, but it had been at a sacrifice.

However, she had passed a key point, and after that she
egan to go out at night, when some man took her fancy. Her
arents were relieved.

Each time they returned to a village close to the original
ound, Tale Teller took little Death Gift to it to show Dead
agle. The boy remained interested in the things of the dead,
nd enjoyed these trips, but Dead Eagle did not respond. Tale
eller's penance was not yet done, and his apology not ac-
epted.

The priest noticed the boy's affinity for the dead. "I have
ork for such a child," he said. "We prefer to strip the bones
ean as soon as possible, so as to release the spirits from the
aptivity of the flesh. But it is hard to get people to do this."

"If Death Gift is willing, I am willing," Tale Teller said. He

talked to the boy in signs, and the lad nodded; he would be
happy to do such work.

So in the morning Tale Teller would bring his son out to the
mound, and leave him with the priest, and fetch him back in
the evening. The priest instructed Death Gift in the proper
application of the tools, so that the bones were not damaged.
The boy did well, enjoying the work, and the bones were soon
clean. The priest rewarded him with favor, gifts, and more
work. But the bodies were finished before Death Gift's interest
faded.

The priest inquired, and ascertained that there was similar
need at other mounds. Tale Teller and his family went to a
village where there was such a need, and while he told tales
Death Gift worked with the local priest. His reputation
spread.

Requests for the boy's service became too numerous for them
to accommodate. Tale Teller had regular villages to visit, and
these were not necessarily associated with mounds in need, for
deaths did not come often. They discussed the matter, and
finally Wren offered to take her brother to the villages in need.
She was not at ease about leaving the family, but Death Gift
was family, so it could be done.

They tried it, experimentally. Tale Teller and Tzec remained
in one village, while Wren and Death Gift went with a warrior
from a nearby village in need. Wren was obviously nervous,
and not from any fear of the warrior, who would surely be so
wet clay in her hands. It was the separation from her parents
that concerned her. They returned three days later. Not only
had Death Gift done an excellent job with two dead old bodies,
Wren had made two live young bodies perform in another
manner.

After that they split the family when the need arose, and
Wren became more confident. The demand for that part of the
family grew, for it seemed there was interest in what both
brother and sister had to offer.

When Wren was ten and seven winters, which was old for
a maiden, she did something daring: she went to the lodge of
the uncle of the Chief of Atafi, who was the younger brother
of the former Chief Slay-Bear. His wife had died several months
before, after bearing him three girls. His name was Deer Head

Wren treated it as she would any visit, showing up in the evening with her honey. The man, startled, took her in; he had never thought of her in this fashion, for she had traveled widely and seldom remained long in this village. He was an older man, well respected but not possessive of young women.

"I have seen your mark," she told him. For he had a discoloration on his back that had been there all his life, in the general shape of the head of a deer. It had marked him for contact with the spirits, but he had never claimed to know their ways.

"My mark appeals to you?" he asked, surprised. "Most people find it ugly."

"Now I will show you mine." She dropped her moss skirt, stepped out of it, and turned around, presenting him with the tribe's fullest and finest set of buttocks.

He stared at her mark. He had not known of it before. Then he stared at the body it was on. He was not so old as to fail to see that it was the most beautiful body of the region.

"My mother married a man with a mark," Wren said. "I will do the same."

"I make no promise of marriage!" he protested.

She turned and came to him. "Then let me please you for a night."

Flattered by her approach, and smitten by her body, he agreed. She did what she understood so well, which related to the hardening and softening of penises. By morning Deer Head was in love. He too was soft wet clay in her hands.

They agreed to marry at the First Moon Ceremony, which was coming soon. Among the tribes to the near north it was called the Green Corn Ceremony, and among those of other regions it had other titles, but the Toco did not grow corn, so they gave it its proper name. It was the celebration of the turning of the year, from which the ten and three moons were numbered. At this time marriages were initiated or continued or terminated. Impurity was cleansed. Grudges were settled. Names were changed. Boys became men and girls became women. Most important, the spirits were honored. It was by far the most important Ceremony of the year.

Tale Teller and Tzec had been through it many times, but

this time their daughter was to be well married, and it was
special. They were thankful for Wren's good fortune, and this
was the occasion to express that thanks.

The priest decided on the exact day for the Ceremony to
begin, when the moon would be full. He split cane into tiny
splinters, counted these into several bundles, and gave them
to messengers. Each splinter represented one day until the
Ceremony. The messengers went to every village invited to the
local celebration. Each chief would discard one splinter each
day, and when only one remained it would be time to set out
for the assigned place.

This year the Ceremony was near Atafi, in a section of the
forest recently burned so as to clear it of brush. This meant that
the ground was firm, but there were few dry branches for fires.
However, there was an unburned section nearby, and good
water also near. It was a good location.

On the day assigned, the river was filled with canoes, and
families took the easiest route. But those from the closer places
walked, carrying their things. It was a time of great anticipation
and excitement.

They converged on the ceremonial site. The people of Atafi
had marked it plainly, and made trails leading to it. They had
also hauled in supplies of wood and food for those who needed
it. The center was laid out in a great square; that had to remain
clear, for the main activity would be there. The visitors immediately made temporary lodges outside the square, several
families sharing each, and built fires for great numbers to use.
Men from different villages worked together, doing what had
to be done; this was a time of peace and amity, and any who
shirked or picked a quarrel would be shamed.

As night approached, they ate hugely. This was because the
fast would follow. They finished every scrap of food they could
hold, but nothing from any current crop; it was all old food.
They dug out the region for the central fire, threw in some
tubers and tobacco leaves and kernels of corn, and filled it in
with clay and white sand to make it level and clean.

Women were present, but of special status during this time.
No adult man could touch any female, not even an infant, until
the Ceremony was done. He would not even use the word for
"woman"; he had to say "food preparer" or "lodge carer" or

something similar. The women in turn had to speak in quiet voices and preserve harmony.

From the evening of the first day until the sunrise of the third day the men fasted. On the day of fasting they drank the White Drink in large quantities and vomited it out again, in this manner purifying themselves. There was nothing covert about this; they shot great streams of liquid from their mouths onto the ground in the center of their circle. The head priest was the purest of all, for he had fasted for three days before the Ceremony started, and was notably thin and weak. In this manner they ensured happiness and well-being during the coming year.

The priest brought out his most sacred medicine bundle and laid it out for the others to see. It was wrapped in a deer skin with the hair side out, and inside it were many smaller things wrapped separately. One of these was his magic crystal; another was a collection of pieces of the horns and teeth of several animals; another was an enormous rattlesnake skin that unfolded impressively; another was a group of special stones that could strike sparks and make the sacred fire. This bundle was the collective soul of the tribe, and had to be treated with the utmost care and respect.

On this day, too, the men did their best to settle any serious differences or crimes. Everything had to be pure for the coming year, and bad feelings were a kind of impurity. Everything was brought out into the open, and all grudges were settled. All was well.

This was the occasion for Deer Head to declare his marriage to a small bird, if no man objected. None did. "Marry any bird you choose," his nephew the Chief said with a smile. "That creature will not be harmed in my village." The men laughed, knowing how pleased the Chief was with this particular liaison. Only Deer Head would have access to her without the honey; that made it all right.

Yet there must have been some grievous error, for there was to be terrible punishment before the next First Moon Ceremony. Tale Teller did not know this at the time, but later he was to realize that he should have been better alert for it. The threat to the tribe he had been warned about was approaching, and he did not see it.

On the third morning the women cooked plenty of food, set it just outside the square, and returned without pause to their lodges. The men were hungry, but did not rush to eat; it was bad form to seem too eager, since the fast was for the purpose of purification. However, every bit of food was gone by noon.

At noon the Chief of Atafi announced that the new fire was about to be made. The women and children were required to extinguish all their old fires and to remain quiet in their lodges; any failure here could lead to dire consequences.

The priest, painted red, fetched special dry-wood lengths, fixed one a bowstring, and worked the bow to twirl it against a piece of wood held between his knees. This was the hard way to make a fire, compared to the punk pot—but this was a new fire, while the pot was merely a saving of the old fire. When it got hot and began to smoke, he put small chips near, and continued until they caught fire. He set the fire in a pot reserved for it and placed it in the middle of the sacred square. The new fire had been started!

They added wood, and built it up into a good blaze. The priest walked three times around it, invoking the good spirits. Then Tzec, honored among women, brought a few new fruits and vegetables to the square and retreated. The priest threw bits of fruit and a few drops of the White Drink into the fire. He added an herb that caused it to hiss and send up white smoke. With this it was done: all social wrongs had been expiated, and all crimes other than the unwarranted killing of a person were forgiven. Those who had been socially restricted could return to normal relations.

Now the women were allowed to participate. They came to stand around the outside of the square. They were clean and neat and pretty. Wren was beautiful, and Tzec was elegant. All had a suitably serious look on their faces, but Tale Teller knew that some were humoring the menfolk, and did not really believe that the welfare of the tribe depended on a ceremony that mostly excluded women.

Now the priest made a speech to the warriors. "I remind you of your responsibility to remain pure in spirit and body and to do your duty in all things. You should be especially brave in warfare, and be dedicated hunters. You should be a credit to your tribe and your clan and your family. I know you will do honor to the name of Toco.''

The priest addressed the women. He spoke much less politely. "If any of you other creatures did not put out your old fires, or if any of you are not pure, you must get away from here immediately, or the pure new fire will burn your soul *and the souls of your family*. You must serve only pure food to your children, lest they get worms or evil spirits infest them.'' The priest frowned, and he looked like an avenging spirit himself, because he was haggard from his rigors of the Ceremony. "Most especially, do not break the rules of marriage or of sex on this hallowed occasion. Do not try to pollute any brave warrior with your honey, for however sweet it may seem, it is completely bitter to your soul and his at this time. *Wait till the Ceremony is over!*" He glared around at them, and the women looked suitably chagrined, though the truth was that it was not they but the men who were most eager to resume sexual relations at the earliest legitimate moment. The priest's ferocity was really directed at the men. The men suspected this, which accounted for their somewhat shamed silence, and the women were sure of it, which accounted for their muted, demure aspects. In fact, Tzec caught Tale Teller's eye for just a moment. She was four tens and three winters old, and her skin was wrinkled and her body stooped with wear, yet he longed for her and would have sought her honey this moment had it been possible. Beside her, Wren stood tall and buxom, and he knew that Deer Head was looking at her and feeling similar desire.

Now the priest addressed everyone. "All of you, think about the new, pure fire I have brought you, to purify our society for the coming year. You must do your utmost to remain pure, lest the spiritual fire take vengeance on us all. If you behave properly you will enjoy good health, and our ceremonies will bring plenty of rain, and our hunting will be successful, and we will be victorious over our enemies in war. But if you fail to hold to the rules, you will spoil it all. Then we can expect drought, defeat, captivity, humiliation, evil spirits, severe illness, and death!" It was rhetorical, but completely true, for the coming year was to see the destruction of these villages. If only everyone had known!

The speech was done. Attendants took fragments of the holy fire and set them carefully in pots and took these out of the square to the women so that they could light new fires for their lodges when they got home.

Now the festivities of the occasion began. The priest summoned six of the oldest and most prestigious women for a dance. Tzec was the first of these, though she was not the oldest, because of the great respect she had earned through her travels and her healing. There was hardly a family who had not been touched by her in some way, whether it was a child who had been cured of a fever-making evil spirit by her magic crystal, or a man who had been strengthened by an herbal drink she had shown his wife how to make, or someone who had appreciated the manner in which she had made the onset of a death in the family bearable. More than one of the married older warriors had been initiated into sex by her, learning their confidence so that they became attractive to young women. If the truth were known, she was probably a more popular figure than the Chief himself—and it was to the Chief's interest to leave it that way, because her daughter would now be part of his larger household. Who would have foreseen this when the young Throat Shot first encountered the nine-winters-old mute girl? She had indeed changed his life, and that of the tribe.

The women were dressed in their finest skirts and paints and shawls, bedecked with bead necklaces, rattles on their ankles, and additional beads in their hair. Six respected old men joined them, and Tale Teller was one of these. They too were well dressed, their long hair bound back and decorated with colorful feathers. Each carried a branch that had been partially burned in the new fire, and pure white feathers.

The drums started beating, and the musicians joined in, playing their pipes and gourd rattles. The dancers sang as they moved, completing the ritual music of the occasion.

The priest led the dance, circling the fire, making quick short steps, stamping his feet. The other men kept pace, and the women made their smaller circle inside the men's circle, going in the opposite direction. This dance concluded the ceremonies of the day. After that the women went home, or at least to their temporary lodges, to ignite their fires, and to cook huge quantities of the new vegetables and freshly caught mussels for the feast on the fourth day.

On that following day the women proudly brought some five tens of different dishes, the most splendid array they could manage. There was dried deer meat, which counted as new rather than old food for this occasion, fish, beans, pumpkins, gourds, and many varieties of wild fruit. They served it to the men in strict order of rank: first the Chief, then Deer Head, then the most respected warriors beginning with the oldest. Tale Teller was included in this number, though it was obvious that he was no longer a warrior; his first kill as Throat Shot was still remembered, if only because it was one of the tales of himself he told.

Later that day the warriors put white feathers in their hair and formed three circles around the fire to dance. They sang as they moved, accompanied by the musicians, and the drumbeat seemed to shake the whole world. After that they decorated themselves with war paint, brought out their weapons, and fought an impressive mock battle. Some had to "die" in this encounter, and there were those who had a special talent for agonizing mortality. It was a great pleasure to watch.

At last the younger women were asked to dance. In fact the priest declared that any woman who refused would be severely penalized. There was almost a laugh at this point, for the women were dressed and eager. They had pendants in their ears, their hair shone with bear oil, there were strings of white shell beads around their smooth necks, their breasts were full and gleaming, and there were tortoiseshell rattles on their ankles. Wren was outstanding among them, phenomenally proportioned; yet Tale Teller saw in her mainly the echo of Tzec when she had been young. Indeed, Wren had completed the missing years of Tzec for him; he had seen her grow and mature and use her first honey, as he imagined Tzec had done in his absence, and now she would bring to Deer Head all the delights Tzec had brought to himself. They formed three circles around the fire, facing in, then turned outward so that the watching men could appreciate the full splendor of their skill.

Finally one of the assistant priests came to the center to make an announcement. "The First Moon Ceremony is done," he said. "All of us have been made pure. Now all of you must paint yourselves and follow the senior priest."

Immediately every person, man, woman, and child, got to work with the clay paints. They removed their clothing and used the paints as clothing, becoming something other than naked. When they were ready, they followed the priest in single file and in a set order. First came the assistant priests; then the beloved old men according to their seniority, with Tale Teller third among them following Deceiver of Enemies, whom he had known in youth as Alligator; then the warriors according to their reputations; then the women in their own order of seniority and association with ranking men; then the children; and finally those who had committed minor infractions and were therefore to a degree impure despite the general cleansing wrought by the Ceremony.

The priest walked down the path to the water of the lake. He waded in, up to his knees, his hips, and his chest, washing off the paint. The others followed, and the clay paint dissolved away, the last symbol of past impurity, and they were completely pure. They emerged naked, as if all of them were mere children, which was permissible for this occasion.

Then they returned to the square to don their clothes again and dance, with every person participating. The First Moon Ceremony was over, everything was pure, and the new year had begun. None of them realized how close their doom was looming.

Wren finally left her family, for she would be making her own family. She was now held in high esteem, for it was seen by all that she had preserved herself in order to be ready for the uncle of the Chief. By Toco custom, the Chief had sexual access to the wives of his relatives, and the Chief was extremely pleased with his uncle's choice for his second wife. Wren prevailed on Tale Teller to move with his family to Atafi so that they would not be far from her. Her husband was glad to agree, for all the members of this family were highly respected, Tale Teller, Tzec, and Death Gift included, and it seemed only proper that they should live in the most important village.

There was no one to conduct Death Gift to his appointments. But he was now, by their judgment, ten winters old, and able to travel by himself. He still had no fear; they had kept watch on him because it was dangerous for a child to have no fear, but now he understood the reasons for caution, and agreed to be careful.

Tale Teller and Tzec went as a couple to tell the tales. He was now an old man of four tens and nine winters, and she an old woman of four tens and three winters. His arm remained only partially operative, but that had long since ceased to be a problem. Tzec was wizened and sunburned in the normal manner, but she remained his love. He still saw in her the child of nine winters whom he had not dared to love. They faced the coming ending of their days together, placidly. They had had full lives—more than full!—and the realm of the spirits was becoming more attractive.

But one thing bothered Tale Teller: he had not yet had Dead Eagle's acceptance of his apology. His original mission remained unfinished. He had never found the Ulunsuti, and the threat to his tribe remained. Was that threat empty, or had his failure allowed it to come in its own time? He could not be certain.

Wren was soon swelling with a baby, who well might be a future chief if male, for the Chief had no offspring. To Tzec it seemed only right: she was of chiefly stock among the Maya, so her grandson should be chief again. If it was a girl, she would be beautiful, as all her line were.

Wren's time passed, and in the spring of what the Castiles would have called the year 1550 she bore a perfect baby boy. Deer Head was pleased; he had thought his days of siring offspring were over when his former wife died, but Wren had revived his manhood and given him his first son. There was a great celebration in the village, and all paid honor to the mother of the future chief.

A trader came, and they all went out to meet him, for traders always brought interesting things. He brought not only trade goods, but news: the spirits were attacking the villages of the tribes across the Little Big River. The villagers nodded; they had always known that those villages were not living in proper harmony with the spirits, and deserved their punishment. The trader remained for several days, then got ready to paddle elsewhere—and fell ill. The spirits had attacked him, so the priest did what he could to drive them away.

When the trader broke out in ugly small spots, Tale Teller became afraid. He had no fear for himself, but he could fear for others, and now he feared for his daughter. For he recognized the type of spirits that had attacked him and his family of the Principal People. The ones the Castiles called small pox.

"Get rid of him!" he warned. "Put him in his canoe and float him away. Do not go near him, for he brings terrible spirits!" The Castiles had told how such spirits could be carried from person to person, and he had seen how the Castiles fought off the spirits better than the natives did, just as the Castiles fought battles better. The Castiles had seemed to believe that the merit of a particular person did not matter much, and that the evil spirits simply infested anyone they could reach. If the Castiles were right, it might be possible to get rid of the spirits by getting rid of the trader.

The priest did not agree with Tale Teller. "Since when are you the authority on the nature of spirits?" he demanded, and continued his rituals to drive the spirits from the trader. But in a few more days the trader died.

Tale Teller went to his daughter. "Wren, you must leave here with your baby!" he urged her. "These are terrible spirits, worse than the ones we fought off in the Castile camp. The magic crystal may not be able to prevail against them. Do not let them catch you!"

She understood his urgency, but could not oblige. "I cannot leave my husband, or travel well with my baby."

Tale Teller went to the mound. *O Spirit of the Mound! I fear the evil spirits are coming to our village! I beg you to forgive me my trespass, and tell me how to save our village from them.*

Now at last Dead Eagle answered. *Foolish man! There is no way! Only the magic of the Ulunsuti can show us how to stave off this disaster, and you did not fetch it. There was no point in talking to you after you had failed, for you had sealed the fate of your people.*

Tale Teller was appalled. *But I would have gone again to fetch it, if you had warned me.*

I warned you three times. First when you were here and I took your fear. Second when you began to forget, and I showed you the nature of the threat, there among the Principal People. Third when I showed you the source of the evil spirits: the Castiles. When you ignored these warnings and still did not fetch the Ulunsuti, I knew it was useless to talk to you, and I did not do so again. Now go away; what will happen will happen.

Now at last it all was clear—too late. Dead Eagle had indeed warned him, and he had been blind to even the most forceful warnings. He had always known what he had to do—yet he had renounced his mission. The evil spirits of the small pox were too powerful to be balked; only the Ulunsuti could have shown the way. Sun Eagle had finally located it—and Tale Teller had refused to go to fetch it.

Now his people would pay the terrible price of his failure.

CHAPTER 21

☙

MOUND

O Spirit of the Mound, I have told you of Wren and of our lives with her, and how I finally realized what was the nature of the terrible threat to my tribe—too late. Now I will tell you the last of it, and you will judge what it means.

The evil spirits came as they had among the Principal People. The running noses, and the high fever, and then the spots, and then for many death, and for the rest, near-death and disfigurement by the spots. But the spirits came much faster this time, infesting most of the village of Atafi at once. Because of this, there were not enough people left to take care of the ones the spirits ravaged, and they suffered worse. The priest himself was attacked, so could not help others. The evil spirits knew how to make it worse.

Tale Teller made sure there were supplies of food in his lodge, and jars filled with water, so that they would not have to go far to fetch them. The evil spirits had come for him once, and would find him again, and this time might make sure of him, just as they would make sure of his village.

He hoped the spirits would spare Death Gift, because he really worked for the dead, but they did not. He hoped they would spare Wren, but they did not. He hoped they would spare Tzec, but they did not. The only one in the village they spared was Tale Teller himself. Because he wore the magic crystal, which Tzec gave back to him the moment the siege began and which the others refused to accept from him. It had learned how to protect him from the smallpox spirits, and they could not get into him.

But he had seen how the spirits went after others when they left the first ones they attacked. They could be saving him for last. Then they might all gather together to overwhelm the magic crystal and destroy him. So he did what he could for Tzec and Death Gift, and also for Wren and her husband, Deer Head, bringing them water and such food as they could eat. He changed their cloaks when they sweated, and wrapped them again when they chilled. But he knew it was not enough.

Death Gift died. Tale Teller did not tell Tzec, for she was too ill herself to be grieved further by this news. How tired she looked now!

The Chief died. Deer Head died. Wren's baby died. They had not even named the boy yet.

He tried to avoid telling Wren, but when the men came to carry the bodies out, she knew. When they came to take her baby she tried to cling to it, but she was too ill and weak to make more than a token protest.

"Oh my father," she gasped. "Hold me!"

He put his arm around her fevered body, and she wept briefly, then sank into sleep. He let her lie back, knowing there was nothing more he could do for her. The demons had to be cast out from within. He went home to watch Tzec, who needed him too.

"Oh my love, what of my daughter?" Tzec asked. "What of her husband and son?"

"Her husband and son are dead," he said numbly, wishing she had not asked. "She is still living."

"Go to her. Keep her alive." She forestalled argument by sinking into sleep herself. She looked so old, like Twice Cursed. He realized with a start that she *was* as old as Twice Cursed when she had died. Tzec had been aging all the time. Only he himself seemed to be an unchanging age, and he knew that that was only from inside. Others saw him as an old man, though he felt much the same as he always had.

He returned to the Chief's lodge. All through the village he saw the bodies being hauled away, and heard the wailing of those who survived.

Wren was dead. He had missed her dying by returning to his wife.

He went back to Tzec, and found her dead also. He had missed *her* dying by returning to his daughter.

He was angry at being deprived of both their deaths, though they were his two deepest tragedies. Tzec, who had changed his life with the Tale of Little Blood, and then again by marrying him. Wren, who had endured the Castile captivity with him. His woman, his child. So like his two wives of the Principal People, mother and daughter, dying with their sons. No Spirit, Halfway Stream, Death Gift, the nameless son or grandson, gone.

The evil spirits had done it again. They had taken all his family from him, and deprived him of all whom he loved.

Those who had not been infested by the spirits at first were caught later. Now those who had survived the first attack tried to take care of these later ones, but they were no more effective than the others had been. The deaths continued. By the time it was done, half the people of the village were dead, and the survivors were weak and scarred.

Only Tale Teller had been spared. The spirits had not attacked him at all, this time. The magic crystal had protected him, yet this was also the cruelest possible punishment. Before, among the Principal People, he had been recovering from illness himself, and the deaths of the others had been somewhat muted. This time he had been fully alert throughout, knowing what was happening yet unable to prevent it. This time he could not retreat into the belief that his family was only working outside the lodge, and would soon return. This time he *knew*.

There was nothing to do but bury the dead. The bodies had been taken to the charnel platform at the mound by canoe; the traffic had been constant for half a moon. When the last one was there, it was time for the burial ceremony.

Every person of the village, male, female, and child, went to the mound, for otherwise the job would not have been possible. An assistant priest had survived; he was not qualified to handle the ceremony, but there was no one else, so he had to play the part of a full priest. The recent bodies were not properly prepared; there had not been time, and Death Gift was among their number. Even had the boy survived, there would have been far too much for him to do alone.

It was worse than that. Three tens of tens of people had died, half of all in this region, and many of those who lived remained weak. It was not possible to carry all the dead to the distant mound, or to bury them there; the job would kill the living from exhaustion. So most of the dead were simply hauled to the nearby marsh and dumped in, and some dirt was tossed on top to cover them. It was an ignominious burial, but better than no burial at all. The assistant priest did a ritual for them all, more than two tens of tens of them, and with that their spirits would have to be satisfied. Tale Teller thought of the bodies of the charnel platform near the Wide Water, their spirits enraged when they were dumped in the charnel pond, and only some of them pulled out and buried. This was like that, only this time it was by design. This marsh would be a terrible place for a long time, because of the justified rage of the spirits of those so poorly buried.

In some tribes it was the responsibility of the families to bury their own, and if an entire family died, the bodies were left lying where they were, unburied. But that could make a village uncomfortable, because of the smell. In any event, it was Toco custom to bury the dead, and if the family could not do it, others would. But the meanest bundle-burial in the mound would have been better than this marsh dumping.

As it was, the job of taking eight tens of bodies to the mound was awful. The bodies were decaying, and smelled bad, and they did not look very good either. Flies swarmed in to bite them. This was all right at the charnel platform, but not pleasant in the village. They put four in each canoe, and two paddlers would take it down the river, while the crew loaded the next canoe. Women and children worked at this as well as the men; there was no other way. Tale Teller did his part; he was able to lift an end of a body, and to paddle.

When they put Deer Head and Wren and her baby in a canoe, they also put Tzec and Death Gift there. That was the one Tale Teller paddled, with a tired young warrior at the front. They took the canoe along the familiar course down the river without talking.

Tale Teller stared at the bodies. They were dressed and wearing their most precious possessions, to accompany them to the spirit world. Deer Head had a necklace with ten and one valuable silver beads, another metal bead, and ten and nine shell beads. He could have traded these for many things in life, and might do so in death.

Wren had two tens and one shell bead strung around her neck, and three silver beads, and one blue glass bead on her clothing. Her baby, more important to the tribe than she, had six tens of silver beads, two fine gold beads, and a number of others, all strung around the body. If wealth was important to the spirits, the baby would almost certainly be a chief.

Death Gift rated inclusion among the chosen because he was a member of Wren's family and had served well in preparing other dead. He had two small silver beads and ten small purple seed beads. He had treasured them all in life, and surely would continue to value them. Tale Teller knew the boy was at home among the dead.

Tzec had traded or given away most of the beads she had gotten from the Castiles' buried horde, but she retained her most precious possession: a piece of iron from Castile armor. She wore ten and two shell beads around her neck, and a bead made from a bit of that iron which had broken off. She wore her best moss skirt. She was old, and dead, but she still looked beautiful to him, for he saw through the changes to the girl she had first been, who still lurked in the sunken outline of her face.

His second family, taken from him by the evil spirits who had taken his first. Now, again, painfully, in Tzec and Wren, he saw also Twice Cursed and Laurel, just as he saw his first two sons in his adopted son and natural grandson. Had he understood the message of the good spirits in time, and fetched the Ulunsuti, he could have saved his second family. Certainly he had been warned! How could he have been so foolish?

Numb, Tale Teller continued paddling.

They took down the charnel platform and smoothed the top of the mound, making it level. They brought the ceremonia bowls and pots and threw them down on the surface, breaking them, so that these dead utensils would serve the spirits. Then they laid out the bodies in rows, orienting each with its head to the north and west, as was the custom so that the spirits would not be confused as they freed themselves from the bodies and would know in which direction to go. The bundled bodies which had collected from the past ten winters were set around and between the primary burials; each new member of this mound would have several experienced spirits to help show the way or to perform routine chores. The spirits could not depart the region of the bodies until those bodies were formally buried, though all their flesh was gone; they had simply had to wait. Some other tribes killed servants for this purpose, but the Toco understood that those who had died normally would be willing to wait until a chief joined them, and then serve him. In this case it was the Chief and all his family and friends and their families, but the earlier dead would understand. The Toco were close in death as they were in life.

Tzec, well respected in the tribe because of her chiefly Maya ancestry and the kindnesses she had done for so many others, as well as for her birthing of the woman who had birthed the likely next chief in this or the spirit world, was given special honor in burial. She was placed in a sitting position, only her legs flexed back because there was no room for fully extended burials, and the iron plate was held in her right hand. She looked regal—yet still there was that girl of nine winters hiding behind the old body. She had changed Tale Teller's life in so many ways, and now she had left this world—and he could not join her.

Wren and Deer Head were set opposite, their heads pointing to the east of south, because of their spirit markings. The spirits of ordinary people would follow the ordinary course, but those marked by the spirits would receive special attention from the chiefs of the spirits, if properly identified. Their positions identified them, for the marks on their bodies would no longer show when their flesh was gone. Had Tale Teller been buried here, he would have had reverse orientation too, because of the mark Dead Eagle had put on him. But of course that was not to be. The spirits had made his unworthiness clear by refusing to take him when they took his family. The magic crystal had protected him, yet the final siege by a war party of spirits had never come. They had not even tried.

The burials should have been fully extended, but there were so many to do and there was so little space on the mound that it was necessary to flex the legs backwards at the knees. This was not normal procedure; indeed, as far as Tale Teller knew, it had never been done before. It was one of a number of serious compromises they had to make in order to get the job done. The few weak survivors simply did not have the strength to enlarge the mound enough for fully extended burials. They might not have the strength for even the reduced mound to be made.

When all of the bodies had been placed, the top of the mound was entirely covered. From a distance it might have seemed that a band of people had camped there, and were sleeping.

Now it was time for the hard work. A crew had been clearing the brush from two areas beside the mound, and women had been making special baskets with carry-straps that were strong enough and tight enough to hold sand. There were piles of loose sand in the cleared areas. The men, women, and children took up their baskets and walked to them. Tale Teller joined them; he could carry a basket well enough.

There were only a few good, big wooden scoops, so these were given to people to fill the baskets of the others. A line formed, but it was not long. In a moment Tale Teller was having his basket filled by a woman who scooped in the sand while he held the basket in place. Then she helped him heave it up across his back so that he could catch hold of the strap and keep it there. He walked, and he bore the heavy burden around and to the edge of the mound.

He paused as the man ahead of him dumped his load of sand and went on around the mound. The priest had set up the path in a circular pattern so that there would be no confusion and no colliding. All the workers were grief-stricken, as was Tale Teller; it was best for them to focus on their own thoughts and just follow the ones in front as they worked.

Tale Teller dumped his load beside the last one. The sand fell on the face of a woman and trickled down around her head and neck. It seemed cruel to cover her like this, smothering her. Yet of course the dead could not smother, and the spirits needed to have their bodies properly interred. This was what gave the spirits their freedom.

He shook out his basket and turned to the right. This brought him to the second pile of sand, where a boy was ready with his scoop. Most of the carriers were men and most of the scoopers were women and children, because they were not able to carry as much.

Tale Teller heaved up his basket again and walked on. This time there was a low ramp being formed at the end of the mound. He went to the end of this and dumped his load, then stepped off and walked around to the first pile of sand, completing the circuit.

He lost count of the circuits he made, being aware only of the diminishing size of the piles of sand on the side, and the increasing size of the central mound. The day grew hot, but the work continued. Those who became too tired changed places with the scoopers or took lighter loads; no one stopped working.

Some things stood out from the rest of that dreary day. He blinked at one point to discover that the body he was covering was that of his wife. Tzec was facing him, her eyes closed but perhaps seeing him. Because of her posture, her head remained in view after the rest of her body was covered. "Oh Tzec, I love you," he breathed.

I always loved you, Tale Teller, she replied. *I want you with me, here.*

"No! I am unworthy! I failed to fetch the Ulunsuti!"

Dead Eagle says the northern spirits made a mistake, she said. *Your family was supposed to be spared, and especially Gray Cloud, to help you fetch it. Without him, you could not get it.*

"But I renounced the spirits!"

In that you were wrong, and it is the root of your failure. But the spirits were wrong first. Dead Eagle will accept you here at this mound. Your spirit can join ours. We can remain together.

But he wasn't sure. He turned, and saw the woman who followed standing behind him, waiting with her basket of sand. Embarrassed, he started to apologize, but she shook her head. "We all understand," she said. "She was a great woman, and your wife." Then she dumped her sand, covering part of Tzec's face.

By the time he had completed the next circuit, Tzec was hidden. His mind returned to numbness.

By nightfall the job was done. The central mound had expanded hugely, mountainous compared with the original mound, and the piles of sand at the sides had become broad, shallow pits into which the water was seeping. A broad ramp led to the top of the mound, which was flat.

Now they started the ceremony. This was normally limited to males, with the women making and serving the White Drink, but there were not enough strong males to do the dead proper honor. They allowed females, but took only those who wished to do it, and who had labored on the sand hauling. They cut off their hair in the same fashion as the mourning men, so that they were now symbolic men. "They have done the work, they have shorn their hair, they grieve as we do," the assistant priest said. He turned to Tale Teller. "You have communed with the spirits. Do they dishonor women who come to honor the dead?"

The priest was plainly wrong on protocol, but right in the necessity of the situation. "There are female spirits too," Tale Teller replied. "My wife has said nothing to oppose a woman who will bear the burden of a man. But if there is objection, let the women honor only the female spirits of this mound."

After that there were no objections, for Tzec was the most respected woman of the village, and she had always been outspoken about the rights of women. They knew she would accept the honor of living women.

So the women donned shawls, covering their breasts, and with their shorn hair they lacked any female appeal. They painted their faces and stood erect, in the manner of men. The other women were put in charge of the children, who went to a temporary lodge made nearby, where they ate and slept.

The mourners walked to the east side of the mound, and faced it. The sun was just setting; the timing was important. Four men brought out bows. The priest had a basket of arrows. He drew one out. "Two whom does this arrow belong?" he asked.

There was a pause. A warrior knew all of his arrows, but

others did not. So many warriors were dead that it would be impossible to know to whom each of these belonged. By agreement, they belonged to no one, until this moment.

Then a woman spoke. "It belongs to my cousin the Chief. I will take it for him."

"Take it," the priest agreed.

She approached, and he gave her the arrow. She carried it to the nearest bow-man. "I bring you the Chief's arrow, to salute him and to be with him in his death, that his spirit may have it for good hunting."

"For the Chief, I shoot his arrow," the warrior said. He strung it and drew it back and fired it toward the sun, low, into the east side of the mound. The head was embedded in the sand, but the end of the shaft showed.

The priest drew out another arrow. "To whom does this arrow belong?"

"It belongs to my wife, Tzec, from the land of the Maya," Tale Teller said, for after the Chief, she was the most respected person buried here.

"Take it."

Tale Teller took it and brought it to the second bow-man. "I bring you my wife's arrow, that her spirit may be protected by it."

"For your wife, I shoot this arrow." The man fired it into the sun and the mound.

So it continued, until every arrow in the basket was gone. There was one for each of the primary burials, whether extended or flexed, but not for the ones from the prior winters. They had had to wait until a chief died, and their honors had not been forgotten, merely postponed. But they were not worthy of individual attention at this time, having had it at the time they were brought to the charnel platform. Because there were more burials than people participating in this ceremony, some had to go twice. It didn't matter; what mattered was that the ritual be observed for each person buried, and that he be named and honored and receive his arrow.

When it was done, the east side of the mound had so many shafts projecting from it that it resembled a huge cactus. But every person had been named, and everyone had his own arrow.

The sun was down. It was time for the next stage of the ceremony. They walked around the mound to the opposite side, where the ramp had been formed. It had not been for the sand-haulers to use, but for this aspect of the ceremony.

They formed into a line to the west of the mound, with the fading glow of the set sun at their backs, and marched to the ramp and up it to the top. They stood at intervals, facing the center, forming a pattern.

The group sat cross-legged on the flat surface of the mound, in a circle. The dead were close beneath them, but that was the point: it was time to do the spirits further honor, so that they would rest in peace. Torches were set in the center of the circle, lighting the faces of those opposite. The people smeared themselves with bear grease containing the repellent herb, so that the mosquitoes would not come.

The women came, bearing cups for the White Drink. It was black in color, of course, but that meant nothing. It was called white because it symbolized purity, joy, and harmony. The women brewed it from the leaves of a variety of holly which they cultivated for this purpose. While the men and male-women had labored with the baskets of sand, the others had brought the leaves and twigs that had been roasted before, and boiled them in water until the liquid was dark brown. Now it was ready, and they dipped it out and poured it through a strainer into the cups to cool. One woman tested it by pouring it over her fingers. It did not scald them, so it was ready to be given to the men.

Tale Teller accepted his cup, and waited until the last person had been served. Then they all slowly lifted their cups and sipped the hot brew. It was bitter, but bracing.

When a lot of White Drink was taken, it made people vomit. But that was for purification. This time they were here to honor the dead, having been purified already by grief and labor. Also, there was not enough White Drink to allow them all to consume enough for vomiting.

He saw the person on his right glance at his cup. It was the woman who had followed him during the day, waiting while he talked with Tzec the last time before burying her. She had never participated in this ceremony before, and was uncertain how to proceed, so was watching him for guidance. She was now a mock man, unattractive with her hacked hair, and like a man, could not admit confusion or ignorance.

He lifted his cup again, slowly, and sipped. She did the same. He lowered his cup, closing his eyes, savoring the bitterness. It was an echo of the bitterness in his heart for the loss of all he loved.

The night deepened, but Tale Teller was not cold. The White Drink invigorated him and gave him warmth; in fact he was lightly sweating. His mind clarified and his thoughts were heightened. He now gained perspective on the course of his life, and the lives of others, seeing them all as cords in the greatest of baskets, each one necessary to its stability, yet each one beginning and ending within it. His own cord was longer than those of most others, five tens of winters, but without the intertwining cords of the Trader and Tzec and Beautiful Moon and Gray Cloud and Twice Cursed and Laurel and Tzec again, his own cord would fall out of the basket and be lost. Now those other cords were ended, and his had no reason to continue; the basket was complete.

With this realization came the revelation of his proper course. He would remain here to make his apology to Dead Eagle, and tell the Spirit of the Mound about those cords, so that the nature of the basket might be known. He was the Tale Teller; it was his job to tell the tales, and this would be his final telling. Once he had done that telling, his life would have no further significance.

The dawn came. Somehow the night had passed, though his thoughts had seemed to occupy only a brief time. The faces of the others around the circle seemed similarly surprised. It had been good, communing with the spirits of the dead, and there had been no evil consequence because of the presence of a few women in the circle. The spirits had indeed understood.

The priest got to his feet. His legs, like those of the rest of them, were evidently kinked, and he swayed a bit before getting his balance. "Now we must perform the dance of death," he said, lifting his empty cup.

The others got up and lifted their cups. They stood in their places in the circle. Then they began to move, circling slowly to the left, the direction of undoing, stamping their feet. It was a solemn dance, showing their grief. The heaviness of their footfalls derived from the heaviness of their hearts.

The priest moved to the center, signaling the final stage. He drew two lines in the sand from north to south, marking a broad path across it. He stood in the center of this path. "I have drunk from this cup in honor of the dead," he said. "Now I give it to the spirits. I kill it, that it may serve them as it served me." He flung his cup down at his feet, so hard that it shattered and the fragments scattered. Then he turned and walked slowly down the ramp, away from the rising sun.

The others followed his lead. They flung down their cups so that they shattered. Indeed, these were special cups, made to be delicate so that they would readily break. But many of the people had used shell cups, which would not shatter, so they merely set them down within the spirit path and left them there. The spirits knew what would break and what would not. Soon all of the mourners were down the ramp and away from the mound.

It was done. "Fetch the women and children," the priest said. "We will return to the village."

The women and children were ready to go, having watched the concluding ceremony from a distance. They had put out their fire and taken apart their temporary lodge; it too had been killed, to serve the spirits of the mound. They brought the large empty bowls used for the White Drink, and these too were broken in the path.

It was done. The sand covered all the bodies, though it was not as deep as it should be. The ceremony of the night had been completed, though not as well as it should have been. The spirits might have some difficulties setting out on their journey, and the aspect of those spirits that remained here at the mound would not be allowed to be completely comfortable, but it had to be enough. It was better than those dumped in the swamp.

It was done. It was done.

They walked east to the river where the canoes were. But Tale Teller lagged, and slipped away when no one was watching. The others were so tired they probably would not miss him; each would assume that he was in some other canoe. By

the time they verified his absence, he would be finished here.
For he alone was not yet done.

He made his way back to the mound. He walked up the
ramp and sat on the center. "O Spirit of the Mound, I am the
Tale Teller," he said. "I am dying..."

"And these are my tales, O Spirit. I beg you to accept them,
and to accept the good people who have joined you in your
mound, for they are blameless. They would not be here now,
had I been true to my commitment and honored your mission.
I was fallible, I misunderstood, I was weak and tortoise-headed
and foolish. I renounced you and failed to fetch the Ulunsuti.
But I beg you also to let me die here, though I cannot be buried
here, so that my spirit may at least see the spirits of my loved
ones as they set out on their journey west to the land of the
spirits, and yours, O Dead Eagle."

A day has passed, and a night, and a day—I have not
counted them, for they do not matter. I have been intent only
on telling my tales. My tales of the Trader, and the Cacique
of the Calusa, and Heron Feather, and Beautiful Moon, and
Doña Margarita, and Gray Cloud and Black Bone, and especially of my wives and children. They were all good people.
I have told also of the bad people, the Castiles with Chief de
Soto, and the one good man among them, Juan Ortiz. I have
told of the message of Sun Eagle, that we not tire the land
and make it desolate. I have not eaten, and have drunk
nothing since the White Drink. Now my vision is blurred and
my voice is hoarse and my body sags; I am dying, but my
tales have been told, and my loved ones are known. I have
done what I can do.

"I beg you, O Spirit: now let me complete my death, here
where at least for a little while I can be with those I love. With
Tzec and Wren, and through them with Twice Cursed and
Laurel. Let me do this, before the animals drag away my body
and foul it, and doom my spirit to eternal shame. This much
done, O Spirit!"

Give me the magic crystal.

I lift it from my neck and over my head. I try to stand, holding
on its cord, but my legs will not respond; they have no feeling.
Here, O Spirit." I hold it out.

Bury it.

I lean forward and scoop out a place in the sand before me. I make a hole. I set the magic crystal in it, and cover it up. Now I can die, for the crystal no longer protects me.

The threat to your people was greater than I knew. The threat was to all the people of this land. I thought the Ulunsuti could abolish it, but it would have saved only your village, not the others, and in the end the result would have been the same. The failure was not yours alone, Tale Teller; it was mine, and all the people's and all the spirits'. Our way of existence is doomed. I accept your crystal, and I return to you your fear.

"I thank you, O Spirit."

I accept your body here.

I looked up. "But I cannot be here, O Spirit! There is no one to bury me."

Gaze into the sun.

I look toward the west, where the sun is setting. It is blindingly brilliant. Then I see a motion; the trees are swaying as if being pushed by some giant creature, but there is no creature. There is no sound, yet something huge seems to be there. Then it comes into sight. It is a monstrous serpent, as big around as a great tree trunk, with rings of color along its length.

"The Uktena!" I breathe. "I did not find it—so it has found me!"

The serpent turns toward me. It has horns on its head, and its scales glitter like sparks of fire. On its forehead is a brightly blazing crest.

"The Ulunsuti!" I cry. "The transparent crystal!"

But I cannot have it. It is too late; the evil spirits have killed all those I know and love. I would have had to kill the Uktena to get it, and I know now that I could not have done that ever in my health, even without fear, because I was not a warrior. Now there is no chance at all, for the Uktena has come to kill me.

Terror rises up in me as the giant snake slithers toward me, but I cannot flee. My legs will not work. I cannot fight the monster. My arm will not work. I cannot look away from it. My neck will not work. I am dazed by the brilliance of the crystal, and I can only wait for the jaws of the Uktena. It slides up on the mound, its mouth gaping. Its great teeth glisten with saliva.

Yet even in my terror, I feel a deep background joy. *My fear is back! I am whole again!*

I scream. Then all is light.

AUTHOR'S NOTE

Tale Teller believed that he would not be buried with those he loved, and that his body would be dragged away by animals and his bones ignominiously scattered and lost. That his vital spirit would be humiliated and dissipated because of his lack of burial. But this was not the case.

We can reconstruct from the evidence of the mound what happened to him. The others of the village realized that he was missing, but assumed he had gone to some other village. Only when they compared notes did they realize that he had never returned with them. Then a small party went back to the mound, fearing some desecration. Several days had passed.

They found Tale Teller's body hunched on top of the mound, facing west. There was no mark on him, but he was dead and his magic crystal was gone. Since there was no evidence of any other presence, they assumed that the spirits had killed him and taken back their crystal. But the spirits had not removed him from the mound, so it meant he was supposed to remain there. This was not surprising, since he had been an honored member of the community.

They dug a hole in the south side of the mound, where there were no burials to be disturbed, and dragged him to it. They flexed his body tightly, knees brought up to chin, to take up less room, but it tended to unfold, perhaps because he was too freshly dead and had too much flesh on him, or possibly because the spirits were interfering. So they shoved him in on his left side, compacting him by the pressure of the sand of the interior, and filled in the hole. It wasn't much of a burial, and the position was wrong, but it had to suffice. They were warriors, not priests, knowing no better. At least he was with his family, and his spirit should rest.

They returned to Toco Atafi ("Old" Toco village), which de Soto had mispronounced as Tocaste, and reported. The priest shook his head at the blundering manner of it, but agreed that they had done the best they could. There were other things to attend to, for the people were leaving their ill-fated village. They had to, to escape the malice of the shamefully buried spirits in the swamp. Some were going south by foot, carrying their belongings, to join relatives in villages which had not been destroyed by the evil spirits. Some were packing their canoes, to travel by the water to villages closer to the coast. They never returned. Atafi and Ibi Hica ("River Village") were deserted, and their locations remain unknown at this writing. Indeed, Tatham Mound itself was unknown until recently, and the neighboring Ruth Smith Mound was rifled and finally flattened by bulldozers, its history lost. That was the one used by the villagers of Ibi Hica, and others of that region. Tatham Mound was the only one to remain to demonstrate the presence and tragedy of these people.

Archaeologists had believed that the Safety Harbor culture did not extend this far north, until these discoveries. We do not even know their language or cultural affinities. I assumed for the purpose of this novel that the Toco, known to history after a village in the Tampa Bay region of Florida as the Tocobaga (Toco Chief Baga's village), were affiliated with the large Timucuan family of tribes of northern Florida. The word "toco" means "come out" or "withdraw," or even "desire" in Timucua, which suggests that they did indeed come out from the larger group, desiring to go their own way. The meanings of the few native words I use are derived from the Timucuan dialects. I assume further that the Timucua were more loosely affiliated to the larger Muskogean group of tribes who occupied what is now southeast United States, and that their culture represented a variant of this. We simply do not know—because there are no Toco survivors today. Apparently the white man's diseases wiped out all of them, leaving the region empty until the Seminoles, who were of Muskogean stock, moved in. Hence my description of Toco ways is limited and general and largely borrowed from the ways of other tribes, because I did not want to go beyond what could have been.

Actually, much of what we do know, in the popular sense, is wrong. The names of tribes and groups listed on the maps are seldom the ones the people used for themselves. Often we took as their names the insulting epithets their enemies gave them. Even our innocent ignorance would have been funny at times. For example, the Muskogee group of tribes we call Creek—because one tribe lived near a creek, of all things. But the designation Muskogee is no better: it means swamp. In truth, these were the People of One Fire, because they shared the ceremony of rekindling the sacred fire each year. They were cultural heirs to what is archaeologically the Hopewell Tradition, with its elaborate ancient temple mounds. The Hopewell culture was fading by A.D. 400, but some striking mounds were constructed thereafter, such as the complex at Cahokia, which Tale Teller saw in a historical vision as the Pyramid of the Sun. We know of the phenomenal trading empires of such cultures only vaguely, and choose to believe that North America was inhabited by primitives.

Tale Teller's incapacity of the shoulder was not evident on his bones. It was actually an injury of the tendon, scarring it so that it adhered to the flesh around it and became inflamed, reducing the mobility of the arm. With modern surgery he could have regained the full use of that arm. Because the eagle-shaped external scar marked him as a person set apart by the spirits, he should have been buried with his head to the east-southeast, but the warriors who found him did not realize that. This shows why a thing as important as a burial should not be left to amateurs. (Actually, archaeologists do not know why some burials were "backwards," but I am free to have it my way here.)

The others named are also in the mound, as described, along with the pottery and arrowheads. (The arrow shafts were of wood, and soon rotted away, their possible traces obliterated by the digging and sifting of the archaeological crew.) Tzec still clutched her metal sheet, and Wren's son, buried with her, retained his fine collection of beads, including the two gold ones. Even the archaeologists marveled at the contours of Wren's "gracile" skeleton.

For archaeological purposes, the skeletons were numbered, roughly in the order of their being excavated, which may have been opposite to the order of their being buried. Thus they are listed in the records approximately as follows:

Tzec—#7 Elderly female, interred in sitting or reclining position, arms folded across abdomen, knees flexed. (She was only forty-four, but had aged rapidly in the last decade; I'm not sure whether it was a slow illness or genetic, but the effect was to make her seem older than she was, through to the bones.)

Tale Teller—#16 Adult male, flexed on left side, intrusive burial. (He was the opposite, seeming younger than he was. At fifty, he was among the oldest of the tribe.)

Deer Head—#58 Adult male, legs flexed over chest, head east-southeast. (Opposite the majority.)

Wren—#66 Adult female, supine, legs flexed over chest, head east-southeast. (Opposite the majority.)

Baby—#73 Young infant or full-term fetus recovered adjacent to pelvic bones of Burial #66.

Death Gift—#79 Approximately eight-year-old (based on dental eruption) child, supine, legs flexed over chest. (He was two years older, but retarded by early privation.)

The other burials are similarly listed, and represent rather dry reading for non-archaeologists. The collections of beads associated with each burial are as described.

What of the original mound, and who was Dead Eagle, with whom Tale Teller had communion? This is an interesting situation. What was originally thought to be a single mound, when Brent Weisman found it, turned out to be two: a smaller, older mound within the larger new one. Thus it existed for centuries before being augmented by the Toco tribesmen we know of as the Safety Harbor culture. There were only about twenty-four burials in that mound, compared with more than three hundred in the later mound, and it seems to have been a burial place for the elite. It also seems, like the later mound, to have been a single-episode interment: that is, all the bodies were placed there at one time. This does not mean they all died at the same time; as the novel shows, bodies were normally saved, defleshed, bundled, and buried only when a chief needed to be buried.

Attempts to date the lower mound precisely have been frustrating; with all the sophisticated modern methods, there was little general agreement. Therefore I make a somewhat arbitrary ballpark assignment: this mound dates from perhaps the year A.D. 1200 (the radiocarbon date from one artifact suggests as early as A.D. 1,000), compared to perhaps A.D. 1550 for the later mound. At least one of the burials was flexed at the knees, in the manner of many in the later mound. That was probably another "intrusive" burial, actually associated with the later group. What makes this unusual is that nowhere else among American Indians is this mode of knee-flex burial known. The orientation of the bodies differed, too, appearing to be random; Burial #102 had the head pointing north, and Burial #105 the head pointing south. The latter seems to have been fully extended, with three hundred and thirty shell beads on the right wrist and the legs, and a copper plume ornament at the right shoulder, a copper ear spool at the head, and a second cranium by the chest: perhaps part of a trophy skull. This was evidently a person of extraordinary significance, and the probable identity of Dead Eagle.

A large circular copper plate was between #105 and #102, more than a foot in diameter. Beneath it was the body of an infant (Burial #133). The situation seems obvious: Chief, wife, and child. Copper was rare and precious, and was not wasted on low-status burials. The other burials could be of servants, or of prior bodies from the charnel structure.

The problem is that initial examination suggests that both #105 and #102 are female. Could Dead Eagle have been a woman? Then where was the father of the baby? These bones were placed a long time ago, and are poorly preserved, so the sexual persuasion is not obvious. Further studies are being done, and in due course we may have the answer. In the interim, another arbitrary decision: Dead Eagle was a man. Certainly he presented himself to Tale Teller as male.

It is chancy at best to extrapolate an entire culture from one of its burial mounds. I, as author of this novel, had to make many fundamental assumptions, some of which may be ludicrously inaccurate. What, for example, was the population of the region served by this mound? We cannot simply count the bodies in it and make an estimate from that. We do not know the turnover: if the people lived long, fewer bodies per year would be produced than if they tended to die young. We do not know how many mounds there were, because developers and farmers tended to erase them as impediments to progress, so there may be no record of many that once existed. The significance of Tatham Mound is that it was discovered intact and untouched, so that its precise nature could be determined—and even then it turned out to be a considerable challenge. We do not know whether it was one of half a dozen serving the local population, or whether it was limited to some special segment of that population, or whether bodies flocked to it from miles around for the honor of residing in it.

I assume that the site of the old mound was reactivated immediately after de Soto passed this region, because the other burial site was obviously bad medicine after such an occurrence, resulting in the displeasure of the spirits. I am assuming that it was the principal burial site for the village of Atafi for the years 1539–1550, and that all villagers came to it in due course. With one major exception: the impossible situation resulting from the plague. At such time as a cache of two-hundred and twenty bodies is discovered in the muck bordering Lake Tsala Apopka, I will stand vindicated on that.

As I make it, the village of Atafi had a population of about six hundred men, women, and children. They lived an average of thirty years. This may seem low, but one reference claims that few lived to the age of forty, and life was harsh compared with what we know. Many children could have died young, and women in childbirth, and men in war. A man could live to the age of fifty—Tale Teller did—but he would be a patriarch. At any rate, a community of this description would produce about twenty bodies a year, and in eleven years about two hundred and twenty would accumulate. Those are the bundled burials. I assume that the smallpox plague killed half the population of the village. That was typical of its devastation. About eighty bodies were conveyed to the mound for formal burial along with the accumulated bundles, and the rest were shamefully dumped in the muck. Thus the tally actually found in the mound.

Another assumption: the existence of a contraceptive herbal preparation, universally used. The Indians had wholesome attitudes about natural functions, and there were no bad words in this connection. Thus a man could be named Bear Penis without embarrassment, and a child could watch her parents copulate, learning how to do it. Young women were generally encouraged to make free sexual use of their bodies before marriage, and in some tribes, after marriage too, with such men as they might choose. Their clothing was conducive: bare breasts, and the "moss" skirts, which were fashioned from what we call Spanish moss, an air plant dangling from trees in the southern states, especially Florida. They could weave this moss into a fine fabric, or wear it loose; either way, we can be sure it showed precisely as much young flesh as they desired, in a most intriguing way. Men generally cooperated, indulging in sex with any young women who expressed the interest, and not forcing any who did not. I have avoided euphemisms, such as "making love," or use of the ellipsis, and have told it as I believe my Indian Tale Teller would have: penis into cleft. Why conceal the details of an act which carried no negative onus and which the participants enjoyed so much?

Before marriage, it seems to have been the women who made the choice about sexual indulgence; after marriage it may have been otherwise. But it was important for babies to be legitimate; it was an insult to be accused of being without a father. How did women avoid getting pregnant in the unmarried state? I assume that the Indians knew several times as much about herbs as we credit; perhaps the moralistic Spanish and English missionaries suppressed any such information, so it did not come to us. A bitter herb topically applied might have done the job, and to mask the bitterness it was mixed with honey, and this had the coincidental effects of making the act easy and conducive: the odor of honey in a friendly young woman became aphrodisiac. Who is to say it was not so? I think they must have had similar potions against mosquitoes and biting flies. We now know that some of these supposedly spurious remedies did work; there are books on the medicinal qualities of particular plants. Because my protagonist was not a priest, this information was not his right; he depended on the priest in much the way we depend on the doctor, knowing little about the origin of the pills we are given.

I did not wish to confuse my readers, but there was no way

I could use modern names for places. Thus the Mayaimi was not the region of Miami, but Lake Okeechobee by its earlier name. The mounds of that vicinity shown in Chapter 7 are now known as the Fort Center complex; otherwise they are and were as described. This is associated with the Belle Glade culture, an evident precursor to the Calusa in this region but probably not of the same stock. The spirits' misfortune is our fortune, for the burning and collapse of the charnel platform resulted in the preservation of the marvelous wood carvings, demonstrating the nature of this prehistoric Indian art. Fish Eater River is now Fisheating Creek, except that access to it is now more difficult.

Time was another problem. As far as I can tell, the Indians had months (moons) and years (winters), but not weeks or hours or minutes. There are thirteen moons in a year, but that's close enough to what we use. They also did not use our measurements of miles and feet or kilometers and meters. They surely did have units of measurements, but not what would be familiar to us. Thus I was constrained to develop the awkwardness of "the time the sun would have taken to move one finger in a ten-finger sky," or a bit over an hour, and to estimate the height of a mound in terms of several heights of a man. I had two cultures in mind as my audience: the one I was trying to represent, and the one of today, and I did not want to be false to either.

I like games of all kinds, and they come into my fiction frequently. I had several books of Indian games, one of them a detailed manual of eight hundred pages. Alas, my protagonist did not share my fascination, so they hardly show in this novel, except for the organized ball games. Should I ever write another novel of this type, I will draw on those neglected references. It is one of the frustrations of research that only a fraction of it can be used, and not necessarily the most interesting fraction.

In some cases I had to choose between differing versions of things described in the research books, and sometimes I had either to elaborate or to simplify. This is, after all, a novel, and clarity and interest are important. An archaeologist cares about whether a potsherd (that's sherd, not shard) is Pasco Plain or St. Johns Check Stamped, but the average reader cares about whether de Soto made it with the Lady of Cofitachequi. (Yes

I don't know how to pronounce it either; I settled on COF-it-a-CHE-kee.) For the record, the pottery described in the novel is Pasco Plain, which was by far the most prevalent found in the mound. And as for the Lady—as far as we know, Hernando de Soto did like the look of her, for she really was a lovely creature, but he did not touch her sexually. She did escape in the manner described. I elaborated by having my characters Tale Teller and Wren advise her on the need to escape, and I simplified by deleting reference to what happened to her thereafter, because I regarded it as unsubstantiated rumor. The story was that several slaves escaped on the same day she did, one of whom was Moorish, and that she was seen living with the Moor as his wife. The implication is that he helped her and she rewarded him. I prefer to remember that she was an acting Chief, the niece of a female Chief, and believe that she would have hurried back to resume her duties at her home village. That does not exclude the Moor, of course, but why take a slave who doesn't speak her language when she could surely have her pick of native warriors? I suspect the rumor was intended to discredit her reputation with the white man.

This business of taking the Lady and other Chiefs prisoner, after they had befriended de Soto, needs explaining. Other Spanish explorers had little success in Florida, but de Soto was more professional. He knew that the natives would not give up their houses, food, and women without objection, no matter what they said before they appreciated the full price of the Spaniards' visit. He knew they were not innocent children without means of striking back. Columbus had left a garrison when he first came to the New World, only to discover it destroyed when he returned months later. The men had annoyed the natives, probably by stealing their food and women, and the Indians had retaliated by killing the offenders. So de Soto routinely made friendly overtures, then took the Chief hostage so that the Indians would not attack the party. He would let the Chief go once he was safely through that Chief's territory; it was time to take a new hostage. If the natives attacked anyway, then the life of the hostage was forfeit. This was hard politics, but effective; it led to real trouble only when de Soto got careless or when he was misinformed, as we have seen.

One spongy area was the location of the Cherokee tribe. (The

Principal People, as they called themselves, are known to our history as the Cherokee.) I have de Soto passing through its region and encountering several villages, but authorities differ on exactly where the Cherokee lived at the time of discovery. They were culturally affiliated with the Iroquois to the north, but had been separated for some time. Was it decades or centuries? My judgment is the latter, so I feel de Soto did encounter them, though there is no firm record of this. They were the largest individual tribe of the Southeast, but relatively gentle, so there were no significant battles in their territory.

The Spaniards, and later the British, were experienced in war, and they almost invariably prevailed when it came to pitched battle. On occasion the slaughter of enemies on the battlefield or after their defeat was tremendous. Many captives did die because of harsh treatment. But by far the greatest devastation to the natives was because of a factor the white man did not realize at the time: disease. The Indians were not acclimatized to European diseases, so were more vulnerable to them. Estimates of pre-contact Indian population have varied widely; I believe I once saw one of 300,000 in all of North America, which suggests perhaps a million in the western hemisphere; but the *Atlas of Ancient America* says there were about forty million. It has been claimed that the western continents were thinly populated, the implication being that this was a waste of good land that needed the fulfillment of European colonization. It was thinly populated only after the white man's diseases decimated it. The actual reduction may have been to five percent—that is, nineteen of every twenty Indians died.

Here is a partial listing of the responsible diseases: smallpox, measles, bubonic plague, typhus, mumps, influenza, yellow fever, and vectored fever. (That is, a disease transferred by a vector, such as mosquitoes, perhaps malaria.) My judgment is that smallpox was introduced by the explorer Alonzo Alvarez de Piñeda, who ranged the coast of the Gulf of Mexico in 1519, causing a five-year epidemic in Florida which probably spread to the interior undocumented. It may have been introduced again by Lucas Vasquez de Ayllon, who founded a colony in what is now South Carolina in 1526; he and many colonists died, and it probably spread inland through the Indian tribes. Thus in 1529 I have it reaching the territory of the Catawba and the Cherokee with devastating effect. There is no historical record of this particular plague, but there is reference to plagues of the past which wiped out entire regions, and I believe my case is credible. As we have seen with the settlement near Tatham Mound, such destruction of population can extirpate all historical reference to a region, so that it is assumed to have been empty. But for the evidence of the mounds and the shell middens—the refuse left from settlements—and spot references to the region by the chronologies of the de Soto expedition, we would not know these people had ever existed here.

There had been measles or typhus in Florida in 1528. I assume that it was what took out the captives at de Soto's winter camp in north Florida in 1535–40. An unidentified plague did occur in 1535–39 with high mortality. So I gave my characters measles, which they survived, though few other Indians with de Soto did. Bear in mind that measles is not necessarily a minor childhood disease; it brought me as a teenager as close to death as I have been, and without intravenous feeding I might not have survived it. For the Indians, chained and hungry and inadequately protected against the winter, it would have been worse. Then in 1550 I show smallpox, finishing the story. That disease was known before and after, and was probably traveling slowly through the Indian population, wiping out just such communities as this one. Certainly some disease was responsible; the abrupt onslaught of bodies and subsequent abandonment of the mound and villages indicate that. The reason Tale Teller alone was unaffected was that he had been exposed to smallpox before, survived it, and was now immune. He died of exposure and dehydration, not of the attack of evil spirits or the monster horned serpent. At least this is the interpretation our culture puts on it, as our mythology differs from that of the Indians. We suppose he would have died even if he had not removed the magic crystal.

Speaking of mythology: I wanted to provide information not only about the everyday lives and interests of these people, but also about their framework of beliefs. Thus I presented several of their stories and myths, ranging from brief references to the fifteen-thousand-word adaptation of the Quiché Mayan "Little Blood," from the *Popol Vuh*. I used our common terms for things where they seemed applicable, even in the stories, such as "buffalo." What point to insist on the technically correct "American bison" when both the red man and the white man knew these great animals for what they were?

Readers will have to make their own judgments about things like the Ulunsuti crystal. Two quartz crystals were found in the mound, and these were indeed regarded as stones with magical powers. Many Indian tribes in what is now southeastern United States treasured such crystals, believing them to have the power, among other things, to show the future. Similar crystals are available today as jewelry, and I suspect that some folk who wear them are conscious of the powers the Indians ascribed to them. They are about one inch long, translucent, and hexagonally faceted. The lesser of those in the mound is the one I think Twice Cursed gave to Tale Teller, and that he finally gave to the mound so that he could expire. It had preserved his life and his youth to a considerable extent, but it was time for him to die. To what degree belief can make a thing real we do not know, but the so-called placebo effect makes a case for it. Our culture has legends about the powers of the chalice known as the Holy Grail; the magic crystal known as the Ulunsuti seems as reasonable as this. Was fetching it an impossible quest? Was it really Tale Teller's failure that prevented the Toco from foreseeing and avoiding the evil spirits who destroyed them? Who can say?

Did Tale Teller really talk to the spirits of the dead? Our culture would say he was deceiving himself or suffering visions. Certainly he waffled some on exactly what the spirits told him, interpreting it first one way and then another, according to his personal desires. But this is human nature, and does not reflect accurately on the validity of spiritual communion. His culture might say that our information about the death and resurrection of Jesus Christ and the occurrence of miracles in His name are of similar validity. Certainly there are many today who say they receive messages from the dead, and these too can be subject to self-interested interpretation. It behooves us not to be too critical of beliefs which are serious in other cultures. I, as a complete skeptic about the supernatural, nevertheless appreciate the power of faith: what a person truly believes may indeed be true, for him. Thus if he believes he has no fear, then he has none. If he believes the spirits speak to him and show him history, as did those of Cahokia Mounds in what is now Illinois near St. Louis, then perhaps they did.

Some may question the reference to scalping in the first and sixteenth chapters. Scalping was not a general practice among the Indians originally; it was spread across the continent mainly by the efforts of the white man. But it did exist in one region: the Southeast. So the Toco might have practiced it, and surely they knew of it. Certainly the practice of cutting out beating hearts existed among the Maya and Aztec (Mexica), as described.

There is one major thing I did to which purists may take exception. I gave my characters a roughly contemporary outlook and feelings. That is, Tale Teller's thoughts and reactions are very much like those a modern person would experience if he found himself in similar situations. The same is true for Tzec and the other major characters. Now, I do believe that all human beings are essentially similar, once the trappings of their particular cultures are stripped away; all love and fear and seek their own advantage while believing that they are in some fashion superior to others. But it is more than that. This is a commercial novel, which means it is intended to appeal to a wide readership. The average reader does not relate well to characters who do not in some way resemble that reader. So, unable to determine the true inner nature of the folk who were buried in Tatham Mound, I elected to make them much like us, in the hope that this would lead to a better understanding of their situation than would otherwise be likely. If you felt joy and grief when the characters did, and cared what happened to them, then this effort has been successful even if it is not precisely true to what actually happened. I do believe in the humanity of my subjects, here.

Reference was made in the Introduction to the financing of the excavation of the mound by the parents of one of the participants. Archaeologists have a real problem obtaining funds for their work, because our culture seems to be more interested in organized spectator sports than in scientific research. Any person who is interested in helping archaeological exploration should get in touch with the nearest university; the people there will be glad to clarify what is going on and to accept any contribution. As it happened, there were several projects in Florida at this time. One was across the state, where actual brain tissue had been found. But Tatham Mound was in a relative backwater and related to an obscure culture; it lacked the interest of more dramatic discoveries. Its chances for adequate financing were relatively poor. Except for chance circumstances that would represent poor plotting if written into fiction.

I married the smartest woman I could catch, so that I could have smart children. One daughter was in college, and the other was doing very well in high school and pursuing many interests. We make it a policy to support our children's interests to the degree feasible and appropriate. Also, I had resolved when I was poor that if I ever got rich I would use my money for more beneficial purposes than those to which I saw others contributing. Increasingly, I am doing that. Thus it was that when Cheryl took an interest in archaeology, her mother went with her on "digs" and took her to the meetings of the Withlacoochee River Archaeology Council, abbreviated WRAC. As I put it, WRAC among the ruins. They helped rescue what artifacts remained in the Ruth Smith Mound of Citrus County, Florida, which is our neighborhood, before it was dozed into oblivion. Actually, it had been dozed before: this was merely a remnant.

Cheryl came home one day with news that a major new mound had been found. It would surely have great archaeological interest, but its excavation was uncertain because of the cost. My wife and I discussed it, and decided that this was a worthwhile project. Not only would it support our daughter's interest, it would benefit the world, by making the information in the mound available. So we approached Brent Weisman after a WRAC meeting and discussed it. We were prepared to donate $10,000 toward the excavation of Tatham Mound. Brent thought that should cover it. It would be a gamble, because there might be little besides sand in the mound. On the other hand, there might be a great deal in it. So we visited the University of Florida and talked with Dr. Jerald Milanich, Chairman of the Department of Anthropology, and we made the donation. Our only stipulation was that this donation be considered anonymous, because we did not want to be deluged by requests for money, and we hoped that our daughter Cheryl would be allowed to participate to the extent feasible in the excavation. Children are not necessarily the best workers for something like this, but Cheryl was extremely bright and responsible, and I suspect that the authorities were glad to have her participation. At any rate, had she not taken an interest in archaeology, and had we not been in a position to afford substantial support, the major part of the financing of the excavation would have been delayed, perhaps for decades.

The excavation was supervised by Jeffrey Mitchem, whose doctoral dissertation is my major reference on the Safety Harbor culture. He was assisted for the first season by Brent Weisman, whose separate research had led to the discovery of the mound. I regret that the study made by the specialist in bones, Dale Hutchinson of the University of Illinois (that's near Gray Cloud's original home), was not completed in time for this novel; I run the risk of error in my adaptation of the various skeletons. Some literary license may have to be invoked.

At first the mound did seem to be mostly sand and arrowheads; they were excavating that section. But when they came to the center, it turned out to have several times as much significant material as had been hoped for. For example, there were one hundred and fifty-three glass beads of Spanish manufacture associated with the burials, the largest assemblage of early-sixteenth-century Spanish trading beads found in any North American Indian site. Since some of the "Nueva Cadiz" beads were manufactured only before 1550, they helped date the burials. Some may have been found only in Tatham Mound. Certainly these Indians had contact with the Spanish, and surely that contact was with the de Soto expedition. The copper artifacts could not have been mined or manufactured locally; they had to have been traded, perhaps from a region as far away as the Great Lakes. Thus early commerce was confirmed. In fact, the study of what was found in Tatham Mound may result in a redefinition of the extent and nature of the Safety Harbor culture. This may have been a backwoods region, but it is now a known region.

It finally took larger crews and three seasons to excavate and curate (that is, sort out and classify) it all. Cheryl went out there regularly to work, though sometimes the temperature was freezing and sometimes it was bakingly hot. Slowly the mound was reduced and the artifacts removed until almost all of it was gone. We continued to contribute as necessary, for in this period my success as a writer of light fantasy was burgeoning, making this affordable, and we also contributed to the work on the de Soto winter camp in northern Florida, and to the investigation of the neighboring Seminole Indian camp of a later date. By the time it was done, we had donated approximately $75,000 to these efforts. But this project did indeed help rewrite the archaeological map of Florida, and two doctoral dissertations will be based on it. We regard this as money well spent.

But I like to make use of whatever I encounter. After all, this was a significant discovery right here in Citrus County, Florida, where I live. I have done a good deal of writing set in Florida, and I like the locale. So I decided to write a novel based on this information. Of course, it could not be limited to the mortuary rites revealed by the excavation; there is more to a culture than death. So I researched more widely, and this book is the result. We funded the excavation for personal and philanthropic reasons independent of the novel, but it is my hope that the novel will in time earn enough to match or exceed the amount we put into this research. My money comes mainly from light fantasy, but it would be nice if a more serious project like this one paid its own way, as it were.

It would also be nice if this project alerts a wider range of people to the nature and significance of archaeology, and to the kind of history of this land not found in school texts. I doubt that many people realize the true nature of the de Soto expedition; I hope that now my readers do. I have portrayed it as accurately as is feasible, given disagreement among scholars about details, and the route I describe and the battles along it are pretty much as they occurred. Juan Ortiz was a historical character, perhaps the real origin of the Pocahontas legend; he really was the captive of Chief Hirrihigua (one source says Chief Ucita), tortured, then saved by the Chief's daughter, and he did join the de Soto expedition eleven years later. Even de Soto's dog, Bruto, is historical, as depicted.

The mound was on the property of a large forested ranch for Boy Scouts, which was a fortunate coincidence in several respects. First, it was protected from casual molestation, which makes it almost unique in Florida; access was controlled, with a closed gate and combination lock, the combination known only to those authorized to enter, and changed periodically. Second, there were cabins on the property, representing an ideal place for the working crews, who consisted mostly of students from the University of Florida, to stay. Third, this property was managed by the ranger for the Scout Reservation, Paul Anderson, whose competence and helpfulness greatly facilitated progress. Overall, this was about as good a place for such a project as could be imagined.

I made penciled notes when I visited the mound, and though these are unscientific, some samples may offer a notion of the manner in which such a project proceeds.

1–13–85—@ 2:20 P.M., to padlocked gate, combination. Past Community Center. Narrow dirt road, overleaning brush, palmettos, small live oaks, sand pines, bay laurel, sparkleberry. Road like a river, winding through open marsh, grassy. Birds—heron, buzzardlike.

Wooden bridge of planks, palms with woven-basket trunks, magnolias, larger live oaks with branches like tangled tentacles. Bumpy, up-down road, endlessly winding. Hog wallows, holes.

More groves of tentacular live oaks, pretty. Patches of palmetto and wild oats, in turns and admixtures. Large grassy swamp. Overgrowing brush scrapes car. Violently holed road.

Suddenly 3 cars, 25 minutes later, 5 ½ miles deep.

Start excavation from east side, proceeding across mound to west. Ten-foot (3-meter) trench. Every shovelful sifted through screen. Two screens, two sifters each. Cheryl and Andrew on one. Screens suspended from tripods, red/white colored poles, piles of sifted dirt below. Roots in the mound, making digging hard. Lisa, in red sweatshirt, using clippers to snip out roots. Pottery sherds start about 10 feet in. All Safety Harbor, so far.

Mound cleared of most trees; about 6 remaining, 4"–6" diameter. First 3-meter section dug down 3"–6", smoothed over for a picture. Day pleasant by mound, maybe 60° F. Cleared out the peat.

Initial 3M × 1M trench goes deeper, showing layered peat, then white sand, so first stage merely clears the recent accumulation; next stage will get into the real stuff.

Stakes and string marking. Little level-glass on string, to obtain elevations. Jenette using that, in yellow sweatshirt, blue cap. Dry paintbrush used to dust off sherd still in place. Map on tripod at top of mound; can be oriented in any direction.

The "towers" are wooden ladders with top-landings, anchored to the small trees.

Because I am poor with names and faces, I noted names and clothing to identify who was doing what so I wouldn't embarrass myself by addressing someone by the wrong name. Sometimes the folk would talk to me or show me something, and of course I circulated, asking questions. I was there nominally to pick up my daughter Cheryl, and as an interested member of WRAC; I did participate in a number of WRAC events. The fact that I was financing the major part of the job was supposed to be unknown, but I was accorded unusual courtesy, so some folk did catch on.

As these notes show, this was deep in the jungle. We have color pictures of it, and of the initial stages of the excavation. I appear in some, and Cheryl in some. My wife, Cam, suffered the usual fate of those who take pictures: being left out of them.

Cam and I took a WRAC tour on a hay-wagon that showed the region and the site, and when we came to the mound with the people working on it, there in the foreground was Cheryl brushing off some bones, with a headband and flowing dark hair, looking exactly like an Indian maiden. It was coincidence, but my imagination lent it significance. Probably Wren looked somewhat like that, in life.

Indeed, my life comes into this novel, because my imagination and my hunger for information and insight cause me to have an emotional involvement with everything I write, whether it is light fantasy or heavy history. Critics who talk glibly of Anthony "potboilers" are either ignorant of my attitude or deliberately malicious; I do write for money, but never *only* for money. Thus the main character of this novel is Tale Teller, who today would be called a free-lance writer, with an incapacity of the arm similar to what I experienced during my bout with cat scratch fever and later with tenonitis. I believe it is the first time I have made a writer a protagonist in one of my novels, but I didn't do it as an analog of myself or because I lacked the wit to invent a better character. I did it because I believe that the tale tellers were the entertainers, educators, and historians of prehistory. Indeed, I believe that a significant aspect of man's nature derives from tale-telling, because this is where the human mind appreciates not only what *is* but what *might be*. It is man's art that sets him apart from the animals: his imaginative vision. Tale-telling is perhaps the first art. In short, here is the font of man's imagination, one of the major things that sets him apart from animals. I believe that our species will be remembered less for the manner in which it builds edifices than for the quality of its imagination, however it is expressed.

The process of excavation was not always dead serious. Indeed, humor could lighten the somewhat tedious labor. I doubt that Dr. Milanich quite appreciated my remark "What do archaeologists eat for a snack? Mounds." There could be an all-but-festive atmosphere at times, and a stranger might almost have thought the people were playing on the beach. But they were not. My notes of 1–27–85 describe several three-meter squares, with people working with clippers, trowels, and paintbrushes—clipping out roots (can't just pull them; they would disturb bones), painstakingly digging out sand, and brushing the bones and artifacts clean so they could be photographed in place. Every item in the mound was surveyed in, so that it would be possible to put the entire mound back together with every bone and sherd and arrowhead where it started. Once they encountered the burials, they dug by the trowelful, not the shovelful, proceeding with excruciating care. They set little red flags by each discovery, to map it, then excavated it carefully after marking off a territory around it. Every bone was precious, every bead, and every sherd. So the site resembled a collection of castles in sand, complete with banners, each person with his own little territory. Once I saw the word "DIGROS" sketched in the vertical sand wall of one of the excavation squares, and inquired. It was a pun, of sorts: rather than call themselves "diggers," which resembled a racist term for black folk, they tried to make a nonracist version.

Here is a sample from my notes made immediately after returning from my visit to the mound 10–4–86:

> Jeff Mitchem showed me the beads that were associated with the fetus burial, remarking that the mother had few beads with her. I asked whether she could have been a woman of low status married by a chief, so that the baby would have more status than the mother, and he agreed. I asked whether the bones

indicated an attractive young woman, and he said that the pelvis seemed outstanding. That seems to be it, then; she may appear in the novel.

One young woman brought something up for Jeff to check, but it turned out to be only solidified sap. "Makes you feel sappy," I remarked, and she agreed. We talked about how they tell male from female bones; it seems that the elbows of women bend back farther than do those of men, and indeed so it seemed with those present. I remarked how there is the trick, stepping back from a wall and picking up a chair, that men can't do yet women can. Another young woman knew of that, and leaned forward as if picking up a chair to demonstrate, in the process showing a deep flash of bosom. Do they do it intentionally? I, as a typical male, treasure such flashes of anatomy.

Years later, I still wonder how many of the ways of women are intentional, and remember that there was more than bones to be seen on that mound. It was easy to flesh out the skeleton of the young woman who was to become Wren, since similar examples were there with their flesh. Meanwhile, Cheryl got to know the participating students at the University of Florida and considered going there, but colleges and universities all over the country were soliciting her—she had made one of the highest SAT scores ever seen in north central Florida—and she attended a summer session at Harvard and then went to select New College in Florida. At this stage it seems unlikely that she will go into archaeology, but it was a nice facet of her education, and of mine.

The mound was found in 1983, and Jeff Mitchem's comprehensive doctoral dissertation, which is about the size of this novel, reached me in 1989. This actually represents fast progress, because so many things came together: the discovery of an intact burial mound in a good location, the involvement of WRAC, the presence of an advanced student of the Safety Harbor culture, the involvement of my daughter, and my ability to do what I felt appropriate, financially. In a sense, my Xanth fantasy series paid for the excavation of Tatham Mound. Well, Xanth is a parody of Florida turned magic, so perhaps it is fitting.

This project was, for me, worthwhile on several levels. I enjoyed learning about the American Indians. But I discovered that I am not really suited for the research novel. I am interested in just about everything, but my success with light fantasy has spoiled me, and I no longer care to spend hours ferreting out whether the potatoes used by the Wild Potato Clan of the Cherokee are the same as those we know today. I concluded that they are not; ours do derive from the New World, but not from North America. What the Cherokee harvested was actually another kind of tuber. So I chafed under the frustrations of research: I'm not cut out for this. I have little patience with hours of diligent searching that produce nothing I can use, as was often the case. I eased the situation by hiring a research assistant for this novel: Alan Riggs, who enabled me to save about two months on this novel. That was a blessing! For those who are curious: with the considerable help of the computer I can do a Xanth novel in two months; *Tatham Mound* took about seven months, spread out over about five years. It could have taken far longer, had I had the patience. I work harder and faster than do most writers, and do not tolerate slowdowns well.

Even so, there was no way I could utilize all the material I had collected for this project. I had a story to tell, and beyond a certain point detail becomes tedious for the reader who wants mainly to be entertained. Some promising references turned out to be irrelevant, and there is one I never even opened; it remains sealed in plastic, because my research took another direction. It relates to Florida's prehistoric stone technology, and my protagonist never got into stone chipping. I also collected references on the medicinal and magical uses of plants— but my protagonist never got into that aspect either. Some other novel, perhaps. I hate to see such good references wasted on an indifferent researcher like me.

There was also a private embarrassment: a decade or so back, as background research for a major historical fiction project I have not yet gotten to work on (but have patience; I still have it in mind), I read three books on European prehistory. I thought they would be repetitive, but to my surprise they barely overlapped each other. My memory indicates that one of those references gave a surprising origin for flint, the special rock which is so good for arrowheads: it was petrified bat guano. I mentioned that to Dr. Milanich, who gently gave me to understand that I might be mistaken. So I dug out my books—

and could find no such reference. Did I dream it? Was I taken in by someone's facetious invention? I may never know. Meanwhile I'll just mention that what they had locally for arrowheads was not flint but chert, which is not as good. You have to make do with what you have.

There were many people involved in the work on the mound and in support of the effort. I regret having to slight them by not mentioning them here by name, but the mere listing would require pages, and this is a novel, not a text. Dr. Mitchem's dissertation does list them, so those who wish to follow up on this should check for the published version of *Redefining Safety Harbor*. I will say that there seemed to me to be a real spirit of community in this project, with nice people at every level, and I'm glad I met them.

I hope that this novel has helped to make people aware that those who lived here before us were real people, and that their life-style was as valid for them as ours is for us. As I said in the Introduction, their way was worthy of respect, as is our own. This is fiction, but perhaps their actual life histories were as interesting. These people, destroyed by our advance into their territory, should not be forgotten. In our ignorance, we did not treat them well.

NOTE: Piers Anthony now has a "troll-free" number for those who wish to get on his mailing list as a source for all his books and projects. Call 1–800 HI PIERS.

BARRY LOPEZ

DESERT NOTES: Reflections in the Eye of the Raven and RIVER NOTES: The Dance of Herons

71110-9/$7.95 US/$9.95 Can

"Barry Lopez is a landscape artist who paints images with sparse, elegant strokes…His prose is as smooth as river rocks."

Oregon Journal

WINTER COUNT   58107-8/$3.95 US/$5.50 Can

Quiet, intoxicating tales of revelation and woe evoke beauty from darkness, magic without manipulation, and memory without remorse.

GIVING BIRTH TO THUNDER,   71111-7
SLEEPING WITH HIS DAUGHTER $7.95 US/$9.95 Can

In 68 tales from 42 American Indian tribes, Lopez recreates the timeless adventures and rueful wisdom of Old Man Coyote, an American Indian hero with a thousand faces—and a thousand tricks.